The Syndi-Jean

JOURNAL:
Year 3

The Syndi-Jean

JOURNAL:
Year 3

BCK KWAN

PARTRIDGE

To order additional copies of this book, contact
Toll Free 800 101 2657 (Singapore)
Toll Free 1 800 81 7340 (Malaysia)
orders.singapore@partridgepublishing.com

www.partridgepublishing.com/singapore

To all family, friends, fans and followers...
Thank You for the support.

In memory of dad.
-b

Preamble

Syndicessca Jeannie's third year at The Facility was perhaps her most difficult year on a personal level. It was also a volatile year as all manner of chaos descended around her and, by default, The Facility as well.

Rules were broken.

Not just The Facility's rules for its trainees.

Rules of all manner were broken throughout the year.

Her first two years may have had their challenges where her life was concerned. She had struggled with her education and managed to pull through. Her social life had rocky moments as well. The incident with Sophie, the previous year, in particular, was extremely rough on her; damn near broke her heart. Yet, their friendship prevailed when it could have easily shattered beyond repair. Unlike most of the other trainees, she had endeared incredible trust and loyalty from those she calls her friends, even going beyond conventional means to protect them from any repercussions of her own actions.

In dealing with a young and powerful telepath/telekinetic called Ethan, she defied a Guardian/Counsellor in ways that were unprecedented. It even threatened her standing within The Facility; and yet, she managed to gain the trust of a few of The Facility's governing board members. She was even given privileged information in regard to The Facility; more than any other trainee ever had.

She pushed more boundaries by entering into a relationship with the Exchange Participant, Walker just as the year turned. It was, as with everything she had done thus far, an unprecedented move as there had been no mixed pairing within The Facility before. She would also continue to dictate terms on how the abilities of the Telepaths and the Telekinetics would be put to use, challenging the members of The Facility's governing board. In turn, the application of those abilities within given situations would also be tested.

All that paled as Jeannie was pushed to her limits in dealing with the events that came about in her toughest and darkest year. She had to face more than just the consequences of her actions from the previous years. Repercussions from events and actions stemming from further back came to the fore. The walls and fabric of reality broke down as I was personally witness to, and her mind teetered on the brink of insanity even as she pushed her telepathic abilities to the limits in helping her friends and others. Dreams and nightmares more than came to life.

She had confronted the darkness within herself, but her past continued to haunt her in more ways than one. Her past may have also proven to be her salvation. She discovered her strength, and her true spirit revealed itself. For as much darkness resides within her, it is only in true darkness would there be the brightest light as Jeannie would discover. It was a year she would have her happiest moments and hardest losses.

And in that, she would discover her potential, and herself.

-- Remington C_.

JANUARY

Jan 10

A customary recap is in order, in case you're coming to this fresh as a daisy.

For the past couple of years, I've been studying, training and living at a place I can only refer to as "The Facility", located somewhere within the vicinity of New York City. The Facility has a proper name, of course, but it's regarded as restricted information and known to certain people who are supposed to know. Just to ensure I don't share information I'm not supposed to, these journal entries get vetted by an editor before that person will let it out for public consumption.

This "Journal" was started to keep my mom apprised and informed of my activities/life in The Facility. It started out as letters and morphed into what it is now. Whoever my editor is at The Facility, he or she had set up some blog website to post it there, so it's actually an open journal. I was encouraged to slowly divulge information about the courses, the training I go through and the people I mix with as well as bits about myself. Things do veer into the unusual at times, so do keep an open mind, okay?

How unusual do things get? Well, Becca, my best friend and suite-mate at The Facility, is what we term a Foreign Exchange Participant. Think of it as an Exchange Student Program, except she comes from another planet. I'm not even sure where this planet is, but apparently we have been having visitors to our planet since way back. Nowadays, it's more for educational purposes. We learn from them, they learn from us and about us.

Now, the thing is, I ended last year getting into a serious relationship with an F.E.P. called Walker. Relationships and me haven't really been the best of company and I've had some serious missteps in the past. My track record with relationships isn't quite the best. The last one ended up with Mikey, and I fell out of love with that guy. Oh, we're still friends; we still connect for Mikey's sake, and if Mikey has a future in that area, I want that option open to him. I suppose that should give an idea of who and what Mikey is to me; and if you knew more about me, you'd understand why I wouldn't want to really say anything out loud on that topic except, Mikey is very important to me.

Walker and I connected fairly early on in my time at The Facility. I like swimming, lounging in the pool or being in water, and so did he since his people practically lived in water. Well, not quite lived "in" water, but more like their lives and livelihood revolved around water. He's more comfortable in water than he is on dry land, I suppose. We're at the pool almost every night and he got me into this practice of what I've been calling "aqua-acrobatics". It's partly a form of exercise for me, but more a meditative practice for him the way some people would do yoga. To be as good as Walker, I'd probably need the lung capacity of a dolphin.

Otherwise, it's a specialised diving suit, like the one he's been working on with another F.E.P called Ehrmer, who designs and builds environmental suits and exo-skeletons like the one he uses to get about at The Facility, and just about anywhere else. His physical being isn't suited to our environment, so he's got this suit he uses. I've got a point here, so bear with me.

As my budding relationship with Walker was getting on, I left The Facility and headed home for a week's break. Becca accompanied me as a chaperone. It was the same as last year right down to the camping trip with Becca, Lian and Mikey in tow. Lian's my best friend ever since I started schooling at CGL, and she's the only one among my Penang friends who knows all my secrets, like my true age and my 'special' abilities.

Aside from that, I also caught up with my other friends, or at least, those who were still around Penang.

So, that was how things were for the first few days of my 'vacation' until Remington showed up on the fifth day with Walker, Ehrmer and Sophie in tow. Also with them, but not from The Facility, were Steven, Becca's boyfriend, who works at the IASC - International Administrative Space Coalition; and Charlie, who's basically my personal doctor. He's mom's friend from her school days. Walker and Ehrmer brought along the upgraded diving suit. This suit is supposed to allow a user to dive without the use of air tanks, drawing breathable air from the water itself the way a fish would with its gills. Don't ask me to explain everything though, that's Ehrmer's speciality. I'm just the 'test pilot'.

Remington is my former Guardian/Counsellor at The Facility, but he still keeps tabs on me at mom's request. He footed the bill for a boat we took out a little off Muka Head. It was isolated enough for us to carry out a few test dives, and one other activity. Becca and Steven didn't join us, opting to have a little time to themselves on the beach. The boat was still pretty packed with Sophie, Walker, Ehrmer, Lian, Remington, Charlie, mom, my brother Rick and his friend Karen who lives with us and helps to look after Mikey while I'm at The Facility. Of course, there was Mikey and me as well.

The differences with the suit since last year and now were subtle in appearance. There was a nice metallic sheen to the fabric-based suit that made it look like some kind of robotic exo-suit. Lian commented that it looked like it came out of some anime. That went over really well with Mikey, especially once I got the faceplate on. It was far easier to put on without help than the previous suit, and it felt much lighter as well although Ehrmer said the weight difference was really negligible. This "Mark III" had what he called, "kinetic based hydraulic micro servos" that allowed the slightest movement to maintain a kind of power for the suit to carry out it's primary function of drawing breathable air from water. The servos also aided with the movement of the suit, making it feel lighter. Basically, the more you move, the more power you generate. Yes, there's a battery too. Still lighter than carrying around an air-tank on your back.

Whatever it weighed, I didn't have that sinking feeling like before when I got into the water. Walker accompanied me using an air tank and equipped with the camera. We dived deeper, stayed under-water longer than we did last year, and all the while I gave feedback over a much improved comms system in the head gear. There was a foam like lining on the interior layer of the suit and at no time did I feel the water pressure bearing on me, no matter how deep we dove. There was still a slight sense of light-headedness after about twenty minutes, which Ehrmer attributed to the air mixture. I attributed it to the giddy experience of using the suit and diving with Walker.

We then went through an aqua-acrobatic routine. Sophie took over handling the camera at that time and described our routine as "erotic" despite that it's no different from any other routine we practiced at The Facility's pool. Well, I didn't have to keep gasping for air every time we broke the surface. She was teasing, of course, given the status of our relationship, which she says is big news among the other trainees back at The Facility.

Once all that was done, Charlie did a cursory check on me to make sure there weren't any ill effects of using the suit. Once he cleared me, Lian asked to try on the dive suit. Remington seemed reluctant, but Ehrmer was more than willing to have another test subject. I know Sophie did a test as well, last year. He walked Lian through the suit's functions and she had no problems getting it on herself with some instructions. Despite making the suit to my specs, it still fit Lian snugly. She couldn't help striking a few poses that came out of some anime series – original *Bubblegum Crisis* came to mind. She got me to snap some photos, too. Then, Walker assisted her with the dive. It didn't take her long to adjust to breathing with the suit while underwater.

Lian didn't go deeper than about twenty feet, and she was out of the water in less than fifteen minutes feeling exhilarated, like a kid who got to play with an expensive new toy. Mikey and I were also in the water at the time. No one else joined us. It was after Lian got back on the boat and out of the suit that we broke for lunch of typical fast food; easy to buy, pack and keep for a while.

Sophie and I didn't eat that much. While everyone else was resting, we got around to our practice. Both of us are alike where particular 'special' abilities are concerned. While we have our telekinetic abilities, Sophie's a latent telepath whose abilities suddenly bloomed. I've been helping her with both, although recently on the telepathy thing. There are others like us at The Facility. Not a lot though, and even fewer of us who actually have both 'talents'.

While we have our usual training in class, I've been helping Sophie do other things not covered in training, particularly flying. At it's basic level, telekinesis is the ability to move objects with the mind. In class, each of us has a different method of applying our TK abilities, so it took a while to get Sophie to even levitate herself, much less fly. Remington helped to let her come to Penang last year and she got to try out flying in the open. It was more distance than height then as we 'flew' away from the boat and then back again.

This year, we headed up and out, taking the chance that no one was going to notice two girls in swimsuits flying about. Sophie is daring enough to try anything within reason. The highest she could get up to was no more than twenty feet within The Facility. This time, the sky was the limit. It was more like levitation, heading straight up and she had a decent rate of climb, slowly moving outwards so that we weren't directly over the boat. She started first and I followed behind her. When I felt she was slowing down after about maybe fifty feet, I moved past her and encouraged her to go higher.

Like I said, each of us applies our abilities differently. When it comes to flying like this, Sophie's concept was more akin to pushing away from the ground. In her mind, she was more or less still connected to the ground. The higher she went, the appearance of less control showed up. Even moving laterally was a slight problem at that height. It was more a change in perception in how to use her abilities as it was a matter of endurance. I don't even think technique factored in. It's like how all of us know how to write, and each of us has a different handwriting style. I had to get her to not just follow my handwriting but to also handle the pen my way. The most I could do was to keep explaining my process to her, but the likelihood of her adapting to my style was low. It would be better if she could find her own way of doing things with her ability, knowing that certain things are possible, like flying.

4

I kept pushing Sophie to take full advantage of the open sky we had, doing more manoeuvres and testing her speed. We ended up flying circles around each other, settling maybe thirty feet above sea level.

In all, I think Sophie did pretty well, lasting far longer than she has ever managed. She still ended up physically and mentally exhausted, but said it wasn't as bad as last year. Charlie advised her to have a check up with Ms. Phillips, The Facility's resident health care specialist, and even got Remington to ensure it would happen.

By the time we headed to the beach where we left Becca and Steven, it was probably close to five in the evening. The boat couldn't get too close to shore; we had a little dinghy for that. Remington and mom stayed on the boat while the rest of us headed to shore for a spell. I swear, Charlie actually seemed relieved to be on solid ground. Lian ended up keeping Ehrmer company. I think she was grilling him about the diving suit as well as his own exo-suit. Rick and Karen were off on their own. Sophie took a nap on a blanket under a tree. Walker also kept me company as we took Mikey out for a swim. For some reason, the jellyfish kept a respectable distance from Walker – and us by default. I usually see the jellyfish floating about in the water, but it was the first time I've actually seen them move away.

It was close to eight at night when we finally left Muka Head and closer to midnight by the time all of us got home. I was amazed our visitors lasted the day due to the travel time and time difference. Sophie zonked out on the sofa when we got into the house. Lian went home soon after and Charlie also headed off on his own. Remington had two rooms at a hotel, Becca and Steven took one room while Remington shared the other with Ehrmer. That left Walker with me for the night, and man, did we have some stuff to catch up on and work out.

We're still navigating the messy waters of what our relationship would be, how it would work, and what we can or can't do in our relationship. All I've got to go by as a reference is Becca and Steven, but Becca is nothing like Walker and I'm nothing like Steven, so there's no guarantee that we could have the same kind of relationship. Also, I'm not entirely sure about pursuing a physical relationship at this point, but let's face it, that's going to come up some time down the line in one way or another. We already have a physical relationship of sorts with the swimming and aqua-acrobatics. That puts us in pretty close proximity already, with about as little clothes between us as possible, going on for almost two years now. I've also had far less on around him occasionally and it's never bugged him or me. I go skinny dipping in the open at my campsite; I'm not shy nor ashamed about it.

Anyway, after I put Mikey to bed, Walker and I spent a little time talking things out. We didn't have much to cover. No bridge to cross because we hadn't gotten to it yet. We agreed to let things flow and tackle each issue as it came about. We kissed a little, but we didn't go so far as to even make out. We shared my bed and he fell asleep shortly after that. His arm was around me and I could feel him breathing. It was soothing rhythm and a huge sense of comfort being there with him. It wasn't like he was holding on to me, and he was asleep after all.

I don't sleep much. When I do sleep, it's usually a couple of hours or less. It has to do with my physiology or biology, or whatever physical thing it is about my body's system that also causes a few things to seem out of whack. We'll get to that stuff as it comes about.

So, there I was in my own room, in bed with my new guy and watching over Mikey. I did fall asleep in the end, but I was also awake before anyone else. It was a warm morning, even before the sun was up. I checked on Mikey first and then I had a shower. By the time I got out of the shower, Walker was awake and feeling dehydrated. I got him to the shower and he livened up almost immediately under the running water. Whether he had enough sleep or not didn't matter much once he got under the shower.

Sophie also found the heat and humidity of the day a little stifling, even after a shower. Remington and the others got back to the house in time for lunch, which was ordered in from a Chinese restaurant. I even skipped over to the shop-lots nearby to pick up some hawker food for the others to try out before we settled in for lunch. Walker and Sophie were adventurous enough to try some of the more spicy food while Ehrmer stuck to the more conventional dishes from the restaurant. Lian managed to drop by towards the end of lunch. She knew we were leaving after that.

Of course it was hard to say good-bye to Mikey but I told him I would keep trying to meet him every weekend in the dream-world like before. Karen would still watch over him, and Rick would help out as well when mom is off doing her own work, or isn't around for whatever reason. I know Charlie will also check in on Mikey at least once a month, so he's in good hands.

I've been back at The Facility for a day or so now, getting back into the groove of things. This is pretty long as it is so I'll get to the other stuff next time once I figure what I want to write about and how to get about writing without repeating anything I've covered before. Plus, I wanna head off to the pool for now and work some of this slight tension that's built up since I got back.

Jan 11

A couple of days before the others arrived in Penang, I got a haircut; my first in probably seven months, give or take. My hair was pretty long down my back by then, past my shoulder blades. Lian had introduced me to this place where they use discarded hair to make wigs for cancer patients. Since I wanted to have my hair short again, it was easy enough to lop off a considerable amount. In the end, I got that really short spunky look back. Helped a lot when I went swimming in the sea.

Walker didn't pay any mind to it though. It was obvious he did notice when we met up in Penang, but he didn't say anything. He has hair and it's fairly short like a military styled crew-cut, but I don't think I've ever seen it grow, come to think of it. Maybe it's not an important factor among his people, but having never met anyone else like him, I couldn't really say. It seems like such a minor trivial thing to bring up with him given our relationship, and I don't want to seem like I'm fussing over a new hair-do. Not that I'm doing it here. Just saying, I had a hair-cut.

Of course, Carol thinks I got the hair-cut because of Walker. Helen thought it was more becoming of me to have it short than long, while the others at the lunch table had nothing to contribute. I didn't bother justifying anything except to comment that I had barely been back two days before Carol started up with the rumours and the gossip.

Among my other friends at the table were Becca, siblings Keiko and Keitaro, my TP partner Jenny, as well as a pair of TP trainees, Kevin and Bastian, who decided to join us for lunch since Jenny and I were in class with them before lunch. I had worked with Kevin before, but we hardly mixed around until lately while Bastian has been with The Facility since July last year.

Since getting back to The Facility, it's mostly catching up with the week's work I missed out; checking in with all my tutors, seeing what I need to do. There are no real breaks with the training because that's just the way life is around here. My weekends are still free which let's me keep Saturday for connecting with Mikey, like yesterday. My Friday dinners with Sophie are off the calendar for now (she says), since I'm mentoring her in TP.

I also checked in with Tommy at the Operations Center and he told me to settle all my training and classes before I start working there again. There has been nothing new in terms of progress with the data stream we've been monitoring and decoding from the probe.

There were some boxes outside my work-room, stuff I requisitioned through my current Guardian/Counsellor, Linda, for my computer project. Colleen, my computer with a functioning A.I., has been dormant while I was away and she complained like crazy, saying I abandoned her, despite knowing I had gone home for a break. This is what I get for programming a personality to an A.I. matrix. I've got quite a bit of upgrading work to do over the next few weeks; and to think I started out using leftover obsolete junk parts. She's not elegant, but she's got two interface panels, four display screens, voice recognition and interface, and a mini interactive holographic heads-up display. That, too, is not perfect, but I had to make do with what I could get and what was available to me; like the best of what's left.

Then there are the other activities such as my flight simulator training, which I need to beef up on my own time. I've consulted with Keiko to continue kendo practice as well as our sparring in other forms of martial arts and self-defence. She's eager to continue our weapons practice with the various wooden replicas of several typically bladed weapons. She can kick my butt with hand-to-hand, but somehow I'm wiping the floor with her when it comes to the 'weapons'. It does not count kendo, in which she is a master. However, if we break the rules of kendo and she let's me handle the *shinai* or *bokkun* as I like, I can put up a decent fight.

The last couple of days have been like that, getting to classes, checking in with the tutors and trainers, working out my social calendar and checking in on Mikey. While it's the weekend, there are classes and training going on for those who need to do some catching up with the tutors and trainers. That's life around here.

I'm heading for the pool now to unwind.

Jan 14

Mr. Hardy, the Theoretical Physics and Quantum Sciences tutor, was not too particularly pleased with my progress after the attempts at catching up last year. To be fair about it, I was just getting the hang of all that Theoretical Physics stuff and barely scratching the surface of Quantum Sciences when the trip home occurred. Coming back to class feels like I got tossed into the deep end of the Quantum Sciences and my brain felt like it wanted to explode across the various planes of possible spatial existence unseen by any observer... or something like that. Carol recommended I watch an old TV series called "*Sliders*" for a quickie briefing on the subject of parallel worlds – not that I didn't have grasp on the concept. I watch anime; I occasionally read comic books and manga; it's a common idea that floats around in both forms of media.

Ah, well... I don't want to get too much into it, but I will say it isn't just learning the theories, but pushing the limits of imagination in the possibilities of application, or even if such theories are even possible. Carol's pretty good with all this, so conferring with her helps. It's just that she sometimes has a repayment system involving the rumours.

While I still spend every night at the pool with Walker, we haven't really been doing anything too spectacular that would even be considered "boy-friend/girl-friend" activity, I think. I even suggested she talk directly to Walker if she felt I wasn't entirely forthcoming. It's all because of my decision to neither confirm nor deny any of the rumours that come my way. It hasn't been particularly helpful to Carol's "news-worthy" ways.

The rest of my classes have been steady and I think I've got a grasp on the catching up part. Electrical Engineering has been helped by working alone in putting Colleen together. Programming has been helped mostly by working in the Operations Center with Tommy. There's still a little struggle with Mechanical Engineering with dashes of architectural designs suddenly thrown in yesterday, but I've got Helen to help me out on that. Then there's the TK and TP training which are not really problematic for me. Miss Tracy, who runs both training, comes up with some of the exercises she would like us to try out, and we practise what we can to accomplish those exercises. I have no problems there as I'm more like a Teaching Assistant in the TK training, but I've got my own work keeping me busy in TP training.

Jenny is still working the Learning Network with Callie and Toni, who's Callie's TP partner. Because of my relationship with Callie, I'm in an advisory capacity. The network idea was Remington's, but creating the network and putting it to practical use was something Jenny and I worked on. In other areas, as mentioned before, I'm also working with Sophie to develop her TP skills and preparing her for the other Communications Network system I want her to try out. It links the thought centres of any participant enabling direct communication. It's something Remington suggested working on although we haven't had any official opportunity to put it into use as yet.

Then, last night, I dropped by the Operations Center. I've been eager to get back to work, but Tommy knew exactly what I was eager about. The glitch in the signals we received late last year was still under analysis by Mission Control at the IASC. There's still no fixed consensus about its validity. He said it was most likely Mission Control did have a preliminary result based on the software I had provided them, but they didn't want to admit they were wrong. It seems some members of the Mission Control team agree with my analysis. It's frustrating.

Just a little explanation here. Early on in my first year at The Facility, Remington got me talking to an astronaut named Tomas who was working in Space, alone, and preparing for a very long haul mission. We bonded over a love of David Bowie music. When Tomas got beyond basic reception and the only signals we could get from him were the constant stream of data that his ship was collecting and transmitting, I suggested a gamble by sending him a rhythm sting of a Bowie song; a tapped out rhythm following the opening of "Under Pressure". Late last year, the data stream had a glitch that appeared as "empty pulses". Of course I had to suggest that the glitch might have been Tomas' response, and I even had my own program, loaded with a bunch of Bowie songs from my own collection, doing a comparison search. There was no particular reason to think Tomas would use music from any other artist, but the folks at Mission Control gave that argument anyway. So for the last few weeks, they've been running their own analysis while Tommy and I continue to work the incoming data stream that was coming from Tomas' computers, and then passing on reconfigured data – from the stream of numbers and symbols to something more readable – over to Mission Control. That's basically the job I have been doing: code analysis and reconfiguration. Nothing really spectacular.

I officially start again next week, so Tommy says.

On a more personal note, I should probably mention that I haven't slept much these last couple of days, clocking in barely an hour each night, if I actually fall asleep. I can't really tell. I may have dozed off while trying to sleep or I may not. It's not impacting my daily activities though. I've gotten by on way less sleep.

I guess that's about it for now. I'm heading off to the pool to unwind; catch up with Walker.

Jan 16

Familiar strangers. It could be an example of an oxymoron, but it's the best description to illustrate the situation where you come across a lot of familiar faces although you don't really know anyone. You know a few who might become your friends and the others are the familiar faces of strangers who are there, filling in the gaps on a daily basis.

Since I don't know everyone in class or training, there are faces I've come to expect to see. We know when someone new arrives or if someone leaves for whatever reason. While the number of F.E.P. within The Facility is small, I don't know all of them simply because they're dabbling in fields outside my course of training, with one exception – Sociology.

While there aren't any fresh faces in TP or TK – suggesting that The Facility hasn't picked up any new potential psychics – there are a couple of new faces in other classes. It's something I thought I'd mention but I won't get into that unless I end up mixing with them.

One person who seems to be missing is Yumana. She, along with Sunee, got interested in the aqua-acrobatics Walker and I were doing, and ended up getting some lessons from him in that area. Sunee said Yumana had gone back to India, attached to an advanced environmental science organisation, working in environmental restoration and preservation. All I knew before was that they were working in what was dubbed, "Nature Technologies". It has something to do with taking what works in nature and applying it to various technologies used in anything and everything. Walker referred to it as "bio-mimicry".

After all this time, I'm just getting her name right – Yumana. I kept calling her "Yamuna" – and looking back, I wrote it that way for almost two years – and she never corrected me. Then again, aside from the pool and the occasional get-together, we never really mingled.

Since the F.E.P.'s are part of an exchange program, we tend to see some trainees disappearing from the classes as they partake in the exchange program. I don't know how long the program lasts because I've been around for two years now and I've known Becca, Walker and Ehrmer for all of those two years. I don't know about Ehrmer, but Walker disappears for a week or so at the end of September for his 'ritual'. Becca has never really left my sight, so to speak.

Yeah, can you tell there isn't much for me to write about? Most of my week so far has been catching up with classes, filling in friends and generally keeping busy with my projects. I have notes from various classes to review and then consult the tutors to clarify what I don't understand. There is something to be said about not having to sleep much at night. It gives me extra time to do the reviews and clock in some time in the flight simulator.

There is one bit of news actually. Both Remington and Linda came looking for Becca and me. There's a new F.E.P. coming in a few days from Becca's home, so she's supposed to liaise with the newcomer and help that person adjust. Since I've been learning and can communicate fairly well in Becca's language, I get to represent The Facility. As far as we know, it's the usual student exchange bit, so there isn't any need for formalities. I'm not required to dress up or anything.

It's about dinner and I'm meeting Walker; our first official dinner together as a 'couple'. Maybe I'll put on a dress. I know Helen will get a kick out of that.

Jan 18

It's Sunday evening now, and just after dinner – alone. It's been a pretty busy weekend with the dinner on Friday night and catching up with Mikey on Saturday (that took a while), clocking in some time with Colleen and catching up with training, studies and whatever else, while dealing with Carol and her 'news'.

The dinner on Friday with Walker was a pleasant experience. I didn't plan on dressing up, sticking with my usual ensemble of jeans, collared t-shirt and a light shirt over that. Nothing fancy at all; even Becca was disappointed I wasn't making much of an effort to be presentable, or more precisely, ladylike. I countered that I would rather be comfortable in what would likely be an awkward situation than to add to the discomfort by dressing up. After much persuasion from her, I ditched the jeans and borrowed a long skirt from her to wear. I had to thank her for forcing the change because Walker made the effort to not wear the usual casual shorts. He looked like he came straight out of training, but he admitted to making a last minute change as well.

Dinner was unique as he got me to try something new, supposedly some kind of delicacy from his home, or a close approximation. It seems there are some flavours that can be considered universal, like we could agree when something is supposed to be sweet or salty or even sour. Maybe that joke about strange stuff that, "Tastes like chicken," may not be so funny anymore. He wouldn't tell me what it was supposed to taste like, although I was pretty sure it was made with some kind of fish.

We also talked a little during the dinner, and didn't have any plans beyond dinner. He admitted to consulting with Becca who suggested some activities, running through a number of suggestions. None had any real appeal to either of us, beyond providing a decent laugh over it.

We ended up in the garden making plans about what we could do on our dates, which would be fixed to Friday nights for now. Aside from hanging in the pool, we didn't have much else in common except where our work was concerned. Walker has a brilliant mind. He's way smarter and analytical than I am, but I don't want to constantly pick his brain every time I have some kind of road-block on my projects. However, it is great to talk things out with him in those situations because he does get me thinking about the problems in different lights. I wish I could do something like that for him in return.

We've got maybe the next three or four activities laid out for the next month and I've got to come up with some suggestions of my own aside from only watching a movie. Being in The Facility limits our choices. It's not like we can go window-shopping or something. Also, we agreed to be as casual as we liked, which meant no more dressing up. I had to ask him then if he liked me in a dress to which he commented that it was nice, but I also appeared uneasy with it. I admitted as much and added that I didn't mind as much as it would seem.

The dress thing also came up during lunch the next day with Helen saying that I should be wearing more dresses instead of jeans or pants all the time. I complained about the feeling of being half-dressed and she said, "That's what stockings are for." I don't know about the other girls at the table, some of whom made faces at the remark, but that was coming from a guy who likes to dress like a proper lady – and looking damn gorgeous at it too. It was already common knowledge I didn't possess that many dresses in my wardrobe. I only had one (just in case of... whatever) and I wore that the first time I had dinner with Walker a couple of years back.

The most anyone was talking about was the lack of making out. Carol was disappointed about the lack of action on my part because after we left the garden on Friday night, he walked me back to my suite, dropped me off and headed back to his room. After a quick change, I went to work on Colleen for the rest of the night.

After the lunch-time interrogation, I headed to the Infirmary for my weekly visit with Mikey in the dream-world. For some reason, the link took a whack out of me and despite spending about a couple of hours on the dream-plane, it took the better part of four hours plus on the outside. The time dilation occurs often, although seldom stretching on the side of reality. These trips don't often end with me feeling drained, physically and mentally. It's just that there was a huge feeling of fatigue and lethargy coming out of the dreaming this time.

I did whatever reviews I could manage after dinner but zonked out by about eleven last night. I woke up after half past two feeling famished. Caught up with Tommy briefly in the café while looking for a midnight snack; he was on his break. Even he noticed I seemed a little off. I attributed it to the week's activities and readjusting to the hectic life of The Facility.

After a morning dip in the pool, most of today was spent finishing up a fortnight's worth of review materials. Hopefully, the rest of the classes will go on smoothly and I won't have to worry too much about keeping pace with everybody else. These are the times when I feel like I'm in way over my head. What helped me relax in the end was a kendo practice session with Keiko. Just going through the motions of doing the strokes properly helped take some of the edginess off and got my head to focus properly. I can't really explain it any other way. There was a sense of serenity that descended with each stroke of the *suburi*.

So, we're caught up to speed right now. I'm gonna clock in some hours with the flight simulator again tonight and see if I can get some shut-eye later.

Jan 21

It's been a busy couple of days playing host to the new F.E.P. with Becca. It should probably be noted that since "Becca" is only a close approximate of her real name, we had to work a bit to come up with a close approximate for our new friend. If I were to write out how their names were actually pronounced, it would look like a string of consonants randomly strung together and look completely made-up, even though they're not. Their spoken language doesn't lend easily to our limited range of letters. So after much discussion with the new girl, who's a touch shorter than Becca, we settled on Kadi as being something easy enough for others to remember and recognisable enough for her to use. Of course, between her and Becca, they'd be using their real names. On my end, Becca introduced me as "Jnz'a" – yeah, I think that's as close as I can manage to spell it. It translates to 'box' or 'container', a vessel of sorts. Everyone else still calls me, "Syndi-Jean."

I did eventually learn what my name meant in Becca's language or rather what it meant in the way she pronounced it, and I'm not going to share it. When she told Kadi the name she first used for me, they had a pretty good laugh over it. That doesn't say much, but you get the idea.

While Becca's training has been more on the social intricacies of our culture and a little on the science side, Kadi is more a student of biology and physics. She's interested in plants and talked a whole lot on terra-forming while asking how the plants of our world thrived in the wake of what she called, "rampant civilisation." I guess even environmental concerns can be universal. I was thinking at the time that it was too bad Yumana had left.

Aside from Kadi, there were only four new trainees who were introduced this year, one of whom was returning after a few years in the exchange program. The others were, as usual, from countries around the world that are supposedly part of the IASC, and they're all easily way smarter than me. One of them though, this guy from... wherever... is into artificial intelligence and robotics, so he's one I'd like to get to know.

Anyhoo, Becca and I spent the first day with Kadi going through the motions of showing her around The Facility; through the registration process, keying in her vitals into the security systems and such; then getting her checked out by Ms. Phillips. After that, it was to her suite and her suite-mate, a girl called Rain, who is in the same mechanical engineering class with me. Their suite is across the hall and a door away from us, close enough in case Kadi needed to consult Becca. She was also given a comms unit. I guess I should also mention that Remington is Kadi's G/C, which made sense since he is also Becca's G/C.

It wasn't until yesterday we introduced her to the rest of the gang at lunch. They were accommodating enough to help her feel welcomed. Even Walker, Ehrmer and Corogi were there, probably at Becca's request. It was mostly the same as when I helped get Callie acclimatised to the environment of The Facility. Kadi connected easily with Carol on the physics stuff and even Keitaro got into the groove with the physics of mechanics and robotics. I did as best as I could with some of the translation, falling back to Becca for the more complex stuff. In the midst of all that, Becca thanked me for helping out. I thought it was weird because I felt like I had done nothing much. She said it was a big deal, particularly with the language barrier. Kadi had a basic grasp of our language already, so the translating bit wasn't as much work as I thought, but Becca said certain things didn't translate well, and that was where I helped.

"Okay," I said with an uneasy smile because I really had no idea what she was talking about then. It seemed to me that she was doing pretty well on her own and I was more or less a sidekick. It was only this morning she admitted she had been feeling nervously unwell throughout yesterday and that translating a lot of stuff had put a strain on her. Becca is usually pretty easy-going and I don't think I've ever seen her in a stressful situation before – if yesterday was actually that.

She admitted that she had been worried about serving as a kind of ambassador to Kadi, enough that she hadn't slept the night before. It seems almost such a trivial thing, but now that the last couple of days have passed, she's much better as things are going back to normal. I still offered to do whatever I could as her back-up to helping Kadi around, and with learning the language although Rain should be doing that.

Ah well, back to the grind for now.

Oh, and I did get an idea about spending time with Walker. I wonder if he'll be up to it though. I'm going to discuss it with him later and then we'll see where we go from there.

Jan 24

Becca mentioned before what it's like to be a mentor; not an easy thing since it takes a lot of your time. For someone who's as easy-going as Becca, it's been stressful for her to mentor Kadi. She knew what to expect, particularly with Kadi having to adjust to the environment and the food. I'm doing what I can to help her. Becca's done quite a lot for me over the last couple of years and I don't think I've ever seen her so swamped in dealing with one person. Was I ever that problematic for her?

Yes, I'm concerned for my suite-mate. It does seem like she's got her hands full with Kadi. I did make only one suggestion so far but Becca hasn't agreed to it, preferring I bring it up to Remington instead. That's what I did today. I managed to get a meeting with Remington and Linda, as well as Kadi, Becca and myself.

The idea was simply this. Becca has the experience of being at The Facility, having lived through it all. Aside from the food issues, which we agreed Kadi had to get used to, a lot of the knowledge could be shared via a network session between Becca and Kadi. It was simply a matter of Becca accessing the memories and sensations needed for Kadi to acclimatise herself to The Facility. I was confident I could pull it off as well, but like I said, Becca hasn't agreed to it.

Kadi was a little skeptical as well although Remington pointed out that it was a feasible idea. Becca's argument was it would be better for Kadi to experience things as they came along. While I agreed, there were other things I felt could be passed along; certain bits of knowledge could be shared, like language. A lot of how I learnt Becca's language was because of the time we spent in the dream-world. Granted it took a few days in terms of experience, but it was about a day in real time.

Remington was supportive of the idea so long as both Becca and Kadi were in agreement, but also stressed the importance of taking things slow with the orientation period. Linda felt it was good I had taken some initiative, perhaps even for the right reasons, but agreed with Remington on the matter. She also reminded me that it was about the learning experience and not just 'downloading' information into the brain. Becca only said she would think about it.

After we left Remington's office, Kadi voiced her curiosity about the network and I did my best to explain it. Suffice to say, she was intrigued.

Elsewhere, I think I've gotten into a fixed routine now with my classes and activities. I'm back working at the Operations Center from midnight until four in the morning, only four nights a week. I still get in some kendo practice with Keiko and we spar every other day, exchanging notes on our different styles. She picks things up fast once she sees me doing something new.

I guess things are about as steady as can be, which feels like a rarity.

Jan 26

Before I head out for the day, let's catch up on the last few days.

To start, I had dinner with Walker on Friday night, although we were joined by Sophie and Will. While no one said it out loud, I'm pretty sure it was a "double date". All we did was have dinner together and talk – a lot. It was mostly Sophie trying to get a grasp on the status of the relationship between Walker and me, to which Walker gladly obliged her questions. For most of the first two years, Walker and I have been acquaintances, to swimming buddies, to something he described as "kin". While I had actively tried to avoid getting into any kind of relationship with anyone, somehow, we've evolved beyond the whole "kin" bit and are now something of a couple.

Yeah – I can't really bring myself to confirm it to myself, can I?

He constantly reminded me it wouldn't be him to break that kinship, and it would probably be true I made the first few moves. I don't know when or what I did, but it was a mutual decision to move forward.

Sophie admitted it made sense I would end up with Walker despite the pursuit of John or the pining of Keitaro, or the few others who might have even vied for my attention, to which I vehemently denied. Even with all the gossip Carol would report on.

"From so early on, all you guys could talk about were the guys I would mix with," I said. "You've been with Will for a while now, not even Carol talks about that at lunch."

"You think maybe Carol had a thing for you?" asked Will.

"Some kind of weird fixation on my love life, maybe," I said.

"I don't think that's what he meant," said Walker.

Sophie was the one who broke into laughter first and it took me a moment longer to join the dots on that one. It wasn't something that actually crossed my mind. Then again, I was pretty sure Carol wasn't interested in me in that way. Also, I had no idea if the concept of same-sex relationships occurred among Walker's people, but maybe it did considering he picked up on the innuendo.

Through most of dinner, it was mostly Walker and I discussing with Sophie and Will, the intricacies of navigating a relationship within The Facility. They had a few weeks jump on us after all. I also did bring up my idea about Walker and I spending time together – alone. Sophie questioned the sensibility of that idea considering everything that happened over the last year with her. I haven't really done that with anyone since. Walker was quite willing to go through with my idea, putting his faith completely in me that I wouldn't let anything bad happen. I countered I had equal faith in him; he wouldn't let anything bad happen to me in the pool.

"That's a pretty good basis for a relationship right there," said Will.

We went our separate ways after dinner with Walker and I ending up around the pool area. He asked me when I was planning to put my idea into motion and I said I was good to go anytime he was ready. He would need to work through his schedule so that we could try it next week.

After lunch on Saturday, and this was after the meeting with Becca, Kadi, Remington and Linda, I spent my afternoon in the Infirmary as usual, off in the dream-world visiting Mikey. Despite appearing to be sleeping, the readings taken by the bed would suggest otherwise because my mind is not really getting the kind of necessary rest it needs when I'm off on a dream-walk. Or maybe it is.

Anyway, I don't know if it's the weekly sessions with Mikey or if he's being moody, but while he did turn up, he seemed a bit distant this time. It was as if he wasn't half as excited to see me as he used to be on previous sessions. I hope he wasn't viewing meeting me as a chore. This was my attempt to keep in contact with him as best as I could manage even if I wasn't there for him physically. While I was happy to be with him even for that short period, I couldn't help but feel a little let down by his lack of enthusiasm. On hindsight, I could have asked him if anything was wrong.

Okay, Becca just checked in on me, which means it's time for breakfast. Nothing much to write up about Sunday anyway.

Jan 28

Some news from Remington, but via Jenny. While Jenny is officially my TP partner when I'm supposed to be in class, my time has been spent coaching Sophie. I still practise with Jenny from time to time, but we've got two or three network systems to work through. One being why Remington was looking for us.

Jenny said he handed her a list of names for the next field trip in March and going over the list, we had our work cut out for us. Aside from Ehrmer, there were three other F.E.P. listed with Kadi already making the list; Corogi also. Add three other first timers and that's six newbies in a team of twelve participants this time, more than any we had carried before. John was still on the list though, but so were Sophie and Helen as well as Resh and Sulli who joined the network last year. What bugged us most was Carl being on the list.

Jenny had asked Remington about it and was told we had to accept it. Carl was there on the first field trip – the one where we worked on but didn't use the network because of the 'leaks'.

Man, has it been a year since we were on this field trip to the colony at Mount Olympus? We had two trips to the colony in my first year, but last year really had me running around. I haven't heard anything where the colony was concerned. I wonder if Peter is still okay there...

One other bit of news Jenny shared. Since I have been working with Sophie, Jenny's been tapped to partner another TP, Ethan! It seems Remington is going to be his guardian, so that's a good thing.

Given what happened last year, I'm surprised he decided to come back. Since he left last year, I had not heard from him in any way. Sophie wasn't too pleased with that bit of news – she was with me in class when Jenny came looking for me.

Since I'm on this track, I should note that Sophie's been making pretty good progress since we started. She's gotten used to communicating via her TP, establishing a strong link with me during our practice sessions, unlike how I started out with Jenny. She's also been practicing on Will, linking with and sending him thoughts and such, and then picking up only his thoughts in return without 'hearing' from anyone else. Even I didn't pick up on those side sessions, although I wasn't really 'listening out' for her. Also, it's not like we trainees haven't done that with our friends. I used to do it with Becca when I started here.

Telepathy is a tricky thing to control at times and it is not unlike normal listening; hence all the typical words that are usually associated with hearing or listening. Except for us "teeps", it happens directly in our head instead of our ears. No one really knows how or why it happens, not even the geniuses here at The Facility. It's not like we chose to have this... ability. We just have it, like almost everyone has the ability to hear. While we grow up learning not to listen to every single bit of noise that comes to our ears, we have to train ourselves not to 'listen' in via our TP.

Thinking on that, there might be a solution to a concern Jenny and I have about the number of people on the network. It's not that we aren't able to carry the network of twelve, or fourteen if you count Jenny and myself. I've managed the network on my own for brief periods, but we have quite a number of F.E.P.'s on this upcoming network and that alone would pose a problem. Not so much with Ehrmer, but they do have different mental functions from us. That will be my part since I have dealt with other F.E.P.'s on the network before, and Jenny could have a go at it. If I take up the four F.E.P.'s there would still be eight others, three of whom are first timers. They might be problematic if they're resistant to the network. At best, I figure we need one more person to help and I've got an idea about that.

I'll have to discuss that with Jenny.

The rest of the day has been pretty normal. Had kendo practice with Keiko. She's got me helping out with the juniors now, letting them whack on me for practice, but I get to hit back if they make a mistake. My normal practice with her after finishing with the juniors is more on sparring. After that, she goes over the intricacies of my style in detail, pointing out any mistakes and discussing the moves I did correctly. It's more of a refinement practice since she decided I didn't need anymore formal training. I was fine with that, but I still enjoy practising kendo with her or even Keitaro.

Well, I'm heading off to the pool now.

Jan 30

Just to follow up, I caught up with Jenny over lunch to share my idea of having Sophie learn to work the network, thus making herself available as a back-up to either our network or to Callie and Toni's network, should they need an extra hand. Jenny was apprehensive but not reluctant to the idea. I still need to consult Remington, since he's still the "program manager" for all the network systems we've developed. I've made an appointment to meet with him on the matter tomorrow.

In the meantime, I caught up with Ehrmer and Corogi in his lab last night after dinner. It was to discuss having them on the network, and to lay out the process of determining Corogi's learning centres in her brain, something that might take a number of personal sessions. I did the same thing with Ehrmer a couple of years back, so he backed up what I was explaining to her.

Did the same with Kadi earlier today. I had Becca with me so she could assure Kadi about my intentions. Kadi heard about the network already and was keen on it. Becca reminded me not to use the network for the same idea I put forward the other day, and I promised her I wouldn't; Kadi would be like any other participant on the network.

While I was doing all that, Jenny had to catch up with some of the others to fix a schedule for our test runs. I have yet to approach some of the other newbies and that other F.E.P. on the list. Maybe I'll get Walker to help set up an introduction or something.

Aside from all that, the rest of my classes are getting along as is my work in the Operations Center. It is a little frustrating working there because we still haven't gotten an actual confirmation from that other team about Tomas's signal. Tommy has me back at the usual work of running through the signal feed and putting it through the paces. He did ask what I would do if they would verify the signal was from Tomas. It could only prove Tomas was alive and conscious enough at some point to send the signal, but given the delay of the signal in reaching us, it may not be the case now.

"You should settle for the fact your idea worked," he said. "You came up with a signal that could easily be sent and he responded in the form you expected. Never mind if those guys don't want to believe you. Go with your gut on this."

I had to at least admit that Tommy's argument made sense.

Since Yumana had gone off, Walker asked me to help out with Sunee, who's still interested in practising the aqua-acrobatics. I obliged the other night and will probably do so again later tonight. It's not like she's practising every night. Besides, I still get my own practice with Walker. His reason for asking me was simply this, "I'm trying to avoid giving birth to any rumours that would arise if I were to perform the exercises with her."

Given some of the rumours that went about when I first got into doing the aqua-acrobatics with him, it was reason enough for me, and even Sunee understood. She was willing to have me as a practice partner, and like practising kendo with the juniors, it's something that allows me to practise all the earlier movements. I don't get to do that often with Walker since we've gone so far past all that.

Tomorrow's going to be pretty busy for me, meeting with Remington and then with Linda. Since it's Friday, I have a date with Walker. For now, I'm going to spend some time with him in the pool.

Jan 31

I have some time before my dinner with Walker, so I'm going to cram as much as I can before I have to go. Let's start with last night.

After signing off on my journal, I headed to the pool, expecting to have another aqua-acrobatic practice with Sunee. She wasn't there. Instead, Walker was giving some pointers to Corogi and he asked me to practise some movements with her instead, to which I obliged. It was a different experience. I don't know much about her biology, but Corogi can last underwater longer than I can.

After Corogi and I were done, I did my laps and then had some practice with Walker after Corogi had left. It was almost midnight when we finished and had the whole pool to ourselves. I floated about in the middle of the pool for a while and stared at the night sky above, feeling pretty relaxed and serene, letting all the problems of the day slip away for that brief moment. I then closed my eyes to shut the world away.

What I didn't realise at that point was that I started floating upwards and out of the water, rising above it. I don't know how long that happened, but when I suddenly heard Walker softly calling my name, I opened my eyes and fell into the water. He was there to catch me though. I don't think I was under water for more than a brief moment and next thing I knew, I was in his arms and had mine around his neck.

He asked if I was alright as we moved to the pool's edge and he then told me what happened. It was a weird thing to happen. We both got out of the pool and pretty much brushed off the incident, but it stayed on my mind. It was a first. First time my TK got away from me like that, if it was that. Anyway, I didn't sleep last night and it's not for the lack of trying either. I ended spending the night in my work-room tinkering on Colleen's A.I.

I didn't take in a morning swim and after breakfast, I just headed to class. After class, before lunch, I met with Remington to discuss the possibility of having Sophie train as a back-up on the learning network. It was within his plans to get more of the TP trainees to learn the network. He reminded me that Kevin was also quite willing to learn operating the learning network, although Jenny and I had planned to have Kevin and his TP partner, Bastian, learn up the communication network. Still, it wouldn't hurt to have a third team learning to operate the network.

"Why don't you take Callie and Toni to the next level while bringing on Kevin, Bastian and Sophie at the introductory level," he said. I've been very protective of the network because of the potential problems, but Callie and Toni are ready to move on to guarding for leaks and hacks. So, it was back to discussing that with Jenny.

I really should coordinate all these things better instead of running back and forth.

After lunch was my monthly review session with Linda. She asked how I was getting along with my classes while juggling my activities, my projects and working at the Operations Center. She also reminded me that the work was supposed to be part time, I wasn't required to be there every night and when I did work, I was allowed time-off during the day to recuperate.

Her concern was that I was pushing myself too hard since coming back from my break, going so far as to note that my sleeping pattern was erratic at best. "While you may be sleeping, it's not consistent," she said pointing out that I have been noting the lack of sleep within my recent entries. I used to clock in a few steady hours, maybe two to three hours a night, but it used to be nights in a row. Now I was lucky if I did clock that much two nights in a row, but it wasn't happening, even with the dream-walks I take on Saturday.

I admitted feeling a little stressed, trying to not just catch up but also keep up with my training, jumping around the classes as I needed. She felt therein was the problem. We were both quiet at that point and I tried to recall my schedule of late, the mess of activities and the lack of thought in getting things done, like running around on the whole network thing. She asked, "How are you feeling?"

I looked up into her eyes, pondered a moment and then nodded. I knew the significance of that question around here; a means to evaluate a state of mind. My mind was a bit of a mess right now. Becca has been too busy with Kadi to notice that I was a little off, and making sure I would take time off when such a situation arose.

"You're planning that dreaming thing you do with Walker, aren't you?" Linda asked, and again I just nodded.

"Tonight?"

I nodded. Then, she nodded in return. I knew what she was thinking given the things that happened last year, and to her credit, it was something that didn't need to be said. What she did say was a touch surprising. There was a serious, yet smirky look on her face as she said, "Have fun tonight then."

With that she pretty much dismissed me from her office.

When I got back to my suite to get ready for my dinner with Walker, I noticed an envelope with my name on the kitchenette table. In it, I found twelve new requisition forms and a note that said "Use wisely, -L." I had finished the first set of requisition forms Remington had given me to get new equipment for use on Colleen, and I really hadn't expected anymore. Linda said she would try to get me six more, but it looks like she managed a year's supply.

Right now, I still have about half an hour before I'm supposed to meet with Walker. Better get ready, so… signing off for now.

FEBRUARY

Feb 2

Well, that's one way to get around the rumour mill even if not entirely. There is a lot of speculation going around because... well... what's everyone to think when you follow a dinner date with a trip to the Infirmary to spend the night there? Of course there would be questions.

I had a quick change of clothes before heading out to dinner, borrowing one of Becca's shorter skirts which seemed long enough on me. I still had a slim pair of shorts on under that. Before I left the suite, she took a customary picture – every time I've put on a dress or skirt.

Walker and I met at the café, and he commented that I didn't have to always wear dresses for every date; I didn't last week. I'm sure he recognised the skirt, but didn't say anything. I countered by saying that he didn't always have to wear longs, which he always did to our dinners this year; he smiled and agreed. We'll see what happens next week on that front. He then handed me a single red rose and said, "Here's to tonight going well."

I took the flower with a slight smile and then gave him a peck on the cheek before we sat at a prepared table. I noticed Hank and Carol having dinner together a few tables away and threw a sly smile their way. I had no idea what they expected, but suspected they may have picked up our plans from Sophie. She was there with Will last week when I suggested the idea to Walker. I really tried to be discreet about this idea.

Anyway, dinner was simple with a mix of dishes like before. He's been introducing me to some dishes from his home. He also had the chefs prepare some of the usual food I would have but in smaller quantities in case I couldn't get used to his food. While it didn't look like any kind of food I had ever encountered – and like before, I couldn't really tell what it was made from – I was quite willing to try and actually enjoyed it. It also got me thinking about why I usually see the F.E.P. dining alone during lunches and occasionally during dinner. The sight of the food, while edible and made from our usual range of edible stuff, would probably turn a few appetites off. In Walker's case, so far, a lot of the food may look strange to me, but it's mostly seafood and the occasional poultry; often duck instead of chicken.

During our dinner conversation, he asked if I stopped having dinner with other guys just because I am in a relationship with him. Before the whole relationship bit came about, I was having dinners with a few different guys on rotation, including Keitaro, Paul and Tommy. That was also when I was adamant I wasn't going to pursue any kind of steady relationship with anyone. I told him, when people get into a relationship, they would stick with that one person.

"Is that common, or just you?" he asked.

"I think it's different for each situation or each person," I said. "But I always thought that when you're in a relationship, you don't play around."

He knew I was unsure about all this and it was verified thanks to Hank yelling from his table, "That's crap!" to which I responded by yelling back, "That's rude!" Walker laughed before saying he was okay if I wanted to have dinner with other guys because they were my friends as well. Given that our conversations were being eavesdropped on, I suggested that we hold off on anything else of a sensitive nature until we got into the dream-world, and again, he laughed. We kept our conversation to our projects from that point until we were done with dinner and ready for our first dreaming together.

At the Infirmary, Will had prepared a second bed for Walker next to my usual one. Ms. Phillips wanted to monitor him in case of... anything that might happen on the inside. Will had also set up a privacy screen and said he would be on watch and we would not be disturbed. Walker and I thanked him as he started to apply the patches to Walker so that the machines would monitor him. I didn't need any because the bed I have been using all this time has the function to monitor me. There were some sensors in the bed itself that would monitor my vitals, feeding those readings into a display unit on the extended head-board. There was even a port so that the data could be off loaded to another console, but that's all not really important except to Ms. Phillips and Charlie.

Walker was a little apprehensive because it was the first time we were doing this. I've taken others into my dream-world before and with maybe the exception of Sophie, everyone else came out unscathed. In the year and a half I had been doing this, Walker only asked about it once, but I had never once taken him in until now. It was a strange thing it never happened earlier. There was barely an inch between the two beds so I could reach over to take his hand. I didn't need to, but it felt like the right thing to do in order to comfort him.

I asked him if he was ready. He nodded once and closed his eyes. He didn't say anything but I could feel his hand relax in mine. It felt like he put his trust in me completely, but without saying it out loud at all. I closed my eyes and we were off to my dream-world.

On the flip side of reality, that being the dream-world of mine, we arrived outside of Kinstein's Kitchen. Walker was a little disoriented at the new location and it took him a moment to take in the sights and sounds of the land around us. He was amazed that we had travelled so easily to a whole other world – exactly what he asked me about so long ago – and, technically, we hadn't really travelled. Physically, we were still at The Facility, on the beds within the Infirmary. It was our minds that were linked into a particular environment of my design, for the most part.

Despite saying it's a dream-world or a dream-land, I honestly have no idea how it truly exists, because exist it does even when I'm not sleeping or dreaming. For all I know, it existed before I even came along to create my own world here. That's beside the point in any case. I've never really tried explaining this before.

So, there we were, outside the Kitchen and Walker's trying to get used to the idea that we were in some strange new land. I was a little beside myself at his sense of wonder. It took a while before he even realised we weren't wearing the same clothes we had on at dinner. I was in my typical garb that matched the world and he had about the same, almost a reflection of my clothes. I told him that we had a lot of time to check the place out and I would show him around, but to get started, I had to drag him into the Kitchen and introduce him to Kinstein.

As Kinstein could make anything Walker wanted, he tried by asking for a particular dish, which turned out to be something we had a couple of weeks back. While waiting for the food, Old Crans came up to us with an errand, and it was suited to Walker's talent. We were to retrieve a town leader's pendant from the bottom of a lake. Before we set off, Walker got his dish and found the food to be as good as if it came directly from home. I told him that it would always meet his expectations because it was from his own memory.

Once we were done with the little snack, we set out for the village which was quite a hike away. Once there, determining the location of the pendant was way trickier since that nearby lake was huge. Walker suggested getting some equipment together to create a sort of scope to look into the lake without having to dive in at all locations. He found it quite exciting to work with such "primitive tools" to create something that would have not really belonged within the world. We got a general idea about where to look from that town leader, hopped into a small boat and did a systematic search from the surface. Once we found the pendent (didn't take long), Walker dived to retrieve it.

When we were done and returned the pendant, we had some personal time to ourselves, swimming in the lake. Being in the dream-world, certain rules didn't apply, so when we ended up doing some aqua-acrobatic routines, I could keep up with him without having to constantly break the surface for air, and that was fun. No TK to help me keep up and no specialised suit to help me breathe, I could keep pace even when he picked up speed. The only time I faltered was when he did something new that I hadn't learnt yet, but we didn't mind.

By sunset, we were sitting under a nearby tree, drying off and watching the skies. We talked, and he asked about the time factor. I said it was variable. We had spent about half a day so far but on the outside, it could have been an hour or so, or more than a day, but I felt it was unlikely. It was a lovely evening. We decided to spend the night there and only headed back to the Kitchen at day-break.

The fact that Mikey was there waiting for me meant it was at least Saturday afternoon in the Infirmary. I asked Walker if he wanted to 'wake up' but he said he would stay with me. Mikey was happy to see me and was not as moody as the last couple of visits. He was also happy to meet Walker again. We ended up spending a bit of time together. Mikey told me about what's been going on at home and with his new kindergarten. If I had to guess, he was having problems fitting in at first and was now just getting along there. I'll have to check with Karen or mom on that. I should also note that he's still stammering a bit, searching for the words, but there is a marked improvement. His grammar's not perfect, but it'll get better.

He was also quite taken with Walker and instead of hanging around the Kitchen's back room or the garden out back, we headed down to the brook. Normally I wouldn't, because it is too deep for Mikey but since Walker was with me, I decided the two of us would be able to watch over Mikey better. I, for one, am glad Mikey can get along with Walker.

It was hours later before we finally got back to our reality. Ms. Phillips and Will were there to greet us and the lights were still low in our corner. She was a little concerned because of the length of our 'trip'. It was close to four in the afternoon on Saturday; we had started a little after ten the night before. She checked out Walker first and aside from being a little dehydrated, he was fine. Will led him to the Infirmary's shower so he could freshen up. Once the boys were gone, Ms. Phillips then turned her attention to me.

She asked what went on in the dreaming because as it turned out, some of my readings went a little out of range at some points. It could have been the aqua-acrobatics with Walker. While I had done some swimming within the dream-world, I had not done anything like breaking conventional rules such as breathing just to keep up with Walker. She then pointed out that while Walker's readings were generally stable for the most part, there was only a slight spike at the same time my readings went a little off the scale. She surmised it was a typical stress reading but then commented that I was moaning slightly during that period.

I blushed and then admitted we made out a bit after our swim, but that was as far as we got. As far as I'm aware, it was rare anything that happened within the dream-world would manifest in the real world unless it was traumatic, to say the least. I guess now, the opposite might be true too. Thing is, there was no outward indication of what I went through during that time I was in that coma a few years back. The readings might indicate something happening in the dream-world, but it did not always reflect exactly what is happening. This is the first time I had to suggest a more... heightened... experience to explain the readings to Ms. Phillips. For everything I went through last year, she never once brought up any issues about my readings.

Ms. Phillips needed to verify against my previous readings and while it would be in her report, she wouldn't say anything to anyone about what I admitted to her. In my case, I'm putting it down here and it'll be a while before anyone else reads this, although knowing Carol, she just might get wind of it somehow.

Walker and I left the Infirmary together after his shower and he was still ecstatic about the whole experience. We had a late lunch and talked about our little sojourn before the conversation veered back to the issue about me having dinner with other guys. I guess I was concerned about how that activity would impact our burgeoning relationship. I remember him saying it was all new to him because this kind of relationship just doesn't happen among his people. In a way, it's a break of tradition for him, and I know how important those traditions are to him.

I raised a point he mentioned before, about how when it came to connecting with a partner among his people, it was with a single person and for life with the purpose of procreation. He countered that since he was here at The Facility to learn not only about the science but culture as well, this was as good as any learning experience in the way we, as people, would connect with each other on a more personal level. My feeling, and I said so to him, was that I was probably not the best example for such a situation, but it didn't matter to him. It was the experience and I had often been his consultation point on these matters over the last couple of years. To think of it, it's almost two years since I tried to explain the intricacies of dating to him on our first 'date', if I want to call it that.

We left it at that in the end. He recommended I carry on with my friends as I have, including the occasional dinner with other guys. We would still do the typical couple things like a fixed dinner date on Fridays. I don't know if the swimming with each other every night counts as we've been doing that since... well, I can't remember when we started. We still met up at the pool later in the night. I think it was obvious to Sunee that our dynamic in the pool had changed dramatically. In helping her with the aqua-acrobatics, pulling off demonstrations with him had a different air. Even I felt we clicked better, and he was smiling at me quite a bit after some of the demonstrations. Heck, I wasn't too shy about giving him a kiss before we got out of the pool for the night.

The rumours were pretty light today. No one really bugged me about anything; not about the date or the dream-walk or even our little pool antics the night before. Carol and Helen were teasing a little, but I haven't really said anything to them. The only person I shared with so far is Becca, and even then, I kept it as clean as I could manage – pretty much what I've written so far – without too many embellishments.

I'm off to the pool for some laps.

Feb 4

It's been a busy few days although I think I'm doing okay enough in classes. It's gradually getting tougher with all sorts of equations and theories getting longer and more complicated, but I'm managing. I think. Every time I take a little break, I always have hard time catching up and I think by now, I'm there... again. I just have to keep pace, ask questions where I need to and consult or rely on my friends on occasions. They helped a lot last year and they know I'm not as bright as they are, but I've got some smarts in other areas – programming and A.I. – so I'm not quite the moron I constantly appear to be.

On the flip-side of the learning, I'm apparently moving on to teaching now. I've been working with Sophie for some months now, helping her to control and apply her TP. Well, now I'm going to take her, Kevin and Bastian onto the Learning Network. I'll still be working with Jenny on that while she's still supervising Callie and Toni on their network, and taking on Ethan as her trainee. On that end, I'll be only advising Jenny there and I was told to turn Ethan away if he ever skipped out on Jenny in favour of getting my help.

It has gotten to a point where Miss Tracy is leaving all that to Jenny and me in order to focus helping the few other TPs. Taking everyone into account, Jenny and I have six TPs in our care, that leaves Miss Tracy with the remaining five. Yeah, it's an odd number considering we're usually paired up, but that lone wolf is Carl who no one really wants to partner with. Both Sophie and Ethan are technically without partners, although Ethan was paired with Carl last year. After that mess, well, Remington's not having them paired up again.

All of us have issues with Carl, and I guess I'm partly to blame. He's also the reason I've been slightly reluctant about having more people on the Learning Network. However, as Miss Tracy, Remington, Linda and several others have told me, I've got to have some trust in my colleagues to have the sensibility to do the right thing.

So, I guess I should mention that Ethan's officially back at The Facility since Monday. He's got some of the normal classes like Sociology as well as TK, but he's got some personal tutoring going on because everything else is mostly too advanced for him. I think they have him on basic Biology, Chemistry and Physics; and if so, I wonder if I can get in on that. I could do with some refreshing on the basics.

Anyway... Walker and I still connect at the pool every night, but we've been keeping things clean and civil, more out of courtesy I would say. There aren't a lot of people in relationships within The Facility – like Will and Sophie; or Jenny and Kevin, who have only been seeing more of each other recently – so we're not trying to rub it in, so to speak.

Well, that's about it, I guess. I know everything is generally in broad strokes and I'm also leaving out quite a bit. I've been maintaining a steady two and a half hours each night so far since Sunday, so I guess that's good.

Gonna dip in the pool now and then check in at the Operations Center later.

Feb 5

Ethan appears to be fitting in and he doesn't seem to be giving Jenny any trouble. He's joining her in his original class, the same one with Callie and Toni. Despite being separated for most of the time, Jenny and I still try to catch up, and confer with Miss Tracy on our trainees. We've haven't had any practices between ourselves for a while now, not since developing the Communications Network. Thing is, we're doing quite a bit with our trainees, particularly with

Sophie for me and Ethan for her, that we're in no real danger of slacking off our own TP practice.

Since Tuesday, Jenny and I have been going around getting in touch with the potential network participants. We needed to put together a schedule for the test sessions preceding the actual run. Given how Callie and Toni ran their test sessions last year, we determined that it wasn't necessary for everyone to make it to each session we were planning, but we needed at least two sessions at the end where everyone had to participate. That was more for Jenny and me than for the participants. At this point, we've got almost everyone save for three more. While Jenny had approached John, neither of us is willing to approach Carl about getting his available times.

While Carl was there at the beginning in helping us develop the network, he has not officially been part of any network that we've run. At least, not in the current incarnation of the Learning Network. Some people are aware of his involvement at the beginning, and I wonder, if they know he's on board now, would they still be willing to participate?

Meanwhile, I did get in touch with the last F.E.P. on our list, with a little help from Ehrmer. She's called Laurie – yes, it doesn't sound very alien and even I was taken by surprise at first, but then Becca and Callie's suite-mate, Jo, have got fairly normal sounding names as well. One F.E.P. I knew but who has since left, was called Fred. Anyway, it's an adopted name and her real name is far different, and unpronounceable; I tried. She had heard about the network and is a little apprehensive, but willing to give it a try after some encouragement from Ehrmer. I explained the need to map her thought patterns and learning centres, and aside from Ehrmer, I would be doing the same with the other F.E.P. on the network.

I've got my work cut out, diving into at least two unknown minds. Kadi's mind should be similar to Becca's so while I will have to map her as well, it shouldn't be a big problem. Still, shouldn't take for granted it'll be a cakewalk just because I've done it before.

Anyway, once we get everyone's schedule, Jenny and I need to work out a timetable to get as many people involved in our test sessions over the next month and a half, especially the first-timers. The field trip is scheduled for March 25, and I'm going to start with the F.E.P participants first, from next week. That's on top of the other TP activities I have to be involved in. In a way, I guess it's also good I'm managing well enough in my other classes right now.

At Linda's suggestion, I'm also fixing my time at the Operations Center to three times a week to balance things out; Sunday, Tuesday and Thursday nights – or Monday, Wednesday and Friday very early mornings, if you want to be finicky. It keeps from clashing with my Friday nights with Walker or Saturday with Mikey. Tommy's agreeable with the schedule, reminding me that I'm supposed to be learning and working there on a part-time basis.

The thing about the data stream, before I started out last year, it was a singular burst accompanied by a code locked message for me. At the time, it was the only signal from Tomas. Since I started at the Operations Center, the burst was confirmed to be from his computers, not his normal communications system. There have been additional bursts of data from time to time. So, based on that, I asked Tommy if Mission Control did have some kind of link to Tomas, or if they actually had a lock on his supposed location, especially if they are receiving data transmissions.

He confirmed that Tomas's ship was back on the telemetry scope but there have been no actual communications from Tomas directly beyond the 'glitched' response late last year. Redundant independent onboard sensors were programmed to take external readings and stream the data back to Mission Control. He also mentioned that no one is really willing to make any changes to the programming unless it was absolutely vital to the mission. It again made me think about how Tomas might be viewed as just a component in the overall scheme of things; a component that may have malfunctioned but has not adversely impacted the rest of the mission.

"There are others who are worried about him as well," Tommy said. "Leave that worrying to them and you focus on what you need to do."

When I think back about it, it's kinda monumental. I got to know Tomas... it's been two years now. That means at best, he's been out there, on his own, for over two years. The likelihood of getting home is minuscule to impossible, maybe even not at all. As far as I know, it's supposed to determine if we humans would ever be capable of truly making it out there on our own, alone in the darkness.

And I have to wonder if this is my future...

Feb 7

Let's do some catching up.

Jenny met with the last two first-timers, accompanied by John. He had been helpful before with getting reluctant participants on board, so I suggested having him along. On my end, I asked Remington to accompany me in approaching Carl. He refused, saying I should be able to keep a handle on things there and not let anything spiral out of control. Well, it went as well as I could hope, picking lunch in full view of witnesses as a time to approach him. He already knew he was going to be on the network for the field trip so he knew we had to approach him some time. He was really smug about it.

He knew why I was meeting with him. I asked for his available times in order to work out a schedule with the other participants and he said he would be readily available for whatever times I chose to schedule the sessions. I repeated my request for his available times stating that everyone else was required to do so and I walked away with my lunch. To be honest, I hoped he would pull something like a mind probe or a mental blast, but he didn't do anything. It would have been a nice excuse to drop him from the sessions though.

Jenny joined us for lunch yesterday when I approached Carl in the café, and thanked me for including John in the 'recruitment', saying he was a big help. She ended it all by saying, "You should do something nice for him," except she didn't recommend anything.

"Can't really think of anything," I said, and Helen suggested giving him another rematch. "I should thank him by beating him up?" I asked.

"That last rematch didn't quite get started, did it?" she said. "I mean, if I recall correctly, it wasn't really him fighting, or didn't you write that down somewhere."

John and I had two fights last year and both technically resulted with no winner. I was not curious to find out who is the better fighter. I spend enough time doing that with Keiko every other day except Saturday.

Anyway, we left it at that and I guess John will have something in mind in the end. I don't think Jenny told him it was my idea to get his help. It was only after lunch when Sophie approached me about her and Will joining Walker and me for dinner. I told her I was fine having dinner together and had already shared my suspicions with Walker a couple of days back that it was coming; he was fine with the idea – so there.

Dinner was more a small gathering of friends than a double date. Walker and me on one side of the table, facing Sophie and Will on the other side. Food was nothing too fancy, mostly at Sophie's request. It seems she wanted to try out more Penang food via our chefs. Good thing I've got a high metabolic rate and a fairly active lifestyle, because she went a little overboard even by my standards. Walker stuck to the safer stuff, which were mostly seafood, although he did try some chicken curry with rice.

To her credit, she steered clear of any discussions about our activities last week, but she did bring up the whole dream-world trip thing. I haven't taken her back there since the incident last year. Until now, she hasn't really asked me about going back for another trip.

"I know we got up to some pretty weird stuff over there, but no one really knows anything about what actually happens unless you write about it," she said. "Even when I was on my own doing my own thing, you really didn't know what I was up to, right?"

It was the first time she talked openly about that particular time, but I said she was right. I didn't want to push the issue. Things do happen there I'm not normally aware of. I could be late to Mikey, and I wouldn't know what he would be doing while waiting for me. I suppose if I really wanted to, I could know but I'm not even sure if it's possible. Even Walker chimed in, arguing that while the whole dream-world could conceivably exist within my own mind – if it actually did – the possibility of knowing one's own mind completely is currently inconceivable.

Sophie wasn't too interested in all that. "Actually, I'm more curious about the sense of privacy over there," she said. That was when it hit me what she was actually asking for.

If she really wanted to take a trip back to the dream-world, I had to make sure she remembered the rules. "You know how it works over there, right? If you are required to do something, you really have to get that done, or there will be some consequences," I said.

"So, if we get a little task to do, get it done and out of the way first," she said.

"She really wants to do this, doesn't she?" Walker asked me directly.

"Do what?" Will asked.

At my urging, Sophie laid out her plan. Will seemed partly intrigued at the notion. I think he understood what was being proposed to him. After all, he's the one who usually watches over me whenever I go on my dream-walk within the Infirmary on Saturday afternoons. To him, it was more of a meditation session instead of what I claimed it to be. Whether he believed I was in another world was a whole other case, and what Sophie was asking him to do was to take that leap into the unknown, at least from his point of view.

Walker offered that it was quite an experience and encouraged Will to give it a try. My concern was not the 'experience' of the dream-world or the privacy Sophie is after, but more on the activities and nature of that world. I sure as heck didn't want another incident that would... scar... another friend. I suppose that's not quite the right word. Sophie got lucky, and maybe in some way, so did Ethan.

In any case, Sophie getting Will to agree to a trip to my dream-world was also contingent on me agreeing to take them along, not to mention what Remington, Linda or even Ms. Phillips would say about it. The whole dream-walk exercise was something for me to get a hold of whatever mental issues I had, be it with the sleeping problems, my mood swings or even concentration in certain aspects. Some of the dream-walks had specific purposes, albeit metaphorically, to help me adjust to either physical or mental problems. Occasionally, running off to the dream-world was similar to taking a break from the confines of The Facility. Taking people along sometimes helped, but if they got caught up with the tasks I had to perform, lack of completion usually led to more problems. It wasn't always the case.

I had to spell it out for Sophie, reminding her how important it was to make sure any task handed out by Old Crans, if he had any, required attention.

"So long as it doesn't require your help, I'll gladly do it," she said. "Or if I have to help you and maybe return the favour?"

It was the way she said it, with a grin that made me remember exactly as she said it. I was all the more willing to let her take her 'revenge' if it came to that. It's water under the bridge now and hopefully it'll never flow this way again.

We arranged for the trip next weekend. It's probably a little too far off for Sophie's liking, but it was the best time since I usually have a light Saturday. It also gives us some time to negotiate our G/Cs and Ms. Phillips, who will not be too pleased. We then caught a late movie before calling it a night.

After the movie, Walker escorted me back to my suite. I invited him in, but he declined, saying it would give rise to too many rumours and speculation, but I didn't care anymore. We were officially a couple, so it shouldn't matter if he did come over or not.

He smiled, saying it was late and perhaps next time. He leaned in and gave me a kiss, leaned his forehead against mine (I had my eyes closed) for a moment, and then said good-night.

After he left, I tried to get some sleep, but couldn't. A quick change of clothes and I headed off to work on Colleen for the rest of the night. Yeah, I didn't sleep last night or this morning and I don't feel any different. I'm gonna head out for breakfast now and then take in a revision class. Still have my dream-walk later to catch up with Mikey.

Feb 9

Classes go on every day at The Facility and including the weekends. Most of the trainees take on a lighter schedule during the weekends so most of the classes do a weekly revision. It's useful when you need to do a catch-up or check in with the tutors or even ask for clarification in my case. I take in a morning review on Saturdays and then my afternoons are spent with Mikey.

On Sundays, I take in whichever classes I can manage and treat them like any other day of the week, it's never the same classes each Sunday because of the number of classes I have to cover.

Except last Sunday afternoon because I caught up with that new guy I mentioned before, that A.I. expert from wherever. He was in the programming class on Sunday morning and I snagged him for lunch with the gang. The first thing that got me mixed up at first was his name, Nikolai, but he goes by Nik around here. I figured he was from one of the Russian federations but he's actually Malaysian born. His mom is Malaysian. He didn't share anything much in that area during orientation.

I asked him why he was taking the programming class on the weekend since he was supposed to be working in A.I.. He was trying to get into the flow of The Facility's programming language. I mentioned I was working in A.I. as well and then asked him to join me for lunch. I didn't mention there were others as well.

I ended up introducing him to Carol, Helen, Keiko, Keitaro, Callie, Jo, Toni and Ethan, and then left an open invitation for him to join us any time. We chatted over A.I. systems, traded a few ideas and methodology. He's using C-sharp in his programming which would allow other common systems to adopt his A.I. if he wants to get it out there. My learning The Facility's programming language was more in order to configure some of my own programs to be of use on The Facility's system. It was his purpose as well. In all that, I kept Colleen my secret.

After lunch, I checked in on Colleen and did some tinkering. The few ideas Nik shared had potential if I could adapt them, I guess. Then again, I don't want to use his ideas on my system without letting him know about Colleen in the first place.

The new and authentic heat sinks and cooling systems have been installed into Colleen although some of the heat sinks I made last year are still working well enough. Some of the newer projectors I got are doing a far better job with the holographic interface than what I had to work with before. I probably need more holographic images to be sure because all I've got are the few images from Francine and those of Mikey. They don't look as good as what I've got on my mini-projector that's in my room. Still, based on what I've got right now, crude as it is, it's actually functional enough for some basic purposes of interaction.

I caught up with Jenny for dinner to work out a schedule for our network test runs. I think we've got something decent worked out to accommodate everybody, including Carl. The first session is a week and a half away but at best, I'll be working with Corogi first by Thursday.

I'm heading for breakfast now and then it's off to classes.

Feb 11

Word's been getting around about this new pseudo-superhero movie playing in our internal mini theatre. It's not a typical superhero movie but it had people with psychic abilities. It's brought up some interesting discussions in TP and TK training, after I was dragged there by Sophie and Will. Sophie will latch onto any new uses for her abilities and this movie focusses on some varied uses of TK and TP abilities.

Most of what turned up on screen are general perceptions of what we can do with our abilities, and some beyond like those tests I wasn't keen on taking last year. I don't think we can use our abilities to rapidly heal people, and I've been tested on precognition too. The use of TK was flashy, enhanced by special effects. While there were some ingenious applications featured, we know from some experience not all of them will work in real life, like a TK shield, not to the extent in the movie.

Sophie may want to try anything she saw in that movie, but I think she's sensible enough to not go off in that direction. She hasn't brought any of it up though, so hopefully it hasn't crossed her mind to try. I would hope the same applies to everyone else in TP and TK training although I can't guard over all of them, even if I'm currently partly responsible for training most of them now.

Speaking of which, Ethan's been showing some progress in the TK department, so it looks like he's regaining some control back. After the mess of last year, it appeared his TK had gone temporarily dormant. It's back to normal now. Jenny's had nothing but good things to say about his TP training. As she reported, he's been performing quite well with the given exercises and is also allowing her to monitor him when he's practising blocking; that's when he's supposed to block out other people's stray thoughts or excess noise and not eavesdrop. He appears to be fitting in well enough and seems to have a decent aptitude for the basic sciences. I don't think I've seen him more relaxed or comfortable being at The Facility.

I'm still sparring with Keiko. Despite saying she wasn't going to teach me anything new in terms of my proper kendo training, she has been sharing some new moves and techniques, and has me sparring with Keitaro more often; both sessions this week so far. In terms of ranking, he's far ahead of me. I don't know if he's holding back, but I seem to be holding my own during the sparring. Although Keiko said I wasn't really required to vehemently stick to kendo rules when sparring with her brother, I did my best to stay within what I was taught, occasionally trying something new I picked up from either sibling.

I think it was more for Keiko to observe my style of fighting because as far as hand-to-hand or kendo is concerned, she is still, by far, better than me. When it comes to weapons sparring, I'm still trouncing her butt; kendo being the exception, and that's a bit of a puzzle she's brought up before. I can beat her with other weapons – granted we are using wooden replicas – but not with the *shinai*. At best guess, we have different mentality association with the weapons we are using.

"I know you're supposed to be something like a grandmaster in kendo, so maybe I don't expect I can beat you," I said. "When it comes to the other equipment, I don't know what you're good at, but I know I can handle those."

"Knowing is half the battle, but that doesn't really apply here," she said. "We both know what we're capable of ourselves and what the other is capable of, but you still constantly surprise me."

In any case, we both had the same suspicion and I've asked Jenny to assist in tomorrow's sparring session. She's agreed to monitor Keiko and me when we spar to see if I'm actually reading her moves or not. I doubt it, even on a subconscious level. It's also not likely Keiko is projecting her moves. At best, if I'm right, Jenny's going to find both our minds to be totally blank during the sparring session.

I'm heading off to the pool now to unwind, clear my head a little.

Feb 12

Keiko and I did more than simple sparring today. I should also note I'm writing this from the Infirmary where Ms. Phillips insisted on keeping Keiko and me for the night. More precisely, it was Keiko who needed to spend the night for observation and I was encouraged to do the same, if anything, to keep her company. It wasn't that our fights were brutal, but we did whack each other pretty hard. After all, we were wearing the kendo gear for all three fights, or portions of the armour for the last two fights. It was as close to no holds barred as we could get, but we really needed to determine if what we guessed would happen was really happening... and we got some interesting results.

For the record, I wasn't reading her mind and she wasn't broadcasting any thoughts. Jenny confirmed that during the various fights, both of us were not even thinking, at least not in the conventional sense. Between the fights however was a different case as we were apparently assessing ourselves and each other. Jenny said she picked a lot of concern from me, especially after each sparring session.

We covered kendo first followed by hand-to-hand and ended with weapons sparring. Jenny was particularly impressed by the way our minds would clear when we take the ready positions at the start of each round. She likened it to an old CRT television being turned off when all the sound, all the noise would switch off and there was a singular focus to the moment at hand. That was soon followed by an awareness encompassing everything. That's all she could verbally describe. She said it was an amazing transition, unlike anything she had ever encountered. I suppose is something unique to trained fighters. I wouldn't particularly call myself that, but I know the mind-set we get into when we fight, and she got to glimpse that in Keiko and me at the same time.

Just to be clear, we checked in at the Infirmary after the fights because despite the protective gear, we were pretty tough on each other. I may have been a little rougher during the last fight and bruised Keiko in the ribs, striking her a little past the *bogu, again!* Ms. Phillips did a preliminary check on her first and once she felt Keiko was fine, she did a check on me while Keiko took a quick shower in the Infirmary's bathroom. When it was my turn to use the shower, Ms. Phillips did a more thorough check on Keiko and confirmed the bruising I gave her. After Ms. Phillips finished with her examinations, Will brought in some dinner for all of us to share. We then got to analysing our little experiment as Jenny shared her observations.

During the kendo sparring, Keiko's focus was more on me and simply watching my movements. She was more attuned to the little nuances in my movements with particular attention to the tip of my *shinai,* while being focussed on me overall. It kinda helped to understand how she was reading an opponent's movements in kendo. Apparently, there was more to it that even Jenny couldn't fully articulate, but between Keiko and me, we understood what she was getting at. On my end, she said I was equally focussed in almost the same way Keiko was, but not as attuned. My concentration not only focussed on my opponent, but all around as well. It was like I was aware of being observed but not quite to the same point of being distracted by my surroundings.

During the hand-to-hand fight, Jenny said our awareness and focus were almost aligned. In a way, it seemed both of us were equally attuned to each other's movements, reading each other's moves, foreseeing what was likely to come next and adapting to changes as it happened. It would account for my being able to hold my own against Keiko these days. Keiko maintained that I am still a defensive fighter, but admitted I have improved in taking the offensive position. We traded quite a few blows, but she still landed far more punches than I did. For this fight, we had removed the *men* and *bogu* portions of the kendo armour but kept the *koté*.

When it came around to the weapons sparring, things changed. She was using her *bokkun,* something she's exceptionally skilled with, while I settled for a control baton, the one with the cross handle, in my right hand, and a kukri replica in my left. Keiko also put on her full armour while I took off the *koté* so as to have a better grip on my weapons. According to Jenny, this was where things went a little weird. While Keiko basically had the same mentality and focus during all three sparring sessions, mine changed through all three sessions. While I appeared to have some focus during the first two sessions, Jenny said that I blanked out completely during the weapons sparring. Simply put, it was a situation where Keiko could not read any of my movements, and I was apparently a mindless fighting machine from Jenny's perspective. I was more on the offensive and despite her own skill with her *bokkun,* I apparently pounded her pretty badly in retaliation for the first two rounds.

Of course, I wasn't a complete mindless fighting machine, I just seemed that way. Jenny said my mind was all over the place and nowhere at the same time. She found it really difficult to describe what she saw or felt. Even at Keiko's urging, the most she could come up with was that I was running on pure instinct while sensing everything around me. She didn't pick up any signs of my TP abilities kicking in at all.

Jenny confirmed I wasn't reading Keiko's mind during the sparring and Keiko wasn't broadcasting any movements in advance. I always thought that she, like those old samurai warriors, would consider a fight in her head before making a move, picturing the battle being won before even the first strike is made, but Jenny didn't pick up on that. So, consequently, if I were to face off against John again, he can at least be assured I wouldn't be using my psychic abilities to win the fight.

In the end, Jenny found the experience quite illuminating. She had never willingly scanned two minds the way she did with us – even with our permission – just to see how we think, act, react and focus during our sparring. It wasn't going to make her take up any kind of fighting skill though. The issue about my mentality during the final round was the only mysterious quantity with no real answer to why I was like that for that one fight and not the others. Keiko, for one, is very curious to find out if I could actually apply that mentality to either kendo or our hand-to-hand sessions. *"Mushin,"* she muttered, without explanation. We talked things out at length after Jenny left and she thinks that I may be a far superior fighter than she is, but only in a given situation.

I hoped she wasn't going to manufacture that particular situation simply to test me.

I'm pretty tired right now. I guess the fight took quite a bit out of me, so I'm gonna knock off for now. Still pretty early though. It's barely midnight.

Feb 14

Before I get on with today's planned trip to my dream-world, I want to write about this. When I signed off last time, it was just about midnight on Thursday, and feeling pretty worn out. I had powered down my console unit when Walker dropped by. I hadn't gone to the pool and I didn't tell him about the experiment Keiko and I planned on, but he heard from Jenny that I was in the Infirmary. Apparently she dropped by the pool to inform him and I was appreciative of it; I told her so when I got out of the Infirmary yesterday.

Anyway, Walker dropped by the Infirmary that night to check on me and to find out what happened. I did my best to explain what Keiko, Jenny and I were up to and why. It wasn't quite what I had written in the journal, missing out on a ton of details, but he understood. He rephrased it as a social experiment dealing with perception within the intricacies of a duel, adding that there was no real benefit to derive from such an experiment except to the fighters. I could only smile in response because it was just like him to find the experiment and learning experience in every situation, trying to analyse my actions.

Tired as I was, I didn't chase him away, but we kept talking. When I tried to stifle a yawn, he started to excuse himself to let me sleep, but I asked him to stay. More precisely, I asked him to lie with me and keep me company for a while longer. I shuffled over a little to give him some space on the single bed and he let me cuddle up to him. I slowly laid my head on his chest and he put his arm around me. I admitted I hadn't really had a solid night's sleep in a while.

I haven't been writing about it, but up to that point, my sleeping times have been pretty irregular. The most I managed in the few days since my uneventful dream-walk was no more than an hour to maybe ninety minutes, tops. It didn't matter when I was trying to get to sleep or when I actually did fall asleep. Even after Ms. Phillips ran her tests on me, there was no real indication anything was wrong.

Walker didn't say anything in response to my comment, but instead he started stroking my back. I closed my eyes and listened to the slow and strange rhythm of his heartbeat – if it was his heart that I was hearing. For as much as his physiology may seem similar to ours, I had no idea if he was anywhere as biologically similar. All I know is there was this steady slow rhythm pounding away in his chest that didn't sound like a normal thump-thump heartbeat rhythm. That, added with the gentle stroking he did, somehow made me fall asleep. I don't know how long it took, but I may have been really tired from the day's activities.

Solid deep sleep for close to maybe seven hours.

When I woke up, he was gone. I still don't know when he had left during the night. He only asked how I was feeling when we happened to cross paths on the way to class. I was feeling more refreshed than normal and I said so adding, "Thank you for keeping me company last night." He smiled in return and then said that he would see me later for dinner – it was Friday after all. We were off to our respective classes then when he turned and asked if we should call off dinner for the night. When I asked him why, he reminded me Saturday was Valentine's Day. I was aware of it, and we did plan on spending some time in the dream-world, away from prying eyes.

"Nothing wrong with dinner tonight and again tomorrow night," I said. He took a moment to consider and then agreed that we would stick to our normal plan for dinner.

The rest of the day went as normal. There was not even a peep from either Carol or Helen about Walker and me in the Infirmary together. Keiko didn't say anything, which made me wonder what time she woke up, and if she did see Walker. I filled Becca in over lunch, but spoke to her in her own language, totally forgetting that Kadi was there. She had questions for Becca about Walker and me, but at least she didn't ask the others or even tried to practise her English that way. I'll have to be a little more careful next time. Kadi's a new factor to consider.

When dinner rolled around, Walker had a topic of discussion all ready. I suppose I should have seen it coming given it was the first Friday thirteenth we were sharing. I'm not one for superstitions, but I did my best to answer his questions about the day and why people deemed it such an unlucky day. I admitted not knowing the origins or reasons for the day and the number. My offer to look it up for him seemed redundant as he had done his own research.

I managed to tell him what little I know about how the Chinese people don't like numbers involving number four. It was common enough around Penang, so I had some passing knowledge on that at least.

For no particular reason, I filled him in on my session with Corogi on Thursday morning. It was a little problematic to lock down her learning process, and I had to schedule another session with her on Monday. Her thought patterns were also extremely guarded, which was unusual because it would indicate some mental abilities in her, but no one has actually said anything in that respect. I asked him if he heard anything about Corogi being potentially psychic, and he suggested I ask her directly. He didn't seem too eager to go in that area. It was just talk.

I'm about to run late for my dream-trip. I'm dropping in to see Mikey as usual, and Walker is coming along again. I'm also supposed to take Sophie and Will along, but I've got another plan for that at the moment. People have found their own way to my dream-world before, so maybe it's time I helped Sophie do that instead of me taking her each time.

Back later.

Feb 16

The dream-world, or the dream-land, the dreamscape, or whatever you want to call it; how and why it exists is beyond my knowledge. I didn't create it, but I moulded it to my needs. It's there, and there is a purpose for its existence, at least for me. People have found their own way there before. Ethan did it on his own last year, maybe Sophie could do it too.

Ms. Phillips wasn't too pleased with our antics but agreed to let us be as long as we used the beds and monitoring devices. We ended up using three beds while I took the chair, so she was only left with two spare beds. I can go in to the dream-world and basically get out again at any time – although it's not usually a good thing. What I had Sophie do was to monitor me as I went in once and came out again on my own. This allowed her to 'feel out' my process, so to speak. I arrived outside the Kitchen as usual and then 'woke up' almost immediately.

Then, I monitored her as she took Will in. To make things a little easier, they both got into separate beds first and I had them hold hands. He closed his eyes first as if he was going to sleep and then she would dive into the dream-world, taking him along. Essentially, she would only be guiding his thoughts towards the dream-world. She knew to picture the Kitchen as her target point and I would meet her there. That's a conscious act, as much as it can be defined and why, in my case, I'm not usually considered to be asleep during my trips. When I was sure she was off, I took Walker in with me. It's not to say it would have worked because for all I know, she could have landed in her own dream-world, one of her own making.

Thankfully – really – she was at the Kitchen when I got there with Walker. Will, being the newcomer, was naturally amazed at the situation noting that everything had a specific texture, from the feel of the clothes to the wood grain of the furniture and even the smells of the tavern itself despite the knowledge that it's just a dream-world that he got taken into. While he talked things out with Walker, sharing notes and all that, I did a little checking of my own with Sophie. Once I was sure she was okay having made the trip on her own, and giving her a means of contacting me in case of any problems, I checked in with Kinstein.

As far as he knew, everything was fine and while Old Crans had been dropping by once in a while, there was nothing in particular for me to take care of. It happens on occasion. Not every trip I make requires me to fix something. He also informed me that Mikey was already waiting for me. I asked Kinstein to take care of Sophie, Will and Walker, and then went to check on Mikey.

I spent a while with Mikey alone in his room at the back of the Kitchen, catching up with his progress at school and how things are at home. It's great that we get to talk instead of him struggling and babbling while I do most of the talking. I still have to mind my own vocabulary though. He said Karen is letting him watch his favourite cartoons with all the giant robots and such. I'll leave it to her to be sensible about the content because those series tend to get pretty racy these days with their fan service. He's taken a liking to *Eureka 7* and their sky surfing robots – out of my own DVD collection – although he still likes the Gundam robots.

When we finally came out of the back room to join the others. Sophie, Will and Walker were still there having some drinks and snacks. Walker was having something that didn't look like anything familiar, which I guessed was something from his own memory. Mikey greeted Walker and Sophie properly but he wasn't familiar with Will.

Since Old Crans didn't turn up, Sophie and Will headed off on their own. I gave her a general direction to a lakeside village; not the same one Walker and I had been to before. That left Walker and me with Mikey for the duration. It was probably a couple of hours more before he headed home and then it was just us. Walker was enjoying himself with the food in particular, even with the realisation it wasn't as real as it could be. The taste of it and the sensation of eating it was somewhat valid to a point, although he would be hungry again when we left the dream-world. At that time, it was a satisfyingly full meal.

I told him there was something else I wanted to try, but it would take some effort on our part. He was curious, but I kept it a surprise then. When we left the Kitchen – and still no sign of Old Crans, which meant no little side job – there was a pair of winged horses waiting outside. He was a little nervous about riding them, but I assured him that it was safe. I couldn't hold his hand all the way nor could we really share a horse. Once he seemed comfortable enough, we took to the skies.

I suppose I could have flown us, even without any psychic abilities because it is a dream-world after all, but it was nicer to let the winged horses take us. It's been ages since I rode them and taking flight like that was so much fun. They do have a mind of their own at times and they're not always accommodating. Like the jellyfish, even these animals seemed to have some kind of respect for Walker, nervous as he was around them. I told him such creatures did not exist in the real world, not that it gave him any comfort. He's very much a land-based person, uncomfortable in the sky.

We headed towards a border that seemed like some empty land. The closer we got to it, the more the empty land began to resemble an ocean, even though there never was any in the first place. We landed on the beach and then the horses left. We took in the sights and once Walker felt comfortable enough, I explained what I had planned; my little Valentine gift to him. He was a little taken aback but was willing to give it a try.

With his eyes closed and a slight probing of his mind, I had him imagine what his home was like; the one in his dreams. He previously mentioned about living near water, so being near a large body of water like this sea served my purpose. I didn't have it in mind if his home would have been on the coast or out on the water itself, but once he imagined it in his mind, I had something to work with. The more details he could give me, the more accurately I could recreate what he had in mind. I'm no real architect but when I was done and he opened his eyes again, he was pretty impressed I had a piece of his world sitting on the edge of mine.

What was once an empty beach now had a cliff face reaching out into the water. Partly etched into that cliff face was the dwelling sitting partly in the water. I said, "Go ahead," and he ran out into the water, dived into the waves and swam towards the dwelling. I coasted over the water, flying behind Walker. He moved so fast in the water and I suspect it's his natural speed, which means when he's in the pool or when he's pacing me, he's really slowing himself down.

The rest of the trip, well... let's just say that we frolicked about in the water, made out a little under the stars and generally spent the night at the dwelling doing a little intimate exploring without really getting to the down and dirty – I know it was Valentine's after all, but that's no excuse to go all the way either. Intimacy was a bit of an issue at the moment and both of us still don't feel all that comfortable to go to that next step. I'll admit there's a part of me that's curious enough, and at the same time I'm trying to be cautious about it. I also know he's got some issues about being in that kind of intimate relationship because there's a different connotation among his people. One thing we did agree on, given the short period of time we've been officially together, our relationship is, on all accounts, an experiment. Because Walker is a F.E.P., we couldn't really be in this for the long term. Sooner or later, he will be heading home.

We didn't spend the whole night at the dwelling. We spent a long time together, but we didn't sleep there. Walker felt hungry so I flew us back to the Kitchen and then left the dream-world. It had been barely five hours since we left, despite spending more than twice that time on the other side. Walker gave me a slight kiss before heading off to the Infirmary's bathroom for a quick shower. While he was gone, I asked Ms. Phillips if I showed any signs of inappropriate behaviour like last time. She said I appeared to shift restlessly in the chair, but that was it; no little moaning like last time.

Sophie and Will were still in their beds, off in the dream-world. Since they weren't back yet, I told Ms. Phillips I would check on them later. I wasn't planning on heading back to the suite tonight anyway as I had already arranged with Becca to leave the suite to her and Steven. Before I left the Infirmary, Ms. Phillips asked if I could do a quick scan on Sophie to determine if she was still in the dream-world. While I could try, I wouldn't know for sure what to look for.

"Whoever you had to scan me before while I was off in the dreaming, that's who you would need," I said. I then asked if Callie had ever done it, but no one had actually scanned me when I was off on my trips according to her. While the scanners Will and Sophie were hooked up to were showing they were in the dream-world, she said she would feel a little more comfortable if there was some way to know for sure. I told her I would help to keep an eye on Sophie and Will if they still weren't out of their little dream trip by eleven that night.

Walker and I headed off for dinner then. We had some light dishes this time, like some salads with fruits and soup instead of the usual meat dishes I would tend to order. Walker wanted to hit the pool later. He would probably have a slightly heavier snack before turning in.

He thanked me for the gift and apologised for not having anything prepared this year. He also reminded me that it was our third Valentine's dinner together, and it made me think back to that first dinner. It was a coincidence that we happened to have that meal on that day, and it wasn't really as a couple, just two trainees who were alone and decided to share a meal after a swim. Honestly, I wasn't keeping track. We spent most of our after dinner conversation reminiscing about some of our close calls – usually my fault – and some of the more tender moments that would eventually bring us together.

It was more than an hour later when we finally parted ways. He headed to the pool and I headed back to the Infirmary to check on Sophie and Will. It was nearly eleven when I got there and they were still in the dream-world. I was a little worried, not a lot but concerned enough, wondering if this was how Ms. Phillips or the others felt when I took this long – or longer – when I was on my dream-walk.

I didn't really want to disturb Sophie and Will, but with Ms. Phillips fretting away, and probably planning to not let this happen again, I decided to head back into the dream world to check on things. At the time, I was also hoping I wouldn't be intruding on their little getaway, but my best bet was to actually check in with Old Crans. Anything and everything that happened within the lands would reach him for sure. It's only a matter of whether he was willing to share.

I got back into my usual bed which Walker had used earlier, and slipped back into the dream-world, arriving at Kinstein's Kitchen as usual. I headed in and while Kinstein was there like always, as were a few other denizens, Old Crans was still missing. It was a touch troubling because even if he didn't have anything for me to do, he would still be around. When I asked Kinstein about it, he said that it has been a while since Old Crans had dropped by. Even by his reckoning, from the time I left the Kitchen with Walker until now, it has been a few days. While that kind of time has passed for Kinstein, it's not necessarily the same for Sophie and Will, although it is possible as well. I asked around, checking with some of the other patrons, but they had not seen Old Crans for a while. I thanked them for their help anyway and then headed off to try to find Old Crans, starting with his home.

I don't often cheat when it comes to travelling around my own dream-world. I would usually walk when it was required of me to do so as instructed by Old Crans, or I would use a horse, maybe hitch a ride with some travelling merchants. Flying on my own steam was for some occasions but kept to a minimum. What I did this time was more akin to actual teleportation. Well, not quite, but close enough. It was more like I left the Kitchen, picked a big wide tree and, with one hand on the tree, my eyes closed and thinking about Old Crans, I walked around the tree. By the time I made one full circle, the Kitchen had disappeared behind the tree and Old Crans shack came into view in a small clearing. Like I said, a bit of a cheat. I could probably do the same with Sophie, but I still wasn't ready to disturb her yet. Old Crans hiding away was a more immediate concern for me.

I approached Old Crans' shack with a little caution and knocked on the door. Old Crans himself greeted and invited me in, all without doing any funny rhymes or his usual elongated poems. I know he doesn't always have to speak in rhymes, but it's still odd to hear him speak like a normal person.

I asked him if there was anything wrong and why the change in his way of speaking. He complained having to always speak in rhyme because it made him extremely long winded and too enigmatic. He then got to the nitty-gritty and I learnt a few things about my own dream-world I wasn't entirely aware of before.

There have been 'visitors' before, like those other dreamers I mentioned finding their way to my dream-world. According to Old Crans, they have been more like spiritual visitors; apparitions or ghosts even. Until Ethan, no one had really set up their own presence in my 'lands'. While that has been taken care off, his so called 'Dark Kingdom' still sits just off the borders of my 'lands' blocked by the range of mountains he called the "Terror Range". Since they appeared, no one has ever crossed the range. He couldn't even tell me how the range got that name.

Then he told me of how Sophie's self-entrance into the lands had upset a balance. If I had brought her in like always, then it wouldn't have been a problem because I was the buffer. I practically gave Sophie the keys to the kingdom in a way because she didn't enter the lands via a normal dream like other visitors, she took my path in. When I thought back a little, Old Crans hadn't been to the Kitchen since Sophie arrived with Will in tow. While this is affecting Old Crans, it wasn't affecting me in any way, at least, so far. It would catch up with me sooner or later.

He went on about the other strange bit of land that popped up off the coast that didn't quite match the rest of the lands, and how it was affecting the 'flow'. When I said that I made that place, he still said the land itself was in turmoil, has been for a long while. It wasn't one thing but a lot of little things, and not just the little errands he's had me tackle.

I know it's difficult to make sense of all this. The land has its own kind of rules and I always thought my own well-being was tied to the land. The way Old Crans went on about some of the problems, and how some of them didn't affect me, the rules didn't apply. Even my own construction of Walker's dwelling was having an adverse effect on the lands now, something that had never happened before. I still can't work out how Sophie's presence was a bad thing either. Before I left his shack, I asked Old Crans to try to determine the underlying problem to everything within the lands. His reply was even more enigmatic. He said he would see me once more with my task and if I was successful with it, he wouldn't be needed anymore. He pretty much chased me off after that.

I know I'm writing a lot about all this; stuff I've hardly written about before but it's to help me keep track of whatever is coming. Looking back over this entry – long as it is – I'm mixing in a lot of things here.

Anyway, once I was done with Old Crans, I tried looking for Sophie and Will but couldn't find any trace of them within my dream-world. I headed back to the Kitchen and left the dream-world from there.

On the outside, it was already Sunday evening. Sophie and Will were gone by then. Ms. Phillips told me they came out of the dreaming barely an hour after I went in, saying they didn't even cross paths with me. Since the bed readings showed I was in my dream-world instead of sleeping, she let me be. I got her to run a full set of tests on me and asked her to share the findings with Charlie. I wanted to know if there was anything else going on, aside from my odd sleeping times, anything I wasn't entirely aware off, especially after that meeting with Old Crans. She was a little skeptical but she obliged me. That took almost two hours.

I sent Sophie a comms message after that, but there was no reply. I checked in with Walker first and then with Tommy, to let him know I was taking the night off after a really long weekend. I got maybe a little over an hour of sleep just now, and since I couldn't get back to sleep, I've been writing all this up.

It's just past five in the morning now. I've still got some time before breakfast, so I'm heading off to the pool.

Feb 19

It's been a pretty busy few days and the journal has suffered a little neglect. My focus has been on my work, particularly TP. With Corogi and Kadi on the learning network, I've got Sophie on the communications network as well as the learning network. She's handling both quite admirably. Where the learning network is concerned, I had her with me during the sessions with Kadi and Corogi. I took her through the process of determining the learning centres for both Kadi and Corogi and I'm thinking of letting her try with Laurie tomorrow.

Meanwhile, Jenny is conditioning our newbies by having them join Callie's and Toni's network practices. Seems that they're managing with the network with the typical complaints about headaches, easily taken care of with a couple of aspirins from Ms. Phillips.

Speaking of whom, she hasn't gotten back to me about my tests. It's making me think that there actually is something wrong, but then, Charlie would have called by now if there were.

Following up on that, I haven't been sleeping much for the last few nights – except last night – and I can't attribute it to anything. Some might say it's stress related to the class work or maybe I'm worrying too much about my medical report. My usual activities haven't changed in any way so it's business as usual. Aside from the little bit of worrying over the network, I don't think my moods are out of whack. No one has said anything over lunch, not even Becca. In fact, the only person who has noticed anything is Walker.

He brought it up last night when we were in the pool together. I mentioned not sleeping much, but that was about normal for me even before I started at The Facility. Back then, sleeping half an hour to an hour every other night barely bugged me. Nowadays, it's some kind of issue that might or might not be something serious. Even now, I'm wishing Ms. Phillips or Charlie would have something to tell me.

Anyway, since we were in the pool, Walker could feel whatever vibes I gave off in the water and it seemed the vibes were off. He couldn't narrow it down for me and I couldn't articulate anything on my side. He asked when was the last time I had a good night's sleep and after thinking back a moment, I could only come up with that night in the Infirmary almost a week ago, when we shared the bed. I fell asleep listening to his heart beating. He suggested trying it again, which we did, but in the garden instead.

We got out of the pool and had a quick shower (separately, of course) before meeting up in the garden. This was probably shy of eleven at night; I noticed the wall clock when I left the changing room. There weren't a lot of people around, maybe one or two at the café. We sat on the grass under a tree instead of the bench so I could stretch out a little and lay my head on his chest. His arm went around me like a gentle hug, more to support me. We quietly looked out over the city. I broke the silence in the end.

Even if this worked, I couldn't always go to him just to get some sleep. He said to try to get to sleep and not to worry about next time. I closed my eyes and listened to the steady rhythm of his heart. I did fall asleep but I don't know how long it took for it to happen. It must have been a pretty deep sleep because when I woke up, I was in my usual bed in the Infirmary and it was almost six in the morning. Ms. Phillips wasn't there, but one of the other assistants was watching over the Infirmary that night. She told me Walker carried me in around midnight and then left, saying he didn't want to disturb me. I didn't know what to think, but I thanked her and left, heading back to the suite.

I've been typing this up since then, feeling a little... I dunno what I'm feeling. I'm not quite tired, but yet not quite rested either. My head feels a little light but there's no headache, almost like I'm in some dream state.

We'll see how the day goes.

Feb 20

Because the trainees hardly ever leave The Facility except on some special occasion, The Facility does provide some amenities such as the mini theatre, or the pool, or the gym. I've also mentioned the little sundry shop where we can get some basic necessities, or make requests for specific items not readily available from them. The DVD library is sadly lacking in anime fare while a lot of older films and other shows are available in a digital format. I may have mentioned a hair-salon where Helen has a weekly appointment, and the four-lane bowling alley, but yesterday I was told about the spa. Never knew we had one at The Facility.

It only came up because I caught up with Walker during lunch to thank him for helping me the night before. He apologised for leaving me at the Infirmary. I said it was okay, and thanked him again. The little bit of news I couldn't get to sleep without Walker was kindling to the likes of Carol and Helen. Even Keiko and Becca chimed in with their own theories, and that's beyond the obvious sleazy or snarky remarks from Helen and Carol. It was Jenny who said if I was feeling stressed out, I could take in a session at the spa. Of course, I had to say, "What spa?"

Heck, even Callie knew about the spa and said it was next to the hair-salon, one of those amenities I don't make use of. When Jenny brought it up, the others also thought it would be a good idea for me to take a spa day to unwind.

"I've been curious to try it," said Walker, which took me by surprise.

"Then you two can make a date for that," said Helen. "Make it a couple's session."

"If it's meant to relax me and help me sleep, a couple's session would defeat the purpose," I said.

"It would be more like he could help keep an eye on you in case you fall asleep," said Becca.

I looked over to Walker, who smiled, and I nodded. "I'll take it under advisement," I said.

I discussed it at length with Walker over our dinner tonight and then we went looking for this spa which was several floors below the suites. Turns out, like everything else, the spa runs all day every day. Walker and I signed up for a session on Tuesday afternoon, an afternoon where we could both take a class off. We then managed to catch a movie. Sophie and Will were there as well.

Sophie mentioned the movie to me earlier during class when I had her working with Louise to determine the learning centres of her brain. Sophie did it quite well. Louise is one of the F.E.P.'s who has been at The Facility for a long time, so that made it easier. They tend to be more acclimatised and their brain patterns are somehow more similar to ours, or rather less... unusual. By next week, our test sessions begin. I don't expect there will be any problems with maybe one exception; Carl. The most I can hope for is that he'll behave himself.

One other thing though; I did catch up with Sophie about the whole dreaming bit. I tried to explain the concerns presented by Old Crans last time. She didn't quite understand what I was getting at and I couldn't think of how to explain it more simply. I'm still heading in tomorrow as usual. Frankly, I'm not sure what I'm going to find there although I'm hoping everything will remain the same.

I'm kinda tired so I'm gonna sign off for now.

Feb 22

I dropped in on the dream-world yesterday for my weekly session with Mikey and nothing felt out of place as far as I could tell. While I didn't see him, Kinstein said Old Crans was around. I'm still a little nervous about his words the last time I saw him. They had such a prophetic ring to them, like something big is going to happen.

Anyway, meeting up with Mikey is always a high point in my week. It lets me catch up in different ways now, picking up on how things are at home and how he's doing in kindergarten. I advise him on whatever problems he has and, as best I can, inform him about what I get up to at The Facility, occasionally sharing what I've learnt. It's generally what we talk about when we meet up.

He asked about Walker and I told him that we were friends. I'm not sure how he would take it as yet, but he seemed happy enough hanging with Walker the last couple of sessions. Mikey's been my only steady guy since he entered my life, so sharing another guy with him is a really tricky proposition. I have to take into consideration that Walker may not be in my life for the long run. Even with that consideration, I'm going to enjoy this relationship as much as I can, if only I knew what exactly I'm supposed to be doing.

After Mikey left, I met with some needy villagers who were looking for help. I wondered at the time if this was how things were going to be if Old Crans isn't going to be around. I followed them to their village to confront their problem and it was a first; a troll-like creature roaming about. Despite other mythical creatures existing in the dream-world, trolls were never part of the menagerie. Getting the villagers to rally together and build the trap took a day. They chased it away in the end. It felt wrong.

By the time I came out of the dreaming, it was roughly six hours later. Almost two days spent on the other side. I left the Infirmary after tidying up the bed, resetting the monitoring devices and making sure the readings were saved. Ms. Phillips wasn't around and I still haven't heard from her as yet. Aside from the one night, my sleeping times have been no more than an hour each night.

I've been using my extra hours to focus on my studies, especially applying the theoretical to the practical as best as I can. That means working on my Virtual Rocket via the flight simulator and also working on Colleen. I also made up some hours at the Operations Center. Yeah, haven't been writing much about that, but there hasn't been much to write about. The fellows at the IASC Mission Control are still working on the signal without much agreement on the result. I think they overloaded my software with every conceivable piece of music they could throw in there to make sure the analysis is thoroughly exhaustive.

Most of today was spent catching up with review classes. I know I haven't really covered much where my life is concerned and there's a lot of criss-crossing on several things, lightly touching on each bit. It almost feels like my head's as scattershot as my journal entries lately.

I'm going to keep this short because I've got to get ready for dinner. I'm meeting with Sophie and Jenny to work out our game plan for the upcoming Network sessions and a contingency for Carl. Maybe he's already screwing with my head, which might account for the scattershot thoughts. We'll see what happens later. I've gotta go for now.

Feb 24

Following the dinner discussion the night before, it was agreed I would connect Carl to the network since Sophie's still in training and Jenny didn't want anything to do with Carl where possible. But then, Carl didn't show up for the network test run. It wasn't really a requirement for him to be at every one of the test runs as long as he came for at least a couple. We had everyone else though so it was a pretty good turn-out.

The test session was in the VR Arena with a simulation of the colony running, so we had participants hanging out in the areas they would be in on the field trip; Remington assisted since he has the assignment list. I would be hanging with Peter again and I can't wait to see him. I didn't have much to do during the test session except to watch over Jenny and the network. I took Sophie through the process of watching for leaks while she was linking Laurie on the network. I linked the other F.E.P. as well as Helen. Carl would round out my five while Jenny had the other five which included John and the newbies. Sophie would be wary about the leaks because she was affected by them on the first network. It's how we met.

We had a two hour session using personal materials. Only Sophie and I had our own thing to do, as mentioned above. In that respect, we had a pretty good run with no leaks even with the newbies on the network. It was surprising. Then again, we're using the refined system Jenny's been practising with Callie and Toni. It was easier connecting everyone and was also less of a strain on us maintaining it for two hours. Sophie definitely felt so.

A roundtable Q&A session followed. Questions were traded over each person's personal topic of study to see how others would respond. No one missed a single answer. Even Remington was impressed. I gave credit to Jenny, Callie and Toni since they were responsible for refining it over the last year. It's been a year since I've been part of running a network.

John approached me after we left the VR Arena to ask about Carl being absent and I said that it was his choice. He had the time-table and it wasn't required of him to attend if he didn't want to, as long as he turned up for the field trip itself.

"Do you need me to talk to him?" he asked, which took me by surprise.

"I'm sure he'll come around," I said. "He knows not to mess around with this."

John only eyed me quietly, nodded his head and left.

Jenny, Sophie and I continued our little network review through lunch, and that little meeting with John quickly became a talking point around the lunch group. Carol led the way as usual filling that little encounter with all sorts of innuendo because John has some kind of thing for me. Helen, surprisingly, was the one who came to my defence, pretty much firmly establishing my relationship with Walker for everyone within earshot.

Today, Walker and I met up after our morning classes were through and headed off to the spa together. I admit I was a little excited and I wasn't really sure what to expect.

While it wasn't quite the same as the VR Arena, the spa had a similar system to create any kind of pleasant relaxing environment. A default setting was one where the walls projected some kind of tropical not-quite-jungle environment during sunset complete with a waterfall not too far away and the sounds of birds and insects all around. The lighting source was from the sunset itself, partially obscured by leaves. It was all video images on the walls and ceiling, enhanced by the decorations of actual plants around the room. Even the beds, well, the frame of the beds – not counting the mattresses – looked like they were made of rocks and logs.

We couldn't make any changes to the room's practical aspects – the plants, the bed, the other equipment all around – but we changed the visuals to something more to our liking; an under-water scene with whales, dolphins, and other marine life swimming about. Dolphin chatter and whale songs could be heard in a distance. I was told that we could request a desired environment next time, so it was something to consider, not that I minded the default setting.

So being in the spa is like being pampered, I guess. I got a facial – felt weird – and a full body massage from head to toe during which I fell asleep. By the time I woke, I was lying face down and Walker was rubbing some kind of scented oil down my back. I asked him why he was doing that. He had inquired about the techniques and how it affected the physiology of a body, and then figured he could try it because it looked easy when the masseuse was doing it to me. He then told me I had been out for about over an hour and asked if I felt rested. I realised that I was feeling worn and physically tired, but it was also remarkably relaxing the way hands worked my back.

The room was pretty warm, or at least, I was feeling pretty warm with his hands moving all over my body. We spent a while more in that room together – and I'm sparing the details here – before we headed off to that jacuzzi massage and by then, I was wondering what I had signed up for because I was getting hungry. There was no concept of time in the spa. By the time we left, I felt extremely light, mentally and physically; I could say I was practically giddy.

He walked me back to my suite after dinner and we kissed good-night, which given everything else that happened today, it was pretty tame. I don't know when, but I'm definitely up for another round at the spa sometime. Right now, I'm really tired and I hope I get more than an hour's sleep; nice prolonged happy sleep.

Feb 26

At best, I'd say it was seven hours that night and another five hours last night (or this morning); the most I've had in a while, and I'm feeling good and rested. Becca had to wake me for breakfast.

Anyway, when I got back to the suite that night, Becca was asleep already, so I only filled her in over breakfast. She promised to keep it a secret as it was sharing stuff in her language. The most I let out to the others over lunch was admitting that I did fall asleep during the massage, as Helen had suggested would happen.

It was also during lunch that I got a comms message from Linda, asking me to drop by her office. All sorts of stuff ran through my head at that point and I was nervous about this meeting. Enough time had passed for events of the last few days to reach her, and she would have read the last journal entry by then. I finished what was left of my lunch and then hurried off to her office, much to the curiosity of the lunch group.

Ms. Phillips was there in Linda's office, which made me think back to the tests I had her run on me some time back – almost two weeks or thereabouts. When I arrived, Linda started making a call to Charlie and then the discussion about my test results took off from there. Charlie started by asking about my sleeping patterns and if I had been having any mood swings. I filled him in by saying that aside from two particular nights – a week ago in the garden, and the night after the spa treatment – I've been clocking just over an hour each night since the tests. I also told him what happened on those two occasions. My daily activities were fairly normal otherwise.

Ms. Phillips did check up on me the night I spent in the Infirmary last week. She even had the bed monitor my readings, which were then shared with Charlie. The most they could confirm was that I'm under-going some biological changes again and nothing to be too concerned about, according to Charlie. After the last check-up, I was told that the gap between my actual age and my physical age had shrunk, which Charlie believed was my body's way of adjusting itself to a peak setting, or as Ms. Phillips put it, I had hit my prime.

Now it seems that the gap is widening again, based on the current readings. The bombshell came from Charlie saying some of my hormones were reacting as if I were going through puberty. Given that situation and the 'setting' I was supposedly in from a physical standpoint, everything else was going a little out of whack.

That was when Linda brought up the issue about Walker and me. Now, it's not like I haven't been through all this before. I mixed around through high-school and I've even gone beyond that; I've got Mikey after all. I don't think the relationship I have with Walker is any more serious than my last one, but it is causing some "chemical unbalances" (Ms. Phillips' words) in my system. From the way they were explaining things, it seemed Linda had already been discussing my relationship with Ms. Phillips and Charlie. Ms. Phillips pointed out that the occasions where I had more than an hour's worth of sleep usually occurred after I had some extraordinary contact with Walker, that is, not just swimming in the pool. She put forth the supposition that the dream-walks which included him didn't count either. Charlie, bless him, didn't pry about the relationship even after he was told about Walker – they had met, after all.

I asked Charlie if any of these changes that I was currently going through would affect my dreaming, but he couldn't draw any conclusions there. There have been links between my physical or mental health and my dream-world, but Charlie has never been able to do any tests that would successfully link the two conclusively. Whatever is happening in my dream-world may or may not be related to my current condition, but there was some hint, maybe, that made me decide to ask Ms. Phillips for the test that day.

So, something that I've got to ride out for now. Charlie still wants me to mind any other changes and report to Ms. Phillips who will report back to him. With that, we were done. Linda hung up the phone and asked me to stay back. After Ms. Phillips left, she asked me about the spa session with Walker and if there was anything that she would have to be concerned about.

"Like what?" I asked.

"Are the two of you getting hot and heavy?"

"Is that really a concern?"

"Your situation is unique," she said. She explained that for as long as the exchange program has been running, no one has ever had a relationship with an F.E.P. out in the open within The Facility. Becca's didn't count because Steven was working elsewhere. "Remington is concerned, as am I," she said. "We have no real idea what to expect, even if you don't count a biological standpoint. I am worried if these changes you're going through is a result of your current relationship."

I understood where she was coming from and I assured her that Walker and I are equally aware of our current situation. As good an admission there, I guess. It may seem to others that we are 'fooling around' and 'getting hot and heavy', but we are also addressing the biological and cultural issues. I've had my share of experiences of difficult relationships, being a 'mixed breed' myself, so I have an inkling of what to expect.

I caught up with Walker later at night to fill him in on the day's meetings and he seemed overly concerned about my well-being, even after I told him it wasn't that big a deal. I asked how he viewed me in the context of our relationship, and he said that I am a potential mate. It was also why his actions seemed to accommodate my needs. It was his way of reciprocating my actions that have complemented him over the last few years. He even went further by saying it was an honour for him to cater to my needs, simply because I was worthy of such attention. I was dumbstruck by his declaration that my only response was to kiss him, in the middle of the pool, surrounded by witnesses.

It was surprisingly quiet today. Lunch was uneventful with most conversations turning to class work, weekend plans and barely addressing any new rumours my rash actions gave rise to. I'm sure even Tommy will have something to say. I'm signing off for now and heading off to the Operations Center.

Got a bit of work to catch up on.

Feb 28

It was my monthly review today. Despite meeting Linda a few days back, she held off on the review session because she hadn't gotten all the reports from the tutors yet.

We touched on my classes and training, taking particular note on how I'm involved with the training aspects where TK and TP are concerned. I have been doing as best as I can manage with the other subjects and Linda said that the tutors are taking note of my efforts. While I feel like I'm struggling trying to keep up, I am actually progressing faster than it was expected according to my tutors. Even Mr. Hardy had some good notes in his report.

I've stopped writing about all that, unless it's relevant or I have nothing else to write about. I don't know how to keep what I learn in class relevant, because it's me, learning things and keeping up. With the TK and TP stuff, it's not just about me learning stuff. There are the networks and me training others.

What came up lacking is mainly my work at the Operations Center. It suffered a little bit due to me missing a few days here and there. I also couldn't really focus the other day because I was so tired that I had to ask Tommy to excuse me while I headed off to bed. Just for the record, sleep the night before was about four hours and last night was under four hours worth. Maybe it was the spa treatment or hanging with Walker, but there's no real link to either unless I take another spa treatment to see if it has the same effect on my sleeping. Anyway, it seems that my sleeping hours are tapering off again.

So, back to the meeting with Linda. She expressed a little concern about my relationship with Walker (again) and how it might be affecting me. Basically, I haven't slacked off on anything where my classes and activities are concerned, with maybe the exception of the Operations Center, and I told her so. The concern was more towards my well being as a whole. Sleep has been affected, and the biological changes I've been going through could be associated with the progression of this relationship. I reminded her again that Charlie said not to worry about it for now. We got into a whole semi-argument over this, going round and round until I said, "If anything strange happens, I will be checking in with Ms. Phillips and Charlie."

"My worry is that the 'anything strange' that does happen will be something we may not be able to take care off," she countered. We pretty much ended it there after she got me to promise I would do as I said. I don't think Remington would have done that, but I shouldn't compare. If she needs the occasional promise, I should accommodate her.

Before I left her office again, I handed in another requisition form for some additional parts to fix into Colleen. I know I'll never get to the scale or complexity of the VR Arena's holographic displays, but I wanted to improve Colleen's holographic platform enough for me to interact with it on a smoother level. That was my justification to Linda. I also agreed to have her check on Colleen, and we arranged a time. It's always nice to have different people interact with Colleen.

Between yesterday and today, there's nothing much to write about. Walker and I had our dinner date as usual last night and things seem to be moving along smoothly so I've got no complaints or worries. We hung out by the pool after dinner and had a late night swim before calling it a night. That was it.

I'm signing off for now. Really short entry this time, and I really should keep them like this when I can. I'm heading to the Infirmary, off to my dream-world and catch up with Mikey.

MARCH

Mar 3

It's been a busy few days since the meeting with Linda and the biggest concern bugging me is that Mikey didn't make our usual hook-up. Linda has since let me call home to check-up with Karen and as far as she knows, Mikey went to bed as usual on Saturday night and there was nothing unusual. What bugged me even more? Mikey didn't want to talk to me.

Back tracking a little, the dream-walk was at the same time as usual, and this was after the meeting with Linda. When I got to my dream-world, there were major changes even though Kinstein's Kitchen looked pretty much the same. I had to take in the sights around the Kitchen itself before going in because while there was a sense of familiarity, it was also different. Some of the trees appeared deformed even if they were still lush and green. The hills in the distance appeared to have barren spots that moved about. Clouds were heavier and darker than normal. All of it seemed to suggest a reflection of my well-being, perhaps.

There were no changes inside the Kitchen save for the lack of patrons. Kinstein greeted me in his usual cheerful manner, like I had been gone for a long time. I greeted him back and started heading for the back room. He said Mikey wasn't there. Just to be sure, I opened the door to the back-room and instead of finding the usual room filled with toys and throw pillows, there was the dark back-room with brooms and brushes. Kinstein then said that there haven't been as many visitors or patrons for a while. It seems the lands have become too dangerous to travel. Given how time passes in there in comparison to out here, it was hard to determine when it started.

"What about Old Crans? Has he been around?" I asked.

Before he could say anything, a couple of villagers wandered into the Kitchen looking fairly alarmed, saying their village was under attack from fire breathing creatures. I don't want to say 'dragon' because what I saw didn't look like any dragon I could ever imagine. For as long as there have been some strange magical creatures like flying horses and unicorns in this dream-world, there have never been dragon-like creatures or – if what I got from other villagers is true – trolls, ogres, gargoyles and some strange large beast with the head of a lion on a buffalo's body that walked upright on hooves and had a snake for a tail!

Since Old Crans wasn't around to say anything, I followed the villagers to take care of the creature terrorising their home. I had to rally the villagers to help trap the creature. That took a couple of days. Couldn't stop them from killing it though. It was another day before I left the village and headed back to the Kitchen.

Once I was away from the village, I took to the skies to survey the land. From on high, I could barely recognise the land. It reminded me of the time last year when I was in pain and the land reflected some kind of block in the flow of energy, but it wasn't the case this time. I then noticed the mountain range that separated my world from Ethan's. It was higher and darker than I remembered, and I wondered if there was some influence flowing from there. I looked towards the other borderlands and even then, some of them didn't look right. I couldn't tell if there was some influence spreading from my land into theirs or if it was from their lands into mine, or if it was all a natural change that was affecting all the lands.

I flew higher to get a wider view, but as high as I went, I couldn't see beyond the other lands that were on my borders. It was something I hadn't done before. Even then, everything looked the same. It seemed that no matter how high I got, I could never get high enough to see everything. After a while, I stopped and looked down again. It looked familiar but nothing looked right at the same time. I really don't know what to make of it and that made me feel a bit sad for some reason.

Back at the Kitchen, there was still no sign of Mikey or Old Crans. With one creature vanquished, Kinstein had a few patrons again. If this was any indication of how things were, each trip into the dream-world was going to be harrowingly busy until Old Crans decides to pop up again and tell me what needs to get done. I hung around a while more to talk to the other villagers to get a feel for what was going on in other areas.

By the time I came out, it was Sunday afternoon – a whole day – and I was feeling the worse for wear. I still tidied up before heading off for something to eat. It was way past lunchtime so there wasn't anyone else at the café. Food didn't do anything to replenish my energy and I actually felt worse. I didn't finish the food. I headed back to the suite and plopped into bed... and slept. Becca had to wake me for breakfast on Monday morning and asked if I was okay. I was still feeling worn, barely rested, but relatively better than when I crashed. I got better as the day moved on; as I moved about and had a shower, breakfast and all.

Right before class, I sent a comm message to Linda requesting to make a phone call home. That only happened today, and it made me miserable that I didn't talk with Mikey. Linda tried to be supportive about it, suggesting it was just a one off thing and everything would be back to normal by next weekend.

I zoned through class after that. The last couple of days haven't been all great, and my mood was reflective of that. Becca knew and shared it discreetly with a few others, but not Carol. Walker's been equally supportive in his own way by keeping me company in my slight misery. Otherwise, I don't think I would be composed enough to write this out.

For now, I'm off to the Operations Center to clock in some hours.

Mar 5

It's been a couple of days since the last entry, and there is the little moody air around me. While it was possibly not as toxic as earlier in the week, it wasn't the kind of mood to carry onto the network during yesterday's run.

Prior to that, I still had to mix around with the others, and especially Sophie in TP training. Moody or not, I still had be involved with Sophie's training primarily and some of the others as well. So, aside from Becca, Sophie was quick to pick up on my moodiness, but she kept it quiet after I explained the reason for it. Most of the discussion happened via our network practice, and I also prepped her even more for the Learning Network. When the test run came up yesterday, I had her linking up two people instead of the one she had last time.

Our second field trip test run was in the VR arena again with Remington in the control room watching over us. There were only eleven of the participants there for this round and Carl was not there again. All our F.E.P.'s were present, so that was good. I managed to hold myself together for the duration of the test run. Jenny, who easily picks up on my mood whether we're sharing thoughts or not, kept asking if I was okay before, during and after the session. I don't think Remington noticed anything.

The test run lasted over two hours followed by a questionnaire. At best, we got a ninety-eight percent high, courtesy of John, and as low as eighty-eight. Sophie held up pretty well, and she was excited with the results, especially since the person with the lowest score wasn't one of the two people she linked to the network. We still have three more test sessions before the actual field trip on March 25. Sophie asked if I was going to have another 'sneak attack' test like we had last year. I didn't think Remington would approve considering how things turned out then. I doubt Jenny would want to go through another sneak attack either. While it was successful to a point, it still fell to me to fix everything and it wasn't a nice thing to handle in the end.

I caught up with Jenny to check on the progress of her team; Callie, Toni and particularly Ethan. They've formed their own little lunch group, often when they have a class – three times a week. Jenny reported that Callie and Toni have been practising the communications network. Ethan has been progressing with his training, establishing connections with her and trading prepared information with ease. He asks about me every now and then, but she advised him to approach me directly. He hasn't made any contact with me in a while now. I've got my own concerns about him again, but I'm not sure how to approach the matter for now.

Outside of that, my sparring sessions with Keiko have wound down a little, again, due to my mood. It was easier to focus on kendo instead of full-fledged sparring. Additionally, it does get my mind off my mood. So, it's an hour or so where my thoughts aren't quite on Mikey. Keiko's has me be a sparring dummy for our increasingly skilled juniors over these last couple of days. I watch for their strokes and help correct them, making sure their swing is centred properly and their strikes are hitting the right places. It helps me at the same time since I have to be aware of the movements they make and then I have to be extra aware of my own movements during my demonstrations.

My flight-trainer has me flying a Gulfstream G550 in the simulator now. It has some kind of infra-red vision system and the visual panel is pretty different from the other models I've flown so far. Even the control panel is so different, but I guess that's a given for different companies even if some things are the same. The handling is way different from the Cessna, which is the one I'm most comfortable with; the one I started with. As far as my instructor is concerned, I'm pretty set if I want to take on an actual jet although I still won't be allowed to fly one alone. Yeah, that's been going on a while now and I really don't think I'm getting that chance any time soon.

Aside from that day, I've been clocking about an hour each night for sleep and spending the rest of the time between the Operations Center and tinkering on Colleen.

I'm heading for the pool now.

Mar 7

Since Ethan came back with Remington being his guardian, it felt like he wouldn't be the problematic troublemaker he was last year. One of those problematic things was the way he crept off into the dream-world and built his own world there. It started small like a little village on my turf and has since moved off to the border-lands, separated by this really massive mountain range that even the denizens are afraid to get close to.

There are other lands that border mine, probably created by other people. I don't know for sure if those 'lands' have creators or owners. As far as I know, Ethan's the only one who's created his own land on the dream-plane. I confirmed that with him just now after my last trip in. I actually scaled the mountain to take a peek into his land and when I set foot on it, the very essence of Ethan flowed through me signifying it was his land I had stepped on. I didn't linger and left once I was sure it was Ethan's land. It was not a good experience being there last time. Since then, I think Ethan's gotten some control over his own land – and his psyche, I think.

So after I got out of the dreaming, I tracked him down to a little chat. He confirmed building up his own world and staying on his side. I explained being curious about the mountains and admitted to stepping over. Before we parted, he mentioned Sophie talking to him about building her own world on the dream-plane. It was puzzling news to me because she didn't say anything over dinner last night. I'll get to that in a while.

The dream-walk was a disappointment again because Mikey didn't turn up for the second weekend in a row. I've sent Linda a message asking to let me make a phone call home again, but she has yet to respond. I hope it's nothing too serious and that he's not just avoiding me. To top that, there were more creatures to deal with; another fire-breathing creature, a cyclopic brute, and a bunch of trolls. I tracked one of the trolls to the mountains. That was when I decided to get to the top of have a look at Ethan's land. In all, I spent like a week and a half on the inside, but somehow less than five hours on the out.

Before all that, I was actually feeling much better and looking forward to the dream-walk. Friday was pretty good and I was quite myself again. I had a sparring session with Keiko and spilled it all on her. Of course, Keiko enjoyed herself since I was putting up quite a fight after those few days of moping about. I didn't win, as usual, racking up a bunch of bruises. I gave as good as I got, which surprised her because she's usually reading my moves and getting the blocks ahead of me.

Then, the usual Friday dinner. Walker and I were joined by Will and Sophie, where she didn't say anything about talking to Ethan or about creating her own dream-world. Instead we covered our burgeoning relationships, comparing notes. I seldom see Sophie and Will together around The Facility and she hardly talks about it, unless we're together at dinner, like last night.

They're even conspicuously apart in TK training. On my end, I'm with Walker every night in the pool. Then again, that was going on even before we were a couple.

Dinner, talk, food and chit-chat; that was it. After Sophie and Will went off for a movie, Walker and I hung out in the garden. He asked about scheduling another spa session, and I figured waiting until after the field trip. He only nodded in reply and we sat quietly with me leaning on him a little. I think he knew when I was about to fall asleep because he nudged me a little and then suggested turning in.

An hour or so later, I was up and about, clocking in some practice on the flight simulator and tinkering on Colleen. That brings me back to Saturday, and I guess I'm done for now. Heading off to the pool first and then I'll be checking in with the Operations Center.

Mar 9

Finally got Sophie to open up about setting up her own dream world. She's got her own reasons, of course, and she understands that consciously accessing the dream-plane doesn't happen when one is asleep. Thing is, the way she going about this puts the whole dream-plane thing into a different perspective now. The way it exists and functions raises all kinds of questions, mostly from her and some from Ethan as well. Questions I can't answer like some expert on the topic.

The dream-world was a place that kept me occupied from time to time when I wasn't sleeping much. I built it over time, long ago. How and why it affects my psyche or physical well being from time to time is a mystery even Charlie can't crack. I guess it's because he's never been to that side of my reality to do any real examinations. Come to think of it, I can't even think of how he would carry out any examinations on me in both worlds at the same time.

There is another strange thing about this dream-world I may have mentioned a long time back. Despite the dream-world not really existing in any sense of reality, I have pulled inanimate objects from there to here before. I have no idea what happened to that flute though. It was with me for a couple of years, and yes, despite not mentioning it before, I can play the flute. The year before coming to The Facility, it went missing – probably somewhere in the chaos that is my room – and I have no idea if it's still in the real world or if it vanished back to the dream-plane, if it still does exist in the first place. I don't know how that works either.

66

I'm not going to mention that to either Sophie or Ethan, otherwise they might start pulling stuff out of their own dream-world. Okay, got a chill out of that thought, particularly what Ethan might pull out from his side. I don't think he reads this journal, but I think Sophie does.

It was over TP training I got Sophie to open up. I caught up with Ethan over lunch. That meant I was sitting at the other table Ethan shared with Callie, Toni, Jo, Jenny and a few others. It was to clarify with Ethan about what he discussed with Sophie. Once I was done, I excused myself, took what was left of my lunch with me to my usual table with the usual lunch group. They knew I was partially supervising his training, particularly in TP, but they were still curious about the meet.

Sophie's part was yesterday and Ethan was today. After lunch was another network test run for the field trip and while there were only eight participants this time, Carl still didn't come along. The only person who seemed agitated by this was John, who came complaining to me again. I reminded him that Carl wasn't obligated to attend every test run. He was only requested to attend at least one test run before the actual field trip so we could have a feel of him on the network and how he would actually fit in. Of course, John wasn't buying that.

"Well, you can drag him to the next one then," I said.

"Maybe I will do just that," he said with a sly smile.

The test run this time was held in the café with Remington watching over us there. Sophie still carried her two participants. Ehrmer was absent this time around, so I had one less. Jenny had the rest, but with the absentees, she had it light too. It was a good opportunity to get Sophie to practise watching for leaks although we really didn't have any. I guess it was pretty cool that the test run was uneventful. Then again, we didn't tell any of the newbies about how the leaks occur, only they are likely to happen. It's amazing how everyone is so dedicated to their work.

Instead of a questionnaire, we had a little Q&A with each person taking turns to ask two questions and anyone else could up and answer. One interesting factor is the process of not just learning facts through the learning network, but the capability of reasoning with the facts to come up with the necessary answer. It was John who asked the kind of questions that needed deductive reasoning based on his study materials. Even I picked up a little on what everyone else was learning. It'll be even more interesting if anything I gleaned off the network will help in classes.

Jenny and I were not part of the Q&A because technically, we're not part of the actual learning team; we're running the network so that everyone else can learn. It's not like we can't be. Callie and Toni integrate themselves into their network, and Sophie is a part of this one. Even with Sophie helping out, we're doing pretty good and I think we'll have no problems handling the large number of participants for the allocated time of the field trip.

A lot of it is keeping my mind off Mikey, who still doesn't want to talk to me. Both mom and Karen assure me that he's okay and he's sleeping like normal. Linda suggested letting it be for now and she also said that Mikey might be going through a phase and needs a little time away from me. I thought he always looked forward to meeting me, but maybe it's not the case for a while as Linda is suggesting. She also told me she's working with Remington to let me take a couple of days home after the field trip. That's eased my mind a little, and she wants me to focus on work.

That's about it for now, I guess. I'm heading off to the pool.

Mar 12

Sometimes, there's the feeling everything is going well, things are just peachy and nothing can go wrong, then out of the blue, the universe turns around and bites you on the ass. It hasn't actually happened. Things have been moving along smoothly, but the feeling is that it's coming. Okay, maybe except with Mikey, and maybe that's the turning point down the line

So, things have been going smoothly. Classes are fine. I'm managing with my studies and activities, getting a kind of balance going. My tutors are okay with my progress. Even Mr. Hardy has said so as I was walking out after his class. The most feedback I get is from Miss Tracy telling me I'm doing great helping Sophie and guiding Jenny with Ethan. I want her to give Jenny full credit for Ethan, Callie and Toni. It's a whole other thing with the TK training though, coming up with some other exercises in which we can use our TK abilities.

There's still that small window between dinner and me hitting the pool when I catch up with Becca. I talk to her in her language, she replies in English, and we correct each other as best we can. She's still mentoring Kadi although not so much these days as Kadi seems to have gotten into the groove of things and adjusting to the food. Becca made sure she started off easy – that's from her own experience – before handling the more common food served in the café.

Aside from that, I think Walker and I are making some progress. We get together every night in the pool and the tension of our relationship being on display has worn off quite a bit. It's business as usual whenever I'm at the pool with him; help coach Sunee and Corogi with the aqua-acrobatics before it's my turn to practise with him. Then he paces me as I do my laps. By that time, it's Walker and me in the pool. We tend to play a bit before calling it a night. I've also been trying to learn a few phrases in his language.

Finally is my sleeping pattern, as per Charlie's request to keep track. Since the last dreaming trip, and aside from that Saturday night, I've been clocking about an hour on average over the past few nights. Whatever is going on with the dream-world of mine, it's wearing me out a bit and I slept for over five hours, but just that night.

At least, that's my reasoning. My head's in a pretty good place – no mood swings or melancholia or depression setting in – and aside from the slight concern over Mikey, I think I'm doing good. After all, I get to see him at the end of the month, so there's something to look forward to.

So, I guess that about covers me in particular. We have one network test run tomorrow and one more next week before the field trip. Maybe for once, it won't be such an eventful year, not that the last couple were eventful except for a couple of incidents. Then again, it's a matter of perception, isn't it?

More later.

Mar 14

I suppose I had this coming.

During the field trip test run last year, I got Sophie and Ehrmer to conspire testing our network security measures in monitoring for leaks. I didn't tell Jenny or Remington about it. Sophie and Ehrmer got together with almost everyone else to "hack" the network. That sent Jenny into a panic, and I had to take some extreme measures to close off the network without burning out someone's brain. I promised Remington I wouldn't pull anything like that again without informing him first.

So guess what happened?

Sophie worked it out with Jenny and Ehrmer to have them pull off the same thing so that she could have the experience of actually tracking a leak. Jenny in turn checked in with Remington about it and decided to leave me out of the loop. To make matters worse, guess who decided it was time to join in on the network test run? That gives you an idea what I had to deal with on the test run yesterday. Let's get back to the beginning.

We had ten participants on the test run with Kadi sitting out for once and surprisingly, John was absent too. Instead, we had Carl. Since I had agreed to link Carl into the network, I briefed him as per our protocol even if he already knew how it all works. He looked like he was tolerating me. He guessed I would be the one linking him onto the network.

"No one wants to link with the pariah," he said, "so you're making the sacrifice as usual."

"No one thinks of you as a pariah," I said. "You just decide to act on your own and tick everyone else off."

"And you still think your methods are the right ones."

I decided not to retort. Whatever I could say or do where our abilities are concerned, it wasn't going to change his mind about how to use his own abilities. Given what he pulled with Ethan last year, he has the tendency to push the limits of things we really shouldn't do. However, I have to admit, it takes some imagination to do what he did.

We were back in the VR Arena with the colony simulation up and running. Things moved along smoothly for the first ninety minutes and then a couple of 'leaks' happened.

When that first leak occurred, Sophie was the first to react, as if she was aware it was coming. I paid it no mind at first since she did as she was supposed to, isolating the person first by blocking him from the network, and then informing Jenny and me about it. Then came a second leak from one of Jenny's 'terminals', but she also handled it as expected. These were small issues, and those two were back on the network fairly quickly.

Two leaks in succession after weeks and numerous sessions being trouble free? I got the feeling something wasn't quite right, and I wasn't the only one. Carl also picked up on the leaks. I was paying particular attention to him, in case he would try something, but he stayed focused on his own work for as long as he could manage as the little leaks continued. Some of the F.E.P.'s were involved as well.

Then the hack happened, and it wasn't quite what I expected. Unlike the mess last year where several participants poked around at each other, there was something of a coordinated move this year. It started on my end with the F.E.P. dropping off the network. Even Carl picked up on it. It was like they closed their minds and wouldn't let me re-connect them – not that it was impossible. It was usually best when everyone was a willing participant, but that was usually agreed upon before we even start with the test runs. No one had ever backed out of the network while it was running.

Once the F.E.P.'s were 'off-line', I tried to ask Ehrmer if there was something wrong. Then I felt a surge from Jenny. It was like one massive mental wave of information overload. When I looked over at her, she seemed to be smiling at me. Then I felt Sophie drop off the network taking Laurie and Helen with her. I could 'hear' Carl ask what was happening, but I didn't have an answer for him as the mental wave hit me. I could feel Jenny and her linked participants aiming for Carl.

I then felt Carl hitting back, and I was caught in the middle being the link that connected them all. It took me a moment to get my bearings and then I put up a block between Carl and everyone else. While I closed off the link between Jenny and me, I kept Carl linked, in case he didn't want to stop after I put up the block. While we weren't linked, I could still sense Jenny – it's that bond we share from being TP partners in training – as she slowly took her participants off the network link. I was keeping an eye on her the whole time too because it felt like she coordinated the mental attack on Carl. As much as I was wary of him and anything he might have tried, I wasn't going to let him be a target either.

Sure, I was pretty pissed at the time, but I kept myself in check. I looked over at Remington who was in the control booth watching over us. He didn't seem as ticked off as he was last year, which made me suspect he knew something was going to happen. It was about then when I felt Carl's hand on my shoulder from behind me, and I nearly took his head off because I was a little jumpy at what happened.

"I think you can get out of my head now," he said. After I 'disconnected' from him, he added, "I don't need you to protect me. I can take care of myself." And he walked off before I could respond.

We still had the Q&A session after that, but without Carl, we didn't have a conclusive analysis. After all the participants left, save Ehrmer, I was then informed of Sophie's little plan, and how Jenny embellished it as a sort of payback. They got away with it because they had shared the idea with Remington. Carl being there was 'a happy coincidence.' He then recommended scheduling an extra test run for next week and said he would make sure everyone would attend that last test run. At least we would have one test run with a full complement.

He stressed that there would be no more acts against Carl, and Jenny agreed. He would also remind Carl not to act out during the network tests or the field trip. I would still have to watch over him. I suggested letting him know that what happened was more directed at me than at him. I felt he would most likely hold a grudge.

"Why would you want to do that?" Jenny asked.

"He made a comment earlier about being the pariah no one wants around," I said.

"I'd say that's a fair assessment," she said.

"And I'm still obligated to make sure he gets treated as fairly as everyone else on the network," I said. I think she understood where I was coming from. Even if we didn't feel comfortable with him on the network, it was best that even he gets fair treatment for the sake of the network. Sophie then reminded me about all the other times he tried hacking the network and the events of last year. Remington said he would still have to talk to Carl about the next test.

We parted ways after that. Sophie said she would see me at dinner that night. Apparently, she cleared it with Walker and I had to verify that with him over lunch. He would meet me at the pool after dinner.

So, dinner was just Sophie and me, like it had been months ago. We caught up on a few things, and the real status of our relationships since the guys weren't around. She seemed really happy about where she was with Will although he's apparently a tad ambivalent about what kind of relationship he's in, at least, according to her. I asked if she even defined the relationship with him and she put the question back to me as a response.

"It's an exploration for both of us," I said.

"Three months now, isn't it? And you're both still exploring?"

"It's not like we can compare with any other relationship around here," I said.

"And how many do you think there are floating about?"

I admitted that aside from her and Will, there weren't any other relationships I knew of within The Facility. The only one I could relate to was Becca, although Steven wasn't working within The Facility, so it couldn't count either. She then told me of at least two other relationships involving people I know. Given how I try not to partake of the daily gossip around the lunch table, she said it was understandable that I was aware of such things.

"If you need advice, there are others you could talk to," she said.

"I'll keep it in mind," I said. "So it's your turn."

She felt that she and Will were not perceiving the relationship in the same way. She talked, in broad aspects, about their getting together and what they get up to. There's still the small sense of competition between them in the use of their TK abilities, so they tend to push each other a bit to improve their skills, something I've seen more in Sophie than in Will simply because I hardly see him do anything with his abilities outside of class or the Infirmary. Her concern was more on the issue of intimacy, or the actual physical lack of one.

On that front, the most I could do was lend a supporting ear because for as much as Walker and I would make-out or find ways to 'pleasure' each other, we haven't exactly been as intimate as Carol would like to suggest from time to time. I won't go into too much detail here because it does wander into the personal affairs of two other people who weren't there to discuss things out with us.

I caught up with Walker and talked things out with him after that. Not so much Sophie's side of things but rather where he and I stood in relation to the discussions I had with Sophie. I told him I wasn't complaining and that I was happy with what we had. We even talked about the intimacy issue, particularly about the possibility of such a thing. He asked if I would be happy if we could "be intimate", and I said I was happy either way simply because we were together.

I really have no idea what he thinks when I say things like that. While I am capable, I don't read his thoughts or even allow them to get into my head. I have extra guards up when I'm around him because I don't want to let any stray thought or emotion he has for me leak into my head, and I don't want to inadvertently influence him in any way. It's a really tricky situation. But we are as open with each other as we can manage and I know he tries to do things that will keep me happy. I want to do the same for him as well.

Yesterday was pretty eventful, and today has been a bit of a breather. There are a few things, but comparatively, it's nothing significant. This has been pretty long and I'm off to the Infirmary for my dream-walk now.

Mar 16

Mikey did drop by, but I didn't get to see him. It seems he turned up at the Kitchen and Kinstein catered to him as usual, but Mikey didn't even wait for me. He had already gone off – or probably woken up – by the time I got to the Kitchen, at least that's what Kinstein told me. Granted, I was disappointed, but at least Mikey came. I hope everything is okay with him, at least.

Meanwhile, it feels like things have gotten worse with more strange creatures roaming around the land. I don't know if I want the job of being a monster hunter or monster killer. Killing them is something I try to avoid but that reputation is growing even if I haven't actually killed any of the creatures I helped capture. Even the denizens of the land are changing in their attitudes as well since the creatures appeared. There's some kind of bloodlust going on, and I'm hoping it's not something that's building up in me, if the dream-world is reflecting any part of me.

Anyway, all that extra activity is wearing on me so I've been having some solid sleep on Saturday nights for the last couple of weekends. None of my other activities have knocked me out that way lately, be it the swimming or aqua-acrobatics with Walker, or even the sparring with Keiko. I don't think what goes on in the dream-world would be considered physical activities. Or would that be mental activities? I can't tell if I'm physically or mentally tired when I knock out, I'm just tired. We'll see how things work out during the rest of the week on that front.

While on the subject of activities, I got to interact with Nik quite a bit. It was his first time dropping by the gym, checking out the place. After Keiko and I were done sparring, he asked if I had practised *silat* before. I dabbled a little in high school, getting through the basics and a little more before I changed schools. He practised as well, although it's been a while. At Keiko's encouragement, Nik and I went a couple of rounds. It took me a while to settle down to sparring with strictly *silat* after going free form with Keiko for so long. We drew a bit of a crowd again because I don't think anyone else had actually seen *silat* before.

Silat has a kind of fluid swaying movement that would look strange to the lay-person. Even I thought it seemed like some kind of strange dance at first, but the movements have a purpose. The tumbling and the strikes, while subtle for the most part, are pretty real and effective, especially as you pick up speed. It also comes across as an art-form, much like kendo, but it does have its real-world application. Even the army and police force back home make learning it as part of their training. As far as I know, *silat* is typically Malaysian – and Indonesian – in that it's a hodgepodge of moves liberally borrowed from other martial arts that found their way to Malaysia from so long ago.

Nik and I talked about our styles and while I perceived his as the usual style (*gayung*, I think), he referred to mine as "*silat angin*". Keiko was fascinated and knowing her, she's capable of picking it up by watching, even if Nik and I declined teaching her anything. If she watched us practise a bit more, she'd have some of those moves in her repertoire.

I left an open invitation to practise with him if he wanted, but we would have to work out a time because my sessions with Keiko come first. He said he would consider it. I don't know if it's him, or if we're from the same country or if he's cautious from a religious perspective, but there seemed an uneasiness about interacting with me. If he's from one of those devout communities, he would be wary about interacting with a member of the opposite sex in a social environment. I could be wrong about that. It could be he's heard things about me and he's simply wary.

I had dinner with Keiko and she asked more about *silat*, but I didn't have much to share with her. It was just another martial art I picked up while in Penang. I've been typing this up since finishing dinner, so I'm off to the pool now.

Mar 19

Classes are getting along; the tutors are happy with my progress – such as it is – in that I'm keeping up with stuff I'm barely comprehending. It really does seem like I was brought to The Facility for my abilities than my smarts, or lack off, so keeping up with every one else is something of an accomplishment.

My flight instructor is happy with my progress on the new simulation, so that's another jet I can pilot, simulatedly. (I know, it's not a word.)

Colleen's coming along nicely with the new parts I've been getting although I'm also using whatever little spare parts I have left. I've been thinking about what I'm going to do with Colleen down the line. If I have to leave, I can't quite take her with me. I can probably save her primary A.I. to a portable hard drive to take out. I have to leave all the hardware behind. If I'm not leaving her behind, she is stuck in the room now, isolated and disconnected from any other system or network.

Tommy's also pleased with my progress learning and working in the Operations Center. Granted it's mostly collating data, but I've also come up with some programs to help out in that area. The concepts took a while to design, but the programming was easy enough. He's told me that extra credits have been added to my programming class and he's sent a note to the tutor and Linda. So that's one up for my progress.

Everyday is a challenge and I have time to fit all that somewhere without getting too stressed. For the record, I've been clocking just under two hours sleep each night since Saturday. I'm feeling fine; no mood swings or headaches or any strange behaviour like unconsciously floating above the pool. Until then, there's still the field trip for this month.

And with that, let's get to the extra network test we had on Tuesday. We still have one scheduled for Monday next week before the field trip itself on Wednesday. This one was pulled together at the last minute by Remington to make up for last week's session. Given what happened, I guess it was no surprise

Carl didn't turn up for this network test. Heck, even John turned up, which means Remington did get the notice out.

With how things turned out last time, both Jenny and Sophie are uncomfortable with Carl being on the network. We talked it out with Remington after today's session where I agreed Carl might be a disruptive influence, especially given that Jenny managed to get willing participants to partake in a mental attack on him. Still, I already decided to give him the chance and link him into the network. I seriously doubt there would be a repeat occurrence during the field trip.

Remington didn't make a decision on the spot. He took a couple of days to consider it, consulting with some of the other participants. Got that from Helen, Resh and even Ehrmer. Jenny and I had a brief meeting with him just now and he made it clear that there is some animosity towards Carl for a variety of reasons. The only person who spoke for Carl being on the network was John. Remington said his final decision would be based on how the last test run turns out. Carl is expected to attend that and if he's too much of a distraction, he would still be a part of the field trip – that can't be changed – but not part of the network.

He also had to get Jenny to agree not to do anything disruptive again and maintain the integrity of the Learning Network. That's still a few days away and in between, I've got my dinner date with Walker, hopefully catching up with Mikey and a bunch of monsters to take care of, probably.

For now, I'm heading off to the pool to unwind a little, coach a little aqua-acrobatics and spend a little alone-time with Walker.

Mar 22

A few days to catch up on, so let's start from Friday. Pretty quiet day, but an eventful evening. I had my dinner date with Walker as planned and he had some news. I knew, going into this relationship, this moment would come. I thought it would be later in the year, like sometime after June or July. Instead, he's going to be working at the IASC department from April 4 (that's a Saturday) with no end date. That depended on how much work needed to be covered. It's the same department he's been liaising with over the last couple of years, so they know him there and they're aware of his unique status.

At best, we've got two weeks before he goes off and we've got at least one spa session together on the cards. Somewhere in the middle of all that, I'm supposed to get some time off after we're done with the field trip; a day to actually catch up with Mikey

It got pretty emotional throughout the evening. Every time we moved on to some other topic of discussion, my thoughts kept pulling me back to the point that Walker wasn't going to be around. I kept asking him all sorts of questions about his work, where he would be staying or even if there was going to be a pool for him to use; he confirmed there is. Every time I steered our conversation that way, I got a little bit depressed, and he kept turning the conversation in another direction. By the end of our dinner, he had to ask why I insisted on making myself miserable by dwelling on something I had no control over.

I didn't have an answer at the time, and it was something that stayed with me through the weekend. I mean, he's going off for a month, and we would be together again after that.

His way of cheering me up was to take me to the spa and schedule our next session together so I had something else to look forward to. That's on March 31, a day where we could afford to miss a class in the afternoon. We then ended up at the pool to relax, fully clothed and in the water, even if there wasn't anyone around by then. We could probably have been comfortably stark naked in the pool, but that would have raised too many issues with the G/C's and way too many rumours overall. Even though he could, Walker didn't take his shirt off. It was close to one when we called it a night, and after a quick shower and a change to dry clothes, I clocked in some time on the flight simulator before working a little on the virtual spaceship.

On Saturday, I managed to catch up with Mikey, but only briefly. It was like he was leaving as I arrived, with no idea how long he had been waiting. While I did not ask him why he's been staying away, the most I got out of him was that he didn't like coming around any more. I told him I missed him a lot, and he barely responded. It's the feeling something was off. I got to tell him I loved him very much, and then he was gone from the Dream-world. It felt like he isn't coming back and there's nothing much I can do about that except wait until I get home.

Again, there was chasing monsters, and goblins, and whatever strange creatures there were all over the Dream-world. I've got to find out where these creatures are coming from and why they're popping up all over my lands. This monster business is getting tiresome. They shouldn't be there in the first place. I still think it's Ethan's doing but I can't be sure. Maybe when Walker isn't around, I'll set up a session with Ethan to check out his dream world – with Remington's and Linda's permission.

By six in the evening, I was done with the Dream-world. Will thought my readings were a touch unusual and Ms. Phillips got called in to check on me as I was coming out. She insisted on making sure I was okay before letting me go. I was zonked out for the rest of the evening and I fell asleep around ten until about just before five this morning.

Most of today has been light as I took in some revision classes in physics and mechanical engineering, asking questions where necessary. Some people get testy when I do that, slowing everybody down because I need to have things clarified. The tutors don't mind it as much as the trainees though. After all, that's why they're revision classes.

So, that's the weekend in a nutshell. I had a short chat with Becca earlier when I got back from dinner and she's doing well. Kadi's fitting in, so there's less stress on her these days. I'm off to the pool next to unwind. After that, I've some work to get to in the Operations Center.

Mar 24

We had the last network test yesterday with a full complement, and yes, that included Carl and John. It was held in the VR Arena and ran for a full three hours. The cool thing is that not one of us (Jenny, Sophie and me) was stressed out from running the network. If the field trip runs a full four hours like before, we shouldn't have any problems maintaining it. At least, that's one of the main concerns tackled in these test sessions. The other is to make sure that people who are linked to the network actually learn what they're supposed to learn.

While we averaged out in the low 90 percent range, given that we had newbies and a few F.E.P.'s to contend with, it was considered a pretty good score. The test session itself was not as smooth going as it could have been. Sure there was some animosity, an ephemeral negative vibe flowing through the network, probably stemming from the simple point that Carl was on the network. I couldn't determine who was giving off the vibe, and it seemed like it was everywhere.

Suffice to say, I did my best to block off as much of the negative vibes. I couldn't be really sure if Jenny and Sophie did the same, but I have to take it on faith they did, as part of their own function on the network. All that was shared with Remington after the network test was done and I think in the end, he might leave Carl out of the network. He hasn't said anything yet, but given how the feeling was on the network, it would seem the best course. If I want to say how bad the vibe was, well, even John felt it, enough to have his recall rate drop to 93% from a high of 98%.

As to the test session, we agreed things went smoothly enough. Jenny's 'stamina' is good and Sophie seems to be handling herself well. If all goes well, particularly with Sophie, it'll be proof that we can get Bastian and Kevin to start their own network as a team with Sophie still as back-up.

I'm looking forward to the field trip and particularly catching up with Peter. He'll quiz me a little on Mechanical Engineering and it'll be a good opportunity to put some of my lessons to the test. We'll see if I can figure out more of the machinery they're using there and how they work.

I know Ehrmer and Corogi will look at the suits used at the colony while John and Sophie will inspect the robotic systems running there. Helen will be surveying the new structural additions or improvements in both the work areas and living quarters. Kadi and one of the newbies are digging into the farms – aeroponics and hydroponics in the greenhouse, and the normal one that uses 'natural fertilisers' as well as the treated soil. That's what I've been told. I'm not quite sure what Carl or the others are studying at the colony, but operating systems – like electrical and basic utilities – are being included as well as the general work and studies that are being done at the colony. I know Resh is hopping across three different areas and Laurie is flipping between two areas.

I also expect Will and Ms. Phillips will join us again like last year even if they're not linked into the network. Neither of them has said anything. Given what they were doing last year, they might be included.

I haven't written about this lately, but Keiko has picked up a couple of new students in Kendo. The first joined a week back, and the other is Kadi. She accompanied me to the gym the other day and after watching the juniors train and the sparring sessions between Keiko and me, she wanted to try. Keiko was a little apprehensive at first, but since she had one other newcomer to her group, Kadi could be paired with him in practice. It falls to me to do some extra translating to help Keiko coach Kadi. It's a different kind of revision for me.

Kadi's English is okay, but with Keiko, a lot of the Kendo training is done in Japanese – like counting, commands, the name of strokes and strikes – and not everything can be translated easily. It takes a while and I have to find a roundabout way to explain things to her. It's only been a couple of classes now, but I think she's getting the hang of it. Becca has since been duly informed; she gave her blessings, and sympathies. Since we were a little short on the *shinai*, I let Kadi use my spare.

Well, I guess that's about it for now. I'm off to the pool. I know I should get some rest for tonight but I don't know how much sleep I can get. In any case, I've set my hardly-used alarm clock for six tomorrow morning, just in case it's the rare occasion I crash for more than a couple of hours.

Mar 25

Here we are after the field trip and I'm trying to decide what to write about. This has to serve as my journal entry and my report for Remington and Linda on the day's events.

Honestly, I'm feeling pretty sad about the whole thing more than anything. Let's take this from the start.

I was up before the alarm went off, clocking in just over an hour or so of sleep, but I was pretty ready to go. I hit the pool for a few laps before breakfast. Sophie was also there unwinding her nerves in her own way, gliding in circles above the pool. We greeted each other and didn't say much. I guess we were both nervous about the day. On my side, it was simply if Carl was going to be on the network.

We had breakfast together. She was excited about the field trip and running the network, and I only said she would be fine. I reminded her not to push herself too hard because she was also part of the learning team. She could contact me if she had any problems and I would back her up if she got tired. After breakfast, we headed to our suites to change for the trip.

Like before, we had a quick get-together with all the participants for a briefing, complete with snacks and drinks for anyone who skipped breakfast. It was then we were told that Carl wouldn't be part of the network. John protested the decision, and then asked if there was any way to link Carl and him without affecting the rest of the network. Of course, Carl offered to do just that. Remington disagreed before I even said anything, like wanting to remind John about the last time Carl got into his head. And since Carl made the suggestion, I got tapped to ensure he didn't start using his TP during the field trip. Heck, even Jenny or Sophie could do that; even John, should he decide to speak up if he felt Carl linking up with him.

Carl seemed smug about the decision. John grumbled audibly while the others seemed ambivalent. There was also a sense of relief. With a group of that size and tension in the air, you don't have to be psychic to notice when some relief sweeps through several people.

As expected, Ms. Phillips and Will joined us as last minute additions. There was no announcement made about them joining us as they were not part of the educational aspect of the field trip. Sophie didn't even acknowledge Will being there.

Sophie followed my lead since we didn't start the network right away. We gathered in the VR Arena first and the colony's image was brought up around us. The images of the colony's residents followed. The thing I noticed was how incredibly thin and dark they looked, taller than before too, but it could have been the VR imaging or my memory playing tricks on me. It has been a year after all.

We had the usual 'meet and greet' as the newer members of our group were introduced to the colonists and then we were split into our designated little teams. That was when we started linking everyone up to the network, with the exception of Carl. I was happy to see Peter again, but I was also worried about how he looked, almost listless and tired. It was as if he hadn't been taking care of himself or the colonists were having nutritional problems. When I asked him about it, he said he – and everyone else – was fine.

Everyone had gone off except Ms. Phillips, Will and myself. Peter took us to check on the children. That was Ms. Phillips' primary concern. To my surprise, there were three kids now, the youngest being about four months old. The oldest should be just over a year old, but she was walking about without much support. The second child was probably about eight months, but you wouldn't be able to tell by his size either. Will put forth a theory that had to do with gravity, and Peter agreed with it, but there was no real proof beyond the obvious fact of the colony being where it is. As far as Ms. Phillips was concerned, the kids were all hale, hearty and healthy, despite looking a little on the thin side, to me, and not taking their age into account.

While Ms. Phillips and Will were checking on the kids and their mothers, Peter took me around the colony's infirmary and attached labs, showing off some of the newer additions, most of which looked like they were cobbled together with whatever spare material on hand. It was a lot like my own work when I was first putting Colleen together with all the discarded computer hardware in that store room. We discussed how he had put together those varied pieces of equipment to create what had been requested by the other users in the labs. It was fun that we could troubleshoot like that, trading ideas on how best to use the discarded equipment.

I recognised a couple of pieces used before in the perimeter units that watched out for oncoming storms. He said that some of those units were torn apart by the storms, so whatever could be salvaged ended up being used in this way instead. There were still some of the sensors working out there, but not all of them were reliable enough and there was no real way to get all of them fixed. Going out was a risk, which was why Ehrmer and Corogi were now looking into improving the suits again. It was about then when Ms. Phillips called for Peter to have a check up, and that got me a little worried at first.

It turned out Peter got caught on the outside in a storm some time back and his suit couldn't keep out the dust. Some of it got into his lungs and so, he got exposed to the elements. It took a while for Ms. Phillips to get through with him and the prognosis was not too good. It was like mild radiation poisoning. He could carry on as usual but somewhere down the line, it's going to catch up with him. He laughed it off saying it's the price of leaving home. It's something I've heard before, the risk all astronauts face with prolonged exposure in space.

As long as he's still capable, there's still a lot of work for him to do around the colony and there wasn't really anyone else to cover for him. Everyone has his or her place and function to perform.

I spent almost two hours in or around the Infirmary before Ms. Phillips finished her work. During that time, there was only a slight snag in the network with Resh feeling a touch bored. Jenny was on that quickly. Even Sophie picked up on it – a very slight reaction from her 'echoing' through us controllers. Resh was 'off-line' for no more than five minutes and then Jenny reconnected him to the network once she was sure he got past that momentary lapse into boredom. We had the same problem with Resh last year. Anyway, it's reasons like these why Jenny and I aren't counted among the actual participants. The network is our first priority while for everyone else, it's the learning. Not that we aren't learning a little as well.

Will opted to stay back when Ms. Phillips left the VR Arena, following Peter and me through the colony. Peter pointed all the new stuff that had been put together over the last year. He then got me to explain to Will how each of these things were supposed to function; all those little intricacies that provided light, heat, water and air to each of the colony's living and working areas; how they were processed and recycled. Even as I rattled off as much as I could recall from my previous trips, adding on what I now know from my classes and training, Peter was suitably impressed as was Will.

Will asked about how the water and air in particular got provided to the colony in sufficient supply. It was something he said he was curious about since last year, but never gave it much thought until today. I did my best to answer his questions and Peter only corrected me when I missed a detail or two here and there. It felt cool I could do that. Once that was done, it was Peter's turn to ask questions of us, turning our attention to what we did on our last visit a year ago.

Briefly, Will and I accompanied Peter last year when he was making a routine maintenance service on one of the air scrubbers. Will first started trying to move one of the tools with his TK ability. I then did that crazy stunt, using my TK to simulate giving Peter a hug and it practically knocked me out momentarily. Peter already knew I'm a telepath. He still wears that crystal I gave him in the dream-world. I had to explain about being a telekinetic as well and he deduced that Will was a TK too, but had to ask if Will was a TP as well. Will admitted that he wasn't. I had to explain that what we pulled off last year was pretty stressful, and while he didn't see it, I had quite the nose-bleed from pushing myself too hard.

"I'm a man of science and I have my faith as well," said Peter. "The scientist in me finds it difficult to accept without proof, while the religious side might be willing to take that step into believing the unseen. What the two of you are able to do with your minds, it is truly astonishing and a little beyond belief if I hadn't experienced it myself."

Will admitted he wasn't very religious and said, "I find it difficult to reconcile science and religion."

"I can't speak for others but for me, religion is a guide to living your life," Peter said. "That is why it requires faith. Also, there are just some mysteries that even science cannot explain, which is why some of these things remain as theories."

Peter than asked me if I had any religious following. I admitted I had none, but believed in a higher power or supreme being. He nodded and said it was enough to acknowledge the existence of God.

All that went on as we kept walking around the colony. We even passed some of the other trainees. Sophie nodded to me, probably acknowledging Will was with me, or that she was holding up well enough with the network. She didn't seem stressed and I think it was almost three and a half hours by then. We also passed by John as well as Carl at different points. Carl appeared to be behaving himself and not messing about with the network. Everybody else seemed really busy while Will, Peter and I walked by having our little semi-philosophical discussion.

We ended up at the control room for the holographic projectors, the one that controls the cameras recording the colonists and sending the data to the VR Arena so that we can 'see' them. Alternately, it also receives information from the VR Arena so that our image is projected around the colony via their little projectors. It turned out that their holographic projectors are almost as bad as the ones I was using on Colleen when I first fixed the available projectors on her. So, the image of me Peter was looking at was, according to him, extremely gauzy and occasionally transparent while I had an almost perfect image of him within the VR arena.

Peter then asked Will to let us have a moment. Will looked over to me first, and I simply nodded. He left and it was just Peter and me in that control room. He explained briefly how the system was working and admitted that what was being sent to the VR Arena was a slightly altered image of each member of the colony. He then pulled up the specs for his image explaining he had lost a couple of fingers and some toes to frostbite when he got caught on the outside during a storm. As he depressed a key on the keyboard, his image shimmered a bit and the last two fingers on his left hand disappeared.

"I didn't want to hide it from you," he said.

He looked gaunt, like there was absolutely no body fat. His sinewy looking muscles could be seen under skin that seemed almost too translucent and dark, and I was quite fearful about how he really was. He assured me he was healthy and that the physical changes were a result of the diet they were all on and a result of adapting to their environment over the last few years.

I should note at that point, I felt contact from Sophie and Jenny asking if I was all right. I immediately apologised to Peter, closed my eyes, took a deep breath to get my emotions under control, and checked in with them. Jenny did a brief and momentary block on me, and then said that most of the others were done. She offered to take up some of the F.E.P.'s, shared off the others with Sophie and I dropped off the network.

By the time I got back to focussing on Peter, he had readjusted his holographic image. He apologised for causing me distress. I said that it was okay, but I should be a little more careful with the network itself. I then asked him if everyone at the colony was the same.

"In varying degrees," he said.

"Is Ms. Phillips aware?"

He nodded. Ms. Phillips and others were being kept apprised of all their conditions. He then told me not to worry too much. It was about then when I got the call from Remington informing me that the trip was over and everyone else was already gathering to leave the VR Arena. It was the strangest feeling actually, but I don't want to put it into words here. Right before we signed off from the colony, in front of everyone, I gave Peter a hug right there even as his image, and everything else, faded away.

I only had a slight nose bleed then – not as bad as last year – and I had a handkerchief ready. I noticed John eyeing me from one side and Carl doing pretty much the same from the other side of the group, with even a little bit of a smirk or a snort coming from him. Everyone else, pretty much kept their distance for a moment until Jenny stepped up and took me aside. By then Remington and some of the other G/Cs had come down from the control room for the debriefing. Jenny handed me over to Remington and I turned myself towards him, hiding away from everyone else. Remington just put his arms around me and I heard him giving instructions for the others to carry out the debriefing elsewhere.

I'll admit to crying a little and I know Jenny was hanging around a while even after everyone had left. Remington didn't say anything for a while; he held on to me and we stood there. He mentioned when Linda arrived at the VR Arena, and then said, "Keep in mind what he told you about faith."

Very slowly, he pushed me towards Linda and then said, "We really should get you some red or black handkerchiefs if this is going to be a common occurrence." It got a little bit of a laugh out of me. When Linda asked him what happened, he said that I found out about the status of the colonists. That got Jenny's attention, but Remington took her aside and escorted her from the VR Arena saying they had to get to the briefing.

Linda looked me over and asked if I was okay while acknowledging that what I found out was something that's been kept quiet. There is a huge concern about the health of the colony and the changes the colonists have been experiencing. It's a huge deal for all kinds of doctors; that is, how we are to adapt to the rigours of the environment where the colony is. Earth is unique as we are unique to the Earth, so leaving all that behind for a future in space, especially in the long term, can be hazardous. We may be adaptable for the most part, but not as adaptable as some, like the F.E.P.'s who have been with us for extended periods.

"What was that thing Remington said about faith?" she asked.

I admitted that I wasn't really sure, but figured it had to do with trusting the unseen, like the future. She felt I had some thinking of my own to do and advised me to take the rest of the day off to unwind. I insisted I was okay, but she said to do it anyway, suggesting I catch up with Walker. I ended up doing that and spent the afternoon relating the morning's events to him while we sat by the pool.

Even he experienced some changes adjusting to life, not just at The Facility, but on Earth as well. The most he could offer was that, "Humans are a resilient species. Your own history shows that even in the face of greatest adversity, you find ways to survive and thrive." I guess that's where the faith thing comes in.

Walker kept me company through my afternoon of reflection. When I was ready, he escorted me to my suite where Becca was waiting to take custody of me. Apparently, she was informed by Remington, and several others over lunch, about what happened and she said she was instructed to make sure I wasn't left alone for too long. If anything, I guess someone was trying to prove that I have a support system here at The Facility. She also told me that Remington wanted me to write up my report.

So, I guess that's about it.

Mar 27

Maybe I was too hasty with the last write-up. I wasn't feeling all that great when I was writing it and I know, after meeting with Linda over a few details, I missed out a few things. That's my memories and emotions clashing over each other and some things got lost in the mix, I guess.

For example, I left out the lost supplies Peter mentioned. The crate from home missed its landing zone, and they lost over a third of the supplies in the crash. The devastating part was that most of what was lost was meant for the garden to help them grow more food. Seeds were lost to the elements, blown by the winds while others just got wasted in the freezing environment. Even when the Pilgrims crossed to the New World, they could at least find crops to start their own farm. Such a prospect was not viable for the colony. It's another eight months or so before the last of the pre-planned 'care-packages' reaches them.

The other thing was about scavenging for materials. A two-person crew headed North for some additional ice and picked up pieces of the lost probe that supposedly crashed in that region. Peter said they're keeping tabs on some current programs so that when the missions are over, they might pick those units up to see what's left that they can use.

Those are some of what I didn't mention before among others, but it's not really that important I guess. I should have asked the obvious question about how our link and communication with the colony worked without any lag time. Meanwhile, I'll try to catch up with what happened since that night.

Even after I finished up the last entry, I couldn't really unwind my head. I didn't even feel like taking a dip in the pool. I spent most of the night talking it out with Becca – which made it a second round, after Walker – and she didn't say anything. When I think about it, it really kinda makes Walker a typical guy – giving advice and trying to make things better. Becca just listened, asked for details and then kept pretty quiet most of the time. Even after I was done, she stayed up with me and kept me company while we watched TV.

Walker dropped by a little after midnight and took over keeping me company while Becca turned in. He didn't say anything but sat next to me on the couch, his arm around me. After a long while, he asked when I was heading home. It was set for Saturday, but Linda hadn't mentioned any details like if Becca was coming along to keep an eye on me again. I don't know if it's a day out in the city or a trip home. All I know is that I really, really want to catch up with Mikey.

We still had the TV on with the volume turned down to a point that it was white noise in the background. I fell asleep in his arms again with my head on his chest. I don't know for how long, but when I woke up, he was asleep and it was still dark on the outside. Whatever and however I was feeling before I fell asleep, it was still there, but not as strong. People get to sleep things off, but I don't think it works with me.

I tried not to wake him up, but did. He asked if I was okay. I said I was and that I couldn't sleep anymore. I offered him my bed, but he decided to head back to his suite instead. I walked with him halfway and then headed to the Operations Center. I know I set a time-table for work there, but I ended up agreeing with Tommy to at least three times a week. So if I miss one night, I drop in on the next and then try to adjust back to my schedule.

I discussed the day's event with Tommy. He knew about the colony and the problems they were facing, but said it wasn't part of his job scope so there was nothing he could do about it. The most he could do was to follow what's going on and, as with everything else, hope for the best. It's the same with Tomas. It's all out of our control. If I were religious, I suppose I'd consider prayer, which is simply to say that everything will hopefully turn out for the best.

I got through the rest of the day well enough with only lunch-time proving the road-block to an otherwise normal day. Then again, having Carol and Helen bugging me about the incident in the VR Arena would be considered a normal activity at lunch. Becca and Jenny had my back, but I was game enough to answer their questions. Helen was among the field trip participants but she wasn't keeping track of me. The others who were with us at lunch, while curious, were not too inquisitive.

I caught up with Jenny and Sophie today before TP training, had my meeting with Linda about my last entry and well... look at the start of this entry. There hasn't been anything different or strange over the last couple of days that really needs me to recap. I'm still feeling a touch of... I don't think it's depression anymore nor is it melancholia or even real sadness. I've gotten over much of it through the last couple of days, focusing on my work and activities.

Right now, I'm gonna be a late for dinner with Walker, so I'm off.

Mar 30

It's been a pretty long weekend and that should probably be counted from the dinner with Walker to Monday morning. I've been up and about for the whole stretch unable to get some sleep, and I am feeling a touch worn out. I did try, but kept tossing and turning about, unable to settle down enough to fall asleep.

I was a little late for dinner with Walker. I apologised without giving any reason and he gave that smile of his that reflects his understanding and tolerance at my odd quirks. Since I was late, I passed the opportunity for ordering our dinner over to him and make do with whatever he decided to order. It's a good thing I'm not too fussy about my food and I do enjoy most of the dishes he gets the chefs to cook up.

While we were waiting for the food, he told me of a meeting with his G/C as well as Linda to accompany me on my trip home; he confirmed that for me. His argument? Since he was going to be working on the outside with the IASC for a month, what was a couple of days with a friend?

The first thing that popped into my head was, "You know we don't really have a pool, yeh?" Again, he smiled in response, and I smiled back, adding, "I'm really happy you did that. I never even thought I could ask Linda to let you come with me. I've never asked for anyone to come with me."

He reminded me I did request Sophie accompany me one time. but I reminded him that it was for an experiment associated with her TK training.

It was in the middle of dinner when both our comms unit went off, informing us that Walker would be accompanying me home. Once we got that notice, we started planning what we were going to do. Most of my time would be spent with Mikey and maybe catching up with Lian and whoever else was around, but it would mostly be with Mikey. I've had some concerns about him lately.

Since I can't drive, I couldn't say at the time what we could really do or even plan. Walker was pretty understanding about it and even the prospect of being cooped up with me for a couple of days seemed intriguing. He referred to it as a social experiment where he would observe me in my natural home, away from the activities of The Facility.

After lots of talking through dinner, we headed to the pool to review some of the aqua-acrobatics. That's so I can carry on with Sunee and Corogi next month. I had taken to using my TK on myself to mimic Walker's movements, more for precision than actually doing them. He says I'm good at it, but most of the time, it's the limitations of not being able to stay underwater as long as he can. I should mention that Corogi is almost able to keep up with Walker on that end while Sunee has the same problem as me, although I can hold out longer than she can.

It was nearly one when we finished and he walked me back to my suite. After a quick change, I headed off to the flight simulator, clocked in some practice first, unwound with some Viper simulations and then worked a bit on my virtual spaceship simply because I didn't feel like sleeping. It was around half four when I finally decided to head back to my bed. I'm pretty sure I didn't get even an hour's worth of sleep.

By about six, Becca was looking for me. Apparently she had already been adjusting herself to Penang time. Walker knocked on the door soon after that, with a small bag all packed. We met Remington and Linda at the main elevator by half six and Remington was the only one who escorted us the rest of the way.

We got home (in Penang) in time for dinner. Walker bunked in my room, and he had full use of the bed for the whole weekend since I barely slept. We did cuddle a little, but I'll get to that later... maybe. Karen's been bunking in with Rick so Becca had the spare room.

Dinner was out at the hawker centre. Lian managed to join us once I called her. Becca and Walker seemed okay with the food and blending in with the crowd. The small part that didn't work out too well was Mikey. He wasn't as happy to see me as I was to see him, and he was a little distant during dinner. It was almost like he was a little scared of me. I wasn't quite sure but I felt... kinda dejected.

Lian didn't hang around after dinner, saying that she had a date of her own. There was nothing to complain about since Walker and Becca were around to supposedly keep me company, but they ended up chatting with mom who had a lot of questions. On my end, I caught up with Karen to work out what was wrong with Mikey.

It was a bit of an effort to get him to settle down to talk. Mom kept telling me to be patient with Mikey and even said that both Rick and I had moments of alienation from her when we were growing up. That was even when we were always together with no actual distance between us like there is between Mikey and me. The most I got was that he didn't want to go to the dream-world anymore. Frankly, I don't really blame him given how things have been over there.

I spent much of the night trying to connect with him, but Mikey was somewhat reluctant to talk, occasionally running off to Karen instead. Karen, bless her, kept sending him back my way encouraging him to talk to me. At one point, even Walker came over to keep me company after watching Mikey avoiding me every now and then. He didn't say anything; he sat next to me, as if to lend some support.

By eleven at night, Mikey started nodding off, so I took him to bed. Remington, who had been with us the whole way from when we left The Facility, through dinner and all, headed for a hotel – I think, no one really said anything and he was back the next day. Mikey had his bed in my room so that's where I was for most of the night. Walker stayed up as long as he could with me. We did cuddle a little and he asked if I was okay because I seemed so distracted by Mikey. I admitted being worried about Mikey's behaviour – not that it was bad behaviour – and to his credit, he didn't offer any words of wisdom or try to help solve the problem. It was simply a problem he couldn't take apart and put back together like all those machines, systems or theories he usually works with.

After Walker fell asleep, I checked on Mikey. I even did a little scan to see if he was off in my dream-world because this would be about the time when we would meet up over there. Like before, with Sophie, I couldn't really sense anything. It's strange that even as a TP, I can't read a person's thoughts when he's asleep. It's not like the mind completely shuts down during that time, but the mind and its thought process behave differently when a person is asleep… I think.

At around four in the morning, Karen came out of Rick's room and we ended up talking about Mikey. I was reading one of my old copies of *Frankenstein* when she came by. She told me about how Mikey was faring in kindergarten and some of the habits he had picked up; the bad ones outweighed the good by more than a bit. "At least he's not selfish," was one of the better things.

Her main concern about Mikey, as it is a concern with every kid his age, was the lack of an attention span. He likes what he likes and completely ignores everything else. When Mikey sits to watch his cartoons, he's learnt to use the fast-forward to get from one robot scene to the next, skipping over the story completely. I observed that myself. He has no patience for TV shows because he can't skip to the good parts. He gets to bed between ten and eleven at night (at latest) and is usually up by half six in the morning. He does have a short nap in the late afternoons as well. At least his sleeping pattern is far more regular than mine.

"Your mom, and even Charlie, said not to worry about it," she said. "He'll eventually settle down, start getting curious about other stuff and his focus will shift."

"I'm more worried that he doesn't want to connect with me," I said.

"Yeah, he's kinda scared about meeting you. Something about monsters and ghosts trying to get at him there."

"I don't blame him about that. My dream-world isn't as idyllic as it used to be." I thought a moment, then said, "Do you think that he's associating me with all that monster stuff? Is that why he's a little scared of me?"

Karen didn't even need to think about it. "You have to ask him yourself, Jeannie," she said even as she tried to stifle a yawn. In all, she spent maybe just over half an hour with me and I suggested she get back to sleep. The last time we did anything like this was the night before I left to study at The Facility.

On Sunday, Lian came over around ten and Remington came back in time for lunch. Most of my morning was spent trying to get Mikey to talk to me about why he was scared and what we could do about it. I had a suggestion, but I needed him to want to go back to the dreaming, and I would help him fight whatever monsters he thought were going after him. He had to be ready to go back, and I asked Karen to remind him from time to time. Whatever else I can do about it is down to Mikey. I didn't want to force him to hang around with me if he didn't want to.

While lunch was something of a family affair at a Nyonya restaurant, Mikey ended up going home with mom, Karen and Rick while Becca headed back with Remington. That left Walker and me in the company of Lian, who played chauffeur and guide for the rest of the day. I asked Mikey if he wanted to go to the beach with Walker and me, and we also planned to hit the forest reserve, but he seemed somewhat reluctant. I didn't push him. Maybe I should have. It would have given me the time I wanted with him, but by giving in to him, I think I screwed up.

The beach wasn't anything much, but Walker and I took a dip while Lian took some sun. It was the forest reserve that really got to him because while Central Park was the closest thing to The Facility that had all kinds of trees and foliage, it wasn't as lush and dense as the forest reserve. Walker was quite amazed with the trees and flowers, and the green that was everywhere. It was one of those little things I love about Penang.

While we walked through the forest reserve, Lian kept asking me about my relationship with Walker; where I stood with him, what my plans were as well as how it would affect Mikey in the long run. Even with Walker there, I couldn't bring myself to admitting I had thought of such things from time to time. Walker wanted to know as well. In his case, it was if I wanted him to stay beyond his exchange program, or would I go with him when he had to leave, or if we would just end things at that point.

Lian has always been practical with me. She has had me confront some of my life choices in hard ways, and for that, I've always been open and honest with her. When she questions me about my relationship with Walker, even with him present, I had to face up to it. I had to consider such things on the spot. I openly admitted that I did have feelings for Walker, but I couldn't say if I loved him. I admitted to him that since the last guy years ago, I've become mindful of how I should feel towards any person It's why I tried to avoid relationships for the last couple of years when I started at The Facility. What I had with him was something I was trying out, something that I was willing to work at. I also admitted I liked the way he made me feel and the way he cared for me. It's something I really want to reciprocate. It was the closest I could describe to being in love with Walker.

Walker, for his part, had to ask what the word "love" meant. Apparently, there was no translation for it in his language. I could understand that because of how he had described people getting into relationships where he's from. While I couldn't explain "love" to him due to a lack of reference of his customs, I had to explain to Lian why he would not know what "love" meant.

I simply said to her, "Not everything is as universal as it may seem. Some things that are culturally common here are unknown in some parts of the world."

It did feel strange that I had to have this conversation with Lian and Walker practically on the eve of him leaving for a month. We've been a couple for three months now and I'm still feeling my way around, trying to figure out which way I should go – the short term or the long run. While I hardly write about it – simply because everything is in the process of being worked out – I have talked with Walker at length about our potential problems. His approach, so far, is to take things as they come because he, too, has no point of reference for our relationship; not from any of his own experiences or his own customs. As far as I know, we're both in uncharted territories, making things work as we go along.

All in all, thanks to Lian, Walker and I worked out quite a bit about our relationship during that little trek through the forest reserve. We probably couldn't come up with a more relaxed, serene and romantic place to do it. Thing is, we've got maybe a week to work on it before he goes off, and I'm feeling a bit bummed about that. That's the way it goes with me, isn't it? I decided we would be a couple a day before taking a week off from The Facility and now, as we're about to move forward, he'll be gone for about a month.

It was close to six by the time we headed home, and Lian didn't stay. Mom was out; called on a job. It was only Karen, Rick, Mikey, Walker and me left at home. Karen and Rick walked out to the hawker centre to buy some food and I called for pizza take out. So, dinner was at home and there was a lot of it. Walker focussed more on the hawker food although he did find the novelty of the pizza with a local chilli and anchovy (or *sambal ikan bilis* topping) enticing. It was something that was locally unique. I was a little worried about him handling the chilli though, but he seemed to manage well enough. I don't think it was too spicy for him. He turned in for a nap after dinner.

As for Mikey, I gave it one more try to connect with him, but he was distracted and distant as he had been the whole time I was home. I ended up putting him to bed around a quarter to eleven. Karen and Rick would drop him off at the kindergarten on the way to school the next morning.

After Karen and Rick turned in, I ended up watching over Mikey again and Walker woke up around one in the morning. He was feeling a little off, saying he hadn't eaten so much in so few days with a lack of swimming to burn off the excess energy that he's been building up. To help him with that, we ended up making out in the a shower together for probably close to half an hour.

I saw Mikey off in the morning, left a note for mom, who wasn't back yet and then sent off a comms message to Remington. By the time Walker and I got back to The Facility – escorted by Linda who met us when we arrived; she said Remington was unavailable – it was just after dinner on Sunday night. I know for those of you who are calculating, the travelling time doesn't make much sense, but really, it is what it is due to some unique travelling methods that I can't really disclose fully. I think I may have mentioned something about it before though.

The moment we got back, Walker and I hit the pool the first chance we got. A little supper followed and then he turned in for the night. I did a little review work first and then, feeling a little restless, checked in at the Operations Center. I came back to the suite around five in the morning, but couldn't get any sleep. Since I've now come back to beginning, I'm gonna take off for now, get some laps in before breakfast and it's back to the grind.

APRIL

Apr 2

Linda called for the monthly review yesterday and in all, I think it went well. Before meeting with her, I reflected on the month that was. My focus was mostly on my work, and the network for the field trip. Aside from the issue with Mikey, I didn't think I had any problems or issues where my work or life in The Facility was concerned.

Linda wasn't too concerned with my work or studies as everything was considered to be better than expected. My progress across the board was good and it seemed like I was balancing my studies, my work, teaching and extracurricular activities well enough, at the cost of my sleeping time. I did tell her – and she was aware of it – that I hadn't been sleeping much, but it hadn't impacted on me in any particular way as yet.

"Have you had any steady sleep since you got back from Penang?" she asked.

I hadn't had much sleep since the trip. While I didn't sleep over that weekend, I had gotten an hour or so the last couple of nights; last night too. I may have even dozed off during the spa session the day before that, but I couldn't be sure. Only Walker could verify it since he was with me. More on that in a while.

Linda asked about the incident during the network test, that hacking and attack against Carl, and how I felt about it. By this time, it's just something that happened and I wasn't dwelling on it. It wasn't something I could guarantee wouldn't happen again because of who was involved. I have tried to 'make nice' with Carl since then, but he still harbours some animosity towards me. Once that bit was out of the way, she asked how I was feeling with regards to the teaching aspect of TP and TK I had taken on. While I felt Sophie was coming along impressively with her TP practice, I couldn't comment on Ethan since Jenny was training him. I hadn't talked to her about it in a while now.

"You might want to check in with her," she said. "Seems she's having some problems with him."

Linda told me that Remington wasn't around, so she met up with Ethan the day before for the monthly review. He complained a little about Jenny's methods, and was also having some problems sleeping lately. I plan to drop by her training session with Ethan tomorrow to see how things are going there.

It was probably one of the shortest and easiest monthly reviews I've had. It was a good month, and I felt good about it with the exception of the issue with Mikey. It feels like something nasty is waiting down the line, but it could simply be paranoia.

So, as to my Spa date with Walker; it was fine. Since we had made a request for a particular environment in advance, we got just that. The room was laid out with the beds appearing to rest on some coral structures. The walls gave off a soothing cool blue hue that set the mood nicely and there were plants around that looked like they belonged on a sea bed. There was even spot lighting that looked like sunlight, or maybe moonlight, breaking through the surface of the water high above. Added to that was the whale song playing faintly in the background and it was bliss.

We had a full body massage each and I think that may have been when I dozed off. I remember feeling the strong hands working down my back but I'm not sure when it stopped. The next thing I was aware of was Walker rubbing down my back. I couldn't really say if he wasn't the one doing it all along. He did it the last time and he knew I enjoyed it then. I may have heard the other masseurs leaving the room. I'm pretty sure it was the girl rubbing me down earlier.

His hands on me felt amazing, and his touch was both firm and light. We had robes going into the room but had them off for the massage. We were lying face down though, so that was the position I was in when Walker was rubbing down my back, partly massaging and partly layering the scented oils. Since it was just us in the room, I rolled over and it wasn't long after when I pulled him closer. We kissed lightly at first and I moved his hands to where I wanted him to touch me. It was the closest we've got to actually having sex, but we didn't. I want to say that Walker is like any other guy, and physically, he's close.

In terms of his physicality – the sleekness of his body, the sheen of his skin with the very fine hair and all that – is more akin to a dolphin that looks like a person. I don't want to say it out loud for sure but that's the closest comparison I can come up with although it's just me. I should tell him that's what I think; see how he feels about that.

Anyway, enough of that. It's not really my place to comment on his anatomy while I may have some say about his physicality. After all, he's my boyfriend. I've got a couple of days left with him and I intend to make full use of them. Our spa session was an amazing time and I have fond memories of that to carry me through the next month. I want to build a few more memories before he goes. Tomorrow night is out last dinner and I really intend to make the most of it.

So there.

Apr 4

Well, that's that for now.

Walker's gone off to his new living quarters at a IASC facility somewhere in South America. I was not told exactly where. It might be the same facility I've been in contact with in regards to Tomas' mission. It would take him a day to get there and another day or so before setting to work. We agreed to keep in touch either through e-mail or a video conference, or something else because this month of his at the IASC is a trial run. If things go well enough and there's enough work to hold his attention, it could be more than a month.

As much as that thought puts a slight bit of depression on me, I'd rather play over our last few hours together as an antidote. Friday was focussed on work during the day, and night was spent with Walker.

The work bit had me touching base with Jenny and Ethan. While Jenny feels that Ethan is progressing, Ethan feels like he isn't. I went over the lesson plans with both of them and then tried to explain to Ethan why it was laid out that way. Each portion is to build his skill and stamina, and as expected, it's something he's not likely to notice unless his skills are put to use. I related how Jenny and I had to run the network for four hour stretches and how those would wear both of us out by the end of each session.

With his permission, I did a brief scan on Ethan to check how he was at blocking out excess thoughts, keeping things quiet in his head as well as inadvertently broadcasting his own thoughts; all this while he carried on a lesson plan. I had done this with Sophie as well while she practised with another TP in class. I pointed out every time he slipped a little. This was to show that while his skill was there, he needed to improve to a point where he wouldn't unconsciously slip up at any time. At his age, he would be a touch impatient at things moving too slowly. Using the "learning to walk before running" analogy would be wasted on him.

Via a TP network, the three of us came up with some variations on the exercises so that Ethan wouldn't find the sessions boring. We'll have to run some of those exercises pass Miss Tracy for approval first, so Ethan has to continue with what has been planned. He excused himself after that to get some sleep. It wasn't my call as Jenny was his tutor and class hadn't ended. She agreed, saying he looked like he needed it. After he left, she also said that she didn't sleep well the night before.

"And I thought I was the one with the problem of sleeping through the night," I said as we left the class. I did notice Callie practising with Toni, although Toni looked as if she was falling asleep as well. It could have been her way of intense focus though; closing her eyes to concentrate of something. Even I do that from time to time in both TP and TK, so it didn't strike me as anything unusual. It was the timing of it, with both Ethan and Jenny saying they hadn't slept well the night before.

During lunch, Sophie asked if we could meet over dinner. It was the last dinner with Walker before he went off, so we agreed to push it to later. I'm meeting her in a while actually. After lunch was Theoretical Physics with Mr. Hardy and then I had my dinner date with Walker. It was more of a picnic in the garden under a tree.

We had mostly finger food even though we had forks at our disposal. Over dinner, we discussed the channels we had to keep in touch with each other. As long as I was working in the Operations Center, I had a link to him. Our personal consoles can't connect to the world outside, not in the free and easy way one would normally expect. I had considered using the dream-world as a way for us to connect, but given the state of things there at this time, I was reluctant to bring it up then.

I related what I wrote earlier, comparing him to a dolphin. He laughed at it and said it was a compliment to be compared to such an intelligent creature. I offered to stop writing about our relationship in my journal from this point if he so desired, but he didn't mind. It's not like he's trying to hide things.

It was almost ten when we finally hit the pool, and about half twelve when we finally left. We ended up at my suite and I showed him my last couple of entries. It wasn't the first time he's been to my room, although I've never been to his. We ended up spending the night together, making out and cuddling a little. I listened to his heart beating steadily, and then I fell asleep. He woke me up around six this morning. We had a shower together and then headed out to breakfast. It wasn't long after that when he left.

I went through the day as normal; took in a review class in the morning and the dropped in to the dreaming to check if Mikey had come by. He didn't. After waiting around for a while, I left without doing anything else. I've been writing this up since then. It's a rare occasion where I've got some time to spare before dinner and I miss him already.

Apr 6

I guess I've been a little preoccupied over the last week not paying much attention to other things beyond my studies, activities, and Walker. That dinner with Sophie? I may have been a touch tired to understand what she was getting on about. I thought it had to do with her problems in her dream-world, the way she went on about having bad dreams. It didn't occur to me then that it was bad dreams keeping her awake. It was also the second time someone told me about bad dreams.

The reason why I didn't write about this sooner is because it didn't really register when talking to Sophie. Our dinner was basically catching up with each other and me listening to her talk out her problems with her dreams, thinking it was about her dream-world.

What triggered it all was early this morning during my break from working in the Operations Center. There were quite a few people in the café. After looking around a bit while munching on a toast with butter and peanut butter, I made a casual comment to Tommy that I hadn't seen so many at the café at that time before. He said the number of people had been growing lately. I took his word for it because he's at the café every morning at about the same time. According to him, the number of people practically doubled over just a week. To be fair, "doubled" was increasing from four to the eight people I saw this morning. Among them were Kevin, Toni and John, who I probably shouldn't count given that I have seen him around at this time before. Will was also there, but he was probably working the night shift in the Infirmary. I wasn't sure about the other four although I see them in classes.

What caught my eye was that some of them looked like they were actually too tired to be there in the first place. The kind of glazed look suggesting they hadn't slept much at all and they couldn't get back to sleep. I didn't think about talking to any of them at the time and I didn't make the connection to Sophie or Ethan either. The one thought that came to mind was that some people were working really hard or that they were worried about some project.

Now, despite not doing much on the last trip into the dream-world, I ended up sleeping that night. Like I said, I was tired when I met with Sophie for dinner and the moment I got back to my suite, without changing or washing up, I crashed into bed. It was almost half five when I woke up, so at best, it was five hours worth of sleep. I took a morning swim and found Sophie floating around the pool area. I couldn't tell if she had gotten any sleep. At best, if she did, she had gotten as much as I did.

The current plan is to get along with classes as usual and if I notice anything out of the ordinary, like someone not getting enough sleep, I should take note or talk to that person. I should also check in with the lunch group to see if anyone else is having the same problems. Most likely, no one has shared anything with anyone. Everything has been mentioned in passing like it's no big deal because everyone has a bad night once in a while, right? Everyone has a nightmare or two once in a while. Not everybody talks about it every time.

I first heard about Ethan from Linda. Jenny mentioned it later, but not quite in the same way, and then said she hadn't been sleeping well. She did say that bad dreams had been keeping her up, but it didn't really register then. Sophie talked about bad dreams but I thought it was about something else. It's a long shot but maybe, everything is connected. I don't have to speculate about '*if*' they're connected because chances are, they're connected. It's the way my luck goes sometimes. If it keeps going that way, I'll be somehow responsible too, and I'll be the one who may have to fix it.

Like I said... It's the way my luck goes sometimes.

And Murphy's Law would reverse all that because I wrote that down, right?

Apr 8

No one wanted to talk about their sleeping problems, and the most I can confirm is... there are people with sleeping problems.

I tried to get them to talk at lunch; I really did. What I got were awkward silences followed by Carol complaining about me not being forthcoming enough with details about Walker and me in my journal. The rest chimed in as well once Carol got it out in the open and I ended up defending myself for the most part, insisting that nothing happened beyond what I had written. After all that time, I really didn't have sex with Walker, but it's something Carol refuses to believe.

Among those at lunch yesterday, it seemed to me that Carol, Keitaro and Sophie didn't get enough sleep. Sure Carol seemed energetic enough to complain and argue about my journal entries. The subsequent discussion was equally energetic, so while they may have seemed a little tired or worn when lunch started, they sure weren't by the end.

Becca felt I was lacking things to do since Walker left and was poking around to fill that void. I miss Walker, and more so when I'm at the pool at nights. I still have to supervise and advise Sunee and Corogi with their aqua-acrobatic practice. It makes me wish he was around even more. I also try to make sure I leave when the last person to get out of the pool makes me the only one there.

So much for letting my thoughts flow. Reading back on what I just wrote, and deciding to leave it that way, makes it seem a bit disjointed. I used to be able to do this; to keep track of my activities and write. Since Walker left, things seem mundane. Is my life really that boring or have I made it out more than it actually seems by writing this journal? Sure, things were interesting when I first started, it was something new and fresh. I had problems to face and work out, but now...

Maybe Becca's right. I'm just looking around for something to take my mind off Walker, and all the studying and projects or activities aren't working as well. I was happier being with him and a touch lost on my own despite the friends I have around me. And it's not like he's totally gone.

Anyway, I'm gonna keep this short and stop here for now. Time to report to the Operations Center.

Apr 11

Just when I thought things were a little mundane, I get a royal kick in the butt for it. There are two things I need to touch on, one is why I went missing a day and a half from The Facility.

Very early Wednesday morning, during the break with Tommy in the café, I noticed there were more people there than before – that's two mornings prior. Some were doing their studies, either going over notes or using their consoles, others were there having a hot drink; I could see the hot vapours coming from the cups. A couple appeared to be sleeping with the heads resting on folded arms on the tables. In all the times I have been at the café during those wee hours, and we're talking like three or four in the morning, I had never seen more than three people at a time, and that was a rare occasion. The most was four people, but even that was like when one person was just sitting down for a midnight snack, another was leaving a couple of minutes later.

I asked Tommy about the night before. "I just figured there was some major test coming or something. Then again, I've been working the graveyard for a few years now and nothing like this has happened before," he said.

I shared the few stories I heard about people having problems sleeping lately, but no one has actually said anything to confirm or deny it. At best, whatever was going on at the café in the early hours was probably an indication of that.

Kevin and Toni were there again, although Toni was one of those who appeared to be sleeping. I didn't see Will this time around, Ethan was there and one of those guys from the recent network, Rex. That made three people technically under my supervision in TP training, leading me to wonder if there really was a connection. All three of them were sitting far apart from each other though, which could have meant they weren't there together.

I excused myself, telling Tommy that I wanted to talk to Kevin for a while. He said to take my time and reminded me to clock out of the Operations Center later. I nodded and then walked over to Kevin. I greeted him, asked how things were and how he felt about TP training. He and Bastian are learning to work a communication network, but not the learning network as yet. Then I asked, "Having trouble sleeping?"

"Bad dreams," was his reply, which suggested that it was something that was getting around.

"You wanna talk about it?"

"It's silly. Don't really wanna talk about it."

"You aren't the only one with bad dreams lately, you know?"

"Like who else?"

I kept quiet and glanced around the rest of the café.

"Must be something going around," he said with almost a hint of a smile, like I was not privy to some little secret. If anything, it almost seemed like he was suggesting I should have an idea about what was going on. I decided to talk to Ethan and excused myself.

Ethan was surprisingly tight-lipped even when I asked how things were in his dream-world. I was a little concerned about the creatures from his lands creeping over to mine, but he didn't say much. He said he hadn't been dropping in there a while now because of the time factor. His last few trips took much longer than he expected even though he spent only a little time on the other side. When pressed for more information about the creatures, he said he wanted to get back to sleep. I let him go.

By that time, I was pretty tired myself so I returned to the Operations Center to clock out before turning in. For some reason, I slept through most of the night and had to be woken up by Becca. She was surprised to find me asleep at half nine in the morning. I must have clocked close to four hours by then. She asked if anything would cause me to sleep like that. I recounted the night while taking a shower. There had been no changes to my activities, I didn't do anything out of the ordinary lately and I doubt talking to people in the dead of night counted. She didn't know if it was a good or bad thing I got as much sleep as I did without any real reason. Even I couldn't say so myself.

She came to wake me because Remington was looking for me. Right after I got dressed, pulling my jacket off my bed, I checked my comms unit and sure enough, there were notices from Linda and Remington. I had slept through the comms signal. I put on my jacket, pocketed my comms unit and followed Becca to Linda's office.

Becca stayed long enough to make sure I made the meeting and then left. Linda, Remington and Jenny were there. Without addressing my tardiness, Remington said we were putting the communication network into play. Jenny was eager, but Remington's demeanour gave me pause. Something wasn't quite right. My first concern was the number of people connected to the network. Remington said at most it would be no more than five. Then he dropped it; he wanted me to connect with my mom.

The last time I saw my mom was at the end of last month. She went off on Sunday for some job, and I guess everything went well as I would expect. She's quite professional about the things she does. I didn't hear from anyone at home that she hadn't been back for a couple of weeks. This, in itself, is not really a big deal. Rick and I are pretty self-sufficient kids, and she made sure we could take care of ourselves, financially, too.

I mentioned before that when we were growing up, we travelled a lot. At that time, mom was a little directionless, following Mac around and dragging us all over the world to various hot-spots. Mac was a soldier who became a mercenary and later worked in some security firm. He had contacts he introduced to mom, and us by default. Strangely, we were treated well, or the reputation of mercenaries is grossly misrepresented, or maybe we met only the nice ones; maybe it was out of respect for Mac. Rick and I learnt a lot of self-defence from these people. Mom ended up doing reports and articles for newspapers – and three books in all – about the mercenaries, their lifestyles and the occasional mission from the inside, all under a pseudonym; their names were changed too, of course. She still gets royalties off those books.

Over the last few years, she's been working from time to time as what some people call a "retrieval expert", making use of the contacts she had made as back-up, surveillance and resource, sometimes for a particular non-monetary fee, often not. Apparently, something went south with this latest job and she was stuck behind the lines with no communication options.

That's where we come in, according to Remington.

While our relationship has been steady over the last couple of years, pretty much amicable, I make it a point not to get involved with my mom's business or her jobs, simply because it's her thing. I knew she wasn't going to be happy with Remington pulling me in on this one. If mom really needed help, she could have reached out to me although I'm sure I wouldn't be her first choice. There's someone else she would contact, but she might have been working on this one with Remington from the beginning. I didn't ask him though and he didn't say anything about it.

It's difficult to write about this. Out of respect to mom and her client, I can't give out any details about what she was doing, why, and where. However, I can write about what Remington had Jenny and me carry out. Instead of recapping the briefing in Linda's office and what we did, I'll skip over all that. Linda, in the meantime, would cover for Jenny and me at The Facility, informing our tutors, and in my case, people I train with.

Remington escorted Jenny and me to the airport where a private jet whisked us to a location I can't disclose, but it took hours getting there. Since we took a private jet, I got curious enough about flying it. The pilots were accommodating to let me try it out, and since I'm not naming names here – and I'm not even mentioning what kind of plane – it's as clandestine as it gets. I got to pilot a real jet for a short period without the autopilot. The pilots were impressed that I could give them an accurate reading of the entire control panel. They even gave me a few pointers I can't wait to try out in the simulator.

It was just turning night when we got to our destination. Remington introduced me to the extraction team I would be accompanying to get my mom and her package out of the hot zone. Using Jenny and me for the communication network meant they could lay off the radio, which they suspected was being monitored. Whatever mom had with her, the people after her wanted it back; obviously. Jenny remained with Remington at the control centre, keeping in contact with me and the field captain to relay Remington's instructions. I would scan for and keep a bead on my mom. That was the network... well, four people connected to coordinate an extraction. At no time did Jenny nor I connect with Remington directly. All of his instructions came through Jenny.

I was given a really heavy triple layered bullet-proof vest to wear and a chintzy helmet, which didn't feel as safe as the vest did. Remington said it was, "just in case." Even Jenny felt nervous when she saw me wearing the vest, wondering out loud about the situation I was going into. I told her, "Don't worry. I've been in worse," but it didn't ease her nerves. It probably got her thinking about what other situations I have gotten into that would be worse than flying off with a bunch of "security experts" into a "hot zone".

Technically, I didn't need to go out with these guys, but Remington felt that it would be easier for my mom if I was with them. There were four guys on the Hawk and one of them had the job of watching out for me.

So, here's what we did. I took a moment to call out and connect to my mom, reaching out telepathically and hoping that she would answer; which she did. Cut one lecture away and I relayed Remington's plan. With her feeding landmarks, we could determine her location on a map and direct her to a rendezvous point where the Hawk would be able to pick her up. She wouldn't have too far to go, depending on her package. Once she was okay with that, I linked up with Jenny, who in turn, linked up with the field captain. He found it a little strange at first, but I told him to think of it as a constantly open mike between him, Jenny and me. He just had to guard his thoughts a little.

We loaded up on the Hawk and then it was in and out. All the while, I kept in contact with mom, tracking our progress and reporting it to Jenny who would relay to Remington. Any changes in orders from Remington would come back to the field captain and me. Under the cover of dark and a half moon, we got in there, picked up mom and her package, and got out without those "security experts" having to do more than watch our perimeter. We were well off the ground by the time a couple of shots came out of the dark, but it sounded like pop-guns over the din of the blades. Chances of them hitting us in the dark were practically nil.

I know it sounds way less exciting than it actually was, but as I said, I can't write a lot in detail about this. The communications network worked better than we hoped given that we had at least one person who was completely unknown to us linked in. That was always the worry, how that unknown individual would react, and the field captain was all business; no stray thoughts. He understood clearly how the network operated from our little briefing.

My mom had the idea of what we were doing the moment I connected with her. We are alike in most of our abilities, which was why Remington had wanted her to join The Facility. She chided me briefly about flying in with the extraction team saying it was an unnecessary risk, despite being decked out with safety gear and having one other person guarding me. This was while we were in the Hawk heading back to where we started. I think she continued her concerns later, but with Remington instead.

In the few hours before we parted ways again, I caught up a little with my mom. It was her chance to get me on my own without being distracted by Mikey or Lian or even Walker. I told her about how life at The Facility was getting along, basically stuff I had written already, but I left out the bits about the dreams and people not sleeping well.

She left shortly after we were done, because she still needed to deliver her package. I know Jenny slept a little on the way down, and a little after we were done with the network. Once she was awake, we headed back, taking the same private jet. She slept again on the flight back while I had a brief chat with Remington as he reviewed the use of the network, asking about the progress with the other trainees. He also touched on what he had heard about Ethan lately and asked if I had heard anything. I mentioned that early morning meeting, but he was not sharing any information. I informed him about the few people who had sleeping problems, even pointing to Jenny at one point. She seemed to be sleeping a lot all of a sudden.

Before arriving at our original departure point, she woke up and I asked if she slept well. She said it was the best she had in a while even if it was in short periods. I tried getting her to open up about her sleeping problems, and she only attributed it to bad dreams. When I asked her about it, she couldn't remember any dreams while sleeping during this little outing.

It was just past half eight on Friday night when we finally got back to The Facility and the first thing I did, after a nice hot shower, was to check with Sophie if she was interested in having a late dinner. She obliged joining me for my dinner, but had a juiced orange only. I asked her about her sleeping issues and dream. This time, she told me about the monsters that plagued her dreams, from being chased around in her own worlds, to monsters lurking around The Facility, and wherever else she might dream of. She couldn't describe the monsters themselves. When I pushed a bit more, she admitted that she couldn't remember because she might not have actually seen them, but there was the sense that the monsters were there.

If I understood what Sophie was getting at, it was likely no one else wanted to talk about their dreams filled with fearful stuff like invisible monsters. It was more the feeling there were things lurking, a sense of fear permeating through, but nothing really manifesting. Just the sense of it is strong enough to make people wake up from their sleep with the feeling that something is wrong, but there's no determining what it is; all just a bad dream; nothing to talk about because... there really is nothing to talk about.

Personally, I don't know how dreams work. I'm less clear on why we dream in the first place and I was never curious enough to learn about it; not even trivially. I think I do dream even when I've slept for an hour or so because I do have a vague sense of dreaming when I wake up. My own dream-world has got nothing to do with actual dreams or dreaming

When Sophie asked me to go into her dream with her, I wasn't sure if it was possible. I barely know how the brain works in a conscious mind that I would attune to as a telepath, never mind how a brain works in a dream state. At least, from my perspective.

I would have to consult Miss Tracy, Ms. Phillips, probably Charlie, Remington as well as Linda on the matter, and even with that, I wasn't really saying that I didn't want to do it. I needed to know what I would have to do.

"Couldn't you wait until I do the REM sleep thing and then scan my mind?" she asked.

I told her that I wouldn't know if I were in her thoughts or in her dreams if I were to try it that way. "I really want to help; to do this thing. I just need to be sure about where I'm going in your head," I said. She agreed, understandingly, to let me make my inquiries. I then wondered if everyone who was having sleeping problems or bad dreams were having individual problems, or if they were all connected.

It's almost three in the morning now and I've had a pretty long couple of days. I should try to get some sleep. I've got to catch up on my classes, a few people to meet and a trip to my dream-world later today.

Apr 12

Miss Tracy, as willing as she is to help in anything to do with TP or TK, has no idea about dreams and how they work. Instead, she referenced a movie from the eighties about a group of psychics who would go into people's dreamscape to help them. So, based on that, she figured it was a possibility. Beyond that, she had nothing else to suggest as a course of action.

Linda was a little more open about the suggestion, but she recommended running it by Remington since he was a little more knowledgeable about TP skills. How and why that was a fact was not discussed. Every time I think he might be a psychic, he, somehow, proves me wrong. Then someone makes a suggestion, or he does something, to reinforce that idea again.

Remington thought it would be something worth trying, but there was no way to really determine if I would be going into Sophie's dream or her thoughts. Was there a way to differentiate the two? I guess he's equally blur in that department as I am. He does know there's a difference between my dream-world and normal dreams. He would back me up if I wanted to try this because if it worked, I could possibly help Ethan as well.

He would inform Linda of his recommendation so that she would back me on the matter, if she decided to go along with our plans. He would call Charlie as I requested, who I hope will come in on this. Remington would also consult Sophie's G/C to make sure he would have an idea of the scope of what we were trying, as well as the potential dangers that might arise. This was in case anything went wrong with the whole experiment.

Ms. Phillips, surprisingly, was glad that I brought up the plan and she was more than willing to let me try. She had already seen a few trainees with sleeping problems and was at a loss of what exactly to do. Most of them have been spending the night at the Infirmary, hooked up to monitors to chart their brain activity to determine if there was a problem or not. Again, this kind of sleeping problems and bad dreams is not her field so she couldn't say how things would go. It was likely at this time, that aside from Sophie, no one was going to let me into his or her dreams.

As far as I could determine after meeting with all of them, we're in some uncharted territory. I told Sophie that I was willing to try, but I didn't tell her about how apprehensive I felt about it. Getting into her head and all, especially under these circumstances, was a dicey proposition for me given what happened last year. I think she must have been aware of it as well, but kept mum. I think I'll confirm it with her later, to be sure.

When it comes to being a telepath, we can 'hear' other people's thoughts (never tried animals though), but we don't 'read' people's minds per se. We can sometimes drop in a thought or two into other people's head, so to speak. We might influence how a person might think – maybe, if movies are anything to go by – but it is ultimately up to that person to form the final thought. You don't always act out what you're thinking, right? That's what people are usually afraid of because there is a tendency to think one thing and say another. To lose that sense of personal privacy can be horrifying, as is the idea that your thoughts may not be your own. That's why we are being trained to use and control our abilities, and why I have my own rules about how I use my abilities. Comparative to all that 'basic' stuff, working the networks is a little more complex, but it follows the same basis. It's a matter of training and practice to handle that kind of information flow, that's all there is to it. It still takes a level of trust from our participants.

Dreams tend to be visual, so it's actually a trickier proposition. I don't claim to know how it works, but maybe try this. We can close our eyes and visualise things in our minds. For a telepath to 'see' these things, we need to share the same mind set or 'wave'. It helps to close our eyes too. I know scientists have done something like this. The brain gives off electrical impulses when engaged in certain activities like dreaming. The experiment is where they try to get two dreamers on the same wave-length or electrical impulses by hooking up wires between the two people, sometimes involving a sensory deprivation tank They get to share a dream in that way. It's called fringe science for a reason. For telepaths, it's a matter of 'synching up'. It's how I get to pull people into my dream-world, but it's not in an unconscious state like actual dreaming.

I wish I could explain it better. It really depends on understanding how telepathy works. Even being one, I can't really explain it all. It doesn't always work with the others, but it could be because I'm not just a telepath, and probably not a true natural psychic at that. Or am I actually that? I really don't know for sure because I don't know exactly what that implies. I don't want to say that there are certain rules on how we are supposed to work and then go off to do something that completely contradicts those set rules. It's not some kind of science. There is nothing set. We are learning how our abilities truly work and how we can apply them. That's why we're at The Facility. It's a learning process.

Anyway, Walker made contact and it was really my fault that I didn't know about it earlier. There was an e-mail from him a couple of days back, but I don't always check my e-mail on a daily basis as there was never a need. I took for granted that the software on the console that monitors the e-mail would let me know I had some mail in my inbox, but I didn't have it on. He wrote to Becca asking if everything was okay with me because I hadn't replied him yet. That's how I found out about his e-mail!

In reply, I wrote briefly about the last couple of days events, basically sending him the last journal entry in part. I haven't heard from him as yet.

I'm strangely still worn out from yesterday. The dreaming session I took ended up with me having to help villagers hunt down creatures all over again and Mikey didn't turn up either. I am getting a bit tired of that, but on the bright side, it's getting me to sleep more on Saturday night. I turned in just after midnight having spent time in the pool to coach Sunee with her aqua-acrobatics. Corogi wasn't available. I was worn out by the end of the day and I slept pretty deeply. I don't remember dreaming tho, but I was up and back at the pool by half six in the morning.

It's about ten at night now and I'm heading back to the pool. Corogi should be there tonight, but I'll try to catch up with Sophie first.

Apr 13

Well, I'm a happy clam.

I checked in at the Operations Center and Tommy said there was a call for me. I had to wait for it to be patched through since I didn't really check in on time. When the call got connected, I got to talk with Walker at the IASC Mission Control Center.

We spent close to an hour or so just catching up. I apologised for not writing back earlier, and he told me more about what he's been doing over there. He's mostly working as a theory checker of sorts, looking over their work, poking holes where they're weak and sharing ideas on strengthening whatever systems they're working on. He couldn't go into detail, saying it was mostly classified, and it would be over my head. He actually used that term with me for the first time. I had to explain it before when I first used it in his presence.

When we were done, Tommy commented he had never seen me so happy before. He pointed out that I couldn't stop smiling.

I'm gonna keep it at that.

Have to keep an eye on my e-mail inbox as well.

Going to sleep now. Really tired, but happy.

Apr 16

By all rights, given my sleeping pattern, I shouldn't even dream when I sleep, but I'm pretty sure I do. The weirdest I had was when I dreamt I was at home, sleeping in bed and dreaming something else. It occurred to me that I was dreaming in a dream, but I didn't know what I was dreaming of then. It was strange. At one point, I remember carrying Mikey around my room and then... everything went blank, and I woke up. It was the strangest sensation I ever had.

Anyway, that's a little beside the point right now. Last night was the first attempt at getting into Sophie's dream. When Callie was asked to try to get into what was thought to be my dream last year, she tried to "synch into my frequency". So that's what I tried with Sophie, except I had help from Ms. Phillips to get my brain-waves to synch with Sophie's.

Last night in the Infirmary, Ms. Phillips had Sophie hooked up to one of the monitors first and then had her fall asleep. In the meantime, it was my turn to get hooked up so that Ms. Phillips could monitor my brain-waves. Will was on hand to help watch over the machines. Linda and Miss Tracy were also there as observers, watching over us. Once Sophie's REM started, I started scanning her mind. Ms. Phillips would occasionally say when my brain wave patterns would synch with Sophie's. It was to let me know when I might be in line with her dream or not. It wouldn't make much sense to me, but it did let me know, in some way, what I was supposed to pay attention to in Sophie's thoughts.

First impressions? For someone who was asleep, there was a lot of noise in her head coming from her subconscious. Heck, I could even hear parts of conversations with her from the day playing over again, like her brain was sorting through the day's stuff. Or was it more than a day? Is this what goes on when we sleep, or is it just her? I know different people behave differently, and I would know that no one has the same thought process, but there is an assumption that brains work the same way in a general sense. Still, it was a bit of a surprise to find that amount of activity going on. I wasn't even sure what I was actually looking for. I didn't know if it was thoughts, sounds or some kind of images. It was harder than I expected.

I'm pretty sure I didn't fall asleep even though according to the reading on the monitor, I almost did. Might have been some kind of feedback from Sophie, but I kept trying to go with the flow. Ms. Phillips' voice kept fading in and out, so it became progressively difficult to navigate her thoughts. I think I may have gotten to the point of connecting into her dreams, but I wasn't sure how close I got on the inside, because she woke up. As far as Ms. Phillips could say, I got pretty close to synching with Sophie.

I was willing to give it another shot there and then, but Sophie didn't want to get back to sleep. When I asked her if I was anywhere in her dreams, she only said that she could sense I was around. Ms. Phillips suggested that the only reason Sophie could remember was because she woke up in the middle of her dream. If she slept through her full cycle, she probably wouldn't even remember. In the end, she's willing to have another session. That's later tonight. I think I might be able to get into her actual dream if I take the same route tonight, with Ms. Phillips nudging that little bit more to get me to the right frequency.

Meanwhile, the last couple of days have been smooth. After that chat with Walker, I ended up sleeping for about three hours. I left off the journal entry that morning around half four and by the time I woke up, it was almost eight. I saw Becca on my way out to breakfast and she was surprised to learn I just woke up. Over breakfast, I couldn't stop smiling the whole time as I told her about talking to Walker.

Half a month on and I think I'm doing okay with the aqua acrobatics. I managed to get Corogi and Sunee to work together on one routine and they found that they complemented each other's movements nicely (small 'yay').

I then took them to the next part of the routine which should continue for another few days before moving on again. I'll admit to using my TK in the pool to get the movements down, especially Walker's side of the routine. It's a little cheating on my side since I can't duplicate his moves exactly.

As for kendo, it's been a little different, and yet the same in that I'm helping with the coaching. While I try not to play favourites, I have to give a little more attention to Kadi particularly when it comes to translating Keiko's instructions. The problem is that I'm translating from what little I know of Japanese to either English or her language. It's mostly those little nuances that Keiko use in her kendo instructions that I have to translate.

Probably due to this personal attention, Kadi has been progressing a touch faster than the other juniors, but not quite to the level of our intermediate students. In training them, I've become a little more aware of my own strokes and movements, like self-consciously fine-tuning my own strokes.

Anyway, I should get some rest before my next real dream session with Sophie.

Apr 18

We'll start with where I left off. Once I got to the Infirmary, Ms. Phillips briefed me over the system she had for keeping me informed on which areas of Sophie's mind I was going to scan, and perhaps enter. Last time, I mentioned that I felt like I was falling asleep, but there's a need to keep conscious for me to do what I needed. There was nothing she could give me to keep me awake because my body would counter it almost immediately. It's one of those things with regard to my biology, part of why I heal faster than normal.

So, Ms. Phillips' new idea was to have me use an ear-piece, and she was right in my ear. I didn't think it would work, but it did! She managed to navigate me right into Sophie's dream.

Sophie was a little late. She came in with Will who helped to hook her up to the monitor while Ms. Phillips assisted me. I had to wait for her to fall asleep and once she hit her REM state, I got to work. As before, it was a matter of navigating whatever was in her head with Ms. Phillips guiding me to synch with Sophie's frequency. We got through it a little faster this time and I think I got into her dream because Ms. Phillips told me that our brain-wave patterns matched perfectly.

I don't know if anyone reading this would have the same sensation in dreams. You dream you are doing something or are involved in something. It's kinda like a first person perspective and you're actively involved in whatever you're doing in your dream, but then it suddenly switches and you're also observing yourself doing those things. It constantly switches between first and third person perspective, but you don't interact with yourself. Well, maybe some of you may have experienced that, but from my experience, I've never interacted with myself in my own dream.

It was weird when I hit Sophie's dream and there were two of her. It was like she was occasionally participating in her own dream and sometimes, she was watching herself with me. The strange thing was that neither version of Sophie interacted with me or even acknowledged I was there. It was not for lack of trying to get her attention – short of actually touching her – and trying to register that I was in her dream.

Now, the dream itself was as she described it. She was wandering around the corridors of The Facility, but it was dark, like it was late at night and she wasn't quite sure where she was going, occasionally looking around at something that didn't seem to appear. I didn't pick up on the sensation she said she felt. Based on what she related before, I had an idea what was going on and what she likely felt. I thought it was strange that while I was in her head, I didn't have a bead on her feelings. She had mentioned the fear and paranoia being strong in her dreams, but I didn't feel them. So I figured the next logical step was every time she looked back at whatever was spooking her, I headed in that direction to find what she was afraid of.

The further I wandered into the supposedly scary hallways of The Facility in Sophie's dream, the further I seemed to be moving away from Sophie's dream. At least, that's what Ms. Phillips kept telling me. I was really curious to find out what was scaring Sophie, a person I knew who would have stood her ground to confront her fear instead of running away. The darkened imaginary corridors in her mind weren't any different to the corridors of The Facility at night. I didn't find anything there and I think it's not The Facility itself that's putting some kind of fear in her.

I need her help with this. It's her dream after all, and I think there might be a way around that as well. Also, I wondered if any of the others who were experiencing sleeping problems or bad dreams were having the same dream. I don't know if there's anyone else who's willing to try what Sophie and I are doing

Sophie woke up in the middle of her dream again. I really don't know how describe what it's like to be in someone's dream when they suddenly wake up, but I was out of her head almost immediately. She claimed she didn't see nor sense me in her dream. I described what I saw and she verified it was the dream she had. She said that the location changed on occasion; it wasn't always The

Facility. That portion where I 'caught up' with her was only a small fraction of her dream. We're going to try again tomorrow night; that's Sunday.

I'm trying to keep things on an information level with all this because there is plenty I'm leaving out. It's a lot to cover actually, but I'm sticking as best as I can to the dream and scan stuff. I could mention that Sophie woke up with the shakes, like she was scared of something, or that she eventually got to sleep later, but that's more from Ms Phillips as I didn't observe any of that. I know I would not do too well if my sleep patterns get broken up in this way. It hasn't happened with me lately, but I know the effects well.

I got about an hour's sleep in my special bed in the Infirmary after that. It was around five in the morning when I woke up. The Infirmary was not dark, but dimly lit. Will was sleeping next to Sophie and I left them there. She looked peaceful. There was one other Infirmary staff working there that night; Susan, I think. We nodded at each other as I left.

The rest of the day ran smoothly except Sophie took the morning off. We were to have our TP training, but given what had gone on the night before, it was logical she didn't turn up. I checked on Kevin and Bastian, their progress with the Communication Network and shared some details of our recent application of it in the field.

I only caught up with Sophie during lunch and she looked a little more rested. She relayed that she woke up twice more during the night, and it was after I had left. I asked her if it made sense to her she would be afraid of something in her dream, and she said, "Of course, it doesn't make any sense."

"I just needed to be sure," I said. "I kept heading to the area you were looking back at, and I didn't see anything there." I suggested going to the dream *with* her, but from a conscious standpoint instead of passively synching frequencies. I had made contact with her dream self and was not recognised in any way to help. To counter that, I wanted to establish an actual presence in her dream. She felt it was worth a shot, and asked if it was even possible to do that.

We then descended a into the technical side of things as Will had done a little research into the matter for Sophie. Accordingly, if she were in a basic dream state, her delta waves should have been active on the monitors, but instead, they weren't as active as they should have been given the stage of REM she was in. There was also no way to determine if my moving into her mind during the dream would have resulted in the occasional bursts of beta and alpha waves. When I asked her about it, she explained that the beta waves indicated active thinking while alpha waves indicated a relaxed or reflective state of mind.

It was Becca who made the assumption that Sophie's brain appeared to be working out problems in intervals while in a dream state. "That's only based on what Sophie explained about the brain-wave patterns," she said. It was also saying that we had no real idea what was going on or why her brain was behaving in that manner. When in my Dream-World, Ms. Phillips has recorded extensive activity across the board, particularly spikes in theta activity. While I would appear to be sleeping, the scans would indicate otherwise. At least, that's what I've been told, and it's all beyond me. I know that my dreaming somehow helps me.

The wonder of talking with Sophie about our little experiment over lunch was that it got the interests of the others at the table – Carol, Helen, Keiko, Keitaro, Callie, Jo, Kadi, Will and Ethan. Sophie was open about her sleeping problems and bad dreams, and that got Ethan to openly admit too that he had been having bad dreams lately. Nightmares are common enough among kids his age and it's not something kids share. Mikey took forever before telling me he was feeling scared about going to my dream-world. Once Ethan opened up, Will, Callie and even Carol admitted to having bad dreams lately. Only Carol hasn't been having problems sleeping. She would admit that her dreams of late have been "a touch disturbing" (her words), but she has slept through every one of them.

The strange thing is that there are similarities. The dreams all point to something hidden and unseen that is stalking or chasing them. The location varies tho, so why Sophie's took place in The Facility is a bit of a mystery, but it might actually be completely irrelevant. By the end of lunch, before we headed back to class, Callie and Will were willing to let me into their heads to check out their dreams; see if there are any similarities.

There isn't much to write about over the rest of the day since it went along as usual. Mechanical Engineering in the afternoon, sparring session with Keiko in the evening and then I had to get ready for my dinner with Hank. Helen actually booked a dinner over lunch and since Sophie was there, she said I could go ahead with it. Keitaro, being one step behind, booked the following Friday dinner, which would be the last Friday of the month. After that, Walker might or might not be back. Also, Helen asked but said she would be there as Hank, which meant I had to put on a dress. I took the time to get ready. I have a dress I hadn't even worn for Walker, not that I had to, and I was going to put it on for Hank. Becca was even suitably impressed that she had to take a picture for posterity.

When I got to the café, Hank had set up a special table in the garden and he was decked out in a suit looking remarkably dashing. He barely commented on my dress aside from saying it suited me, but that it would look better without my jacket over it and if I had worn proper shoes instead of sneakers. I did take off the jacket, but then commented that I felt a tad exposed – which was strange considering I wouldn't mind going skinny dipping or wearing less than nothing if it suited me. Wearing that dress flowing below my knees, with its short sleeves, felt weird. I'm so used to my jeans and shirt combos, and I know practically nothing about dresses. I thought this looked okay and it fitted well when I was in the store. Even Lian said it looked good on me, so I picked it up there and then. In retrospect, I should have shopped around a bit more.

Over dinner, Hank asked how things were with Walker and then inquired about the dream problems people were having. He requested I not write about his issues, so out of respect, I won't go into details about our conversation.

The dinner was delicious as expected, nothing fancy. We ate, made conversation and that was mostly it. There was no after dinner activity, but it was a pleasant evening nonetheless. There was so much that went on, so much we talked about and that's all we did, but somehow, it stuck with me that it was such a nice thing to do.

Anyway, that's all caught up. Becca still wants me to unwind tonight given how busy my nights have been lately. It's too late to go to the pool though, so I'm heading to the flight simulator to clock in some flight time.

Apr 19

First things first and going in sequence. Still no sign of Mikey or Old Crans in the dream-world, but still lots of stupid looking creatures that are beyond any actual mythological description. They're getting more and more mashed up, unlike when they first appeared. Taking them down is getting tougher for the most part while some are truly dumb as a post that the villagers do not need my help.

One change is that a community notice board has gone up in Kinstein's place and there are now bounty hunters – or rather, creature hunters or trappers – roaming around. Kinstein's Kitchen is still neutral land which is considered safe grounds, even the creatures don't come anywhere near or block the roads to it. There is some sense of intelligence there, or maybe some new rules have come up. Maybe they know that it's sort of my base of operations, so they don't come near it, but what do I know about how these creatures think or act anyway?

Yeah, I'm trying to consciously label the creatures in my dream-world that way, "creatures" instead of monsters, because I'm trying to keep things separate from the "monsters" that are haunting the dreams of other people. Since they're using that term "monsters," I'll stick to "creatures" for my side.

In any case, all the creature hunting and getting the villagers to set up their own defences has been tiring and it knocked me out on Saturday night. I conked out sometime past eleven, clocking in a solid seven hours or so and waking up just after six the next morning feeling pretty worn out. It didn't make getting through today any easier because I haven't felt this stiff in ages. Good thing about Sunday is that the classes aren't mandatory, although I still did take in extra revision classes in the morning.

At lunch, I caught up with Sophie, who seemed much better and rested, saying that she slept restlessly through the night. She could still remember the dreams being a touch disturbing. On my part, I complained about the creatures that had been turning up in my dream-world and then asked her if she had been experiencing the same. I don't think her dream-world is bordering mine, but I was curious if there were similar problems. She said she hadn't dropped by in a while.

"I hope I didn't start you on the same path as me, that you have to go in once in a while to reset some biological issue," I said.

"You don't have to do that nowadays, do you?" she asked.

I gave it some thought. "It does help me get some sleep, like last night," I said. Every night between each Saturdays, I clock in about an hour so I guess it's still something I need to do. If I pass, I might end up having less sleep, but it's not something that's been playing up as badly as before. "I guess I still need it, but that's just me."

"Do you think it might be me, too? Could my sleeping problems be a side effect of running a dream world?"

"It wouldn't explain the others," I said and she noted that aside from herself, Ethan and me, no one else has the dream-world connection.

We then agreed to give my getting into her dream another try there and then – right after lunch. The idea this time is to mentally synch with her first, create a basic TP network and then she would fall asleep, hopefully taking me with her. We explained this to Ms. Phillips and Miss Tracy, to whom we sent a message via the Comms unit and she met us at the Infirmary. Then, since he was with us at lunch, Will helped to get us hooked up to the monitors.

The brain behaves so differently when a person is asleep and the basic thought process that we TPs sort of 'listen in' doesn't work. Even in developing the learning network, it took a while to learn about the subconscious and cognitive learning areas, and how to access them; yes, it is a slippery slope. Come to think of it, I'm not really getting into her thoughts either, but I was going to experience what it was like for a person to fall asleep and move into a dream state – at least, that was what I was hoping for. It wasn't quite what I got and it was pretty underwhelming.

We had two beds set side by side. Sophie was on one and I was on the other. I listened to her breathing and did as best as I could to match it. She would occasionally check if I was still connected to her and I responded. I could sense her thoughts going quiet, and I sort of followed suit. I could hear Ms. Phillips through the earpiece quietly telling me Sophie was falling asleep. Me and sleep, not always compatible, and while I didn't quite fall asleep myself, I did follow Sophie's thoughts, or what was left of them, into the subconscious and a little beyond into the dream state. It was not quite the process I expected. Everything went quiet and then there was really nothing for a while. I latched onto whatever "essence" of Sophie I could identify with and went with the flow.

It was Ms. Phillips who confirmed when Sophie was in REM and told me that I was still in sync. It was a weird sensation being somewhat semi-conscious and fully aware at the same time. The dream started out of nowhere, not like fuzzy forms coming into being, but like the lights being switched on suddenly and then, you're there. I have no idea when she became aware of her dreams starting. Like before, I found her in her dream, again, occasionally being in two places at the same time. She still didn't register my presence. The location was different though. I didn't recognise the place, but it wasn't The Facility corridors. This time, I could sense the presence Sophie seemed to be afraid of. I just couldn't see it.

I made deliberate contact with Sophie by taking hold of the hand of her dream-self; easier said than done. Once that happened, she acknowledged my presence. It started with her looking at her hand which led her gaze to seeing me. I greeted her and she responded, "What are you doing here?"

It took a while before she could recall what we were attempting to do. Things got a little weird after that because once she remembered, the whole world changed around us. Next thing I knew, we were someplace else, which she said was her dream-world. It was a bit of a surprise that it happened because, technically, we were effectively out of her actual dream. Even she was surprised it happened.

We tried to get back to her actual dream, but couldn't. It was my first time being in her dream-world so I asked how she created it, knowing that she got advice from Ethan. She explained that he took her to his dream-world and got her started by building a small village there before creating an imaginary border that would separate her world from his. It's similar to how he got started off my dream-world. So, she's got her dream-world bordering Ethan's, but not mine.

None of this has got to do with the bad dreams though. There was nothing else for us to do there and since we couldn't get back to the dream, we called it off and decided that we have to try again next time. Still it was a little weird the way we jumped from her dream to her dream-world, which exists on a different level. Ms. Phillips even detected the shift on the monitors and asked what happened. Beyond describing what I wrote, we had no idea what really happened. I suppose that's how dreamers find their way to the dream-worlds.

Sophie, Will and I had dinner together, going over what we think might have happened, but there wasn't much else we could really determine. None of us are experts in this area and we're stumbling along as best as we can to figure things out. Tomorrow, it's Will's turn. I'm gonna head off to the pool for now.

Apr 21

Looking back a little over the last few entries, it's all been about the dreams and the attempts at getting into Sophie's dream. Maybe Becca's right and I *am* looking for something to distract me from Walker's absence. Except that Walker and I have been keeping in touch over the last few nights via video conferencing. It's been an incentive for me to check in at the Operations Center a little earlier than usual so I could have a little time with him before he turns in for the night. The last few nights have been busy, but I do check in with Tommy and Walker, when I can, before heading off to the Infirmary.

And while I've been writing about myself and my so-far-futile attempts at getting into Sophie's dreams, I wasn't the only one checking into dreams. Callie had volunteered herself to our little experiments, but while I had been focussing on Sophie, Callie had been conducting her own experiments with her TP partner, Toni. I learnt about that today when I approached Callie about scheduling a session with her. She was in her TP class with Toni when I dropped by to look for her. I didn't want to do it in the public arena of lunch time.

I confirmed with her that I had done sessions with Sophie. Will was last night; I'll touch on that in a while. Since she volunteered, I wanted to try getting into her dream next. That was when Toni asked how I got in, citing paths via active thoughts as Callie was falling asleep or scanning for any kind of thoughts within Callie's sleeping mind. I was halfway through explaining that I had linked with Sophie as she was falling asleep before I even realised just what she was asking.

"You guys did this on your own?"

"You think you've got the monopoly on all TP experiments?" Callie said.

"No," I said, "But I'm trying to keep things above board where the use of our abilities is concerned. I write about everything I do so that Linda and Remington are kept informed, and with this dream thing, Miss Tracy has also been supervising. I'm trying not to give them reason to fear us by doing things in secret."

Toni said that it made sense and Callie reluctantly agreed, but went on to cite a few examples around TK like teaching Sophie to fly outside of class. We got into a bit of an argument – not the shouting kind – but I think we ended up airing a lot of stuff that's probably been hanging between us over the last year. I know she was never happy about my "ratting" her out that led her practising stuff with Carl, but Carl had the same problem of wanting to do things that even our trainers (and Remington) found to be a little on the dark side. That was also why I didn't want to force my own rules on how I use my abilities on anyone, even if I did share them in the end with the understanding that they weren't hard and fast rules anybody had to adhere to. Miss Tracy was quite understanding in that respect, saying that they were good guidelines on how our abilities should be used. It's partly why I get a little more leeway than most of the others; why I got tapped to assist her with training.

I think, in the end, Callie understood where I stood in terms of how our abilities were being used within The Facility, and by default, on the outside should such occasions arise. Toni picked it up fast enough, but then, she didn't have the chip on her shoulder that Callie was carrying around. Even after all this time, Callie is still a little wary of me and the stuff I do. Sure she gets a little antsy during our 'counselling' sessions when I have to review her activities on the learning network.

I don't begrudge them their little experiments from time to time, but they had to make sure someone of authority, that being Miss Tracy or Remington, be kept informed of their clandestine activities. I was pretty sure at the time that whatever they did, with Toni scanning Callie's dream or vice versa, no one was informed; they admitted as much.

At least, I got them to report their activities to Miss Tracy, including anymore 'sessions' Callie might have had with her suite-mate, Jo, and then arranged a session to get into Callie's dreams with Toni assisting. Callie's dreams haven't been keeping her awake as much as Sophie's, but she admitted to having some restless nights and bad dreams. I was curious if they were the same as Sophie's or Will's.

In Will's case, there was the similarity; a presence that seemed to be haunting him, but instead of some localised area, it came from all over. I wasn't familiar with the initial setting of his dream, and it flit around from place to place. The Facility appeared at one point, but it was not tied to that haunting presence. He also did not acknowledge my presence in his dream. I tried to make the same physical contact I had done with Sophie, but it didn't happen. I was like a ghostly observer in his dream. I accomplished less in Will's dream than I did in Sophie's. Well, maybe with one improvement. It was relatively easy to synch into his dream, even Ms. Phillips was amazed at how fast I managed it.

I linked with him first and then once he started falling into the dream state, it was easy to dive in with his ebbing consciousness. It was similar to what I did with Sophie, although I don't plan to do that with Callie. I'm going to let Toni take the lead and dive in with her; to see how she's doing it and if there's any difference. After all, between Toni and Callie, they refined the learning network to a point where it wasn't a strain to run the network for extended periods.

I have been thinking back to that argument I had with Callie. I wonder if that is something I should share with some of the other trainees in TP and TK, about the openness I'm trying to maintain with Miss Tracy, Linda and Remington. It's not my philosophy in how I behave with my abilities, and I do tend to occasionally push the boundaries, which might paint me as a hypocrite. No doubt, that's how Carl sees me most of the time anyway. I'm not going to turn him around any time soon. But then, I do write about it all, and in that, I'm at least keeping my G/C informed.

In any case, I should bring this up with Miss Tracy; see what she thinks. I'm not usually one to be open about these things, but if Callie is any indication, there might be others who are a little stumped about why I get to do some of the stuff I do without getting told off for it, while everyone else is expected to use their abilities only within classes or with supervision.

Then again, no one else has really complained…

Or are they just scared of me?

Apr 25

It's been a strange couple of days. I'm having problems trying to separate reality from dreams… really, I can't seem to sort things out in my head. I don't know what it is that's affecting me exactly; if it was one too many trips into people's dreams or that insane jaunt through Callie's dream.

I think I'll start with that, but how do you describe fluid insanity in words? I don't think I have the vocabulary to even scratch a fraction of what went on in Callie's dream. And are her dreams always like that? It's not that it was intently scary, like the nightmares I experienced with Sophie and Will, this was so different that, at first, I didn't think it was a related issue. There was that presence lurking in her dream, much like in Sophie's and Will's dream; I felt it this time.

That was on Wednesday night in the Infirmary. Will was assisting Ms. Phillips again as they attached the plugs to both Callie and Toni, while I only got the earpiece since I was using my usual bed which would monitor me. Miss Tracy was supervising as usual. This trip was also a little different since there were three of us linked together. Toni would dive into Callie's dream and pull me along on the trip. It was clear I wasn't going in as a passive observer since my intention was to meet Callie and Toni in Callie's dream; something I barely managed with Sophie and Will.

First of all, Toni's dive into Callie's dream was unlike anything I had tried. It was more invasive almost forcing Callie to dream in a particular way. I could hear Ms. Phillips saying that we were going off course at first. Callie had fallen asleep first, but since Toni was linked directly with Callie, it was more like Toni was initially pulled along. Ms. Phillips mentioned when Callie's brain waves hit the typical pattern right before her REM started, but then, they shifted to match Toni's brain-wave patterns, who hadn't reached REM sleep as yet. I couldn't really tell what was going on in that respect because my vantage point was very different. I could sense thoughts and some visuals in my head, like being aware of being in the Infirmary, but then it felt like I fell backwards into a deep hole as the world pulled away. This was all in my mind, by the way, while I was linked to both Callie and Toni, so I wasn't sure if this was what they were experiencing or my interpretation of it. I was trying to get a sense of what was in their heads as they were falling asleep. So much for trying to be passive.

Somehow, I could still hear Ms. Phillips keeping me apprised of our brain-wave patterns, letting me know when I was in synch or not. For the most part, I was almost in synch, but at the same, not quite fully there either. "Just a phase beyond," was how Toni described it. Meaning while we were in the dream with Callie – and interacting with each other, to boot – we weren't actively in the dream. Only a little out of it so that we could interact and observe, but not participate. I didn't even think if such a thing was even possible. I didn't think such a thing made sense in any way, but that's what we did. I mean, I've heard of lucid dreaming, when the dreamer can take control of the dream, but while that was what I thought we could achieve, it wasn't what we were doing.

I told Callie and Toni about my previous attempts with Sophie and Will, getting right into their dreams, but also lacking interactivity with the dreamers; that my presence in the dream, despite technically being a part of the dream, was not recognised.

"Don't know anything about that," Toni said. "This is what we did and this is where we are."

Where we were was not anything I could readily describe. It seemed like we were inside a generic building, but the walls were all askew and partly transparent we could see outside the building. The sky was blue in patches, night in other areas. There was no sense of time or place, and I wasn't even sure if we were on the ground or not. Callie seemed a little dazed like she was shifting between meeting with us and participating in her own dream. I could recognise some of the tutors wandering around the room, which sometimes seemed like a foyer or atrium, occasionally small, fluctuating to someplace big; sometimes indoors, often not. Floors above and below appeared and disappeared, some like they were partly finished – if they were even actual floors in the first place. It was quite unlike the steady locations of Sophie or Will where we would start with one place and then move around. Callie's was fluctuating all over the place, not to mention nothing was at any proper angle.

Then, there was Callie herself. When she was in her dream state, everything seemed normal to her, like it was all natural, or that was how the world was to her. When she slipped out of that dream state to mingle with Toni and me, her observation of her own dream was summed with a snarky, "Wow, is this trippy or what?" She claimed she never remembered much of any dream except for the occasional residual feeling she got. Lately, the feeling was one of paranoia. That was the only link I had suggesting her dreams might have been the same as the others.

We didn't stay in that one location in her dream; we moved around, not that seemed to make much difference. Every location looked roughly the same, with the same problems with reality, or at least, reality within a dream. I think at one point, even The Facility appeared, or at least, one of the classrooms. Following her through different places, we watched Callie do all sorts of things or talking to people none of us knew. They might have been amalgams of several people because of some vague sense of familiarity. I think there was a thread in the narrative of the dream because it went from checking out a place, to meeting a person at some studio, but it turned out to be the wrong person. Then there was an office that seemed like it was decorated wrongly – the computer on the desk was at an impossible angle, but it was on an impossible table that didn't seem to have a proper place for a person to sit. There was more, but all the while, there was this strange sense that someone was stalking us – not just her, but us. Toni and I felt it and we kept looking behind as if there was someone there. We even stood back to back, so we could watch each other's back.

Fat lot of good that was. When I asked Toni about it, she said it had been there the last couple of times she tried this dream trip with Callie. Callie couldn't remember when it first started, but it's been there a while.

"Should we try to reach for it?" she asked "The three of us, pulling it in."

The moment that suggestion came up, I could hear Ms. Philips saying that something was happening with the brain-waves; that they were 'flattening out'. Honestly, I couldn't figure if it was Ms. Phillips who said it or even what it meant, but things got really weird when we decided to do what Callie suggested. A funny thing I didn't notice at the time was that Callie stopped fluctuating between her dream and us. Maybe it was an indication of something not being quite right, but it didn't register at the time.

By then, we were in some park-like location, and again, as weird there as everywhere else in her dream. We stood with our backs to each other and tried to pinpoint where the sensation was coming from. Callie reacted first, turning around and then reaching out with her hands as if to grab at something that wasn't quite there. I sensed it a moment later and reached out in the same direction, and Toni followed suit. It was like we were reaching out with our TP or TK – although Toni didn't have TK abilities, but hey, we were in a dream world – and we got hold of something there. We pulled it closer towards us, and the reality around us reacted pretty violently, as if something was coming and the world itself was resisting it.

We kept pulling at it despite the storm that came up around us, and we literally ripped a hole in reality! One ripped hole, black on the inside, in the middle of nowhere, ahead of where we stood in the dream, like something poked through just a little. Callie seemed ecstatic while Toni appeared fearful. I felt like something was so wrong and I could barely register Ms. Phillips yelling away in my ear. I couldn't make out what she was saying, but this sense of intense fear and paranoia swept through me as the three of us got sucked into the rip, straight back to reality!

I woke with a start in the Infirmary as did Callie and Toni, all about the same time. Things were moving pretty fast as Ms. Phillips seemed to be angry, disappointed and even impatient as she moved to check out Toni and Callie (with Will's help) while Miss Tracy moved over to me to check if I was okay. The most I could say was that my head was still buzzing, like something in that rip did something, but I wasn't sure what exactly happened. I didn't realise at the time that we were still in the dream.

This was why I mentioned that I got mixed between the dream and reality. At the time, when I first woke up, I really thought we were back in reality. That whatever happened in the dream was something that caused us to wake up, like waking from a nightmare at the last possible second before something bad happens.

I got off my bed and brushed past Miss Tracy, pulling the earpiece out of my ear while heading to the wash-room. Ms. Phillips and Will were busy with Callie and Toni, although I could hear Ms. Phillips call after me, but I didn't make out what she said. I got to the wash-room and splashed some water on my face, and that's when I felt something wasn't right. When I turned around, I was in the wash-room in my suite. I could still hear Ms. Phillips saying something, but it was faint and garbled. It felt like I might have wandered back to my suite, but I was still linked to either Callie or Toni who were in the Infirmary. It never really occurred to me that I was, in effect, dreaming.

A day's events were going by in a flash, but I couldn't determine how or when I was getting around to those things, like attending class, or having lunch with the others, sparring with Keiko and even picking a fight with John for some reason. Things blurred in and out to a point that I felt nauseous enough to check in at the Infirmary. The moment I decided that – I woke up, again.

I sat up in the bed, like coming out of a nightmare as I did before. Things still didn't feel right, like I wasn't quite awake... And I woke up again! I'm quite clear about this, that it happened three times; waking up with a start in the Infirmary, Ms. Phillips and Will rushing to tend to Callie and Toni. The strange thing was I could hear Ms. Phillips talking to Callie to check on her, but I could also hear her voice from another direction. I couldn't make out what she was saying and my hand automatically went to my ear. I didn't feel the earpiece that I was supposed to have, but I did remove one earlier. That got me thinking that I was still in a dream, that I could hear Ms. Phillips in two places – before me and in my head. The one in my head was muffled, though. I couldn't really make out what she was saying. The one in the Infirmary wasn't making much sense either, like no one was speaking properly and all the words got jumbled coming out of people's mouth. I mean, it sounded right, but gibberish at the same time.

Miss Tracy came over to me again and I instinctively recoiled from her this time because I was somewhat sure it wasn't really her. That was when things went askew again. The Infirmary itself began to contort out of shape, like any building or room that was in Callie's dream. The bed I was on changed its shape into something that could barely hold me, and I fell to the ground. I noticed Callie and Miss Tracy reaching for me as I fell. The ground was hard when I hit it, but then it ripped like I landed on a sheet of paper and I fell through again. It was like when I first entered Callie's dream, falling into the darkness, but this time, the world faded and there was no stopping. The sensation was of falling. It wasn't floating or flying, and I couldn't do both. It felt like I was completely powerless and alone in the dark – again.

The sensation was familiar and it was one I didn't care to revisit; it crippled me badly at that moment. I don't know how long I was in that darkness. I couldn't say if it was even the same darkness that haunted me over the last few years, or the same darkness I embraced late last year. It was just darkness and fear and paranoia, cold and endless. Whatever I could sense of Ms. Phillips calling out to me barely registered and I had no foothold on any sense of reality, dream or otherwise.

It was Callie who reached through the darkness to give me a helping hand somehow. I could also hear her calling out to me and it took a moment more to register there was a hand there for me to grab on. I think I was flailing about in the dark and I just happened to make contact, and the world reformed around me all skewed and out of shape... And we woke up.

It wasn't the briefest of moments that I couldn't distinguish between Callie's skewed dream world and the Infirmary itself. I wasn't sure if I was actually awake. My senses were pretty skewed thanks to Callie's weird dreams. Half the time since coming out of the dream, I couldn't tell if I was still in the dream or not, even if there was nothing skewed in reality. The day that followed was not the easiest to get around and the only comfort I had was that it was going by slowly, not like highlights in a dream. Just for control, I got Keiko to practise our most basic steps in kendo. It was something that could give me a sense of focus, and it helped.

A little.

Most of the day, I was jumping at corners, spinning around because I thought someone was following or watching me. Even Becca was worried because I was behaving so erratically. I haven't slept since either.

The most I can say now is that this presence haunting the dreams, there's a person behind it. There has to be; someone who can get in there and exert some kind of control to do whatever he or she wants. It protected itself when it felt threatened, and it manipulated the dream environment as it needed. That denotes will and intelligence, perhaps instinct. Who or why this was going on, I don't know. I don't even know if I can fight this. Whatever is going on with the dreams is something that's starting. Something else is coming.

I think.

It's just a feeling...

I dunno. I've written a lot about what happened, but at the same time, I'm not quite sure which parts are real and which aren't. Part of that is what's getting to me, making me wonder if Callie's insanity is infectious, or if I've been insane all along and it's coming out now. Then again, if I can determine that I am a little on the insane side, isn't that some kind of proof of sanity in the first place?

No. Again – y'see, that's the paranoia sneaking up on me. Next thing I know, the world will spin around again and skew off in all sorts of angles.

I need a break.

Apr 27

It's bad enough that the last few days have been problematic. Getting around like treading on fragile glass planes has been hell on the nerves. Making matters worse is that I completely forgot about my dinner with Keitaro last Friday night. He didn't even try to remind me. While I have been trying to attend classes like normal and joining the others for lunch, my nerves have been jittery at best. Helen said it best when she called me a nervous wreck yesterday.

The trip into Callie's dream shouldn't have been all that difficult, but somehow, things got out of hand and I got caught off guard, badly. Ms. Phillips, Miss Tracy, Linda and Remington are all aware of what happened and they are at a loss as I am about what to do. I need to do something. I need to figure out what to do because I can't keep going around jumping at shadows, being afraid of the dark and not wanting to sleep. I haven't slept since that night. I didn't even get around to the dream-world of mine.

To be fair, it's not at all Callie's fault and I wouldn't lay the blame on her. I was poking about in dreams and she volunteered. It's just the trip into her dream has royally screwed up some of my perceptions. I would be sitting in class trying to focus on the lesson and the room's corners would suddenly go askew. The walls would go transparent, only to show sky that wasn't even outside The Facility, either day or night. The floor would tilt and turn even while I was seated, and the disorientation would set in something fierce. I've disrupted a few classes by jumping about at nothing, like I was waking up from a dream, except that I never fell asleep.

Out of caution, I've also stayed out of the pool. The most I've managed is to sit by the pool, dipping my legs in the water while watching over Sunee and Corogi as they practice their aqua-acrobatics. After all, I still have to supervise them. Just as with Keitaro, I agreed to have a dinner with him. I apologised profusely and agreed to have an additional dinner with him and that he could set the date after I get my head levelled again. He was quite understanding saying that Keiko had warned him off about the date. Add to that my erratic behaviour over lunch lately and I think he knew to bide his time for me to come around. Bless his patience.

Since I haven't been sleeping, I've been checking in at the Operations Center just so I could talk with Walker. I related to him about all that's been happening and how it's affected me. He's been incredibly patient as I rambled about the problems I've been facing, even when it's obviously past his usual bedtime; this was over a few days. He's learnt to listen instead of trying to solve my problems. In fact, the most he offered was his confidence I would handle the problem in my own way. He was also worried about my well-being.

On the downer side, he's been requested to stay back for another two weeks, approximately. He did want to get back to me, but he's also obligated to work with the people at the IASC. I told him I hoped to get things settled on my end before he got back so it wouldn't get between us later. He actually laughed at that. Not a big laugh, but more like a knowing chuckle which was echoed by Tommy.

They know me well enough.

Tommy voiced his own concerns about my well-being since I was hanging around the Operations Center quite a bit. I tried to put in some time in the flight simulator at first or even working with Colleen, but the problem with reality occasionally fading away left me either crashing in the flight simulator – in more ways than one within that little cockpit – or losing grip of the equipment while working on Colleen. Either course was unsafe, much like avoiding the pool for the time being.

All of that was really screwing with me, mentally and physically... and I am getting really tired, mentally and physically.

I really need a break.

Apr 29

It had to happen. It was just after I finished writing up the last entry, saying I needed a break. I was in the kitchenette reaching for the fridge when everything went haywire. My sense of balance went completely out of whack and next thing I knew, I lost my footing, and fell. I think I knocked my head too because it's still aching. In any case, my collapse caused enough of a ruckus to wake Becca. She said she called the Infirmary and they had someone come around to check on me before they decided it was safe to move me to the Infirmary itself.

Becca spent the night in the Infirmary watching over me, saying that I tossed and turned a lot in my sleep. Yeah, apparently, I fell asleep. The few days of avoiding sleep took its toll. Ms. Phillips had me monitored thru the night and much of the next day since I slept all the way through till about lunch. Letting me know that my brain-waves were erratic throughout the dream phase was an understatement. They phased out towards the end and I appeared to be sleeping properly and deeply about an hour before I woke up, according to her.

I won't go into the details of the dream, or even what little I can remember; not the details, but the feelings and sensations stayed on. The feeling of paranoia and fear remained. I haven't had any of the other episodes where the world skews away and reality starts bending in all sorts of direction, but I'm apparently still a little jumpy, although not as much as the last few days. The disorientation is still there but not as severe or as frequent, so I guess I'm coping.

I could also say that whatever was bothering the other dreamers, it's gotten to me as well. If I was on the outside before, I'm now a part of this unique group of dreamers. I wish I could work out what it is that they have in common. Ethan, Sophie and I are psychics with telepathic and telekinetic abilities while Will is TK only and Toni is a TP as is Callie, for the most part. Most of the others that I'm aware of are non-psychics. At least, they're not in either TP or TK training, and I can safely say that I know only a small number of the others in that I share the same classes with them. The rest are the typical familiar strangers I see on a daily basis, but hardly mix with. It's quite a varied bunch.

I decided, for the sake of some sense of normalcy, to try a dream-walk today. I didn't sleep last night, after having been knocked out for close to twelve hours, and since I skipped the last session on Saturday, it was time to try anyway. More simply, I couldn't focus in class- Electrical Engineering. Can't say it was a good trip though.

My dream-world appeared normal at first but whatever was screwing up my perception in reality affected my perceptions within the dream-world as well. I don't know how or why it happened. Things got really weird over there, but in a different way since the perception of reality over there is nothing like reality over here. Up became down in some cases; indoors became outdoors and the creatures that lurked about seemed far more benign than the people. It appeared as if the creatures were the real denizens and the villagers were the creatures that had to be hunted. Whatever that haunted me in that restless sleep followed me through to the dream-world. I still jumped at shadows that hid nothing at all, I still got a touch disoriented and reality, such as it was in the dream-world, still got skewed and twisted.

Coming out from the dreaming felt like nothing was accomplished. I tried to recall as best as I could the events that happened in the dreams and the dream-world, particularly with that moment in the dark. I know I said it seemed familiar, like the darkness might have been the same one that was a part of me, and yet, not quite the same. I'm trying to be clear about that because I think that's the key. If it was my past catching up with me, despite effectively leaving it behind to a point, there was only one person who came to mind. I dreaded to think that one person has come back after..

No, it wouldn't be possible in any way after what I did.

+++

I was contemplating that last bit for quite a while when Becca knocked on my door saying that Callie and Sophie had come by to see me. It wasn't to check on me, they had something else to discuss. Considering it was the two of them together, I had a hunch what they wanted. It was Sophie who said it; they wanted me to do one more trip with them in order to confront the presence that was in their dreams. I agreed, but said I wanted to get as many people involved this time, to create a larger network with the other dreamers involved.

"If it took three of us to find this presence and have it react against one of us, it might be good to have strength in numbers," I said.

"And if it goes after one of us again?" asked Callie.

"Let's make sure it's going to be me," I said. I only had a rough idea of a plan and it wasn't guaranteed to work. Among the three or maybe four of us, if Toni was willing to join in again, I think there would be enough strength to hold everyone together even if one of us got attacked by whoever or whatever was out there.

When I asked about Ethan, Callie said he was still coming along fine like things were normal except for seeming a little worn out like he lacked proper rest. I knew he was having bad dreams, but it didn't sound like they were the same as what we were all having. I wondered aloud if he might be connected to all of this. Sophie surmised it might have to do with the creatures in our respective dream-worlds. Callie pointed out the numerous times I mentioned that the dream-worlds and actual dreams are two different things. For me, they were two different things, even if the dreams had seeped into my dream-world on the last trip. For Ethan, the two worlds might be connected.

"Remember how we got pulled into your dream-world when I made contact with you in your dream?" I said to Sophie. "Your world was built based on advice you got from Ethan." One thing that did occur to me, and I brought it up then, was that Sophie could point out Ethan's dream-world from her own place, as I could point to Ethan's dream-world from my own, but I could not sense Sophie's dream-world from mine, despite having Ethan's dream-world bridging us.

While Callie had problems following my thinking, Sophie had it easier. Maybe it's growing up with fantasy and the like since she reads a lot of comics and books where such convoluted realities existed. She could make the assumption that Ethan's dream-world might exist on a different plane from mine and hers, and yet exist in both or more realities of the mind. I try not to use the word "assumption" but in this case, it's all we could do because we don't know how it all really works. All we knew was that there was a vague connection at best and even that is unproven, not unless we get Ethan to join in the session.

I'm really hoping he's not the cause of all this, though.

I'm catching up with Callie and Sophie later along with the others who can't sleep – the few who have been haunting the café during the witching hours – and then I need to work things out with our G/Cs, Miss Tracy and Ms. Phillips. I want this to work because I'm really tired of the disorientation. It's making look really stupid, falling over for no reason and being jumpy all the time.

I need to take control.

Whatever happens.

Apr 30

Clearing things with Miss Tracy, Ms. Phillips and more importantly, Linda, was easier than expected. The fact that we're getting more people involved was a tricky proposition by itself, but by approaching Ms. Phillips first, she advocated our plan and agreed to let us try mainly because she was out of ideas and the Infirmary was getting crowded at times. Miss Tracy was up for anything we wanted to try and my only concern was Linda. She did partly what I expected her to; question our steps, our methods and the safety concerns. Even when I didn't have proper answers, she would push for my next course of action. I knew I couldn't guarantee anything, least of all was safety of a participant in this reckless plan, and the most I could do was to promise I would do whatever I could to keep everyone safe. She felt that given everything that had happened over the last year or so, it was good enough. I pulled through for Sophie and Ethan before and I had always put the safety of our network participants ahead of the function of the network.

I related all this to Callie as an example of why I try to keep things open with Linda and Remington where the use of our abilities was a concern. It allowed us to try risky things like what we are about to do. I think she understands my position now, and I stressed that it's something I intend to keep doing for as long as we are at The Facility. If we weren't, I would probably be a little more cautious about using my abilities.

During my meeting with Linda on that matter, she took the opportunity to review my monthly activities and admitted to being a little concerned about my well-being over the last few days. She understood I was a little nervous about getting to sleep given what I had recorded concerning the events in Callie's dream. She relayed the same thing I heard Remington tell mom some time ago, that if I wanted to help others, I had to take care of myself first. Otherwise, I was not going to be of much use.

"So, are you sure you're up to this?" she asked of the little experiment we had planned.

"Now is good, considering I just got some rest," I said.

She eyed me something fierce, like she was deciding if I was certain I would be able to handle things if something bad were to happen. She didn't say anything and I was a touch uncomfortable, but she went on with my review. She noted that aside from the last few days, I had been doing well in training. I might have to do a little catching up once this little episode is behind me and I've got my focus back, otherwise, it'll be tough going since I can't afford to keep on disrupting classes when my perceptions go haywire.

On a personal aside, I really want to get back into the water. That's reason enough for me to do this.

Also noted by Linda was my excessive time spent in the Operations Center, although she knew the main reason for that. She said it was fine since I was using the video line at a time which was considered off-peak, and so long nothing important came up that required it. She understood why my time was spent there lately instead of at my other projects like the rocket plans on the flight simulator, and Colleen. As mentioned, I have maintained supervising Corogi and Sunee with their aqua-acrobatics even though I haven't been in the water.

Unlike the previous sessions, this one was pretty quick. I still needed to prepare myself a little. Sophie, Callie and I managed to get a few people to participate in our test; Will, Rex and two others whose names probably don't matter here as I've never mentioned them before. Maybe I'll get around to them if something significant involving them happens. It's simply to keep things coherent and simple.

I really wanted Ethan with us, but he was reluctant and I wasn't going to force him into it. Still, I left him an open invitation and I hope he'll turn up later. The other person I was curious about, since he was there in the café last night, was John. He could have been there having a late snack before turning in, as was his habit, or if he might be similarly inflicted by the bad dreams that haunted the other patrons of the café that morning. I couldn't be sure.

After this, I'm going to meet up with Keiko for a little meditation and Sophie is joining us. It's a little exercise to get my head into the game. After that, we're having a little dinner meeting with our participants before we go into the session. Then, we'll see what happens.

MAY

May 8

It's been a while since the last entry and frankly, things did get a little hairy. To explain it all, well... it's a little complicated. We were dealing with dreams, reality and a whole host of abandonment issues. Having it all take place in the realm of dreams makes it a little difficult to put certain things into perspective, particularly from a reality standpoint. In their own way, dreams can make sense, sometimes, but often, the reality in dreams throws everything for a loop-de-loop, so...

And to get down to the bare bones of what happened and why, along with my part in all of this, like I said, it's complicated. Remington wants me to write it up anyway, so here I am, giving it a go with the knowledge that it's not going to make much sense. I will try to put it in some kind of context. I don't want to say it was a 'mess' really. It's one of those things that happened because... I don't know why it happened... actually. Y'see, I kept thinking that it wasn't really my fault that all the bad dreams started, but then, it somehow is also entirely my fault because I just have to be responsible about the whole thing. Especially when we found out what was behind it all.

As far as I know, Sophie, Callie and Toni also have to write up their reports, and for all I know, they probably finished a couple of days ago; I have no idea what they wrote. In my case, this is going into my journal. I've already rambled on quite a bit, procrastinating in a way to avoid getting to the nitty gritty. Add to that I had one extra task to take care of since we all came out of that 'bad dreams' episode. That in itself would suggest that everything that happened was my fault.

I'm pretty sure that the others might start with our little group session and how we got together in the Infirmary to get hooked up to as many machines as there were, and how there weren't enough machines for all of us. I was willing to give up my bed, but Ms. Phillips and Charlie, who got called in at the last minute by Ms. Phillips, insisted I be monitored. For me, the beginning actually goes back about four years or so. That's why it's complicated. It's dealing with a part of my past that I've been trying to put way behind me tying in with that dark period of my life I tried to leave behind when I started my studies here at

The Facility. It's kinda overly dramatic when I think of it; the sins of my past catching up and screwing around with the people currently in my life.

So where exactly do I start with this? I had to explain my part in all this to the others – not all who participated, just Callie, Toni and Sophie... and also Walker and Becca. Yeah, Walker's back; a couple of days now. He came back early, and that one's my fault. Anyway, I've told that story about my past about three times already, and doing it here will be the fourth. Chances are, I'll probably be more detailed here. Perhaps.

Following Becca's advice and going with the flow, I'll skip to the dreaming part itself. It was amazing we managed to link everyone – eight of us – into one dream, and things were really messed up with having several dreams crashing into one. It was a weird sensation and surreal experience. I know I wasn't the one who did it, but somehow we interacted with each other. I guess it might have been Callie or Toni who pulled it off, but I don't know how. I didn't make it happen when it was between Callie, Toni and me, so it wasn't me this time around. I was a passenger for the trip making sure nothing was going to get out of hand.

I won't even try to describe the reality of the dream beyond that it was parts and pieces of the dreams of our participants all meshed together. That's because we started off in the same location – The Infirmary – and while everyone was gathered within the dream, the area surrounding each person was different. It was like the Infirmary had six different designers throwing their nightmarish designs into some sort of mash-up. Really, it's something to be seen to be understood, so it's no point in trying to describe it. It's important that we were making contact with each other, and we managed to attract that presence stalking us in our dreams. Everyone had the same sensation from their own perspective, which made the presence practically omniscient at first; but we did have a plan.

We had laid it out with our guardians – Remington, Linda, Ms. Phillips, etc. – and our participants. The few of us who were psychics would link with our normal participants, but my part in all this was, well... bait. Given what happened last time, it seemed like I was targeted, so we were hoping it would happen again. At least it would attract the presence away from the others towards me. Unlike last time, we were prepared and I had back-up. That was the plan. I was as ready as I could be; just not for what we actually found out in the end, the way it all tied together.

I guess I should also mention those other participants who weren't psychic, Erica and Jim. According to Ms. Phillips, they practised lucid dreaming and were actually quite good at it. It was something that gave us an edge and probably a reason why they were willing to participate. Lucid dreaming is like a psychic power but within the realms of actual dreaming and not like my dream-world. They had the power to control their environments and steer their dreams accordingly to their desires. The haunting presence that invaded their dreams was something beyond their control and that was why they ended up with the bad dreams.

Once each of us could sense that presence watching us, Callie, Toni and Sophie merged the various dreams into one – forcibly, much to my concern – and pretty much pulled the various sources of that presence into one. Rex helped where he could while Will did his best to lend support to Sophie. He stayed by her side as much as he could; it was understandable and good. Erica and Jim did their best to put some kind of control into the environment, holding the "room" together. Yeah, I was kinda passive through this part. Once we localised the presence, tho, it was a whole other deal for me.

As our reality kept getting twisted around us, the presence, for some reason or another, took on a human form. It could have been the possibility that with all of our perceptions focussed on that presence, it might have been understandable why it might have had a human form, but it was a blurry mix of masses and mixtures that seemed constantly in flux. There were no fixed distinguishing features, just a swirly fluctuating mass of... whatever it was. It appeared skittish, like it didn't want to be seen. It also seemed small; almost child-like.

Sophie and I had the same thought, based on its size. We were thinking of Ethan, but it didn't feel like Ethan to me. It's hard to explain that part. Sure, the first impression was Ethan, but unlike many occasions when I get close enough to him to get a sense of him, I wasn't getting it from this presence. Really, if it had been Ethan, I would have sensed it a long time ago, like when we first started all of this. Heck even Sophie would have sensed if it were Ethan. Whatever or whoever this presence was, it was someone new, and yet, particularly familiar to me.

I didn't say anything because I wasn't really clear about it, but I had the sense that it wasn't as dangerous as it seemed. It was a good thing that despite what all of us had gone through with uneasy nights, we weren't some mob looking at something we could get at, and neither were we actually scared of this thing once it appeared before us. We were curious, but it was scared of us instead. It shirked away, it tried to back off or maybe even scatter its image because it kept... I think it tried to break its image apart; turn invisible again. This was when I tired to approach it, reaching out my hand first. I think it did respond, but slightly.

The response was a little strange. The figure didn't reach out like I did. Nothing in particular reached out, but the figure shimmered and a small portion of it sort of extended outward. It was like a flat surface spiked outwards a little before recoiling. It was a strange, brief and subtle reaction that was also noticed by Callie and Rex, based on their reactions. Given my position between the figure and the others, I wasn't sure if anyone else actually saw it, but it was significant in that I got a response. At least, that's what I felt.

Maybe because I was targeted before or that I was simply front and centre at the moment, when the figure couldn't back away, it moved forward towards me. It didn't run or walk, it just moved, parts of it trailing behind. And it was fast too. It moved towards me, and at me before I could realise what it was doing. I only managed to take half a step back when it hit me and moved through me. I wasn't knocked off my feet as much as I was pulled backwards, and when I hit the ground, everything was gone again. I was back in that black void and all those feelings came rushing back – fear, paranoia, isolation, panic.

I found out from Sophie later that when the figure went through me, I faded away with it before anyone else could do anything. No one had time to properly react because the other thing that happened was that everyone apparently got shunted to their respective dreams, at least, from Sophie's point of view. If that was the case, it sure didn't happen to me that way, I got shunted to my worst nightmare.

So this part gets a little tricky. Unlike last time where the sensation was one of falling, this time around, I felt like I had some kind of ground beneath me. Added to that was Charlie's voice in my head, thanks to the ear-piece I still had with me on this trip. It wasn't very clear, but it wasn't completely garbled either. I knew he and Ms. Phillips were monitoring all of us on the outside, and Charlie was probably keeping a closer eye on me than on the others, so he would know if something 'unusual' happened. How much he really knew about dreams and how they work, and all that, I don't really know. He knew enough about tracking my brain-waves. So, the fact that I could hear him meant that something 'unusual' happened, from their perspective. On my end, I was cowering in a foetal position like a lost little girl in the dark, shivering from fear and paranoia, mostly, but not completely, disoriented.

I must had some kind of external reaction because it was Charlie's voice I was clinging to, and although I could barely make out what he was saying, it felt soothing, as if he knew I was in a dark place and he was trying to calm me. I never did verify if it did happen that way, but Charlie became my anchor at that time. It took a while for me to focus on his voice. I slowly set my mind to focus on other things as well, primarily my kendo basics. I was going over the steps and strokes, slowing bringing my breathing in rhythm with the movements in my head.

Yeah, I know… it sounds funny even in writing. Having thoughts in my head while being nothing too real in a dream. Take it as it is, it's harder to try and apply any kind of logic to it. Well, maybe dream-logic works that way. I'm just relaying what I experienced.

Anyway, I don't know how long it took, but I managed to get some control over myself, pushing through all those negative feelings, staying as focussed as I could on my kendo basics. I did that meditation with Keiko before I started this dream session. It was something I had planned to help me build some focus. My worry was that if I got overwhelmed, I wouldn't be able to get my focus together. That's where Charlie came in. It really was by accident. I didn't have any plan that actually involved him talking me through that dark moment, but all that combined got me to a point where I could at least stop shaking and pull myself together, enough to stand on my own feet in that darkness. It took a while and no one came looking for me this time. I didn't have Callie lending a hand in the dark.

As far as I know, while I was pulling myself together, Sophie and the others were trying to regroup. By the time I was on my feet, it was still a long while before I saw any of them again. Wherever they were at that time, I was certain of one thing – that presence was completely with me in the dark.

I can't really say how I knew for sure that the presence haunting our dreams was completely with me and not with anyone else, it's how it felt. In order to keep focus tho, I kept my hands in the same position as if I was holding my *shinai* and standing straight as if in the *kamae* position in kendo. I closed my eyes and reached out with my senses as best as I could, and felt the presence still watching me.

I did what I thought was right and said, "Why are you doing this?" I didn't bother asking who or what, like I knew it wasn't important. I didn't get any response tho.

I opened my eyes, maintaining my position, and stared into the darkness. "I know you're here, so why don't we meet?" I asked. There was still no answer and the silence was really hurting my ears – don't ask how that happens in a dream, but that's how it was.

I reached out even more to try to make some kind of contact instead of just getting a sense of that presence. I spun around because I thought I felt it behind me, and I caught the barest glimpse of a form fading away, like it was scattered by some unfelt wind. I turned again, and the same effect happened. It was like this presence wanted to stay behind me, out of sight. As far as I knew then, that was all it really did in anyone's dream. There may have been mention of monsters or something bad, but I suppose when you get the sensation of being watched, particularly in your dream, it creates a kind of uneasiness one would associate with something bad or even monsters. When that feeling of uneasiness follows you to the real world, every other sense you have either compensates as a defence mechanism (I guess) or, in my case, amplifies those feelings and making things a little uneasy in reality.

By this point, I got a little annoyed at the game. I spun around once more, but this time, I made a gesture to block the presence from moving away and then, with a snap of my fingers, I created a world around us. It was like turning on the lights. The world appeared and, of all things, it was exactly like being in the forest of my own dream world. This was me taking control with little regard to any kind of safety protocol I had come up with. It was a forcible move to bring light to the presence. The presence before me was also as clear as our surroundings, and she looked like a little girl who was trying to find a place to hide. She couldn't have been more than six or seven, maybe.

And she looked like me. Black hair that was a little longer than I thought I had, green eyes and a slight Asian complexion with that flat button nose – at least, that's how I view myself in general. In any case, she didn't look like that for long. She looked like me and then the features shifted a little and then she looked like a younger version of Callie before shifting and looking like a younger version of Toni. Her appearance kept shifting about, but her height and relative age remained the same.

I tried to placate her because she seemed panicky and scared of being unable to get away and hide from me. I kept saying things like, "You don't have to be afraid," or "I'm not going to hurt you." I probably already hurt her in some way and was scaring her as much as she had done to me. Saying those things felt silly. Never thought it worked in the movies so why should I have thought it would have worked then. To be fair, it didn't really work, but it did let me get closer to her. Close enough to reach out for her. In hindsight, probably not the best idea, but it was something that proved to be the right thing to do.

In making contact, I got flooded with all sorts of emotions and sensations, like everything, every memory, in that little girl poured into me. It was so overwhelming that I jolted awake in the Infirmary. My head was bursting with all sorts of stuff and it was pounding like crazy. Charlie told me that it was a moment of panic in the Infirmary and my readings were all off the scales. I was thrashing about for a moment and then I passed out again, sort of falling back to sleep. I might have still been connected in some way because that same moment I fell back onto the bed; Jim, Will and Toni woke up, seemingly in a panic. At least, that's what Charlie told me.

It took a while more for me to sort out my head, get through all those feelings and sensations that got pushed into me. There was a myriad of memories passing through, mixed with all sorts of thoughts and associated emotions. It felt like I was spiralling through a life – short as the life was. By the time I finally came out of it, I dropped to the ground, back in that forest where I started. The little girl was like, squatting a little distance away from me and eying me as if I was some strange creature. I propped myself up as best as I could and looked over to her, but with a whole new perspective about who I was dealing with. This was the realisation that hit me like a brick truck ramming into me at high speed. I couldn't even believe what I had in my head, what I had learned.

I looked at her... hard, and her appearance stopped shifting. She stared back at me and it really hit me what... who I was looking at. It didn't make much sense at the time, but I had to accept what I had learnt, hard as the realisation was; as complicated and as difficult as it seemed. I really couldn't believe just who I was looking at because all my logical senses told me it wasn't possible for this person to rightfully exist.

Sophie, Callie, Erica and Rex then turned up, like they had come out of the nearby trees with Sophie leading the way. They found me on the ground staring at the little girl squatting before me. Erica was the one to ask if the girl was the one who had been haunting our dreams, and I quietly nodded.

"And you know who she is?" asked Callie

"I know who she's supposed to be," I said, "but I don't really know her."

Sophie pointed out that at this time that the little girl looked a little like me while Erica said that she looked more like Callie.

"It's complicated," I said. "I think... She's supposed to be my daughter."

That got everyone's attention. This was where I went into the complicated history of how we got to this particular situation, and I guess I have to relate all that here again. This goes back almost four years to that dark period in my life when I was held prisoner in my own dream-world for what seemed like a long time. I had no real sense of time, but it might have felt like a year, but closer to almost four months on the outside. The circumstance that led to that situation isn't important here, and I really don't care to relive it or even write about it. What I wasn't aware at the time was during that period, I was in a coma – it was the second time I was in a coma – and I was pregnant... with twins.

In fighting for my freedom and my life at that point within the dream-world, I was stabbed through the gut with a sword. Because I wasn't aware of the pregnancy, I wasn't pregnant there in the dream-world, so once the fight was over, I healed myself. After I broke free of my captivity, one of the things I did before leaving the dream-world was to restore it from the ravages my captor had inflicted upon it and on me. No, I'm not naming him and despite his current state in the real world, which is my fault, he still frightens me. For a brief moment, I wondered if he was the one who was stalking our dreams. I already wrote about this some time back, about my past catching up with me, and in a way, it has. Anyway, in restoring the dream-world, I poured a lot of my energy into the land itself. I placed my hands onto the ground and imagined a wealth of energy pouring through my hands from within me into the ground, spreading outwards and restoring the lands to what they were meant to be.

I felt wasted and drained, and that's when what was going on in the real world at that precise moment hit me... I was in the middle of my very messy delivery. Because of my condition, Charlie couldn't operate on me and I had to go through the process naturally. Mikey was first, and his sister was stillborn. As far as Charlie knew, she was fine until those last few moments when everything went haywire before I came out of the coma and right into the process of giving birth to Mikey.

And that's the short version with a lot more details left out.
She was simply named Michelle and I never met her...

I'm pretty sure I rambled on more when I was explaining things with the others, and I was probably more detailed when I related the story to Becca and more so with Walker. If I were to write out everything, I could probably fill a book with that part alone, and I don't want to revisit all of it again.

Back to that moment for now. When I finished doing my best at the time to explain how Michelle came about, I also had to put forth the fact that her existence was an impossibility. When I was asked how I could be sure about Michelle, I related stuff from whatever pieces of memories from her that had been crammed into my head. The first memory I could access was one of the night sky. This was followed by a lot of memories of observing me from a distance and a few other things. There was a lot of observing people from distances and I could, at the very least, verify that she had been jumping from dream to dream. How she actually did that, and why, was still a little beyond me.

Once we got past all that, I made the suggestion for the others to leave and at least check if the everything was okay on the outside. Sophie offered to report our activities to our guardians while I stayed back because I wanted to deal with Michelle. Once everyone else left, I reached out an open hand to Michelle. It took her a while, but she reluctantly took it. I then took us to my dream-world and straight to Kinstein's Kitchen. Once I did that, I could hear Charlie's voice in my ear saying that Sophie had explained quite a bit. He also asked how it was possible that the little girl who died at birth could even exist in a barely existent world. I couldn't answer then, nor now. Not for certain.

I won't go into too much about what happened next. I spent close to a day in the Kitchen trying to communicate with Michelle, but she never said a word. I think she could understand me, and I managed to persuade her to stay with Kinstein. He agreed to watch over her. If anything, this was really going to put the existence of my dream-world to a real test, to see how relevant its so-called existence is to me. Through it all, some of the villagers still dropped by asking for help, but I needed to focus on Michelle at the time.

I was about finished with the arrangements with Kinstein when Sophie dropped by. Apparently, a couple of days had passed, and Charlie had left. For me, it was barely a day ago. Sophie also informed me that there had been no reports of anyone having bad dreams, especially among our participants. She also confirmed that the café was relatively empty for the last couple of nights. She then said that Ms. Phillips wanted me to come out of the dreaming so that I could get some proper rest and food.

I gave Michelle a hug and Kinstein gave his assurances, and with that, I finally woke up. It was already night in the Infirmary. Ms. Phillips, Remington, Linda and Will were there. Will was at Sophie's side. She was awake by the time I woke up. Remington asked if I was okay, to which I nodded lightly in response. He then gave a slight gesture at the entrance, and both Becca and Walker came in. I was really happy to see him then and I gave him a huge long hug, holding him so close. He didn't say anything. He just held me. Remington excused himself, saying he needed to update my mother.

The next few days were spent in some depression. I talked things out with Becca and Walker, and considered perhaps that time when I was trying to heal my dream-world all those years ago… the energy I was pumping into the ground, had come from me and perhaps from Michelle. In some weird way, I had infused her into the lands, but there was no way to know for sure if that was it. For all I know, I was in the dream-world throughout the pregnancy. If you're working it out in your head about the timeline, factor in that my unique biological condition forced the pregnancy to run it's course in almost half the time. Maybe she dreamt her way into the dream-world at the time and then got stuck there when she was supposed to have been born.

How and why she ended up there, if she's as real as I want her to be, or as real as she wants to be, I really don't know. All I know is that she's there, and she's real enough to go hopping into other peoples' dreams and causing problems. How and why that happened, I don't know. During the time I spent with her, she didn't say anything. Given how time passes over there, it wasn't hard to see why she seemed older than Mikey.

Wow… The moment I wrote that, a memory of hers of when she met Mikey flashed in my mind. Not just observing him, but actually making contact with him. I don't know why it didn't happen before this, but it seemed like… they looked at each other curiously for a moment. I can't even be sure of when that happened, but it might have been at any time when I was supposed to meet up with Mikey and I was late.

Anyway, from that time when I came out of the dreaming, I haven't gone back in. I'm planning to do that tomorrow, as usual on a Saturday, and see how Michelle is doing over there, I don't think I can even bring her out into the real world. For all intents and purposes, she belongs in that world.

Everyone has been supportive, and no one is really saying anything though. As far as most people know, the bad dreams have abated for now. The others who were there when I spilled the tale have kept things quiet for the most part including Rex and Erica. Becca and particularly Walker have been my anchors, and I started swimming again yesterday under the watchful eyes of Walker. He commended me on handling Corogi and Sunee's aqua acrobatics training. I apologised so much for pulling him away from his work. He kept assuring me that it was mostly done anyway and he has been keeping contact with the others through the Operations Center.

Speaking of that, I haven't caught up with Tommy yet.
And speaking of people I haven't caught up with yet, what the heck am I going to say to Michelle's father?
I'm tired… we'll leave it for now.

May 9

Linda asked if I was willing to make things a little less vague by filling in the blanks in my writing. The idea that I had a life before I started at The Facility, before I started writing this journal, does put a few things out of whack such as stuff about my biological condition, the whole dreaming exercise, my abilities,

Mikey and me, or just plain old stuff that happened to me that is impacting my life right now. I told her I would think about it and in a way, I'm also letting her know now that – No, I'm not about to go into such details about my life in this journal for everyone to see. It's not really the point of this journal anyhow. Coming to The Facility to learn was supposed to be a fresh start, but then, no one really gets that kind of fresh start without having something from the past cropping up at some point.

This was meant to keep my mom apprised of my activities at The Facility, so retreading my past that she already knows is redundant. For everyone else, it's probably easier to go with the flow and fill in the blanks. Sure I have kept my relationship with Mikey a vague point without saying who he is to me, that is until that last entry when there is absolutely no doubt that he is my son. Throw in the little fact about my actual age as opposed to by biological age – which is how everyone else perceives me – and it's an incredibly sensitive issue to tackle. It was entirely my thing and there's no one to truly blame for that one, and the only regret is that I didn't experience the actual pregnancy, just the birthing.

Speaking of the kids, I did my dream-walk earlier today and while I had hoped that Mikey would turn up, he didn't. I spent my time trying to bond with Michelle instead. I really want Mikey to meet her so he doesn't get some crazy idea that since he hasn't been turning up, I suddenly went off and got another kid to replace him.

Michelle still wasn't saying anything and Kinstein said she has been equally quiet with him. She has stayed with him though and she does behave like a normal child. She eats and sleeps and does everything else in between a normal child her age would, with the exception of talking. I tried encouraging her by doing simple things like identifying a cup or a table or even my name and her name, but she watched and looked without saying anything, or even trying. I really want to know exactly where she came from; how she came to exist in this dream-world. I also want to know how she managed to hop around in dreams, knowing when someone was actually dreaming and then going into it. Those dreams and this dream-world exists on two different levels as far as I'm aware, even though they do cross occasionally; unless everything Charlie has told me about what he could figure out about my dream-world is wrong, which would make everything else I ever wrote about my dream-world wrong too.

Apart from the dreaming stuff where I didn't get anything accomplished and didn't fight or capture any creatures, I've been trying to catch up with some of my classes. The whole week has me being a touch depressed from the whole episode, and my focus in class has not been too good. When I was feeling particularly miserable, I skipped class and soaked in the pool. The days leading up to that episode, I was hardly in the water, and the days since I've been slowly working my way back into the water, not always with Walker's supervision

The effects of being in Callie's dream are still wearing off, and I'm still a little on the jumpy side. The more rest I get, normal sleep or even with the dream-walk, the more I get away from the weirding of the world; the skewing of reality. I really wonder how Callie gets through the days if her dreams are like that. I don't know if Toni is similarly affected. I should ask her to be sure. In any case, it's taking me a while to get the effects on my head toned down, or thrown out altogether. It wasn't Michelle who put that into my head, so it simply might have been from spending time in Callie's dream.

I'm still going to take in some revision classes tomorrow and hopefully I'll be back on track and back to normal by Monday. I'm also going to try getting permission to make a phone-call home on Mikey's birthday. That's coming up soon, I'm not saying exactly when. Remington would let me make the call when I needed, but with Linda, I'll have to do things differently and give her some advance notice. I've accepted that.

So, here's to things getting back to normal and keeping things a little shorter than usual.

May 13

The last few days have been me trying to adjust to normal reality while trying to calm myself in those jumpy moments that still creep up from time to time. I've managed to squeeze in some sleep each night, ranging an hour to hour and a half. At least, it's some rest each night. I get to bed after finishing at the pool and shower. Once I'm awake, I check in at the Operations Center to catch up on work, except for last night when I was on my Spaceship project. I also clocked in an hour with the flight simulator before heading back to the pool.

I've filled Tommy in on the recent events. He probably thinks it's all a lark, but then queried if all these dream-worlds were alternate realities, only accessible by us dreamers. We had a small discussion on the matter, and I used up what little I could remember from Theoretical Physics (and Quantum Sciences) in less than fifteen minutes. He was ragging on me about it for the next couple of nights.

One other matter I needed to deal with was the date I owe Keitaro. I considered having it this Friday, which would have gotten it out of the way sooner, but he preferred to hold on to this debt for another day. I wasn't sure what to make of it at first. He apparently wants to make something special of it, but hasn't told me what the plan is. I tried asking Keiko over lunch the next day, and again during kendo practice, and repeated that the following day (yesterday), but she still hasn't found out what his plan is.

Speaking of Keiko, we've been going through the motions with kendo over these last few days simply because it's helping me with focus. That's something I need for now, to keep my mind from drifting due to the diminishing effects of Callie's dream. Keiko wants me back to sparring by next week. She says that I've laid off long enough and if it was focus I needed, the sparring would help get my focus sharper. She feels once I get to that, I would slip back to fighting mode where I become acutely aware of my surroundings in that particular way. A part of me isn't looking forward to it because I get the feeling she's just waiting to whack my head right again.

Meanwhile, things around the lunch group have been interesting. The rumours were about the so-called dream virus that was going around, but only in whispers. No one ever admitted to getting it, but someone always knew someone else who had problems sleeping. While no one would take anything from what Sophie or Callie were saying in way of explaining what really went down, they would apparently listen to either Rex, Erica or Jim, even if he wasn't there for the later part. From what I've heard, there's a version floating around that wasn't quite what happened either, but it sounded a lot more interesting and exciting since they kept the idea of a monster of some sort stalking through people's dreams. It takes the spotlight off me, and I think it's something that was intended by all involved. No one has said anything about Michelle, at least, no one from that little group left at the end.

The other rumours swirling around me had to do more with Walker and me; how he came running when I was in some trouble and in the Infirmary for a couple of days. We have been pretty close over the last few days, more because he was watching over me in case I might flip out while in the pool; didn't happen. He's also been with all of us at lunch so there is the impression that he's being overprotective, but he really isn't. It's more concern than protectiveness, because everyone else in the lunch group can attest that the last thing I need is protection, unless it was from myself.

Another concern of mine has been Ethan. I haven't seen hide nor hair of that kid since I asked him to be a part of our group. Toni said he has been turning up for his TP training and that's about it. She mentioned he looked like he still hasn't gotten much sleep, but I've got nothing on that. If he was connected with the others where the bad dreams were concerned, he should have been over it by now. Unless his bad dreams were not the same as everyone else's, in which case, we have a different problem there.

And I guess that's about it where my social stuff is concerned. I'm off to the pool for now and then to get some rest. It may be a few days, but that's the pattern as it is.

Come to think about it, one person who's been relatively quiet through all this is John. I haven't even noticed him in the gym lately...

May 15

It's about two years now since I started with the spaceship rocket design. The original idea was for it to help me get a sort of physical reference point for all the theoretical stuff I was learning. Since then, it's taken a life of its own, occasionally falling by the wayside whenever something else grabs my attention. While I can't physically build the spaceship, I have the flight simulator to use as a core base and design the whole ship within the flight simulator's computer. This wasn't only the flight deck of the spaceship, but the whole ship itself.

Elements of my training that have contributed to the spaceship included the engineering courses, Mechanical and Electrical, Theoretical Physics and even Astronomy along with some Celestial Sciences. There are also some of the structural stuff like accommodations, amenities and services such as air, water and waste recycling, power systems and even a garden.

I'm mentioning all this because I've been asked to do a review in order to see how far I may have fallen behind given my absences from classes and the constant need to catch up. It's probably also due to the fact that I've been struggling with my classes all week, with the exception of TP, TK and Computer Programming. Then again, skipping on those to catch up with the other classes was probably a contributing factor as well. Still, it's something that was coming a while now. Anyway, that's for next week.

Apparently, I need to meet with the tutors in each of my classes – with the three exceptions – and go over the aspects of the whole spaceship, its functions, operations, systems and whatever else with respect to the class that tutor teaches. I will get quizzed along the way about what was used within the design and what was bypassed, and I have to give reasons. Linda reminded me this is not a test of any kind, just a way to gauge where I stand in relation to my training. After that, it will be determined if changes need to be made, probably in the sense if I need additional tutoring to catch up – like I did last time, getting help from my friends – or in a more severe case, drop back a couple of months to join the newbies, some of whom actually jumped ahead to the classes I am in.

I'm beginning to wonder if Remington had got mom to join this Facility as he had hoped, what would she be doing? I doubt she would be going through classes like this. Even Callie isn't having this much trouble with her classes, whatever they are. I don't really see her in any of the classes I'm in, not even TK and TP.

Anyway, I did get to make that call home on the day I wanted to wish Mikey a Happy Birthday. I persuaded him to visit me in the dream-world tomorrow. That took a while, but he agreed. I hope it'll be a nice surprise that he gets to officially meet his sister, although from my recollection of her memories, they have met, albeit briefly.

The issue of Michelle has been getting some mileage around the lunch group, more with Helen and Sophie asking about how she would or even could exist in the first place. The reasoning came from Sophie stating that the dream-world was a figment of my imagination, so by all rights, Michelle would be a figment of my imagination.

Helen, having been to the dream-world, had a different opinion as she reminded Sophie about how the dream-world would continue to exist even when I wasn't active in it, therefore, proving that it existed of its own volition. The inhabitants, like Kinstein and the villagers, had their own lives regardless of how often I visited. Although, there is a suggestion that the health of the land also depended on me.

Becca then chimed in on the aspect of time being a contributing factor in relation to perception because of the time she spent there with me a couple of years back. It may have been a few days in real time, but we spent weeks together where she managed to improve her English and I learnt her language. It was not possible to truly learn things in dreams and have them retain in reality. Even she would admit to having dreams that didn't carry into reality upon waking from a normal sleep. It was an interesting point she shared considering she's an F.E.P.. I considered asking Walker if he dreamed.

Everybody had an opinion. This included others like Ehrmer, Corogi and Walker, and I don't think it's going to let up anytime soon. Not all of them have been to the dream-world, but the idea of how it might be a parallel world, and the way it functions, was something of interest. Helen's interested in making another trip and Keitaro voiced the same desire although he doesn't want to consider it as a replacement to our missed date as yet. Carol is still a little reluctant while Becca preferred to remain non-committal on the subject, saying that someone needs to remain grounded for the time being. Keiko, Toni and Callie had no interest whatsoever. Sophie's got her own world. Even Erica has shown an interest in how that world happened, if I was a lucid dreamer, and if we could share some notes or thoughts on our process.

In all, it's been surreal actually. Good thing those episodes where reality goes screwy have tapered off considerably, and I haven't felt jumpy at anything for the last day or so.

Well, keeping it short again. I have to get ready for my dinner with Walker.

May 17

That was quite a busy weekend, from the dinner with Walker to the dream-walk and all that happened today. Individually, they are what they are; typical events that take place on their usual days. As a whole, they do make up an active and interesting weekend.

On Friday night, I was getting ready for dinner with Walker. It was a bit of a surprise that he came to the suite to meet me instead of us meeting at the café like usual. It was our first official dinner together since he's been back, although we have had meals together since then. There was really nothing special about the dinner tonight, but the way he paid attention to whatever I said or did, without being too obvious at first, was endearing. Once I noted that he was doing it, he pulled back a little. It was more the typical way he would observe something; applying that analytical eye to the most minute of problems, trying to see if there have been any changes to my behaviour while he was away.

When I asked, he pointed out a few minor shifts in the way I sat to the way I ate. Not that there were many variations in the first place, but there were, according to him, some changes in the last month. I then asked if there was anything that actually remained the same, and he said I was still the same height, had the same eye colour, and I still adjusted my glasses with my right hand (I'm left-handed), handling the frame by the bridge of my glasses – like I actually noticed I did that in the first place.

I asked if it was important that such changes happened, and he said it was something he observed in humans, that certain habits stay the same while other habits might change to accommodate a certain adjustment to one's life. At best, some of the changes I've made, no matter how minute, might have been affected by the events that occurred over the past month. One overt example is how Callie's dreams might have affected my overall sense of balance for a while, and after a period of adjustment, according to Walker, I'm listing a little to the left when I swim my laps. I protested at first but he said that if I wanted, I could simply track my own path the next time I was in the pool. I start as close to the wall on my right as I could manage and then see how far I'd drift off by the end of the lap. I tried it this morning, and he was right.

After dinner, we sat in the garden and he told me more about his time at the other facility in South America. I can't really write about what we talked about (classified stuff) until whatever they are working on is officially announced or actually happens. It was nice and relaxing to listen to him talk about all the strange and unique things about us that we take for granted, like those little things about me he pointed out earlier.

We ended up in his personal suite after that and I spent the night there. We slept together, and well… nothing happened beyond that. Then again, given the imaginations at work within The Facility here, what I say isn't really going to matter with the others. I ended up sleeping about an hour and a half or so, and then I watched some TV while waiting for him to wake up a few hours later. It was quite liberating to kick back and unwind like that. I got back to the bed before five in the morning, and lay there next to him. He only woke up about half an hour later.

I took the dream-walk in the afternoon and caught up with my kids. Mikey did turn up and I introduced Michelle to him, explaining how the situation came to be. He confirmed that they had met on occasion. No words were exchanged between them. I caught up with Mikey and how things were at home. He asked if there were still creatures lurking about and I told him there were, but added that I had a plan to help him with that. I just needed him to come back next week. At first he thought I was trying to trick him, but I said I wanted to get some help from Keitaro to work it out. I hadn't asked him at the time. The idea came to me while I was watching TV in Walker's suite.

After Mikey left, I caught up with Kinstein to get the lay of the land, and then told him of my plan and how it might cause some changes to the 'world'. I was going to introduce some form of advanced technology, but at the same time, keeping it within the tone of the world. On his end, he told me about whatever little progress he was making with Michelle, treating her like an adopted daughter and having her help out within the Kitchen itself, teaching her to cook and clean a little. She's taken a shine to her new 'duties'; something that keeps her occupied without complaint.

Again, nothing too special, but the kids got along well enough. The situation with them reminded me of my relationship with Rick. Although we are twins, I only appear older than him even though on a maturity level, he's probably savvier than I am. Because of the unique nature of the dream-world and it's unique time-flow, Michelle has turned out to be older than Mikey, but he's more 'matured' than she is. Then again, until Michelle opens her mouth and begins to speak a little, I won't know how much she actually knows aside from those sparse memories of hers in my head that are slowly dissipating.

Once all that was settled with Kinstein, I took on one job to help some villagers track a creature that's been poaching from the farms. That took the better part of a day. Added to the time I spent in the Kitchen, it was close to two days, but only five hours or so on the outside. I managed to catch a late dinner with Keitaro and filled him on my plan to help Mikey. Suffice to say, Keitaro was willing to help so long as it was understood that it still didn't count as a replacement date.

That leaves today, mostly spent in review classes trying to catch up with my lessons. What was cool was that I got to discuss openly with the tutors about my upcoming review tomorrow. I managed to clarify some of my notes – they were suitably impressed, at least the three I met with today – and explained a bit of it in relation to my spaceship project. If I coupled it all with the review tomorrow, I should be fine, which one of them said so. It gave me enough of a confidence boost actually. I've managed to secure some time with Ehrmer tonight to go over the finer points of Mechanical and Electrical Engineering. He'll tear some of my notes apart, but it'll be a good thing to make me really sure about my stuff.

I should get going.

May 20

I suppose I could have gotten back to this a little sooner, but I wanted to wait for the feedback from Linda. I had to go through the review, meeting up with each of the tutors when they weren't having a class in session. Following that, they would make their reports to Linda, in her capacity as my G/C. She would have a review with her superiors and others who might be tracking my progress and then she would let me know of their decision. That happened about an hour ago and it was as I had hoped.

Basically, I wasn't too far back and I had the capacity to catch up again, I only need to get some help from my friends again, those who might be willing this time around. Let me back-track a little…

I spent much of Monday and a little of Tuesday getting around in order to catch up with my tutors. It wasn't meant to be split over two days but some of the review sessions got long and I had tons of questions to answer that we didn't finish everything on time. It gave me a little opportunity to prepare for the Tuesday session which included Theoretical Physics – probably my weakest subject, because it's a lot of theory and limited hard evidence. I even got to check some of my facts with Carol, and she offered to continue helping me if I needed.

The general feeling I got at each of the review sessions was anxiety at first, but I got more relaxed and confident as the sessions went on. My tutors were not too hard on me, and they were quite accommodating and understanding. Even Mr. Hardy said that he could tell that I was trying to do as best as I could manage during my review with him. I think he was suitably impressed in the end, at least, that was the impression I got.

Most of Tuesday, after the last review before lunch, had me in a bit of a relaxed state. The slight worrisome tension I had in facing the reviews lifted a lot by then. I filled in the others on what I went through with the review, and what I thought the tutors felt how I might have done. Helen said there had only been one other case like mine before. She couldn't say who that person was or what happened to that person either. It was something she heard. It didn't make me feel all that great, but Becca said that if there was anyone who was going to beat the odds, it would be me. The others agreed with her even citing an example or two from the last couple of years, like when I fell behind the last time and had to catch up.

Tuesday afternoon was spent catching up with TP training, checking in with Jenny on Callie and Toni's progress. She also reported that Ethan's been attending his training, progressing normally although he does have signs of fatigue and insufficient sleep. I didn't see him then. I haven't seen him in a while now. Much as I want to look for him, I have to hold myself back and let him have his space or it will look like I'm interfering, even though he's one of those I'm watching over in TP and TK, but not outside of classes. If he stops turning up for his training with Jenny, only then can I make an official report to Miss Tracy and go looking for him.

By the evening, I was back to sparring with Keiko and as expected, she went all out with hand-to-hand. A part of me was glad to get back to that kind of sparring because after the two days of review, I really needed to let out some pent up stuff. It wasn't quite anger or frustration but some leftover bits of frayed nerves. Keiko was right about that too; sparring was a good tonic to the edginess that had plagued me since the trip to Callie's dream.

Of course, I got whacked up a bit, but still held my own. Still can't beat her outright when it comes to hand-to-hand sparring. I think she's only this tough when facing me because she knows I can take it and heal up faster than anyone else. In any case, it gave me a good night's sleep – 3 hours solid – after which I spent catching up on my work in the Operations Center.

I had the meeting with Linda this morning after breakfast and, as I said, it's as good as it gets; I don't have to back-track too much, but there's a lot for me to catch up, and it's not for slacking off or anything. It's mostly the two Engineering classes and Theoretical Physics, as expected. I'm cruising through Computer Programming, there's nothing much to be said for either TP or TK, and I'm doing well enough in the remaining classes so I don't need any extra tutoring there. I may not be as smart as the other 99% of the trainees here, but I've been holding my own and even Linda is suitably impressed by my "persistence," as she called it.

Anyway, I better cut this short. I'm heading off for lunch and then it's back to classes for me.

May 22

Over the last couple of days, with the sparring and kendo in between, the after effects of visiting Callie's dream have pretty much worn off. Frankly, it's the kind of experience I really do not care to go through again.

Dreams are weird places to be and how they actually work is really a mystery. Some say that it's our brain's way of sorting through our day's events, and if we don't dream, we go crazy or worse. There are also cycles during our sleep during which our dreams occur, but as far as I know, I don't sleep like a normal person, but I do recall having dreams, even if I sleep for an hour or so. That's supposedly not really enough time for an actual sleep/dream cycle, but what do I really know anyway.

I've been doing a lot of catching up over the last couple of days since I've gotten the clearance to continue instead of falling back. In the middle of all that, I got into a friendly argument with Nik over some of the A.I. programming systems yesterday. It was in the middle of the computer programming class, and we were comparing notes. I mentioned one thing about how I was setting my system and he was saying that it was an illogical system and that it wouldn't work. Of course, I had to defend my system, which I knew was working because of Colleen, and it was more her that I was defending.

Our argument carried over from class and into the lunch group and I didn't realise it at first until Helen asked what language we were arguing in.

152

Apparently, my Malay wasn't as rusty as I had thought because at some point, our argument ended up in that language. I had to learn it when I was schooling in Penang. It was a requirement, and I hadn't really had any chance to use it since I last met up with my friends. Even then, the Malay girls would usually speak in English, which was more common when we girls got together in or out of school. I guess in some way, it gave them the opportunity to practice their English. When Helen pointed out our conversational language, that was when we stopped arguing.

I admitted that I wasn't even aware when we switched languages and he was grateful to have someone to talk to in Malay. He even complemented me in being able to carry on an argument in Malay revolving around computer science, no less. Following that, I explained to the others what we were arguing about. Carol had to tease about us having private and secret conversations that I didn't want Walker to know. No one would be able to corroborate what I was explaining to them in any case, it was my word that the argument between Nik and myself was really about A.I. systems.

In any case, Helen backed me up, informing Nik she had seen my concepts working in Colleen. I had to tell Nik more about Colleen and how I was using my own programming language, a factor as to why my little idea worked better than he would expect in his preferred programming language of C# (C-Sharp). The catch was that I couldn't expect it to work within The Facility's programming language and obviously, modifications would need to be made. It also took me a moment to realise that Helen could follow what we were talking about in terms of the technicality of our A.I. Programs. I didn't get around to showing Colleen off to Nik though.

I hadn't noticed if Nik mixed around with anyone else. He always seemed quiet and focussed on his work, but then again, that's pretty much how everyone generally is around here. Even those in our lunch group are like that when we aren't together, at least, based on my own observation during the classes that followed.

Anyway, since my focus has been on my classes and my studies, there hasn't been anything else that's really occupied my attention. I still spar with Keiko and had kendo practice yesterday. Last night was spent partially on my Spaceship project, took an hour with the flight simulator before checking in with Colleen. I got a couple of hours sleep before all that.

And before I sign off, I want to mention that dinner I'm heading for is with Sophie and not Walker. She asked for the dinner a couple of days back over lunch – the same lunch with Nik – and I told Walker about it that night and he was okay with it. She didn't really say why she was requesting the dinner, but I guess it was more for us to catch up since we haven't had dinner together in a while.

Well, that's about it, I've cooled down from my session with Keiko and I need to get ready for dinner.

May 24

The dreaming trip yesterday was pretty much a success. Keitaro was successful in creating what I needed and we had help as Sophie came along too. When we got to the Kitchen, we were a bit early and Mikey hadn't arrived yet. That was a bit of a surprise and I was really hoping that I hadn't missed him, but he was a little late.

I introduced Michelle to Keitaro and Sophie (again), but the kid still wouldn't say anything. Kinstein said she was doing quite well in helping out at the Kitchen, but she has not said anything to him either. It was obvious she could understand us though because she would follow his instructions. At least there's that.

So this idea I had that required Keitaro's help was to create a pair of robotic guardians for Kinstein's Kitchen, except that they'd be made of wood and maybe a little iron. We didn't have to set out to gather any of the materials needed. I got a list of what Keitaro figured we needed and I made them appear. It's more like, I opened the back door from the Kitchen and we stepped out to a clearing with all the necessary materials on hand already.

I didn't need a robotics expert as much as I needed someone who could design a pair of kick-ass robots that can be operated individually or linked up. The actual working mechanisms weren't really needed; we're in a world of imagination here. So with Keitaro giving directions, Sophie and I used our TK to assemble the pieces as he saw fit. It took us the better part of day putting together two eight feet tall robot replicas. One was for Mikey and the other was for Michelle. I sure couldn't make one because I have two kids to cater to now.

Mikey arrived when we were about three-quarters way through, and Kinstein brought him out. He marvelled at the structures and while they did appear bulky and a little skeletal, he immediately got the idea of what we were doing. After we were done, Keitaro helped Mikey with his 'robot' while I helped Michelle, teaching her how to make the whole thing move; powered by imagination. We didn't get into how the two separate robots could merge into one, but we did get into the firearms of the robots. They didn't shoot energy blasts, but small arrow like projectiles, decent enough to keep the creatures at bay and not kill.

I got Mikey to agree that he would only use the robot when Kinstein allowed it. When not in use, they would stand guard as totems watching over the Kitchen. This was to prevent Mikey from simply dropping in to play with his new toy, not that I minded it, but it would prevent him getting some proper sleep if he drops by every night. I wish I could follow up with Karen and Rick at home, but they wouldn't know if he dropped by the dream-world or not when he went to sleep. Still, they would know to watch out if he didn't wake up on time like normal. I should drop them a note to have them contact me if that happened so that I can drop in on the dream-world to make sure Mikey isn't sneaking off on his own. Kinstein has some power there in any case. I did have Keitaro ensure a 'locking mechanism' that Kinstein could control in my absence, like being guardian of the keys.

Once the kids got comfortable enough with their toys, we took it for a little test drive to a nearby village that was supposedly beset by a couple of creatures. Mikey seemed a little gung-ho, but it served its purpose in fighting off the creatures. Michelle was a little more reserved in her actions, pretty much a complete opposite of Mikey. She did enjoy herself with her own toy though, she even laughed. It was probably the first time I heard her voice. Mikey doesn't feel too scared about coming around and he was quite eager to meet up again next week.

Another giddy kid among us was Keitaro who was quite ecstatic to see his robot designs working despite having no actual energy source. The designs had been simplified, so while there is robotics at work, it's mostly braces and levers, pulley functions; basic mechanics at works. They shouldn't really work, much less with kids handling them, and in the real world, they probably wouldn't. Still seeing them move about was something to behold. Keitaro's designs were pretty slick and streamlined, even if they were made of wood and a little steel.

Once we were all done, Mikey headed home and I sent Keitaro back to reality while Sophie and I had other business to attend to. When we met for dinner the night before, she asked for some help with her own dream-world. At her request, I'm not writing about it beyond all this. A lot of what I write about revolves around me and how my friends revolve around me, but they have their own lives too. They have their own problems, and in this particular case, one of them has asked for help.

By the time we came out of the dream-world, it was Sunday morning, over fifteen hours since we started. We had spent over a day in Sophie's dream-world. Add to that the day spent with the kids and I suppose the hours would have racked up. Of course, there have been cases where the adverse has happened. I managed to only grab one extra class after lunch before getting into a sparring session with Keiko.

It was during that training when Keiko told me how Keitaro was gushing over his robots. We had a bit of a laugh over that and I shared more details over dinner

Now that I've killed some time letting the dinner settle, I want to spend some time in the pool with Walker, so I'm off.

May 26

It's just not over.

Someone, somewhere, didn't want to open up and say that they had the same problem until it comes up big time. I suspected Ethan had sleeping problems and I did want him to join us when we tackled the problem. According to Jenny, that bit of sleeplessness has caught up with him and he's slipping during his training with her. She only brought it up today during our review on our TP charges. It's part of the training system I'm supposed to be covering.

The other person I suspected having the same problems, but was never proven or brought up, was John. It was John's friend, Peter, who came up to me saying that John's been having problems sleeping. He wasn't clear if it was bad dreams or not, just that John had mentioned about not getting enough sleep. He didn't have any more information. He requested I check up on him because of all those stories that had been going around about what we did with the last group of people with sleeping problems.

Yeh, that's not really clear, is it? It's like I'm rambling away there. It's this thing with John. Even when he's not physically around and I keep my distance, he still gets in my head by having one of his friends ask me to check in on him. In all honesty, I'm a little reluctant to approach him about this when he hasn't confided in anyone beyond Peter. As far as I'm aware, he has been attending his classes and no real problems have cropped up, aside from maybe looking a little tired from time to time.

I think ever since my being with Walker became public knowledge, he has been keeping his distance, although I sense his eyes on me every now and then; especially in the gym during the sparring session more than during the kendo training. It's that feeling he wants another rematch, but then, he might have other things on his mind where I'm concerned, that is, if the rumours constantly shared by Carol have any truth to them. Let's just say that if I wasn't with Walker and was a little more loose, we just might end up together. In some parallel world, maybe we are together.

Peter approached me as I finished up kendo practice with Keiko and the others. I was apprehensive about his request and Keiko noticed this. After Peter left, she asked me what I intended to do. I was a little reluctant to simply take Peter's word that John needed help, and unless John actually asked, I wasn't obligated to do anything.

"You know you're going to help him," she said. "Even I know you're going to help him whether he wants it or not."

"What makes you so sure?"

"What makes you think you won't help him anyway? It's in your nature," she said. "You can't leave it alone."

It was something like that and, just to spite her, I did think of leaving it alone. I'm catching up on my studies. I'm getting help where I can and the last thing I need is another jaunt into the dreams of others that's going to knock me back again. At least, that's my official excuse. Part of the whole 'help' thing is that they should want my help as well. That's on John as well as Ethan, and neither has officially asked. Not to mention that they do have options in asking help from Callie and Toni, who did pretty well with the last group.

There it goes again. Every now and then, when it comes to John, I get a little carried away on writing about or around him. Yerghs!

Problem is, that was the highlight of the last couple of days. Things have been going along as normal as can be. There hasn't been any change as to how I've been carrying on with studies, and activities, and sleep over these last few days. I wasn't really sure if I had anything to write about at first and I really didn't want to reflect on Peter's request.

But there ya go. A pretty quiet two days. I'm off to the pool now.

May 29

Keiko was right. I poked around and inquired about John's supposed condition. Even Carol picked up on my little reconnaissance and asked over lunch today if there was something going on that got me so interested in John all of a sudden. In return, I asked her what she might have heard or noticed about him lately. She noticed his occasional lack of attention in class lately, like he hadn't gotten enough sleep.

"Is there anything to be concerned about?"

"Just a feeling that he might be having some of those sleeping problems that were going around," I said.

"I thought you guys took care of that already," said Helen.

"I thought we did, but maybe he's got some other kind of problem. I'm trying to determine if it's really my help he needs or not."

"Yeah, we know which one you're hoping for," said Carol in jest.

While Carol may play up the rumours and constantly force the issue of matching John and me, the others around the table at lunch are well aware of my feelings regarding to John.

Anyway, while I have no hard evidence to the contrary, it would seem that John is having some sleepless nights. It might be bad dreams, or he might be worried over work, or more likely worried over other girls; hopefully, not me. I've got myself into a nice groove rotating all my activities while keeping pace with my studies and work. The less distractions I have, the better. My days are pretty packed and I've more or less got a regular sleeping schedule. Granted it's down to no more than ninety minutes, but at least it's been steady these past few days. Working on either my spaceship design or on Colleen is like my own personal quiet time because there's no one else around to bother me in those wee hours. Well, I still chat with Colleen to help her improve her vocabulary, not that she actually needs it. Her learning curve is getting steeper every time I check on her.

If my classes were hard before trying to understand stuff when I was starting out, it's gotten even tougher putting everything into a kind of theoretical practice. Walker and Ehrmer have been helpful with the tough parts, and I think Ehrmer has been more than gracious to help in return for my helping Corogi with her aqua-acrobatics. She has been eager to continue with her practice so I've had to step in to practise with her as Sunee has not been turning up lately due to some project work. It's some new ground for me as I get to practise Walker's side as he supervises and corrects us.

Between Walker and Ehrmer, I get put through the paces of applying the theories to possible scenarios. They're aces at what they do. Even Becca and Kadi have been helping out a bit, which has made me realise that the only non F.E.P who is currently helping me is Carol. She's still aces with the whole physics thing; theoretical, quantum or otherwise. She did question me on the whole multi-system propulsion function on my spaceship. I've got up to four systems backing up each other from typical atomic force, to particle agitation propulsion, to a highly probable teleportation system. That last one could be viewed more as an artificial wormhole system. She was more like, "What are you thinking putting those systems there?"

Tommy also helps in some areas during our down time, while making sure that I'm keeping up with my work and everything else I'm supposed to be learning there. I still keep hoping for some kind of sign from Tomas that he's still out there, but there hasn't been any other sign since that rhythmic pulse the IASC Mission Control is still running through some program or other.

The only distraction I have is Walker; more to help with my unwinding than a distraction. I've got a dinner date with him in a while and, well... I don't have much to add to that. Our relationship is moving along. I don't want to write too much about it and I'm happy enough to keep things quiet in that area. We're in a pretty happy place; well, I'm in a pretty happy place with him. I hope he feels likewise.

I should ask him later over dinner.

May 31

A few things to get through since it was a busy weekend. Friday's dinner was fine with pleasant company, and there's nothing too spectacular to comment on, so... that's that.

Saturday was spent catching up with studies at first, but after lunch, it was time with the kids, watching over their use of the wooden mechas. They are getting quite adept at controlling their individual mechas, but they're not doing too well when they have to merge, like they can't get in synch with each other. Michelle is progressing a little faster than Mikey at using the mecha. I wondered if Kinstein was letting her have soma extra time that Mikey isn't getting. Then again, Mikey could be dropping by on his own to get some practice without me knowing for sure. Still, I'm sure that given the chance, they would find some way to have a go with their new toys. At least, I'm sure Mikey would try. I'm not too familiar with Michelle's behavioural patterns, so I can't anticipate her or what she would do.

We headed out to a nearby village that needed some help with the creatures. By all rights, I really shouldn't be taking the kids into such situations, but this isn't the real world. The rules are different enough that I can control the level of danger if needed. If needed, I can step in to take control of a situation to keep the kids safe, but it was not necessary for this little errand. I've got a decent system working to trap these creatures so that we can safely confront the creature; or creatures in this case.

In all, it took me close to a day on the inside and less than four odd hours on the outside. I had a little time for a break before dinner, which I used to unwind a little in the garden doing some meditation. I sat on the grass and faced the city, the sun setting over to the right. My concentration got broken an hour later by the comms device going off. It was Linda requesting I meet with her the next morning (this morning actually) for our monthly review.

I was pretty free after dinner so Becca and I caught a movie. It was a nice little traditional sci-fi that had only one actor in one location, that being the moon. It was a brilliantly made movie and some of the others had been talking about it over lunch, and even in class. Some were going on about the mining operation and the A.I. robot that was looking after the mining facility, while others were going on about that plot-twist. I won't spoil it here. Of course, there was that complaint about the gravity issue. Given that it was set on the moon, gravity looked pretty normal. Overall, a nice diversion and really fantastic little movie. At least the rules following how an A.I. works is fairly true.

After about four hours of sleep, I decided to work on Colleen. I ended up discussing the movie with her, more from the point of the A.I. in the film and how much of its actions – or programming – would ring true with her. We got into a discussion about how much 'free will' she might have as opposed to how much free will a normal person would have under certain conditions – socially, religiously and so on. I kept in mind to have the same discussion with Walker, Becca or Ehrmer. Would really like to know what they think and what it would be like where they're from.

Colleen reminded me of my meeting with Linda, giving me enough time to get some breakfast. I got to her office on time so things got off to a good start, I felt. She covered my classes and more importantly, my progress of late. Apparently, the reports from the tutors have been positive, so despite the extra problems with the dreams and such earlier in the month, I managed to keep pace with my studies.

As I was keeping up with socialising and other physical activities – the kendo practice and sparring with Keiko or swimming, for example – she didn't have much to say in that respect either. She did ask about my relationship with Walker and how that was progressing, noting that I had not written much about it lately. I admitted to not letting out too much, citing the tendency for rumours getting out of hand. She respected my decision on that.

She then touched on the issue of John and asked if I had decided on taking any action. I was surprised as she hardly ever referred to my journal entires. I'm not sure if she followed everything I wrote. Regardless, I shared the results of my inquiries, including some I had done lately since the last entry. Nothing really points to John having problems with his dreams. I did catch sight of him a couple of times, once in class and once at the gym. He seemed utterly exhausted and perhaps suffered from a lack of proper rest. I've not talked to him, so I haven't really decided to help him or not.

Linda suggested I consider talking to him, just to be sure. I asked her if she could confer with his G/C (whoever that was), as I'm aware there's this "check and balance" thing where the G/C's could check up on each other's charges. I felt if she could get some real information instead of the second-hand reports I've been collecting, that John's problem was indeed psychological, then maybe I could do something about it. Otherwise, I'd technically be interfering where I should not. At least, she agreed with me on that point. Unless John made a request for me to intervene, I really didn't have to do anything in this case. I learnt that dealing with Ethan last year.

Once that was done, she informed me that Remington wanted to talk to me, and she gave him a call. While waiting for him, she said she had shared the last few entries with him, particularly about Michelle. She had asked him about her and he confirmed that I had lost a baby before.

When he came in, the discussion focussed on Michelle, if she was who I thought she was and how she got into other people's dreams. He asked me what my particular plans were for her and if I had informed my mom about her. On that last point, I admitted I hadn't gotten around to informing her personally, but assumed she was still getting the journal in advance of having it posted online. The rest of his queries were answered no differently from what I had written before in previous entries. I'm working through it as I go along because I don't know of any other way to handle this particular issue at this time. He said that he and Linda were open to me if I needed any advice.

"Well, how do you deal with a daughter you never knew about, who may or may not rightfully exist in reality?"

They had no answer for me. I mean, as far as I know, Remington has no kids and I don't know anything about Linda's private life. I wasn't sure myself if I wanted to tell mom about Michelle because it's not like I can get the two to meet without pulling mom into my dream-world – and why would I want to do that?

Anyway, Remington voiced his concerns, and if I was going to start taking up more time on my trips to the dream-world in order to deal with Michelle. So far, I get to spend a day or so with the kids, but it's no more than a few hours on the outside. If it stays that way, it'll be fine. I'm more concerned about when Old Crans is going to pop up with some unimaginable errand for me to carry out. I'm also wondering if Michelle's sudden appearance is going to tie into that!

Everything is in under consideration right now; informing my mom about Michelle, anything else about Michelle, helping John (if it's needed), details about Walker and me that Linda wants me to share... I think it's more to do with the relationship between us, with me being human and him... not so much. That's the concern than the actual relationship between us. I didn't discuss anything with the others over lunch, although I did mention a little of it to Becca just now before I started writing. She knew I was a little bothered and writing things out was her suggestion, although I probably would have gotten to it on my own.

So that's the weekend in a nutshell. It almost feels like I really have no time to spare anywhere, but for a few moments here and there where I can squeeze some personal time. After all, I'm heading off to the pool after this to spend some time with Walker, after helping with the aqua-acrobatics and doing my own laps, of course. That's personal time right there.

And it's calling me, so I'm off for now. Wonder if he's interested in watching that movie. I don't mind a second viewing.

JUNE

June 2

The more Carol goes on about how beautiful and elegant physics is, the more I grow to hate it. Nothing makes sense. I mean, there is the general basic physics that we know, the kind where we get to perform experiment after experiment to prove those equations, like Newton's three basic laws of force. Those are physical laws that even Walker and Ehrmer would agree exist where they came from. The further I've gotten with Mr. Hardy and now with Carol, the more things fall apart.

Case in point, when I started here at The Facility, Gravity was something pretty solid and understandable. It was the force that held us to the ground, and kept the Earth in orbit around the sun simply because it keeps falling at that particular angle, the same way a satellite is constantly falling towards Earth just beyond the horizon and is thus in orbit around our planet. Now, Gravity isn't quite what it used to be because it seems strong enough to hold things down, but weak enough for us to move things about, even on Earth.

It's kinda hard to get around really explaining this, but my feeling is like… if Gravity is strong enough to hold us down and we need such extreme forces to escape it, like a rocket blasting to break away from Earth's gravity, how is it that I could even lift my own foot off the ground? I then figured that maybe Mass plays a part in the whole thing, so the more massive something is, the harder 'gravity' holds it to the ground and thus, more force or power would be required to move it. However, if Mass is such a factor, why doesn't something with less Mass, like a piece of paper, gets pulled towards the gravity of a building that obvious has more Mass, or do you have to be as small as an ant for that to work? But then, an ant would could still cling to something as small and light as a feather, so maybe Mass doesn't quite factor in there.

I struggled through Theoretical Physics at first, and then came to learn that, "Theoretical Physics," is an oxymoron. To me, Physics is an experimental and observational science, and I've had a tough time coming to grips with all the theoretical stuff, especially pushing into Quantum Mechanics, or Quantum Physics, and Particle Physics. I can accept that atoms were once thought to be the smallest things ever and then it was discovered that inside these atoms were electrons, protons and neutrons. And within these tiny 'balls' are quarks, which supposedly have been proven to exist, but not in any kind of visual sense. The assumption that if quarks had a sense of matter, what was inside the quarks? That's apparently where the whole other bit about Strings come from that could actually explain Gravity, Electro-Magnetism and those forces that hold neutrons and protons together or split them apart; or maybe not.

Carol had other ideas where I was concerned, and my particular relation with Gravity. For one, I could break Gravity all on my own because I had the occasional habit of flying thanks to my TK abilities. She used that as an example of how weak Gravity actually is, not to count the number of objects she had me physically pick up from the table. The fact that I could also manipulate objects via TK was also proof that Gravity isn't as strong as most people would make it out to be. She pointed out that stronger still was this Electro-Magnetic force inherent in all objects and that could be the force that attracts and repels things. In one way, this EM force would be like gravity in that particular way where one massive object might attract another object and hold on to it, but at the same time, like with magnetic forces of opposing power, push back just enough to not create too strong a hold. The strength of this particular force could also be determined not only by the Mass of an object, but also by the composition in relation to another object.

For example, people in general would have enough magnetic force that would result with being pulled towards the Earth but enough opposing elements that would give us the ability to push away at the same time, so with enough strength, we can jump or push away from the Earth momentarily. An ant might have enough elements that would attract it to all kinds of objects, thus allowing it to be upside down on a piece of paper held by me, but enough opposing particles between that ant and other elements or objects that would allow it to move.

Again, this was just a possibility – a theory. It was not necessarily the truth of the matter that would fully explain the nature of Gravity or Electro-Magnetism or how Quantum Mechanics would fit into all of this and how it would also relate to Einstein's theory of General Relativity.

Still having me use my TK ability, she had me ponder the possibilities of extra dimensions. She had me agree – and I could easily agree – that we live in a four dimensional existence. There are the three basic dimensions that we see and the fourth dimension of Time. That, I could live with, but there was that whole deal about parallel worlds. She went on about additional unseen dimension and how three dimensional objects can have two dimensional shadows and four dimensional objects might have three dimensional shadows (whatever they may look like), and then she went on to explain something

164

called a tesseract or a hypercube – take a three dimensional cube, which is a square extended into a third dimension, and extend it into another dimension. The other example where she got me to use my TK was to have me float to and stand on the ceiling, so I was upside-down. At least, to her perception, I was upside-down and to my perception, she would be the one who was the wrong way up and thus within one environment, we had additional dimensions from two different perceptions.

My general reaction was, "That's silly." That didn't stop her from pushing on until my brain was feeling pretty mushy. Walker said that while he could follow most of our Physics, there were vast differences into what was being looked into among the scientists or physicists of his world. The same thing applied to Ehrmer who admitted to finding the theories we had to be fascinating, but it didn't have much impact on his work.

Y'see, all that is why I don't really want to write about the classes anymore. I felt I needed to share part of the difficulty I go through in learning all these possibilities; of things that might or might not actually exist, especially with all this theoretical bits. I'm managing better with the Engineering materials because I have a place to apply what I learn, even if it's a virtual spaceship. I can't do anything of that sort with all that theory. There are no experiments, and Carol confirmed this, to either prove or disprove the existence of Strings, so it's not something I can dismiss because the theory alone could explain how everything fits together. My question to her became, if these so-called Strings were basically energy forms that vibrated and thus controlled the behaviour of other elements that would eventually make up the building blocks of, well, everything, what were these particular Strings made of? The energy had to come from somewhere or from something. If there was one constant that was true (supposedly now), energy is something that exists and can only change from one form to another, it can never disappear altogether, like water on our world.

Her reply? "Maybe you can come up with, and contribute, a new theory."

Anyway, I've got a bit of a headache now thanks to all that. I'm off to the pool.

June 5

Things have been pretty normal to an extent that it might seem like there's really nothing to write about. After the last rant, it does seem like nothing much is happening. Fact is, I have been trying to keep a lower profile since my meeting with Linda and focus on my studies. After all, the last time I went poking around, I ended up getting my head screwed around downside up. So, in keeping with that plan of maintaining a low profile, I've been quietly attending the lunches with the others, but keeping as quiet as I can while listening to and ignoring the usual gossip.

My classes have been moving along, as have my other activities. I've managed to maintain my flight hours in the simulator. I kept up with the Spaceship design, looking more into the drive systems as well as keeping up with working on Colleen. Time with Keiko is now standard as is pool time with Walker. Supervising the others in TP and TK is as good as it gets without having to follow up on Ethan. Jenny's got a hold on that for now. Overall, life is just peachy keen and as low profile as I can manage.

Carol is still helping me with Physics, and I also discuss those things with Walker or Becca. Walker also helps out more with Mechanical Engineering, as does Ehrmer while Corogi is quite good with Electrical Engineering. I get around in sociological discussions with Becca and Kadi – keeps me in practice with their language – and occasionally with Rain while helping her with the language barrier. When it came around to computer programming language, I would talk things out with Nik either in or after class, but we don't go further than that. It's not that he's a devout Muslim, and we're not back home, but I'm with Walker and I don't want to give out any vibes for Carol to pick up on. We happen to have a couple of areas of interest, that's all.

So, that's the plan for the foreseeable. Keep things on an even keel and do the work. There's still that part-time work I have in the Operations Center and Tommy is a great one to bounce some ideas off when it comes to my engineering or even my spaceship design work. He's also pretty good with the physics stuff so I can talk things out with him. As much I could just about keep up with the theories, I still couldn't wrap my head around the equation of some of them.

One last thing I should probably write about. The TP network training with Sophie, Kevin and Bastian is coming along and we've gotten five people to volunteer for their network practice. We've had one test run and they did well. No one had any problems and we had no leaks or any kind. I ran back-up, watching the network flow and for any kind of problems. I had Sophie watch out for leaks as well, basically getting her to work as a back-up to either Jenny or myself. She did much better than I expected, and I believe she's more than ready to manage a full network wth the advantage of catering to the F.E.P.'s. After all, she was co-running the network with Kevin and Bastian while watching for leaks and problems. Only Kevin came out of it with a slight headache from pushing himself a little hard, but he was fine after a while. I even made sure he checked in with Ms. Phillips, to be on the safe side.

There's another network test run next week with different volunteers, so we'll see what happens then. I don't expect any problems given how the last test went.

And that's about it, I guess. I'm off for dinner with Walker and we're gonna watch that movie later.

June 7

A couple of things to cover, but we'll take things as they happened. Picking up on Saturday, I took a trip to my dream-world with Walker in tow. I wanted him to meet Michelle and briefly told him what to expect with her, the fact that she doesn't talk and was a little odd.

I usually start around three in the afternoon, to make sure Mikey gets some proper sleep before he gets to the dreaming, but we started a bit earlier this time around. I wanted a little extra time with Michelle before Mikey arrived. It wasn't meant to be playing favourites between the two. We got to Kinstein's Kitchen and there were already some villagers waiting to meet with me. That was quite common these days on each trip, but Kinstein managed to work out some kind of schedule where they can meet with me after I've had some time with the kids.

Michelle was still helping out in the Kitchen, mostly with serving and bussing the tables, occasionally sweeping the floor. Nothing too tough for a kid her age (whatever that age is), and given the world she's living in, I'm not complaining about the work she has to do. It keeps her busy and Kinstein makes sure she has some studies to do as well, so at least there's some education going on for her.

Walker and I got to the Kitchen and we first met up with Kinstein. I also greeted Michelle before heading off to the private back-room where I usually hang out with Mikey and that's now expanded to accommodate Michelle as well. It was there I properly introduced Michelle to Walker and while he greeted her verbally, she still didn't say anything. She smiled. While Kinstein's been teaching her to read and write, she has not spoken in any way during the lessons; not to read aloud or even ask questions.

It wasn't long before Mikey turned up and the moment he saw Walker, his eyes lit up. He ran to embrace Walker first, obviously happy to see him, and

---

that got me a bit worried, particularly if Mikey gets too attached to Walker. I mean, I'm glad Mikey can get along with Walker, but I have to consider that Walker and I may not have much of a relationship beyond the next year. It's only an assumption since all the F.E.P.'s return home at some point and Walker's been around even before I was at The Facility.

Mikey started talking a mile a minute, and it was more than what he shared with me of late. He talked about how some of his friends at the day care/kindergarten talk about having big brothers or big sisters who help them out, and how he's now got a big sister who can do so much more, like pilot a mecha with him. Since she's here and he's in the real world, he can't prove anything beyond making a few simple drawings. At least those drawings are getting him some friends, or so Karen said. Just to be clear there, I only told Mikey that Michelle was his sister, I didn't tell him that she is supposed to be his twin sister.

Walker seemed to get along with Mikey and Michelle at the same time, but Michelle never said a word the whole time. She would respond when being talked to or being called, and she would follow instruction, but she never said anything to any of us; not a single peep. Even when all of us headed out to help a nearby village with its singular creature problem, she was cool under pressure. She followed instructions and didn't over-react even when the creature charged her. That got me worried for a moment, but I didn't have to because Keitaro did a fantastic job on those wooden mechas. Even after that, when the creature was taken care of, I asked her if she was okay, or if she was scared, the most she did was to nod or shake her head.

After we got back to the Kitchen, Mikey headed home – or woke up if you prefer – while Michelle got back to her chores. Walker and I set off for the little 'home on the sea' to unwind. We ended up in a discussion about Michelle's state of being and other things that I'll try to explain. It has to do with the concern of Michelle's state of being and if she actually exists, or if all of this – including the world we were in – was simply a figment of my imagination made manifest and shared across other people's consciousness. It became a question of which of the perceived realities was the real one. If both worlds could be accepted as real, which would take precedence where I was concerned.

I made the argument for the point that the dream-world was always something I dreamed of and made real to a certain extent. I even cited examples and moments when I did pull something from that fantasy world into reality just as much as I could pull other people from reality into the fantasy world. Granted that normal rules of reality didn't apply in the dream-world, so to that extent, it couldn't be as real as when we would wake up. Then he posed a stumper, "If everything here is within your control to change and manipulate, why are there so many things that are beyond your own control?" He cited the villagers, the creatures and even Michelle as examples. Then he took it one step further by asking, "If you were to die in the other world, would you continue to exist here? Or would this whole world cease to exist?"

We got into a whole 'perception of existence' argument – things exist because we see them existing, and so the world might actually cease to momentarily exist when we sleep because we don't 'perceive' it while sleeping – and the thought of dying in either world was not something I was keen to ponder. His reasoning was that if the latter occurred and the world ceased to exist, then nothing in the dream-world truly mattered and hence, Michelle was utterly irrelevant. If the former happened, then the possibility of the dream-world being something akin to a parallel world could be considered. In that scenario, Michelle would be very relevant indeed, and deep in my gut, she is definitely relevant to me at this time. Just like I knew by looking at her that she is my daughter.

It occurred to me though, that if the dream-world is really within my control, I really should be able to determine for sure the nature of those creatures that have been causing problems. Something to try out next time, if there is a next time considering that other matter that came up; I'll get to that in a minute. It could be I've never wanted to exert too much control over that reality myself. Probably the thought of playing God – not that I haven't been doing that anyway on occasion over there – was not something I was aspiring to when I first dreamt up that world. Maybe it is something else to consider when Walker brought that issue up, but I didn't really give it that much thought then. Maybe it only occurred to him when he brought up the matter then.

Anyway, we spent some private quiet time together after all that discussion. He said that whatever I decided to do, I had to see it through. He offered to help out if I needed him to. The issue remains, I don't know how long this situation will play out, and I don't know how long Walker can stay in the long run.

It was way past dinner by the time we got back to the Infirmary and we were met by Ms. Phillips, who wasn't there when we left earlier in the day. She requested a brief meeting with me and I agreed to it, but after Walker and I got something to eat. She made the oddest remark then saying, "Sounded like you guys got really active, I'm not surprised you need to recharge." I didn't notice it at first, but as we were leaving the Infirmary, I realised that our beds were surrounded with drawn curtains.

I returned to the Infirmary after dinner and had plans to meet Walker at the pool later. Ms Phillips asked about Ethan's activities in his own dream-world, to which I didn't have any particular knowledge. She then laid out the situation; Remington got reports from some of the tutors about Ethan nodding off in class, with one particular exception. He checked with Ms. Phillips because he was aware of Ethan making trips to his own dream-world, but not how frequently. If Ethan was making frequent trips to his dream-world, he wasn't doing it in the Infirmary and therefore, out and away from any supervision whatsoever.

"Do you know if Ethan's been dropping by that dream-world every night?" was what she asked me in the end. I admitted not keeping any tabs on him beyond the TP training, and even that was covered by Jenny. I was kept apprised of his training and made reports for Miss Tracy where that was concerned.

She then asked if I could sense if Ethan was off in his dream-world right now or if he was actually asleep. I didn't answer right away and it was a moment more before voicing my reluctance to scan for him without Remington knowing about it first. I felt it would be better if there were someone else of authority around, and I told her so. She was, at least, understanding about that and she respected my decision.

So she asked me to wait while she called Remington in. I politely tried to refuse but as she insisted, I ended up sending a comms message to Walker letting him know that I was not likely to make it to the pool as agreed.

While waiting for Remington, she asked about our trip to the dream-world. I related about the kids followed by the discussion Walker and I had, before having some 'intimate quiet time' to ourselves. It was then that she mentioned an external expression of our activities and it became necessary to put up the curtains around us. It was the second time such a thing happened although as far as I could recall there had never been any external reactions to events that happened to me while I was in the dream-world. Such things that happened to me had a habit of externalising only after I came out of the dream-world, and usually if it had been some kind of extreme injury. I didn't think it was likely that my emotions would seep through in a 'dream-state', and I said so to Ms. Phillips. She suggested I ask Will about it since he was on duty when it happened earlier.

I think I might have turned a shade when she said that because I felt my ears heat up like crazy, and I'm not one to be embarrassed easily. I kept quiet after that. Thankfully, Remington got to the Infirmary right then.

When the situation was explained, Remington easily surmised that he was there to cover my actions should I do as Ms. Phillips requested. I could have gone on more about the morality of the situation, but I didn't. Remington knows where I stand on such an issue.

His solution was for us head over to Ethan's suite and check on him. If he was asleep, I would do the scan as briefly as I can manage. On the bright side, he wasn't asleep when we got there so I didn't have to do the scan; big whoop! The four of us got into a bit of a discussion to ensure that Ethan would get some proper rest and not go off to the dream-world every night, even if he didn't admit to doing that. We also agreed that I would check on him once in a while to make sure of that, and he would have to be in the Infirmary if he wanted to drop in on his dream-world, just like me.

Another change that Remington wanted was for me to have more direct involvement with his training and progress at The Facility. This meant that I would take over his training from Jenny, and she would now get Sophie as a TP partner. In effect, I would be his mentor much like Becca has been for Kadi. This was a bit of a turn-around from before because Remington didn't want Ethan to get too fixated on me at first, and I agreed with that assessment. I was a little apprehensive this time but it did seem that he wasn't adjusting as well as Remington had hoped. My apprehension stemmed more from the fact that I was barely keeping pace with my own training as it is; hence the low profile over the last week or so. He said he would discuss the matter with Linda to work things out with her as well as my tutors if need be.

In following the rules, I agreed to be Ethan's mentor so long as Linda was agreeable. Remington moved pretty fast on that because I met with Linda today and she wanted to be sure I knew what I was getting into. I've been helping Becca with Kadi, so I had an inkling of what was expected of me. She felt it would be good for me to do this and I should go to her if I need some help.

"Don't try to solve every problem with him on your own," was her key advice.

I caught up with Jenny first to let her know of the changes, to which she seemed relieved. She never once voiced any problems with Ethan before. Then with Sophie, I had to let her know of the changes as well, that she would be training with Jenny, although still helping out Bastian and Kevin on their network sessions. Also, I informed her that if she wanted to take any trips to her own dream-world, that she best do it in the Infirmary and keep Ms. Phillips informed. It was only then she said that there was only once when she slipped into her dream-world unintentionally while asleep in bed. She was somehow aware of what happened, but made the most of it, instead of 'waking up' immediately. She hasn't made any trips since then, but she also didn't say when it happened.

At least I did my part in keeping her informed about that. I only started writing all this up after dinner, so I guess it's pretty long now. I wanna hit the pool, so I'm outta here.

June 9

There are times when things somehow come together within moments of each other. Whether it's a good thing or not always remains to be seen.

So the situation is that I may not be working in the Operations Center for a while. I guess I need to explain a bit about what I've been doing at the Operations Center and I have to skirt around the details a bit, as usual.

Just for background, the IASC has a deep space probe out there and it's sending back tons of info. That info is shared between the IASC and the Operations Center at The Facility to be processed. The data streams in as what might look like gibberish but each set of data has a particular code to identify it as either an image from one of the multiple cameras, or a reading from the sensors, or telemetry or whatever else. The computer basically separates the data according to the code markers that precede each clump of gibberish looking data, then part of what I did was to verify and isolate any particular discrepancies, merely as a double check. As good as computers can be, they're only as good as the programming, and every once in a while, errors can occur from somewhere. Yeah, it's really nothing much, but data is data, and it's something that needs to be sorted and verified in order for it to be valid for these guys.

In between all that, Tommy would teach me about the other work the Operations Center would do in conjunction with other agencies around the world, and I would occasionally help out in that respect as well, to learn the processes and systems in place. I would also learn about the other agencies. Primarily, my focus was on the space probe data.

So, what happened is that the data that's been streaming in was all messed up and the computer didn't know what to do, leaving it to us and the folks at Mission Control to work out what's going on with the data. There were all sorts of speculation such as radiation interfering with the signals – which was just as quickly dismissed as it was suggested – to a break down in one of the

172

transmitters. These space probes are meant to withstand a heck of a lot and last much longer than expected, but this particular probe has been having its... problems. To me, it didn't feel like the data stream getting junked up was actually as big a problem as they thought, but apparently, I don't have an opinion since I was some lowly 'tech' who's part-timing in helping with data verification. My guess was more that they're still miffed over my previous efforts with the 'glitched signal' from last year.

On my last night (or just now), after I was 'requested' by Mission Control to take an extended leave from the project, I took a break with Tommy and shared with him what I thought the issue was with the current data stream. To me, it looked like the data stream was overly compressed and messed up. In effect, what was supposed to be an image would only come out half-completed, peppered with numbers or figures that would either be a telemetry reading or something else. I reported it first as per protocol, then checked the data, like I was supposed to do. That meant verifying the files for what they were supposed to be by comparing the code markers. The code markers identify the type of data batch and the source, like a camera or sensor, as well as a date stamp of sorts along with where and when it was taken in relative to Earth. All that metadata would essentially allow us to pinpoint exactly where the probe would be at that particular given time, give or take half a degree. It's not perfect a system, but it works well enough.

I told Tommy that I noticed a messed up image with two date markers while another set of supposed telemetry readings showed two sets of telemetry in one, as if the probe was heading in two different directions at once. Even if I was not great at the figures, I had been doing this long enough to figure out what it all means when I look at it. I felt that there were overlapping signals. I only had maybe five or six 'files' to work with, but I got him started on the same track. I posited that there wasn't really a glitch in the data stream and that there were two or more signals coming in on the stream we were receiving. He said that if we accepted that theory, then there would have to be two or more probes using the same broadcast wave.

This was me playing up my minimal sci-fi interests, and I suggested that perhaps the probe was sending a signal from much further away, but it had been boosted somehow. Tommy felt it was too easy a solution, but accepted the hypothesis since we already knew of advanced civilisations out there, even if other people aren't ready to accept it yet. Of course, he also knew the movie I was referencing and said that it wasn't going to fly with the folks at Mission Control.

"It's a good idea though, and the possibility is there," he said. He then said he would look into the matter, keep me posted and I could still drop by once in a while as part of my continued training, but I couldn't work on the project anymore for the time being. He would also inform Linda and Remington about the change in my status. Given the recent changes on the day side of things, they probably wouldn't mind this change on the night side. It's simply another change for me, as many in about the same number of days. At least, it feels like that.

Anyway, it's been a pretty downer of a night and I couldn't really sleep with the extra time I had on my hands. Been typing this up since I got back to my room and the rising sunlight is starting to peek through the curtains of my room. Think I'll take in some laps before breakfast.

June 12

Being a mentor is really not easy, especially when Ethan is the mentee. There have been conferences with Linda and Remington to work out the reporting bit. Remington is Ethan's current G/C and my previous G/C. Since I was handed off to Linda, I'm not supposed to meet with him at any time alone, although there have been off-cases, such as the network training. The coverage on Ethan requires a lot more than one little consultation with him for a couple of minutes in class.

Over the last couple of days, I've had to memorise Ethan's schedule so I know where he is and what class he's supposed to be in at what time. I also have to know about his activities, which apparently, he doesn't really have any. So, I have to guide him towards some activities, maybe wean him off the whole escaping-to-the-dream-world bit, if he was really doing that on a nightly basis, and put his focus somewhere else.

Anyway, I think we've got a system in place where I can report to either Linda or Remington, preferably both at the same time, though that's going to be difficult. Becca's got it easier since both she and Kadi are under Remington's guardianship. The easiest thing for me is to report directly to Remington all things regarding to Ethan, and to inform Linda every time I do so. Easy to say and plan, but we'll have to see how things go when the actual reporting needs to be done. Ethan was also informed of this arrangement although I assured him I wouldn't be completely invading his privacy even though I would be scanning for him every once in a while. I did say I would keep it to an absolute minimum if I could manage; my preference is to not do it at all.

I had one TP class session with him already, mainly to gauge where he stood regarding the training he's had with Jenny. I can say he's pretty good and confident with his skills where sending and receiving is concerned. He's also maintaining his blocks really well so that no stray thought enters or escapes his mind. His control has obviously improved over these last few months and I made sure to inform Miss Tracy about this, ensuring that Jenny gets the credit she deserves. For my part, I would continue the training, try to refine Ethan's control a bit more and see if he can be ready to get onto the whole network training as well. It's really nothing much, but it does give me the opportunity to 'talk' to him about his activities.

I did arrange to have him take me to his dream world sometime next week. I don't want anything to get in the way of my own dreaming trip tomorrow (Saturday). If I don't over-do it, I wouldn't mind getting to his dream-world on Sunday, see what he's been up to over there and then have him work out a schedule for his own trips. Part of it is to help him have some other activities outside of classes and that's a bit tricky. Ethan's already the youngest teep I've met, which also makes him the youngest at The Facility. The second youngest person I know at The Facility, not counting myself, is a good nine years older than he is. Basically, there's really no one close enough to his age to mix with. It's no wonder he's probably jaunting off to his dream-world every night, not that it's been determined he's doing that as of this writing. I haven't done any scans to confirm it either. He's promised to get some proper sleep over the last few days, and he already looks better.

Wish I could get some proper sleep myself over the last few days too. It's been getting less and less since I stopped going to the Operations Center. I barely got about twenty minutes this morning before the restlessness kicked in and I just couldn't fall asleep. Didn't even feel like writing anything so now, I'm rushing this a bit. I spent one night clocking in some hours on the flight simulator, trying out a different plane from the usual one I've been practising on. I picked one at random that had more or less the same specs as the one I've been 'flying'. I can't even remember the make and model of either plane right now.

Another night was spent tinkering on Colleen while last night was wasted trying to study, but I couldn't focus. Despite the lack of proper sleep, I'm not feeling any effects like being tired, wired or having a headache of any kind that would normally be associated with the lack of sleep. We'll see how things go after the dreaming tomorrow. I usually get a pretty good night's sleep on Saturday nights.

Meanwhile, stopping here and I'm off to meet Walker for dinner.

June 14

The more time I spend with Michelle, the more I want to spend with her, to get her to open up in some way and know her better. I even had to reason it out with Mikey, telling him that I had spent years with him while he was growing up and I was never there for Michelle, and I think he understood. I explained to him that I needed time to figure out Michelle, who wasn't cooperating as much as I could hope. She pulled away every time I tried to reach out to her. She knew what I wanted to do and while she didn't say yes or no, her actions suggested she didn't want me in her head.

Since that time when her memories poured into me, they have been fading away almost immediately and what little I can recall now isn't helpful in understanding her. These few memories, albeit in fragmented form, are mostly from those few days when she wandering around in other people's dreams. My intention of linking with her is to try to understand why she doesn't want to talk and learn more about where she came from or how she came to be in this place; the dream-world. As much as I've learnt about her, she is still a considerable mystery to me.

Kinstein's sure she can read and understand things we say. He does his best to educate her and keep her busy, taking care of her as if she were his own. How she would react to that, I don't know and I hope she would at least regard him as a father figure. As much as I would want to, I can't spend all my time with her within the dream-world.

Something else came to mind concerning Mikey. I hadn't considered it before because I was busy with other things like the bad dreams and Michelle popping up, but with a little extra time on my hands and a little less activity to busy my brain, my thoughts wandered back to this thing. When Mikey stopped coming to visit me in the dreaming, I thought it was because of the creatures and the mysterious presence that turned out to be Michelle. While he does come around these days, there's still a sense of apprehension about him, like he's still nervous about visiting the dreaming. I thought the mechas helped with quashing his fear of the creatures, but these last few visits, it's the joy of riding the mechas that's bringing him back. When he's in that thing, he has no problems with the creatures, and the creatures themselves haven't been as dangerous as when they first appeared. It was a subtle shift, and even most of the villagers have managed to tame a few.

With Mikey still being a little nervous, Michelle appearing and not wanting to talk, add to that Old Crans who still hasn't turned up with that last job he said he has for me, things still are not quite right in the dreaming. I've been so wrapped with concern over Michelle that I hadn't stopped to consider the situation until now. Before I left the dreaming yesterday, I got a sense there was still something askew and it sent a shudder through me. Depending on your perception of 'reality', even taking what Walker suggested about the nature of the dreaming, it's either something is brewing or there's something going on in my head. For anyone else who's been reading this, the latter is probably the most likely, and that probably isn't anything new where I'm concerned.

The trips have been pretty routine of late. I get there, catch up with Kinstein, try to figure out Michelle, hang with the kids, take care of some creatures for the villagers and then spend more time with Michelle after Mikey goes off. It is unlike when Old Crans used to throw out those off-beat and strange errands like hiking off to find a piece of rock, or shift a stick a little to the left, unclog the flow of a river, help out at a farm – things like that. Maybe doing those things actually helped with my head in some way, and since I haven't been doing those things, maybe something's stuck somewhere.

Anyway, I got some sleep last night too, clocking about a solid four hours between one and six this morning, and it felt way less too. This was because I checked the time before I slept and after I woke up. I was a little worn when I woke up, but it was more a stiffness that got worked out with a nice morning swim. Most of today was spent catching up with classes, and I had lunch with the others as usual. I'm still doing as best as I can to ignore all sorts of rumours that come mostly from Carol and Helen. Granted, the rumours surrounding me are less now that I am with Walker, so speculations over who might like me or who I might like have subsided a lot. Their rumours have shifted to some of the newbies who came in this year, but aside from Kadi, none of them have actually joined our little clique. Even Callie drops by once in a while either with Toni or Jo, never by herself.

Well, it's time for me to get to the Infirmary. Ethan's taking me on a trip to his dream-world to check out what he's been up to there.

We'll see what we'll see then.

June 16

So, uh… couple of things to cover, since some things tend to pile up on one another. Starting where we left off, the trip into Ethan's dream-world was quite an experience. He has done something a little different, but I guess that's to be expected. The landscape's not all that different, which wasn't much of a surprise considering the proximity to my dream-world, but it was more of the functions and the way some things work around there. All said, being in his dream-world was a little freaky to say the least. There was an uneasiness that seemed to sweep over me and that feeling stayed with me throughout the whole trip. I tried to pin it down but there was no real way to do it since the overwhelming sense of it was pretty much all over the place.

Anyway, the task at hand with Ethan was to check out his dream-world; see what was taking up his time in there. This is what I found out.

The nature of his world is different from mine and I don't really know all the ins and outs of it yet, but from what little I could see, he focussed a lot on building up the village. There were farms for food and animals, so there are supplies for the villagers, not that it was an actual issue. What he had was a major community going on and he was apparently busy getting things working in the way he wants. It was almost like the village he had in my dream-world before he left it and started his own. There were some elements that appeared modern although with an old-timey semi-medieval twist, yet not quite Steampunk. The village was not that large if you only counted the residents and the homes, but it's pretty large when you take in the farm lands and the nearby dam that provided the water flow.

Just as I had Old Crans advising me on some matters, he had someone advising him too. I didn't meet that person who moved around in a hooded cape. He only met with Ethan once, whispering something out of earshot from me. Ethan then went about fixing a few things around his little village. I spent my time watching him at first, and later took a walk around the surrounding landscapes. The mountains separating his lands from mine were quite a distance away, but visible from his village. There was no real direction to speak off, but I guess, it was a day's walk to the west of the village.

I didn't wander that far from his village always keeping it in sight since I wasn't familiar with the landscape. If his place was anything like mine, lose sight of where you are and you tend to get lost.

When I got back to the village, I helped Ethan on a couple of errands, to get them out of the way as quickly as possible. I took the opportunity to talk things out with him a little more and asked him about the mysterious hooded man. Ethan said that the man, like most of the villagers, came about as the village grew. The man came up to Ethan one day, started talking about particular problems around the village that needed to be resolved. As each problem was tackled, the village grew or improved. The man would occasionally send him into the mountains to move a rock or gather some plants. He didn't think there was anything wrong since I talked about doing the same thing on occasion.

When I asked him to describe the hooded man, Ethan said that he was an older man with 'long wiry hair, moustache and beard', but he could never make out the face that was often obscured by the hood. Ethan simply called him 'the old man'.

Once we had everything done, I suggested we head back to reality, and promptly woke up in the Infirmary barely two hours since we started, much longer on the inside. While Ms. Phillips was checking him out, during which he fidgeted a lot, I kept trying to work out why he was spending more time than needed in the dream-world. It wasn't that he was needed because he appeared to be more like a handy-man for the village than anything else; I didn't say that out loud to him. I asked him about the time factors and if the jobs were commonly like what we had experienced. He said that the longer trips usually had him leaving the village for the mountains.

When I asked about the creatures, he said they mostly stayed on the mountains and hardly ever roamed the forest, as far as he knew. They had never bothered his village. It seemed strange to me, but my focus wasn't quite on it... actually, my focus since going into his dream-world had been a bit fuzzy, especially when I try to clarify some of what we talked about.

Anyway, I changed tactics a little and compared his activities in his dream-world to that of computer gaming. He picked up on that analogy and understood when I said that his little jaunts into his dream-world to build-up his village and all was akin to gamers who spend time on the computer games, building armies and empires, to a point that they forget the time and don't get enough rest. I haven't done anything like that, but I've had friends from CGL who did get into gaming and their school work suffered badly as a result.

I told him that going off to the dream-world to work on his village was okay as an activity, but he wasn't like me in that he didn't have extra hours in the day to spare. Even I don't drop by my dream-world every day and I do make an effort to get some proper rest each night. Ms. Phillips backed me, telling him that he was getting unhealthy and if he didn't get some proper rest, he wouldn't do well and he would have to leave in the end. That was something he wasn't keen to do, so he agreed to put his 'visits' a little further apart. We also got him to agree to make his visits to the dreaming in the Infirmary only, and I said that I would be monitoring him from time to time.

I understand it's difficult for him to mix with any of the others, but I had an idea which I ran by him first. I asked if he would be interested in doing some martial arts, perhaps pick up some skill with which he could use to defend himself. I even hinted that it would be useful in the dream-world because he could protect the village even better. It got him interested enough to consider trying, but he wasn't interested in kendo; I didn't even recommend that one to him.

I figured it would be easier for Ethan to bond with another guy over self-defence and few people came to mind. The first was Keitaro, but he declined unless Ethan was willing to join the little kendo group. I briefly considered Nik, but he had mentioned he wasn't interested in teaching silat. If he's a traditionalist with that art, he would rather have a master train Ethan instead than to take the responsibility himself.

The other person who came to mind was John. He is a good fighter, there is a discipline to his style, and he could be a good teacher. Since he favoured a mixed martial arts style, it was a little looser and not too fixed to any one particular style of fighting, picking off the best techniques from various styles. For someone like Ethan, it seemed like an exciting style to pick up, if we didn't take into account the grappling bits.

I caught up with John the wee hours this morning when he would grab a small snack before turning in for the day. I couldn't help noticing that he was not looking too good himself, almost like Ethan actually – like he wasn't getting any proper rest. I think he was a little surprised that I approached him in the café this morning because we have generally kept our distance. He still puts me on edge, and from what I heard, courtesy of Helen and Carol, he's been keeping his distance out of respect that I've chosen Walker over him. No one actually confirmed that and I doubt he would either.

Anyway, it was about two in the morning, and because he looked haggard, I didn't get around to asking him about Ethan. He seemed really tired and worn out, as if he had been struggling to stay awake during normal hours and could not get any sleep when he needed to. Maybe it wasn't really a good idea, but after I asked how he was doing, I shared with him the few rumours about his current predicament. He practically flipped, getting all pissy and frustrated. It took a while to calm him down and have him open up. At no time did he feel like a threat. I related the previous problems other people had with their dreams without revealing their identities, and what was done to help them. I then suggested he check with Ms. Phillips. If she needed me, or if he wanted me to, I would help him with his dreams.

Thing is, he doesn't remember any dreams or dreaming at all. It's not that unusual if someone doesn't remember dreaming even when it does happen every night. Still, I told him that his best option was to check in with Ms. Phillips. She had been monitoring all the others during their problems and there was some good coverage to be done if he was willing to participate. He made me promise to help if it was required, and I agreed. I didn't ask for anything in return; though the reason for meeting up with him this morning had slipped my mind. I'll have to follow up with him again later.

I'm getting kinda tired and I wanna head off to the pool, so I'm stopping here.

June 19

Being a mentor is a extremely time consuming thing, so much so that writing this has fallen aside while my nights are spent doing review work and plain old catching up where I can. It's been quite a few days since the last time I wrote, so there's quite a bit to cover right now.

First off, I informed Walker that I offered help to John if he needed it. His response was diplomatic, saying it would be just like me to help the one person who puts me on edge; the one person I would least likely to have anything to do with. He added that if I knew John truly needed my help, I would step up because it was in my nature to do so. Given the history between John and me over these last few years, I was worried there would be more of an issue. Then again, maybe Walker is right, and there truly is nothing to worry about, that me going into John's mind, where there might be all sorts of thoughts about me, is not going to be that bad.

Anyway, there hasn't been any call from either John or Ms. Phillips so either he hasn't gone to see her as I suggested, or they felt it wasn't necessary for me to step in. Besides, there are other options such as Callie or Jenny who would be able to help out in that area.

Ethan's been taking up much of my time lately as I tracked his progress and activities through the week. I've gotten him to join our lunch group and the others have been accommodating, including him in our conversations. I think he might feel like he has friends who would listen to him and ask after him now. From what I gathered so far, I don't think he communicated much with anybody else, so he tended to head off to his dream-world instead.

No one among the lunch group has criticised what I've been doing with Ethan, even when they are aware of our history and the incidents. While they've been accepting of him being in the lunch group, it feels like he connects more with Callie and Toni, than any of the others. That could simply be because he already spends so much time with them that training with me gave him something to talk about with them. Another person he seems to be getting along with is Kadi, which is a surprise. They don't even have any other classes together except Sociology, at least, as far as I know.

I thought there would be more to write about, but that's really as much as there is since my time is spent in that way lately. I've been doing as best as I can to maintain my pace where my lessons are concerned. Like I wrote earlier, I've been doing most of my catching up at nights and it's mostly taking place during those hours when I would have been in the Operations Center. In a way, I've sort of balanced things out and it might have been serendipitous I had to step away from there, although I do miss working with Tommy and the others. And since my personal study time is taking up that time I lost from the Operations Center, I haven't had to give up on either working on Colleen or clocking in with the flight simulator.

My nights are still spent with Walker in the pool. He paces me for my laps, I help him with the aqua-acrobatics and then we're swimming around before we call it a night. There hasn't been much change there. We're having dinner with Sophie and Will tonight. No particular reason, we're just getting together. I've got more time than I expected.

June 21

When I mentioned that Walker and I were having dinner with Sophie and Will, I didn't mention that Sophie was the one who asked for the dinner on Thursday afternoon (during lunch). She felt since I'm not training her directly as I'm training Ethan now, we could do with a dinner to catch up with each other again. At least, that's the reason she gave me.

We got off to a normal double date and it was mostly Sophie and me catching up with each other. Then she mentioned being asked to help scan John a couple of days ago – which makes it the night before she asked for the dinner. I was a little surprised she brought it up with Will sitting next to her. Given that he was working part time in the Infirmary, he should have kept the matter quiet. If anyone were to bring the matter up with me, it would have been Ms. Phillips and not Sophie or Will.

But it didn't stop either of them, and Walker was no help. He asked about John's condition, which Will was more than willing to share. It felt odd that they were all behaving this way. And I can't believe I'm doing this as I need to write a little about what we talked about, given that I have to step in as requested. That's not because Sophie had problems with John.

So, John did drop by the Infirmary as I suggested and went through at least one sleep session there. Sophie was called in to scan his dreams. Apparently, even while John was showing signs of REM and the EEG showed that he was actually dreaming, Sophie could not pick up anything. She did nothing different from what she experienced before and easily found her way into his dream, but found nothing there. If there was any indication John was dreaming, it didn't show up in his mind. She said that she made three attempts to get into his dreams to determine what kind of problems he might be having, but each time was met with blank darkness.

"It was like walking into a darkened room with no windows and no light switch," she said.

Will verified that as far as the machines were concerned, John was dreaming and rather uneasily. The REM was the physical sign as was the restlessness of his sleep. He wasn't startled awake, but he woke up less than two hours into the session, not wanting to try again. A discussion between Sophie, Will and Ms. Phillips followed on whether to involve me, especially given my history with John. If they made a decision then, I didn't know about it till today, but I'm cutting ahead.

It was Sophie and Will who decided to fill me in on the situation, what happened and the problems that came up, and then asked if I would talk to John again. I thought it was the most insane thing ever, getting me to talk to him about a private session, and even Walker backed me on that point. There was quite a bit of discussion about the ethics of the situation I, and Walker by default, had been put in while Sophie turned it around saying it was my idea that John check in at the Infirmary in the first place. To be fair, I was expecting Ms. Phillips to call on me to scan John's dream, I didn't expect her to go to Sophie. Callie or Toni would have been a better choice in this.

So now, cutting ahead to today, we managed to set it up so that Ms. Phillips would meet with John and call me in to consult based on Sophie's recommendation of having someone with more skill to tackle the problem. Needless to say, John was disinclined to have me poking about in his head, and it did seem like this was the first time it was suggested to him. Ms. Phillips laid out the problem about how Sophie found darkness and that I would be more likely to determine the cause.

I brought up the fact he told me that he could never remember what he was dreaming, and how there might be an actual cause for all this. "Wouldn't you like to get to the bottom of all this and get a good night's sleep?"

"You can't hold whatever you find in here against me," he said while pointing to his head. The way he said it that made me feel he was still obsessed with me, and probably not in a good way. In any case, we were in agreement that I would take the dream-dive tomorrow night, and frankly, I am a little nervous about what I'll find there. It's John after all.

I told Walker about this just now and he *is* a little nervous about me getting into John's head as well. That's despite the assurance the other day that it was in my nature to help if and when I was asked to do so. He even shared his reasons – that I would get overwhelmed with anxiety again like every other personal encounter with John; that I would have to face another kind of darkness that might bring out my darkness; that I might get caught in some maze of a dream for days. None of his reasons doubted my skills though and they were valid reasons based on previous encounters with John and situations I've been in over the past couple of years.

"I think everything that I've gone through was meant to help me face this particular problem," I told him. I also decided there and then to have Sophie as my back-up, which did assuage his concerns, a little. He wasn't going to stop me or hold me back, and he wouldn't ask me to step away either. He already said it was my nature to help and he wasn't going to do anything to make me go against that.

Over the rest of the weekend, I checked in with the kids on Saturday, except that Mikey didn't turn up. Kinstein said Mikey did not drop by anytime before I arrived. While I could have pulled Mikey into the dream-world, I didn't do that. If he's staying away again, I have to respect that decision and check with Karen later to see if everything was alright. I still haven't made the call home at this time. I probably won't unless he doesn't turn up again next week. I hope he's not jealous of Michelle.

As for Michelle, I spent my time the usual way, trying to coax her to speak up. I kept talking, telling her about her father and Mikey, about myself and how I felt about the situation. I did the same things as I did with Mikey, using the toys in the room to test her recognition skills – those toys that had blocks that would fit through frames, like putting a cube through a square hole. Although she is still a kid, technically the same age as Mikey, I can't help but treat her more like a curiosity than the daughter she's supposed to be. And I am treating her differently than Mikey, not just because she appears older than Mikey. Well, she is older, in a sense.

Since she still didn't want to talk, I tried to get her to write things out, but she didn't want to even try though I think she might be capable of doing so. I asked her simple questions that had "Yes" or "No" answers, thinking she could reply by nodding or shaking her head. She didn't go for that either. Kinstein saw my frustration and said he hadn't had much success in getting her to open up either. As much as he works her, she obeys without complaint and doesn't even refuse in any way. I feel there's something odd about her from time to time when we're together. I never gave it much thought until this trip because I didn't have Mikey to split my attention.

I went out on one errand after all that, taking Michelle and her mecha along. I considered not involving her at first because Mikey wasn't around, but I felt we could use some solo time together. As Kinstein said, she could take instruction without complaint and she did really well on her own. Even when I thought she was in trouble, she didn't cry or call out. She hunkered down and tackled the creature to the ground and then stepped away for the villagers to take over as we had planned.

These little errands tackling the creatures have become less, as the villagers are getting adept at trapping and domesticating them. I've only had to deal with the more dangerous ones and even then, I try not to involve the kids when it comes to a minotaur or some sort of hydra like creature. Those take a while to bring down.

One thing different happened. As I was leaving, saying good-bye to Michelle, she gave me one big hug, the kind that kids are wont to do. They grab you with both arms and hold on tight. I hugged her back and we held each other for a while. I felt emotional. When I looked at her as we parted, her face was as blank as ever; expressionless. She stared at me with those big curious eyes that never changed even when I gave in and smiled at her. The only reaction there was a slight tilt of her head, almost catlike. She then turned and walked back towards Kinstein, picking up a couple of dishes from an empty table along the way.

I nodded towards Kinstein, who nodded back with a slight wave of his hand, and I left. I got washed over with a huge melancholic feeling once I woke up in the Infirmary, so I sat there on the bed for a while. The on-call nurse came to check on me, I said I was okay. She quietly checked the readings that the bed-sensors recorded and smiled before walking away. I guessed that everything checked out as normal. It was a while more before I got off the bed, tidied up and then left.

The feeling stayed with me through most of the night and Sunday itself, which made concentrating in class a little difficult. I did as best as I could to focus, I wasn't as vocal as I usually was during the revision classes and even that was noticed by the tutors. Then again, I wasn't the only one who was feeling bogged down and tired in those classes, I just wasn't my usual inquisitive self.

It was after lunch when I got the comms message to meet Ms. Phillips in the Infirmary. It was to discuss the dream-dive for John. That got me out of the slight funk I was in. I passed on dinner and headed straight to the pool after that meeting to talk things out with Walker. We had supper later even though I still wasn't really feeling hungry, and we retired to his suite.

I slept for about three hours and couldn't get back to sleep after that. I managed to wiggle out of the bed without waking him. He's aware of my sleeping patterns so it's not a big deal that I'm not there when he wakes up. I came back to my room and I've been writing since that. And that's the weekend. ...

I'm hungry now.

June 28

The session with John took longer than expected. It was also stranger and tougher than expected, and it's taken me a little longer to recover from it, to get over some of that. I'll try to get through it as best as I can. To be honest, I did contemplate what to write because I would really like to skip over some stuff, what with being in John's head and all, but Becca suggested that I stick with what I've always been doing.

I'll skip the preliminaries and start at the point where I got into his dream. It was unlike any of the other dreams. There was no visualisation, no environment; there was nothing at all. It was just black, like being blind I guess. There were sounds, so there was activity around, but I couldn't see anything. In that, it was different from the darkness that used to haunt me in my own head. Yeah, I was a little on edge when I first got into his dream with everything being... well, black. But the odd sounds, like there was something normal around, was what eased my nerves a little. And to be fair, I was a little prepared for it based on John's descriptions of his dreams beforehand, what little he could tell me and what I had gathered from Sophie.

The other thing that swept over me was this weird feeling; a sense of arousal at first and then the sensation of admiration. Given it was John's head, or rather his dream I was in, perhaps it was something he was projecting. I was dead wrong about it, but I didn't find out until much later. Still, it was a disturbing feeling and one I couldn't shake off. It was extremely distracting and disconcerting, lending to the sensation of being observed by someone in the dark and that person was projecting all that emotion. It was the arousal bit that threw me off because it really felt dirty and lusty. It raised certain feelings in me I had tried to suppress a long time ago – and it's got nothing to do with what I've got with Walker now. It was not a good feeling and it was there only for a moment before that other sensation of admiration kicked in.

I did as best as I could to shut away the feelings that were wheedling their way into my head, but not completely. There was a rotation of emotions and feelings, most of which were nasty bad ones, at least to me. Once I blocked out what I could, I turned my attention to the next two problems; the darkness around me and locating John within his dream.

I tried a few tricks to tackle the darkness problem, from whipping up a box of matches, pulling a torch-light out of my jacket pocket, to creating floating balls of lights around me. There was a floor I was standing on, so things were not as invisible as it appeared to be. So instead of lighting things even more, I tried a different tactic. I put out my arms to reach into the darkness. My hands disappeared into the black. I closed my eyes and then parted my hands, imagining I was parting the curtain of darkness.

When I opened my eyes, I was in his dream. It was a little surreal, as dreams would be. There was no one fixed locale. The environment fluctuated fluidly so it appeared to be indoors one moment, outdoors the next; day one moment and dusk the next. The locations were not any place I was familiar with, but that was a given since it was his dream. I think that in dreams, we tend to venture and remember places we've been to, places we've missed or places we want to be, and it's often based on an amalgam of locales we've seen in one form or another. I don't know enough about John to know the places he's been or even where he came from.

There was minimal urban sprawl and more small town locations with vast open spaces, no city-scapes or even The Facility coming into view, just low two-storey buildings, no more than three floors at most, sparsely arranged. None of what I saw would suggest anything about John unless these were places he wanted to be in. There was a sense of some threat, though; as if something or someone was watching over all of this – the town, the almost faceless people that wandered the streets like normal denizens going in or out of whatever places I kept flitting through.

I tried to focus homing in on John, attempting to make some kind of contact, but I couldn't find him. It was almost as if he dreamed of places, but did not 'see' himself there. I figured he was back in the dark place since that was what he described as his dream, but there was more going on. I didn't realise it then. So, I'm gonna speed through this a bit here.

I headed back into the darkness to start again, with the intention of finding John first. It took a while and a few tries and tricks. From there, I brought him out of the dark and back to the dream where there was light. Things went a bit haywire after that. It appeared that John had scampered to the dark, or at least wrapped the dark around himself to shut the 'world' away because of something 'out there' that spooked him. That, in itself, was odd because John didn't seem to be a person who got spooked easily, even in dreams. It didn't seem to me that anyone was taking control of John's dream, but more like someone was hovering around the dream and manipulating things. If he was hiding away in the dark, why did dreaming that become a problem for him?

I managed to get him to talk to me a little about where he came from, and if anything in the dream's locations that seemed familiar to him, or if anything was out of place. I tried to convince him about thinking (or dreaming) of a place he didn't want to go to, or some place he couldn't access. Such blocks usually represent a problem to be faced, but it was also something we would run away from and would rather not face. If John wanted to get to the root of his problem in there, he had to get to that place that 'spooked' him. This was when the dream's environment stopped fluctuating and started to coalesce into some dark urban street at dusk in some seedy town, and well, it got pretty embarrassing for both of us. Well, it might have been embarrassing if I had let it get to me.

Going into this, John had warned me about it and I knew he had a bit of a fixation on me, but what was going on around us at the time was taking things a bit far. The locale we were in was like a red-light district except practically every other girl around us was me in various state of undress, with boobs and butts of various sizes. Granted, almost all of them didn't quite have my body even if they had some semblance of my face. There were girls writhing away in display windows and girls walking the streets, and I really didn't want to think about what else was going on inside the buildings itself, but I had a pretty good hunch about it. There was one building that attracted attention – the theatre. I was most curious about it because it was the one that John didn't want me to go into. He didn't really want me to go into any of them, but it was the one building that he also didn't really want to step into.

The theatre's marquee lights were on, but there was no title on display. The rest of the lights for the booth in front, for the hallway or even at the displays were off which made the theatre seem truly ominous. The marquee lights gave it an eerie glow, much like what you'd expect of a haunted house in some bad horror movie. Even as we moved towards it, John kept advising to stay away even going so far as to say, "This is the part of the movie where you know it's a bad idea going in there."

"This isn't a movie, this is your dream," I said. "You do have some control here."

"Not in there. That place is not mine." I remember nodding when he said that, like he could identify what was and wasn't part of his own dream.

"All the more reason to check it out, don't you think?" I said.

I had the hunch someone had snuck into John's thoughts and took up residence in his dreams, looking around at first and then establishing something a little more semi-permanent without actually taking over any thoughts or actions. An observer, much the way Michelle had done with the others. The thought didn't occur to me at that time, linking the two, but I've had time to think about it since. I know if you're reading this, you've made the same conclusion. I'll get to my thoughts on that in a while.

We entered the darkened theatre. It felt weird that I was leading the way and he was straggling behind me given the bravado he's often shown in the gym. I didn't point it out to him. Even the bravest of guys would have something to be afraid of and maybe this was it for him.

The theatre hall was huge, much larger than it appeared from the outside. The screen was blank and nothing was projected although there were a few people seated, spread out around the theatre. The design was pretty classic; an old-fashioned looking theatre that hardly exists anymore with lush looking red seats and carpet, gallery boxes flanking each side and balcony seats above us but only towards the back of the theatre. The seats themselves looked wide and spacious unlike the cineplexes of today. John and I walked down the left side of the centre mass of seats. When we were more than halfway in, the lights started to dim and the sound of the projector running could be heard.

I stopped and turned, looking up towards the projection booth. I was about to head back up the aisle when John put his hand on my shoulder and stopped me. I looked at him and noticed he was fixated on the screen. I turned to look and it hit me hard enough for my legs to give out under me. It didn't even occur to me that I was scurrying backwards a little. The theatre suddenly went darker, like whatever lights were on at the time got turned off and only the glow of the screen filled the theatre. I could hear laughter from the few members of the audience, but it wasn't disgust that grew within me, but more the fear and shame.

What was on screen was my horror, the deepest darkest moments of my life being replayed; stripped naked, raped, violated all at once. Given what was displayed on screen, the perspective of it, I knew who was behind this, but my mind didn't want to accept it then. The sense I had was that what was happening was impossible. Then again, I was drowning in fear, anxiety, confusion, but mostly that paralysing mind-numbing block-everything-out-of-your-head fear that sent me into a blind panic. I think I might have screamed, but I have to take John's word about that.

From this point, I have to rely on other people's perspectives, information I picked up when I had to go around apologising. Whatever was going on inside the dream, I was reacting like crazy on the bed, tossing and trashing on the bed. Will tried to hold me down and I apparently slugged him one. That punch had me twisting about on the bed and when I fell off, I blew off one TK blow that sent my bed flying into the other bed where John was and knocked him off. The wires that were taped to him got yanked off his skin. He got caught before he fell off the bed.

I guess it might have been luck that the machinery in the room was not damaged, aside from a few dents and scratches. I think I was out of the dream by then, but probably not in my own head because I have no recollection of what happened at the time. I was told that I scrambled into a corner with my arms covering my head and I was part screaming and part wailing, ending up in a foetal position. There was also a TK bubble around me. It might have been the same one that burst out of me earlier and I pulled it back, or it might have been a second one I threw up as an instinctive protective bubble no one could get through at first.

Sophie was in the Infirmary at the time, but she couldn't get through to me. Both Remington and Linda were called in, but they couldn't get through to me either. So, Becca was next, followed by Jenny, Callie and even Toni – anyone who's had close contact with me via TP. None of them could get through the bubble. Even John gave it a try. It was Becca's idea to call Walker. By the time he got to the Infirmary, I was apparently all balled up in the corner whimpering and crying, still covering my head with my arms and keeping everyone at some length by my protective bubble. It had been hours since we started and even the Infirmary's assistants who could manage, had left. Will was escorted to his room and watched over by Sophie and even John was sent off by Linda. Only Ms. Phillips, Remington, Linda and Becca stayed back watching over me.

No one was clear how he did it or what he said, but Walker breached my bubble. Remington said he briefed Walker on the situation first and then left it to him to try anything. It was the idea that since I had been spending a lot of my time with him on a personal level, it was a guess the personal connection between us would give him the extra edge in getting through to me. Becca said he got as close as he could manage and called out to me softly. He then started muttering something no one else could make out, but his hand slowly got through. That allowed him to move slowly towards me, and I didn't flinch when he finally put his hand on me. It was only when he carried me that I put my arms around him. Becca said he quietly carried me out of the Infirmary and all the way to the pool, followed by Remington, Linda and Becca. Carrying me the way he did was probably not the easiest thing given how far the Infirmary is from the pool.

He jumped into the pool with me in his arms, making sure my head didn't go below the surface. I think the water made it easier for him to hold on to me for as long as I apparently needed it, long enough for Remington to send Becca off, leaving Linda watching over Walker and me. She said that Walker kept talking to me, but softly enough for her not to hear what he was saying. She noticed when I loosened up and the protective bubble – small enough to surround me even in Walker's arms and keep the water away – disappeared. My clothes got wet and I cuddled closer to Walker. Linda then felt I was okay with Walker and she left, asking him to keep her informed about my condition. From that point, I have no idea what happened and how long he stayed with me. I don't think I was actually aware what was going on and I probably fell asleep in his arms.

When I next opened my eyes, the world came back to me, I was in my bed feeling utterly worn out, drained, miserable, afraid and all cried out. I then felt that Walker was next to me, one arm around me from behind. I had barely twitched when I opened my eyes, and he sensed I had woken up because he asked how I was feeling. I could barely answer. He must have sensed it, assured me it was okay as he stroked my hair. I didn't go back to sleep, but we lay there on my bed for what might have been another hour or so. I rolled over to look at him, and he smiled first and then said, "You're hungry." I only nodded in reply, but even then, we didn't get off the bed straight away. He waited until I was ready to get a move on.

It was only during the meal when I realised it had been a couple of days since the trip into John's dream. My voice was a little sore and low so I didn't talk much, but I apologised as best as I could for keeping him away from his classes. He only smiled in return. I thought about it for a while and said I wanted to tell him everything about what happened and what was going on. He had to ask if I was certain, and I nodded. Up until then, no one really knew all the details about what happened during that dark time in my life. Even Callie and the others had a mere glimpse of it a couple of years back, but not the whole picture, and they've kept things quiet for my sake. In telling him, I went into some explicit details.

I could see his demeanour change throughout recounting my past. I could see the flashes of anger and of horror come out and fade just as quickly, like he was keeping himself in check. I wouldn't blame him if he flared out at me and the things I was telling him. I wasn't sure if he had any frame of reference within his culture to fully understand the depravity I went through, but based on his reactions, I was sure he knew what I was talking about. It might have been about four months in real time, but it was closer to a year of being constantly raped, tortured, beaten, abused and violated by that maniac. The violations were the worst, it made all the other stuff seem tame and if there was ever a clear cut case of outright abuse of being able to get into a person's head for plain evil purposes, this was it. I had to cite examples of the violations to Walker so that it was clear why they affected me more than the other things. But even that was nothing compared to what happened once I got free. That part, I had hinted at before but told no one until now.

As Walker listened to that part, I could see the fear rising within him, and I couldn't blame him for that. It was something that I was afraid of myself, that darkness I referred to from time to time. By the time I got to talking about feeling brain matter squelching in my hands, maybe I was being way too explicit. I paused a moment and then apologised for being too detailed. His response scared me a little. He said, "It's not what you did, it's in your telling and you were projecting a certain pleasure in recalling these events."

I kept quiet at that, and I felt flushed with shame. I knew what he meant and it was something I didn't realise had surfaced. It might have been some residual feelings since I opened myself to that same darkness late last year. I knew it was going to change a few things about me, but revelling in that part of my past was, admittedly, a bit surprising to say the least. I barely noticed that I had my head down and tried to avoid looking directly at Walker, so I didn't know he never took his eyes off me. Despite learning of that dark period in my past, he's still by me. I think he has relayed whatever he needed to Linda, but he has kept what I shared with him a secret.

The rest of that night... He stayed with me. I caught up with everybody else over the next couple of days, even John although I had no real explanation for him. I kept things really short with him because he kept looking at me funny and it was extremely uncomfortable. After all, he's seen things no one else has seen, and it's not just my body although it was what he did seem to focus on. I'm going to have to deal with him some time soon. I think he's told a few of his friends already, what with the feeling of other eyes on me.

Other things... I got Linda to help me put a call through to a particular person so I could check on... yeah, I'm not going to write his name here. In any case, that maniac is still in a brain-dead coma so, I'm guessing that the playing field where he's concerned has changed. This guy was the first truly powerful psychic I have come across outside of family and he found ways to use his ability to literally take anything he wanted, whether it was from me or his own country. His current state of being was the result of my actions. If his presence is hovering in John's dream...

Really, I have no idea. I'm just putting some thoughts down. That thing about the way Michelle was jumping from dream to dream? I've been thinking about it and how it might relate to this current problem. I'm still unclear about how Michelle came to be, but she is a presence that lives in that world. If she's a presence that could manifest itself, it's likely that he managed to pull himself together. I'm hoping on the unlikely, but I'm guessing it's a really bad bet. If he's back and coming for me... could be why he picked John... I'm just spitballing. I need to work some of these things out a little more, and it's something I really don't want to think about. Afraid of where it might lead me, especially if it's down that dark path again.

Anyway, I've also been catching up with my classes, putting in time with my projects, doing my laundry, catching up with my friends and filling them in with as little as I cared to share about what happened. It's time spent recovering from the 'shock to the system,' so to speak and Walker's been incredibly patient and helpful; Becca is a close second.

It's been a long week and this has been pretty hard to write. Lots of things to cover, plus my own thoughts on some of the matter while trying to keep things simple and as short as I can manage without going into too much detail about my past. There are some things I don't mind sharing, but not all of it on a public forum. Girl's got to have some secrets.

June 30

Something I didn't get around to writing about was the trip to my dream world. Mikey didn't turn up again. Walker came along to keep an eye on me and we spent a little time with Michelle. I didn't do anything more than that. No little monster hunting job, no wandering around with Walker, no side trip to the beach; nothing beyond spending a little time with Michelle and hoping Mikey would drop by. I've been doing my best to keep my appointments, but things are getting askew in that respect. Mikey has skipped two sessions now and I'm getting a bit antsy and maybe partly depressed, but that could also be due to the trip into John's dream.

Suffice to say, despite taking some time to recover from 'the encounter,' I've not exactly been feeling any better. There's still the sense of dread somewhere in me, and there's the fear that he is out there waiting for me. I can't seem to get over that, even when I'm trying to work it out of my system with Keiko. She's racked up some nasty bruises over the last couple of days, and she's quite happy about it. I tried to have a normal sparring session, but I kept moving into some brutal and almost insane territory, maybe succumbing to plain mindless violence. I don't know what I was doing in some of them, I needed to lash out a bit and she seemed like a convenient choice, being able to defend herself.

Meanwhile, of all people, Carol's been leading some kind of rumour control action against John's little tittle-tattle. It feels like it's John being himself by sharing the bits about what he saw in that theatre, but at the same time, it's the kind of malice I wouldn't expect of him. The gang around the lunch table have been somewhat supportive in their own way, but they've all done their part in helping Carol. Of course, she has had some conditions to which I've complied by explaining the circumstances and providing some paltry details surrounding the events that John's been sharing, and that's to the lunch group. Still, aside from Becca and Walker, no one's got the whole story, and it should be that way.

I'm beginning to understand why it is encouraged by The Facility not to share our past, and instead focus on our future. Carol's a little happier to learn about my past, although she did squirm about the details. Helen's being a touch sympathetic and insists that not all guys are bad. I stressed that I was in a relationship with a guy, and girls can be far meaner when it comes to being bad. Keitaro's treating me like glass while insisting that my honour should be defended. Kadi, Ehrmer and Corogi are more curious than ever about further details – which kinda suggests that such crimes are pretty universal and not entirely eradicated as one might think. Only Keiko, Callie, Toni, Jo and Jenny did not seem to react any differently. Well, to be fair, Callie, Toni, Jo and Jenny already knew something of this from a couple of years back. Kadi's suite-mate, Rain, was with us as well but she didn't say anything. A few of them are regarding me differently now. I don't think I've ever noticed so many crowding around our usual table at lunch before. Sophie wasn't there, but then, she hardly joined us for lunch.

Then today, I got a comms message from Linda informing me that I would be having a day off tomorrow. She only mentioned that Mom's coming into town and, perhaps, so will the others, including Mikey.

It's been a long while since I've been out with family. Remington made sure I got some time with Mikey in person every three months. I guess it's been that long, but it sure feels much longer this time.

I guess that's the way things are right now. Sooner or later, I've got to deal with John, and that includes, confronting my past... again. After all these years, I guess I'm not over it. Then again, something that leaves such a scar on the soul is not something one gets over so easily. I have to understand exactly what I'm dealing with this time, if it's really a person or some kind of essence that's not going to go away.

Or maybe, it's some remnant of a memory…
Something I need to work out.

For now, I'm off to the pool for a good soak.

JULY

July 2

It was a really nice day, if it weren't for that little incident. It sometimes feel like some things just wheel out of control at times or I'm getting into some strange predicaments. It might be a family trait though, given the things we've gone through, be it my mom or even myself.

Since that day when Walker carried me to pool and I fell asleep in his arms, my sleeping pattern has been more or less erratically normal, in that when I do get to sleep, it's for no more than an hour to ninety minutes; erratic in that I haven't been sleeping as much as I used to before going into John's head. I only slept a couple of nights and when I didn't sleep at night, I dozed off a couple of times after lunch while resting in the garden. That night when I got the comms message from Linda, I ended up not sleeping. Instead, I was working on Colleen and chatting with her, working on some ideas and plans to carry on to Francine. I ended up hitting the pool around half past five in the morning, and Walker came by a little later to get some laps in before we headed out.

It was about half past six when we gathered at the main entrance. The group included Becca, Callie, Linda, Remington, Walker and myself. We headed down the main elevator to the basement where a van was ready for us. Remington drove us to the Crimson and we got there just after seven in the morning. Mom and the others were already waiting in the lobby and strangely, Lian looked sleepy. I greeted mom, Rick and Karen, gave Lian a hug and then hugged Mikey. He didn't seem as enthusiastic to see me as I was to see him. In fact, he seemed downright fussed out and crotchety. Karen said he had just woken up and probably didn't get enough sleep.

Walker was extremely polite with mom and the others. Lian kept asking him about the progress in our relationship as we headed off to a private room for breakfast. She then turned to keep Becca occupied; it was nice of her to do that. Remington and Linda ended up briefing mom about what my recent activities I caught up with Rick and Karen regarding Mikey, who had dozed off in Karen's arms. Callie's mom turned up a little after eight and joined us for breakfast. After breakfast, Callie left with her mom.

I found out that Lian had a few days off and flew in to see me instead of using the previous method. She had been in the city for a couple of days now. Rick accompanied her while Mikey and Karen came in with mom the usual way. Lian said that it was nice to have an official stamp in her passport. It took her a day to get over the jet-lag and then had a day wandering around some of the nearby shopping complexes. Rick complained about the trip and wasn't looking forward to the trip back as it takes way too long. Lian responded by saying that he's been a prince while accompanying her. It would be a day before she would head back, but for the time being, it was one trip where she wouldn't have to crash in the afternoon due to the time difference. When she said that, I was thinking about Mikey who was still sleeping by the time we finished breakfast. Karen did wake him up to have a little something to eat before we left the room.

As much as I wanted Mikey to stay with me, his moodiness resulted in Karen and Rick taking him up to the rooms reserved for us. Lian had one for herself, courtesy of mom. Remington left with Becca, probably to meet with Steven. Linda stayed with mom, but they moved to the bistro. Walker, Lian and I headed to see Francine.

From the state of things within that facility, it looked like mom hadn't been there in a while; perhaps since my last trip. Francine was happy to be accessed again after so long. I got Walker to take position within the scanner and then made a holographic image of him, which was projected off Francine's projector. He knew what I was doing with Colleen was barely a fraction of what I could do with Francine given the materials I have to work with. It was something to show-off.

Lian kept him company after that while I did some work with Francine. It started with comparing aspects of her operating system to Colleen's and then I started making some adjustments and moved on to other stuff. While I was focused on my work, I could still hear Walker discuss our relationship with Lian. It was slightly over an hour by the time I was done. When I turned back to Walker and Lian, she said, "Finally. You're supposed to be on a break and you're working instead while I chat up your boyfriend." Even Walker laughed at that.

I asked Lian what she had done so far in the city and then we headed out. She voiced a concern about Walker at first, but with him decked out in sweats and a cap with a decent pair of sun-glasses, he appeared as normal as any other fellow on the streets. After all, he had even less back in Penang and he got by okay. Of course, it was our luck to get caught in some little robbery.

It was really being in the wrong place at the wrong time. We had done the park every time I had the chance with Mikey, but since Mikey wasn't with us, we wandered the streets – and it seemed safe enough with so many people around. No one really gave Walker a second look although both Lian and myself got a few glances. Still, two Asian looking girls around town isn't that rare. Also, Lian said she wanted to find something nice for me as a birthday present, but I kept insisting that within The Facility, anything considered essential was provided. Still, she insisted.

So we went from store to store for the better part of a couple of hours. It felt really nice to walk along the streets, hanging on to Walker from time to time. Public displays of affection are not really easy for me, and he was pretty accommodating. I wouldn't have gotten away with anything like that back in Penang. It was about lunch when we happened to walk into a little convenience store to get some drinks. So, we were in the back where the drinks were when a pair of robbers came in to rob the store.

One of them focussed on the store-keeper while the other moved inwards. He was halfway up the aisle when we heard the commotion up front. I stepped in front of Lian instinctively and Walker suddenly appeared in front of me. We backed up a little, trying to stay out of sight as a stock-boy came out from the back room, right into the line of sight of the gun-man heading our way. Luckily, the gun-man didn't fire off a shot, but whacked the stock-boy with the gun instead. Unluckily for us, Lian let out a gasp that attracted the gun-man's attention. He turned his sights, and his gun, on us while shouting some obscenities and orders at Walker. To his credit, Walker didn't even flinch. He must have known what the threat level was with a gun, but if he did know or not, he didn't show it. My own instincts took over from there.

I slipped in front of Walker first, using my TK to block the gun that was pointed at him, basically pushing it aside. I moved as quickly as I could manage, closing the gap between the gun-man and me. I was barely aware of Lian calling out my name. I could sense Walker moving to cover Lian, like he was aware of what I was doing. I reached the gun-man to land one lucky undercut blow just below his solar plexus and the gun went off as he went down. The bullet shattered the glass window of the refrigerator. That drew the attention of the other robber who started coming towards me. I threw a TK punch at him, which worked, knocking him off his feet, but he got a shot off that grazed my side.

Walker moved fast after that, and grabbed a ball of string off a shelf. He tied up the first robber. The shop-keeper picked up the other gun and covered the second robber. I dropped to my knees, grabbing my side. Lian reached me, asking if I was okay. The stock-boy got to his feet and picked up the first gun and then headed to the counter to call the cops. I knew we couldn't be around for that, and Walker definitely couldn't be around to meet cops. I wiped up what little of my blood was on the ground with a handkerchief from Lian, while telling her to have Walker leave the scene. I requested the shop-keeper to keep any mention of us. Thankfully, he agreed – probably out of gratitude – although I don't know about any video surveillance he might have, not to mention the other three witnesses who were in the shop at the time. We moved out as quickly as we could while I was holding the handkerchief over my graze. It wasn't too long before it stopped bleeding and healed up. The gunshots did draw a small crowd of lookie-loos, but we managed to get past them.

By the time we were halfway back to the hotel, I was walking like a normal person again. I did my best to conceal the blood stain on my clothes but mom and Linda noticed it, and we ended up telling them what happened. I mentioned the possibility of video surveillance and the other witnesses. Linda went off after that to check on that shop. We were instructed to stay indoors until she got back. I took the opportunity to have a shower and change to the new shirt from Lian. Walker had a shower after me while Lian used a different bathroom.

After my shower, I checked on Mikey who was still with Karen and Rick. He was still a little stand-offish; best I could describe it. Even Karen had nothing to contribute for his behaviour. She suggested that it might be a phase that Mikey was going through. As much attention as I tried to give him, it made me feel like it wasn't enough.

Rick left the room after a while leaving Mikey with Karen, Walker and me. Lian came in soon after Rick left. It felt like a strange little afternoon what with our incident followed by me trying to reconnect with Mikey. We were all sitting on the floor and Mikey only wandered about between Karen, Walker and me, but he spent more time with Karen who kept encouraging him to walk over to me. I asked if he was scared of the dream-world, if he was scared of me, or if he was scared of something else, or if there was something disturbing him while he was sleeping; things like that. Even Walker asked a few of his own questions once he understood the direction I was taking. The last time Mikey stopped meeting me in the dreaming was because he was scared of the creatures that had suddenly turned up, the same ones I've been trying to deal with. I thought the 'mechas' Keitaro helped to build dealt with that, for a while.

The idea, that Karen and Rick raising Mikey might result in his estrangement from me, was disconcerting. It's not like I wasn't warned about it either, but I thought I could have made it work, especially once we got around to meeting in the Dreaming. After all, a weekly contact was better than no contact for prolonged periods. We were doing okay, at least until earlier in the year. I don't know if I did something or if something changed. Suddenly, he stopped coming around for extended periods. Whatever the reason this time around, he was not telling me. Or maybe he didn't really know himself, and couldn't say it. I couldn't push him for stuff he didn't have the skill to talk about.

It was close to six in the evening when Linda finally got back saying that she got some 'damage control' done. She didn't give any details beyond some witnesses describing, "An asian chick doing kung-fu." Rick came back a little later saying that we were to head down for dinner in a private room at the restaurant. Mikey went with Karen and they were followed by Lian. Walker and I brought up the rear and we took a moment to hold back. I did motion Lian to go ahead first.

The moment that we were alone, I thanked Walker for trying with Mikey, and over the incident at the shop. I thanked him for having my back. He said that it was expected of him since I was considered to be his spirit-partner or spirit-kin – I think I translated it right. I know it's not 'kindred spirits'. My response to that was to kiss him, and we held that until the comms unit on my belt went off. It was Linda asking what was taking us so long. Walker and I laughed at it and then exited the room. Along the way, I asked him if there was anything I could do to repay him for the last few days. He has been a real rock for me through this past week.

Dinner was a little grander than I expected given that it was to celebrate Rick's and my birthday. The surprise was that Remington brought some of our friends over from The Facility including Sophie, Will, Keiko, Keitaro, Jenny, Carol, Hank (not as Helen) as well as Ehrmer and Corogi. That was considered as 'a handful of your friends' according to Remington. It was cool having them around although I think it might have overshadowed Rick since he only had Karen with him.

Lian and Carol got along like gang-busters, as expected, like the last couple of times they met. Rick and Karen took to Ehrmer and Corogi first while the rest of us mingled around, but it was mostly mom catching up with everyone else, which kinda left Walker and me to ourselves. Still, it was nice having everyone around. It was also kinda odd too because the last couple of years, this has been a family affair. I didn't know Remington had planned this and it would have been cool if he asked me about it first. We have lunch with each other every day and that's not to say that I don't want to hang with them on my day off. It was just odd, I guess. Despite all the little idiosyncrasies, I had a wonderful time at my birthday dinner.

The best present was Mikey agreeing to meet me in the dream-world for the weekend, even if it was Karen persuading him to do so. Linda let me stay the night at the hotel with Lian while Walker followed the others back. He felt I needed some personal time with Lian, given how she had been preoccupied with everything else during the day. So, through the night, we talked about how everyone else was getting along – at least those that she was still in contact with, either in person or through one or two social networking websites. And when I say we talked through the night, we really did that. At around five in the morning, she started packing her stuff, but that didn't really stop us either.

Rick knocked on the door about half past six and then we headed down together. There was a car to take them to the airport. We said our good-bye there, agreeing to meet in about three months. That had been the pattern after all. With that, Rick and Lian were off to the airport and I took in some breakfast before heading off to work with Francine. My mom was already there, expecting me.

Normally, anything with mom, I don't bother to get into the details because this journal was started to keep her informed of my activities while at The Facility. Our talk covered a multitude of topics and it became clear what Linda and Remington have been sharing with her. It was sort of gratifying to hear that in discussions between Linda and mom, Linda kept the personal stuff aside for the most part. My relationship with Walker was not discussed, but the incident with John made the bill.

Maybe the air between mom and me has cleared a little in that we were okay during the whole talk. I agreed I was in a fairly solid relationship with Walker. Would I have called it 'love'? I don't know if I can even say it out loud, or to him directly. There have been times when I thought I was in love, but it did not turn out that way. So maybe I've never been in love, not even with Mikey's father. That was a tough one when it hit me that I didn't love him.

We ended up having lunch together and that was when Remington turned up to ferry me back to The Facility.

So, on this outing, I got to clear the air with Mom; had some time with Lian; had one heck of a birthday with only that incident being the black mark. I managed to get some more work done with Francine. I got back to The Facility in time for the afternoon classes, and I caught up with Walker at the pool as usual. Everybody else acted as if nothing unusual happened, and that was fine by me. I caught up with Linda earlier today for our monthly review. Despite all the incidents over the past month and the occasional absence from classes, I have managed to maintain my pace and am doing well enough. She didn't touch too much on the extra-curricular activities this time, but she shared what she covered with mom.

Anyway, this is long and I am feeling tired. Maybe I'll get more than an hour of sleep this time.

July 5

Well, Mikey turned up during my trip to the dreaming but he was still a little apprehensive. Even with Walker there, Mikey wouldn't give any explanation for his behaviour. I played with the kids, went through some educational help with them, spent some time with them and more as best as I could manage. And that was the easy part of the trip.

Mikey wasn't the only one who turned up after an absence. Old Crans dropped by the Kitchen after I got back from a little errand. I dreaded the meeting because he said before that I would see him one last time with one last important errand. He went away just as the creatures started appearing and I figured that when he reappeared, he would have an answer to why the creatures came about. There was an oddness to him and his reappearance. It was the way he moved and spoke that didn't seem like the old Old Crans. There was hardly any rhyme in his speech, and he moved a little more spritely than normal.

He spoke about the energy flow of the land, the sudden influx of creatures and then he talked about the sudden appearance of Michelle. I felt a chill run through me and I feared, at that moment, about where Old Crans was heading; I was not wrong. Old Crans said I needed to take Michelle to a plateau on the very mountains from where the creatures come from, and she would have to be sacrificed. There would be an amulet within her that would need to be destroyed. If I permitted Michelle to survive, the creatures would not stop and perhaps grow in strength. Then, before I could even argue the point, he disappeared. He didn't wisp or fade away. One blink and he was gone, leaving that dreadful choice. Worse still, it happened in front of the kids, Walker, Kinstein, and a number of his patrons who might have been from nearby villages that are plagued by the creatures. It really wasn't long before whispers of witchcraft could be heard.

When Old Crans disappeared I turned to Michelle and Mikey was the first to speak up, asking if I had to 'take her away now'. I explained that I had to think about it; that there had to be another way. My intention was to seek out Old Crans for clarification. He had never been proven wrong about such things, although there have been misinterpretations. There was one occasion where he was manipulated into saying certain things in a certain way. Part of his character is to speak in rhymes even if it wasn't a hard and fast rule. He could break that aspect of his character at any time, not often when it was dispensing an errand. Of course, explaining that to the kids or even the rumourmongers in the Kitchen at the moment was not going to make things any easier.

Thankfully, Kinstein promised that no harm would come to Michelle while under his care. During his time in watching over her, there was no evidence there was a relation between her and the creatures, and he would continue to watch over her. I gave him directions to another hut that I knew of in case he needed another safe place; better safe than sorry.

When I was about to send Mikey home, I asked him if I would see him next week. He shrugged noncommittally, and vanished, heading home and back to normal sleep, or maybe waking up. Walker and I left the Kitchen after that, waking up in the Infirmary a good five hours since we started. Walker didn't say anything then, but I knew what was on his mind. The same thing was on my mind – what was I planning to do next? And I had no answer at the time. I still don't after a day of contemplation; nothing beyond finding Old Crans and trying to get a clarification.

When he saw me today, still preoccupied with my conundrum, he said, "No matter how deep you get, find a way to take a breath, even if it means going back to the surface and starting again." Trying to work that one out gave me pause, but I understood what he meant after a while. I did my best to settle back into my normal pattern of activities. There was nothing much I could do about Michelle until I got back to the Dreaming. I had to wait a while. I had my schedule and I had to stick to it.

Then there was the issue with John. I'm not quite ready to get back to that as yet. I need to figure a few things out first. I need to get some things in order before I tackle anything else. For now, classes and lessons take precedence, and I have to focus on the grind.

July 10

Things haven't been going too well. The little bit of sleep I've managed to squeeze here and there hasn't been restful enough. Add on the bad dreams I've been having lately. It's that damn theatre that's creeping into my head every time I close my eyes, and in retaliation, I must have blown that theatre apart twenty times or more now. That wakes me up and I don't get back to sleep again. I do try, but it doesn't help that I'm always back in that theatre watching myself get abused over and over. It's been going on since that last trip to the Dreaming. My head is getting royally screwed these days.

Despite not needing much sleep, I still need to get a little every now and then, but it's not helping when that little bit isn't restful. I've been keeping myself as busy as I can, putting in more time with Colleen and taking extra flights in the simulator. I haven't said anything to anyone, but Walker and Becca have already noticed something is wrong. The occasional screaming when I wake up in the middle of the night wakes Becca. And Walker, well, he feels it in the water whenever there's something wrong with me, and he adjusts his attitude accordingly to be as supportive as possible.

I think the others are beginning to suspect something and Carol has been picking up some rumours about me dozing off in classes and waking with a major start (true), picking fights in the gym (not true), wandering the halls in the middle of the nights (well, I do that every night anyway, it's surprising that's become a rumour), and that I've been sneaking around a few other rooms that belong to a few other guys (no comment). One thing I would add is that Keiko changed our training yesterday to have me focus on doing the kata and then made me meditate on it for an hour or so. It might have been the closest to getting some sleep

Despite it all, I'm still keeping pace with my classes and lessons. I am aware of some major problems going on if my head keeps getting into this place on a regular basis. That thing with Michelle isn't helping matters much either, because what I'm expected to do is nestled in my mind. I don't know what the implications are in this case. It's not the same when I had to do it with Sophie last year. That was meant to free her from something bad. This thing with Michelle, Old Crans is asking me to kill her... again, intentionally.

From my point of view, as the situation stands, Michelle belongs to that world; to that land. She is more than just a part of it, and maybe more than just a part of me in that world. I lost her once saving that world, I don't think I can do it again.

To top it all off, I'm really tired and I know I need some real sleep. I don't want to go back to that theatre again. I need help... but to ask for that means I have to lay everything out – stuff that I've not shared with everybody. I don't think I can just let loose bits and pieces, it won't show the whole picture. Everything I've shared over the last three years is barely the tip of the iceberg that is the whole of my life. I mean, it's obvious, isn't it? This life here was

meant to be a fresh start and I figured I was doing well, but the past is just not letting go and nowattttttttttttttttttttttbataaaaaaaaaaaaaaaaaaaaaaaaaabb;;;;;;;;;**
<input error _ initiating autosave>

<system alarm & report>
<initiating shutdown>
< _ >

July 13

Halfway through writing that last entry, I collapsed on the console and seemingly passed out. At least, it's how it appeared to Becca when the console's alarm went off, and she came in to check on me. She didn't panic and made a call to Ms. Phillips, who came by to check on me, accompanied by Linda. I was then taken to the Infirmary by Sophie, who carried me by using her TK. It was only there when Ms. Phillips could determine I was off in Dreamland, or what I thought was my Dreamland. What happened was... weird... and disturbing.

I arrived outside of Kinstein's Kitchen as usual. Everything looked normal although I was aware of what had happened; I didn't arrive of my own volition. I was curious how it happened, but I knew I wouldn't get any answers in that respect. I headed into the Kitchen anyway. Everything looked fine from the outside, but when I stepped through the door, it was like stepping out of the Kitchen. I doubled back through the door, but I had no luck getting into the Kitchen. I then tried to move around the building to the rear entrance, but oddly, the back of the Kitchen looked exactly like the main entrance.

Either someone was trying to keep me out of the Kitchen or this wasn't the real Kitchen. I knocked on the door, but there was no answer. I pushed the door open, but looking in through the door was like looking out. I was momentarily baffled even as I scanned my surroundings. There was a sense of doubt that crept into my mind. Since I was in the Dreaming, or maybe something close enough, I decided to try looking for Old Crans. I headed away from the Kitchen towards the trees, picking the nearest largest tree to walk around.

Like before, I placed my hand on the tree and walked around it. I closed my eyes, imagining Old Crans' shack coming into view, except when I opened my eyes, only the Kitchen came into view. My second attempt was to take to the skies to get a view from above. It became obvious I was not in my own

Dream-world, but some strange facsimile. The higher I flew, the more obvious it became as a blank void appeared to surround the piece of land where the fake Kitchen stood. Next thing I knew, the world turned upside-down and I crashed – hard – to the ground.

Painfully, I picked myself off the ground and looked around, and I was back in front of the Kitchen. I looked upwards and it was just blue sky. It was about this point that I started to worry, short of a full blown anxiety attack. I kept looking around for a way out. I even tried to wake up. The more I tried to find something that didn't work, the more the anxiety built up. I was really getting wigged out when, much to my relief, Sophie turned up.

I was fully aware I wasn't in my own Dream-world, so the fact that she found her way to me took me by surprise. When I asked her how and why she was there, she explained that my readings changed from what appeared to be me in a Dreaming, to one where I was in a normal dream. My other readings also changed, showing panic and anxiety, similar to some of the other dreamers. She took the chance to link into the dream. Of course she wasn't too pleased to hear that I hadn't found a way out.

Even before we decided what to do next, we were surprised by rustlings in the trees around us. We turned and looked everywhere around us. Sophie suggested leaving and I didn't disagree; I didn't have a way out. I figured if Sophie made the way in, she had the way out and it was the best chance we had. I told her to focus on leaving, but she got distracted by creatures suddenly appearing at the tree line. They were critters about the sizes of little puppies or house-cats, and the appeared to be scurrying in panic towards us.

We looked at each other, I grabbed her hand and we closed our eyes. I felt one of the critters reaching my leg at that moment. Then I felt the air change and I opened my eyes. I was back in the Infirmary. I first felt a hand in mine, which I thought was Sophie's (and I wasn't wrong), but then I felt the clothes. I sat up and noticed that I had the Infirmary gown on me, but I didn't feel that. I felt the same clothes I had on when I was in the Dream-world. Ms. Phillips and Will were watching over Sophie first while one of Infirmary's assistant's moved towards me, but stopped short as I sat up. She noticed it too.

The clothes I had on in the Dream-world were on me, under the Infirmary gown. The assistant called Ms. Phillips who turned her attention to me, but even she stopped short when she noticed the clothes, as I got to a proper sitting position. I pulled off the gown and then noticed something else. There was some movement in the left leg of my pants, that caused me to jerk my leg. I felt the fur brush against my leg as the critter dropped out and started scurrying about. I quickly reached out with my TK and grabbed it, lifting it off the ground. It was unlike any creature on Earth, perhaps only in legends and mythology, but everyone was looking curiously at it.

Ms. Phillips reacted pretty quickly by emptying out a box of supplies for me to put the creature in. Once it was in, Ms. Phillips closed the lid and the little creature dashed madly around the box. Then everyone looked at me.

The word 'magic' got bandied around quite a bit among the Infirmary staff. A new little critter comes into existence out of nowhere, 'magic' comes pretty close to describing the event. The thing is, I have crossed-over things from my Dream-world to reality before, but I've not had one follow me out. And it wasn't even from my Dream-world. And it wasn't my way out either. The only thing that I crossed-over that lasted for more than a year was the flute.

For now, Ms. Phillips has taken custody of the creature with no name or description in order to study it. I got half a day before getting a comms message to attend a briefing today. The message said, 'review and briefing', not 'debriefing'. Just to be clear on the timeline though, I might have been in the dream for maybe half a day on the inside, but by the time I came out of it, it was Sunday evening. I had missed my appointed session to meet the kids. I managed to have a late supper, caught up with Walker, spent the rest of the night doing reviews on work I missed and by Monday morning, my presence was requested at a briefing. Whoever sent the message gave me only a floor and room number with no directions. Since this comms came as I was sitting to breakfast with Becca and Walker, she offered to inform everyone else if I didn't make it back for lunch.

The briefing didn't seem to be any different from the review committee last year. There were familiar faces there including Linda and Remington, as well as board members like Pete and Sonya (I'm going with that, right or not). There were three others; one I recognised but did not know his name while the other two were new to me. I wondered if there had been changes to the board since I kept seeing new faces.

It wasn't a big room even if there were quite a few people there. As I entered, I saw the layout and sat in the chair that was obviously prepared for me. Sonya started things by asking if I had any questions. I replied that I wasn't the one who called for this, so it wasn't on me to ask questions. I noted that there was more than one person who was scanning my mind at the meeting, and I knew it wasn't any of the other trainees. It confirmed my suspicions they had other TPs in their employ. I noticed both Pete and Remington let out a little smirk each, like they expected that of me. One of the other guys clicked on some device in front of him, and I felt the invading minds leave. I kept my guard up anyway and decided to do some additional blocking of my own. Sonya confirmed that it was simply to determine if I would be truthful or not during the 'review'.

From there, they got into the nitty gritty, which didn't only involve the little creature that crossed-over. They got into quite a few things that I've avoided mentioning in this journal. There were those rumours where I was sneaking around to several people's room, but had no comment to their validity. Well, I wasn't quite sneaking around, but I do wander about at nights doing my own odd things and getting into a few places I'm not really supposed to. It's been that way since my nights were free as I didn't have to report to the Operations Center anymore, or when I couldn't sleep. That's just one of the things; there were others.

Naturally the issue about helping out with the bad dreams came up and how it might have affected my studies and attendance. Linda stepped in saying that my tutors have reported I am keeping pace with everyone else in my classes, adding that I have been more active by asking questions on parts I missed. The issue of the bad dreams that plagued a few people still, probably a few that I'm not aware off because they aren't in my circle of influence. On top of which, I may be the latest victim of the problem given the events of the last couple of days. From a different view-point, I might even be the cause of the problem... indirectly.

That topic of discussion then led into some weird territory. I was asked about my Dream-world and about the dreams of others, and how we managed to interact with each other in those dreams. As far as I was aware, it was simply a landscape on which my mind would perhaps function while being in a state of rest of some kind. It was already determined that the Dream-world and normal dreams were two different things.

There was speculation that I might have, as one of those unnamed board member put it, "Pushed your consciousness into a parallel reality to inhabit an alternate version of yourself."

I'll admit that it was a little far-fetched for me to even consider it during that briefing, but the idea stayed with me. It might even give 'credible' explanations to a few things. Perhaps that critter does exist on another world, and I did cross-over something very real. Of course, it would put whatever abilities I have in a whole new light. It doesn't explain why I always start in the same place and how I might take 'passengers' with me from time to time. I made a mental note to have a discussion with Mr. Hardy about the idea. Right now, though, I think I need more people than just Mr. Hardy, if I want to tackle this particular problem of mine head on. But let's get back to that briefing for now.

Pete brought up my relationship with Walker, asking how things were going on that front, and that I be utterly honest about it. I asked, "How open?" He replied with a question, asking point blank, "Have you two had sex?" With equally point blanked frankness, while hiding how fazed I got by hearing that question, I admitted that we had slept together in the same bed, and we had "made out vigorously" on occasion, short of having copulation. I mentioned that we did have sex within the Dream-world on two occasions.

"Would that count, if it wasn't in this reality?" I asked.

Remington pointed out that Walker was most likely headed home by the end of the year. It's been almost six years since he first arrived. The other unnamed lady asked if I was still thinking of a long term relationship with Walker, to which I admitted that it wasn't entirely up to me.

"And if he has to leave?" said Pete.

It was something I had considered but at the same time, I had not given it much thought. I preferred to enjoy the moments as they came along. Ultimately, it would be something I had to discuss with him personally. Remington said that it was a 'fair enough' answer and the issue was dropped from that point onwards.

Sonya changed tacks and asked how I was managing with the training with the other TPs, from a personal level and not what Miss Tracy had to contribute. I know this is something I haven't written about in a while now because things have been going smoothly with no real complaints on my part. Jenny's managing her group while I'm managing mine. We're both working to develop more networks.

Pete asked about Ethan, and I commented that he was doing fine. He has taken to doing some basic martial arts training with John's group. I think he enjoys being one of the guys. The incident with John has had no impact in that area. I also mentioned about the times when he's been off in his own Dream-world, but I don't monitor his activities there. He only goes in twice a week now and usually on Wednesday and Sunday afternoons. Ms. Phillips could verify that for me if they asked her. With him being a staple at our lunch table, I've been able to check on him during the day as well.

Despite everything else, I'm managing to keep up being a mentor to Ethan. It helps that we're currently TP training partners. I only briefly mentioned that I've gotten him to be a back-up to Kevin and Bastian's network test sessions. It used to be Sophie, but they adjusted to Ethan just as easily. Remington seemed pleased.

Then came the issue about my security breaches, and I commented that it was about time they finished dancing around with my activities. I had been sneaking back into a few secured areas and I really hadn't been bothered to mess with some of the surveillance cameras. Pete was mindful of the fact that I could avoid being caught if I truly wanted to. Remington knew this as well, but they both kept quiet. No one actually bragged that their surveillance system was so great or that I was so careless; we knew where we stood. The question was simply why I had gone 'exploring' again after almost a year of behaving myself and abiding by the rules. That's also not to say I was being all that 'good' the whole time either.

I explained wanting to make sure, from time to time, that Mikey was being kept out of the records, and that there were no new files being created in one form or another with alternate fake names or something of the like. There was maybe a slight hint of guilt that came across the face on one of those nameless guys. Remington and Pete seemed to know what I was getting at, but said nothing. They knew, from last year's incidents, that if I wanted to do some extensive nuisance, I was definitely capable. However, I had kept my 'illegal' activities to a minimum this time. I found the full surveillance facilities this time around, added to the environmental controls and records facilities from last year. There are a few other things, but out of respect, I'm not going to mention any of that… yet. The one place I hadn't wandered into this time was the Operations Center although I did catch up with Tommy on only one occasion, and that was when I went looking for a snack around four in the morning.

By this point, it might have been almost two hours since the review started and I was getting a bit tired about the whole thing. It felt like things were moving along a little pointlessly. The review was mostly verifying information that they could have gathered from my Journal entries or half the rumours that are floating around. Given the phrasing of the request, I was wondering when they were getting to the briefing part. So, I decided to bring the matter to the fore. I mentioned that despite everything, and answering their questions, it really felt like there was something they wanted to ask of me.

The room fell silent and there were a few concerned looks darted across the room. Remington had his head bowed slightly almost as if to signify that he didn't seem to agree with the others. Sonya broke the silence by saying that it was good I managed to balance my activities and my studies. She further went on to say that on two noted occasions, I performed 'admirably' under extreme situations. What came to mind were when I went with Remington to help my mom, and during that robbery. By then, I blurted out, "I have a right to refuse, right?"

"I think, we would rather you hear us out first," Pete said.

I settled back into my chair. That unnamed guy I remember from last time spoke up. There had been requests from some organisations, including one I knew of, to have me assist in some operations, and this was based on what happened with Remington. It might have been one of those soldiers who was watching over me, who reported to someone else somewhere who might be working for an 'organisation' or two that might be interested in me now. It might have explained the look on Remington's face at the time. I thought it might have been disagreement with the others, but it could have been guilt for getting me involved.

I was also informed that it was typical for trainees of two years or more to start 'interning' at selected organisations like the IASC. I'm aware that Ehrmer has worked with some medical organisations as well as some movie effects companies. That's playing to his strengths, and mine happens to be my TK or TP abilities. They told me of the few organisations that had expressed an interest and that I consider the opportunity. Remington said I could also consider taking on none of the opportunities and then reminded me of the promise he made to my mom.

There was a condition put forth as well. I would have to sort out my personal issues first. If the dreams I was having did become a hindrance, it might interfere considerably with any work that come my way. I thought that the timing of it all was a bit odd given that I just had an 'episode' resulting in some strange occurrences. Also, Remington would be overseeing any external activities. I thought it was unusual considering he was removed as my G/C last year and was not supposed to have any say in my current training, unless this 'internship' isn't part of actual training. In any case, all files pertaining to the organisations would be transferred to my console for perusal.

I know; it does seem a bit of an anti-climax given how close this sudden 'review and briefing' was to the recent events – maybe given the amount I've written so far as well. It might have been a coincidence that the two events are that close. Linda didn't give me any advanced notice, which she should have as my G/C. In any case, I've got some information to consider and some choices to make.

At the end of the meeting, I was dismissed, but instead, I sat there for a while. Pete asked if I had any questions. I said I didn't. I was mulling some things over and considering the situation I was presented. Some of the board members decided to leave, but Pete, Sonya, Remington and Linda stayed with me in that room. Pete asked me that question, "How do you feel?" In reply, I gave him a look of semi-frustration. It's not my favourite of questions.

Finally, I said it felt wrong that I had to go through the questions about the classes and the training, or at least the way the 'briefing' happened. I couldn't see how it was relevant to the 'opportunities' that were offered to me. Sonya offered that it showed how I was managing my time and the maturity level at which I would face the decisions I had before me. When she mentioned my 'maturity level' I glanced over to Remington, who gave me a nod. It served to remind me that despite how I looked, I was still much younger. She said, "You do surprise us, proving you are capable beyond your years."

"She has lived much beyond her years," Remington said while eyeing me. "And she has much more to live. In her own way, and her own time."

Linda suggested I head back to my room, or at least, back to my friends. It took a moment still before I decided to move. I caught up with Becca and Walker first to let them know what happened. It was close to dinner by the time I was done, obviously missing my session with Keiko. Becca and I came back to our suite where I looked over the files. I was asked not to write about the organisations in question, so I can't mention them here. Before I can consider anything, I do have my own problems to take care of.

I'll need Linda's help to get a few people together at some appropriate time when everyone would be available. I have been giving this some thought since I started and I know I need to consult Mr. Hardy on the possibility of the Dream-world being an alternate reality. As a back-up, I could do with Sophie and Callie as first choice where TP is concerned. I know there are others who would be willing to help, but I wouldn't ask them directly. The Sociology tutor would be good to talk to for some ethical issues I have in my still free-forming and hazy plans… maybe. Remington, of course, since he knows more about me than others, and in case something goes wrong, he'll have to inform mom. Either way, she'll have to be informed if this crazy idea of mine goes ahead. That also means having Ms. Phillips and Charlie as well. I wonder if I can get all these people together or if I'm going to have to approach each one on their own time.

This entry is way long and I'm in need of a good soak. Maybe it'll help clear my head a little more and get some of that free-forming stuff into clearer view. I don't know if I want to involve Walker in this though.

July 16

So just maybe Colleen will behave herself this time as we try this again. It's about a quarter to three in the morning and I'm recording this entry instead of writing it out, mostly due to Colleen's insistence we try this again. The last time we did this, she ended up submitting the entry before I could go over it. I'll admit to being a little reluctant to trying this again. Anyhoo, the way this should work this time is that I voice my thoughts verbally; Colleen records and converts it to text. From there, I'll transfer the file myself. I know I've mentioned that Colleen is a stand-alone, but I'll leave it to The Facility's people to work out the whole network thingy which was my own design. After all, it took a while to figure out ways to link my own programming language to The Facility's individual systems.

I am trying to keep my speaking style to something neutral as best as I can manage, without falling into my uh... local lingo. As much as I try when talking to my friends here, I tend to slip once in a while.

So, the last couple of days have been kinda busy what with trying to find ways of arranging time to get certain people together. Linda's been helping out as well, but getting those people I want to talk to together is not easy. I may have to approach them individually, at least the tutors. Not so much the others. I can always catch up with them over lunch or something.

There was this other thing which I'm a little reluctant to mention because I'm not sure exactly how... what... wait-wait-wait-wait-wait...should probably try to...uh... It was actually just now when I was walking over from the simulator, and I swear I saw some kind of shadow darting across a corridor not more than forty or fifty feet away. I know for sure it wasn't a person. I barely saw it for maybe a second or two as it moved really fast. It was probably no taller than three and a half, maybe four feet, and not really broad either. It might be considered sleek in the way it was moving.

At first, I thought it might have been one of the new F.E.P.'s at The Facility. I noticed a couple of them during Sociology, but haven't had the chance to meet them properly. I don't know if any of them might fit the shape I saw, but if we stick to the guidelines for the F.E.P.'s who come around, I doubt they would look too strange... and I'm sure none of the new trainees would look too strange either. Haven't gotten to know any of them, so I don't think it was any of the newcomers I saw.

I tried to go looking for the shadow or whatever it was that cast it, but I didn't find anything at all. The strange thing was that the corridor I saw the shadow moving in... it ended in a dead end. No doors, just walls and a sealed window. I tried looking for other passageways that might be large enough, but I didn't find anything. I didn't quite dismiss it completely, but I came to my lab here. It's just that... I couldn't quite concentrate on my work. I considered working on my journal, but my thoughts sort of drifted to the other stuff and I started to talk things out with Colleen. That's when she suggested working on the journal with her. And of course, we're back to the beginning with me being a little reluctant to begin unless I could be sure she wasn't going to mess around with me again.

So, to recap… In trying to get a few people together to work out my plan, I've hit a snag in getting said people together because their time isn't as flexible as I thought. I might be hallucinating and am now jumping at shadows in the dark. And I guess Colleen is behaving better now with her A.I. getting streamlined the more I get to work on her. And finally, despite everything I wrote last time, I still have a few secrets I'm not sharing in these journals. I'm sure those tech guys or security personnel would love to interrogate me on some of my other uhm… shall we say, 'clandestine' activities in these wee hours. Y'know, like how I'm gonna get the text file from Colleen back to my room console and have it posted when we don't have pen drives or when Colleen is basically not on their network and all that. Hope they don't think that little bit I made up last year about having Colleen sending data through electrical wires was true… or was it? (winky face.) *Aiyoh!* No emoji in this system…

So, that's it *lah.*

End recording and convert the file.

July 17

Okay, so maybe I'm not hallucinating and it wasn't just a simple shadow I saw – it was a critter not unlike the one I crossed over; except this was bigger. Much bigger.

I was heading back to my room from Colleen's lab. The corridors were still dark and I was feeling a little tired. When that shadow crossed in front of me at the junction, I didn't hesitate to run after it this time. Despite being a little worn, my head cleared fast enough to try seeing what I was looking at. Of course, there weren't many places to run even though the floor space alone is pretty big. I should mention that while it wasn't the same floor as last time, it was roughly the same area. You could almost say that this was a localised phenomenon.

I might have been stomping about a bit, or maybe not many people were asleep yet – or maybe they had already woken up – at half four in the morning, but some of the other trainees came out of their suites calling out after me for running around. In all fairness, I might have knocked about a wall or two with my TK when I tried to use it to reach out and grab the 'shadow' that kept evading me. From what I could make out then, it moved like an animal, bounding on all fours. Gravity didn't seem to affect it because it ran, surprisingly quietly, up the walls and even bouncing off the ceiling at one point when it was evading my TK bubble. It took a while, but I managed to capture it.

It was a rather large critter, unlike the small one that followed me through from wherever I was last time. This new one was about the size of a chimp or a medium dog, but that wouldn't really give anyone reading this a real idea about the size or shape of this creature. It didn't stand straight on its hind legs, or even on all fours. It appeared to default to a crouched position so at best, it might have been two maybe two and a half feet based on its 'hands' to its head. The face appeared to be almost cat-like with a short button like nose instead of the long nose you might see on a dog. It didn't appear to have ears, but there was a lot of fur.

Some of the other trainees who came out of their suite due to the commotion were staring at the creature and asking what it was. I only said that I saw it running around and managed to catch it. One of them asked why only I seem to be around for these strange occurrences. He might have been there at a few other incidents, so it might appear to be more than coincidence to him. Wish I had asked his name. Anyway, I decided to take it to the Infirmary and turn the creature over to Ms. Phillips. I had to wait while she could find something big enough to contain the creature. In that time, I noticed the creature appeared to be nervous or scared even, but it also seemed to observe its surroundings while suspended in mid air by my TK bubble.

We studied each other pretty intently in that moment.

Anyway, once it was in Ms. Phillips' custody, I came back to my room to write this up. I am worn out, so, I'll keep this short for now.

July 25

It's been a while since the last entry and there are a few things to cover. I don't think I'll be getting to them all. It's not like last time when I was off doing a few things while staying quiet, but there were some events that were intentional. I've been a touch busy chasing down a few things that I haven't really gotten around to writing them up. At the very least, I've made one phone call home to let mom know that I was okay and she didn't need to come barging in. She said that she wasn't likely to do that anymore, preferring to leave it to Remington to sound the alarm if necessary.

Anyhoo, first thing I want to touch on is that guy who made that comment that night, about how things seemed to happen only when I was around. I found him in the café the next day during breakfast. I was heading to the table where Becca was sitting when I saw him, so I stopped there for a moment. I placed my tray on the table across him, sat right down and looked him in the eye. It took him the briefest of moment to look up and notice me.

"You asked about why strange things happen when I'm around," I said and he nodded. "It's only because I don't sleep much, so I'm simply awake and you're asleep when these strange things happen, okay?"

Again, he only nodded. I replied with one firm nod, got up, picked up my tray and rejoined Becca. So that was that. It was a little piece of satisfaction for me to do that.

On Saturday, I was a little reluctant to head off into the Dreaming, but I did promise the kids to make it when I could. So, in I went with Sophie in tow as a back-up. She was quite willing to do that when I asked over our dinner the night before. I was really glad to have her along. Walker has been a fantastic and supportive boy-friend through these last few days and I really owe him so much, but I didn't want to bother him too much. I don't know where or how I can even reciprocate in what feels like a heavily one-sided relationship.

The Dreaming trip was thankfully uneventful. I was a little uneasy when Sophie and I arrived in front of Kinstein's Kitchen. After all, the last trip to that other DreamWorld was very much a head trip that did get to me. So, I was nervous when I opened the door to the Kitchen. The weight that lifted off my shoulders was probably felt by Sophie as well.

Everything seemed okay in that Kinstein wasn't having trouble looking after Michelle. There hasn't been any sighting of or even the remotest word from Old Crans although there were whispers about his warning among the folk who were dining in the Kitchen. Kinstein has been having Michelle work more in the back than in the dining area during the normal hours, mainly to keep her out of sight. He directed me to the back room where Michelle was. Mikey was also there, but he appeared uneasy being there. I greeted them both and asked how things were. I apologised for missing the last trip and tried to explain what happened. Mikey didn't seem interested while Michelle seemed like it didn't matter. She still appeared as impassive as usual.

We spent most of our time in that back-room. The kids didn't ask any questions and Mikey barely said anything. Michelle didn't say anything at all. And I got a little... I don't know what actually, but I was hoping for a little more reaction from them.

Mikey admitted that he didn't feel comfortable going into the Dreaming anymore. Sure I felt dejected. I tried to make it easier on him by saying it was okay with me if he didn't want to drop by as often, and that it wouldn't change anything; I still loved him all the same. I wasn't going to force the issue anymore if he really felt uncomfortable in the Dreaming. In any case, I did talk to Karen during that phone call home, asking her to watch over Mikey as usual; not pressure him into meeting me if he didn't want to. I didn't mention that I would still be dropping by the Kitchen every Saturday as usual. I'd still meet with Michelle and try to figure out this situation that Old Crans had put me into.

As I mentioned earlier, I managed to talk to my mother and filled her in about the Mikey situation and to let him talk to his father when possible. She promised to take care of it so that I didn't have to worry. But just as she would worry about me, I worry about Mikey and I think she knew that.

I know I'm skipping all over the place. Other activities such as kendo or swimming or even the meals have been going on like normal. I am spending more time with either Keiko or with Walker in their respective environments. During the nights, I'm tinkering more with Colleen replacing lots of old stuff that I recycled from the old computers that were in the store room that is now my lab. Just the old bits that needed to be replaced first. Anything else that was still functioning stayed in its place no matter how old it was, like those fans I made or the reconfigured hard drives that serve as RAM memory. I have installed newer hard drives of the PetaByte variety in order to boost Colleen's capabilities. Wish I could get better parts for the holographic projectors, but they're beyond my set budget so I have to make do with what I've got.

And in between those wee hours, I've been a little busy as well. That critter I caught last week wasn't the only one lately and while I have bagged three more over the week – two of them in one night – there have been sightings by others about 'moving shadows' or 'giant rodents' and even simply 'shapes that dash about in the dark'; always at night and often in some dark corridor around the suites in any of the three floors. Any trainee who tends to study or work late in their own labs and are heading back to their own suites have reported spotting at least one or two of the critters, even John. The café is abuzz with all the sightings lately, and as usual, most of the suspicious looks are coming my way again, probably because I crossed over the first one.

I'm pretty sure they're not all from my Dream-world or my dreams, but they are from dreams, possibly from parallel worlds, but the nature of these critters kinda rule out that possibility. Some of the creatures look familiar, like a dog or a cat, but the features are slightly distorted, like when you're trying to remember how something is supposed to look, but maybe the eyes are a little too far apart or a little too close together, and the nose is a little too large for its head, and the ears are not quite right, and the body is that little bit off.

Ms. Phillips has started storing these creatures in a room by themselves now and some of her assistants are also taking care of these things. It's like some mini zoo facility of strange and unusual creatures. Others have contributed to the collection as well. I dropped by the Infirmary to ask her about the creatures, but she says that she hasn't gotten any concrete conclusion yet. Not all of them have internal organs. Those that do, have them in some strange unworkable order, like they've been put together by a child who has no comprehension of how it all works, not to say that I know for sure myself. How they exist or survive is a huge mystery. If my guess of them being creatures of a dream-world holds, then it doesn't matter how they exist as long as someone – anyone – wills them into existence via a dream. Then again, it also doesn't explain how they continue to exist even after the dreamers, whoever they are, wake up. Assuming, of course, that the creatures come from the dreams.

Anyway, I'm worn out. All those nights of wandering about and, in a way, avoiding sleep is beginning to take its toll. I'm gonna have to crash soon. If only the bad dreams wouldn't keep waking me up. Going into the Dreaming doesn't count. I just need one really good restful night without any bad dreams.

July 27

That idea I had about getting a few key people together to discuss some plans to tackle the problematic dreams proved pretty difficult. I had to make do with what I could get. That is, I brought up certain points that I wanted to discuss with said people during class, or more specifically, towards the end of class.

Like last week during Mr. Hardy's class, I brought up the possibility of the dream-worlds being parallel worlds. I had to go into an elaborate description of what some people were experiencing and what had been done about it, especially since it wasn't only me who made the trips into certain people's heads to help take care of the bad dreams. I managed not to name names to be sure I wouldn't spill any private information. We got into quite a discussion when I put forth a theory that our consciousness would enter a realm or parallel world, where we would normally not have any recollection of our existence in this world; and when we are normally awake, we can barely recollect anything from the dream world. In either case, there was no way to know for sure which existence would be the real one simply based on the fact that in either existence, we would simply perceive the other to be nothing more than a dream. Even as the discussion began to heat up, I posed the question about what would most likely happen if our consciousness was, in effect, killed while in a dream. Most of us have had at least one dream that came close, and normally, we would awaken suddenly; such as falling from a great height and you wake up just before you hit the ground.

There were some arguments put forth about the nature of dreams and how they were not likely to be parallel worlds, while some of the other trainees did agree with my theory. Like all theories, though, there was no way to actually prove them all. Given that I raised the topic at the end of the class, we didn't get to finish any discussion. As I was about to leave the class, Mr. Hardy asked why I brought up the idea about the dreams and parallel worlds, and if it had anything to do with my own Dream-world.

I explained what I had in mind in brief points; the plan I was trying to put together. I won't elaborate on that, yet. My concern was more on how much an impact my actions might have on either reality, be it my own or for other people.

He listened intently and looked me over when I paused. He then asked, "How long has it been since you last had proper sleep?" I admitted I couldn't remember for sure. He said it was amazing that I seemed to be remarkably coherent in my thoughts despite looking, "like a ragged doll running on empty. It's in your eyes." He'd seen the same look in various trainees who would burn the candle at both ends. In any case, he tried to provide some answers, but stressed it was all theoretical.

He felt given the way my consciousness would flit between worlds, it came down to a matter of perception. As long as I was true to myself in whichever world I was in, that was the only reality that mattered because whatever my actions, the consequences would still rest with me. "Our existence might just be the dream of someone else, and we may exist so long as our dreamer or observer would keep us in sight. For all I know, I merely exist because you see me existing before you, but then you might be existing because I'm observing you," he said. "But in all that, we are our own individual being with our own perceptions and our own thoughts, our own consciousness. Wherever you go, whatever world you find yourself in, that becomes your reality, but you still will remain yourself. Keep that in mind when you plan your next move."

Yes, it was quite a speech he gave me and it did stick with me even after a few days. It gave me a few things to think about, from the things that happened in my past to the stuff I'm planning for. Even in spending a little time with Michelle, I contemplated what her perception of reality might be. For everything that existed within the Dream-world, she was basically the oddity. As far as I was concerned, everything that existed was something that I created, and in particular effect, so was Michelle. Except, she came into being over there. So, was she a creation of my imagination?

I've discussed things with Sophie and Becca as well as Walker. I know I have to include John at some point. He's the key. It's not really his fault though, but it might have been due to his obsession over me in the years before. Sure he's let up a bit since late last year, but based on what I experienced in his dream, I know he still has me on his mind in whatever fantasies he can concoct. And I have to go back into that to tackle my demon. Can't say I'm looking forward to that.

Anyway, I've got a few more people to meet up with, and I'm trying to get that done with by the end of this week. I want to really try to tackle this.

July 29

Keiko pulled a bit of a change during kendo and had me practising with the *bokkun* instead of the *shinai*. We usually use the *bokkun* for the kata, but she had us doing a whole different set of exercises instead of the usual *keiko*. I'm pretty sure it wasn't quite kendo, but it might have been more *kenjitsu*, but she didn't say when I asked. The swings we were doing didn't quite seem as controlled as in kendo, but at the same time, they also did feel pretty controlled. It was similar to what I had seen Keitaro doing during his time in the Dream-world. While she didn't explain the change or what exactly we were doing, she did say that it might prove useful for what I was planning, whoever told her about all that.

Still, it was an interesting practice session and we were making pretty close to killing strokes instead of trying to hit for marks. After that, she got me into sparring with her using what we had just practised. She knew I had some experience with weapons so she told me to use the *bokkun* as I would any other sword, but keeping in mind what she had shown me. I managed to hold my own against her, improvising along the way, but she kept telling me to really focus and 'be one with the sword'. Mind you, we weren't wearing any of the kendo armour, so any hit that did make contact stung like hell. The wood the *bokkun* is made from may be lighter than handling a *shinai*, but it's hard and solid – and it really hurts. The *bokkun* is shaped like a katana so it has one represented cutting edge, just as the *shinai* has the string (or *tsuru*) to represent the flat top of the katana. I'm mentioning this because while I was using my *bokkun* like a sword that it represents, Keiko's hits weren't with the 'sharp edge'. She kept slapping me with its broad side instead of making actual hits, so I ended up with broader bruises.

While she was focussing on me, I caught a glimpse of Ethan following John's instructions, and it did occur to me to consider if there was a connection between them. It was a momentary consideration if Ethan was, on a subconscious level, connecting to John's thoughts. It was only a thought in the end.

After our sparring, Keiko got me to have dinner with her and over that, she went on more about how I needed to feel the weapon to be an extension of myself. It wasn't anything new to me and aside from kendo in general, I've always been that little bit better than she is in weapons sparring. If I didn't stick to her rules, using either the *shinai* or the *bokkun* in my own way, I probably might have really done some damage to her. I asked her again about why she was suddenly so focussed on getting me on this track, but she kept going on about how I should focus while facing an opponent and channel my concentration. She seemed to be worried about my sense of focus, and then stressed that I really needed to get some proper rest. She insisted that we take in a meditation session after dinner. I usually take a rest for an hour or so after dinner, so sitting in the little garden under the tree was as good an after dinner rest as any.

Try as I could, I failed to get into a good meditative state. Why she wasn't telling me anything kept bugging me and my mind was wandering on its own quite a bit. There were too many things to put together and consider, and I guess it might have shown because she complained that I was barely trying.

One of those things on my mind was tackled a little during Sociology today. As in Mr. Hardy's class, I brought up one little scenario that led to a discussion, but my intention was to play out a hypothetical. I was basically asking about the ethical and moral consequences of having to perform what might be regarded as a no-win act. It was more like, if you came up against someone who was completely evil, could you still be compelled to kill that person for the greater good, but doing so would compromise everything else that you stand for? Of course, it was completely hypothetical because the person in question might not be real, but if Mr. Hardy's suppositions were true, the act itself would still impact upon the person performing the act, right?

Part of the arguments that came up among the trainees was that there are always options in talking things out. It was surprising – maybe a little disturbing – that the act of killing was actually acceptable among more than half of the trainees, if it was for 'the greater good'. Or as the newbie who insisted on following the tenets of Star Trek put it, "The good of the many…," while another trainee argued that it was only applicable to self-sacrifice. No one asked why I posed such a situation to the class, although some of the F.E.P. who were there seemed to eye me curiously. They listened to the arguments but never contributed any suggestions.

I've always liked the Sociology tutor, but I think she was a little wary about how the class was going when I posed my scenario. Sure, we skirted around Ethics and Morals as well as Philosophy. I asked about how one might recognise the nature of evil when no one in their right mind would ever consider themselves evil. Heck, I'm sure even Hitler never thought of anything he did as evil. We probably went into some uncharted territory.

It was strange that the F.E.P's. never participated during those last few minutes of class. Perhaps they held themselves to a different standard. I asked Becca and Corogi about it, since they were there. It was interesting to listen to Corogi's perception on the concept of evil and the way her people would tackle the issue, or at least, from her point of view. There was no such thing as a 'necessary evil' among her people. She had never known such a situation to arise among her people or in their history, but then, from talking with her, evil doesn't really exist among her people. At least, not the way we would perceive it. They have a different word (which I can barely pronounce and have no idea how to spell it), which has a far layered meaning to it.

As for Becca, she gave the same spiel as Mr. Hardy, saying that it came down to me and how I would live with my decisions and my actions. She didn't have anything to contribute to my hypothetical and she didn't even try to explain what the concept of evil meant to her or her people. It was clear she understood what I was getting at, which at least, tells me she understood what 'evil' meant. I was honestly losing track of its actual meaning myself because I don't think it's just the act of doing something bad, but it is much deeper than that. Destroying or killing off something perceived as evil... wouldn't that in essence be an act of evil itself? Do you have to become the very thing that you're trying to destroy?

Would I be my father's daughter after all if I go through with this?
Would I be my mother's daughter? She's as deadly after all.
Besides, I've done this deed once before, and I swore I wouldn't do it again. But now that I might have to, can I, in effect, pull the trigger again?

July 31

Taking into consideration the events of the last few days, such as what happened in the classes and how the last journal entry ended, it was going to attract a particular kind of attention. There was the editor, of course, but obviously both Remington and Linda were keeping an eye on the journal too. Sure as heck several members of the board would also be keeping an eye on the journal entries. Most of them have their concerns about my genes and given what I wrote the last time, it probably raised some flags on their radar. I did as best as I could to prove them wrong about me last year, and now I may have turned around and proven them right; that I might have that capacity for doing the nasty things they were afraid of. I guess, in the end, I wasn't *that* surprised when I got a request for a meeting on my comms unit a day after submitting the last entry.

Initially, I thought it was Linda requesting for a monthly review. The only thing that made me reconsider was the alternate location mentioned in the comms message; Remington's office. In any case, the meeting was scheduled for nine in the morning yesterday and it took up quite a chunk of the day. I still haven't been sleeping much even after Mr. Hardy's advice to do so. I worked on Colleen for most of the night, caught up briefly with Tommy in the café before heading back to my room. I honestly did try to get some sleep, but I was too on edge to do so. I ended up studying until about six when I decided to catch up with Walker at the pool. Sophie was there practising her flying. Becca joined the three of us for breakfast and when everybody else headed off for classes, I had that meeting to get to, after a quick shower and a change of clothes. Despite how things are, there is still some sense of normalcy going on.

Linda was waiting for me outside Remington's office. We had to wait for a while and she took the opportunity to catch up with me, asking about my sleep (if I was getting any); my thoughts on the origins of the creatures as she knew about two more that I caught but did not mention in my entries, to which I still had no real idea of their origins; then she asked how I felt I was getting along in my classes. Everything was quick and brief, and I wasn't sure if there was any real purpose to it except to make conversation. For all I know, she was making notes for our monthly review.

Remington popped out to call us in and I had this sudden flashback of being called to the principal's office. No idea why that happened. Stepping into his office was not quite unlike those other times when I ended up meeting with the board members. There were some familiar faces; Pete was there, and Nakato, and a couple of new ones again. I've pretty much given up trying to keep track of who's who. All I know is that they are among those who run The Facility and they have some pressing need to constantly keep an eye on me whenever there's a remote possibility that I might be starting some kind of trouble. Or conversely, when they have some particular problem that only I can take care of.

I was asked if I knew why I was called in for the meeting, but I said I didn't. I got a knowing nod from Remington, so I simply said, "I do have my own concerns about what I'm capable off, but I'm not that curious as to take another string of tests." Pete smiled at that response and looked over to his fellow board members, almost like he was giving them a 'I told you so' look. That gave me the hint that all this was merely a formality, but we got into much more than that. I was asked to give an explanation to my recent actions and how it would relate to my questioning the morality of killing someone who might not actually exist.

Remington said I didn't have to say anything about my past if I didn't want to. He knew part of the story. He's part of the story itself, but his role in those events is hard to define. In any case, I nodded in acknowledgement to his advice and then said that I was expecting to have to deal with this issue at some point. Ever since that incident with Callie and Jo, I knew my past wasn't going to be ignored no matter how much I wanted to leave it behind and not have it affect my future. I took a moment to compose myself before going on to relate about Phillip.

The first time I ran into him, he had set himself up in my dream-world as some kind of ruler, imprisoning (in a way) anyone who didn't agree with him. I was informed of the situation by Old Crans and, long story short, I managed to stop him. Of course, I shared a few more details with the others in that meeting, but I don't feel like I need to spill everything else here. What's important is Phillip.

Phillip was powerful in both TP and TK. Maybe he was born that way or maybe he learned to develop it all himself, but he was exceptionally skilled when I went up against him that first time. The people he 'imprisoned' were dreamers who found their way to my Dream-world through their own dreams (I've mentioned this before) and in real life, they were mostly kids, each one in a coma. In 'freeing them' they awoke from their coma, and it happened all over the world. If you know what to look for, you might find the connection across several worldwide news reports. In my confrontation with Phillip, I got badly hurt. He stabbed me with a dagger and ran a sword though me from the back, and the pain has stayed with me after all this time. It's the same pain that flared up that day when I was in John's dream. It was the first time an injury from inside the Dream-world had an impact in the real world. When I managed to defeat him, I ended up treating him the same way he treated his prisoners; I imprisoned him within the rubble of his castle, encasing him in a pile of rocks. It was only weeks later that I found out who he really was.

I was in a relationship at the time. While I did mention his name to the board members, I'll use a nondescript 'X' in place here. X and I met by accident, I took to him and we became pretty serious together. Mind you, I was even younger then. It might have been a crush or some weird little fantasy playing out in my head given who he is, and I even thought it was love. But we're not together anymore even if we're still friends for Mikey's sake – yeah, that would make X Mikey's father, and it would make him my 'first'. When X had to go home (he lived really far away) I followed him. That was when I found out that Phillip was X's brother. Despite explaining everything to X, and why his brother was in a coma, I ended up agreeing to help bring his brother back, which meant releasing him from imprisonment within the Dream-world.

I did my best to avoid Phillip, but he wasted no time in toying with me. We knew about each others abilities and so did X, but none of us told his family. So when Phillip made his move and attacked me, defending myself ended up destroying a sizeable portion of a beach. It was a fight I lost and Phillip took the opportunity to show off his superiority and break me that little bit more. Let's just say that the identity of Mikey's father was in question for a while. By the time I managed to get back to X, he had to choose between siding with me or his brother who had spilled everything about my abilities to his family, turning me into some manipulative villain. His family being what it is, X ended up on their side and I was told to leave. Suffice to say, things did not go well for me at that point.

Before I go on, I want to be clear that I'm trying to avoid writing about specific details because I'm choosing not to dwell on certain things. I've long since come to terms with what happened and as I said, X and I are still friends. I did hate him for that moment because he knew what kind of person his brother was, but he got manipulated into that position of siding against me. This was the start of that dark period of my life.

Things weren't going well at home and mom was having problems of her own. I felt incredibly alone and abandoned at the time, hurting like crazy from all angles. That was the time when I decided to 'run away from it all' by escaping into my Dream-world. On the outside, it looked like I tried to commit suicide and given the situation I was in, it was the best assumption. No one knew for sure what really happened. I hadn't shared anything with anybody but there was the knowledge that something bad had happened. No one was sure exactly what that was, at the time.

I don't know what happened in the real world after that, not even that I was pregnant. Until yesterday, no one, besides Becca and Walker, really knew what happened in the Dream-world during that period. Phillip was what happened. You might think me a coward for not going into the salacious details. You might think that he raped me, but the connotations of that word is really inadequate to even suggest what I went through because that was the least of what he did. Words I used before include 'violation' and 'humiliation'. When he captured me, he chained me to a bed and kept me naked. I was used and abused in every which way he could imagine – which was far more than physical – for what felt like more than a year. Over a year of pain and fear, but in reality, it wasn't any more than roughly four months. Because of my unique physiological condition – you know, the way that I can heal faster than normal – my body treated the pregnancy like something invasive it had to deal with as quickly as possible. At least, that was Charlie's way of simplifying the explanation of why I went through the whole pregnancy in half the time it would take a normal person. It's a bit of a digression though.

As bad as things got, it was only a small part of the darkness that started to fester in my soul. The rest of it built up from what followed when my mom, Remington and X tried to rescue me. X did end up confronting his brother, but I was the one who got hurt over and over again. Because of Phillip's skill, he managed to warp the reality of the Dream-world enough to end up with X running a sword through me when he thought he was attacking his brother. I really felt like I was dying by the time my mom reached me and it was her, making contact, that jolted me enough to take some control over the Dreaming, to freeze whatever else was happening around my mom and me – enough for me to have a confrontation with her. That's still private between her and me, and not too relevant to what followed.

When we were done, I sent X, Remington and my mom back to reality, so they never really knew what happened next, that is, until that meeting where Remington is concerned. My confrontation with Phillip was massively destructive and violent, equally to us and the world that was around us. All the fear and pain and rage within me was unleashed without much care for the consequences that might befall me. I released a torrent of both TP and TK energy at Phillip, and did everything to ensure he would suffer as much as he had inflicted on me while preventing him from leaving the Dreaming. I practically tore him to pieces over a substantial amount of time and I was violently ruthless about it all. By the time I was done, there was barely a semblance of a person before me, his head in my hands, begging me to finish it all. It was the slightest of gestures and I blew him to bits in the most painful way I could imagine; crushing him in my hands and dispersing his being to the winds. His scream echoing into eternity and forever ingrained in my mind.

That I was capable of such things, such brutality, it was never a second thought while it was all going on, but when it was over, it was a cold darkness so overwhelming that surged within me. The realisation of what I had done still didn't dawn on me. I drew whatever energy I had left within, plunged my hands into the ground to 'fix' the land and restore it to what it was meant to be. When that was done, I finally let myself return to reality, and paid the price for my actions. While it might have been, perhaps, days in dealing with Phillip, it was mere minutes on the outside, and I returned right into the midst of delivery. My mom and Charlie did the best they could to guide me through the delivery and I barely managed the first of two. I passed out when it was done. It was only days later when I finally woke up that I learnt Mikey survived, and I had lost a girl.

I took it as a sign, the loss of an innocent child – my own baby – as the consequence of my actions. I started to consider everything that had happened to me and what I had done in return, and I felt the darkness present itself. I swore to myself that I would never go down that road again, that I would never let it rule my life. What I did would remain a secret and no one would ever know. The only other person who was involved was gone and while the memories would remain – his dying tortured scream that would still echo – I would push it all down and bury it all. My abilities would never be used in such ways again. I made the rules to guide me and I did my best to follow them. Never again would anyone die by my actions.

I would never kill again.

When I was telling all this, in far greater detail, to the board members as well as Remington and Linda, I knew I was as emotionally distant as I could manage. I knew I had to get through all that, giving them the details of that dark time, and I really had to do it all without flinching. I sort of flipped whatever switch I had in my head that connected my feelings to that time. I wasn't sure if I could do it, but somehow I managed it. Linda said that I was completely apathetic when I started talking about what happened from the point where Phillip captured me. Remington described me as being 'utterly detached from reality' and being almost robotic, speaking in a paced monotonous voice. Funny thing is, I think I might have leaked some emotional information as well. When I finished doling out my tale, I barely noticed the time that passed. What I noticed was Linda wiping away what looked like tears. Nakato also had his hand over his face.

Like I said, I wasn't aware of the time but I was feeling hungry. Pete put in a call for some food to be brought to Remington's office. Everyone else was quiet. I took that opportunity to turn to Remington and requested he not say anything to my mom. She had hints before about what might have happened, but never the details. As much as I've written here, it's also a quick summary without the grim and gritty that I shared in that office. They agreed everything I shared would remain among them and not leave the office without my permission. I know they'll be reading all this as well, and I know they'll be aware of how little I'm actually sharing here.

I need a break, so… to be continued… later.

AUGUST

Aug 1

Touching on a few more things that got glazed over.

When Phillip was going through the insanity in The Dream-world, there were real-world consequences. This is from third hand reports, filtered through X and what he heard. It seemed that Phillip suffered what appeared to be epileptic seizures and by the time they got him to the hospital and did scans, he was considered to be in a vegetative coma. The doctors couldn't determine what happened because there was no internal bleeding, no sign of any stroke, no aneurysm, nothing to cause the sudden loss of all brain activity. Aside from that, his body was still functioning normally as if by reflex. As far as I know, since then, he's been on life-support of some kind, constantly being monitored, watched over. The last couple of times I called X, he confirmed that there had been no change whatsoever.

Anyway, when I started writing last night, I knew it was going to be hard, at least on an emotional level. Going in to that meeting, I was ready and willing to share all that, but at the same time, this being my journal, I wasn't going to be so sensational about it. It might feel like a cheat or I might be 'glossing things over' as one might say, but my past is my past. I had to share a lot more in that meeting with the board members, and honestly, I wasn't sure if I was capable of doing that at the time. I know all this started out as a journal to keep track of my activities and to keep my mom informed, but looking back over the year so far, I was surprised things have gotten a little more introspective. I've been focussing a lot more on my personal activities and thoughts. With what I wrote yesterday, it went to a whole new level of personal. I don't know if there is any objectivity anymore, or if there was any to begin with.

I remember writing about 'embracing the darkness' last year. Maybe that had something to do with me being ready to share that dark history of mine. In any case, spilling it out to the board members the way I did was a bit of a surprise to me because I was always cautious about sharing my past.

After the food was ordered, Remington and Linda checked on me. That was when I was told about how I appeared while telling my story. Remington said if I wanted to stop, I could, and even Linda backed him up on that. I only said that I was hungry.

Linda then did the strangest thing. She reported that I was doing well in my classes according to the reports she got from the tutors. I gave her a confused look, and she smiled in return. There was a bit of a pause before Remington asked if I had been sleeping. "Not much, and you know why." He nodded and then said that I should try to get some rest anyway because it really showed that I wasn't getting any sleep. It wasn't much different from what Mr. Hardy had told me the other day, and it's not like I haven't really tried.

Once the food came, I dug into my burger a little more heartily than I should. The others were watching me for a moment before they started on their own meals. Pete didn't eat tho and neither did Linda. Remington had a sandwich, Nakato had some boxed lunch and the others had their own orders as well. It wasn't long before I was already halfway through my burger when Pete decided it was time to continue asking me if I was trying to find same way to justify my forthcoming actions. The question did get to me, enough for me to slow down eating and suddenly, I was very aware that I was chewing at a deliberate pace.

My silence and concentration on my food was pretty much all it took to confirm his suspicions. "She hasn't quite made up her mind yet," Remington said. "I think she's looking for options."

"I would think so," said Nakato.

"He's after me," I said. "He's going after my friends and he can hurt them. He would do it too, just to get at me." I put the reminder of my burger down and looked at them. "What do you think I should do?"

They looked at each other in silence and one by one, looked at me. Given everything they knew, based on everything I told them, they should have reached the same conclusion I got to; that there was only one way to stop him. And it would be down to me to do the deed.

Of course, they tried to offer alternatives; like talking to him and showing him a different way or maybe restraining him again, or offering to find a way back to reality for him. If they present those options to him, and he accepted, then I wouldn't even have to contemplate what I have to do. To me, there was no other way to deal with him. After all that time I had spent with him, I was sure he was not likely to change his ways. He was one of those who discovered a power that he could wield in any way he chose, and he made his choice which path he would take. He's high on that power.

Seriously though, if you were faced with an evil having that kind of power, a person that would never be contained, how many options are there to pick from?

One of the other board members (don't know her name) pointed out that there was no actual proof any of my friends have actually been hurt, aside from some bad dreams which may or may not have been attributed to Phillip. The only person who had any indication of Phillip's presence is John, a person who I didn't care too much about. They only have my word that any of what's happened did actually happen, which means that they may not believe that Phillip exists; even Remington never met Phillip, he only met X. Since nothing happened in reality, I technically didn't kill anyone; it was all just a bad dream.

Linda picked up on the last bit adding that if Phillip was technically still physically alive, and his consciousness is supposedly floating about in the dream-world, I couldn't really say that I killed him that first time. "It is a matter of perspective," she said in the end. None of it made me feel any better because it didn't change the things that happened.

Despite the food, I was feeling pretty drained by then and I really wanted it to end. Remington picked up on that vibe and remarked that it was getting late – almost half three in the afternoon – and added that I could go. One board member wanted to protest, but Pete raised his hand and nodded in agreement. He then said that whatever I decided to do, I had to keep Linda and Remington informed for now. I didn't say anything else much, I got up and left quietly. Right before I closed the door, I heard Remington telling me that I should get some proper sleep.

I did try to get some rest after that since I had time to kill, but it didn't take. I got into some kendo practice later but even Keiko knew I wasn't on full form. She sat me down for some meditation instead, leaving the juniors to Keitaro. Even though I haven't mentioned anything to her, she seems to be aware of what I needed in that moment. By the time I caught up with Walker at the pool, I only mentioned that I was caught up in a meeting all day. I did my laps and then headed back to my room after that. Becca's was still awake. I related the day's events, and briefly took her through the tale. It was through her encouragement that I shared a little more with everyone else at the lunch table. They were curious as to my absence and probably got a whole lot more than they bargained for.

I didn't give them the same long version I shared with the board, and it was probably shorter than what I've written so far. Sophie reminded me that I didn't have to share anything about my past. Every time I do something like this, open up myself a bit more to them, their perspective of me changes, and

I suppose that's expected. Even Callie, who had joined us for lunch, seemed to look at me differently. She and Jo had a glimpse into that dark part of me but I don't think it was ever in context like this before. I guess I should mention that among those who were at the table included Helen, Carol, Becca, Walker, Callie, Jo, Sophie, Will and Jenny. Keiko and Keitaro were not there. I kept things as low-key as possible because I didn't need to share it with the whole cafeteria. It was Jenny who asked if I was going to put it all into my Journal, and Becca said that I should. If anything, it would help to put things in perspective and act like a 'cleansing' as she put it; a catharsis.

Doesn't make me feel 'cleansed' though. Doesn't make me feel 'dirty' or 'dark' either. If anything, I'm not feeling anything at all. Almost like it doesn't matter anymore.

We'll see how the day goes though.

Aug 3

Took the trip to the Dreaming on Saturday as usual with Sophie in tow, and honestly, I was still a little apprehensive. Anyway, Mikey didn't show up again, so it was down to Michelle and me. Kinstein has somehow managed to keep things peaceful around the Kitchen, noting that there was only one incident when some random villager caught sight of Michelle and loudly declared her, "The cursed one."

Thankfully, no one paid him much mind in deference to Kinstein. I hope that will remain the case and that Michelle will have some protection under Kinstein, especially since I can't watch over her myself for prolonged periods. Michelle herself does seem aware of the situation she's in and tries to keep out of sight when she can manage it. She still may not have said anything much, but she's smart about some things. Besides, some of the people in various villages in the outlying region know she helped with taking care of the creatures that have plagued their homes. I even took her along on the new job I picked from the 'problem board' that helps me keep track of which situations were the urgent ones and which could wait a little. It's different from when I had Old Crans feeding me jobs, but it suits its purposes.

Michelle is getting pretty good with her 'mecha' to a point that I don't have to constantly watch out for her. She was also quite adept at keeping herself hidden within the cockpit so that none of the villagers would see her. Sophie managed herself quite well too when we were dealing with what looked like a cross between a massive Minotaur and a giant angry troll that took a liking to the goats of this particular village.

After we left Michelle back in Kinstein's care, I decided to try looking for Old Crans again. I haven't been successful in finding him in the last couple of visits to the Dreaming. His shack isn't where it's supposed to be, so I've been flying around in specific areas, one area at a time. Sophie's been enjoying these flights because she doesn't get many opportunities to go all out with her TK flying practice. She made full use of our flights to try different ways of flying, different manoeuvres. In any case, it was another fruitless search for me. I'm reluctant to carry out his last set of 'orders' without a little more information. I have this feeling that something isn't quite right with this situation.

When we came back to reality, it was just after dinner time, roughly six hours since we started. We ended up having dinner together and she asked more about my past.

For her, she found it unusual that I had such fear of Phillip. She said that given my past, the training I had gone through during those early years of following my mom around the world, and even taking into account that dark period in my life, I had proven myself to be quite stubborn and resilient in the way I faced certain challenges in my life over the last couple of year she's known me. She even went so far as to call me, "Fearless."

I shook off her compliment, feeling that it wasn't really appropriate. I've tried to do things as best as I can manage and the best way I know how. I don't think any of it would be regarded as 'fearless' in any way.

"You're one of the bravest people I know," she said. "And this guy is just another guy, much like John."

"Not like John. Not like any other guy. He's ruthless and evil, and he's strong. Maybe even stronger than me," I said.

"You said 'maybe'," she said. "And you did beat him before. That means you can do it again."

"I'm worried about what doing that again will cost me," I said.

Sophie understood what I was getting at. She asked about other options I had, including those from the board members. I even asked her if she'd come across any such situation in her many comic stories. She agreed that in most comics, villains weren't as ruthless as I had described Phillip, but there were exceptions outside of the anti-heroes who didn't necessarily have such strict moral codes.

She cited two examples. In the first (I won't name the characters involved, but I will say that the two examples came from the same comic company), the heroes ended up wiping the minds of the villains, turning them into nothing more than supposedly harmless versions of who they were. The end results were not good because when the villains did regain their proper minds, the retribution resulted in major escalations on both sides. She said she would lend me her copy of the trade paperback.

The other example she cited involved a major hero being mind controlled into doing bad things, and in order to save him from doing major destruction against his will, the other hero killed the villain by snapping his neck. Pretty cold blooded and the consequences were dealt with for a while after that.

She also noted that lately, in the comics, the villains have been raising the stakes in their evil deeds with cities being destroyed and victims reaching into millions, and the heroes are pushed to the point of making that kill-decision. Some heroes have actually crossed that line too, it seems. Well, I haven't been reading comics in a few years now and it sounds like the landscape has changed. Even that last JLA book Remington had me read last year seems to have a different world than what Sophie described.

Over lunch the next day, I asked Helen, Will and Keitaro if what I had discussed with Sophie regarding the changing landscape of comics was true. Keitaro didn't have an answer because he reads his manga while Helen admitted to not really reading comics. Will said he didn't read much superhero comics, preferring the fantasy genre, citing *The Sandman* and *Fables* as his choice reading. He also recommended I read something called *"Bone"* saying that it had some similarities to the Dream-world I created.

Sophie reminded me that while certain aspects of the world may go dark, even with the superheroes in the comics, it is crucial that I hold on to the values that are important to me. Whatever I chose to do, I have to make sure it is something that I will have to live with.

None of it made my choices any easier. There was something that Sophie said that stuck with me though; one thing that she was right about.

I beat him before. I shouldn't be scared of him.

Aug 6

Got some time to kill and didn't feel like being anywhere else. Besides, it's been a couple of quiet and fairly normal days that this may be a good opportunity to catch up in some other aspects of my life. This little bit of extra time came about because I didn't make it to class on time, and that's because I overslept. Yep, all those night of short sleep finally caught up in a big way, but it's probably due to a few little things that came up over the weekend.

My lack of sleep has been due to bad dreams where I don't have the power or ability to save myself. I know it's a common enough dream and there have been others where the situation I'm in is far more dire or troubling. But since the weekend, my sleeping period has been increasing. I didn't get much sleep on Sunday night and ended up writing that last entry, but the next couple of nights, I managed close to an hour or so each night. Not quite up to my usual times, but at least a little more restful than before.

Last night, however, after my swim and going through some aqua-acrobatic sets with Walker, I did feel pretty zonked out so much so that after an hour in the flight simulator, my vision was getting a tad blurry and I knew I was drowsy. So I headed back to my room to crash. It might have been about three or so in the morning and maybe Becca decided to let me sleep in since she didn't bother to wake me for breakfast. She left a note saying she hoped I got a good night's sleep and that she would let Walker know why I didn't make it to the pool for my morning dip. By the time I finally stirred out of bed, it was about a quarter to eleven in the morning and I felt wasted. Of course, I did rush about until I saw the note from Becca and decided it was really too late to bother rushing to class; computer programming anyway. I had a nice if lonely breakfast, sat a while thinking about what to do until everyone came out for lunch, and then considered I should catch up on the journal... except the last few days have been relatively normal.

But there are a few things here and there to catch up on, stuff I hadn't touched on in a while.

I had a session with Ethan yesterday and my mind wandered a little during our session. It caused him to ask why I was thinking about a 'churliak' to which I admitted that I had no idea what it was. He said I was thinking about it and started describing that last creature Michelle, Sophie and I squared off against during that trip to the Dreaming on the weekend. I never had names for the various creatures and asked Ethan what he knew about the creature.

One thing he confirmed was that he didn't name it, someone else within his dream-land told him what the creature was called, and there were herds of them roaming about his dream-land. While they were there within his lands, he didn't consciously create them. But then, he could have unconsciously created them since they came from his dream-world.

I described a few other creatures I'd come across and they've all appeared on his lands too. He knew some but not all of their names. Come to think of it, I should take him to the little zoo of critters and see how many of them he knows. I don't even know if he's even seen them yet. We have kept things a little on the quiet side. Some people may have seen some these critters but aside from a few of us TK trainees who usually do the capturing late in the night, no other trainee has physically come in contact with the critters.

Aside from that, Ethan's been doing well with his training and studies. He only goes to his dream-world on Sunday afternoons now. It's mainly because he's found his schedule a little packed and often tiring after his exercise with John's group. They treat him well, behaving like a squad of big-brothers. After all, they know I'm keeping an eye on them and I can kick their collective butts if they misbehave.

I also had an opportunity to catch up with Tommy. I haven't been back to the Operations Center for a long while now. One thing of interest is that he has been keeping a tab on that 'glitched signal' over which I got taken off, and he said he was 90% certain my initial guess was right – there was an overlapping signal instead of an actual glitch. He said that the signal was still coming in, stronger than before, but still no one is sure what to make of it since the computers can't properly analyse the signal.

I spent months visually verifying the signal before feeding it through the computers, reading the data and checking out the markers, and then double checking the computer's results. It was a lot of work but to me, it was a bit like sifting through computer code, looking for particular syntax markers.

Tommy said that the computer's analysis program has undergone some changes to try to accommodate the 'glitches' but the results still aren't making sense. He has been comparing the little bit I did verify with the current data as well as with the current signal. The most he could manage was to verify certain marker positions but could not prove anything else. Since all that wasn't really within the purview of his tasks, he doesn't really have much time to devote to it. He would prefer to have me back in the Operations Center, and he did make that recommendation to his superiors. The final decision is out of his hands. Still, nice to know I could be needed somewhere after I'm done with my studies.

I also caught up with a few others like Ehrmer. I don't spend as much time with him since I've stopped using his facilities, like the furnace. He's stopped working on the diving suit since it was a side project and not really part of his work. As far as I know, he's got Corogi going over the diving suit to see if she can make some improvements on it, sort of a teaching project for her. After all, he is mentoring her.

Then there's Nik with whom I've been trading notes in computer programming; strictly professional. We sparred once in Silat when Keiko needed to focus on the juniors. Nothing going on there, hence no writing.

I still check in with Jenny to chart Callie and Toni's progress with their network. They're coming along, with a couple of study groups asking them to help out. On my end, Kevin and Bastian are also coming along with their network training although all we have done are test runs with small groups. They haven't had any field experience the way Callie and Toni have. I did let Jenny know that if there were other volunteers looking to use the network for learning purposes, to send them my way for Kevin and Bastian to work with.

On the TK side, things are progressing as we are tackling harder and trickier situations where our TK might be useful. As mentioned, some of them have taken to helping corral the critters. I have also openly shared some of the rules I've set for myself, as I did with the TP class, and thankfully, the others are in agreement that the rules are good. Almost all of them have adopted most of these as guidelines on how to use their abilities while the others have their own variation.

There are still rumours about me floating around, the most interesting of which is how I turn into some kind of spirit to wander the residential corridors at night to haunt them. The truth is that I do wander the halls late at night or early in the morning, depending on how you look at it, taking a slight detour back to my suite, but to check for critters.

And I guess this is good a place as any to call it quits for this entry. Classes are letting out about now, so the others should be settling down to lunch soon. I'm sure there'll be some questions as to my absence from the morning class.

Aug 8

Aside from oversleeping the other day, I've still managed to catch up and keep pace with my studies. It is different now as to when I started a couple of years back, struggling along most of the time. The classes aren't any easier now, but I suppose since I've been more open and asking questions when I need clarification, it hasn't been as difficult as it used to be.

For example, I always wondered why when astronomers look into Space, they can never find other worlds with life on them despite knowing for sure life-bearing planets do exist. And why is it possible, that when you look deeper and farther enough, you can conceivably see our own planet Earth from several millennia ago. Well, finally figured it has to do with the speed of light. In trying to figure out propulsion for my spaceship, there's a need to find a way to achieve a speed that was faster than light, or more often referred to as FTL. The speed of light is the fastest speed we know, supposedly. Even the light given out by our sun takes up to eight minutes to reach Earth. Simply put, if we're looking at the sun, we're always looking at the sun in the past, always eight minutes in the past, never at the present time. Its past is our present. If the sun were to vanish from its location in our Solar System, we wouldn't know for at least eight minutes.

So if we take into account the planets around other stars oh-so-far away might have life on them, we wouldn't really know until perhaps a few thousand years from now because what we may be looking at could be thousands to perhaps tens of thousands or even hundreds of thousands of years in the past. Humanity has only been on Earth for maybe the last thirty to forty thousand years and we've only been looking into really deep space, probably during the last hundred years or so. Galileo started looking through the telescope into space back in the 1600s, or so I was taught.

So, that possible little image of Earth that we could conceivably see out there in the deepest portions of Space might actually be no more that a mud-ball of primordial goop that's yet to even produce its first single celled creature. Should it be any wonder that we can't find any inhabited planets out there?

It one of those things where classes are concerned.

Anyhoo, dinner with Sophie last night had an interesting discussion about dreams and my Dream-world, particularly how she compared the two. To an extent, I have a certain amount of control over the Dream-world itself, being able to manipulate the sense of reality there. But I've also acted in accordance to some set of rules which made her question how much control I supposedly have. She brought this up because I mentioned the other day how I 'healed' the land after that showdown with Phillip all those years back. She also pointed out how it was I had to perform certain set tasks to ensure the 'health' of the land even though I didn't have to if I didn't want to. That's just in the Dreaming.

In an actual dream, however, there has to be the realisation that you are in a dream before you can take control of the dream, i.e. lucid dreaming. Although the state of mind in both cases are completely different, as Ms. Phillips can attest to, the state of conditions are pretty similar in that reality can be manipulated – to a certain extent, wholly dependent on the dreamer. The trick, of course, is getting to the realisation that you are dreaming, while in a dream.

She didn't follow me into the Dreaming today, which was something she wanted to clear with me over dinner last night. I was okay with it. I couldn't have her accompany me every time because of a one-off trip that didn't even really take place in my Dream-world. I went on alone.

Mikey didn't turn up again so I got to spend some time with Michelle, taking her for a camping trip that lasted a couple of days; no more than roughly three hours plus in reality. I wanted to see if she had any abilities so

I showed her a few small things, like moving little objects around and then asked if she could do the same. Mikey hasn't displayed any such abilities, but Michelle occupies a wholly different reality. I guess I was trying to see if she was a dreamer who was unaware that she was in a dream, or maybe get her to realise that particular potential.

She didn't say anything through the couple of days we spent together and every time we stopped to take a break during our hike back to the Kitchen, she tried moving a little twig or little stone with her mind. I think she managed to roll a small stone a little, but I couldn't be sure because I barely caught a glimpse of it happening. I asked her if she managed to do something with the stone, but as usual, she didn't respond in any way.

I briefed Kinstein on what we did together. It's in case she continues to try moving things, but with objects around the Kitchen. I gave her a big hug, told her to pass my regards to Mikey should he decide to drop by on his own to visit her, but what were the chances of him dropping by and her saying anything?

I guess that's about it for now. I'm getting a little hungry and it's about time for dinner now.

Aug 11

Have you ever gotten into a situation that was so surreal, so freaky, it feels like it could only be a dream... but it isn't? It becomes something that would completely unnerve you because it's just on that side of what should be real. The flip-side of it is that all of what happened really happened. I'll have to fill in some gaps first though.

First, John's been warded in the Infirmary. It took a while but I finally found out that it was due to exhaustion. Through Carol, I learnt that John's exhaustion was due sleep deprivation. He had to be sedated, but his readings are constantly spiking despite being unconscious. It was a safe bet that he was still having bad dreams, although given that last trip into his dream, it was more a nightmare for me and almost a wet dream for him. There's still something else haunting him in his dreams. I know I'll have to deal with this soon.

So, John was warded a couple of days ago and it took a while to gather the information. In between was that surreal freaky moment that really got way under my skin and chilled me to the bones. Since that day when I slept through breakfast, my sleeping time has been clocking in just under two hours of peaceful restful sleep each night. For some reason, whatever happened before wasn't bothering me lately. Maybe I've got some kind of unconscious defence system set up now, but it's a bit of speculation. In any case, my nights are basically back to normal. It didn't really come to mind until that incident gave me pause to think why it happened.

After clocking in some time with the flight simulator, I spent a little time catching up with Tommy – no particular details to share here. An almost typical late night for me and one I experienced with ease, something I didn't quite realise at the time. So I was feeling pretty good when I was heading back to my suite, taking a slightly longer route that had become a bit of a habit of late; checking for critters, the numbers of which seem to have dropped off a bit. This meant that I was walking around half lit corridors late at night where other trainees were staying. So, imagine how freaky it was to turn that last darkened corner and see the residents standing there outside the door of their respective suites, most in their pyjamas or whatever they slept in, like semi-robotic sentries standing guard.

Imagine them staring blankly straight ahead, barely looking at each other. The dim lighting made everything seem surreal and dream-like and for the briefest of moments, I wondered if I was dreaming because only in a dream do you come across such a scene. It stopped me in my tracks. I recognised some of them, including Bastian, Hank, Kadi and Rain. Others I recognised from various classes and in all, there were eleven of them lining the corridor. Since this was the same corridor as my suite, only Becca was missing from the line-up.

I looked at all of them and could see that their eyes were open, but there was no overt sign that any of them was awake. I then looked up behind me where there's a surveillance camera and then wondered if what I was looking at was being recorded. No one was going to believe me if I were to tell this to anyone. Not being too sure what to make of it all, I decided to chance walking through the corridor anyway. A few steps in and right before reaching the first person, all of them suddenly turned to face me. The look in their eyes gave me pause. It felt like they were all staring deep into me. If I wasn't freaked out enough, they started muttering, almost chanting, in unison in practically teasing tones.

"I'm waiting, Jeannie," they said together. "Your friends are waiting for you. Come and play with us." Then they kept repeating, "Come and play, we're waiting. Come and play."

Over and over in some baiting playful half-asleep tone, "Come and play." I even backed away and felt the fear rising within me. Like I said, surreal and freaky, definitely unnerving to say the least. Thinking back on it now, it feels like I stepped through the fourth wall and into an episode of *Doctor Who* or *The Twilight Zone*. Sometimes, the simplest things can be pretty scary.

It took me a while, as they say, "to gird up my loins." I knew who I was facing up against and I knew John's condition was somehow his doing as well. I closed my eyes and pushed down the fear. I played a scenario out in my mind, of what I wanted to do. I opened my eyes, made a gesture, throwing my arms forward as if I was throwing knives, sending out a psychic blast right down the corridor in an attempt to bring everyone out of a dream without shocking them awake. They say you should never wake a sleepwalker and I felt this was that situation, except I needed to get that controlling presence out of their dreams. I was trying not to wake them up and hopefully send them back to their rooms, but that meant getting into their heads and controlling them, something I didn't want to do. I didn't have much choice in that area.

So imagine if you went to bed, had a nice rest and had a nice dream or whatever, and suddenly, you're awake, standing outside your apartment in your jammies along with a whole bunch of other people looking at each other and all around that dim corridor, wondering what the heck was going on. Of course, being the only one who's not standing in front of her own door, everyone looked my way again looking for answers. Thankfully, by then, a couple of the G/Cs and tutors (who probably are G/C as well) turned up to help sort things out. Guess the surveillance cameras were working, but the response time does leave something to be desired.

I checked with Kadi first because she was the only F.E.P. of the bunch, and I could, at least, reassure her in her own language. I was really curious how Phillip would have gotten into her head though. From my experience with Becca, it wasn't that easy getting into her thoughts, much less try to exert some kind of control there. Phillip pulled off something massively powerful though, getting into the dreams and minds, and then controlling them the way he did. I did as best as I could with Kadi and Rain before Becca came out due to the commotion. Remington was a little late getting there. He only had to give me a look and I knew what he was getting at.

Things were getting out of hand. I had to accept Phillip's invitation and I had better damn well be ready to face him.

Aug 13

The last couple of days were spent in preparation for what needs to be done. I don't think I've ever had this much time to get ready to do something so potentially dangerous, if it actually is dangerous. Honestly, aside from having to face up to Phillip, who could be seen as my nemesis, I have no real idea what I'm heading into or what the threat or danger level is. So, I made a few calls.

First call was mom, to let her know what I was about to get up to. There was a worst case scenario on my mind, and Mikey still has to be cared for. She did let me know that he was fine and doing well in the kindie getting along with the other kids. She assured me that Karen was doing a fine job helping with Mikey. She relied more on Remington to keep her apprised of my activities than to follow my journal on-line. She also reminded me that I could still turn to her if I needed help; I only needed her to make sure that Mikey would be okay if things came to a head and the worst happened.

I then called X to inform him what was going on in greater detail than I had shared with him before. I explained what I was about to do and he questioned if it was a wise decision to take on Phillip where he would be most powerful. He also offered his help, but I only needed him to watch out for his brother. He would hear from my mom if things didn't turn out the way I hoped.

I tried calling Lian, but no luck. It might have been a timing thing and I don't expect her to call back since The Facility's number isn't going to show up on her hand-phone.

Sophie thinks that I'm being morbid and have already psyched myself to expect the worst; a bad way to go into an unknown situation. I had to impress upon her the negative force of nature that is Phillip. She even offered to help. I preferred not to have to watch out for her, reminding her what happened when we went up against Ethan's darkness. Things did not turn out well for her and I had to pull some drastic stuff in order to save her. She actually winced at the memory. I told her that facing up to Phillip was going to be a lot worse and far more traumatic. Chances were, if I needed to save her again, it would be far worse than stabbing her with some imaginary statue.

That was enough to put a little fear into her. Then again, she's one who tends to face her fears any way she can.

Aside from the phone calls, I've done as best as I can manage to keep everyone else informed of my plans. Like Sophie, a few of them asked what they could do to help, and I gave them the same answer I gave Sophie. Walker did voice some concern saying that I should do what I needed and, "Come back safe."

I thought that was sweet, and I said that I would definitely want to come back safe. I spent most of the night with him. He fell asleep and so did I, but only for about an hour or so. I couldn't get back to sleep after that. I gave him a peck on the cheek – it didn't wake him up – and I left to come back to my room. I've been typing this up ever since. There isn't really much to cover because my focus has been on getting myself ready for later. I didn't want to get into John's dream at night. I figure there would be less people at risk if everyone was awake and in class while I tackled this. If Phillip was jumping through other people's dreams, it would give him less dreams to jump around in, perhaps confining him to John's dream.

Ms. Phillips hasn't been keeping John sedated for the last couple of days, but he hasn't woken up. Hopefully, that will change if I'm successful, but I don't know what it is I actually have to do. All I know is, right now, I'm going into John's dream, draw Phillip into a confrontation, and take him down again. How exactly I'm going to do that? I really don't know. I just can't put it off any longer.

So, after this, I'm taking in a swim to unwind my nerves, take in some breakfast with my friends, make sure that they're all there and awake, and tell them to try not to fall asleep until I came back to reality. Once all that is done, I'm heading to the Infirmary and back into darkness.

Event status report.
Filed Aug 14 by Remington C-

On the morning of August 13, Syndi-Jean went to the Infirmary to begin her session. The intention was to create a psychic link into John K's dream and confront a person she believed responsible for a spate of night terrors that have plagued several trainees over the past few months. She detailed her intentions and plan with her G/C Linda, Ms. Phillips, the Infirmary's resident doctor, and myself. We understood the risks she was taking with this endeavor.

On a personal note, I had my reservations about what she planned to do. I had not met the person she was going up against, but I was there when she escaped his grasp several years ago. I saw the repercussions and the effect that episode had on her and I understand her fears. I voiced my concerns, but she insisted that she had to face this Phillip on her own. To be fair, I knew where she was coming from. Perhaps it was a trait she picked up from her friend, Sophie – the need to confront her fear alone and not wanting anyone else's neck on the line if things go south.

The last 35 hours have been eventful. The major concern, at this time, is that Jeannie has yet to surface from the link, and John's condition has been upgraded to critical. What exactly is going on in the mindscape, no one knows. Ms. Phillips has inquired if we could ask one of the other TP trainees to do a scan on John and Jeannie, to better understand their status. I have discussed this with Linda and several other members of the board. While I could name a couple of trainees who would be willing to assist, it would not be in the best interest of The Facility to put our trainees into a dangerous situation without a clear exit. Also, it would be against Jeannie's wishes to have any of her friends to step into this particular fire, even though they would be more than willing to do so to help her.

For the first twelve hours or so, things were quiet but soon after, it appeared that things took a turn for the worse. John started convulsing at first and was soon followed by Jeannie. Ms. Phillips focused on John and after a harrowing half-hour, he was stabilized, but had to be intubated and put on a respirator to help him breathe.

While Ms. Phillips focused on John, I stayed by Jeannie's side and kept watch on the monitors. I called out whatever readings Ms. Phillips asked for. While I was concerned, she kept assuring me that her readings were well within the given parameters supplied by Charlie, Jeannie's personal physician. Jeannie stopped convulsing some time before John did. It was almost as if he stabilized simply because she did.

That was the only indication that they were linked in some way, and that something was occurring on a level unseen by any of us. The most we can do is to keep faith that Jeannie knows what she's doing and that it is the right thing. That's my faith in her.

At least for twelve more hours.

If she does not surface by then, a different course of action needs to be taken. We will have options by then. It might not be the kind of options we want to take.

Event Status Report
Filed Aug 17 by Remington C~

While the event being reported here is basically over, there are certain incidents that would need to be covered. Both Jeannie and John K have woken. However, Jeannie's friends, Sophie and Keitaro, are now regarded as being in comas.

Following up on the previous report, over eleven hours had passed when Ms. Phillips, Linda, John K's G/C and myself began to discuss our options on how to revive Jeannie and John. We could not fully determine the mental conditions of both patients, but the EEG's readings suggested that they were both mentally synchronized. Jeannie's readings showed a slightly elevated sense of activity, while John's basically matched her readings, but at a fractionally lower scale. Ms. Phillips cautioned that neither were in a typical dream state, based on the readings.

The suggestion to have one of the TP trainees link in was brought up again, and preferably one who had joined Jeannie on a previous dream session. I was reluctant to allow it, but knew that it was the most viable option to determine exactly what was going on in their heads. Linda was equally reluctant to put any other trainees in danger, but John's G/C pushed for it, saying that it was a perfect test case for our trainees to prove what they were capable of.

"What are we training them for if not to handle situations as these?" he asked while pointing out that it was often Jeannie taking point on these situations, not giving much leeway to the other trainees to even try.

Ms. Phillips was willing to let another TP trainee link in, but she insisted that it had to be someone who was completely willing to take the risk. I knew that wasn't a problem given the TP trainees Jeannie has endeared herself to. They'd be willing to help. We boiled the list down to Sophie, Callie and Toni; the three who worked together in dealing with Callie's dream. Carl's name was brought up, but given the animosity between Jeannie and him, it was agreed that he was nowhere near being an ideal choice. Then again, given the relationship Jeannie had with John, it was surprising that she agreed to get into his head a second time.

Sophie was approached first and she agreed with only one condition – she wanted Keitaro along as a bodyguard. I am aware that Jeannie had taken Keitaro to her dream world on occasion, and he was there when she had to help Sophie last year. When we approached him, he was more than willing, eager to help in any way. I had to caution both of them, that it was not the same as taking a trip in the dream world. As far as we knew, this was John's dream and I stressed, "The rules are different. We are in dangerous waters here."

Sophie appeared confident, as did Keitaro. They were briefed on all the dangers I could think of where this situation was concerned, as well as the person they might have to go up against. That was the most we could do to prepare them. Ms. Phillips gave them a rapid rudimentary check-up before hooking them up to a variety of monitors as they got into the two remaining available beds. It took Sophie a while before she could settle herself in order to link with Keitaro, or so she said. Then within seconds, she and Keitaro appeared to be in a dream state, according to the monitors. The EEG readings for Sophie and Keitaro did not take long to start matching those of Jeannie and John. It was the only sign we had that the synchronization had occurred. From then, we were waiting again for any signs of activity beyond the various tones given out by the machines monitoring the sleeping participants. When the beeping tones started changing, things were truly moving from bad to worse, and there was nothing we could really do about it.

Barely two hours after Sophie and Keitaro linked in with John and Jeannie, almost fifty-four hours since Jeannie started, and the best I can describe the situation in the Infirmary was chaotic. John, Sophie and Keitaro all went into various convulsions, their biological readings were spiking in all the wrong places. Ms. Phillips and her standby assistants moved with utmost urgency, trying to stabilize the three. The only one who gave no outward sign of trouble was Jeannie. Whatever was going on in the dream, I would have guessed then that things were getting out of hand, and Jeannie would be struggling to get things under control.

Sophie went into a massive seizure. Ms. Phillips had me try to keep her down and prevent her from biting her tongue. I did as best as I could, and I wish I could have done more. By the time I got her arching body down to the bed again, she seemed to have an epileptic fit. Ms. Phillips pushed me aside to take over. I backed off, accidentally knocking into John's bed, and he jolted awake. The assistant immediately moved to check on him and remove the intubation. Keitaro also appeared to calm down.

Just when it appeared we managed to get things under control, one anguished scream came from Jeannie. We all turned to her, and even a few passers-by came running into the Infirmary. I turned my full attention to Jeannie, moving over to her bed. She collapsed into sobs as I got to her. I could feel her shaking and shivering in my arms as she wailed into my coat. Ms. Phillips tried to sedate her. I knew it wouldn't work, but she tried anyway. Sedatives or not, it took a long while before she even calmed down and Linda managed to get her to get some proper sleep.

Tomorrow, we start debriefing John. Ms. Phillips insisted that she wanted to keep John and Jeannie under observation as they rested and the Infirmary has been declared off-limits to non-essential personnel. I am confident that we might get some information from John. I doubt Jeannie would be in any condition to actually share anything.

But that's for tomorrow.

Event Status Report
Filed Aug 18 by Remington C~

Ms. Phillips has listed Jeannie as being in a state of shock. She has also restricted us from pushing Jeannie for information as to what happened. In the brief period I spent with Jeannie, she appeared depressed and refused to talk about anything. She has not really changed position from being curled in a fetal position. A few of her friends dropped by to visit her but even they could not get her to open up.

I have kept Jeannie's mother apprised of the situation and will continue to do so until Jeannie is able to talk to her mother herself. Beyond this, there is nothing else to do for either of them. I have asked Becca to check in on Jeannie as well when she can.

Meanwhile, John K was debriefed earlier today by his G/C and Linda W, overseen by Peter B. The following is a portion of the transcript from the debriefing. At this time, this is the only record we have of what happened.

(Declassified segment)
G/C – We need you to recall, as best as you can and as much as you can.
John – Look, a lot of it doesn't make sense. I mean, how much of a dream can you actually remember once you wake up, huh?
G/C – We understand, but we need you to try to recall as best as you can. Syndi-Jean is practically catatonic and two others are in comas, like you were.
John – There was this guy, okay? And he had some kind of beef with Syndi-Jean. I don't know why he was always in my head, in my dreams. Believe me, the last thing I want to dream about is guys she used to hang out with.
G/C – How do you know he was someone from her past?
John – Because he kept bragging about how he had her, had his way with her, raped her, hell, he bragged and gloated about every which way he fucked her. The guy was insane; he even had video clips of it all playing in some dingy cinema. I wanted to kick his ass for what he did to her.
G/C – And did you?
John – I couldn't even get to him, he kept somehow... he kept just out of reach. I kept going after him and like when I was about to hit him, he seemed just out of reach all of a sudden. I don't know how long... I mean, y'know, time doesn't mean anything. There was no night. There was no day. No nothing. I couldn't tell if it was day or night even. I don't know how long I chasing after him. I'm not even sure when she turned up. All I know is, suddenly, there she was.
G/C – So she just appeared.
John – Yah, like just out of the blue she was just there. I can't recall much... she kept saying things, maybe trying to explain things or something. And maybe it made sense then but I can't recall what exactly she said. All I know is we had to do something to catch this guy.
-break-

John – *Y' know, things got pretty insane, now that I think about it. But it really seemed like it was normal the way the world around me just seemed to go ballistic. Destruction everywhere like you wouldn't believe. It was a war zone! But like I said, I didn't really think twice about it then. It really seemed like it was the most normal thing in the universe. There was a sense, somewhere, that it was insane and yet... not.*

G/C – *Can you describe what she was doing?*

John – *I... I don't know for sure. It wasn't quite a normal fight and sometimes it was a normal fight. I just can't be sure what was going on. I know I wanted to do something but for some reason I just... I couldn't do anything. I know I wasn't paralyzed or anything like that... I just...*

   -break-

G/C – *Do you know when the other two turned up?*

John – *No, no, I couldn't tell you when they did, but they did suddenly come out of nowhere, that girl who's always hanging with Syndi-Jean, Sophie, and that Jap guy she practices kendo with. I know for sure I didn't dream them up. I mean, Sophie maybe, but why would I want to dream about that guy?*

G/C – *Can you recall what exactly happened to them?*

   -break-

G/C – *John?*

John – *I... I don't know, I just... She said she... She was there to find out what was going on. That's all it was. And then... Then, it was... Everything was just... I... I don't...*

   -break-

John – *That guy, Keitaro? He saw Syndi-Jean struggling in her fight and he dashed in like some kinda hero. He was wearing some kind of armour and that sword... It just kept getting larger and larger. It was ridiculous, the size of it... So big that no one could actually lift it, but he did. And when he swung it there was this massive force the carved a path of destruction at that stranger... And it never touched him.*

   I think Syndi-Jean got distracted by him, like she wasn't expecting him. And then Sophie ran in after him and things just got worse.

G/C – *And what did you do?*

John – *I went after her. Stupid move. Well, stupid in hindsight. Should have known better than to stick my neck out in the middle of some crazy fight that even I had no hope of doing anything. Probably did know better but I couldn't just stand back while others were going in to fight some bad guy in my own dream, could I?*

G/C – *You said things got worse.*

John – *Yah, things got real bad. Maybe it was Syndi-Jean getting distracted, maybe it was those two turning up that did it, but somehow, she wasn't up to handling* *that guy she was fighting. Don't get me wrong. I mean, I know she can fight, but the fighting they were doing was way beyond anything I could imagine. It was stuff you see in some Japanese cartoon or kung-fu movies where they're throwing forces of energy at each other and the whole world around us just gets blown apart.*

Keitaro got in front of Syndi-Jean and for a moment, he was blocking off all sorts of stuff that was heading our way. It was like wind and debris and everything you can imagine being thrown about in a hurricane like storm, all that, being focused into one, single… almost bullet-like force bearing down on her, and Keitaro swung that big sword of his knocking aside that bullet. And he did it twice, maybe three times.

Then that guy, all he did was (gesturing with hand) and the whole ground crumbles around us. Keitaro started to fall into a crevasse that just kept getting wider and larger. I managed to grab his arm as he fell over the edge, and it was a struggle just to pull him up. When I was looking down, lying on the ground, it looked like a massive canyon opened up below us, and we were on top of some… pillar or something. I don't really know what was going on then because I was trying to hold on to him and hoping to hell that the ground wasn't going to give way anymore. At least he wasn't holding on to that crazy-ass sword. By the time I managed to help him back up, we noticed that this guy, this… maniac who was attacking Syndi-Jean was floating just above us, and we had this small piece of elevated ground that felt like it was miles up from solid ground.

I could hear, and I remember this for some reason, I could hear Sophie telling Syndi-Jean that she was better and stronger than that guy. It sounded like simple psychology, psyching yourself into believing that you could be better than your opponent, y'know? I could see on her face though that it wasn't working. Whatever this guy did to her, well.. those scars ran deep. And then…

-break-

John *– And then, Keitaro pulled his sword out of nowhere, nothing. It was like he just pulled some imaginary sword from behind him and suddenly there it was again. Anyway, he had his sword and he took a semi-defensive stance, ready to defend and ready to attack… and that guy laughed. Syndi-Jean tried to get Keitaro out of the way because he was still in front of her, like he was trying to defend her. And that guy did another (gesturing with hand) and… and… it was insane, man. I mean, the sword AND his arm just sort of blew apart, scattered into the wind, and there was blood everywhere. It… I… I was j-just stunned… by what happened. Keitaro was screaming and collapsed to the ground… and next thing I knew, I suddenly stepped on nothing, like the ground gave way below me.*

I remember falling and… it was Sophie who grabbed my arm. I couldn't see what was going on next but I could… He screamed and he screamed. I could see it in Sophie's eyes, just how bad things were. I mean… I… I didn't see it, but between the screams, Syndi-Jean trying to calm him, Sophie's tears and that guy laughing… it… it was insane, y'know? It was… just insane…

-break-

John *– I was just… I was trying to get a hold on the ledge and Sophie… Sophie was trying to help me back up. I don't think I was relying on her too much, but she was screaming even as I was pulling myself up with a little help from her. I got my arms up, y'know, like this (motions arms) and I could at least look… I had my head above the ledge and see… That's when I noticed that Sophie's legs were gone, nothing but bloody stumps… and she…*

I'm sorry, it was just… it wasn't like what happened to Keitaro, I could see… it was like… her legs… the flesh on her legs were slowly coming off, flying apart… it was…I can't imagine what she was going through then, the way… y'know you watch those war movie where you see people's limbs being blown apart? It was like that, but in extremely, slow, motion… and it moving up her legs towards her body. I could feel her fingers clawing into my skin as she was holding on to me on that ledge.

G/C *– What was Syndi-Jean doing?*

John *– Oh, that was crazy… She… She was trying to… she was scrambling to pick up pieces of Keitaro's arms from the ground and trying to mold it back onto him. I think that was what she was trying to do, I couldn't really tell. She was covered in blood. It… there was… there was another splash of blood and screams, and I could hear… like, "Stop It! Stop It! Stop!" over and over. I just…*

S-somewhere in all that, Sophie managed to pull herself closer to me… This I can remember vividly. I know it's strange with all the stuff that was going on… I was still hanging over the side of the ledge… and even with that pain in her voice, in her eyes; there was still this fire in her to keep going, to keep fighting. It's such a clear moment that everything else seemed to fade away. Her words were so fierce… and she was saying, "This is your dream! Your world! You have power here! Take control!"

Then she lost it and started to scream right in my face… and that fire was gone, erased by the pain and fear that overwhelmed her. It was all over her face. I… I…

-break-

G/C *– It's okay, John. What happened after that? What happened with Syndi-Jean?*

John *– I think she lost it…She heard Sophie screaming and that was probably when she saw what was happening to Sophie… and she lost it. It looked like she jumped up at the guy. And she was screaming, like rage and fury…so primal, so out of control. I thought I'd seen her out of control before, but not like this… not like this.*

They were like, fighting each other, floating in the air. And the punches resonated hard, y'know? If you ever thought sound effects in movies sounded fake, this was just insane... like the force behind each punch they threw at each other broke the sound barrier each time. Boom boom boom.

I managed to pull myself up and found my footing to watch... just for a moment. I saw her literally rip his arm off and throw it aside... and that bastard grew another out of nothing! Like it never even mattered to him... and I just felt like there was nothing I could even do. I didn't know how to take control, like what Sophie had said. All I could feel was this fear and anger. I knew I didn't want him to win and I seriously wanted her to beat his ass to hell. And that was when one blow she did sent him flying into a mountainside. And she didn't let up... She went flying in after him.

I looked at Keitaro and Sophie who were on the ground. I could see Keitaro was still barely breathing even with half his body blown apart, like some bomb went off inside half his body... and Sophie was still slowly being blown apart, but she was still somewhat conscious... When I turned to her, I could hear her repeating, like some mantra, "Your world, your rules. Your world, your rules." But she was fading... I did get the message. My world... my dream... my rules...

I made a clear-cut decision, firm in my own belief, and the next thing I knew, I was in between Syndi-Jean and that ass-hole, with my fingers around his throat. I have no idea what she thought, if there was any thought in her head because she was still trying to get at him even though I was in her way. I ignored her, and focused on him, still with the single thought... that single decision – and I firmly told him to get out of my head. The weird thing, was that the bastard still smiled as his body started to... I guess, it dissipated... like the atoms came apart and dispersed in the wind. Syndi-Jean wasn't happy with what I did, screaming at me, berating me for what I did, so I told her to go home, to leave my world... and I woke up...

The last few parts, that's the clearest, but I.. I can't really even be sure any of it happened that way anymore. Like a dream fading away now...

G/C – *What about Sophie and Keitaro?*

John – *I dunno... I figured they were okay once I got rid of that guy and woke up.*

-break-

John – *Wait, wait, wait... don't tell me they're still in my head? Are you fraking kidding me?*

-Segment ends. Reminder is classified-

Event Status Report
Filed Aug 20 by Remington C~

It looks like Jeannie is on the mend in more ways than one and surprisingly, it would be thanks to John.

According to Ms. Phillips, Jeannie may have actually gotten more sleep in the last few days than she had in well over three months. Charlie was even called in to check on her, although that was more for her mother's benefit and assurance that there was nothing physically wrong with her.

Jeannie's friends have dropped by to visit her, but she never spoke. Walker has spent the last couple of nights by her side. He mentioned that she cried in her sleep and, on occasion, seemed to shiver in fear.

Then, last night, he apparently got into a conversation with John, who dropped by the Infirmary. This conversation proved to be a turning point for Jeannie. The following is an excerpt of their conversation from the transcript of the Surveillance Footage.

Begin Transcript Excerpt

John: *Is she awake?*
Walker: *She should be, but I think not. Is there something that you wish to convey to her?*
John: *Uh, no... I'm not really sure why I came by.*
Walker: *You have something to say, otherwise you wouldn't have come.*
John: *Look, you know... you know what happened, right? You probably think it's my fault that she's like this right now.*
Walker: *I do not. Neither should you.*
John: *Right, okay... sure... maybe you can tell her friends that because, well... They think I am anyway.*
Walker: *They do not think that. You only blame yourself because you do care for Syndi-Jean as much as we do. Syndi-Jean cares for her friends. She is this way because of what has happened to Sophie and Keitaro.*
John: *Well, not quite. Look, you weren't there... but I know what she went through with that guy. Stuff like that, you don't walk away from... it stays. It's burned in her to her soul. That's part of the problem, y'see?*
Walker: *No, I don't...*
John: *Look, look... this thing that happened to her... It's... It was something that happened over a long period of time and it was bad. So very bad. You could probably imagine the worst possible thing and it wouldn't even come close to what this guy*

252

did to her. He didn't just break her... he scarred her deep... he took her beyond her own limits, showed her the darkness that was within her and gave it breath...
Walker: *Compose yourself, and be clear. Define the problem.*
John: *That's you, isn't it? Always cut to the problem and face that. You think you know her? You think you can fix this problem?*
   -break-
John: *Y'know...? Maybe you can. You have to understand, I've faced Syndi-Jean in a fight and I can tell you that this girl... she can be fierce and fearless..., but not against this guy. This guy has something else on her... something in her...*
Walker: *She fears him.*

John: *No, she doesn't. That's the thing. She doesn't fear him... She fears herself. She's afraid of what this guy is capable of making her do. This thing... this idea, is what you have to get through to her. She won't listen to me, but you... You make her believe that, face that... and she can take this guy.*
Walker: *But what you say is that in 'taking this guy,' she would have to do something that she is afraid to do.*
John: *Yeh, well... there's your problem then. Fix that.*
   -break-
John: *Look, you know as well as I do... sometimes, some situations... there's just that one thing that needs to be done and there are no other options, no other way in dealing with it. She does this, does what she needs to do... it will change her, and she has to accept that.*
   -break-
John: *Think... think of it as a... a rite of passage, y'know? Something she has to go through to become the person she's supposed to be.*
Walker: *That would compromise who she is. This is your solution...*
John: *It's really up to her, isn't it? C'mon, I just want her back to her normal self so that she can get these two out of my head... if they're still in there. I know... I can feel that something just ain't right in my noggin' I just... I'd like her to just clean up after herself.*
   -break-
John: *Look, you just... you talk to her... figure it out yourself what you want to tell her... Just... just let her know, I'm ready... When she's ready, I'm ready... She can... she can jump back into my head and do... whatever it is she needs to do, okay? You tell her that.*

John leaves the Infirmary.

End Transcript Excerpt

Walker didn't need to convey much to Jeannie because she apparently heard everything that John had said. She acknowledged to Walker that John was right about her fears. She told him that with that fear, she had lost before she even began to fight.

While he did stay with her through the night, sleeping next to her, I noted that she did not sleep, not right away. When I checked in on her this morning, I told her what I had seen and heard over the Surveillance Footage. It is not common for us to share with our charges, it gives them a sense of security of not being constantly watched, but Jeannie knows better. She said that she would take one more trip into John's mind to try bringing Sophie and Keitaro back.

I offered to go with her this time, if she would be willing to have me along. She agreed. John has since been informed and we're going in by eight tonight. Charlie has been asked to attend and Jeannie's mother has been kept up to date as well. She said she felt better that I would be accompanying Jeannie in this.

We'll see what happens next and hope for a positive outcome.

Aug 24

Remington said it was time for the journal to have its original writer back. It was never his place to keep filling in for me. Given how things have turned out, it was in my best interest to give my own perspective on the state of things. It's not like I really want to talk about it, or even write about it. Considering everything Remington has contributed, I don't really want to retread it. Most of what John gave in his debriefing is what happened, but it is from his perspective. I have no particular desire to go over all that from my own point of view; I don't have much to add to it anyway. I suppose, though, I could start by stating that John was right.

That night when he wanted Walker to talk to me, he said I was more afraid of myself than I was of Phillip. That first time I had to face him, I know I did pretty bad and unspeakable things – even if I did end up telling a few people, but still, not in florid detail. For the longest time, I did think that I killed him. Everything else that led up to it was worse though, at least for me. I really hated myself for it all, and how I felt about it. When it felt like Phillip wasn't quite dead and the possibility that I had to face him again filled my thoughts, a part of me did relish the thought of doing it all again. A bigger part feared that I had to do it again. What really scared me was that I had this little bit of relish, this little sense within that I really wanted to…

No, I've been fighting that for the last few years. I've accepted the past, that I did such things, and I've moved on. I've accepted that it is who I am and I can make the choice not to do it again... but that small part of me wants to. And that small part, it's growing each time Phillip makes himself known, each time he does something that makes me determined that I have to take action. When I was facing him in John's dream, that small part was practically begging for release. So, John was right, I was fighting Phillip and myself at the same time. John felt that if I wanted to win this fight, I had to stop fighting myself.

Admittedly, I was a little on edge about heading back into John's head, even with Remington backing me up. Remington tends to play things really close. I mean, I always suspected that he had some kind of psychic ability, but he's never really shown his hand, so to speak. When he said that he would accompany me on this trip, I wondered if he had some kind of trick up his sleeve. He didn't do anything in particular of any sort though. If he had done something, I probably didn't notice because I was mostly distracted by Sophie and Keitaro while being paranoid and on edge about Phillip's whereabouts.

So we'll cut to the chase here. Remington and John met me in the Infirmary, pretty much where I'd been for a few days. Charlie was there, checking up on me. He already knew what we were about to do. While Ms. Phillips tended to John, fussing a little with Remington, Charlie kept an eye on the monitors on my bed. Because I was a little hesitant, it took a while for me to get my head on right. Remington took me through some breathing exercises to calm me down. John gamely joined in simply to put one up on me, proving that he was far more willing to having me back in his head than I was willing to do so. The breathing got me calmed, enough to link the three of us and dive into John's subconscious. It wasn't his dream, it never was. It just seemed that way.

Heading into a perceived dreamscape with a conscious mind does tend to create a sense of surrealism. Didn't affect John tho. Everything had a sense of normalcy for him, so he was our navigator in getting back to where Sophie and Keitaro fell. From my perspective, things did look different and I couldn't say what Remington thought, although he didn't seem to mind the surroundings. He moved as if everything was normal.

Even I could remember that we were on some kind of elevated platform, a pillar that had risen way above the normal ground level. When we got there, it wasn't any pillar. It was still ravaged ground but no more than some small rise barely a foot above normal ground level. That was what I noticed first. Then I rushed over to Sophie's still disintegrating body. I didn't even think if she was alive because there was barely half her torso left, and it wasn't moving; wasn't

255

breathing. I was equally worried about Keitaro because he was hurt bad, not as badly as Sophie. I mean, I'm not trying to downplay the fact that he had his limbs blown apart and scattered to the winds. It's just that he was probably far more stable than Sophie was.

I'm making a mess of it. I don't want to play it out, who I was more worried for. It's not fair to either of them.

I checked on Sophie first while Remington checked on Keitaro. He called me over to Keitaro only because Keitaro was responsive. I did my best to reassure him that he wasn't dead or even dying, and that I would get him back to reality. John even backed me up by telling him that he was in good hands. He then went on to praise him for his 'insane courage' for standing ground against Phillip. In all, John did real good in keeping Keitaro's focus away from the bigger problem, that I had no real idea what to do with the situation at hand. I mean, I knew I wanted to get Sophie and Keitaro home, back to their own bodies and back to reality. So, that's what I got down to as best as I could manage.

Remington helped by making suggestions as to what I could do, the first couple of which I had already considered and tried, like simply reconstituting both of them – except I wasn't even sure how. And then he suggested getting into their heads to coach them from within, to have them reconstitute themselves. I wasn't even sure it was possible. The idea Remington suggested was to simply point them on the right track and help kick start the process. I gave it a shot with Keitaro.

It was a strange sensation trying to get into Keitaro's mind. I've sort of linked with him before, like when I took him to the Dream-world. The sensation I got this time felt like a part of him was more than diminished, like his mind was just as damaged as his body, even if the body in question wasn't even real to begin with. For all intents and purposes, it might have been because of the reality we were in, even if it was a mindscape, was still a reality as we perceived it. So, yeah, I managed to link up with him albeit in a diminished fashion that didn't really give us a solid link, but it was good enough to make contact.

From my perception, the reality around us simply changed. There was only me crouching over Keitaro, and his body was still damaged, but he was far more coherent and aware compared to how things were in the mindscape. He couldn't move that much though. He was aware of what happened to him and he was aware of the pain, but he could actually focus past it while we were linked in this way. I explained the plan to get him to focus on reconstituting, rebuilding his body as best as he could imagine how to. It took him a while to focus, to make the effort to literally pull himself together. I even suggested a process to imagine his arm simply growing back. I told him to imagine some scene from a movie where a body or body parts grew back, either as a CGI effect or something. I even suggested thinking about the robots from his anime series where the robots pulled themselves together from various bits. In hindsight, that last one might have been a bad idea, but that's the one he choose.

I could see his arm growing back slowly, although it started with the bone looking positively metallic, maybe even robotic. I felt he was on his way and decided to break the link, and the landscape faded into reality. I could see his arm progressing slowly, although Keitaro appeared unconscious before me. I felt a chill run through my body even as I kept watching his arm slowly come back, better than what I was trying before when I was scrambling for all the bits and pieces and trying to press them back into place. I then felt a hand on my shoulder, and I jumped. It was Remington's hand, but it made me aware that I was still jumpy; on edge. In any case, I heard Remington telling me that I had done good and to keep calm, reminding me that I still had to work with Sophie. He said that he would keep watch over Keitaro. John was asked to keep watch of our surroundings, in case Phillip came back.

John seemed confident that Phillip was gone, at least he said so. He kept watch anyway, to put me at ease. So, I turned my attention to Sophie and linked in with her like I did with Keitaro. Her situation was way worse, probably more so than before. One thing that gave me some relief was that she had learnt something for our previous experience. She wasn't entirely unconscious as I thought, but was instead in a meditative state. She had pretty much shut herself down to focus on slowing the process of her body disintegrating, but from within. I only learnt that when I linked in with her. It was quite a struggle for her actually.

I did as best not to distract her too much and once I worked out what she was doing, I did what I could to back her up first. Once that was settled and the strain on her wasn't too much, I got around to explaining what I felt she needed to do. It wasn't quite the same as last time when she was injured in my Dream-world. Different world, different rules, but some things do remain the same, I guess. John's mind, but Sophie's existence as well as Keitaro's, Remington's and mine, we were literally manifestations of our own volition, so we had a certain amount of control over our existence. We also tend to carry certain preconceptions along with us from one state of reality to the next without really establishing what rules that particular reality sometimes has. For example, we would sometimes dream we get hurt and then carry that sensation over to reality when we wake up. Or alternatively, we see what happens when a person gets shot in a movie or even real life and we carry that over to the dream. So, when we dream we get hurt in a particular way, we dream that as actually happening even when we can prevent it. In trying to work out how Phillip pulled himself together, I figure he could control his existence within a dreamscape, but I couldn't understand how he was jumping about the dreamscape of various people at any given time. That's beside the point right now.

Sophie immediately got the idea of what I was getting at and began to refocus her energies to reconstituting herself instead of slowing down her disintegration. She briefly shared her idea of how she would rebuild herself; it was actually quite detailed, like she knew a fair bit about anatomy, and then I backed her up. It's as simple as imagining an energy transfer from my body to hers or simply imagining being microscopic inside her body and rebuilding by hand. In Sophie's case, it was a far more precise process than what I had suggested to Keitaro. The end results were pretty obvious when we got back to reality almost a whole day later.

I was more than relieved to have them both back, but my relief was quickly overshadowed by Keitaro's sudden diminished capacity. He could barely feel the arm he supposedly lost and what little movement he could coax out of it caused him a great deal of pain. The rest of his body ached as well, as if he had suffered some massive trauma that wasn't readily visible. When Ms. Phillips tried to have him stand, he could barely manage it. He stood unsteadily for barely a few seconds before his legs gave way. Remington quickly moved in to help him and said that it was his mind still not completely accepting the reality that he wasn't quite as hurt as he imagined. I knew that Keitaro was mentally stronger than that. If he was having problems of such a nature, it was simply that I didn't guide him properly in healing himself. For sure, I would have to carry out some extra sessions with him, either in his own dreamscape or pull him into my Dream-world and see what we have to work with.

I only suggested something of that sort then, because I didn't really think it through at the time. I've had time to process the situation since, so I think that's my solution. I've yet to discuss this with Remington, Ms. Philliips or Keitaro. I'm not even sure if any of them would let me, but I want to try. I've got to at least try to bring him back completely like I did with Sophie.

Speaking of whom, Sophie's pretty much back to normal as far as I can tell. Ms. Phillips has run her through a full physical and even Charlie helped out in that area, particularly since he's been dealing with me. Because of that, he has a bit more experience with dealing with the after effects of my dream trips, although nothing actually like this. Still, even a little experience in that area is better than no experience at all. At least, Ms. Phillips thought so when she asked him to help out. They couldn't determine if it was an after effect that was affecting Keitaro though.

Guess I'll call it for now. I'm getting kinda tired and there's a lot for me to catch up on given how many classes I've missed. I've got a lot on my plate. I haven't even dropped in to check on Michelle and I find that I do miss her.

I guess I should at least mention something about John before I sign off. We have reached some kind of amicable respect for each other. We've had our ups and downs, and he's often been on the receiving end of some hard knocks from me. I know he'd knock me one for blaming myself, but it is because of me, or at least, his fixation on me. But I think we've reached a pretty good place in the end.

I'll still be keeping a wary eye on him though.

Aug 27

As much as I've tried to let things get back to normal, circumstances haven't really allowed that to happen. In the cafeteria, I'd notice someone, or more than one, looking at me, but when I look toward them, they'd turn away like they're trying to avoid eye contact. That's just one example; it's been that way everywhere with almost everybody, in the hallways, in class, even around the pool and the gym. Aside from my friends, practically everyone seems wary of me, like I'm some dangerous newcomer all over again.

Only today I got confirmation from Carol that people are behaving that way. Apparently, because of her proximity to me, even she was out of the loop for a while and had to probe her sources for the lowdown. It seems there's this strange, vague sensation going around among a lot of the trainees, that the major battle that happened in John's 'dreamscape' was somehow 'broadcast' to several people. It took the form of a residual nightmare for quite a few people. It turned out though that some people dreamed about the battle and some can remember me being there even though almost all of them can't really remember any actual details. It simply started with someone sharing with a friend about the nightmare he or she had, and the other would say they had the same dream, and someone overhearing would think it was a coincidence and they would check with someone else... And it spreads.

From what Carol found out almost everyone was touched by the dream in one way or another whether they actually remember having the dream or not. Dream... Nightmare... Whatever...

Helen had her own sources whose reports included some descriptions of how I supposedly appeared in those nightmares, although there were variations in the descriptions. The most common was how my eyes glowed green – might be a given since my eyes are green – and the glowing obscured most of my face, but they knew it was me. Second most common was how I had energy pulses around my hands and how I could throw energy bolts from them. Some say that I was the one who blew Keitaro's arm apart. Others know it was 'the creature' while some would say I was 'the creature' itself. But that's dreams for you. No one can be certain about what they remember once they're out of it. Still, it was enough for people to share, extrapolate and imagine what it is they actually saw. Helen admitted as much, that she had the dream as well. Given that I came out that first time after Sophie and Keitaro were injured was sometime in the afternoon, I think, it wasn't likely that the battle happened while people were asleep. But then, time fluctuates immensely in the dreamscape.

Problem is that in my mind, it was always less than a day. It's hard to tell with dreamtime because you can dream a lifetime in a nap or a mere hour in a night's sleep. So my sense of time where this is concerned is a little screwy. I thought it was going to take a couple of hours and the decision to enter John's dream during the day was to avoid problems as these. The psychic backlash obviously happened and people were probably drawn into the psychic web to share in the dream.

It's speculation on my part, of course. For all I know, maybe Phillip did plan all this anyway. His way of isolating me from a support system, but I could be over-thinking that.

At least, I can be sure I'm not paranoid. I was right; people were eyeing me and talking about me behind my back while being nervously wary of my presence. I have to hope that that's all it is and nothing more. I am aware that all this could very well jeopardise everything we've built with the networks. So far, they're still in use with Callie and Toni running one while Bastian and Kevin are getting theirs moving along with Sophie assisting them for now. Jenny is supervising Callie and Toni. I'm still in a supervisory position of making sure everything is running smoothly, tackling any problems as and when they arise. None so far, so that's good.

Anyway, I don't want to push my luck.

I've talked to Remington and Linda about my wanting to help Keitaro and they've given the go ahead to discuss my plans and intentions with him. He's been struggling a lot with most of his activities that were so natural before. He can barely even hold on to the pencil when he wants to draw, and it breaks my heart that he's that way. There has to be something I can do, but I have to talk to him first.

I'm signing off for now.

Aug 30

Following up on one thing from last time, we've been pretty lucky so far that there have been a few questions about the still ongoing nightmares and its influence on the network. The team has been able to handle the questions and keep our volunteers and participants calm. The network sessions are still going on, even if I'm not an active participant anymore. I still 'log in' once in a while to check the connections and help watch for 'leaks' although that is a rarity these days.

So stepping back a bit on that; yes, the nightmares are still going around although John says he hasn't had any bad dreams lately. Add to that the critters that are still appearing. I've snared two over the last week while Will has come across one more. The little zoo Ms. Phillips started to observe and study these critters has had some strange activity. While there have been no breakouts as far as we can tell, some of the critters have vanished from their locked and secured cubes, as if they never came into existence in the first place.

I'm pretty sure it's not me giving these critters any form of existence in our reality. These are creatures of dreams, so for them to manifest in our reality, somebody has to acknowledge their impossibility for them to actually exist; to believe in them. In effect, they have to will these critters into existence. Chances are, the critters vanishing could be related to some people not having nightmares. I'm guessing that as long as the nightmares continue, the critters associated with the dreamer will continue to exist. If it does work that way, we could put the critters on display and find out which creature belongs to whom. It is just a guess though.

These nightmares have to be related to Phillip somehow, although in sharing my thoughts with Becca, she reminded me that the nightmares actually started out differently; they started out with Michelle supposedly jumping about from dreamer to dreamer. We never really determined what sparked that one off, but it did get me to thinking about it all. It wasn't something I even considered at any time, about Michelle being the initiating event to all this.

I dropped by the Dreaming to check up on her and thankfully, nothing has changed. She's getting along fine, Kinstein is able to keep his patrons under control and his Kitchen is still neutral territory. And after everything

I've done for the denizens within the Dreaming, they know better than to go after Michelle and tick me off. I wish she would open up and talk to me though. I really need some answers about her and I still haven't been able to find Old Crans.

Now, as to the problem with Keitaro. We're going to link up later tonight and then we're going to see what we can do to get him back to normal. The main obstacle is basically how much a fix he has on reality through perception. Sometimes an idea gets into our head and, sometimes, because of our perception of reality and its physical rules, we find it difficult to exert a force of change on those things. Will have to see how hard a grip Keitaro has on reality, even in his imagination.

So, I guess I should get going then. Will report back later on what happens next.

SEPTEMBER

Sep 1

So I guess I should get to writing about what happened with Keitaro. I figured since this problem started in what was thought to be John's dreamscape, it could be fixed in Keitaro's dreamscape. What we pulled off was more a state of deep meditation than actual dreaming. We didn't have anyone else with us. No back-up from Sophie or any support from Keiko or any of our friends. I did learn that Walker dropped by to check up on our progress although I was deep in Keitaro's mind by then.

Anyway, once Keitaro was in his deep meditative state, I linked into his mind and went in search of his 'self'. I'm not sure how long it took me to find him, but when I thought I did, he was in some kind of zen garden practicing with a katana. From a distance he appeared almost normal but when I moved closer towards him, it didn't quite appear to be him. It was more like an idealised version, the kind where we see an ideal version of ourselves when we dream. I looked around and then noticed another idealised version of himself practicing with a Japanese bow and arrow.

To me, it was like a setting out of a Japanese movie that showed an idyllic life of a samurai. I did wonder if this was what Keitaro focused on. There was no distortion of reality that you would normally find in dreams. Everything was actually quite steady and coherent. I wandered about the area a little more in trying to find the actual Keitaro.

I eventually found him in a nearby shrine; well, a shrine from the outside but something else inside, which appeared much larger. On the inside, it looked like it was part old-fashioned meditation shrine and part modern hall with white walls. He appeared to be meditating at first, but I could see that he was still trying to reconstruct parts of his body. There was this disturbing mixture of flesh with somewhat metallic, maybe even robotic, prosthesis. At least, it looked like prosthesis that was not melding with flesh as well as it could. It looked like parts of the metal was slowly melting away and pulling the flesh with it.

I was cautious in approaching him because I could see that he was still in pain. I mean, it didn't really show but there was a sense of it. I carefully knelt beside him and then noticed that my clothes had changed to something a little more traditional to accommodate the shrine. It was something like my *keikogi*, but seemed less formal. When I turned to look towards him, he wasn't beside me but across, about fifty feet away, facing me. And we weren't facing the shrine, like the whole room shifted just that little bit. That was when he acknowledged my presence by commenting that he had been waiting a long while for me to turn up. I could see it in his appearance, and the inflection in his voice, that he was straining to hold himself together.

"I'm here to help, remember?" I said.

"I remember," he said. "Where do we start?"

"Can you move?"

He shook his head.

"I'm coming over to you, okay?"

I waited, but he didn't really reply. I got up and moved towards him. I couldn't get any closer than the fifty feet that separated us no matter how many steps I took towards him. It was like walking on an invisible treadmill so it didn't matter if I sped up or slowed down. He had to agree to let me get close. So, I ended up maintaining a steady pace, to show I wasn't going to give up so easily. I also added, "You have to let me get close, Keitaro."

Once he nodded, I made some progress. When I reached him, I knelt before him. It took a moment more before I decided to bow and said, "*onegai shimasu*", the same way I would do during kendo practice. It seemed appropriate to pay homage to him in his place of power. Even if that weren't entirely true, he is one of my kendo teachers, and I can come up with a dozen excuses to do that, but mainly to humour him and keep him happy. If anything, that attempt in getting to him proved that he could control my actions to a fault. I had to at least have some kind of cooperation between us. I did as best to explain what I was intending to do, to guide him in his healing process; or at least put him on the right path.

I asked why he did what he did; trying to put in metallic robotic parts instead of imagining his limbs growing back. He thought that when I told him to, "make yourself better," it meant exactly what I said. He thought he was supposed to do that literally. And being the mecha fan that he is, making himself better was to be part mecha. While he could conceive the design of what he wanted to achieve, he was also aware that he didn't quite have the technical skill to pull off what he wanted. So I asked if he wanted to continue with his idea or try to revert to normal. I added that in either case, I couldn't guarantee it would work. He had to want it. It was his mindscape; his world, his rules. He had to break his own perceptions of reality within his own mind;

not the easiest thing to do. I could only guide him in this, I couldn't take him all the way.

I won't say which choice he made, that's his own decision, but once he was ready, I took him through the process of freeing his perception from reality. I began by showing him exactly what I meant about the process of healing within the mindscape; I pulled out a knife and proceeded to cut off my last finger on my right hand. While I could block off most of the pain, it still hurt, and of course, he protested but didn't have much time to actually do anything before I sliced off the top half of my finger.

I then picked up that top half – there was no bleeding simply because I decided not to have any blood gushing. I got him to hold his attention on my finger as I put the severed piece back in its place and let the cut heal. While it was meant to serve as an example, this little act did impair my finger back in the real world. It's not like I use it a lot though. Even when I'm typing, it's my least used finger, and in case no one else is aware, I am left-handed. I could wiggle my finger to show him that I had cut it off and had reattached it. I stressed it was only possible within that environment, and that he could do exactly the same for himself with his wounds, and that I would guide him through it, as best as I could manage.

I took his hands in mine and focused on them healing back to normal. In a way I was basically exerting a kind of energy from within me, through my hands and into his hands that would then start forming back into what they would normally look. It only worked a little bit and even then, the form couldn't really hold and it slowly reverted back to its mangled and semi-demolished, part metallic appearance.

"You can find it within yourself to take it all the way," I said. He said he would try. This was one of those cases that trying wasn't going to be enough, but it was a start. If it was going to be permanent, he needed to be fully committed to the healing process.

I kept talking him through the process, simply to keep him on track with his focus. It took a long time, and that's in an environment where time had no meaning or frame of measurement. I couldn't really tell how long we took, but it was over a day on the outside. By the end of the long process, we managed to get him his arms and legs formed. Parts of his body still needed work and because this was the extent of what we did on this round, it didn't mean that he was back to normal. The chances of that were slim because it had to depend on him.

Even with my own skills, my finger hurt like heck when I woke up. I was constantly rubbing it while being debriefed by Ms. Phillips and Remington.

Remington noticed what I was doing and asked me about it. I didn't really go into detail to explain everything, and he didn't comment. At this time, it's still hurting and there is still some limited movement, but again, it's not like I paid much attention to how I was using it before. I will be keeping an eye on Keitaro over these next few days to check on his progress. He could flex his fingers albeit with some effort and pain, but it was slightly better than before. I told him that it was going to be a slow process, but how fast the healing was going would still depend on him.

"You have a strong spirit, Keitaro," I said. "You can do this, but it will take some time. Just focus on the healing process as you go to sleep and try to be aware when you're in your dream." I didn't tell him that was the hardest part, but I did give him some pointers on how to determine when he was actually dreaming. It takes a while to come to terms with the dream environment. If you don't believe me, try figuring it out yourself when you go to sleep tonight. You have to remember though that when I linked in to Keitaro's mind, he was the one in deep meditation while I was conscious. Even if he fell asleep during our session, I was awake and aware while being in his mind. He and Sophie did the same when they consciously entered John's 'dream' to help me.

Anyway, I'm kinda worn right now and I could do with some real sleep of my own, except that my finger is really screaming for attention.

Sep 4

With everything else going on and dealing with Keitaro, not to mention that things are pretty much at the new normal – some bad dreams being shared and the occasional critter being sighted, if not caught – I've been keeping myself busy with studies, projects and such. It's mostly to keep my mind off the fact that I miss Mikey something fierce. It's been a real long while since I last saw him and while Linda has been letting me get the occasional update from home about his progress, it's not enough. I don't even know if he's actually missing me as much; even Karen doesn't know.

So, taking a step back from all this self-importance that has permeated this journal, I'll catch up a little on the others in my life around here. To be fair, it's not all about me, right? Sure, it's my journal and I just don't want to focus on me for today.

First up, Keitaro appears to be doing better these last couple of days, gaining back some motor skills and the obvious pain he used to express has subsided.

He is able to hold a pencil again, but like a stroke victim, he has to start over retraining himself in some of the simple tasks that are second nature to us. His sister, Keiko, has been helping him through some stuff and I did offer to help further, but they refused. Honestly, I'm not even sure where their suite is.

I guess Keitaro is managing his healing process because I can see his progress over the last couple of days. It's most obvious when we're in the gym and practising kendo. His grip on his *shinai* is getting strong and his swings are getting stronger in comparison to last week when he could barely hold the *shinai*, much less swing it.

Keiko, on the other hand, does get frustrated a little, depending on how cooperative Keitaro gets. She's been taking her frustration out on me, either in kendo practice and sparring, or plain hand to hand combat sparring. I take it though, because I knew what it was all about when she started getting tough over the last few days, especially with me. But it's only in training though, not outside the gym. She's about normal and a little cheerful that her brother is on the mend when we're at lunch.

Speaking of them, given how I've been concerned about Keitaro, the rumours have started to naturally lean in that direction. There have been reports of John's jealous rage and how Walker is internalising in his usual quiet way, none of which happened as far as I know. John's doing fine as I've caught up with him at the gym, while Walker... I'll get to him in a while. Carol's attitude towards the rumours has changed, probably since she found that she could fall out of the loop through sheer proximity to me.

Helen, on the other hand, has her own sources but she hardly shares anything with me unless it's to either agree or disagree with Carol. She does lean more to my defence. She's often checking out the newcomers every six months and then shares what she learns with us. She also invites them to our table once in a while and then we use what we learn as conversation starters. Honestly, unless the newcomers are either a TP or a TK, my interest level kinda bottoms out. I do try to learn about them when they're with us, but not a lot sticks lately.

Between Carol and Helen, we've got a pretty good grasp of social news around The Facility's trainees. It's not necessarily my thing, having been the subject of those rumours for so long.

Callie and Toni join us once in a while, but they have their own little group. Sometimes, Jo will be with them when they join us, but she's still a little wary of me – probably a little more so these days – and she tries to keep her distance. It's probably those rumours that she's picked up, but given recent events, I really wouldn't blame her if she stays away for a while.

The classes have been moving along smoothly with our Network volunteers still sticking by us. There was a sense of wariness before, but so far, the two active learning networks are running with full complements. That's really thanks to John who's been a huge champion of the network. The other TP trainees, who are not involved with the learning networks, are also in various stages of developing their skills. Ethan is still not directly involved there, but I'm working having him be a kind of watchdog, watching for leaks and problems as I used to do. It's a slow step in having him test the boundaries of his TP abilities.

Miss Tracy is also keeping me busy, helping out in the TK training. I am still uneasy with some of the 'skills practice' that we've been doing, but the others are equally aware of the dangers in the application of these little skills we're perfecting.

Moving on to those a little closer to me than most, and not to say the others aren't important – they are – but Becca's been my closest confidant all the time I've been at The Facility. So, it's a little more than heartbreaking to acknowledge that she will be leaving for home by the end of the year. It's odd though because she's been at The Facility for even less time than say, Ehrmer or even Walker. But her 'training' has been more of a cultural exchange than the kind of technological exchange that Ehrmer and Walker provide. The three years, eventful as they have been, have flown by.

We're still spending our evenings together catching up and sharing bits about our lives and troubles. She still speaks English to me and I talk to her in her language. When she leaves, I'll be watching over her mentee, Kadi. I've noticed that while Kadi does speak the same language as I've been learning from Becca, she's got an accent. My 'accent' is even odder to both Becca and Kadi.

I've shared my concerns and problems with Becca and she's done likewise, although she's had more answers for me than I've had for her. She has watched out for me more than I have done for her and I truly wish I could do more. She keeps saying that I would only repay her when she would not be around, and I know she's referring to Kadi, although she's never really said anything to that effect.

And then there's Walker. Throughout this year, he's been my rock and my solitude. He gives of himself so much and he's been supportive, taking care of me in all the dark moments. I don't know how to repay him and I haven't been able to work out what to do. He's still there for me every day and like Becca, I've learnt things from him that I will need to pass on some time down the line. He will be on his 'retreat' soon and I will have to continue training Sunee and Corogi in aqua-acrobatics. They're coming along cohesively as a team and I am amazed at Corogi's abilities in the water, given that she has admitted to not being comfortable with the medium, coming from a highland community.

Sometimes, I do wonder about taking the next step with Walker. Given how things turned out the last time I got into a serious relationship, I am a little wary. It's not like we're not in a serious place now. I mean, we're in a good place; we're together. He's been there for me so much this past year, but at the same time, we're so aware of what's in store for us should we move to the next level. Like Becca, he'll have to leave and go home. I thought it was within this year, but then he went to work with the IASC for that period and…

If he leaves, could I go with him?

Would I go with him? Leave everything here behind, including Mikey?

When we look at stories of love and romance, we normally see the moments; the good parts or the bad parts, the parts that would make or break the relationship; the forces that would drive a couple apart or bring them together stronger than ever. They happen in such 'closed spaces' sometimes that we don't see outside influences, and we hardly ever see 'what happens next' that comes beyond 'happily ever after'.

My life in this Facility is like living in a 'closed space', but the influences that shaped me before I got here are still out there beyond this space. They still affect my life even though I don't see them. Of course, there are those within this space that affect my life as it is right now, be they friends, rivals or other people with their own agenda. That's the variety of life, isn't it? Never easy, never perfect; a hodgepodge of moments that get strung together by all the seconds and other moments in between. We get to pick and choose what we want to remember.

I know I should be writing more about Walker, but not right now. As much as we've been together and learned about each other, he's still a quiet and private individual. His focus is mostly on his work, as long as I don't interrupt it – which I do on occasion. I would say that he does know me a lot better than I know him, but we really haven't dug that deep into each other. For now, that's about it.

Sep 7

It's about half three in the morning and it's not like there's anything particularly pressing that needs to be written down. I just can't get back to sleep and I'm not in any particular mood to study or tinker or watch TV. Besides, I don't want to wake Becca accidentally.

I went for a quick walk, sat by the calm pool for a while, watching the few lights around, dimly reflecting off the still watery surface. I then shuffled over to the little garden for a while. I considered dropping by the cafe, but wasn't in the mood to snack (shocker, I know), and I passed by Operations Center. I greeted some of techs whom I haven't seen in a while. I didn't see Tommy and I wasn't really supposed to be there without permission at the moment. In any case, I didn't feel like staying. That's when I headed back to my room. Sure there were other options like taking a simulated flight, or tinkering on my rocket design or even on Colleen.

Okay, that's a whole load of nothing there. Not that there's nothing to write about; I did take a trip to my Dream-world with Walker coming along. It wasn't planned. He asked at lunch on Saturday if I could do with some company, and I was more than eager to have him along. It's no big deal that he came along; it's that he's never asked before.

To briefly cover the trip, we headed in around half two, after lunch. We caught up with Kinstein first, and then I met Michelle. Mikey still hasn't showed up for a while now according to Kinstein, and as I mentioned before, I really miss him. I could pull him in, but I wouldn't do that to him, if he really doesn't want to go there.

The three of us helped out at a village, it wasn't a creature attack for once, just a busted dam that resulted in a little water shortage. Michelle used her mecha to help with the rocks while I used my TK to control the water flow. Walker got the villagers working with him while doing a little redesigning on the dam to make it work better, even installing a kind of filter system to ensure the water would be that little bit cleaner. It wasn't a big deal kind of job, much like what I used to do before the creatures were so rampant. All things considered, this was pretty lightweight and we were finished in no time.

After that, we headed to the little hut out on the water. I think that was why he wanted to come along; to experience swimming in a vast body of water that simulated a sea of sorts; mostly created from what he had shared with me before about his home. He swam out to the hut, carrying Michelle on his back. I could clearly hear her laughing, but she still didn't say anything throughout the evening, night and morning we were at the hut. It was nice to hear her laugh, though and that's something else Walker's given me, even if it was by accident. Michelle loves the water and she spent a lot of time in it with Walker and me. Maybe her love for the water came from me... but that's speculation – even if I want to think it that way.

We headed back to the Kitchen sometime in the afternoon, and as I dropped off Michelle with Kinstein, he told me that there was still no sign of Mikey. I was bummed by that.

By the time Walker and I woke up in the Infirmary, it was a good nine hours since we started. We had a late dinner together and skipped the pool – probably a rarity for him. I ended up spending the night with him at his suite although I only slept for an hour or so. I lay there next to him for a while, maybe it was an hour or so before I got up and ended up watching some TV at his place with the volume so low I was watching mimes. I didn't want to leave him like I occasionally have when I spent the night at his place. Simply because I can't get back to sleep and it was pointless for me to lie there in bed. I would end up fidgeting until he woke up, not that it has happened that way. He also understood the situation where my sleeping issues were concerned and he has said that he didn't mind if I left in the middle of the night. I would usually catch up with him at the pool in the morning anyway. But I stayed this time, until he woke up and we headed off to the pool together.

Sunday was mostly spent catching up on my studies, doing reviews and such. I caught up with Ethan to follow up on his progress; this has become a typical Sunday activity and it's usually before he goes off on his own Dreaming session. I also checked in with Remington to review the progress of the Learning Network and how everyone else is doing there. He asked if things were going okay with the training and with Linda in particular. It was only then that I realised I hadn't met her for a monthly review over the last week. Don't know if she forgot, because she's usually the one who calls for the meeting.

Then there was the kendo practice and a little sparring. Dinner was with Becca and Sophie followed with a dip in the pool – not right after dinner, but a little later. Walker and I parted ways a little before half past midnight and I was a little zonked, so I crashed into bed once I got back to my room. I woke up a little over an hour later and, well... we're back at the beginning. And it's still early...

I dunno, my mood's not really there.
I'm signing off for now and maybe I'll go chat with Colleen for a while.

Sep 25

If you were to ask, I'm utterly drained. It's been a long while since my last update simply because... Well, I decided to act on this crazy situation and... I... Things got away from me.

I really tried to do the right thing, and things got away from me. Right now, I'm under review for my actions and the consequences. They're deciding if it would be safe for me to continue at The Facility. I've been isolated, but at least I'm confined to my suite instead of some other room like last time. Meals are being delivered, usually by Becca who keeps me company when I feel like eating. Aside from Becca, only Walker, Sophie and John have come by to see me. I guess the others might be scared of me and I wouldn't blame them. The one person I need to talk to is the one person who is actively avoiding me, and I don't blame her. She may never want to talk to me, or even want to see me, ever again.

Honestly, I've barely left my own room and it was Becca, probably with Remington's coaxing, who suggested I get to writing things down. Before that, I was wallowing and crying and have been overly depressed to the point of immobility. Walker's been having the unenviable task of keeping me in check, keeping me from blaming myself too much, and he's been the rock I asked him to be. I told him it wouldn't be easy if what was to happen did happen. We never anticipated this. I know it seems to be a constant state of being for me over these last few months, this state of depression and sadness. But this... hurt...

It's more so these last few days. I just can't get over...

I should start at the beginning, as best as I can recall. It seems so long ago now...

Sept 8 – 12

While it seemed that things weren't as bad as they appeared, Ms. Phillips had been tracking the nightmare cases. I didn't really know about it. I found out by accident, when Bastian brought it up with me before the network practice that day. I never knew he was having nightmares, as well having problems sleeping. He checked in at the Infirmary and when he talked to Ms. Phillips directly, she started asking specific questions as to the nature of his dreams.

While his concern was more towards the possible effects of the bad dreams impacting on the network, I did get him to talk about his session with Ms. Phillips. His dreams switched between two locations: the dark halls of The Facility where the shadows were more than daunting; and a dark forest filled with strange creatures stalking him. Ms. Phillips showed him the menagerie of critters and asked if any of them appeared familiar. He identified a couple and asked where they came from. She told him that I caught most of them. That gave him reason to ask me about the nightmares, particularly if the creatures came from me and onto the network.

As much as I've monitored the network, there was no sign of any such occurrence and I told him so. Sophie had been my double check, and she didn't detect anything that might have come from me. In any case, this little chat led me to inquire with Ms. Phillips about how widespread the nightmare problem was. Not everyone was sharing that particular information with me, even among my friends. I only managed to catch up with her the next day after dinner. She wasn't available throughout the day. She wasn't too willing to share any details at first but after I argued that there may be concerns about our volunteers possibly having nightmares while being on the network, I needed to know who might be a potential problem.

According to her, it was estimated that almost seventy percent of The Facility's trainees were experiencing sleeping problems of one kind or another, and almost eighty percent of that were experiencing similar nightmares as a cause. She then said that if there was going to be a problem with the network, it would have cropped up by then.

She reckoned my Dream-world was somehow tied to all this in some way. She admitted she was speculating, but there was the feeling that I was somehow tied to all this. The main connection was the critters.

I wrote before that Ethan recognised some of the critters from his Dream-world, but I never mentioned it to anyone else. It was Remington who shared that bit of information with Ms. Phillips That was proof enough for her to connect the problematic dreams and critters to me, especially since I had a hand in helping Ethan establish his Dream-world.

It felt like she laid the fault on me, but immediately said that her statements in no way suggested any of these things were my fault. I felt I needed to do something about it. Whether it was my fault or not, I felt I had a responsibility in tackling the problem.

Keep in mind though that normal activities and classes were still going on. It took me a day or so to ascertain what I needed to do. I knew I had to approach this from my Dream-world and I was going to have to cross over into Ethan's world. He mentioned that someone else told him about the critters, so that's the individual I needed to find. I was really hoping then that it wouldn't be Phillip.

I kept talking things out with Walker and Sophie on different occasions, figuring out a few angles and scenarios. Sophie was the one who got help from Ethan in creating her world. I needed to get more than an inkling of what to expect, but even she had not been to his world. That was about as much as I got from Sophie at the time. She didn't question my sudden curiosity about Ethan's Dream-world or why I didn't even approach Ethan directly. I was a little hesitant about approaching Ethan simply because if he was in contact with this spook, I didn't want to tip the spook that I was coming for him.

And Walker was a problem solver. If I gave him enough information about what I could expect, he could postulate possible scenarios and solutions, but the fluid nature of the Dream-world posed too many unknown variables. There was a point when even his scenarios got him worried enough that he wanted, almost insisted that he accompany me into the Dream-world. I had considered it at first but he was the last person I wanted with me on this. He had always preferred to think his way out of a problem and he's never really shown any inclination to fighting. Chances were, that was most likely what I was heading into.

So I told him, "I need you out here. I need you out here in case things go so wrong. You're my anchor. You're my way back. That's going to be so much harder than following me in."

He understood what I was getting at, and agreed to my terms. He still insisted I have some back-up, and even suggested I ask John for help. His reason was that if I was going to run into Phillip, John's the first person we knew who got Phillip to back down. I told him that only happened in John's dreamscape, not my Dream-world where the rules would be different.

"Teach him," was his suggestion.

"It would take time," I said.

"He's proven to be a fast learner, and he's somehow more adept at the Learning Network than others."

It was true that John had proven to be intuitive when it came to things involving the TP landscape, so I agreed to talk to John. It would be interesting to see his skills in a world where anything was possible. Since all that took place at poolside way after our swim (and the pool area was empty by then), I had time to catch up with John at the café later, which was…

Sept 13

It was a couple of hours before John to turned up around half three in the morning. I was banking on him being back to normal since we took care of his dream problems, which meant that he would be doing his work until roughly two or three in the morning before taking a light snack and turning in for the night. I told him what I intended to do and why I 'felt' I needed him with me.

He was hesitant for barely a moment – but he was hesitant – before he agreed to have my back. He didn't give any reason for agreeing and I didn't ask. I always believed he would have a motive for agreeing to do anything I asked of him, and I did have a sense that he would ask something of me later. Until now, he hasn't asked for anything though.

I should have also told him to keep things quiet because I found out in an awkward way that he went to consult Sophie about the dynamics of the Dreaming and what he could expect of himself once he got there. Naturally he also told her that I had asked him to help me out, which didn't sit too well with Sophie, who felt left out. She confronted me about it during lunch and my little secret plans came spilling out to everyone. I mean, when I was talking to her about Ethan's Dream-world, I didn't exactly tell her what I was planning to do. She called me crazy, saying it was an unreasonable risk I was taking having John as my back-up. I stressed that given what happened to her and Keitaro, I really didn't want anyone else to get hurt.

"That guy may be magic in there, but I've picked a few tricks of my own since he caught me off guard," she said, and went on to remind me that she was attacked when her back was turned during our last encounter with Phillip.

I stressed that Phillip was not above 'hitting below the belt', if it suited him. After all, in my first encounter with him, the bastard ran a sword through me from behind. And he's probably learnt a whole new bag of dirty tricks since then. It was beyond me how he did what he did to Sophie and Keitaro. I was lucky I could get them back at all, granted in a diminished capacity where Keitaro was concerned.

In any case, Sophie insisted she was coming along one way or another. It meant that if I said, "No," she would drop in on her own anyway; she could do that without me. After all, she learnt how to do it from me.

The bigger problem then was that once she insisted on coming with me, Keitaro and Helen insisted as on accompanying me as well; they were at the lunch table as usual. Needless to say, I was extremely reluctant to have Keitaro along much less Helen, or more likely, Hank. I could keep them out if I wanted, except Sophie thought it would be good to have them along. So even if I decided not to bring them in with me, she would do it herself. She insisted Keitaro deserved a chance at payback, and not hide away in pain, more so since he would be in prime condition within the Dreaming, and capable of providing some support. While I couldn't argue with that, I did have one little advantage on my side. I told them that everything was only in a planning stage and I wasn't quite sure when I was going to go in. After all, I did drop by the Dreaming the day before for my weekly trip visiting Michelle.

In saying that I didn't know when I was planning to make the actual trip, I was telling the truth, and Sophie verified it. I expected she would stoop to sensing if I would lie or not in that respect. She did make me confirm that I would tell her when I was ready to make the trip, and she held me to that. Before anything else then, I got a call on my comms from Linda. I figured sooner or later, it was going to happen.

So after lunch, I headed over to her office, and sure enough, Remington was there as well. I guess when I start making plans of such sort, it wasn't going to escape their attention. Once I took the centre seat, Remington started by asking what was going through my head, reminding me that despite everything that has happened, none of it was my fault. I didn't need to take any kind of responsibility or action on my part, or so he said. I responded by saying that in some small part, I was responsible for some of the recent problems with the nightmares and critters. Probably more so if Phillip was truly behind all of it.

Remington wanted to focus more on my proposed action, so I shared my basic plan with them. It wasn't much different from what they already knew based on the surveillance data they were given. Simply, it was to go into the Dreaming, hop over to Ethan's world and find the spook who's been in some way teaching Ethan about his own world.

It was just that. It should have been that simple.

Remington asked if I had any precautions planned and I told him about having John along, while Sophie and the others volunteered. I also stressed to him and Linda that I didn't want them along given what happened last time. I know I keep repeating this, but this is what happens when you need to share your plans and reasons with different people at different times. If the spook wasn't Phillip, there wasn't much else to worry about. But if it was Phillip, I had concerns, because I felt I could barely take him down without resorting to some actions I'd rather avoid.

Linda asked about having controlled conditions, and I honestly couldn't think of any way to have that. Since Sophie admitted that she hadn't been into Ethan's Dream-world, we were going in blind. The little bit I know from my one visit is like knowing one baseball diamond in Central Park and not seeing the rest, much less the entire city beyond it. The situation as it was then still presented too many variables, and that was one of those things that even Walker was worried about. Given that, Remington wasn't keen on letting me go through with my plan, but he also knew that by telling me not to do it wasn't going to stop me in any way. "You're too much like your mother in that respect," he said with a smirk. "You did the same thing three years ago and you remember how that turned out for you?" This was followed by a really uncomfortable moment of silence.

"If it's going to be as dangerous as you think, you know you can't even guarantee anyone's safety," he finally said, breaking the silence. I stressed again that I really didn't want anyone else with me on this and he reminded me that I wasn't going to be able to hold them back, just as he wasn't going to be able to stop me. "It's the quality of your friends, Jeannie. You've got to convince them of the danger. They have to know the risks. They have to know what's at stake and what the cost might be. After that, you do your best. Understand?"

I did as he told me, and really tried to make things sound as scary as possible when I caught up with the others after my meeting with Linda and Remington. This was a rare occasion because we never got together at night as a group. It was always lunch when we would gather. Anyway, for Sophie and Keitaro, scary and dangerous was all the more reason for them to back me up, despite my worst fears. Helen was apprehensive, but was still keen on coming along. Sophie brought up the issue of involving Ethan, and I told her that it was better if he wasn't included. I decided there and then that I would go in the next night. It would give everyone a day to prepare. It would also give me a day to try to convince the others to not follow me in.

Sept 14

Of course, even with Walker's help, as well as Becca backing me, no one backed down.

My concentration in classes wavered throughout the day; my focus wasn't quite there. I reached out to Keiko hoping she could persuade Keitaro to step away, but said that she never did have any control over his actions. The most she could do was advise him, but he was dead set on helping me in any way he could. I stressed again about the dangers and the possibility his condition could worsen.

She only nodded without saying anything. I know she holds me responsible for what happened to Keitaro, and it was evident in our kendo *keiko* or even our normal sparring sessions. She's been taking out whatever frustrations bottled in her out on me, and I've been feeling it too. We left it at that and I did hope she would get Keitaro to not come with me. I had decided not to take him in with me and I did try to persuade Sophie to do likewise, even if he insisted. But she had promised not to leave him behind.

The only person I still intended to bring with me into the Dreaming at that time was John; Sophie knew that. Of course, in hindsight, I could have handled things better. I could have taken her and John in with me at the beginning, and that would have prevented her from bringing the others in, but I didn't think of that at the time. It didn't even occur to me to consider that until we were in the Dreaming, when it was too late. And the one thing I could have done, should have done – call it all off – was the one thing I didn't do. And because of that, I am responsible for everything that happened next.

It was about ten at night when I made contact with John as previously arranged. We were in our own rooms by then, since I decided not to use the Infirmary for this trip. Once he confirmed he was ready and in bed, just so he wasn't going to collapse in some awkward place when I pulled him into the Dreaming with me, I got to it. I expected some of the other TPs to sense my activity. We can't help but notice, but unlike Jenny, they wouldn't really have any sense of the exchange between John and me. I also knew this was the trigger that would set Sophie rounding up the others who she would pull in after me.

I linked up with John and dived into my Dream-world, pulling him along. For him, it was like closing his eyes one moment, opening them again within the Dreaming and looking at some medieval tavern in the middle of a clearing of a forest. He wasn't quite prepared for the transition; few are on their first trip. It took him a while to orient himself. Once I assured him that everything was okay, his nerves eased up a bit. While I had imagined him in some simple clothes suited to the environment – shirt, slacks, boots and for some weird reason, a cloak – I told him he could change his appearance to suit himself. He decided to let it be, saying it felt comfortable enough.

We didn't head into the Kitchen, but into the forest in the general direction of Ethan's lands. I did a lot of explaining along the way about how the Dreaming world worked and what he would be capable of doing, to a certain extent. He was curious enough to ask how Phillip could be 'breaking' the rules and doing anything he wanted if there were such limitations within the Dream-world. I didn't really have an answer, but John intuitively realised that said rules of the Dreaming were simply my own, imposed by myself to keep me in check.

"If you truly wanted to, you could break your own rules and take this guy out. You don't really need me or any back-up," he said. "After all, this is your world. You can do anything you want."

"Part of it is that I don't lose control," I said.

"If you can't let loose in here where everything is as contained as you say, where can you let loose?"

"It's not that simple," I said. I went on to explain what happened the last few times I faced Phillip, letting loose with my powers and abilities, and the darkness of my acts, and the price that had to be paid.

"You're over-thinking it," he said. "I'm sure one thing didn't really have to do with the other."

"You didn't go through any of it, so you don't know," I said. "You don't know what it's like to live with these kinds of mistakes that can ruin other people's lives."

"Maybe I have lived through exactly that, but decided to not let it get me down. What's done is in the past, and we've got to live in the now for the future," he said.

"Maybe that's where we're just different," I said.

With that, he stopped in his tracks and said, "Send me back."

I turned to face him. "What?"

"You've got me here to do your dirty work, to fight this Phillip guy only because you're too much of a chicken to face him yourself. That's only because you're afraid to do what you have to do. So you got me along to do... what? Take him down? Beat him up? Kill him?"

"It's not... I don't want you to kill him!" I said. "I don't know what I have to do with this guy, but I've got to do something. Maybe he's responsible for all the nightmares, maybe he's not; I don't know. I don't know what's going to happen when we get where we're going. I just need you to help keep me in check."

"Any of your other friends could have done that."

"Maybe so, but they aren't fighters like you are," I admitted. "In here, they're playing heroes, but that won't cut it against this guy. I tried to warn them off, but I know they're coming after us as well."

"In which case, we're back where we started. You have to step up to do what needs to be done," he said.

"That's what I'm trying to do," I said. "I know I can't do it alone. I..."

"You're really not good at asking for help, are you?"

I shook my head. "I have major trust issues when it comes to situations like these."

"Then say it or send me back."

I really felt like I was put on the spot then and there. Admittedly, I didn't ask him before. I told him that I wanted to take him into the Dreaming to possibly take care of the nightmare problem, and that he might be the key to solving it. Since I helped him before, I presumed he was eager to help, and he did agree to accompany me. With this, he actually had me figured to an extent. It was with some difficulty on my part when I finally said it, "Will you help me?"

He smirked and shook his head. "You've got me here already, chickadee." He picked up his pace, walking past me, continuing on the path we were on. "And you suck at asking for help."

As we continued our little trek, I continued to explain the ways in which he could manipulate his appearance. He tried out a few things on the fly, like changing the colour of his cloak, or the type of boots he was wearing, all the while we were walking and talking. He didn't ask to stop or pause to try out something. For instance, he asked about weapons and I asked him what he would have preferred, and he simply brought his hand out from under the cloak handling a dagger with a beautifully crafted handle. He played with it briefly, twirling and juggling it deftly in one hand and, just as quickly, pulled it back into the cloak.

I was impressed by his skill at handling the blade and even thought he might be better than Rick. Of course, I'd have to see how he handles the blade in reality, to be sure. Throughout our little sojourn, John quickly developed and honed some skills at a rate that amazed me. He's a really quick learner, and it made me consider that maybe his successes with the Learning Network may not be quite the oddity or fluke we always thought. I already know he's quite intuitive when it comes to our TP activities, but when he pulls off something like this, adjusting so comfortably within my Dream-world, the possibility of him being a latent TP came to mind again.

By the time we reached the base of the mountain, John's confidence about his abilities was palpable. His clothes had also changed subtly from what he started out with, although he kept the cloak. When I asked him about it, he said it was handy. I shrugged and said that it looked odd on him. That's when he pulled out this hat from under the cloak. When he put it on, the ensemble actually looked good on him. That air of confidence more than doubled and there was an aura of mystery with the get-up. It reminded me of some movie character, the visual of it; I couldn't be sure what character in which movie.

He looked up the mountain's slope and asked if we had to climb. I said there was a faster way and asked for his hand. He was suspicious, pausing a moment before slowly and reluctantly letting me take his hand. Once I took his hand, I asked if he was scared of heights. He shook his head, "I don't think so. Otherwise I wouldn't be living and training in a high-rise."

"Well, yeah, but you don't look out the windows and look down often, do you? As far as you know, The Facility could be no more than three floors high," I said.

He conceded the point and realised why I asked about a fear of heights when I started to float off the ground. To his credit, he didn't show any hint of panic or worry... or even excitement. He asked why we didn't do this bit earlier. I explained that there wasn't a real need for it earlier and we needed the time to let him get used to his surroundings and abilities.

He seemed nonchalant about my answer. As I took us higher, he looked down until we cleared the trees, and then he looked up at me. It was a while before I noticed that he was looking beyond me and up at the mountain. I turned my gaze from him, following his gaze upward at the mountain that towered over us. I picked up the pace and we were more than flying up the side of a mountain.

I noticed the various caves on the mountainside that looked cold and empty. I had to wonder if the creatures had truly come this way before or if what I had been told was wrong all along. This mountain range separated my Dream-world from Ethan's. Did the creatures and critters roaming about use these caves to cross over? It was a little cursory thought that crossed my mind then, but I didn't dwell on it.

It took minutes, or what passes for minutes in a dream reality, for us to reach the top, or rather high enough to cross over into Ethan's Dream-world. There was a plateau where we could land and survey what was before us. It wasn't quite what I had seen before because it changes every time, but it was generally a countryside that had some dense forests, few wide open spaces and scattered sign of life.

In a blink of an eye, there were subtle changes in various locations, like the land was still in flux. I took it as a sign that Ethan wasn't around, or he wasn't really thinking about his Dream-world. John voiced a concern about the shifting landscape and I told him that certain areas do remain stable. As long as we followed a stable path, we would be fine.

"And how do even begin searching for this person you're looking for in a place that's changing?" he asked.

"Let's just get down there first," I said

As long as it took us to fly up to the plateau, it took much less time to get down on the other side of the mountain. We were more like sky-diving from the plateau, free-falling down the side of a mountain, partially gliding away from the surface with the aid of my TK – or what passes for it within the Dreaming. John didn't mind the free-fall and it said a lot about his trust in me. He didn't even seem to panic, much less worry as we approached the ground. I slowed our descent and even as I righted myself to land on my feet,

John followed suit. There wasn't much of a clearing where we were, but there was something akin to the beginnings of a path; some flattened grass that marked it, like someone else had been around this area before.

I let go of John's hand (didn't realise that he held on so tightly) and started walking. John followed close behind me. As we made our way along the path, John asked how I could know that the path we were on would take us to where we wanted to go. I didn't really have an answer for him, but I explained that since Ethan was still in a partial world-building and learning mode, whatever path we were on would lead to only one village. It was an assurance that we wouldn't get lost along the way. It wasn't much of an answer, but it led him to ask about how I started my Dream-world.

I explained it was by imagining places I wanted to go to, based on stories I had read or was told or saw in some movie, and then slowly filled it with creatures one would find typical in a fantasy world. I kept doing this over and over, every night for a long time. I used to enter in different ways too, but eventually decided that it was good to always start in the same place whenever I wanted to visit this imaginary world of mine. And that was all it was: an imaginary world. Every visit was a conscious act. I started making visits whenever I felt bored and on occasion, I would try something new, like pulling an occasional object from one reality into the other. Often, it was only one way, like taking in something from the real-world simply by imagining that I had it with me when I go in.

My mom found that when I made these trips, it appeared like I was asleep, but she couldn't wake me. That was when she got Charlie to start doing some tests, to make sure I was okay. By then, my body had adjusted to whatever each session was and it took the opportunity to rest, much like what happens when a person would go to sleep. That's where the whole idea of it being a Dreaming Session came about.

I honestly don't know how it evolved to the point where normal people, while asleep, could somehow drop in. It was usually by chance and often enough, they would have no more of a recollection, other than to suggest that it was simply a dream to them. So, my day-dream imaginary fantasy world became a Dream-world. How and why it exists independently, I don't know. I think that it's taken a life of its own, sustained by other actual dreamers who find their way there.

"For me, it's a conscious thing," I told him. "Things and events that happen here can have effects in reality, like any skills you pick up. It's how I learnt Becca's language so quickly. Well, to everyone else, it seemed like I learnt it really quickly. We were here teaching each other for days."

"You're saying that whatever skills I pick up here, I can do them when I wake up?" he asked.

"To a certain extent and as much as reality will allow." When he didn't say anything following that, I said, "We've been wandering for a while now, probably might seem like hours or even days, but more likely, barely a few minutes have passed since we started."

"Dream-time," he said. "Relative perception."

"Something like that," I said. "There's also a chance we've been out for more than a day by now."

Once I said that, a clearing turned up on the path as we went around a bend and we could see the village. "Was that some kind of trigger? Like when you're tired of walking around, the village will pop up just because you say so?" John asked.

I shrugged my shoulders and said, "It's not my Dream-world. Not quite my rules."

That got his attention. "Wait. Not your Dream-world... so, not your imaginary world. How the hell are we doing this?"

I reminded him that I did not know how these realities sustained themselves, much less exist. There were a lot of impossibilities around us and not everything had an explanation. If there were explanations, the nightmares that most of the trainees were having would have been taken care of the moment they started and I would not have done what I was doing.

"An impossible walking paradoxical conundrum who just refuses to make sense," he said. "That's what you are."

With that, we wandered into the empty village and had a quick look around before we split up to check the huts and homes. I kept calling out to John, asking if he found anything. We both came up empty. I dreaded to think that I would have to pull Ethan in, and I considered it as a last resort. We didn't get to that. John and I met in the village square, fruitless in our efforts. We stood there and looked around while I tried to work out what to do next.

"You're probably thinking that you could do with Ethan's help about now, right?"

John and I turned to see Sophie coming up the path into the village closely followed by Keitaro, dressed as a armourless ronin, and Hank, dressed as a cowboy like he did the last time. I wasn't thrilled to have them around, reminding Sophie the numerous times I asked her not to do this. She shrugged in reply, holding a slightly sly grin on her face. I stressed again the danger that was possibly awaiting us. Keitaro stepped forward bravely, proclaiming that he would defend all of us. When I asked if he was sure he was properly healed and ready, he said that he never felt better, more so than in reality. I decided to take the opportunity to scan him. I had done something similar with Sophie last year when she had been badly hurt within the Dreaming. He probably knew anyway and decided to humour me.

I did a cursory scan on him first and we found ourselves surrounded by darkness, like we were in some shapeless limbo. His appearance changed to reflect his true condition. His attempts at healing himself, despite my earlier advice, contributed to his appearance being a horrid mesh of pseudo-cybernetic implants mixing with his flesh, like he was trying to make himself part mecha. All this also reflected in the stiff robotic like movements he made while gesturing.

I asked him to allow me to try healing his hand, more as an example of what I wanted him to do, and he raised his partially mangled hand that appeared to have some steel protruding out of it. I tried to make it as painless as I could imagine, getting the metal to dissolve into the flesh, the skin covering up the scars, and his normal hand slowly forming into view. If it were a computer effect in some movie, it'd probably look cool or cheesy as the morphing took place. Keitaro winced a little, but the results spoke for itself as he comfortably flexed his fingers with ease. I got him to try the same thing on his other hand and he managed it with some difficulty.

I felt I got him on the mend and I really wanted him to continue with this, but he said he would do so later. On hindsight, I should have pushed him on it there and then. I broke the connection and we 'returned' to the village. I noticed John and Hank talking to each other, Hank showing off the guns he had on him. I found out later that John was asking about the 'skill enhancement' aspect of the Dreaming.

Just when I was about to ask, Sophie drifted down from above. While my attention was on Keitaro, and John was talking with Hank, she took it upon herself to get a lay of our surroundings from on high. She said there was another village with signs of activity not too far away. She pointed in the direction of the village she saw. John took the lead closely followed by Sophie, Hank with Keitaro and I reluctantly pulled up the rear.

Getting to that village didn't take long. It looked almost exactly like the village we had come from with maybe a couple of extra buildings and a functioning well in the square. There was an elderly woman drawing water from it as we approached the village. She regarded us curiously as I wondered if she was another dreamer who found her way in like some of the others in my own Dream-world? Or was she a denizen, created out of nothing by Ethan's sub-conscious?

Sophie took point here and asked to see the, "Wisest person in the village."
The woman didn't say anything, but pointed us to where there were only two rather ramshackle huts were standing. Again, John was the first to move, but I quickly followed second. I cautioned him, saying that we had no idea what was waiting for us in a strange village deep in unknown territory. He replied saying it was no use worrying at that point but to be ready in case of anything, good or bad.

I had to give him credit for the sensible head he had on. It put me a little more on edge, but in a good way. Internally, I was still thinking what I would do if Phillip turned up; how far I would push myself.

John knocked on the door of the shack and called out for the occupant. The door opened and we were greeted by a hooded old man who might as well have been Old Crans, but wasn't. He spoke plainly but his voice had this authoritative quality to it, like the voice of the ages. I couldn't get past the basic image though, like Ethan had made a facsimile of my wise old man for himself. Honestly though, I really wasn't sure what we would find. So I started asking him about the critters we had seen, describing each of them as best as I could. Keitaro took it one step further by roughly drawing them out in the sand on the ground. We managed to determine which were benign and which were dangerous, and thankfully, it was only two we had to be careful with. While we could at least confirm the source of the critters, it didn't explain how the critters were crossing over to reality. So I tried asking him anyway, not expecting much of an answer. He gave a cryptic reply.

He said something like, "The key must be destroyed and the path shall collapse." that naturally led to questions of 'what key?' and 'what path?' from all of us. His response was, "You know the key."

I started describing Phillip, not expecting anything and hoping nothing would come of it; no such luck. The old man said my description 'sounded like' that of a hermit who lived in a nearby cave, and a chill ran down my back.

Keitaro was more than eager to deal with the issue there and then, despite my reservations in not wanting to involve the others in facing Phillip again. John was not as eager, but he wanted to confront this guy who could scare me, because as far as he knew, this was the first person to ever do so since I came to The Facility. Heck, even facing off against John may have made me nervous and edgy, but I don't think I was truly scared of him. I think more precisely, John tended to freak me out more often than scare me.

Well, I could be remembering things wrong, but fear can cloud the mind if it's strong enough.

So, again and reluctantly, I pulled up the rear as we left the village and headed down the path towards this cave where a hermit who could be Phillip lived. I knew I should have been in front of the pack with John. It was Hank who kept me company and asked how I was feeling. I relayed my uneasiness that they were all there with John and me, stressing again the danger that was Phillip.

"You're basically willing yourself into losing to this guy before you even confront him," Hank said. "You may be scared of him but it doesn't mean you have to build him up to more than he is."

I had to agree with him on that, but that was the effect Phillip had on me. Everything that I had gone through where he was concerned, none of it was good and there was no reason for me to think otherwise if we were to run into him here. In the end though, I knew he wasn't the one I was really afraid of, but he was the trigger for my greatest fear.

We found the cave easily and there were signs that someone was moving in and out of it often enough. Enough to suggest that someone was living there too. I brought up the point that we were looking into the issues of the nightmares and not specifically looking for Phillip. John felt if Phillip could invade his dream, then he could cause the other nightmares as well, even if we didn't know how or why.

"Do you think he's even in there?" Hank asked gesturing towards the cave.

Before anyone else replied, a smoky burning stick was thrown into the cave. I turned and saw Keitaro hurling a second burning stick into the mouth of the cave. I tried to stop him, but Sophie joined in. He somehow got a fire going and had lots of burning sticks at the ready. Even Hank threw one burning stick into the cave while John was surprisingly restraint. After a while of watching plumes of smoke pouring out of the cave, nothing happened. It seemed no one was in the cave. At this point, I suggested that if Phillip had been staying in the cave, he could have been hiding out elsewhere like in another person's dream. I suggested we head back. Sophie reluctantly agreed, much to Keitaro's chagrin. John kept quiet about it and Hank suggested heading back to the Kitchen for a meal and drink. He was also eager to meet Michelle. I agreed almost immediately, feeling relief that the others would be out of danger. And in hindsight, we should have left the Dreaming there and then, instead of heading back to my Dream-world.

The journey back to the Kitchen didn't seem as long, because we didn't walk. Between Sophie and myself, we flew everyone back to my Dream-world and straight to the Kitchen. John commented that we could have done the flying much earlier and saved a lot of time. I didn't say anything, but Sophie commented that on occasions when she joined me on certain tasks, we always set out on foot until the task was completed. It was the way things were. It didn't always have to be the case, but it is part of the design of my Dream-world.

We landed in front of the Kitchen and I felt far more comfortable being in my Dream-world. I led them into the Kitchen. Kinstein was surprised to see me, more so at the large gang accompanying me. He remembered Sophie, Keitaro and Hank from their previous visits and even remembered what they ordered before. I had to introduce John. Once everyone was settled and waiting for their orders, I went to check on Michelle. Kinstein told me she had a long hard day washing the dishes and was resting in the back-room. I greeted her and she was happy to see me, smiling and all, but said nothing as usual. By the time I brought her out to the main hall, everyone had their food and drink. John was amazed at the food, saying he couldn't remember tasting a steak so good, and Hank emphasised it was why he wanted a meal before heading back.

I introduced Michelle to John and Hank. Keitaro asked her about the mechas, and she only answered with a thumbs-up. She must have picked it up from Kinstein since I know she didn't learn that gesture from me. Hank quietly suggested that Michelle probably didn't speak because I didn't know what her voice sounded like, making a veiled suggestion that Michelle might be more a figment of my imagination than what I took her for. I dismissed this, suggesting that she was not used to speaking after having spent what might have been years (by her reckoning) being isolated, alone and in silence. He agreed it was a possible hypothesis.

That little bit of down time didn't last long as a portion of the Kitchen's roof suddenly got torn off. Debris fell around us and I instinctively covered Michelle with my body. When I turned to look through the gaping hole, I shuddered fearfully. Phillip was floating above, slowly consolidating whatever debris that was a portion of the roof into some kind of projectile and hurled it in our direction. I didn't react fast enough, but Sophie did, throwing up a TK shield to protect all who were dining in the Kitchen.

Everyone moved quickly. John was ushering some of the other diners out of the way. Hank, nearest to me at the time, checked on Michelle and me. Keitaro drew a Japanese bow and fired off a few arrows. Sophie told him to back down because she had her TK shield up. Nothing much was getting at us, but nothing much was getting out at Phillip either.

"I can't believe you actually came looking for me," he said. "And you did it in such a convenient manner too." One little gesture, and the main entrance of the Kitchen blew outwards, taking most of the wall there, opening up the front of the Kitchen to the elements outside. "You think you have a chance with this posse?" Portions of the stone wall came flying back at us with incredible speed.

I managed to throw up an extra TK shield, backing up Sophie, but even with that, I felt the strain of the force thrown at us. I could only imagine what Sophie must have felt, taking a bigger portion of the hit. There was barely any time for us to regroup and I was worrying more about Michelle at this point. I barely noticed that she had practically zero reaction to the events going on around us. She didn't seem scared or even curious.

Next thing I knew, Hank was covering me, firing his two guns at Phillip. I then realised that Sophie was reeling and being helped by John. Keitaro was also firing arrows at Phillip, but nothing was getting at him. In all that, I wasn't doing anything because I still had Michelle in my arms. I tried to get her to the back where I could see Kinstein gesturing for me to reach him. I could also hear Keitaro swearing at Phillip, daring him to come down to ground level and fight.

And I was running away from it all trying to get Michelle to safety.

I didn't see what happened in that short time I scrambled to get Michelle to Kinstein, who whisked her through the back door. By the time I turned back to the ruckus, Phillip was fighting Keitaro, broadsword to katana, while fending off Hank who appeared to be taking potshots. Either Phillip had a TK barrier up or he was rapidly anticipating each shot and stepping just that little bit out of the way of the shot's trajectory. John was still at Sophie's side and watching the fracas, but I noticed he had a revolver in one hand, holding it ready. I scrambled to him first to check on Sophie.

She was winded by the force she took in protecting us from Phillip. She wasn't unconscious but reeling, and she was struggling to get her bearings. I thought it was amazing that she could hold Hank and Keitaro in the Dreaming still. It doesn't take much, but one massive distraction and we might lose hold on our 'passengers'. I told John to keep her safe until she was strong enough and I told her to leave as soon as she was capable.

By the time I turned my attention to the fight, Keitaro appeared to be wearing down. He seemed to be overly aggressive in his approach, quite contrary to his usual style when I spar with him. Hank seemed fixed in place, but it didn't seem like it was his doing. I made a gesture at him, and he gasped, staggering backwards. Phillip was somehow holding Hank in place while still fighting with Keitaro. Hank didn't even look at me. He started reloading his guns instead, occasionally looking up at Phillip. I imagined a weapon in my hand and for some weird reason, I materialised a *bokkun*. I charged in towards the duel anyway. Keitaro and I somehow worked on instinct and we managed to back each other; covering each other against Phillip. For some reason, my wooden *bokkun* could hold up against the broadsword that Phillip was using. The moment I joined the fight, Phillip pulled out a secondary blade to counter us. And he had this maniacally gleeful look on his face as he threw the shorter blade at me. It was quickly followed by a massive TK force before I could even respond to the blade hurtling at me. The most I managed was to block the blade before I got knocked off my feet and went flying into a table, couple of chairs and the wall.

I scrambled to my feet only to see Keitaro's right arm on the ground, still holding a katana. I looked up and saw Hank holding both guns on sight, slowly moving in careful steps trying to get a clear shot at Phillip who was holding Keitaro as a shield. It was the way he held Keitaro, the broadsword through his gut, so all I could see was Keitaro's back. I couldn't tell if he was still alive because his body seemed to slump towards Phillip, but not too much. And I could still see that sickening grin in Phillip's face.

"You know this is all child's play," he said. "Let's take it to the next level, shall we, princess?"

I yelled out, "Don't!" It was all I managed even as I moved towards him, and I couldn't believe what I saw happen next. The sword withdrew from Keitaro's body and I heard him scream out in agony. I heard shots ringing from the guns handled by Hank and John, but even all that seemed like slow motion. I saw a hand come through the wound that was left by the sword and then it started dissipating. It seemed to glow first and then, like some cheesy CGI effect, the light sprayed apart and towards me. It didn't stop with his hand. Keitaro's body glowed and dissipated as well, like the molecules from both Keitaro and Phillip were being scattered by the wind.

Just before his grinning face dissipated, I heard Phillip say, "Come get me now." As the little dust-like sparkles passed all around me, I swear I could sense Keitaro's essence and anguish, as well as Phillip's presence passing by. My forward momentum faced a quick reversal as I tried to follow both presences, watching the specks of lights speed towards the back of the Kitchen, directly for the back-room where Kinstein and Michelle were.

I remember muttering something like, "No no no no no no," as I quickly scrambled over the debris in my way towards the back-room, John at my side. John got to the door first and slammed his shoulder into it, busting it open. I jumped over his stumbling body and into the room to find that Kinstein was knocked aside, and Michelle was standing there almost directly in front of the door, her arms cradling a large ball of light. I was a little dumbstruck and asked her what she was doing. She only looked at me curiously, her head cocking to one side, her expression blank and emotionless. She then tossed the ball of light upwards as if she were tossing a large beach ball, and it dispersed, like it blew out from the centre. Both Keitaro and Phillip's presence were gone in that instance.

"What did she just do?" John asked.

"I don't know," I said looking about the room, and then down at Michelle who still stood there, blankly staring back at me as if nothing had happened. Even Kinstein admitted that he had never seen her do anything like that before and had no idea what she did. It was about then that Sophie called out to me, and I rushed back to the main area, *bokkun* in hand and at the ready.

Sophie was hanging onto Hank, seemingly unable to stand. He said she was fine one moment and then her legs gave way the next. She said her legs felt like they were on fire, that she could feel the heat. Then, as she said, "We're in the Infirmary," she and Hank vanished, essentially 'waking up' from the Dreaming.

I ran back to the room, told Kinstein to keep an eye on Michelle and then turned to John, "Once you're back in your room, get to the Infirmary." I didn't wait for him to respond, I closed our link and immediately jumped out of my bed in the next instance.

Even as I dashed out of my room, I could hear the fire alarm blaring. Becca was in the living room. She seemed to have just come out of her room as well and it was still dark. I didn't have time to check anything, like how long we had been in the Dream-world, and I didn't even pause to explain anything to Becca except to yell out, "Get Remington to the infirmary!" before I dashed out of our suite.

I ran as fast as I could towards the Infirmary, and it never felt further away than ever before. I knew I was panicking too. I might have been crying a little, but it might have been the smoke that was already filling the corridors. There weren't many others around but I did notice one or two of the trainees peeking out of their rooms, as if to check what was going on. Once I got past the residential area, there were more people, like staff and personnel, maintenance crew. I remember wiping my eyes then, and not slowing down even when someone told me I wasn't supposed to be there. The Infirmary was still a floor away and I was still running.

John had beaten me to the Infirmary. By the time I got there, he was pulling an unconscious Helen away from the Infirmary's entrance. There was smoke pouring out and it didn't look like there were any flames. Sophie was nearby and being tended to by Will, and she seemed unconscious as well. Her legs were burnt and it did look bad at the time in the dim lights. The only person who was missing then was Keitaro. Ms. Phillips grabbed my arm and asked what happened, and why Keitaro tried to kill Sophie and Helen by setting off a fire in the Infirmary. When I responded with a quizzical, "What?" she said that Keitaro woke up, attacked Will and her, then proceeded to toss several bottles of swabbing alcohol around the Infirmary before short circuiting some wiring to start the fire.

It took me a moment to figure it out and I said, "It's not him. It's not Keitaro." I didn't have time to explain it all and said that I needed to find him. This was as Linda and Remington turned up at the scene.

"Please say you're not responsible for this," Remington said.

"Kinda," I said.

"Keitaro started the fire," Ms. Phillips said, overlapping my response.

Linda asked if I was okay, and I only nodded in response. I turned to Remington who was talking to Ms. Phillips, trying to asses the situation, and I said, "It's Philip, he's controlling Keitaro." That stopped him cold and he looked hard at me. "I need to find him."

Ms. Phillips and Linda were looking at Remington and me, probably trying to understand why the situation had suddenly turned serious between us. Then Remington said one word, "Scan."

I nodded and closed my eyes. I wanted to do this. I was going to do this whether he would let me or not. Part of me was relieved that he would agree, so I opened my TP barriers and, in a way, touched every active and inactive, or sleeping, mind I could sense, trying to get a feel for Keitaro's thoughts, or Phillip's presence. I felt both of them when the light passed by me in the Dreaming, so I knew what I was searching for. It didn't take me long, and every other TP within The Facility felt me. I felt 'walls' and other blocks going up, but not with Phillip. The moment he sensed me, I felt him practically taunting me.

And I knew where he was heading.

And I knew what he was doing.

The moment I opened my eyes in a panic, Remington simply said, "Go." And I took off, running again.

I was barely halfway there when I sensed his distress. He woke up to a roomful of smoke and the door was too hot to touch. I could feel it all, the way he tried to head for his door, but that was the source of the smoke. I sent him one little thought – shower. I felt him react to that and he knew it was the right thing for him.

Knowing what I knew then, it shouldn't have been a surprise to see Walker's door in flames when I got there. What took me by surprise was seeing Keitaro standing there in the middle of the corridor. Grinning that sick grin that simply proved to me that it was Phillip in control. He was looking at me, expecting me. I think he began to say something, but with the fire alarms going off around us, I couldn't hear. Maybe I didn't want to hear because I blew out one hell of a TK blast and he went flying down the corridor. Portions of the corridor around him were also affected, but I didn't pay much attention then. I got to Walker's flaming door and forced it open with another TK blast. The door flew off its hinges and into the room, the frame of the door was also destroyed. Only then, with the fire in the room, did the sprinklers go off.

The smoke alarm was blaring away within the room, and the fire alarm ringing on the outside. The water doused the fire quickly enough once it got going. It didn't occur to me at the time that as sophisticated as The Facility was, it didn't have a better fire suppression system.

I quickly stepped into the room and called out for Walker. He came out from his room, already soaking wet and I could see that there weren't any sprinklers spraying anything in his room. When I saw him, I felt a massive sense of relief and I suppose I did let my guard down. I didn't even realise that the way he seemingly dashed towards me was one of urgency. The moment I felt that sharp jab in my lower back, time seemed to slow down. I know I didn't scream, and even if I did, I might have been drowned out by the alarms. But I could hear Keitaro's voice speaking in Phillip's menacing tones about how much he missed having me in his hands. I could feel his spare hand groping me. Then came a twist that sent a shock through my body, and my legs gave way. The last thing I saw was Walker's fist coming straight at my head even as I dropped. I heard the punch connecting as I fell forward and I felt that object in my lower back pulling out, the warmness that followed.

Walker stopped me from hitting the floor, as he called my name. I reached around and felt the small gaping puncture in my lower back. Even with the water raining around us, I could feel the blood flowing out. I couldn't even turn, it was Walker who did it, turning me over and the pain flared insanely. I know I screamed then, but only in that moment. By the time I opened my eyes, I could see Keitaro picking himself up within what was left of the door frame. He had something shiny and metallic in his hand, but I couldn't make out the scalpel at the time. I tried to will my legs to move, to kick, to twitch even, but to no avail. As much as I tried to move, Walker didn't budge. And I didn't even think about using my TK at the time; my head was reeling from the attack and the wrenching pain in my back.

Keitaro barely took one step into the room when he got tackled by John, who managed to knock the scalpel from his hand. It wasn't some spectacular round of fisticuffs, but more like grappling around on the ground. I could hear Keitaro cursing away, throwing whatever punch he could manage, but the close quarters John kept didn't give Keitaro much swing room to build any power. Mind you, my head was still a little fuzzy and Walker made sure not to move me too much since getting me on my side, enough to see what was going on. The few times I've tussled with John, he never fought like this. I had seen this style mostly in MMA or UFC fights.

In one of the grappling moves that looked like he had Keitaro in some kind of locking hold, I could hear John yell out, "If you're going to do your thing, do it now!"

I didn't have any plan or arrangement with him, but I got what he was getting at, even if it took me a second or two to grasp it through the fuzziness of my head. I quickly pulled my focus together as much as I could, and I linked in to Keitaro's head, literally diving straight in at whatever there was of Phillip and kept heading deep.

A dark landscape coalesced around us, there was no sky, just some scary-ass rocky ground floating in the middle of nowhere and no sense of time. We crashed and rolled. I got to my feet fast, but Phillip was already airborne. I reached out with a TK... whatever it was, I reached out and yanked him back to the ground with a hard vengeance. The rage boiled within me and I did struggle to keep my anger in check. Didn't try very hard tho. All that he had done to Sophie, and Hank, and Keitaro, it all flashed on me every time I looked at him.

I stood there watching him crawling out of the crater he made when he crashed. And he was laughing. Didn't faze me. Then he started speaking, saying how much he missed fighting with me. I threw another blast at him and sent him flying into a rock face. Even as he fell to the ground, I walked towards him, closing the gap and not wanting to give him too much ground. He was still chuckling as he picked himself up and dusted himself off.

I got in closer and started throwing punches. He didn't even flinch. He didn't do anything. He stood there taking it all until I held back one and looked at him grinning.

"I've had time to learn to conserve my energy," he said taking a couple of steps back from me. "Time to learn a whole new bag of tricks too."

"Like hijacking Keitaro's body?"

"Oh that was easy. Controlling it took a lot more than I expected, though. Couldn't use any, what's that term you use, TK? Took a lot to control that body. I didn't have much to spare for dealing with your friends, but enough for a few other tricks."

"You've been jumping from person to person in their sleep."

"You have no idea what I've been up to," he said. He then talked about the dreams John has about me, how he saw me in a certain way. "In all that you saw, he sort of respected you in a way." I recalled the variations of me I saw in John's dream, all of which were more or less hookers, and Phillip called it 'respectable'. I began to voice my disgust but he continued. "If you think all that was disgusting, you have no idea what goes on in this guy's head."

"What have you done with Keitaro?"

"I guess I should have let you kiss him good-bye?"

"What did you do?" I practically screamed, hard enough to unleash a TK blow that knocked him back a bit.

His tone and demeanour darkened as he said, "I did what you did. I scattered him to the winds across your so-called fantasy land. I doubt he has the ability to pull himself back together. I know I barely managed it, and it took me a long time to figure it out along with developing some new tricks, like this one." He raised his arms and the ground around me literally broke and crumbled upwards, engulfing me. I struggled to get my shields up, barely keeping the crumbled ground from encasing me when he hit me with a second attack. "You should see what this guy thought of you."

My mind was bombarded with all sorts of mixed images of myself ranging reverential to downright disgusting – the majority of it were so twisted I won't describe any of that here out of respect for Keitaro and Keiko – and it completely threw my focus out the window. My head was reeling from the barrage of imagery supposedly drawn from the deepest recesses of Keitaro's fantasies and I felt the crushing forces of the stones, rock and dirt all around me. If that weren't enough, I could feel what was left of my sense of balance going haywire, the world seemingly spinning in all directions at once. The only thing I felt as everything else seemed to go, was rage. I can't say if it was towards Phillip or Keitaro at that point, but it was pure rage.

Enough to make me lash out with so much force that the mass of ground encasing me practically exploded outwards and I dropped to the ground – there really was no gravity there, only the perception of it – landing on my back. I immediately took off and the ground crumbled to nothingness below me. There was no up or down then, and when I turned to face Phillip, neither of us was the right way up. He was coming at me like a missile. I wasn't really thinking straight by then, or at all. I was going on instinct and fuelled by anger and hatred – rage.

Not a lot of it is clear and it's taken me a long while to recall what it was that actually happened in that moment. I had to come to terms that I became that which I feared. Crazy thing was, everything we were doing in fighting each other, it's mostly all a blur to me. I know he was hurting me and I was hurting him bad, but I was enjoying it in some kind of twisted way. I remember that. And the longer it went on, the clearer and more focussed my head got to that point when I had him, clarity struck. Everything that I had done before, that first time I had to take him down, I had done far worse this time around. What he had done with the ground and the mental assault that started this, I paid it back more than a hundred-fold.

That moment when clarity struck me, he was battered, broken and he appeared drained. I don't remember, or can't remember, when I took his arm off, but he was missing an arm by that point. His other remaining hand was holding on to my forearm, trying to pull my hand out of his chest. And we weren't even standing on any ground, it also didn't seem like we were floating anywhere. There was no landscape around us, no sense of reality. I was painfully aware that I had a grip on his heart, and he didn't seem to flinch or show any signs of pain. He grinned back at me.

"You really can't kill me, you know," he said. His voice was cracked and tired. "Even if you tear me apart like before, it'll just be time before I pull myself back again, and I'll be much stronger."

I knew he was right, and I was sure I couldn't kill him, even if I desperately wanted to do it. I thought I had killed him before. I still believe I killed him before, even though he's somehow come back. I couldn't even begin to explain how he did it, how it happened. So I couldn't do it…

Everything else I had done was bad enough, and it's all worse than killing him, but in that moment of clarity, I couldn't do it. I gave myself so many reasons why I should, from everything he had done to me years before to all that he had done this time to my friends, I could justify it all if I killed him. It might even have been merciful after the crazy insane fight we had, but something still stopped me from that final stroke.

I didn't have anything to say to him. I pulled my arm back, empty handed. I kept looking at him fiercely determined to end him and struggling to hold it back. He laughed, "You just don't have it in you to kill me. That's why you'll never win."

I grabbed whatever tattered remains of his shirt, and I started pushing. Pushing so hard and so fast, and I focussed on the world; my Dream-world. Then I said, "I don't have to win! I just have to not lose."

The Dream-world burst into existence all around us and we were high in the air diving straight towards the ground, and I kept pushing forward, faster and faster. Phillip laughed and laughed. We hit the ground hard, a hill-side, but did not stop. Everything went black again, but this time, it wasn't back to Keitaro's mind. This place was enough to even make Phillip stop laughing.

"What are you doing?" he said and there was a hint of fear in his voice. It didn't slow me down and I kept pushing deeper into the darkness. The darkness I was always afraid of. The same darkness I opened myself to last year when I had to confront it myself. I felt since Phillip and that darkness within me were somewhat connected, I might as well put them together. If I couldn't kill him, I could at least contain him.

"What are you doing?" he said again but with a few choice expletives that I won't repeat here, struggling to break free of my grip. Here in my dark place, he was not as powerful as he could be elsewhere. I still didn't say anything even as I started to slow and eventually let him go. He continued to drift into the darkness and he was screaming after me. Again with expletives but layered with the sound of fear. I stayed in one spot and watched as the darkness engulfed him. I did imagine what was waiting for him and maybe, it is what he would be facing, I truly don't know. As he vanished from sight, I could hear him cursing me before one last scream marked the end of it all. It was the cold darkness and deafening silence all around me.

I don't know how long I was there staring into the black void, more or less in the direction that Phillip disappeared into. Something else stirred within me and I felt pity for him. I can't say why I felt it, but there was also the feeling that this thing between us isn't over. I could wish that it was, but I knew better. In effect, he's a part of me, part of the darkness within me. It just felt appropriate.

With that, I headed back into the light, and woke up in the Infirmary. I was lying on my stomach and the pain in my back flared. Walker was in a chair next to the bed and facing me. Charlie was also there, couldn't see him but I did sense him. If there was chaos before, everything had been tidied up a bit. Ms. Phillips was nearby tending to Sophie who was in the next bed. I could see Keitaro on the last bed, tubes and wires attached.

It was then that I learnt that a few days had passed since I took John into my Dream-world.

Sept 18 / 19

Despite being able to heal faster than a normal person, it still took some time for me to recover from the 'nick' I took to my spine; that's according to Charlie. He also made sure that I wasn't resting too much because he didn't want me to heal too fast. By this time though, I got the feel and use of my legs back. I wish I could say things were better for the others.

Walker filled me in a little about what had been going on since the incident in his room. When I dove into Keitaro's mind – or Phillip's, since he was in control of Keitaro's mind – I apparently passed out in his arms and Keitaro's body went limp in John's grasp. It wasn't too long after that Remington and Linda arrived at that scene to help with me and Keitaro. They had Will and Paul to help get us to the Infirmary, and apparently we were both restrained as a precaution. From there, Charlie was called in to help with me first and then with the casualties.

Sophie was kept sedated the whole time since her legs had second degree burns. Her left arm also suffered some injuries and maybe first degree burns. Her recovery is going to take a while. Hank was luckier in that respect since his burns weren't so bad. Walker was checked, and cleared, for smoke inhalation as was John. Of course, I was most concerned about Keitaro. I got Charlie to check in with Phillip's brother to compare the symptoms and conditions between Keitaro and Phillip. It took another day or so before we got word that they had similar readings. In effect, Keitaro was technically alive, but with zero brain activity.

Remington dropped by once he heard I was awake and then proceeded to debrief me about everything that happened up to that point. I was still a little fuzzy in the head about everything, but I told him as much as I could recall. It got me started in thinking about the week's events, especially the stuff that happened in the Dreaming. Anyway, he said he would keep my mom informed, but also asked if there was anything I wanted to not let her know. At that time, she hadn't been told anything as yet, just that it's been a while since my last update where she was concerned.

Aside from him, only Linda and Walker were my visitors. I didn't really see anyone else aside from Will who was constantly watching over Sophie. Walker said he was keeping Becca informed and said that she was busy with her studies and work. I asked if he had seen Ethan around because I was curious to see how any of this affected him. We did traipse through his Dream-world. Being a little worn out, I didn't really reach out to Jenny either. I could have, but I didn't. Besides, I figured the other TPs would have been wary of me.

It was only after all this when Charlie checked up on me and told me about his talk with Phillip's brother. I decided to make one more trip to my Dreamworld after that, with the hope of finding Keitaro. That was only the next day...

Sept 20

It was in the afternoon when I took the trip back to my Dream-world. I was glad to see the Kitchen had been rebuilt, looking better and bigger than before, and both Kinstein and Michelle were okay. I greeted him, gave Michelle a hug and then had a quick look around the place. He asked how my friends were, and I asked how Michelle was holding up. I was curious if she had done that thing with the ball of light again. He said she hardly ever leaves his sight. But then, he can't keep an eye on her all the time and she does have some private time to herself.

I decided to take her with me when I headed out to get a lay of the land since the fight. I was curious about the creatures or critters that were a problem before. I don't know how long since Kinstein had his place rebuilt, but there weren't any new notices requesting for help on the board he had put up. Either the villages had their own way of handling the critters or there was a massive drop in the creature population all of a sudden. Also, I really wanted to see if Michelle could do that thing again.

We wandered around, moving from village to village, trying to keep a lower profile than usual. Despite how some of the villagers had reacted to Michelle some time back, no one seemed to recognise her. I really wasn't sure if that was a good thing or not. My focus was more towards sensing for Keitaro's 'essence' so to speak, to try and find even the slightest trace if him somewhere. I wasn't entirely sure what I was trying to do, but the hope was if Phillip could somehow pull himself together again, so could Keitaro, with a little help from me. I needed one little bit of a chance, but it didn't come.

We spent three days wandering around and I couldn't find any trace of him. And Michelle didn't do anything weird aside from behaving like a curious child exploring the world around her. And we didn't come across any critters or unusual creatures. All in all, the only thing I got out of the trip was an anxious few days searching for Keitaro and bonding a little more with Michelle. Admittedly, she's still a mystery.

By the time I woke up, it was still the same day and just before dinner. I was feeling better physically, but not so much emotionally. Charlie did one more check-up on me which included standing and walking about – with a little difficulty – and declared that I could recuperate in my room.

I asked him why there and he told me that it was based on Linda's orders, by way of The Facility's board. It was Becca and Walker who ended up escorting me back to my suite later that night and I've basically been confined ever since.

Sept 21 onwards

My recovery sped up a little since there was no one keeping an eye on me for most of the time, but I wasn't entirely idle, lying in bed and wallowing in misery. There was a lot of material for me to catch up on and I could also post questions to my tutors directly through the network they had set up for me. At least, when I felt like it. I guess it's something that was existing for some time though. I couldn't be the first person they've confined to quarters before. And unlike with what happened last year, I didn't really have anyone hovering over me like Owl George did.

Its kinda cool that I could get any food I wanted at any time and it was brought to me, like room service; except it's usually Becca who brings it. I missed the company of friends. I mean, it was nice to have Becca to talk to and help keep tabs on the outside, and Walker was allowed to visit anytime as well, but no one else dropped by. I did get contacted by Jenny through our personal TP link on a couple of occasions, but only to discuss and work out some issues with the Learning Network. I did my best where I could given my frame of mind at the time.

As for others, none of them have dropped by. However, John came by a couple of days back. Apparently, he has a little more freedom than I've got, otherwise he wouldn't have come by my suite, accompanied by Becca. He filled me in on what he had shared with The Facility's inquiry board – and for the sake of the inquiry itself, I'm not mentioning any of it here until that is done. He also told me about Sophie's progress as well as Hank's recovery. Then Sophie came by yesterday.

She was in a wheelchair and her legs looked like they were healing a little faster than I thought. Charlie had apparently sprayed something on her legs, supposedly to numb the pain, but she suspected it might have been something more. I could get more information from Charlie if I got to see him again, but since I was confined to my room, I hadn't seen him or even Ms. Phillips. I could guess what Charlie might have used, and I can't quite share that either. It was great to see her and I was grateful that she was on the mend. She had no regrets about following me in and she didn't blame me for what happened to Keitaro.

"I hope you're not blaming yourself," I said.

"We're all responsible for our own actions," she said. "We all did what we believed was right."

I knew what she was feeling then. I didn't have to use my TP abilities to sense anything from her, but I knew anyway. I shared with her the hope that we would get him back, I couldn't say when or even how right now. She said she would try to find him around her own Dream-world as well. That was the only hope we had – a small, minuscule bit of hope.

I quickly asked her about Keiko, noting that I never saw her in the Infirmary visiting Keitaro. She said that Keiko is going along as normal, pretty much keeping herself distracted with work. If I was concerned about Keitaro, I was doubly worried about Keiko and how she might feel towards me now. When he got hurt last time, she got tougher on me during our sparring. She might be eager to kill me this time.

It was about then Becca suggested I write everything down, saying that perhaps I would recall some little detail about what happened in the Dream-world. Sophie was to meet the inquiry board tomorrow. My turn would probably come after that, so in writing all this out... this is me trying to put things in order and maybe keep a clear tack on how it all goes. Reading over all this, I've tried to keep things in sequence as best as I could manage, putting down as much as I could recall.

Also, I can't believe how much I've written in this sitting. I guess it's been therapeutic because I'm feeling a little better than when I started. Not by much but still, it's a start. Maybe they can refer to all this as part of my statement about the events.

We'll see. I'm just tired right now.

Sep 27

It was something similar that Remington had said, one of those things that somehow got the attention of the Review Board. They talked to everybody involved with what happened, and a few more besides, before they finally called me up. When I got to the Review Board, I recognised all five of them but only knew Sonya, Nakato and Pete by name. Linda and Remington were also there, as my G/C and guardian.

It wasn't any different from before, I sat on a lone chair facing the Board members who sat behind tables on which they had notes and files. Remington advised me not to say anything out of turn and only answer questions when

I was asked. So I quietly entered the room, sat in the chair, quietly eyed each of the Board members briefly, and then looked down a little. The thought I could have worn something better than my usual jeans, t-shirt and jacket, crossed my mind.

It was one of the other two board members who spoke up first, going over the details of the incident, based on what they knew. It didn't seem like they had read my journal entry as yet, but he kept asking me to verify things as he read through his notes. It seemed that they had some of the details, but not everything. It's obvious they had information from John and Sophie in particular. I could also tell which little bits came from Hank, Walker and even Keiko. I'm pretty sure they also talked to the others and I'm sure Becca may have contributed a little. The most I could tell with that exercise was that the information was collected from the others. It was all very factual and to the point.

Then Pete took over by filling in some blanks, directly referring to my journal entry. I was a little surprised and wasn't too successful in hiding it. I mean, I expected it, but still, to have it read back to me in portions. Pete wasn't as firm and fixed to the facts though. He actually encouraged me to speak my mind. I looked over to Remington first. He nodded, encouraging me to go ahead. I'm not going to tread over the same ground here, but suffice to say, I provided a little more insight into some of what I had written, explaining why I tried to keep things linear instead of jumping to the point; for the sake of keeping things in order. The more we went into it, the more detached I became, trying to distance myself emotionally from the things that happened. I didn't want to revisit the rage or the pain of losing Keitaro.

I think it was obvious I got emotionally empty as the questions wore on. They were trying to determine the course of events that happened in the Dreaming and with Phillip. It got to a point where the questions stopped and it took me a while to realise that everyone was just eyeing me.

"Jeannie, are you alright?"

I looked to Remington when I heard his voice, then glanced at the others. "I'm okay," I said.

He asked if I wanted to stop. Nakato said that I could have a break if I wanted.

"Thanks, but I'd rather finish this up. If I'm out, I'd rather be on my way than to wait any longer," I said.

"You're not out," Sonya said.

"We just need to be clear about what happened because to us, a lot of it happened while you were out cold," Pete said.

"I'm not out?"

"You can thank your friends for that," said Pete. I noticed Remington give a sly smile. "We can't fault you for the quality of your friends who would stand by you and fight for you, despite everything that's happened."

"You're not to blame for what happened to Keitaro," Nakato said. "You advised them against joining you, giving ample warning. While you could have kept your guardian and counsellor informed of your actions, you did all you could within your capacity at the time."

I complained that there were other things I could have done, and Pete stopped me there. He said there was no point worrying about what I could have done, that hindsight was only useful for future actions. I would have to think things through better next time. I was also cautioned that it was likely I was going to make the same mistake again. I had to accept that.

It was about this point I got curious enough to ask, "Did Keiko also defend me?" I was told that she did; that I had asked her to stop Keitaro from coming after me, and she did try. Aside from that, I had to talk to her directly.

From there, I was asked to continue verifying their information and filling in more blanks. It took the better part of another three hours and I was emotionally drained in the end. I thought I did keep myself detached from all of it, but in the end, it wasn't quite as successful. I know I cried a little when I couldn't hold back the pain and sorrow any longer, especially when they got to what happened with Keitaro. Remember, I didn't see it all, but I got a fuller picture this time around based on what John, Hank and Sophie reported. I never got a chance to talk to them about all of it.

When all was said and done with the Review Board, there was no change to my status where The Facility was concerned. The board members seemed satisfied with my cooperation. Sonya said that since I had missed quite a bit of work, I was going to be busy enough catching up to get into any kind of trouble for a while. Linda said that Ms. Phillips wanted to speak with me as soon as I could manage, and I had my own things to catch up on, particularly with Keiko who's been keeping her distance.

Pete kept me back a while when everybody else left. He asked me how I felt about Keitaro and what I had done with Phillip. He said that both incidents pushed me to emotional limits and he wanted to know if I needed some time off. I took a moment before responding, and then said that I had hope that I could get Keitaro back.

"Just don't let it become an obsession if you can't make it happen," he said. "Do you understand that?"

"I can't give up on him," I said.

"No, you don't give up on him," he said, "but don't let it consume you either. This could be far deadlier to you than what happened with Phillip. I don't want you lost in your own Dream-world losing track of everything just to try something that may need time and patience. Otherwise, we will have to keep stricter tabs on you."

I got what he was getting at, and said that I would do as he asked. I'd seen enough shows and read enough books to understand the self-destructive power of obsession. He said he would be keeping an eye on me for a while and that I should still talk to Linda or Remington if I had any personal issues. It was something I have to work on. And with that, he sent me on my way and back into life at The Facility.

Outside the room, Remington was waiting for me. He asked, and I told him that Pete didn't want me to obsess over helping Keitaro. "That's a hell of a fight for you," he said with a grin before escorting me to his office. He made the call to my mom and then left me to clear the air with her. He had kept her informed to a point. The least I could do was close it with what happened with the Review Board and their decision. It took a long while and he even had some food brought to me in his office. I also got to talk to Karen about Mikey, who's doing well.

And I'm kinda rambling now.

After the phone call, I came back to my suite and told Becca about what happened today and then I started writing out all this. Walker's next, so I'm heading off to the pool now. It feels like forever since I was in the pool.

Sep 29

It was really great to get back into the pool, and back to aqua-acrobatics; it was pretty tiring. It was a request by Walker that we practise, as I needed to brush up in order to take over for him in about a week or so. I wasn't entirely rusty but I was a little stiff, inflexible even. It's been a while since I did some aqua-acrobatics with him, at least to the level he was expecting of me. It might have been due to my injury. I wasn't entirely worn out but I did get pretty tired due to a lack of mobility over the last few days.

I ended up spending the night with Walker. He was given a new room, and it was pretty sparse. A lot of his stuff got damaged. Some got salvaged, and luckily the stuff in his bedroom were all fine. It was the things in the hall that got wet; those that got hit by the sprinklers. That included his console computer (similar to mine) which had his work on it. He probably lost the last five percent that wasn't backed up yet; some other equipment he was working on; the stuff he got locally, things that he had to work with, that got damaged. It'll take a while to get those fixed. Since he comes from a water-based society, more of his personal items, like some personal images of his home, were fine getting wet.

I apologised to him for the inconvenience, and he said that it wasn't my fault; I didn't start the fire. I argued it was circumstance involving me. He countered that those circumstances could have led Phillip to anyone else. He could have targeted Becca just as easily, or even Carol.

"There are many possibilities and the fact that he came for me was still pure chance," he said. I was too tired to argue after that and he hugged me, held on to me. I felt safe, and calm. I almost fell right asleep in his arms, and he might have felt it because he carried me to his bed. I fell asleep not too long after that.

When I woke up a few hours later and unable to get back to sleep, I moved carefully, shifting sideways, to avoid waking Walker. He woke up anyway, asking if I was okay. I said I was fine and couldn't get back to sleep, so I was going to get some work done. He nodded and went back to sleep. It was probably about half past four in the morning when I left his suite.

I headed off to the café for a quick bite and I ran into Tommy there. We greeted each other and he asked how I was before asking if I was at the centre of the recent incident. I said I was involved. "I guessed as much," he said

Apparently, I was missed by some in the Operations Center. They were still having problems with the data stream that was still coming in from Tomas' probe. He and a few others are still fighting for my reasoning that the signal was dual mesh, but the controller at Mission Control still doesn't believe that, trusting the computers instead. Tommy believes I should come back to the Operations Center to work on the signal. We knew I had to get approval from Mission Control, so until that happened, I was required to stay away.

After that, he had to get back to work. I finished my snack and headed off to my work-room to check on Colleen. I had to do a massive review to ascertain where I left off in her coding. She had reutilised her memory systems to improve her interactive vocabulary, and then there was that little thing I had her working on. I'm still not sharing any of that here; not until I can get it working the way I want it to.

After a couple of hours with Colleen, it was back to the pool for a quick swim – I had left my swimsuit drying in the changing room. Walker was already there doing his morning laps. I also got to greet some of the few morning swimmers.

The rest of the day included catching up with everyone else, but that was mostly over lunch as usual, even though I did meet with some in class. Sophie was mobile but using a wheelchair. Charlie's been checking in on her and she has to report to Ms. Phillips every day for now. The same applied to Hank, who hasn't switched back to Helen as yet. He said he wanted the deal with the scars first, and Charlie's helping on that one as well. I was asked about my own healing and I admitted I was barely feeling any pain in my back. By right, I should still be in the process of healing, but aside from the mild muscular aches from the aqua-acrobatics, I was feeling about the same as before the incident; physically fine, that is.

The rest around the lunch table included Becca, Kadi, Carol, Hank, Callie, Sophie, Jenny and Toni. It was the first time I realised that Keitaro was often the only guy at the table even though Hank was there, but usually as Helen. Keiko wasn't with us, though Carol assured me she was around.

I tried to catch up with her at the gym, figuring she would be coaching the other kendo students. They had been practicing on their own for the last two days and they hadn't seen Keiko for that long. I ended up supervising them and giving a little help here and there with their strokes and form. It was at their request, and technically my obligation as their senior – or *senpai*, which they called me even though none of us were Japanese – and they treated me as such.

I dropped by the Infirmary after that, thinking that Keiko might be checking on her brother, but no such luck. Sophie was there being tended by Will, so I didn't bother them. I thought I could meet up with Ms. Phillips, but she was not around. I set an appointment with one of her assistants to meet her the next day, i.e. today. She wanted to follow up with me on the nightmares that were plaguing the trainees. Since my showdown with Phillip, the rate of trainees reporting to her about sleeping problems and nightmares have dropped, but there were still a few who were having problems. It suggested that Phillip was part of the problem but not the cause. It was difficult to determine the cause when we couldn't even determine when the problem started because no one went to her at the beginning.

Honestly, I was beginning to wonder if the Learning Network was part of the problem simply because of our involvement. Callie had bad dreams at one point and that was when we discovered Michelle. But then, the rumours of the dreams started before that, and not everyone involved with the Networks was having bad dreams then. At its worst, trainees who had never been involved with the Learning Networks were also having them. Then again, I had to consider that it was only happening when people were asleep, and it was only affecting the trainees; none of the tutors, G/Cs or even the help around The Facility. That led me back to the Learning Network because I was pretty certain that only the trainees have been linked in. And again, there have been more trainees reporting the nightmares and sleeping problems than there are involved with our Networks. It's circular reasoning; I could go around and around, and still get nowhere.

And then there were the critters. There was still no explaining that. Sightings and capturing have dropped significantly since the incident. Some got away during the fire, not all have been recaptured and luckily, not the more dangerous ones we learnt about, although a new one was caught two nights ago by the maintenance staff.

Ms. Phillips said Callie helped out with one trainee who was having bad dreams. This was while I was confined to my room. I didn't even notice that happening, but Callie apparently scanned and linked into that person's dream to tackle the problem, much like when we did with her. I wasn't told who it was Callie helped, and she did it alone. She didn't even say anything about it when I saw her over lunch.

Anyway, the meeting with Ms. Phillips took about an hour today and the rest of the day went by as normal. I'm doing as best as I can manage with catching up. I could have done more when I was confined, but I didn't and that's nipping at my heels now. Mr. Hardy isn't letting up either even though I think I'm doing okay there with his class. It's catching up on TP and TK that's a bit of a problem because I had quite a few responsibilities there. Still no sign of Keiko tho. I wonder if she got advice from Callie on how to avoid me.

For now, I'm off to the pool.

OCTOBER

Oct 1

Briefly, Walker's started his rituals; Sunee and Corogi are further along in their aqua-acrobatic routines than expected; and Ethan's been having problems catching up with his lessons. Callie and Toni's Learning Network group has been training for a field trip to the colony – just found that one out and am disappointed I'm not involved. Still haven't found Keiko. And then there was the monthly review with Linda.

It's barely a day and already I miss Walker, but keeping busy has been keeping me distracted as well. The most I've managed, particularly with Sunee and Corogi, is to fine tune their moves, but who am I to really do that given my lack of practice. They're planning a little demonstration at the end of the month. I've got my half down but it's Walker's half that I have to work through with them. So, Corogi is getting the better deal at the moment while I'm drawing from memory trying to help Sunee.

Where classes are concerned, there's still a bit for me to catch up, but quite a lot of stuff to cover for the TP and TK classes. Jenny's been a major help there and she kept really good notes. She also helped out with Ethan during my absence and it turned out to be a little more than she could handle. It's not that hard to forget that he's the youngest trainee at The Facility and most of the classes he's in are often too advanced for him. I've gotten Carol and Hank to help out with his studies, providing a little additional tutoring. He's doing okay with his TP training and Jenny let him try out in supporting a Network session as well. I would have been a little more cautious about that one myself.

I was a little surprised to learn that Callie and Toni were training to link a group of ten for the next field trip to the colony. I thought the colony's field trip was Jenny's and mine. I hope it's not some form of punishment, but then the plans for these things might have been drawn months before I even thought about taking John in and facing Phillip. I need to talk to Remington about it.

The meeting with Linda was today, after lunch. She was concerned about how I was doing in catching up with my lessons, informing me what the tutors thought about my efforts. Some felt I was doing well, while one or two felt I could do a little better. The general consensus was that I was managing. I have been putting in some time with Colleen and with the flight simulator; both practice flights and the rocket design. I know I'm a little behind schedule on that, but I'm doing okay, I think. The shielding design is in place and I've refined the wastes and recycling systems as well. Not too bad for a couple of days work, although admittedly, I did get help from Ehrmer on the shield systems.

Once the classes and projects were out of the way, she asked how I was managing with my friends and the environment in general. I thought she was referring to the situation with Keitaro, so said I was keeping myself busy, adding that I haven't seen Keiko yet.

"I wasn't quite asking that," she said. "I was asking how you're feeling given what's happened."

I didn't have an answer to that because I have been keeping myself so busy, I haven't let myself think about Keitaro and trying to get things back to normal. I admitted being afraid that I would get overwhelmed again if I settled on Keitaro, and I had already spent enough time wallowing in my room by myself. I had other things I needed to focus on at the moment. I informed her that I was told not to be obsessed over Keitaro, and this was my way of keeping myself distracted. I was on the verge of breaking down even as I told her that.

She consoled me a little by saying that it was okay to feel sorrow and regret over what happened. I felt I couldn't allow myself to do that, given everything else I needed to focus on at the moment. She said I shouldn't bury myself this way for too long and that suppressing it wouldn't be any healthier than obsessing. "If you need time, just let me know," she said.

"I've already had time," I said. "I just need to move on."

She said that she understands and she was always open to me at anytime. I only had to contact her through my comms unit and she would come looking for me. I thanked her for that. I still had a materials requisition which she said she would put through for me.

After leaving her office, I felt drained, but I still headed off to the gym to supervise the kendo students. I was hoping Keiko would be there, but still no luck on that. After dinner, time was spent supervising and coaching Corogi and Sunee. I still took in some laps after that, but I was missing Walker's company. I only got back to my room around one in the morning and I've been writing since.

I'll try to get some shut eye, but if that doesn't happen again, I'll check in with Colleen. So, that's that for now.

Oct 4

It's probably the lack of sleep lately, or rather, no sleep over the last three days, that I'm now having hallucinations. Maybe it's not a hallucination but some leftover delayed effect from the whole incident. The last time something like this happened, it was after dealing with Callie's dreams. Reality got kinda screwy and started getting polluted with stuff from dreams... I think. The critters are real enough even though they're supposed to exist in the Dreaming; other people could see and interact with them. Physics and science would determine that their existence is an impossibility, but you couldn't deny the physical evidence. Kinda like that thing about how bees can't really fly because their wings aren't really capable of supporting them, but they fly anyway. When it's something that only I'm seeing, however, it's a whole other case of the crazies... Or maybe fatigue, because I haven't been sleeping.

It's like one of those moments when your focus makes that little bit of a shift and you drift between being awake and being asleep. You catch that little something that just doesn't seem right, and suddenly, you jerk awake. That's what happened, twice today. Everything had been going fine until today.

I haven't had a spell like this in months, but Charlie believes I simply needed rest. He was around to check on me, as well as Sophie and Hank. He took one look at me and asked if I was okay. He knows me well enough to tell if I'm getting enough sleep or not. Ms. Phillips couldn't tell either and she's had lots of contact with me over the last two years or so. Still, his prescription was, "Get some sleep." I do have my concerns if there was some other reason for this sudden round of twisting reality. I simply didn't tell him.

Meanwhile, Sophie and Hank are recovering remarkably well thanks to Charlie's help. Ms. Phillips has been inquisitive about the spray he was using for Sophie, Hank and the other two Infirmary assistants who had some minor burns too. I had a hunch what he was using, probably describing it as an advanced, and more stable, derivative of the original thing that was injected into my mom when she was much younger. That thing mutated within her and is also what's in me. I was never told what exactly it was then and I really don't know its current incarnation, but I know what it does, more or less; stimulate or 'kick-start' the healing process from a genetic level, speeding up the process while 'reconfiguring' the affected areas to its prime default state. Something like that.

It the explanation Charlie gave me about my condition as I remember it; this deal about my rapid healing and why my blood might be dangerous. Whatever is in me is a mutated version of what my grandpa started out with, which is several generations behind what Charlie is using on Sophie, Hank and the others. I'm sure there's a name for it, but I think it's still classified in some way. Otherwise, it'd be out there. Of course, the negative aspect of this thing would be the existence of me, my mom, my brother and even possibly Mikey. In some crazy way, worrying about Mikey and the grief I'm getting now is probably some kind of payback for the kind of relationship I've had with my mom.

Anyway, I'm just rambling here.

I took a trip over to the Dreaming, checking in with Kinstein and Michelle. Still took her out on an errand to see if she would do that thing she did, whatever it was. I have a hunch, but I don't want to say it out loud or put it in writing until I can be sure it is what I think it is. I can think back as much as I want and reread what I wrote, but based on what I saw, it doesn't seem like she had done that before. Or maybe she did more than that one time. That's part of the problem. No one has seen her do anything like that, not even Kinstein. If I could see her do it once more, maybe with one of the critters, then I could be sure that she is what Old Crans and that other old guy might have suggested she is. Until then, I'm holding my reservations.

Everything else has been moving along as usual. I'm keeping myself busy, although I do miss Walker's company. It'll be another few days before he's done with his ceremony. And despite Charlie's suggestion, I don't feel much like sleeping, but I'll give it a shot tonight. No other spells since this afternoon, so maybe I'm okay after all.

Still… guess I could do with some shut-eye.

Oct 6

Strange as it may seem, it took a while before I got to talk to Remington about the upcoming field trip that I'm not a part off. Since he's not my G/C anymore, I couldn't simply meet with him without some prior notice, especially if it's about the educational stuff that doesn't directly involve me. Anyway, he said it wasn't a punishment of any kind, never was.

He clarified, and reminded me, that Jenny and I were never officially part of the field trip teams. Jenny and I were there to run the learning network and we were 'accommodated' for our services. Now that Callie and Toni are able to maintain the network, and I have my hands full with other responsibilities, it made sense for them to run the network on the next field trip. Kevin would be a back-up, being a member of the field trip team. It would also give them the opportunity to check out the colony for themselves, and interact with the colonists.

He also informed me of the field trip participants for this round. Aside from Hank, Corogi (probably stepping in for Ehrmer who's not going this time) and Rex, everyone else was new to the field trip. Some have been volunteers on our test networks and I recognised two others who were part of the Serenity Compound field trips. In any case, I'm not on the roster for this trip, but as long as Jenny and I can run a network, we can still be part of other teams. I'm curious about how Peter was doing, given how things were the last time I saw him. That's part of why I'm disappointed that I'm not going on this trip.

Remington inquired into the other networks as well as how Callie and Toni were doing with their practice runs. Based on Jenny's reports, they were doing well, but I've kept my distance so as not to get in Callie's way. She felt that being my cousin and following me to The Facility, doing the same thing that I started in TP, would make her another me. Something she wanted to avoid and be her own person. As long as Jenny was supervising them and keeping me informed, it was fine and I decided to let her be. Remington was cool with that as long as I could keep tabs on the Network tests.

On the aside, I did get some shut eye over the last couple of nights, just over an hour each night. It's not like I could get back to sleep once I woke up, else I might have tried getting a bit more. On the plus side, no skewed reality over the last couple of days, but my concentration wasn't too good, struggling a bit to keep focus in classes. It could all be due to the lack of sleep, but it doesn't feel like it.

I have some uneasiness going on, like something is not quite right; a kind of buzzing at the back of my head, metaphorically speaking. Like a kind of sixth sense going off. I have to wonder if it's some residue from dealing with Phillip. I didn't have this feeling two days ago.

Otherwise, everything else is going along as best as I can manage. I'm still trying to run into Keiko, but aside from spotting her in her classes, I haven't been able to catch her for a face to face. Over lunch, Hank said to let her be and give her time; Carol and Callie agreed. It's a little difficult to do that. I need to clear the air with her.

In Walker's absence, and with Keiko not there in the gym, I've been talking a bit more to John. At first, it was to check on him, following our little adventure. Then, it was to check on how Ethan was doing with his little band of fighters. Ethan seems to have put on some muscle and has a bit more confidence about him. I guess he's now more comfortable being at The Facility and his life in general. John said he was a quick learner and even got some of the guys to help him out on some of his subjects. Ethan didn't even tell me about it, the last time I saw him. After that, I ended up talking to John out of... I dunno, just to talk to him? I didn't have any particular reason.

In any case, Walker should be back in a day or so. I really miss him.

Oct 9

That strange feeling bugging me still hasn't gone away. There hasn't been any particular incident or event that has risen. Okay, maybe there was one, but a critter sighting isn't something that I would associate with this nagging feeling.

I was heading back from the flight simulator when I came across another critter. Well, not so much come across, but saw it materialise out of nothing. It came out of a shadow. There was enough light for me to determine that it wasn't hiding in some dim shadow that wasn't that dark and then popping out of it. I saw it actually appear, giving me enough time to react and capture it within a TK bubble.

I took it to the little menagerie that Ms. Phillips set up for the critters that have been caught. Even though it was pretty late in the night, about two in the morning, she was there examining one of the critters. She shared her findings with me.

Her biggest gripe was that while the critters, strange and unusual as they are, appear to be breathing and eating whatever they are fed, those related systems are not functioning at all. They appear to breathe but there is no indication of the lungs actually working. They can be fed but there's no sign where the food goes. You can see a heart but it doesn't beat and there doesn't appear to be a functioning circulatory system despite the existence of a simplified version of one; no blood was flowing through it.

She called them inanimate living objects, which brought zombies to mind. She immediately cut me off, saying that there were no such things, preferring to call them 'living dolls'. She then unloaded a lot of info about how unusual these creatures were. Not a lot of it made any sense, but then, to me, they are supposedly creatures from an imaginary world. I don't think they are supposed to make any sense whatsoever. She didn't buy that, saying that if they existed in reality, they should at least conform to some rules of reality.

"I don't quite conform to all rules of reality myself, do I?" I asked her.

"But you exist," she said. "These creatures really don't exist, but here they are."

I left her to her research and returned to my room, thinking about how the critters were coming through; about how Ms. Phillips said that the critters had a biological system, even though that system wasn't working. I thought about Michelle, Kinstein and the other denizens of the Dream-world. I know they're mostly figments of my imagination but I had to wonder how real they are, at least in my Dream-world.

As to that nagging feeling... I wish I could put into words exactly how I'm feeling about this and what it is, but I'm not sure how to go about it. I keep thinking about what I want to say, but it all doesn't sound right. Maybe I'll have to wait and let it play out.

Maybe it's the unresolved issues I have with Keiko. I've asked the others to pass a message to her, that I wanted to apologise personally for not having taken better care of Keitaro while in my Dream-world. I'm still trying to find any trace of him within the Dreaming, but no luck. I wish I could be certain about how she's feeling towards me. I could find out if I wanted to, but doing so would be a violation of my own code of conduct. I wouldn't do that to her. I wouldn't want to do that to anyone, no matter how easy it is.

Otherwise, keeping busy has cut back on my own free time. I got the stuff I asked for, really quickly this time, so I've been putting in the hours on Colleen. I'm going to have to show Linda and Remington what I've been doing with Colleen. They haven't pried and I've been doing a lot of upgrading lately. After the last Review Board, I wondered what would happen to Colleen if I was suddenly ejected from The Facility. She is rather large now and it wouldn't be easy to get her out of the work room without taking her apart. I put in a lot of work on her too, would hate to leave her. I've got to at least have some back-up plan for her.

I'm kinda worn today and I wanna hit the water. Walker's still not back yet and that's getting me down. He'll be back soon tho.

Oct 11

Walker's still on his sacred ritual. I guess he's got lots to discuss with his ancestors. It's not that I'm complaining, I just miss him. I miss being with him and his company. From what I can remember, this ritual lets him get in touch with relatives, mentors and people of significant importance in his life who have passed on. He can seek advice or knowledge from them and they may or may not answer. The more people you have to acknowledge, the longer the ritual lasts. I know he's got a lot on his mind, so maybe it'll take a while more. In the meantime, I'm doing as best I can with Sunee and Corogi, and their aqua-acrobatics training.

The one bright spot is that I finally caught up with Keiko. I had just finished with Sunee and Corogi last night, and was about to unwind with a few laps of my own when she turned up, looking to talk with me. I immediately agreed, not wanting to lose the opportunity. With a towel around my waist, another towel to dry my hair, later using that was a cover while still wearing my swimsuit, we ended up talking in the garden. It's a good thing that the temperature within the building is controlled and it wasn't too cold, despite the cooling weather on the outside. Still, a little awkward.

We walked over to the garden in silence; she led, I followed her. Once we got there, she apologised for avoiding me. I apologised for what happened to Keitaro, but she dismissed it, saying that what happened was truly no one's fault. She had other reasons for avoiding me, but left it at that. Instead, she went on about how infatuated Keitaro was with me, that he was willing to do anything if it meant spending time with me in any way. She even expressed how he had stopped kendo practice for over two years until I decided to try it out. She thanked me for sparking his interest again.

I didn't think I had anything to do with that, and she admitted that she did con him into it. As I recall, she remarked she would train me enough to defeat him. It might have been a sleight and a tease at him, getting him to pick up kendo again. And he was there often enough during training, which I suppose might have been his opportunity to be with me.

She talked at length about her brother and it felt like she wanted to vent a little. It gave me an idea how close she was to Keitaro and it was clear that she missed him plenty. She didn't get emotional, but I could sense that she was. I couldn't tell what kind of emotion, like there was something else she's hiding. I had an inkling of what was going through Keitaro's head, thanks to Phillip. It's one of those things that suggests that no matter how well you think you know a person, he always has secrets that you should never know about. We all put on a façade when we have to interact with other people, and they get to know us from the sum of our parts we put on display. I know I have my share in those deep dark secret places of my soul.

I had a feeling that's what Keiko was holding back, hiding from me. Things she felt might paint Keitaro in a far different light than the person I knew. Then again, maybe I was wrong about that. We talked about him into the night.

For my part, after I felt she was done, I tried to explain what I felt might have happened to him and the circumstances in which it happened. She smiled and commented that it sounded like a true warrior's death. I stressed that I didn't feel that he was dead, that his essence was still somewhere within the Dreaming. I was intent on finding him and told her that I could use her help.

The idea was for her to enter the Dream-world with me, and perhaps act as a beacon for his essence to lock on to. She found it difficult to understand what I was getting at and felt reluctant to consider my idea. I couldn't blame her if she truly didn't want to do this. I think it might also be due to some trust issues she might have with me.

I asked her if she felt we were okay with each other. Her reply took a while and she said, "No." It was an honest answer. She felt things between us were different now and we would have to rebuild our relationship, although we would still have kendo and our sparring sessions. She wanted that to remain as our connecting point.

It was almost three in the morning, when she said she was tired and wanted to get some sleep. She didn't quite say it, but I think she does blame me for what happened to Keitaro. It'll come out when I start sparring with her again. We'll see about that.

It's almost seven in the morning now. Can't believe I'm still wearing my swimsuit. Might as well head back to the pool now.

Oct 13

Quite a few things to touch on, so let's cover those first. Keiko is keeping her distance for now. We cross paths without saying too much. She still hasn't joined us for lunch since she stopped, but she has come back to coaching the kendo juniors. I help out but the most we get to sparring is when she uses me as a dummy to demonstrate the strikes, much like what she did with Keitaro when she was teaching me.

The rumour mill is buzzing about my relationship with Walker as well as with John. I'm guessing the John stuff might be something that Carol is feeding, and I'm doing as best to ignore them. Problem is, with Walker still absent, it's a little hard to ignore the ones that suggest he's returned home on the sly, since no one can confirm anything about his whereabouts. In the years he's been at The Facility, his ritual has never lasted more than a week, ten days at the most, according to Carol's 'information'. We've gone past that, so it's hard to ignore that rumour.

Sophie's wants us to continue our weekly dinners and I was more than happy to oblige. She's doing much better although she's still getting around in a chair. Her muscles and tissue are healing very nicely and I think by the time Charlie's done, the scars will be hard to notice. Hank's much further along than Sophie, but his burns were more superficial in comparison to hers. The other two who are being treated by Charlie are also healing well with Ms. Phillips keeping tabs on their progress.

I've been a bit out of sorts about all this lately. I haven't gotten much proper sleep, not even a Dream-walk. Add in the worrying, and it is playing games with my senses. Sometimes I think I see a critter, but then I find that it's just not so. I'm seeing plants and trees and rocks. I thought my perception of reality was getting screwed over with dreams, but then…

Like I was walking from my work-room to my suite. It was maybe a little after four in the morning. And before I was even aware, the corridor turned into some forest path with trees, bushes, grass and a trodden path. When I realised the environment had changed, I stopped and looked ahead at the darkened path. I swear I could smell the foliage and feel the difference in the air; the freshness you would get from plants. So different from the circulated air of The Facility. I wasn't sure if it was real and there was no one around then to tell me otherwise. I spun around to look back at where I came from, and found myself in the corridor proper. When I turned again to look at what I thought was the forest path, it wasn't there. Only the corridor.

That was one incident two nights ago. The other was last night and it was a little more unusual because it happened in the pool. It was after I was done with Sunee and Corogi. They had left the pool and after I had done my laps, I was floating in the middle of the pool and staring up at the night sky through the dome. After a while, I dived into the water and noticed the bottom of the pool. There were no tiles, no patterned lines. It looked like sediment and the water seemed a little murky. I turned and swam upwards to the surface and when I broke it, the night sky was still above me, but unobstructed. I treaded water and looked up at the clear night sky. Then I looked around and noticed that I wasn't in the pool, but a lake with trees all around. It wasn't a large lake, about twice the size of the pool.

I sensed I had slipped into the Dream-world, but I wasn't quite sure because it didn't feel like I was in my Dream-world. And I was still in my swimsuit, so that part didn't quite make sense if I had slipped into the Dreaming. When I reached the edge, and my hand touched the ground, it didn't feel like ground but the cold tiles of the pool's edge. When I looked up, there was John at the edge of the pool looking down at me. I looked around and found myself back in the pool. If I thought I was hallucinating before, then, so was John.

He asked if I was okay and I said I was fine. "Are you sure?" He turned his hand over to show some leaves he had. "There were trees here a moment ago."

I was stunned. "So it's not just me seeing things."

"This isn't just 'seeing things'. There were trees here," he said. "I could see them, touch them, and these," he held up the leaves again, "are real."

I climbed out of the pool and asked him why he came around to the pool in the first place. Aside from the pool lights, the other lights were already off, so it was pretty dim around the pool. There was no reason for him to even come around to the pool. He said he noticed the odd shapes from the café, which is at the other end of the roof. He figured I was still in the pool and decided to check it out. According to him, he didn't quite see what I saw. While I had a whole immersive sensation of a forest lake, John said he saw a few trees around the pool, probably no more than ten. It took him a while to even notice me in the pool. He called out to me and I didn't respond. He thought I acted strangely, like I wasn't sure of my surroundings. When he saw me move towards the pool's edge, he moved to intercept me and that was only when I actually noticed him. And everything that wasn't supposed to be there, went away.

"You were really out of it, like you were here, but you weren't aware you were here," he said.

"Because to me, I was there in a lake," I said.

I couldn't explain anything and I wasn't even sure if it was something I did. For that, I would need someone like Sophie or Jenny to monitor me, but I'm not about to ask them to do anything like that, yet. I'm not even sure what's going on with all this. Somehow, I don't think a lack of sleep is causing all this. The notion that I missed one trip to the Dream-world would be a reason for this happening also seems unlikely.

Yes, one other notion is hanging in my thoughts, and I know some of you who are reading this have the same idea. But I don't want to say it, or put it down here because if I do so, it might be true. I just don't want that to be true.

I'm still keeping focussed in classes and training. I was asked to advise on linking a F.E.P. to the network and, frankly, I thought Callie had that worked out, until I learnt that none of her volunteer test groups had any F.E.P. She had networked them before, notably Fred during her first year. I don't count Jo, because she's never been on a network group, at least not on an official network. Can't believe I never noticed it before. It was aways an issue to link an F.E.P.

onto one of our networks, I thought that Callie would have at least tackled this problem in her own way. Then again, maybe because it's Corogi, whom I've networked before. Can't help wondering why she asked for me when Jenny's been supervising them and she's equally capable. Sophie's done it as well.

Still, it means I get to be a little involved with the field trip in some way. I have to keep Remington informed about it.

Anyway, it's getting kinda late. I finished up with Sunee and Corogi early today and got back to my room not too long after that in case I started hallucinating again, but so far – nada. On top of it, I am pretty tired so maybe I'll get some proper sleep tonight.

Oct 16

It's one thing when you personally witness an event by yourself and then question its validity. It's something else when you have a corroborating witness even if there's no real proof of such an event. It's a whole other thing when you're told that there's actual surveillance footage to prove you're not going crazy. Of course, when said footage is being used against you for damaging the physical integrity of The Facility, 'crazy' just might be a good defence.

I got a message from Linda yesterday requesting an immediate meeting. This was about the same time Walker finally emerged from his ritual. So, I barely had time to catch up with him as he and the others suggested I go meet with Linda. I had no idea what was so urgent at the time, and finding Remington, Pete and Sonya with Linda raised my suspicion about the circumstances under which I was summoned. As far as I was aware, I hadn't done anything that would require The Facility's Board to come looking for me again. Well, it was all 'at that time' because I was brought up to speed really quickly with a little video presentation.

The footage was from a few nights ago when I had that… experience… in the corridor. It showed me walking down the corridor and how the floor morphed into a grass path. The bushes and trees emerged from the shadows in shapes at first and then became a little more real. It was surreal watching it all with the realisation that there wasn't some computer generated special effect making things happen on screen. From the looks of it, I wasn't even aware of it all happening until I stopped and looked around. When I did that turn, everything went darker, like the shapes filled in the edges of the shadows in the dimly lit corridor. One thing I did notice was that while there were trees, bushes, grass and stones and rocks with the well-tread path, the environment seemed contained within the corridor while I recall being, well, not in a corridor but in an actual forest. So there was one reality that was actual, as caught by the surveillance cameras, and the reality that I experienced. Both happening in the same place.

"Please say that none of that was you," said Sonya.

"I really don't know," I said. "I'm almost sure it wasn't me."

"Does this have anything to do with those little creatures you've been capturing?" asked Pete.

I didn't answer that right away, but then said it was likely. I also told them that something similar had happened twice more, so far. The second time being at the pool while the third... well, that was the early morning after my last entry.

After signing off, I tried to get some sleep and it had been an uneventful night. I didn't get the rest I hoped for and by four in the morning, I was feeling peckish. I headed out to the café and everything seemed as normal as could be. I was pretty wary as I walked through the corridors towards the stairs, trying to be as observant for any oddness that might pop up. Unlike the two times before when those environments crept up on me, this time it was just... there.

I walked up the stairs and when I turned the third flight, I got confronted by a gentle sloping hillside. Looking down where I came from, I could see the staircase leading to the corridors of The Facility. Looking upwards, I was looking up a hill with the night sky above. The only thing I was sure was I had a flight of stairs to the roof. What I was looking at couldn't be real no matter what my senses told me. I closed my eyes, and walked up that hill. In my mind however, I was walking up the steps to the roof, counting the steps as I went along. Yeah, I count steps on staircases. You never know when you need to navigate one in the dark, even in familiar places.

When I reached the top of the stairs, I stopped for a moment and pictured in my mind what I expected to see. When I opened my eyes, everything was as it should be. I didn't feel like I needed to write about that since I felt that one might have been in my head. I didn't have anyone else to back me up on that. There was no one nearby or at the café, who might have even seen anything. There wasn't any particular incident or event like that since, which is one whole day where nothing happened.

Remington asked Pete and Sonya if they could verify the other two incidents from the surveillance footage. Pete said they would look into it. The footage they had was only brought to the Board members the day before. If there was more, perhaps it hadn't been processed as yet, but even I knew it wasn't likely. They – those guardians of the surveillance – probably figured this one footage was enough to raise concerns about what might be going on. I think they are aware that if I didn't want to be seen, they wouldn't have me on any footage.

Pete said I should keep both Linda and Remington informed if it happened again, no matter what time it happened. That meant having my comms unit with me at all times, something I still don't always do. Despite what we had seen on the surveillance footage, the changes affected me in a wholly different way, if I went by what John said of the pool event.

That meeting was yesterday, and no other incident since that early morning. I'm kinda curious as to how I've had three separate events and no repetitions, like there hasn't been another corridor that turned into a forest path like that first time. Each event was pretty unique to the landscape. I'm wondering if that's a factor determining when the next event might occur, not that I want it to happen again.

As mentioned earlier, yesterday was also when Walker came back from his ritual. The meeting took me away from him and by the time I was done, I could only catch up with him at the pool at night. I didn't have much time with him then because he was busy with Sunee and Corogi. I did okay in coaching them, and he wanted to refine their movements a little more and that took most of the evening. Even after they were done, he still paced me for my laps but he excused himself almost immediately after we were done. Since he had been away for longer than even he expected, there was quite a bit of work he needed to catch up on. That carried over to today because I hardly had a moment with him. Keiko cancelled the kendo class with the juniors today, and promptly disappeared, so I thought I could catch up with him. No luck there either, as he was busy reviewing some work with his outside contacts. Since I had time to kill, I've been writing this up since.

I should be getting ready for my dinner with Sophie. I guess with the meeting yesterday, those 'events' and what's going on with Walker, we're going to have a lot to talk about, if she doesn't mind focussing on me. I'd be curious to see if she's willing to hang around with me and be my witness should another event occur. Then again, given everything that she's already gone through, I wouldn't want to impose on her too much.

I should go now.

Oct 18

Dinner with Sophie was pretty uneventful. Guess that's a good thing since we did quite a bit of catching up. Even looking back over my previous entries, I couldn't really determine when was the last time we had dinner together, only the two of us. What happened after, however...

She was escorted to the café by Will, but he didn't stay. He left after helping her get comfortable with the table and her wheelchair. Over dinner, I asked her how her wounds were coming along and she said Charlie agreed to have her out of the chair within a week, two at most. He was using less of the spray and she could sense some feeling coming back in her legs. It's been a pretty painless recovery and she was aware of how painful it could have been. She's started some physical therapy to get her legs back to normal, standing and walking. She admitted to using her TK ability to help her through the PT. The upside that she enjoyed was how attentive and helpful Will has been, the extra attention that he's been 'lavishing' on her.

She then turned her attention to me by asking how things were with Walker now that he's back in my life. To me, it felt like that month when he was away and even though he's back, it didn't quite feel like it because he has been so busy catching up with everything else that got put on hold. She was like, "Ah, just give him some space to clear those things and he'll have some attention for you."

Unlike before, when I could at least talk to him, this was worse in that he's around but at the same time not quite there. Aside from the little time in the pool, we haven't really gotten back together as yet. He seemed distracted by work as much as I was focussing on things to do to keep me distracted from stuff. I didn't have to say it, but she knew I was referring to Keitaro at that time. Of course, I had other things on my mind, like how Mikey is doing back home, if Michelle is doing something I hope she's not doing, and then there's work and projects, and now, there's Walker being sort of evasive when I've cleared things with Keiko.

I'm rambling. But just because I don't write about certain things does not mean that it's not on my mind.

As we worked through our dinner, she asked if there was anything interesting going on. I mentioned my disappointment in missing out on the upcoming field trip, even though I've been helping Callie and Toni linking in the F.E.P.'s who are on the field trip. We're also letting Ethan in on this one so that he can practise with the network a little more. That's because we don't have any other networks in full swing – Kevin being on this trip. Some of the other TPs have been given opportunities to try out but they haven't had the time to fully commit, especially as pairs. It's not necessary, but we prefer to have the TP partners partake together as a check-and-balance, with maybe one other as a back-up. We've had more TP volunteers running as back-up than 'network controllers'. The chances of building new networks are pretty slim right now, but I'm sure Remington could persuade some of the others if need be.

"I was asking about stuff other than work," she said. "Like that thing with John at the pool a few nights back? Something about trees appearing out of nowhere?"

I related the event at the pool and then the corridor before going into the last one with the steps leading to the roof. Even she sensed something was odd and asked why the three different locations. I admitted giving it some thought, but couldn't come up with any kind of connection. I also told her about how disturbing it was that my perception of each event was different from what others would perceive, based on the surveillance footage I saw and John's descriptions of my actions at the pool.

"Could it be that someone else is manipulating what you're seeing?"

"If they are, they're not leaving any traces," I said. "Before you suggest it, it's not Phillip. I've got a small bead on him and he's not capable of anything at the moment. Besides, it's not his style."

"Maybe he's trying some new tricks?"

I shook my head. I was pretty sure it wasn't him and it wasn't me doing it either. I even offered to let her scan my mind for any traces of any intruder. She tried, but found nothing. I admitted to having Jenny scan me first, but without giving her an actual reason. That was after the third event, simply out of curiosity, to see if anything was out of whack in my head. Having Sophie do it was like getting a second opinion.

She then asked if I was taking a trip to the Dream-world on Saturday as usual. I was, since I missed last week, and she asked if she could tag along. She simply wanted to get out to someplace and stretch her legs a little, preferably with some company. "Sure, why not...," I agreed without another thought, to which she smiled.

The rest of the night was uneventful. Will came by around a quarter to eleven to wheel her away after she comm'ed him and I was off to the pool after helping to clear up the plates and dishes. The café staff lightly protested and reluctantly allowed me to help a little. I thought Walker would be at the pool, but he wasn't. I don't know if I had missed him or if he was even there. There was no one else around and the pool was still and glowing. I sat on a bench there and stared at the pool for a while, thinking about going for a dip. I didn't have my swimsuit with me though.

I guess I was waiting for something, anything, to happen. I didn't head back to my room until almost one in the morning. Didn't get much sleep either, although I did try.

I met up with Sophie again in the Infirmary after lunch. Once in the Dream-world, I realised that was her first time back since the fight with Phillip, and probably a site of a defeat to her. I could see it in her eyes. Being there made her a little uncomfortable and it took a while more before she seemed less agitated. We settled at a table and ordered some drinks. She said it was nice to get around on her own two feet without any assistance. Kinstein served the drinks and said Michelle was cleaning up in the back, and he hadn't seen her do anything unusual.

After he left, Sophie asked why Kinstein said those things. I explained that Michelle had done something unusual once and I wanted to see if she would do it again while I was not around. Sophie immediately picked up on what I referring to, asking if I thought Michelle was responsible for the critters and the changing landscape. I wasn't sure and wanted some proof. She reminded me that before the critters, I was chasing shapes around The Facility during the nights, shapes that may have been Michelle in the first place. It was during that time some people supposedly shared dreams.

"If she's crossed into the real world before," Sophie began, and I stopped her there.

"I get the feeling that someone wants me to think that, instead of letting me determine things on my own," I said.

"You're really trying hard not to deal with her, huh?"

"I just don't want to jump to that conclusion," I said. "Do you think she's capable of doing those things?"

"I think she's not aware of what she's capable of, and if she's doing what you think she's not doing, she's probably not aware of what she's supposedly not doing."

That killed the discussion because it took me a while to fathom what Sophie was trying to say there. I know I gave her a confused look and she smiled back at me. Michelle joined us soon after and she seemed happy to see me, smiling the biggest smile I'd ever seen on her. Still didn't say anything. She even gave Sophie a hug as a greeting.

After a while, I checked the 'bulletin board' and found that there were far fewer creature incidents and more of the usual mundane stuff I used to take care of; blocked paths, diverted rivers, a flooding, and an unusual infestation of rabbits in a world where there were never any in the first place. I took a few of the notices and arranged them to determine a path, so we could tackle as many of the problems along the way to that rabbit infestation. Sophie and Michelle tagged along, and it took us about a day to get the list done. It was odd that Michelle didn't seem taken in by the fluffy white rabbits. Sophie thought they were cute, but Michelle seemed… indifferent, as if she had seen them before and didn't care. Sophie noticed it too as we used our TK to round up the bunnies into two large baskets. We counted about forty-two rabbits in all. Sophie volunteered to dump them into her still unpopulated Dream-world.

I didn't see what she actually did with them; she flew off on her own with the two baskets and we met later at the Kitchen. The problem with this only came after we woke up in the Infirmary. Let me track this a little. I got back to the Kitchen with Michelle and spent some time with her while waiting for Sophie. Michelle didn't really behave any differently than any other time. She still seemed curious about certain things and she was quite happy hanging with me. I asked her why she didn't seem happy with the bunnies, but she only gave me that curious look like I was asking something utterly alien to her.

I tucked her in to sleep, and Sophie arrived at the Kitchen. We woke up in the Infirmary around three in the morning. First thing I noticed was the blanket on Sophie when I looked over to her. Then I noticed the blanket moving. She threw the blanket off herself, and all around her and spilling off the bed, were the rabbits. Both of us were stunned by this, as the rabbits scampered about.

There was only one Infirmary assistant on hand and suffice to say, she was not equipped to handle all the rabbits. I sat up and reached out using my TK to keep the rabbits contained. There must have been about twenty or so rabbits running around by then. It took a while more before Sophie finally got around to help corralling them. The Infirmary assistant brought a laundry cart to help with containing the rabbits. It was a strange thing, enough for me to send off a notice to both Linda and Remington.

Sophie ended up sleeping in the Infirmary. I helped the Infirmary assistant to secure the rabbits in the little zoo with the other critters, and only after did I head back to my room. I've got to catch up with Linda, Remington and Ms. Phillips later about all this. I'm really curious if the rabbits are more like the critters, i.e. 'animated dolls' as Ms. Phillips called them, or not, given they were more normal than the odd critter.

It's almost half six now and I guess Walker might be at the pool by now. So, I'm gonna sign off here and see if I can catch him.

Oct 20

It didn't take more than a day for Remington and Linda to respond to my comms message, but I guess they checked with Ms. Phillips first. When I was called to the Infirmary, Sophie was there as well, and the attendant from that night. Ms. Phillips said there were only nine rabbits in the cage when she checked on them the following morning after I secured them, and they were all like the critters; seemingly alive and yet not quite. I was curious why there were fewer rabbits and unless we could view the surveillance footage, we weren't going to determine that one anytime soon.

Sophie had no idea what happened or how the rabbits ended up under her blanket. I verified that she didn't have any rabbits on her when we left the Dreaming. Between Sophie and myself, we didn't have any idea how it happened. Only now, I was sharing the spotlight with her where the existence of these critters and merging realities were concerned.

I raised the point that Ethan was still making trips to his own Dream-world once a week, as far as I was aware. No incidents there; even Ms. Phillips could attest to. I never pried into what he does on his trips, which last exactly two hours. I was trying to make the point that he had some knowledge of the critters, and we even learnt some details about them from denizens in his Dream-world.

It was a thin thread, and it didn't prove that he had anything to do with the critters crossing over. At least, Remington thought so. In the meantime, I continue monitoring things, informing Remington and Linda of any unusual occurrences as before. Though no one said anything, I suppose the others and I could stop making these trips, but there was no guarantee that all the 'bleeding through' that's been happening would stop. And the last time I stopped for too long, well, it wasn't exactly healthy for me.

All that aside, there haven't been any other incidents or events since the rabbits although I have been extremely wary of my surroundings wherever I go. I haven't let down my guard since I was asked to report on any strange occurrences. I did wonder if being extra aware caused the lack of 'events' happening, because except for one occurrence – the stairs turning into a hillside – I was off-guard when the other change-overs happened.

I've really got to find a word to describe these things that happen.

Well, elsewhere then, since all that isn't my whole life. I had that meeting with Remington, Linda and the others right after the morning class, which went through lunch. After a rather late lunch by myself, I caught up with Jenny for a TP review, missing out on the start of the test run for the field trip's Learning Network. I got to observe only, and when it was done, I met with Callie and Toni for a review. I had taken Callie through linking with the F.E.P. participants, and she was holding up quite well. She and Toni have refined their process very nicely and are able to handle large groups for long periods, something Jenny and I struggled with when we started.

After classes were done for the day, I had a sparring session with Keiko. She wasn't as hard on me as expected. She was much harder when Keitaro was injured and not catatonic. It was our first sparring session since our talk. We've been mostly focussed on kendo since then. Dinner was when Walker came looking for me. He joined me for the meal and I asked him if he caught up with his work. He was close enough for now. I told him he didn't owe me any explanations and then asked how his ritual went.

"I thought you said I didn't have to explain." He gave me a sly grin.

"I was just making conversation," I said. "You don't really have to. It's nice having you back."

That's when he reminded me that he would have to return to his home soon and that I had become a part of his life; 'entwined with each other,' was how he put it. He asked if I had considered what I would do about it.

It seemed our relationship was one of the problems he raised during his ritual. "Am I a problem to you?" I asked. He said I was not a problem, but our situation might be considered one. Then again, it was something we considered when we started taking our relationship to this level. We knew there were issues to deal with, and his leaving sometime was one of mine. It felt like it came a lot sooner than I expected even though it's been coming since we started.

He said I had been a major point of consultation with his ancestors. There had never been a relationship like ours among his people and his decision to be with me has raised more than a few issues. He still sees me as kin. I think there's more to the meaning of that word than what I'm aware of. If we were something more than just boyfriend / girlfriend, I thought his idea of 'kin' meant that he saw me as one who would be as close as family, like a sister or more likely a distant cousin. On my side, yeah, I thought of him as my 'boyfriend' and not just a boy-friend.

His busy schedule of late was to catch up with his work, and he was ensuring that it can proceed without him. He wanted all those things out of the way and independent of him, so he could focus on us as soon as he could manage. He's not totally there yet, but his schedule and workload is closer to what is was before he went on his ritual. Another week or so and he'll have more time on his hands. The issue of us weighed on his mind as much as on my own right now.

Throughout most of yesterday, I was in a bit of a daze trying to get a grasp on things between us. I have Mikey to consider, and things are not that great between us right now. I've hardly spoken to him or even seen him in months.

All I get are occasional reports from either Karen or mom about how he's doing. I did consider that if he wasn't in the picture, could I leave with Walker?

All this being on my mind didn't go unnoticed either. I was pretty distracted in class and it was even more obvious during lunch. I was reluctant to share anything at the time, saying that I had some things to work out. Of course, I was also pretty wary of my surroundings especially when walking from one place to another. It does feel a little overwhelming.

I need to talk to Walker again.

Oct 22

There are several reasons why I've avoided getting too closely attached to people. What happened between me and... well, Phillip's brother... we'll use 'M' for now (I know I used 'X' before, let's stick with 'M')... what happened between M and me put me off guys for a while. It was hard to trust anyone again even if he did come for me and faced down Phillip in his attempt to rescue me from his brother. By then, it was 'damage done' and I more than wrecked their family. They forgave me a little later, but in private, mainly for Mikey's sake since M is his father. Publicly however, that's not acknowledged. For convenient political reasons, Phillip was named the father.

It's all a little complicated, given M's family standing in his home country, and I'm not supposed to acknowledge anything, since it has been agreed that Mikey has a stake in the family. Being with M might be every girl's dream, but given what happened between us, it's not this girl's dream. He's no more than a friend to me and a father to Mikey.

It's why I was wary of getting too close to Keitaro at first, keeping him at a distance. Even then, see how that played out. But while I was trying to avoid getting too close to anyone – and I really wasn't looking – I ended up with Walker. Over this past year, we've been close without really crossing that line. As much as we've made out, I've stopped short of actually having sex with him and it's not that I don't really want to; I really do. I admitted to him as much and he sensed my hesitation. I've had good experiences with M, and truly horrific ones with Phillip, both in reality and more in the Dreaming. They weren't the reasons for my hesitation. It was my own body that I'm unsure of. One thing about having a hyper-efficient system that allows me to heal really fast also means that certain things tend to be truly unknown territory.

I was in a coma when I was pregnant with Mikey and his sister. That was my physical state. Mentally, I was trapped by Phillip and utterly unaware of the pregnancy. From the way Charlie explained it, my body accelerated the pregnancy because it was a condition that it needed to 'heal' itself from. So, the pregnancy lasted under five months, and I was 'rescued' in time to face the labour and birth pains. Mikey was born, I lost consciousness and the girl then. We never knew what really happened. I was never told beyond that she didn't make it. Not that it actually mattered to me then. I didn't go through the pregnancy. I didn't carry the babies to term. I woke up and there they were ready to come out, and all I knew was the agony of it all. It's not something you get attached to.

Not something I'm eager to go through anytime soon. That's not to say that having sex with Walker will get me pregnant again, but I don't know what my body will do in that situation. Mentally, I'm guarded against it. I did explain all this to Walker before and he voiced his own apprehension, particularly from the point that we may not be biologically compatible. He is a F.E.P. after all, at least, in the eyes of a general populace. Then again, it may not actually be an issue. There have been other F.E.P.'s who have had relations of our nature and more. Becca and Steven come to mind. They've been together for as long as I've known Becca. All that being said, however, it's not like we haven't tried it ourselves within the safer imaginary reality of the Dream-world.

When I met him the other night, I asked what he thought the future would be for us. If we stayed together and tried taking the next step, he would either stay back with me, or I would leave with him when he had to return home. Where Mikey is concerned, the plan was that I got him for the first six years, then M would step in to do his part in Mikey's upbringing. I could bring all that forward. Mikey does have some contact with his father and he is aware of who M is to him now. While I haven't been having much of it lately, I could still keep in touch with Mikey through the Dream-world if need be. It wouldn't be easy, but it could be done. Walker saw that as "quite a sacrifice" on my part, to be parted from my "cub." Thing is, if I go with him, I don't know for how long or if I would ever come back.

For him, staying meant being tied to The Facility and limited freedom to the world outside of The Facility. We were both aware of our situation and what either future might hold. There was even the contemplation that we would not be together for the foreseeable future. We talked about possibilities and scenarios, and he slipped into that problem solving mode of his, presenting every conceivable scenario he could think of where our relationship might go; if I went with him, if he stayed here with me, if we went our separate ways and everything else in between. In the end, that's really all we had – possibilities.

He left the decision in my hands and said he would abide by my wishes. On his end, it would be desirable to be with me for as long as I would allow it.

And I thought it was a mutual decision.

All that weighed on my mind for the next couple of days, but I did give my almost full attention to my classes and the network test sessions. Callie and Toni are doing okay so far. At this point, we have time for one more test before the trip on the 26th. I really need to keep focus there for now. Even Remington could tell that I had something on my mind that was screaming for attention. Still, we were pulling an average of 92% recall across the board, so maybe he isn't too concerned beyond asking if I was okay.

I guess with all this on my mind, it might have had an effect on those 'events' as there haven't been any slips between reality and the Dreaming for me lately. The incident with the rabbits was the last thing that happened, and the only thing between then and now has been this issue with Walker. I guess it's kept me distracted enough that I haven't had much time for my mind to wander or relax. That said, I have been getting some solid sleep between an hour and a half to about three hours over the last few nights. In a way, I am getting some much needed rest.

Then last night, caught up with Walker again. I thought about our relationship and tried putting things into perspective. It started out as an exploration, but being with me was probably more than he bargained for. He had found a kindred spirit in me, someone that he could relate to enough to form a bond with. I decided not to press him further beyond our discussion that night. After the pool, I stayed the night with him. Slept well too.

I still have a decision to make, tho.

Oct 24

Coming up on the field trip, and the last network test today went along fine given how well Callie and Toni are handling the main functions.

While I'm not officially part of the field trip group, I have been supervising from the control room with Remington while Jenny was 'on the ground' monitoring the integrity of the network. We've stopped saying 'watching out for leaks'. Everything went smoothly and even Remington seemed bored by it all.

I was occasionally scanning only Callie and Toni, monitoring their connection with the F.E.P. team members and even then, for a few seconds at random intervals. Nothing intrusive, really. When I felt they were doing okay, I would turn my attention to my notes or the reports I have to vet, and occasionally, I'd have my own lessons to get through. This time, even with the last report Jenny passed me begging for attention, I couldn't focus on work. And Remington sensed this.

He didn't press me, but it had to come up sooner or later. While I did report it, there was no way an event/incident of such a scale with so many witnesses was going to go by without me having to answer a few questions. Yeah, there was another moment when the Dream-world decided to merge with reality, and it happened in a public place, at a time when there were more than a couple of people. Despite it happening at the gym at its busiest, no one could significantly determine when or how it happened, only that it happened almost in a blink.

For my part, I was sparring with Keiko in kendo. She was being a tad impulsive in her attacks and I was on the defensive for the most part, pushing an attack whenever I could. With the *men* headgear on, your vision tends to be quite straight ahead, and sounds end up being a little muffled. That said, I could tell the difference between our bamboo *shinai* clashing and that of real steel. If I thought Keiko was being impulsive and reckless, or perhaps a little overzealous in her attacks, I really shouldn't have worried because she displayed fantastic control. I had been on the receiving end of several hits that round, especially to the *koté*, and my hand was really feeling it. When I suddenly heard the clash of steel in one block, my focus wavered and she went for my *koté* again, but she didn't follow through. She had stopped short of practically slicing my hand at the wrist. One of our juniors screamed as the strike came down. Our *shinai* had turned into real katana. The blade had cut into my *koté*, but no further.

She lifted her katana with slight effort and then knelt to remove her *koté* and men. I was a little frozen for a moment and only came out of it when I felt her tug the katana from my hands and she motioned for me to remove my armaments. Only then did I notice how close she came to cutting me. While I've had some serious injuries before, I sure as heck wasn't keen to find out if my healing ability would extend to reattaching a severed hand. And given our positions, if she had followed through after her strike, she could have run the blade through me. Also, I realised that we weren't in the gym, at least, not from my perception.

While others could see the other walls of the gym, the mirrored wall was gone. It looked like glass windows, and beyond that, a complete village scene. Most of the gym equipment that were in use at the time remained, while unused equipment either vanished or were replaced by something else. The wooden floor area where Keiko and I were, had a ring made of pebbles to mark our sparring area. John's area where he was sparring with his friends (and Ethan) had the same, as did one other group who were wrestling on a padded mat. Parts of the gym's carpeted floor was now flattened sand with patches of grass. There were huts and a forest beyond that. We could see hills in a distance. For me, it was all open; there were no walls.

Suffice to say, everyone was disoriented by the change, but no one panicked. John, having experienced this before, kept his crew in check and made sure no one wandered beyond where we knew was the gym. He eyed me once and I was equally bewildered by what happened. No one said anything at that moment. I noticed that Ethan was as surprised as I was. Keiko quietly asked me if I was doing anything. I wasn't. She picked up the katana again and examined it before proclaiming that it was a superior blade, practically ancient.

I put my hand on the ground, just to feel it. I'm sure I felt the sand and ground even if, in my mind, I was expecting to feel the wooden floor that we had always practised on. It was about then, the oddest thing happened – the lights flickered. For me, it was like the whole world flickered momentarily, but I was told it was the gym lights that flickered briefly. And in that brief moment, between the flickers, the gym was back, but not everything went back to normal.

Certain items remained, like a few stones and pebbles and some of the environment. A girl had picked up a flower and that stayed with her. On a closer point, the katana remained instead of turning back into a *shinai*. The biggest thing that stayed in the gym was a small hut that seemed to have merged with the wall. It stayed there. In all, the event lasted no more than two minutes, at most.

I immediately grabbed my comms unit to send a note to Linda and Remington. John, Keiko and a couple of others asked me directly if I knew what happened, to which I had no answer. It was the same for Remington when he finally asked me about it in the control room. I could only relate what I saw and what the others told me. I had no real opinions or conjectures.

He asked me if I felt Phillip was responsible, but it was unlikely. If Phillip had any ability to force the merging of reality with the Dreaming, he had to do it through me, making me do it, consciously or not. Either way, there would have been some trace, some evidence in my mind, that I did it. Jenny and Sophie had scanned me before, and found no traces. I had already scanned Sophie, and I scanned Ethan after the event yesterday, to make sure he wasn't the one doing it. As far as I could tell, none of us who make trips to the

Dream-world were causing both realities to merge, consciously or otherwise. This was when he asked if it was time for me to consider Michelle.

"You're running out of options and people to blame," he said. "It's time you should consider what she is. From what I can follow in your journal about her, you're really trying hard to avoid something about her."

"I was warned about something that may or may not be her," I said. "Twice." I couldn't even look Remington in the eyes as I went on. "The one person I need to consult on this, said I would see him once more. I figured that would be when I would be told what exactly needs to be done, but he hasn't turned up, and I've been searching for him."

"You're referring to that Old Crans."

I nodded. "It's just a suggestion that she might be the cause. I was warned about a gateway that could potentially damage worlds. It doesn't specifically say it's her, even if some things are pointing me in that direction.

"Maybe it happened once, but I wasn't even sure what I saw. No one has seen her do anything that would actually suggest that she is the gateway."

"No parent can keep watch on a child at all times," he said. "Even if you think you have someone watching her, they can't do it all the time. You may have to force the issue."

"Maybe it's someone else who hasn't shown up yet," I said, trying to change the subject.

"Then, I suppose, you might want to check with Carl. He's been behaving lately, or maybe he's just lying low," he said. In all honesty, I had already ruled out Carl. I've dealt with him so much over the last couple of years and he has been, as Remington put it, behaving for the most part. Maybe it's a ruse, but I don't think so. I'm not monitoring him or anything, but I am also aware if he does step out of line.

All things considered, I really do have to take issue where Michelle is concerned. I don't want it to be so; for her to be the problem.

I didn't give Remington any answer and he did note that I was rolling things around in my head. That's when he asked that question which made me realign my thoughts. He said, "How sure are you that she is the daughter that you lost?"

I instinctively answered, "I'm not." And that answer I blurted out took me by surprise. I was so sure when I first looked at her, but now...

Remington didn't push the matter. He probably saw that I was affected by the answer. The moment stayed with me through the rest of the day, enough for me to decide not to make a trip to the Dreaming. I was a little apprehensive about confronting Michelle. Instead I dropped by the gym to check on that piece of a hut. A simple rope barrier had been set up with a note that advised people not to approach it. I only realised then that the hut did have a door. It wasn't some piece of wall with a window, it was a portion with an entrance.

Doorways in the Dreaming lead to a variety of places, not necessarily into a room… or a hut. But that's the nature of dreams; reality is never fixed. I remember feeling that I wasn't even sure which world was real.

I'm getting kinda hungry now. The field trip is the day after and I've got stuff to review. But I need some dinner first.

Oct 26

It's been a pretty eventful day. Sure, the field trip took the better part of the morning, but that wasn't the only thing that happened today. I wasn't there for the field trip but I got called in later. I'll get to that.

While I got along with normal stuff yesterday, I managed to catch up with Callie, Toni and Kevin to review their network. Callie was confident that she wouldn't have any problems with handling the F.E.P. on the network for the prolonged period of the field trip. She's done remarkably well on her own, and I've learnt from her in regard to the network as well. She and Toni have made it more efficient and less of a strain on the network controllers. We still require our volunteers and participants refrain from strong emotional expressions, to avoid those 'leak' problems we had before. Callie's method has allowed for passion and excitement for discovery and learning, to enhance the learning process.

All that didn't take up the whole evening. I still got in some kendo practice and took in some pool time with Walker after dinner. Sure, the hut was still there in the gym; its entrance mocking me. Kendo helped take my focus away from it. I really have to fight the urge to step through that door. Even Walker was curious about it, wanting to see what was on the other side; it has to lead somewhere. As far as I'm aware, no one has checked it out. I haven't even heard of any test being carried out, not that I've been poking around on that topic.

Since I wasn't going on the field trip, I didn't need to get any extra rest for the night. I ended up spending most of the late night working on Colleen. I've been upgrading where I am able and replacing parts as they fail, especially where the cooling system is concerned. I haven't thrown away any of those pieces that fell off since I could use Ehrmer's furnace to fix them. It's supposed to be a learning process after all; reusing and recycling, making do with what was available to me. Well, back when I started. Colleen has grown beyond that, where her purposes are concerned. Anyway, that was my night. I snoozed a little while waiting for Colleen to adjust to her new components, rebooting with the new specs. I had to adjust part of the main program a little to accommodate the new equipment. Colleen woke me up when the compiling was done, just before five in the morning.

After another half hour or so checking through some of Colleen's primary functions, I headed back to the pool.

I was surprised when Linda turned up during my breakfast, looking for me. It seemed Remington requested me in the VR arena. She didn't get any other details. I checked my comms unit and there were several message from him. They all came while I was either in the pool or the shower.

So this is what happened...

Ms. Phillips joined the field trip to check on the health of the residents of the colony. She had gone on previous trips, so this is nothing new. Will went as her assistant. It turned out that one particular patient needed a minor operation and the colony's on-hand medical personnel, Mary, wasn't experienced enough to pull off the operation despite having the necessary equipment. Secondary problem was that the colonists appeared to us as holographic projections. Even if Ms. Phillips could relay instructions, she couldn't see what was going on beyond the standard projections, making it impossible to make decisions on the fly. I wasn't clear what this operation was, but it was something that could wait for the field trip. I learnt this after I got to the VR Arena.

In order to tackle the communication problems, Peter asked about using a TP connection. Will consulted Jenny about the possibility, since she was on hand supervising Callie and her team. Will drew from our previous experience about manipulating objects with our TK via the holographic projections. Peter talked about connecting with me through my TP ability through the holographic projections. To be fair, that was when I pulled him into the Dreaming rather than making a TP connection.

After all those suggestions and exchanges, the decision was to create a network between Ms. Phillips and Mary. Jenny stepped up to make the connection, but Remington suggested bringing me in as a back-up. Jenny agreed and I was called in. Jenny and I discussed what we needed to do, and I admitted to her that I hadn't made a telepathic network connection with Peter. At least, not the kind they wanted. We had to also isolate our network from the ongoing Learning Network. We would put the communications network into use, but this would include accessing the visual aspects in the mind. The open nature of this network would also share some thoughts and emotions. Everyone involved agreed to this.

Jenny linked up with Ms. Phillips first while I tried to make a connection with Mary. We started out by naming a few items and asking them to visualise each item in their minds, but with a variation of their choosing. If we could pick up the images through our TP, we were making a connection. It's the same thing I did with Peter before, and I had no reason to doubt it wasn't going to work. To keep things simple, Jenny made the link between Ms. Phillips and Mary. I kept tabs on her while isolating her from Callie's network. There was every likelihood that either Callie, Toni or Kevin would pick up on our little network and then whatever we were doing was going to end up on that network, something best avoided.

The way we had set things up, Jenny would see, hear and sense everything between Ms. Phillips and Mary as much as they would share thoughts, emotions and ideas between themselves. The three of them were, for all intents and purposes, completely open to each other. If you were ever aware of your thoughts at any given time, you have an idea of what was going on here. I had to ensure that this was isolated to just the three of them and no one else, no other TP, was going to pick up on them. For my part, I would get a slight hint of what exactly was going on among the three of them, picking up bits and pieces here and there.

Jenny got a touch disgusted by the procedure as Ms. Phillips guided Mary through it. She could see what Mary saw, as did Ms. Phillips. And in Ms. Phillips' mind, she imagined what Mary needed to do, which Mary did following the images that got telepathically transmitted into her mind via Jenny. Not being a medical student, Jenny got sickened enough that I had my work cut out for me, to ensure she wasn't 'broadcasting' her emotions too much. I know Ms. Phillips and Mary picked them up; that couldn't be helped.

Just over half an hour into it, Mary needed an extra hand to help out. Will was asked to assist. This gave Jenny and me the opportunity to switch places while linking Will into the network. I told him to keep focused on the work at hand and try not to drift to any other thoughts. It was much tougher on him, to participate in the procedure while using his TK ability to manipulate objects over a massively vast distance via the TP link. I backed him a little with my TK while maintaining the network among the four of us. It was no picnic and I felt the strain in less than fifteen minutes in. Even Ms. Phillips felt us struggling with the network.

Peter stayed with us through it all, assisting Mary on his side. When we started out, he gave me a smile on the side and I nodded in response, trying to keep emotions in check. I think he was aware of what we were doing because he kept quiet and had a serious look on his face while we maintained the network. The whole procedure lasted just over an hour. Both Will and I were utterly drained by the end of it while Jenny claimed to be exhausted, but she didn't have a nose bleed from the strain like I did. Ms. Phillips tended to Will first, then gave me a look over. I was okay by then, but had another handkerchief to incinerate. Jenny maintained the 'bubble' around us, essentially keeping us isolated from the rest of the Learning Network, until Ms. Phillips moved on and I was okay enough to put up my own 'walls' again.

Remington said I could hang around until the end of the field trip so long as I didn't get in the way of the others. At best, it was another forty minutes or so, but it was time spent catching up with Peter and helping out (or rather, learning) as he went about servicing the colony's communication array that served the new early warning weather system. I knew a part of the system since Peter had shown it to me the last time we met. He told me that it has proven to be quite useful on occasion, but the sensors always needed to be realigned or repaired outright after each storm.

Through all that, we caught up with each other. I told him about Walker and the problems with the dreams. He didn't have any advice on the relationship front except to say that I should do whatever makes me happy. On his end, the work was getting harder, mainly because the environment where they are is so unforgiving. His physical condition was also getting worse, and while the holographic projection showed us an idealised image of the colonist, I saw what he was looking like now. That's thanks to the network link. Jenny saw the same thing when she was carrying the link. We both saw through Mary's eyes, in a way. Jenny would have been advised not to share that little bit. If it was bad before, it looks worse now, but at the same time, it looked like he was adjusting somehow. I can't get into details on that – not allowed.

It felt like we were on borrowed time, and we knew it. We simply didn't want to acknowledge it. We carried on, keeping things light and enjoyed each other's company. I asked about the kids and he said they were around, adjusting to the environment better than the adults. They also adjusted to the locally grown food better than the others, according to Peter. It took a long period of adjustment for them to get used to the changes that happened to the food grown on the experimental farm.

When the field trip was finishing up, Remington informed me to wrap up my time with Peter and to meet up with him in the control room. We said our good-byes and I fondly wished that we would continue to keep in touch. That's restricted to the schedule of the field trips and perhaps the occasional emergency transmission.

As everyone else was gathering, I felt Callie and Toni closing off their network. I headed out of the VR arena and up to meet Remington while the group went through their review. When I got there, he asked the others manning the VR control room to leave as he needed to discuss something with me in private – I'm writing it here anyway.

He sat me down at a console and said that the security division had brought a footage to his attention. At first, I was wondering if there was anything I did over the last week or so that would warrant their attention, enough for them to raise it to Remington. Then I thought it strange for them to raise it to him when he wasn't my G/C, not in an official capacity.

He loaded the footage and it took me a while to realise it was showing the hut portion in the gym, but the gym was empty. I quickly scanned the screen and noticed the date and time stamp which told me it was from the night before, about the time when I was working on Colleen. The gym was dark save for the little emergency light that provided little illumination. Then the image turned bright green, suggesting a night vision function. It stayed that way for about fifteen-seconds and then reverted. Every fifteen-seconds, the image would switch between the night vision and the normal dark image. This went on for a while and I began to wonder what I was supposed to see. I looked over to Remington. He stared intently at the screen. So I looked back and that's when I noticed it.

A shadow shifted and then extended from the hut, slowly moving outward from the hut's entrance and into the gym. Then the image changed to bright green, but I still couldn't see what was casting the shadow as it stretched even more into the gym, moving past the barrier that was set up. There was no light in the hut, nothing that would cause a shadow to cast outwards. There was nothing Remington or I could see that would be the source of the shadow. But it was a shadow, not too solid black or too light. We could see the carpeted floor beneath it when the image turned bright green. It must have stretched a good seven or eight feet from the entrance when it paused and did something else; it shifted from side to side. It was almost as it someone was looking around to the left and then shifting to the right, and back to the left. After a short stillness, the shadow retreated into the hut again.

"So, you're showing this to me because…" I started, and waited for him to continue.

"You made a suggestion in one of your entries about doorways," he said. "Were you expecting anything to come out of it?" I shook my head. "You also mentioned that the hut resembled some of those in your Dream-world. Is there anything there trying to cross over?"

"I've been chasing shadows for months now, and you're asking if there is something trying to cross-over?"

He nodded at that, as if understanding my frustration at the whole situation. He didn't say anything else, and he didn't have to. I had a hunch what that shadow was, and what he thought it might be. I sank back into the chair and covered my eyes with my palms, pushing my glasses upwards until they nearly fell off. I felt them coming off my head and I dropped my hands. I saw that Remington had my glasses in his hand, holding them out to me,

"You've got to get a grip on this, you know," he said.

"Do whatever I have to?"

"Within reason."

"Like taking a good look at that hut and see where it leads to?"

He gave me a look with a slight smile. I though he was going to say 'no', but instead, "Okay, but not on your own. I'll go with you."

"Now?"

"If you want."

"I'm kinda getting hungry."

"Okay, lunch first." He got off his chair and went to open the door for me. "Gives you a chance to think things through about what we're going to need. No point heading into the unknown without some preparation."

Oddity of oddities, Remington joined me for lunch. That meant he joined everyone else for lunch at the table where curiosities were raised and questions were asked. So, Remington let it slip that we were planning to check out the hut. Out of the blue, Walker sat down at our table and asked what we were actually planning. Then he asked if he could go along. All eyes descended on me then. I reluctantly said, "Okay." Remington smiled and focussed on his lunch.

"Actually, I need either Jenny or Sophie to help out," I said. "Someone to keep track of us from the outside once we go in."

Jenny said she was a little worn out from the field trip. Sophie asked what I needed. I explained that I wasn't sure what was going to happen when we crossed into the hut. For all I know, we could find ourselves in the Dreaming, or someplace else, or nothing would happen at all. So, I wanted someone who could keep in contact with me from the outside in case something did happen. If we did cross over, I wasn't sure if we were going to be physically transported, or if it was going to be some mental projection like my usual visit to the Dream-world. If it was the latter, it was most likely we were going to drop on the spot once we crossed over.

I worked out the finer details with Sophie, that she would keep a link with me as we, that was Remington, Walker and myself, stepped through the hut's doorway. I would keep in contact with her through it all, at least, I would try to. I have no idea if we could maintain contact if our little group does trip over to the Dreaming. We've never done anything like that before. That was all I had planned. No one else wanted to join us besides Walker, at least, no one spoke up when I asked. No one gave any reason for not wanting to go along. Given what happened with Sophie and Keitaro, I guess it wasn't surprising. Remington suggested having someone with Sophie since she would be skipping a class. I asked if she wanted her G/C with her, but she said her G/C would be busy at the time. Remington whipped out his comms unit and started punching out a message, and only then said he was calling Linda.

I wheeled Sophie over to the gym area where Linda was already waiting for us. Walker was beside me while Remington pulled up the rear. Linda got herself a bench and parked herself next to Sophie, who was facing the hut. Sophie and I linked up with a standard network and then isolated ourselves so as to not bother the other TPs. It was standard practice to isolate individual networks in class so no one would pick up our thoughts transmitted to each other.

Meanwhile, Walker was looking over the hut and commented how odd it was that we could not see the wall of the gym through the doorway. I've stared at the entrance and not once did I realise there was only darkness beyond the entrance. I thought it was merely a shadow, but even with all the lights on, and noting how shallow the hut protruded from the wall, Walker was right. We should see the wall, but it was just black. This made me a little nervous. Walker was excited, saying that it was thrilling to truly step into an unknown quantity. For all the scenarios he could probably come up with, given enough information, this particular situation presented him with loads of unknown quantities, and until we stepped into that darkness, we knew nothing. He reached his hand out towards the darkness before we decided on anything, like who was going first.

I took hold of his other hand, and he turned to look at me. He had a smile on his face that reflected genuine excitement. I said, "If you want to go first, at least hold on to me? Just in case?"

"In case of what?"

"If I knew, I wouldn't be so worried and nervous at the same time."

I then felt Remington's hand on my shoulder. I turned to face him, but he didn't say anything, he simply nodded. I nodded back and turned to Walker. Our eyes fixed for a moment, and I felt a calmness wash over me. I gave him a slight smile and he nodded, turning his attention back to the hut. His hand reached out again and he stepped forward.

I watched his hand as we moved closer towards the hut's entrance and the darkness within it. I could sense Sophie's thoughts telling me to keep calm because I was causing her to worry. She filled my head with all sorts of positive reinforcement, trying to instil that nature of hers, to face her fears head on. Then, Walker's hand disappeared into the darkness up to his forearm before he paused. He drew his hand back easily and looked at it, fiddling his fingers.

"It's warm," he said. "There's something beyond this."

I felt Remington's hand give my shoulder a slight push and I stumbled lightly into Walker. He looked at me with that smile and immediately took the next step forward into the darkness. I quickly followed him and felt Remington coming up behind me as we were swallowed by the darkness. I squeezed Walker's hand and called out to him. He squeezed back and said he was still there ahead of me. It was pitch black darkness. I couldn't see or sense anything, I wasn't even sure if we were standing on anything making it really difficult to make the next step forward even if I felt Walker pulling me along. And I still felt Remington's hand on my shoulder. Walker was right, though; it felt warm, but all around.

I then reached out to Sophie, and she responded by saying that we've disappeared into the darkness of the hut. At least it didn't break our connection. She then asked where I was, and I told her that I couldn't see anything, but black. She told me to stay calm and focussed, which was easier said than done. I couldn't see anything, my feet didn't feel like they were on any ground and the only things I felt were Remington's hand on my shoulder and Walker's hand in mine. I asked Walker if he could see anything. He said I should open my eyes. I said my eyes were open. That's when I felt Remington's hand shift and I could tell he moved around from behind to being in front of me.

"He's right," Remington said. "You should open your eyes."

"Maybe try closing them," Walker said.

Even when blinking, I didn't see anything. So I closed my eyes. At least, it felt like I closed my eyes. It was still dark, but then I started to notice a dimness growing, like I could see light through my eyelids. Then everything came into view, and I was sure I had my eyes closed. It was the strangest sensation to have your sense of sight reversed that way. It took me a while to get used to how I had to use my eyes.

I looked around and the first thing I noticed was the hut behind us, the one we emerged from. It looked like the same hut that was in the gym. We appeared to have stepped out of it and into some place that resembled the

Dreaming, but it didn't feel like my Dream-world, somehow visible with eyes closed, as if we were asleep, dreaming. Except, we were awake.

I think.

Remington asked if anything seemed familiar, and I said that it wasn't and yet it was. The landscape did resemble the Dream-world I was familiar with, but it didn't look like any part of my world. I looked around more, moving away from the hut and closely followed by Walker. Remington stayed near the hut instead of following us. While looking, I did my best to relay as much information back to Sophie as I could, both verbally and visually. She reported back that she could see in her mind what I saw. She wasn't familiar with the landscape at all, but admitted that she never did explore all of her Dream-world. So, I could have been in any of the three Dream-worlds I was aware of.

Walker and I explored on our own. He kept pointing out specific landmarks and markers, asking me if they looked familiar, markers such as a slightly deformed tree or an out of place boulder. We appeared to be in a valley of some kind with hills around us. I didn't notice this until Walker was pointing at the hills, asking if they seemed familiar. I realised we couldn't see very far because of the trees. We had walked maybe ten minutes in a fairly straight line, and even the hut and Remington were out of sight. While it was nice to be out in the open with Walker, it was also a tad frustrating that we were getting nowhere. We were looking at a lot all around us, and seeing nothing.

It was a while more before I decided that I wanted a view from on high, and I told Walker so. He said to go ahead, so I took off and slowly headed straight up maybe three hundred feet or so. It gave me a pretty decent view of the world we were in. The view was not good. I leaned forward to look downward and what I saw was mostly all green with trees and hills and open meadows in some areas, a small stream that seemed to flow through the lands, mostly obscured by the foliage. And all that pattern of light and dark greens, resembled an eye. I had to rotate myself a little just to be sure and I had to ask Sophie if she was picking up what I saw. She thought it was a fluke, a trick of light and shades across the landscape. So, I floated higher.

Like some kind of mosaic, a face started coming together. I noticed the pattern of another eye come into view the higher I went. Even Sophie had to admit that it was no longer some fluke, and it was disconcerting to have these eyes staring up at me. I was much higher than I had ever gone before and I still couldn't see the whole thing. I kept floating higher, probably as high as where planes would fly. Sophie pointed out the pattern of a nose before I noticed it; she was seeing what I was. There was a lot to take in. For all I knew, we could be seeing what we wanted to see. I couldn't even see where I started, where I left Walker on the ground, but that didn't stop me from going higher. It was long before we got more details and the sense of recognition hit us both.

"Is that Michelle?" she asked as we stared at the childish face that came into view.

"I think it's me," I said.

There was a tap on my shoulder from behind and I screamed, jerking to the equivalent of jumping out of my skin while floating high above the world.

"Jean... Easy," I heard Walker say. I turned and there he was barely a foot below me, standing on solid ground, where I had left him so long ago. I turned back and found myself looking up at the blue cloud-filled sky. Then I turned back to him and heard Sophie asking what had happened. I couldn't provide any explanation, but Walker said I floated upwards until I was out of sight and a long while later came floating back down while facing skyward. When I came within reaching distance, he tapped me on my shoulder.

Following that bit of explanation, he regarded me a little strangely, looking me over like he wasn't sure who I was. When I asked, he said I looked younger, but not by much. I couldn't see this myself, so we headed back to Remington. Along the way, I told him what I saw from my aerial vantage point. He felt that it made a little sense and suggested that we were indeed within my Dream-world, but somehow physically transposed. If, indeed, we were physically there. As far as I could gather from Sophie, we weren't physically in the gym, so maybe Walker was right about that. Thing is, it didn't feel like it was my Dream-world.

When we got back to where we had left Remington, there was a bit of a surprise. The hut wasn't there anymore, but there was something else. It was the replica of the Kinstein's Kitchen. Remington said he had looked away, looked around, for merely a moment and when he looked back, the hut was gone and replaced by the Kitchen. And I say replica, because it didn't feel like the real Kitchen to me. It didn't even feel like it was in the right place.

"You're looking more your age," Remington said after regarding me for a moment.

I didn't even let the comment sink in. The concern was that if the hut was gone, was our way home gone as well? My next concern was, why the Kitchen? And then I was wondering if we were in that place where I got pulled into and stuck some time back. Sophie had that same concern, since she was the one who had to pull me out the last time. When I told the others that I wanted to go through the Kitchen entrance, Walker argued that we hadn't discovered anything substantial yet and it would be a waste to go back now. Remington reminded me that we hadn't found anything that would have possibly cast the shadow we saw coming out of the hut. I countered that by stepping through the door of the so-called Kitchen wasn't necessarily going to send us back. It had to be there for a reason, and the fact that it was the Kitchen, specifically, had to have some significance.

They reluctantly agreed, deferring to my judgement, since I would know more about the Kitchen than the two of them. I also signalled Sophie to stand by in case what happened last time happened again, that it was all a trap to keep me in this place. I strode over to the door purposefully and pushed it open. Walker quickly came up behind me, closely followed by Remington. Walker, looking into the Kitchen over my shoulder, commented that it looked right, based on his few visits there. I said that if it was drawn from my memories or directly from my mind, it was always going to look right. I was more concerned about what it looked like after we stepped through the door. So, I took a step in.

Nothing happened. The Kitchen was still the same. It didn't do any crazy switch-around and suddenly put me outside again, nor did the interior change into something else. I took another step forward. It certainly felt like the Kitchen on the inside even though it didn't feel that way from the outside. It felt familiar, even though the emptiness of it sent a chill down my spine. It felt cold and forbidding. We kept stepping further in with a degree of trepidation, well, at least, I was. I guess Walker might have felt the same, but with a slight degree of excitement. I had no easy explanations for our situation and he had nothing much to work with, to formulate any reasonable solutions to our predicament. For all he knew at the time, we were stuck in a place that had no way out.

We stopped and stood dead centre within the Kitchen. I realised that some of the windows were open and we could look out, but I wasn't even sure if we were looking at the same place where we first started. Sophie was equally cautious, being there in spirit, but sort of keeping an eye on things through me. She kept telling me to keep calm. While I didn't show it, trying to keep a cool exterior, I was more than a bundle of jumbled nerves on the inside. Even Walker sensed it, eyeing me like he was expecting me to jump out of my skin again at the slightest thing. Turned out I did no such thing when the unexpected happened. It seemed like the lights flickered within the Kitchen, which was strange because there were no electrical lights. Two half-opened skylights provided the basic illumination and the few opened windows provided the rest, but there was a flicker, like in the gym a few days back. And then, there was Michelle standing not too far from us before the entrance to what should be the back-room. And she was holding this black ball.

bck kwan

I cautiously approached her asking what she was doing. She gave me that quizzical look that she also had whenever I asked her anything. Remington came up to me and said, "Try using 'we'."

"What?"

"Instead of asking 'What are you doing here?' try asking 'What are we doing here?'," he said.

I wasn't sure what he was getting at, but I tried it anyway. "What are we doing here?" I asked her. That elicited a sly smile that gave me chills and made me take a step back.

She then held the ball outwards and then tossed it up into the air. I backed into Walker and I felt him take my hand. The black orb rose to the middle of the room and appeared to explode, engulfing everything in blackness. I lost my footing then and fell backwards and next thing I knew, I landed on top of Walker and we were on the ground, in the gym. Remington was next to us, but on his feet. He was facing the wall where the hut entrance had been, looking over it. Judging where we were, it was likely we were exactly where the hut actually was. Linda was quick to help Walker and me to our feet. Sophie was standing, albeit a little unsteadily, wanting to help. There were also quite a few people around by then too as classes were letting out and the gym regulars were coming in for their work-out.

Sophie asked what happened because the last thing she got from me was Michelle smiling and then 'everything went black'. We simply appeared out of nowhere in the same instance the hut vanished, "In a moment of a flicker," according to Linda.

Altogether though, we were fine and it may have seemed like we didn't go anywhere. We ended up right where we started. I did have Walker and Remington on my side for this; so, something did happen. Without a doubt now, at least, for me, Michelle is the epicentre of it all; the nightmares where we first found her, most likely all the critters that have been crossing over and now the merging of realities. I still think there's a possibility that someone or something is using her image to get at me. Then again, it was hard to disprove what we experienced, especially with her there at the end.

Remington has something else on his mind. He hasn't said anything much about what happened except to say, "So, that was Michelle, huh?" There was that odd thing where he asked me to rephrase the question, shifting from the second person reference (you) to a first person reference (we).

He and Linda agreed that we shouldn't talk too much about what happened for now, but said I could write it up in my journal as a soft record. He hasn't told me anything of what happened with him when Walker and I left him alone. I think he has some issue about Michelle; something on his mind that he's not willing to share. When I pushed him, he said not to worry about it and that it was nothing.

In any case, I suppose I should get some rest if I can manage it. There're lots of stuff still rolling about in my head and it's been quite a day. After the whole gym thing, Sophie, Walker and I got together to discuss a few things, despite what Remington and Linda told us. It was more for my benefit to sort out a few things, that whole floating incident being one of them. That really screwed up my head a little.

I guess I should get some rest, so that's about it for now.

Oct 28

It's been a couple of days and things have more or less been pretty normal. The field trip was considered a success after a review of the reports with Remington and getting some feedback from the participants. By default, the Learning Network is an effective learning tool and there was a short discussion to implement it in other areas that have a larger coverage, like project works involving a variety of cross-platform subjects. Building a rocket comes to mind, but I didn't say anything about that.

Jenny got a special commendation as the network supervisor while helping me out with our little side network. We were asked if we could get some of the other TPs involved with the Learning Network. I was fine with it as long as they were willing. The TKs are more willing to experiment with their abilities than the TPs. Getting them to try new stuff isn't easy, especially when it comes to the network where it feels like you're sorting a few too many voices in your head. I suggested Callie as the best person to push the network forward and Jenny backed me on that. Plus, we have that network we pulled off for the surgery, similar to the one I had with Sophie during the excursion into the hut.

A TP, by default, is basically thought of as a mind reader. We hear other people's thoughts and, depending on skill or ability, can do that little bit more. Linking into the visual centre of the mind wasn't that easy. I suppose a neurosurgeon could explain it better; how the light that goes through our eyes gets translated into the images we see, but I also think that we never really 'see' things the same way. Perhaps, by accident, I've proven myself wrong.

Remington didn't push for that, but agreed we pulled off something new that is useful in given situations. The surgery proved that much, and now, Sophie's got a bit of a head start on the others where that's concerned. He didn't quite say I should go ahead and refine it. I still have to help out with both the TP and TK classes, working with Miss Tracy on lesson plans, and dealing with

Ethan from time to time as his mentor. There are my other classes and projects taking up my time. I haven't logged in as much time as I would like with the flight simulator; that's become something I do when I have some spare time, most of which I try to squeeze in with Walker.

I spent some time on my 'spaceship' with Walker doing a bit of a review for me, checking my work and pointing out trouble areas. That was after our swim. He didn't spend too long, just under a half hour and then he went off to sleep. It must have been about one in the morning by then. It was closer to four when I got into my bed and I did get a good two hours of sleep, unlike the restless night before.

Today, there were discussions at lunch about our day-out activities. I wasn't sure if Keiko was going to have the kendo grading again given what happened. She's been grilling our juniors quite a bit while I've been playing the *monodachi*, as she calls it; the one who stands there like a dummy and accepts getting whacked all over. To be fair, she and Keitaro did that for me, so I should do that for the juniors. She hasn't said anything about any grading, and Remington hasn't brought up anything about it either. I'm still going to meet up with Mikey, at least, I hope mom will bring him around. It's been months since I last saw him.

In any case, there were still the baseball games and the clubbing as before. Some of the others are meeting up with their parents. Walker and I don't have any plans yet. I guess it would be nice if we could go to the beach, but that's not likely. Maybe a picnic in the park, by a lake. Honestly, the day could have crept up on me and I wouldn't have noticed this time around. Anyway, I'm simply going with the flow in this.

I got whacked up again during kendo, and I did get some sparring with Keiko after that. I thought about asking if she was planning a grading session for the juniors, but she seemed a little down so I didn't push the subject. She's still teaching me new stuff, but I just can't get all the names of the new stroke movements. It has to do with minimal blocking and attacking, tapping aside your opponent's *shinai* to create an opening to attack (*harai*?) either the *men* or the *koté*. It's two different moves for the *men*, but one for the *koté* though. And she kept complaining that my *fumikomi* – that attacking stomp forward when you strike – was too short, like I was taking a normal advancing step. The way she did it, it was like a giant leap forward, and she did it so effortlessly while maintaining perfect posture.

It was all minor refinements.

There isn't much after that and I want to head off to the pool now.

Oct 30

Ethan's pretty excited about tomorrow and his excitement was infectious too. This was in class when I asked him about his plans. I had to get him to reel in his emotions a little and make sure he wasn't unintentionally 'spreading' it around. He's gotten good at putting up the walls in his mind to keep out the extra noise, but he still projects a little when he gets overly emotional. Most of us TPs pick up on it and it's usually stress related; a sense of frustration more than anything.

Emotional projections like these are quite common, but all of us have learnt to filter it or block them completely. It is tough to block yourself from projecting especially when under such extreme stresses, and yeah, even if those stresses are pleasure related; another particular reason I haven't gone that far with Walker. Then again, it is only under extreme emotional stresses, like when someone gets awfully enraged and affects those around him. It is a little tougher to explain this one away and it is something we TPs don't particularly want to share. People get scared about it, but we are mostly in control of projecting such things and it's more often TPs who pick up on the projections than other people.

A lot of people making plans, and such discussions have become the norm during lunch lately. Keiko has confirmed that she will be having a grading session for the juniors. Her parents will be coming as well to check on Keitaro. She left it to me to either meet or avoid them altogether. I suppose I could explain a little about what happened. Carol felt it was a bad idea when I mentioned it during lunch today. We were discussing what we would be up to on our day-out and when we would meet up for the clubbing. So I casually mentioned the grading and meeting up with Keiko's parents. Helen felt it was a noble gesture on my part and suggested I throw in an apology as well. After all, he did get hurt on my watch.

Not everyone is coming around for the grading this time, while a few expressed an interest in checking it out. I guess there will be transport prepared again and mom's probably secured a hall at the hotel for us. That is, unless something has changed. Most of the audience would likely be friends of the juniors who are taking the grading. Aside from their names, I haven't gotten to know them on a personal level. They're older than I am and in other more advanced classes, but only my juniors in kendo.

So, aside from the TP class and catching up with friends, everything else is moving along like usual. There haven't been any new critters or cross-over events. I kept expecting Michelle to pop out of every other shadow I passed along the corridors at night. How or why those things happened, I don't know and I wish I had answers. If it really is Michelle, I may not have any actual answers in the end especially if she refuses to talk. That smile; that creepy smile. Even now, thinking about it sends chills down my spine.

On that note, Walker hasn't exactly left things alone. He confided that he has been reviewing my journal, trying to find some connection between the events and what happened when we went into the hut. He's also been running some spectral analysis around the area where the hut was, but said the analysis all came back negative. No unusual residual energy to even suggest the existence of anything beyond the gym wall already there. He only asks direct questions when he has any. He's never danced around the subject or tried to weasel any answers out of me the way some others have tried. He still wanted the idea of a parallel world to work, but was also well aware that it was likely all in my mind. Didn't explain much in how it all fell together in his head and my answers barely helped to fill in the blanks he had.

...

Kinda got interrupted there and have lost my train of thought, even after reading through what I've written.

Becca came by asking for help with Kadi, who's not been cooperative when it comes to The Facility's protocols for F.E.P.'s in some cases. Apparently, Kadi is intent on doing some exploring of the city and Becca has her own appointment with Steven tomorrow, so she can't escort Kadi around. Most of the F.E.P.'s tend to take the opportunity to get out if they are able, but often with their 'local buddy' or G/C. Since Remington is also a little busy, he can't be with Kadi. Rain's got her own thing as well, which isn't what Kadi wanted to do.

We have the grading in the morning and meeting with Keiko's parents after that. I intend to take Mikey to the park again with Walker and maybe Lian if she's around. If Kadi doesn't mind that, I suppose she could hang with me. I'm not sure what Remington's busy with though. Becca's the one who needs to clear all that up. She's supposed to get back to me later.

Meanwhile, I'm off to the pool.

NOVEMBER

Nov 1

Yesterday was a full day.

Before we left The Facility, I settled with Becca about Kadi being with me for the day. I briefed Kadi on what we would be doing, but I would also give her some time to do some exploring. She was looking forward to the grading, and hoping to face off with an opponent.

We set out from The Facility at seven in the morning, a bus was prepared for those who wanted to go along. As expected, it was mostly friends of the juniors who were taking the grading, Becca included. Steven was meeting her at the hotel, but she was keen to observe Kadi's grading. The hotel was our grading venue with the same set up. Mom played host again, not as formally as before. It was great that Lian and the others made it, and I got to catch up with them before the grading started.

We did a quick change and did our warm-up. Our guests filed into the hall and took up whatever seats were available. Keiko got me to watch over the juniors and make sure they were ready while she greeted her sensei and other teachers conducting the grading; the same as last year.

The juniors stepped up first, and like before, they had to follow instructions to show that they had the basics down. Keiko had me calling out the instructions though, ranging from footwork all the way to *hayasuburi*. I was particularly watching Kadi who was staying acutely focussed and giving out quite a forceful *kiai* that drowned out the others. She did really well there. I suggested to Keiko to let her try facing another visiting student.

It turned out that Keiko had other plans for me during the grading. I thought I wasn't in for a grading, but ended up with one. She had told me that I would be paired with some of the other students of the visiting sensei because they would need someone to spar with for their grading. So, I was observing for the first part, watching our juniors go through the motions of following instructions and then sparring against each other. Then I had to spar against another *kendoka*. I think he had a higher grade than me, but Keiko said to treat it like a sparring session with her and try to win with a proper hit. That's what I did, giving my opponent no quarter, though he was damn good; not as good as Keiko, so I didn't have any problems defending myself against him. It was a little more difficult to score a hit and there was a time limit to consider. I managed one scoring hit on his *koté*, but that was it. He got me on the *men* but it was a weak hit and didn't score any points. The fight was fierce enough as was his *kiai* and it took me by surprise at first, but like I said, he wasn't as good as Keiko who can really scream a room down.

I felt a little bad that he didn't win his fight against me, but that's what it does come down to in kendo when facing an opponent. It didn't faze me that much when I got paired up against another opponent, another student of the visiting judge. He was also of a higher grade, but didn't seem as experienced because I took him down fast with a *men* hit first and a *do* hit after that. He seemed freaked out after the first hit and appeared quite unsteady as we carried on until time was called.

There were two other pairings after that and in all, the whole thing took almost three hours. While the sensei were tallying up the grades, Kadi got her chance to take on an unknown opponent, also a junior. She did pretty good although both fighters seemed anxious in facing each other. By the time we did our tributes – bowing and thanking the sensei and the hall – it was a little past eleven in the morning. Food was served all around. Like I said, I didn't think I was in for a grading but I got one anyone. Keiko's plan for that was to have me participate, but not have the pressure of knowing that I was being graded. She wanted me to have the fights as if they were normal sparring sessions. So, my grade went up another notch while the two I faced off against were not as successful in their grading. Our juniors got thru their grading, but remained within the *kyu* range. Kadi got to *San-Kyu* and I told her it was really good for a beginner.

I got to meet with the sensei who gave some advice in Japanese, mostly on improving some of my steps and what I did wrong – only ever so slightly – as well as what Keiko could do to take my training to the next level. Keiko translated most of it for me. It was almost the same when I consulted the other visiting sensei. He also pointed out some trouble areas, but had some praise, since it was his students I defeated. It was another hour of mixing around and chatting before the crowd started dispersing. I quickly caught up with Keiko to let her know that I couldn't meet with her parents as planned, and to extend my apologies and regards. She would and thanked me for my concern. She then left, and I turned my attention to the others.

By this point, Kadi was getting restless as was Mikey. Rick and Karen were tired while Walker was talking with Lian and my mom. When I asked them what they were talking about, mom kept mum, Walker smiled, and Lian said it was nothing. It was then that I noticed Jenna hanging with Paul, and they were about to leave as well. Admittedly, I'm glad they're still together even if Paul hasn't said anything about it. I took Kadi to the suite.

Once we were done taking turns with the shower and changed, we headed out with Walker, Mikey and Lian. I told Kadi that the park was the best way to get a glimpse of societal behaviour within the city, and since it was a Saturday, we would get a better cross-section of the population than on a regular weekday. She was a little happier to be out-of-doors, taking in whatever sights she could manage from ground level instead of the aerial view from The Facility. The weather seemed a little on the gloomy side with sunlight barely peeking through some heavy clouds, but it did gave us a nice cool day, even if the threat of rain hovered constantly. We cut through some streets and made our way to the park with Mikey struggling a bit to keep up. He absolutely refused to let me bring his stroller, insisting he was too big for it. He has grown quite a bit since I last saw him, but I can still pick him up and carry him, if need be.

I took the time to catch up with Lian first while Mikey seemed happy to be in Walker's company. Lian filled me in with news from home, and the few friends she was still in contact with. She was more interested in the progress of Walker and me, going so far to ask if I would leave with him when he had to return home. I told her it was still under consideration, and she picked up on the conflict that was going on where that decision was concerned. It was relatively easier catching up with her than with Mikey.

Mikey's able to speak, but he's still finding his way around words, and his sentences are pretty fractured, probably doing really well for his age and we are able to talk to each other. I have to keep my sentences simple so that he can understand what I try to say. There's something here I'll get to in a while.

So our afternoon in the park was spent wandering around, sitting by the lake, checking out the baseball games, letting Mikey go wild around the playground and interestingly, we got almost no second glances despite Walker and Kadi being with us. It's not that they look wildly different form anyone else, but different enough that on a regular day, we might have attracted a little more attention. Well, Kadi did attract a little attention due to her curiosity, peering a little too much at some people and generally being a little too inquisitive. We got away with explaining that she was a tourist.

It was about past three when we decided to head off to a mall at Lian's request. We made one little stop at an ATM so I could get some cash. Once done, Walker said he had a cash card from his G/C for some miscellaneous expenses. Apparently, I could have gotten one from Remington or Linda, but

I never knew that we could. So, he paid for the few items we ended up buying; a shirt and a swimsuit for me, a blouse and skirt for Kadi (picked out and endorsed by Lian), a skirt for Lian, and a pair of pants and a shirt for himself. I paid for a shirt I picked out for Mikey and a little gift for mom. Kadi had a blast and Mikey got so worn out I carried him after a while. He fell asleep on me. It was close to six by the time we got back to the hotel for a much needed rest.

We had the family suite to ourselves again. Lian took a nap as did Kadi, and I tucked Mikey in before settling on the couch with Walker to watch some TV. We weren't really watching TV tho. It was not more than ten minutes of settling on the couch when Rick came by to inform me about the dinner plans at half past seven.

After dinner, I checked in with Francine first. I wasn't in the mood for clubbing because I had stuff on my mind. Walker ended up taking Kadi to meet the others while Mikey and Lian stayed with me. Mom came with me too, because she wanted to talk about some stuff – life, studies, boy – even with Lian present. After the small talk, she dropped the bomb on me. Remington had briefed her about the dreams, the journey through the hut and meeting Michelle.

So here's where I need to fill in that stuff with Mikey. It took me a while to get him to open up, to explain why he didn't want to meet me in the Dream-world anymore. During the whole day, he seemed a little nervous being with me. In his own way, Mikey said he was scared of Michelle. It was a few little things that sounded like sibling rivalry to me at first, but it seemed she was more than a little mean to him. When he was early to the Dream-world, and it was only the two of them there, she would do things like levitate him higher than he was comfortable with, or hang him over the stream. It sounded like she treated him like a toy, but what freaked him out was when she would somehow modify his mecha while he was in it. He didn't quite say modify... it's just the way he described it, like she somehow transformed his mecha into something much less than what it was supposed to be. Thinking back, I hadn't seen his mecha in a while either. Michelle's been accompanying me on the jobs, but even that has settled down a little. I don't know what she did, but I know it's not there anymore, as far as I can recall. Stranger still, its disappearance never really registered until he told me about it.

But that wasn't the real mystery about Michelle. Mom said Remington had made a strange request, asking to see some photos of me when I was a child. When he perused them, he pointed out a few which my mom then showed to me. I honestly could not remember when those pictures were taken, but it was during the time when Rick and I were following mom and Mac around the world to various hot spots and hanging with all sorts of mercs. Mom took a lot of pictures then, working as a freelance photo-journalist, keeping on the move and learning what she could from those people via Mac. She said the pictures were of me, but what I saw was Michelle.

At first, I dismissed it. It wasn't unusual that Michelle would look like me as a child, but it was Remington who suggested that Michelle may be more than an after image of the baby I lost. He implied to her that Michelle and I were the same person. The way he asked me to phrase the question that time… making the reference to first person, it would suggest that I was talking to myself. The way Michelle responded to the question with that smile somehow acknowledged the fact that we were indeed the same person.

Lian had no idea what we were talking about, but it didn't really bother her. She's gotten used to the fact that there are aspects of my life that will never make sense to her, as much as she already knows. I decided to keep the pictures so that I could check with Walker and Sophie, maybe get them to give me a second opinion. Thinking on it, not really sure a second opinion on what. I guess they might tell me if Michelle and I are one and the same, but they also might get to same conclusion that our likeness is a coincidence.

Anyway, mom didn't leave me a lot of leeway after presenting the pictures and sharing what Remington had told her. I need to catch up with him and pick his brain on this situation, and then I'm gonna have to dive in and check on Michelle. Mom felt I should be careful with what I do next, and left me to my thoughts. I explain it all to Lian as best as I could. She already knew that I lost a baby, but that was about it. She just listened with a sympathetic ear.

It was almost eleven at night when we were done. I walked Lian back to her suite. It gave me an opportunity to see Mikey before I returning to The Facility. I didn't wake him, but gave him a little kiss on the cheek as he lay there. Karen said she would continue watching over him with Rick, and I thanked her for it. With that, I got a cab back to The Facility.

I wandered the corridors for a while, watching for any particular discrepancies or twist in reality as well as any critters that might be running around. There hasn't been any such incident, not for a while now, but I still try to keep an eye out from time to time when I move between my workstations – simulator, Colleen, pool – and my room. I ended up at the pool and rested there. I took my jeans off and sat by the pool, dipping my legs in the water. I don't know how long I sat there, looking at the water; at the sky above through the glass; at the city outside.

I only know it was about four when I got back to my room and started writing this up. It's closer to six now. I heard Becca coming in about an hour ago. She's probably going to sleep in for the rest of the day. For now, I'm gonna head back to the pool and try out my new swimsuit.

Nov 3

Sunday was surprisingly quiet, more so than expected. The classes were practically empty which gave me a nice opportunity to have some personal face time with the tutors. I breezed through four different classes in one day absorbing as much as I could from each tutor. The most I found in a class were three other trainees and even then, not for long. We asked questions, covered what we needed to know and moved on. Apparently, everyone was sleeping in after a hard night out.

It was only towards the end of the day, when signs of life were returning to normal around The Facility, I got a message on my comms unit. I expected it earlier, but I guess even Linda needed a break before meeting me for the monthly review. That was yesterday.

The usual stuff was quite brief, covering my lessons, training and projects. Catching up with the tutors the day before didn't factor in, but she had heard about it. The TP and TK classes are always a major factor because I have a much bigger role in them, working with Miss Tracy in developing the others. There's often pressure from Miss Tracy's superiors to get us to try things that really seem shifty, but I do try to find a work-around. They still think we're capable of controlling people's minds – something they're pushing us to prove is possible, especially given what I wrote about Phillip controlling Keitaro – or stopping the operation of a major internal organ of a person. The fact that we can help out in a medical procedure seems of great interest to them. Will is pioneering some stuff there and he has been sharing his progress with me, the results being some spirited discussions in class.

Aside from that, I didn't have any other gripes to share with Linda. She asked how things were with Ethan. He's progressing well enough, busy and occupied with his work as well as some physical training with John. That's working out surprisingly well, and John's been a pretty good influence on Ethan.

From there, the discussion moved on to Michelle and the problems with the crashing realities. Since that trip through the hut, Ms. Phillips has reported a massive drop in the nightmares inflicting trainees. Either something significant happened during that little excursion or the trainees have gotten used to the bad dreams, or maybe the dreams aren't as bad now. Linda gathered that bit of news only a couple of days back, which makes it less than a week after the excursion.

It almost seems as if Michelle may be lying low but I still plan to make the trip into the Dreaming on Saturday as usual. I need to confront her, but before that, I need to talk with Remington, to get his thoughts on the situation. He felt comfortable to share with my mom but he hasn't said anything to me.

"I can't say I understand everything that goes on in your head where this whole dream thing is concerned," Linda said. "I don't even know if telling you to be careful is actually helpful, but whatever you do, I hope you do it safely and come back to us unharmed."

The way she said it was weird. Still, I assured her I would be careful as it's something I have to face on my own. I'm just not sure how to prepare for what's to come. I don't know how she managed to cope with all my weirdness though. She's been sympathetic in light of everything I've gone through under her.

After that review, things fell back into the normal groove. I caught up with Becca to let her know about Kadi's day out activities. I also met with Sophie in class. She's been out of the wheelchair and using a walking stick for balance since Saturday. She asked why I didn't meet up with everyone else at the clubs. I didn't have any particular reasons aside from catching up with my mom. I'm having dinner with Sophie on Friday.

The question of my absence on Saturday night was also brought up at the lunch table, but no one would argue about catching up with one's parents. That would always take precedent over any other group activity. So the question became, why didn't I catch up after I was done with my mom? To that, I had no real answer aside from saying that I wasn't in a party mood after I was done with my mom and Lian, and saying good-bye to Mikey. Callie apparently did have a good time after she was done meeting with her mom and she was not shy about sharing it.

In a way, I'm a little relieved to have things at a pretty much normal state. I still keep a wary sense for anything that might be a little off, especially in the dead of night, but that's also been quiet. So, I'm off to the pool to unwind.

Nov 5

Finally got to meet with Remington today. It's not like there weren't earlier opportunities, it's that he seemed to be avoiding me for a while there. He was barely in his office these past few days, and I tried everyday at various times. I thought he had something going on outside of The Facility, but I saw him yesterday to make an appointment for today.

He seemed reluctant to give me any information, considering how open he was when discussing the hut in the Arena's control room that day. It's almost as if something else happened in the other world which made him a little apprehensive towards me. I had to ask something like twenty questions to get him to admit he asked my mom to dig up those old pictures of me. I even asked him directly if he thought Michelle and I were the same person, but he said, "It doesn't matter what I think."

"Then why bring it up to my mom? Why make me talk to Michelle as if I were talking to myself?"

He didn't answer straight away. He looked at me in some thoughtful way, then said he made a mistake in bringing me to The Facility; that it was too early. "But you're here now and we've got to make the best of it," he said.

That made me regard him with a little suspicion. It was the oddest thing for him to say to me. He didn't even elaborate despite asking him to. It just put me in a mood. I guess it was the expectation that he would have been a little more helpful in light of what I was planning to do about facing Michelle. And I told him so. Instead, he seemed to be putting me down and making me feel like I was in way over my head.

When I think about whatever this deal with Michelle is, I get the feeling that it would have come up, whether I was at The Facility or not. I probably would have dealt with her differently too. Now, however, Remington's suggestion of making the best of it… I really don't know what to make of it or how it applies to this situation. Nothing else he said was remotely helpful, and it still bugs me to no end. There has to be something, some reason behind his words and behaviour.

Anyway, being in the mood I was in, I couldn't focus when I got back to my class. Lunch was not any smoother, and when it became obvious I was in a mood, they left me alone with my thoughts. Only Sophie took a moment to confirm our dinner tomorrow.

Following that, I've hidden myself away in my work room and spent the rest of the day working with Colleen, typing this up on her console. Not really feeling up to writing about anything else.

Nov 6

Remington said I could write this up and he would hold off letting this out until later, like when everything has been settled. If you're reading this, whatever was to happen over the weekend has happened and there have been no repercussions on his end. It's not like he really had anything to worry about, but sometimes, it does slip my mind that there are other things that happen beyond us trainees; that there are other politics that go on among the G/Cs, tutors and board members.

It must have been an hour or so after I finished typing up the last entry when there was a knock on the door to my 'lab'. I wasn't doing anything at the time and I didn't feel like leaving the room. The odd thing was the time. When I heard the knock, I checked Colleen's console screen for the time. It was just past a quarter after two in the morning. I thought it was either Becca or Walker checking on me, so I opened the door.

It was Remington.

Admittedly, I was surprised – and you'd think, being psychic, I should have known beforehand. He asked how secure my room was. I said there were no cameras or listening devices beyond Colleen. He should know that little fact, since my room was initially a store-room and the camera was outside watching the corridor and door. I've gone through every inch of the room and if there were a camera, I would have known. Besides, I've also seen the surveillance layout for The Facility, so I'm sure the room was a private place for me. He nodded, entered, and closed the door.

He apologised for earlier, saying that my activities of late, revolving around the dreams, the dream-world and such have been a sore topic with several board members. And it's gotten worse, given how long the matter has dragged on. The impact on several other trainees was an issue of concern, Keitaro's current state being the major point.

Linda was supposed to bring the matter up with me. While the situation may be considered real for me, as it was already pointed out, there was no evidence of any such thing happening, beyond my word. And given my abilities, it is felt that I may very well be orchestrating everything for some unknown purpose. Any denial I put forth, and Remington has tried on my behalf, is simply my denial; my word that they have to accept.

And my word isn't as strong as it once was, it seems.

Probably one too many freak-outs and too many strange things revolving around me.

"This plan of yours, can you settle it all?" he asked. "Never mind what the others are thinking. I need to know you can settle this and not let it come up anymore. Not in your journal. Not with anyone else. No more bad dreams."

"I don't know," was my answer. And I said it slowly and thoughtfully. I honestly was not even sure I could settle it, short of wiping everything away. Even if I did that, I don't know what the impact is to me or even to someone like Ethan or Sophie who have their Dream-worlds somewhat linked to mine.

"You may have to consider leaving this behind and move on, Jeannie. Take control."

"That would mean doing what I don't want to do. To be who I don't want to be."

"No, you don't. But you can take control. Think about how you handled Phillip. You found another way." He put his hand on my slumped shoulder. "Accept who you are; the good and the bad parts, the light and the dark. Stop hiding and running from it. Take control. You're already on track."

At this point, it was becoming clear what he was getting at earlier. I think it's the same thing John was talking about those weeks back about confronting Phillip. My greatest fear is me, what I'm capable of, and it's the same thing that scares a majority of the board members, I think. All those tests last year...

I then said, "If I do this, I probably should have witnesses."

"What do you have in mind?"

"You," I said, "and maybe one of those board members come along as well." He gave me an odd look and I tried to clarify it. Sophie could step in and carry Remington and the board member as observers so that if anything happened, Sophie could get them out. There was no guarantee about 'safe' given what happened with Keitaro.

He said he would consider it and inform the board members later in the morning. At best they had a day to decide. He then asked if more than one board member coming along would be a problem. As long as they understood the risks, I was more than willing. I only had to clear it with Sophie.

"We settle this then, whatever needs to be done," he said.

"Whatever needs to be done, no matter what it may lead to," I said with as much conviction I could muster within myself. I think he could tell that I was still unsure, but he nodded anyway.

He got up to leave and said, "Get some rest." With that he opened the door and left me to my thoughts. I was feeling really nervous after that, my stomach seemed to be churning and doing cartwheels. I tried to settle my nerves by typing this up.

It's just past five now. I suppose I could take Remington's advice and get some rest, so I'm heading back to my room now.

Nov 7

One last entry before the shit hits the fan – maybe. This is to cover a few things before the trip into the Dreaming. I don't know how long this trip will take given what needs to be done, so this might be the last entry for a while… maybe. For all I know we could be done by tonight. Anyhoo, I've still got a while before jumping into the Dream-world.

After heading back to my room that morning, it took a while but I got some sleep, and was wide awake around half past seven. I dropped by the pool to look for Walker and Sophie, and said I had some news. Over breakfast, I told them of Remington's visit and what the new plan was. Sophie agreed to help watch over our guests, whoever they would be. Walker wanted to join in, but I rather he didn't, because I needed to focus on what I had to do. Whether it meant dealing with Michelle in the extreme sense or not, I couldn't say. I expressed my appreciation for his support and given Sophie's task, I was concerned if we would have too many people to worry about. After all, if Michelle would react the way I expected, she would go after the ones I was closest to. If Walker were to be there, he would be the first target.

He agreed that it made sense. Again, I told him that he would be my anchor to reality, "The one thing that I would fight to return to."

"As you wish," was his reply, ladened with a hint of disappointment.

Sophie suggested that it would be better for me if Walker did come along. "After all, it's more than likely that he would be an equalising influence towards Michelle," she said. "You've written on occasion how both Michelle and Mikey take after Walker."

"And I would still be an anchor for you in there," he said. I responded by saying that I didn't want another incident like what happened to Keitaro. Sophie reminded me that we weren't facing Phillip and I countered that I didn't rule him out entirely in this particular matter. She felt I was being paranoid, and reminded me that I have power and control over Phillip.

I didn't argue anymore and said Walker could come along if Remington was agreeable. In all honesty and thinking back on it, he made sense about being my anchor no matter where he was. And Sophie was right, he does have some influence over Michelle, unless she's as devious as I think she's capable of being. And I may be over-thinking these things a bit over this last day. Sophie, of course, pushed forward her argument during our dinner, for letting Walker come along. I didn't really try to talk her out of it given what happened last time, but I did ask her why she insisted on having Walker come along given what happened last time.

"Hasn't what happened with Hank and Keitaro enough to just give you pause?" I asked.

"You're asking me along this time," she said, "so even you think the situation's different. And I believe you need all the support you can get."

"I'm asking you to help out because you're the best and only option I have in this matter of travelling to the Dreaming. It's just… given everything you've gone through with me over there, why still help me knowing full well how dangerous it could get? You could have just said 'no' and I would have left it at that."

"Because you're my friend," she said. "Even after everything we've been through, I will stick by you and bring as much help as I can manage."

I was taken aback by her response. "But, why?" I did want her to back me up and help protect Remington and the two others who were coming along, but I was also reluctant to have her participate in anything that might actually happen. She smiled, like the answer she had given was all the reason she needed.

I didn't press further into why she was so willing to stand by me and have others back me up. I can't recall anything that I've done to deserve such dedication from her or the others that they would follow me into such fires. Now, it's Walker.

And I could do without inciting some kind of intergalactic incident if he got hurt. That's the least of how I would feel if he got hurt, especially if it's under my watch.

Sometime, when we have the time and there are no incidents to put anyone at risk, I'm going to have another long talk with Sophie about this. And maybe with Hank, because he's also stepped up before and I could never understand why.

I got the comms from Remington saying two board members would be joining us, but he didn't give any names. I didn't tell him about Walker. That's going to be a surprise when we meet up in the Infirmary. Between Walker, Sophie and myself, we've pretty much kept our plans quiet. Neither of them joined me at lunch yesterday or today, and no one asked anything. I stayed focussed on work throughout yesterday. This morning, I took in a short review class, but left early after I was done with my questions. I took in an hour of meditation in the garden to settle my thoughts.

There's one other thing I was hoping to get done as well, if the chance arises. The idea of wiping the slate clean did crop up again and I was wondering what the repercussions of that would be. What it would mean to Keitaro in particular IF Phillip did what he said he did; that he scattered Keitaro's essence across the Dream-world.

Suffice to say, the meditation I attempted was barely calming nor soothing on my nerves. I was, and still am, nervous about this.

These last couple of entries on Colleen are meant to keep until all is said and done. I've got a few tasks for her to perform as well, so we'll see what we'll see on the flipside of this matter. I should get going so... mom, please watch out for Mikey and let him know that I love him very much.

Thanks, and I love you too.

Nov 10

Sometimes, things that are expected to take no time at all drag on forever, and conversely, things expected to take a while zip by faster than one might expect. Then again, dealing with the Dream-world, both cases can paradoxically happen at the same time. There was a plan in place, more or less. I didn't go in blindly and I worked out what I could do in dealing with Michelle. For now, I'm still feeling kinda drained and wasted over the whole thing.

I didn't expect getting back to my journal so soon because I didn't expect the whole excursion to be over so quickly in real time. We spent about five, six days in the Dream-world but a little under forty hours in total.

As to the board members who came along, I didn't know who they were until I got to the Infirmary. So while I recognised Sonya, it was a surprise Walter was there. He's not exactly my biggest fan given the events of last year, so it was a mystery why he volunteered to go along to the Dream-world. I then figured if Sonya was on my side, then Walter might be a counter balance for the board to get a full perspective on my so-called Dream-world, whether they would believe or not. Also, I never knew that Walter was a board member. I thought he was just another G/C like Remington or Linda.

Of course, there was concern about Walker, and despite a word of advice and a reminder of the possible dangers, even for my sake, no one actually said he couldn't go along. No one forbade him to join in, which I did expect Remington to do. Remington gave me a casual look and a shrug after he, Sonya and Ms. Phillips talked with Walker about their concerns, making sure his judgement wasn't impaired or biased. In all, I guess he was made aware of the dangers and the concerns, and the final decision was his to make.

As with the others. I had more than impressed upon them the dangers and my concerns, and still, they followed me into the Dreaming to face Phillip.

It didn't ease my concerns for Walker tho. I had to trust in Sophie that if anything went wrong, she would get them all out.

Linking everyone up was similar to what she had learnt working on the network, and it's obviously not her first time. Again, there weren't enough beds to go around, so Sophie and I ended up using chairs instead. She got the more comfortable cushioned chair while I had the regular upright chair cushioned with a soft pillow and blanket. Will was on hand to assist Ms. Phillips, in case anything weird happened and it wasn't feasible to move us via physical contact. That was about as much precaution as we had.

Once she was settled with everyone linked, I dived into the Dreaming. I could feel Sophie scanning me lightly, then following me in. It was strange that I was so aware of it this time. It's hard to define what it felt like. It's something that stuck in my mind, so to speak.

Kinstein's Kitchen appeared before me as usual and I was alone for a brief moment before the others appeared around me. Walker, Sophie and Remington were dressed in clothes they had worn within the Dreaming before, but Sonya and Walter were wearing exactly the same thing they had on in the Infirmary. In fact, their appearance barely wavered from their 'reality'. Something always changed, some minute little detail would always vary, but that didn't happen with Sonya or Walter. Even Sophie noticed this and asked me about it. I suppose it could have been a personal perception thing, that they saw themselves as being professional in their duty to observe me. I could also say that dreams and fantasy have no impact on them at the time, so their imagination did not really, "go with the flow," but it's probably not that.

I led the way into the Kitchen and they settled at a table. Kinstein took some orders and I suggested some dishes. Walter seemed disgusted by the whole thing, like I was wasting time. He appeared to insist not buying into the world surrounding him while Sonya was a little more open to the experience. Her questions were tackled by Remington and Sophie. Walker and I headed to the back-room to look for Michelle.

Michelle behaved the same as always. I brought her out and introduced her to the others. Walter and Sonya were curious as to her existence and relation to me, while Remington seemed cautious about her. Sophie treated her as usual whenever she followed me to meet the kids. We headed out soon after that with Michelle and me leading the way, Walker behind me followed by everyone else.

It was about five days trekking from village to village. It took a while for Walter to get into the swing of things but Sonya and Remington helped out in each village we visited. Since we weren't sleeping on the ground under the stars, we had to do some odd jobs at each village to get food and boarding. We spent two nights at the third village when Walter finally decided to help out. It wasn't anything difficult like tracking and capturing a critter, just typical farm or labour work. It reminded me a lot of the time before the critters and creatures showed up. Speaking of which, we did see a few from a distance, but we had no trouble with any of them.

Not too long after we left the last village, we reached the mountain Old Crans told me about, so long ago. I was going partly on instinct and partly with Michelle leading the way. It's one of those things about how the Dream-world worked where these 'quests' were concerned. We would end up in the place we are meant to be when the time was right. I headed up the slope with Michelle. Remington and Walter followed while Sophie stayed back with Sonya. At my request, Walker reluctantly stayed back as well. I told him that Remington would watch over me, even though this matter with Michelle was something I had to do on my own.

It was another half a day of hiking upwards, and Walter complained a lot until Remington told him that he could stop and wait until we came down the mountain again. He continued with us, but kept his complaints to a low grumble. I paid him no mind and had no idea what he was complaining about. Just over halfway up the mountainside, there was a plateau with some flat stones piled upon each other to resemble some kind of sacrificial altar. I told Remington that this was the place, and only then did he ask what plan I had in mind. I had been told several times, in various vernacular, that I had to end Michelle's existence. I remember the phrase, "Destroy the key" that came up in Ethan's Dream-world and there were calls early on for me to kill Michelle, something I was trying to avoid.

I told him to stay back and to keep Walter out of the way. They were not to interfere, no matter what happened. He agreed and stood to one side, his back to the mountainside. Michelle and I moved over to the altar and stood facing each other across it. I knew what I had to do, and despite not saying anything to Michelle, she somehow knew it too. I held out my hand over the altar and she took it.

I could immediately feel her invading my mind and my soul. I fought back as best as I could, pushing her out of myself; out of those areas that I felt her trying to get into. I wasn't quite sure what she was up to, but I knew that I didn't want her going into those places, like my consciousness and my thoughts; places that felt like they were essentially... me. From what I could gather, she was a part of me. To essentially remove her from existence within the Dream-world, the idea was to take her into me, but on my terms and in my own way. I wasn't going to let her overwhelm me, which was what I felt she was trying to do. I can say that it was a real fight to not let her win. I had to break her down first to something manageable and then absorb her essence into myself.

I know, it's something I've been doing a lot lately, taking in all these nasty things into myself and tucking them in some dark place. This was just another dark nasty thing I was dealing with, except that it was essentially me.

I don't know what Walter and Remington might have thought at the time while all that was going on. I also don't know what it was they actually saw. It was a real struggle, and obviously, since I'm writing all this, everything turned out a little as expected and I'm here. She vanished from the Dream-world as I took her into myself and there was a little more of a fight with her within me after that. As far as I could sense it, as far as I could tell, Michelle was born of that darkness within me; malicious, conniving, manipulative... I could feel all of that emanating from her and a lot more of the darker aspects of myself. Everything that I've tried to push down and not let it rule my life. And there I was, fighting a manifestation of it all that was trying to become my prominent personality.

As Remington had said, I had to accept all of me; good and bad, light and dark. A lot of Michelle was the dark made manifest, but there was a little good too. The part that could get along with Walker and somehow befriend Mikey at the beginning. Even when we first discovered her, I don't think that everything she did with the dreams was done with malicious intent, but out of curiosity. Then somehow, in all the time she had, she managed to cross worlds, and occasionally send the critters into reality. It was probably out of fun at first, and more likely to get my attention, or maybe to push my buttons. In all of that, though, I really don't know if there was any malicious intent in any of her actions. Maybe it was more out of mischief. Getting down to the nitty gritty, she really had nothing to do with Phillip's return, but Phillip did make use of her to his own benefit. They had nothing to do with each other in the end.

I'm sure of that now.

Even as Michelle faded away across the altar, some odd manifestation of a dark gem-like stone formed on it. It might have ultimately been the key, or not. I picked up a rock and smashed it anyway. The dust was taken by the wind and the few fragments melted away into the alter, which then crumbled into rubble.

Michelle's gone from the Dream-world and in effect, the Dreaming itself is a little diminished. I'm not exactly sure how, but I could sense it. I felt it, as the three of us trekked down the mountainside. Even Sophie felt that something had changed and Walker noted that there was 'less vibrancy in the air,' as he put it. We left it at that and returned to reality with Sophie taking everyone out first and I followed a few moments later. Despite what Remington had suggested about 'leaving it all behind', I don't think I'm done with the

Dreaming, and it's not done with me either. I do feel a little diminished as well after returning to reality. Weary, tired... like something is lost.

I'm aware I'm not going into too much detail with this, but it does feel like there isn't much to be said. I wasn't sure what would happen going in, and yet, here I am writing about it, which does make the outcome kinda obvious for the most part. Any actual repercussions may not arise for a while. When I came out of the Dreaming, I was feeling a little on the low end and I asked Ms. Phillips to run a check on me. I ended up staying in the Infirmary for the duration, heading back to my room sometime after three in the morning. Aside from Sophie and Walker, I haven't interacted with any of the others yet. It might be only then when someone might notice any change in me.

We'll see, though.

I have no idea what Walter thought of the whole experience.

Right now, I don't care and I'm tired.

Nov 12

Few things of note over the last couple of days. According to Ms. Phillips, most of the critters in the menagerie vanished overnight after we returned from the Dreaming. There are only three critters left and Ms. Phillips has decided to move them to a smaller room with the rest of the empty 'cages'. Only one of the critters was regarded as dangerous, and I informed Ms. Phillips so. She said she would be careful with it, even if I couldn't quite say in what way it was dangerous.

There hadn't been any new cases of trainees with sleeping problems. It could almost be said the last couple of nights have been quieter than usual for the staff at the Infirmary. I checked with a few others who were having bad dreams and sleeping problems before. All of them said they couldn't remember any dreams. Most of them have become accustomed to occasionally waking up more than once in the middle of the night. Some of them noted that they didn't wake up in the middle of the night as much as before. Really, there were so many of them that I spent lunch away from the others, hopping around from table to table. Most were reluctant to talk to me, simply because they did know me and were aware of what I was asking about. The others who did open up more, knew I was peripherally involved in some way, and that I had been helping a few others, or so they heard from Callie. Turns out, she knows more people than I do and she's been more helpful to them than I have.

Meanwhile, Ethan came around asking if I had any problems getting into the Dreaming because he couldn't get through to his Dream-world. I told him that I hadn't tried anything since the last trip, and he wasn't aware of what happened. Aside from writing it down in this journal, no one else has actually spoken about it, not Sophie nor Walker. I suggested he may have been a little tired mentally and that he should get some rest. He has been helping out on Bastian and Kevin's network test runs lately, so I attributed his fatigue to that.

As for Bastian and Kevin's network, they have been picking up the pace lately and there were rumblings that since Callie and Toni handled the last field trip to the colony, Bastian and Kevin might handle the next field trip to the Serenity Compound in December. I'm supposed to be supervising those tests, but they have had a few without me present. Either Jenny or Callie have been stepping in to supervise in my stead although I am still being kept appraised of the tests. Callie in particular has taken the initiative to refine the methods even more, since we have been using her methods lately. It really is fine by me that she's gone further ahead with this than the problematic version Jenny and I started with.

As mentioned earlier, I haven't been hanging with the gang, although I still catch up with Walker at the pool. He hasn't inquired about my activities, nor has he pushed for me to open up over the events in the Dreaming. He still paces me for my laps and I match him move for move during our aqua-acrobatics. My focus in kendo and while sparring with Keiko have also not waned in any way. I may be a little more focussed there as well. I think she may have noticed a slight change in me, more in the way she regards me when we're facing off against each other. I noticed John eyeing me in the gym, or at least throwing a suspicious glance in my direction every now and then.

Training-wise, everything is moving along and I've been playing catch-up again. Not by a lot, mind. It's not like I missed out on a week or more, only a few days work and the trainers aren't saying much either. Even Mr. Hardy hasn't said anything about my work and he knows for sure that I'm constantly trying to make sense of the theories he brings up in class. My other projects have also been given due attention at night simply because I haven't been sleeping. At least, not beyond napping for a few minutes in my lab, but I've been clocking in some time on the flight simulator, working on my rocket design and checking up on Colleen.

So, aside from not mingling much with the gang, everyone else seems to be giving me a pretty wide berth over the last couple of days. I should probably catch up with Carol to find out why this has happened. See what the rumour

366

mill is churning out where I'm concerned, not that I'm suddenly developing an active interest in the rumours that are floating around.

PS – missed it by a bit, but still, Happy Birthday, mom.

Nov 20

It's been a while since the last entry (sorry, mom), not for the lack of things to write about. It's mostly due to this feeling of melancholia that came about when helping Becca pack up her stuff. The reality of her leaving next month is really setting in, but then, throw in the fact that Walker is also scheduled to leave at the same time, and you know why that miserable feeling is back. The decision to go with him or not is still up in the air although a lot of what I've been doing lately would suggest that I'm staying put. Things like spending more time with Kadi at Becca's request and agreeing to look after, or take over, some of Walker's possessions because he feels he can't take certain items with him.

Maybe he's aware that I'm not likely to follow him despite what I've said and discussed with him. We've planned a few things that I could do and stuff I could get into, if I followed him to his home. We did look into the process of the "Foreign Exchange Program" and what would be required of a participant. There was an outside chance that I could participate if we didn't strictly adhere to the requirements though. Apparently, it's different from his end, which he pointed out when we went over the requirements.

That funk got deeper when he said he wasn't sure if he would return, and added that if I did follow him, he couldn't be sure when or even if I could come home. That wouldn't be fair to Mikey. It was like taking the decision out of my hands. Consequently, it has made everything else going on seem insignificant.

Although, despite feeling all down in the dumps, I haven't slacked off on my studies and training. It hasn't made my sessions with either Kadi or Ethan cakewalks. We managed to get along although I don't think I was too helpful in dispensing advice, the same for Jenny and the others. I think it got around as to what was up with me, that everyone of them didn't push me on anything and gave me a decent berth, but not too much. Only Keiko gave no quarter, which I suppose was just like her. Strangely enough, kendo was the only time when I didn't feel down in the dumps. Different mentality, I guess.

One of those things I should write about is that between the last entry and this, I did make one trip into the Dreaming. Ethan said he was having problems getting into his Dream-world, so I made the trip to check it out. Sophie hadn't been to her Dream-world for a while, when I asked her. I was never sure if it was all actually connected, but their Dream-worlds were built off mine. And mine had recently undergone some changes. I didn't know what kind of change and how much change until I made that trip.

It wasn't easy getting into the Dreaming as before, and maybe that was why Ethan was having problems. I didn't sense any barriers, but it felt like there was one. It took me two tries to get through to my usual starting point, standing outside Kinstein's Kitchen.

The Kitchen was a sight, seemingly dilapidated and abandoned. Even Kinstein was nowhere to be found. Going through the Kitchen was like walking through some old mansion. The brush was overgrown, outside and in, like the place had been abandoned for years. The back-room where I had spent so much time with Mikey, and later Michelle, looked like a wreck that even the invading foliage could not disguise the hint of physical destruction. It looked like some people worked over the place. I sat in the middle of the Kitchen and took it all in, looking at every nook and cranny that I could peer into from my stationary position. I felt cold, and sad, and lost.

I'm not sure how long I sat there, but I did get moving after a long while. I headed out and looked around. What had once been a forest seemed like a dense jungle just beyond the small clearing in front of the Kitchen. No clear path appeared before me anywhere, so I took to the sky. The sight I got was not any better. Everything looked abandoned. Where there once were villages, were now a few ramshackle huts clustered together. It seemed beyond disrepair.

I also noticed that the mountains that bordered my lands and Ethan's were now gone, but I couldn't see beyond either. It was like the horizon simply ended, that no matter how high I flew or how much closer I tried to get to the border, I couldn't see beyond a certain point. I couldn't say if Ethan's lands even existed anymore. The same was for Sophie's lands, or where I thought her lands were supposed to be.

I then tried heading towards the coast where I had Walker's hut, but I was greeted instead by a desert that reached out into infinite darkness. I'm not sure how else to describe it. It was like an empty dried beach that went on, but the further you looked, it was just black out there; nothingness. No meaning, no significance, no existence... nothing.

So, I left.

I told Sophie and Ethan what I found, and I left it at that. Sophie asked if I was alright, but that emptiness and sadness was obvious to her. Ethan accepted it, but asked if I could do something to fix it. He had spent a lot of time to build up things in his world and he didn't want it to go to waste. Sophie told him that it was never a waste if he learnt things and could apply it to the real world. It did give him some things to think about, and that kept him occupied for a while. He only brought up the matter again today. I guess that got me thinking about the last week or so and the mood I've been in. The last time I felt like this, it was a trip to the Dreaming that helped me out of it. This time, it's mostly staying focussed on work and trying to manage my feelings, especially where Becca and particularly Walker are concerned. So much so that I haven't been sleeping for a few days now. That's not for the lack of trying, I haven't really been able to fall asleep no matter how tired I'm feeling.

I could go on but I guess I should stop for now. I'll try to catch up with some other things next time.

Nov 23

It's getting harder to be consistent here and maybe mood's gotta do with it. It feels like things are going along on autopilot. Maybe it's the now severe lack of sleep, but something's gonna give soon if I don't get some proper rest. It's now going on four days without much sleep. Despite my body constantly adjusting itself accordingly to the lack of sleep, much like the way it adjusts to everything else, there are apparently signs of strains that's evident to several others now, such as the slight dark puffiness under my eyes. Honestly, even I wasn't entirely aware of it until Helen brought it up over lunch. I guess it goes to show how much eye contact I've been avoiding. Either that or no one dared to bring it up. So much for being overly hyperactive.

Well, obviously Walker was concerned more than a week earlier and Becca's been asking each morning if I managed any sleep. It did feel as if Keiko ramped up her speed during our sparring and kendo practice, but maybe it was more me slowing down due to fatigue. My focus, in both TP and TK training, has remained constant, so no real problems there as I've been keeping up with my responsibilities in those classes. It's the slight dip in focus during the other classes that may be an issue. And of course, both Linda and Remington have been checking up on me almost daily over the last few days. If it's not one or the other, it's both of them on the same day, just different times; that's happened twice now, the day before and today. Apparently, Remington wasn't around yesterday. That, I found out from Sophie and Jenny today, because they were out with him.

It turned out that both of them got a little assignment, supervised by Remington. They didn't give me a lot of the details, but they did say that it was involving a kidnapping of a child. A suspect was in custody and Remington got Sophie and Jenny to do a TP probe on the suspect; they are current TP partners after all. They said it was like those interrogation rooms on TV, a darkened room on the other side of a two-way mirror so they could see their subject – Jenny needed line-of-sight – who was being interviewed by an investigator. Apparently, Sophie was the back-up to Jenny, who was to try to pick up any information about where the kidnap victim was held. She would relay to the investigator how she wanted certain questions to be asked in order to get the suspect to think about certain things. Information wasn't going to flow so easily so it did require pushing the subject's thoughts in a particular direction. Sophie, in the meantime, tested herself in determining if the suspect was lying or not. They gave whatever information they could gather to the investigators, but they did not know what the outcome was.

I was pretty sure they weren't supposed to discuss anything with anyone, but they did with me in general terms. Even in writing all this out, I don't think I'm giving away anything about what kidnapping or where. Jenny was more curious about what I would have done, and if I were called to help, would I have done anything differently from her. Given what she told me, it wasn't likely I would have done anything different, if I was willing to do it in the first place. Technically, it would have been against my rules to have probed the subject's thoughts without his permission. Given the situation, and if there was a time factor at work, I probably would have done it anyhow to save a life. I stressed that it had to depend on the situation, and which rule of mine I was willing to compromise. Sophie reminded me of the recent events where my own rules pretty much flew out the window, but also suggested that there were extenuating circumstances. She wanted more to share her experience during the outing simply due to the excitement of helping out in a real life situation. She also wanted to know if she did anything wrong. I told her I couldn't judge under those circumstances. She is technically a newbie teep after all, at least, compared to Jenny and me. She has had a heck of a lot of experience with me tho, and Jenny would have taken her a little further.

It's cool that some of the others get to try using their abilities in such ways, and I am glad that Jenny got the chance. Kinda curious tho if it's only Remington who decides what jobs to pull a TP or TK on. None of the others have gone out on any such things as far as I'm aware, and I'm pretty close with almost all of them, being involved with their training and all.

Like the other day in the TK class, the whole thing about a TK shield came up again and someone suggested that since we couldn't use real guns to test ourselves – which would have been insane to try – the idea of a paintball war was raised. It was the closest we could get to being shot at and better than the super-soakers I used last time. Suffice to say, almost everyone in TK was keen to try it and Miss Tracy agreed to get us some paintball gear. It's been a long while since we've had any real way to put the various personal TK shields that most of them have been developing to the test. Primary inspirations have been the various comics Sophie shared (*Fantastic Four* and *X-Men* mostly) to even *The Incredibles* for visual references. So our paintball war is tentatively scheduled for next week in the VR arena.

I wonder if there's any particular external job that might require our TK abilities. Then again, it's not something we can do discreetly, like using our TP abilities. Well, maybe except for Will, who is improving a lot in using his abilities for medical purposes. I think he intends to specialise in cardio-surgery, although I'm not sure if that's actually it. He's got Ms. Phillips in his corner and she's letting him do quite a bit in the Infirmary. I'm sure I've seen him conferring with Charlie whenever the opportunity came up, usually when he was checking up on me.

Head's gone a little wibbly, so I guess I'll be stopping here for now. Gonna head off to the pool and unwind a little.

Nov 27

That lack of sleep caught up with a vengeance so much so that I pretty much lost over a day and a half. Honestly, I'm not even sure if I was actually asleep or not, I have to take Ms. Phillips word on that, and Walker's, and Becca's, and even Charlie's. And if they're right about me being asleep, then I may have hit a whole different level where the Dream-world is concerned... maybe.

That night after I signed off on the last entry, I did head off to the pool, but I don't think I did anything particularly strenuous. I even declined going through an aqua-acrobatic routine simply because my head wasn't really in the right place for it. I remember feeling tired and mentally drained, but a little more so. Despite Walker doing that thing he did on my back, I didn't sleep that night and spent it working with Colleen instead. By the time breakfast rolled around, I was feeling slightly better. I couldn't put a pin on how I was feeling, it was this numbness, like nothing really mattered. By lunch, I didn't feel like eating, much to everyone's surprise. Instead, I went off to rest under a tree in the little garden, maybe try a little meditation to clear my mind, or get out of the funk I was in. Somewhere in all that, I fell asleep under the tree.

I wasn't really aware when it happened. I had closed my eyes, but I could still see/sense the daylight outside the window through my eyelids. You know how it is when you close your eyes when its still bright, you can still sense where the light is coming from. It was like that. It wasn't like I was trying to get some sleep either. I was focussing on clearing my mind, my thoughts. Trying to blank everything out seeking the darkness, building a faint glimmer of coloured patterns in my mind, something soothing and relaxing. Somewhere in all that, I probably did fall asleep and ended up in a dream. It might have been the Dreaming, but if what Charlie and Ms. Phillips told me is true, then it should have been a dream. It's was just so vivid, like I made a trip to the Dreaming.

I can't really recall how it happened or when. I think it started like a normal dream, but the clearest part seemed to start with The Facility, and the little garden I was in. I was wandering about there, and I was so sure it was the little garden with the rock and the bench and the tree with its little pink flowers. But at the same time it wasn't so little and there was like a whole forest a little bit beyond. I could also see the city just outside the glass and yet there was wind blowing through my hair. It didn't seem odd in any way, like dreams never are, unless you're able to actually think about it. It also didn't seem odd that Keitaro was there.

I know I talked to him, but I can't remember the details of that part right now. I remember feeling sad because I had lost him somewhere. He didn't seem fazed in any way. He led me away from the window and the garden, and into the forest. This part was clearer.

Well… it kinda got a little clearer than what you'd normally remember in an actual dream. While it didn't seem odd that I was talking to Keitaro, the oddness grew as he was leading me into the forest by taking my hand. It dawned on me that Keitaro was not supposed to be there and the further we went on, the more I realised that I was in the forest of my Dream-world. There was even the growing realisation that I was in the Dreaming, and that came to a head when we hit a clearing that had Old Crans' shack in the middle. I don't know when it happened, but 'Keitaro' turned out to not be Keitaro at some point. The build and body seemed similar from the back, but when I looked carefully, I could see it wasn't really him in the end, but there also was the sense that at some point, it had been Keitaro.

Given how things have been throughout the year, the last thing that should be bothering me is dreams. My own dreams, no less, mixing it up with my own Dream-world which I've been trying to let go of these last couple of weeks. But then, Old Crans came out of the shack and after dismissing the practically nondescript guide, he started explaining a few things. Things such as how the Dream-world had fulfilled one purpose; how while it appeared that the Land was ending, it was never truly going away; how nothing hidden in darkness would ever be forgotten or stay hidden; how anything that was lost in the Dreaming would always be found; and even throwing out that, "Nothing ever truly ends."

There was nothing particularly profound, I suppose. At least, nothing I hadn't heard of, or read, in one form or another at some point before. And I could suppose there were some answers in all that rambling. Here's the thing though, as he rambled, the world around us became darker as if the light itself was gong away. As he ended, he took my hands and cupped them, and as he said that last bit, he placed some kind of glowing orb in my cupped hands.

"Last we met, I told you we would meet one last time," he said, burning the realisation that the other Old Crans I met wasn't the true one. "Our time is ended and so, it begins again."

With that, he stepped back and melted into the blackness, leaving me cupping a glowing orb that barely gave enough light to even show me the ground. I wasn't entirely sure what it was I had to do, but like with everything else that had plagued me in this place throughout the year, I figured... it was just another part of me. So, I brought the orb towards myself and pressed it in, taking it into myself.

That might have been a mistake.

I can only say that because it caused me quite a bit of pain at first and it burst its way out of me. It's hard to describe what actually happened and how long it lasted, and that scene from Alien came to mind. Except that it wasn't some slimy little penis-like creature bursting out of me, like in the first movie. It was more like this bright energy poured out of me and everything turned bright. And from my perspective, things went from dark to bright even with my eyes closed. When my focus, such as it is, came into view, it was a beam of sunlight coming through the curtains of my darkened room and hitting me in the eyes.

I sat up in bed and rubbed my eyes to get the brightness down to a slight blur, and only then, realised that I was in my room. I had to stumble out of bed and stagger out of my room to find out that was sometime after nine in the morning. It was a while more before I found out that I had been asleep for over forty hours.

It was Becca who found me after lunch that day and she called on Walker first, then Sophie and the others. Walker was the one who said I was asleep after taking one look at me, and then suggested I shouldn't be disturbed. Becca agreed, although she wanted to take me to the Infirmary, to be sure. Sophie was curious as to how they could tell if I was actually asleep and not off on a Dreaming, and it came down to Walker saying that he could tell the difference. Apparently, Carol added the remark, "Of course you'd know."

In order to not jolt me awake, Sophie used her TK to carry me to the Infirmary. As a precautionary measure, Will used his TK under Ms. Phillips' instructions to run a few checks to make sure I was really sleeping. Charlie was even called in to do some checks since it was his instructions to never let me sleep too much whenever I was hurt or in healing mode. For whatever reason, he agreed to let me sleep it out. When they concluded I was in a deep enough sleep, and after a night of observation, Walker carried me to my room and put me to bed.

So while I was sleeping, certain things continued and it seemed if I still wasn't awake by a certain time, my friends were to wake me up regardless. I beat them to it by a few hours. While I wasn't entirely aware of it, the plans for the Thanksgiving dinner went ahead. The planning and all happened even though I wasn't really aware of it. As I've mentioned before, everyone was giving me a pretty wide berth over the last couple of weeks; even Sophie, Becca and Walker didn't say anything during that time. Given how I was feeling then, I'm not sure if I would have been in the mood for a get-together. Also, given that I had woken up after sleeping for over forty hours, I was still a little out of it by the time dinner came around. Carol said I looked like a zombie, even after I showered and changed. I couldn't wash away the day of testing and questioning by both Ms. Phillips and Charlie while being checked on by a concerned Linda and a worried Remington. I had to explain the whole bit about the dream even though I couldn't explain what really happened then. Not at that time anyway. I would have to make a trip back into the Dreaming to check out what actually happened.

The table I sat at had Walker, Becca and Steven, Bastian, Jenny, Kadi and Rain, along with one of their friends who I wasn't familiar with. One of the cooks was there with us to carve up the roast turkey. The whole dinner had a surreal air to it, at least from my wired perspective. The haze of a dream lingered and everything seemed slow. Things got slightly better as I ate my way through a couple or three helpings and even picked off whatever was left behind. Rain was impressed at the quantity of food I was scarfing down, while Jenny commented that I was making up for not eating the last couple of days. Bastian remarked that what I was doing wasn't very healthy while the cook, well aware of my appetites, told him that it was close to normal for me. Even Walker agreed.

I barely moved about to mingle with the others, but most of my friends came by to ask if I was feeling better. Even Ehrmer and Corogi, and John as well, came by. One person I noticed who was missing was Keiko. She turned down the invitation, although I think it would have been good for her to be with friends. At least, I hope we are still friends and not just master and student in kendo, or sparring partners in everything else. Come to think of it, she hasn't joined the lunch group as often since... well, Keitaro.

By eleven at night, the dinner had wound down a bit. I was feeling tired and I think it showed; it was a bit of an effort to stay focused on things by then. Walker never left my side throughout the whole dinner. Becca and Steven had left much earlier, and I didn't want to disturb them. I haven't asked her how she was dealing with him since she's leaving for home next month.

Walker and I ended up in his suite. Nothing happened. I fell asleep and slept for over couple of hours. When I woke up, he was sound asleep. I lay there with him for a while as I was still feeling lethargic, but I couldn't get back to sleep. I just... watched him sleep, taking in every nuance of his features, committing it all to memory. I don't think I did anything, but he stirred awake and asked if I was okay. I told him I couldn't get back to sleep and then said I would be okay. He nodded and drifted back to sleep. I took the opportunity to slip out of bed.

I ended up in my work room, checking on Colleen and our project, and caught up with a little bit of work, after which I decided type all this up.

It's almost half six now. Walker should be at the pool soon, and I could do with a dip. So... laters.

Nov 29

The last couple of days were spent staying focussed on classes, studies and work. Did feel better once I got into the pool and clocked a few laps, getting the blood moving properly. I have also been clocking close to three or four hours of sleep each night, usually around half past two. I'd wake up a little before six, feeling a little agitated and restless, but that's taken care of by a dip in the pool. I guess something has changed. Yet to be sure if it's a good change or a bad one.

Meanwhile, the little secret side project I've been working on with Colleen works better than I hoped. And I expect that I'm gonna have to meet with

Remington or Linda, and a few other people soon. It took a while to compile and test the program. Looks like I don't have to worry about Colleen if I get booted from The Facility. I also won't have to worry about having my journal vetted by my 'editor' if it comes down to that, but I'll stick to the guidelines for now. I will say that since going operational, only one person so far has detected what I've done, and that's simply because he's been as curious as I have about certain things. To be fair to The Facility, I shouldn't write about what I've done exactly, although it is something I did say, in a bit of roundabout way, that I could do. I've proven that it wasn't impossible, given The Facility's infrastructure within the building.

Yeah, security's gonna have a field day once I submit this entry. We'll see what happens next on that front. I know I've been no end of problems for them, even if I've never written as much about it. After all, this is a public journal, but there are somethings I need to keep secret from prying eyes. No sense alerting them to certain things beforehand.

With the upcoming field trip next month, we're ramping up the test sessions for Kevin and Bastian with Ethan and Sophie as back-ups to the network. Granted, using Callie's system doesn't require a back-up to guard against the 'leaks'. It's more for the peace-of-mind of our participants and overseers. On a more precise assignment of roles; Ethan's learning more about how the network works; Sophie's training to lead and later coach a Learning Network, partnering with Jenny for now. Aside from Ethan, with whom she's reluctant to partner, there's no other TP who can be her partner. Carl's still in the TP program, but no one wants to partner him and he hasn't shown any willingness to change his methods, even if he's sticking to the rules.

Since Remington has already provided us with the list of participants, Kevin and Bastian have reached out to them, and arrange a schedule for the next three weeks leading to the field trip. It's decently paced with about two to three sessions per week. That'll give them and the first-timers enough time to adjust accordingly on both ends.

I had dinner with Sophie on Friday night, and given the massive dinner the night before, we took it easy during our 'date'. I relayed what happened in the Dreaming or in my dream, about how everything got wiped out and had to be rebuilt, but with more details. I still wasn't sure what did happen and most of it had faded away by then; like a real dream fading away after you wake up. She told me about a movie she saw when she was a kid, "The NeverEnding Story", and said it seemed almost similar. In the movie – I think it was from a book – there was a fantasy world that was being consumed by 'The Nothing' and it was up to this young boy to save the fantasy world, called Fantasia. The fantasy world was in a book the boy was reading and it somehow came alive. To save that world, the boy had to call out the name of the Princess of the fantasy world, and the world would rebuild from a single grain of sand. That new world could have anything in it the boy could imagine. Mind you, I'm repeating here more or less what Sophie told me. I never knew there was such a movie. Way before my time; will have to check it out.

I offered there were similarities between that and what I went through. Maybe I did see a part of the movie a long time ago and it's there, somewhere in the back of my subconscious when the Dream-world was created. Or maybe the Dreaming has always been around and it served as different realms of fantasy to the creative dreamers, feeding their imagination and becoming their inspirations for their great works. After all, I know for sure that other people have found their way there and not all the denizens of those lands were figments of imaginations.

After I shared my ideas about the Dreaming, Sophie talked about how we were learning the various sciences and preparing for the future, and yet, I was such a contradiction with my abilities and trips to the Dream-world where none of the sciences could apply. "As much as any scientist would want to understand more about telepathy or telekinesis or even about the nature of dreams and how they really work, you flit about them like it was all second nature," she said. "And we could never learn about how they all work within you or from you."

I was at a lost at that point because I had no explanations left. How or why they worked the way they did for me, I didn't know. She then asked if I was going to make a trip back to the Dream-world and if she could accompany me. We were both curious about what we might find, so I agreed.

The next day, after lunch, we made the trip from the Infirmary, like so many trips before. Except it wasn't quite like any trip before. It took several attempts to get into the Dreaming, for one. It was never so difficult for me to get across before. I would close my eyes, relax and visualise the place where I would want to be, usually Kinstein's Kitchen, and I'd be there. After the first couple of attempts, I agreed with Sophie that the Kitchen was most likely not there. So I tried some of the older ways, such as imagining flying in or walking out of a dark cave and into the light or waking up in a field; stuff like that. What worked in the end was having a forest materialise around us in the Infirmary. And we didn't even have to lie down for that, at least it didn't seem that way.

It's a little hard to 'verbalise' this. Sophie and I were discussing the various methods we had tried. She tried leading a couple of times, unsuccessfully. Then, she suggested merging the Dreaming with our reality, like the way the hut turned up in the gym. So it started small like a rock turning up in a corner, a couple of plants popping up from the floor and the grass growing around it and spreading. Buds grew to massive trees in rapid motion and aside from Sophie and I, no one else seemed to notice what was going on. In less than a minute, we went from sitting on the Infirmary beds to sitting on rocks and logs in a dense forest.

From there, we started to explore. Neither of us absolutely sure we were in the Dreaming for the longest while, until we came across a herd of skittish unicorns grazing by a lake. They scattered when we approached. I had to admit things were different and new.

In all, we spent a few days on the inside exploring the lands. There were no denizens; no villages; no tavern. Only vast forests, grasslands, hills, rivers, valleys; it was a pristine landscape filled with various fantastical creatures. Aside from the unicorns, we did spy a massive dragon skulking near a cave. We didn't get too close, but it looked like a dragon. It had wings too. So did these horses we found. The wings were more leathery and bat-like rather than the feathery bird-like ones on the Pegasus.

We also spotted a couple of griffins and while I didn't see it, Sophie swears she got a glimpse of a sphinx-like creature. The rest of the creatures seemed like the normal forest creatures, such as deer and rabbits. And then there was that firebird streaking through the sky. That was... amazing.

In the end, we found nothing really familiar, nothing from the world before although there was an intense sense of familiarity despite everything being different and, well, unfamiliar. During those quiet nights when I would sit awake by myself while Sophie slept, I could almost sense another presence watching us, but it wasn't some creepy thing like before with Michelle. It felt more... comforting, I guess would be the word. Sophie agreed that despite the various creatures we encountered, there was never any real sense of danger lurking about. We felt... safe.

Despite the few days we spent exploring the Dream-world, it was a few hours on the outside. Ms. Phillips asked if I was actually on a Dream-walk and Sophie confirmed that we were. Apparently, the readings from the bed suggested I was actually asleep. She even showed us the discrepancies against the previous readings. She said she would send the readings over to Charlie for a second opinion. I thanked her for that.

Sophie and I had a quick dinner after we left the Infirmary, and we discussed our trip. I honestly could make neither head nor tail of it all and I don't know what the changes meant to me, compared to how everything worked before. That comforting sensation though was a new thing and while we were being cautious about our exploration, it did put us at ease as well. It was like we had nothing to worry about and it also did allow us to have some solid rest on the inside. I did have one bit of curiosity to put to her though. I had to ask her, "What was it like to sleep in the Dreaming?"

I was curious if sleep worked the same way for her over there. Would you even dream when you're in a Dream-world already? For me, sleep is more often just blackness and a shut-down. I close my eyes one moment and wake up the next a couple of hours later. Sometimes, I dream; often not, at least, not that I can remember. Not quite the same when I sleep in the Dreaming. Anyway, she couldn't provide an actual answer.

It's rolling round to three in the morning now, and I'm feeling kinda worn, which is kinda strange considering I slept in the afternoon. The swim I had earlier wasn't all that strenuous or tiring either, but I'm feeling the need for sleep. So, signing off for now.

DECEMBER

Dec 1

Anything to do with electricity is simply the agitation of electrons; the movement of molecules as they knock about each other, knocking the electrons loose so that they can move along. Data streams using wires are basically the same thing.

Wireless transmissions incorporate all that while utilising radio waves or micro waves and such, but aside that point to point transfer, it still comes down to the agitation of electrons. It's a little easier to play around with electrical signals when you're using fibre optics instead of normal wires which are dependant on their composition and size. Granted, fibre optics rely more on light pulses; the flow of particles rather than the flow of electrons, but the basic concept is still the same. Wires or fibre optics, they are gateways.

At least, in concept, from my point of view. The idea was to make use of The Facility's infrastructure of fibre optic networks to give Colleen a way out, so to speak. It is, after all, electrical signals zooming all over the place. I can't verify anything right now, but if all went according to plan, Colleen's backed up safely with Francine's help. Of course, I'm not gonna go into detail here on how I did it, even if I did share a little more with Linda when she questioned me about it. After all, I wouldn't want to compromise The Facility's security anymore than what I've done.

On the flipside, Linda commended me in pointing out the flaw in their security, although I was surprised no one thought about it before. She pointed out that despite the few so called "bad apples", no one has been more problematic than me, at flirting with the security of The Facility. Most who were invited to train at The Facility likely never took issue with the way things were done, while I've always been a touch apprehensive about certain things despite it being my choice to come here. I do trust Remington, but he isn't The Facility. They didn't quite stick to all that he said he would get them to do.

I'm not going to spill any more here. They are aware of what it is that still irks me. In all fairness, it's more the Board than Security. While Security is having issues with me, it's the Board that has the problem that needs attending.

Unless there's someone else operating between the two, but that would be a bit much, wouldn't it? In the greater scheme of things, it's irrelevant.

Meanwhile, I've been barred from my workroom for the moment. I've handed my key to Linda, and she promised not to turn it over to anyone else without informing me. Will have to take her word on that. Despite the extra attention I've gotten since yesterday, everything else is going along as normal.

Also, while not actual word of my recent exploits got out, the rumours and speculations over my actions have already made the rounds. Mr. Hardy wants to have a chat with me, particularly to check my understanding of wave particles. I had problems grasping the topic in class, especially where the behaviours of seen and unseen particles were concerned. I think I have some understanding of it now, but it is a baffling thing how they can behave in two different forms of existence depending on whether you're observing them, or not.

But let's leave the class topics alone since I haven't been writing about them for a long while now. I'll pass on writing about everything else for now too. It's been a rather busy past couple of days revolving around one or two little incidents and I'm kinda tired from it all. Colleen's technically got her way out of the room, backed up elsewhere and that's what matters most to me out of all this.

Dec 5

Things aren't really letting up, given the issues between The Facility's Board Members and me. It's been a few days since my last write up because I've been asked to keep this thing on hold for a day or so until Remington could verify a few things with me. Now that's all in the clear, I can write about it.

After that 'incident' where I supposedly compromised The Facility's security and Linda sat me down for an explanation, there was word floating around as to whether I was worth training up, given the trouble I've caused over the past few years. So maybe I've had a rather eventful three years (so far) here when you compare me to every other trainee at The Facility. Personally, it hasn't felt so eventful as much as the lulls between the events. Given how things started out, and the constant sparring with Keiko... Then, yes, I suppose it can be considered 'action-packed', but how is that any different from someone like John who also has his own sparring group on an almost daily basis? Or maybe against some regular Joe who plays a game of competitive tennis after work every day? Or some thrill-seeker who would go white-water rafting every weekend?

Anyway, getting back on topic...

About a day after I did the last write-up, rumours started floating around, and I get a comms from Remington to meet him urgently. It happened during an afternoon test session for Kevin and Bastian's network I was supervising. I wasn't the only one who got a call. Sophie was running back-up on the network and she got comm'ed too. We had to cancel the test session and reschedule. Until that point, Kevin and Bastian were doing well with their network and I was considering having Callie start taking over managing the networks, since it's her 'system' in play.

When Sophie and I got to Remington's office, Jenny was already there as well as Paul. Linda and Nakato were also in Remington's office, which made me wonder what was going on. After they greeted us, we were quickly ushered out of the office and towards the exit. Along the way, Remington briefed us.

He said there was a situation already involving several other agencies, and Nakato chimed in saying we wouldn't be in any immediate danger even though it was considered a dangerous situation. Remington stressed we were going to be on site and providing assistance from 'behind the scenes'. I knew then he intended to put our communication network into use, otherwise you wouldn't be having several telepaths in the group. Paul's presence was a bit of a mystery to me at the time, because he was a TK and not a TP. I didn't ask any questions, and listened as Remington continued.

The situation involved several hostages, held by two 'persons-of-interest' in a high-rise building, and it was likely they were heading up a team of at least four gunmen. There had been a threat to toss hostages out the windows unless certain demands were met by a specific time. I can't really go into details, mainly because we weren't told more than broad strokes. It wasn't relevant to what we were being asked to do. When the situation was described, I heard Paul mutter under his breath, "Die Hard," probably referencing the movie given the situation that was described to us. Sophie countered quietly to Paul that the movie situation did not apply unless there was one lone hero already in the building, and no one on the outside was helping. All this as we made our way to the elevator. Linda stayed behind, so I asked her to inform Keiko I wasn't likely to make it to kendo practice.

In the lift, Sophie, Jenny and Paul were given bullet-proof vests as a precaution and really thick jackets, wool caps, gloves and such to put on. As I was familiar with the equipment, I helped Sophie put on the vest while

Remington and Nakato assisted Jenny and Paul respectively with their vests. Remington said I was having something else in the truck, because I was going to do something different.

In the basement parking lot, we climbed into an official looking black van. The briefing continued as we went on our way to an undisclosed location way out of the city. Even if I knew where this building is, I'm not supposed to share it here. The van was nippy and I was shivering, being the one without a thick jacket. I was handed some other gear to put on, which required me to change out of my clothes. Paul respectfully covered his eyes, not that I minded.

Sophie and Paul were on hand in case the 'terrorists' kept to their word about tossing people out the windows. They would back each other, in case it proved too difficult for either one of them to catch a falling person. We weren't told from what height at the time. Jenny would provide a communication network with me like before. Sophie and Paul wouldn't be part of the network, as Nakato didn't want them distracted from their task. Paul admitted to being nervous and excited. Sophie hoped they wouldn't have to use their abilities, because it meant that someone had to go flying out the windows. Catching falling things; it's not something we practised in TK class, but I told Sophie that if she could fly herself, it wasn't going to be any different from catching someone.

"Just don't let them hit the ground if it does happen," I said.

As for me, well... it was what I expected given the dark uniform I put on, and the gear I had on me; padded outfit with a flexible full-body bullet-proof weave over a few strategically placed metal sheets. It'll hurt like hell if I get shot, but it's not likely to penetrate the weave. I had weapons; a baton hanging on the belt; three throwing knives on the back of the belt; each boot secured a knife apiece; padded gloves with metallic caps; an extendable pike-like baton with stun prongs at both ends. No guns. Obviously, I was going into the building. Remington said I would follow an infiltration team in, but later break away to safety and observe. I would provide a 'visual' on the situation inside the building, before any decision would be made for me to make any action needed.

Sophie was worried, but Jenny said I had done it before earlier, in April. "That really was nothing compared to this," I said, which only made her more nervous. I then added, "And this is really nothing compared to some other things I've been through before. Don't worry."

That didn't ease the tension because everyone was now looking at me in disbelief, even Remington was nervous. Well, he didn't really show it, but I could sense it. I think either he knew what I was getting into or he was worried if you would find out, mom. But here I am writing this, so don't worry and don't blame him. We had a purpose for what we did. Nakato even said so privately, but that was later, after everything was said and done.

While it was still early evening by the time we got to the location, it was getting dark and frigid quickly. Right before I stepped out of the van, Remington wanted to make sure that I was clear on the parameters of my role, that I was to simply observe, take no overt action without instruction except in self-defence, and not to do anything else beyond all that. He even reminded me of your condition when I first decided to join The Facility – no wetwork. He also said it shouldn't be any more dangerous than any of the situations I had been in before. That bit actually drew everyone's attention again, so I said, "Guys, I can take care of myself. You know that."

Remington took my glasses off, folded and slipped them into his pocket. "I'll hold on to them for you," he said. I smiled a little absent-mindedly. I get so used to my glasses I sometimes forget I'm wearing them. "Let's get going, I need to introduce you to the team," he said and then he turned to the others. "I'll be back in a while. Be ready."

With that, I stepped out of the van closely followed by Remington. I established a link with Jenny straight away, and we did a quick check with each other. I had her describe what I was looking at, to verify she had a connection. She had to keep her eyes closed to clearly pick up what I was seeing. There was no memory access, so it was quite unlikely for her to get into my memories. In any case, she managed to describe the captain of the infiltration team from head to toe, even pointing out the scar he had just above his left eye; drew my attention to it. She also noted that my vision was pretty good and asked why I needed to wear glasses. I told her to look at details, like words. She could pick up on my astigmatism, and then noted the slight myopia. She said it wasn't so bad and acknowledged I didn't need to wear my glasses all the time. I agreed, and we dropped the topic.

While the infiltration team captain was reluctant to have me on the team, he agreed to let me accompany them on the assurance I would watch out for myself. Unlike before, this team wasn't told about our network. Remington left me with them and headed back to the van. One of the other men made a comment about my not carrying a gun, and I snidely told him I didn't need one. He chuckled to himself.

The team consisted of five men; the captain leading the way followed by his second; a tech man to handle whatever systems and deploy their surveillance equipment; and two others, who were armed like crazy. There was also a sniper somewhere in a building across the street and his (or her) backup who was providing a high view of the situation. This was an infiltration team moving in to negotiate face to face – seemed weird to me – and not a strike team. The hostages were on the second topmost floor, which meant a long climb of the stairs. I managed to keep up with them and not get winded, earning me a little respect from the team. We made our way to where we believed the hostages and gunmen were.

As the team covered area by area of the offices, I took my leave halfway, informing the same guy who was making fun of me earlier. He acknowledged, informing the captain, and I slipped away from the team.

I had been in contact with Jenny the whole time and she relayed information from Remington. She also had the building's schematics, and that gave me a sense of the floor's layout. The area that we were heading for was a meeting room of an office at the other end of the floor. It was one large room; simple layout and easy to control. The door was the sole entry point and there were the windows with the blinds drawn. I got that from the infiltration team.

There were no cameras to hack since they had already been disabled, so we had no visuals in the room. We only had the gunmen's word there were hostages, number unknown. Like I said, we weren't given a lot of information at first. It was partly my job to gather information, and I had to see if I could do better than the infiltration team.

While it was primarily Remington feeding me info through Jenny, I swear I heard Nakato remark, "Let's see if all her sneaking around The Facility pays off."

When I asked for confirmation, Remington said to ignore it while Jenny telepathically confirmed I heard it right. I grumbled a little about the equipment I had on me, took the baton from my belt and left it on a nearby table. I took the pike from its slot on the pants, half extended it to about three feet and kept it in hand instead. It made the pants a little inflexible. I then carefully shifted a ceiling board tile, giving me enough of an opening to float into the space area where all the wires and air conduits were, before shifting the board back into place. Whoever did the wiring in this office, thankfully, had good wire management, so I had some space to 'fly' through. I had to rely on the schematics I managed a glimpse from Jenny's vision, to navigate from where I was to the meeting room, partially following the wires. Jenny reported to Remington and Nakato I was making my way to the meeting room, but refused to tell them how.

I wasn't moving through corridors, but moving through the crawlspace wasn't any easier what with the wires, cables, ducts, et al., filling it. And I needed to be quiet while navigating around, using the pike to shift things out of my way. It took me a couple of minutes to reach the meeting room – after one wrong turn in the opposite direction – shift a ceiling board just enough to get a peek into the room. That's when I noticed that there were two doors, one that was in the schematics and another that wasn't. The room was wide – or long – with the main door at typically the centre point. But there was another at the far end, probably leading to another office. I didn't see any hostages, but noted two gunmen guarding the door. My point of view barely gave me fifty percent of the room. I got lucky they weren't looking upward, or they might have noticed the ceiling board move ever so slightly in the light. In any case, I didn't look for more than a few seconds.

I moved around to the other side of the crawlspace, at least over the space of the room, to get a look at the other half of the room. I positioned myself directly over the two gunmen who were guarding the door. I raised the ceiling board a little to shift it, creating a small slit so that I could look downward at the two gunmen. Made sure they hadn't noticed anything I did; lucky. You usually see these things in movies or TV shows, but you never can be sure if it actually works in real life, but I wasn't going to push my luck either. I could get a glimpse of the hostages huddled together on the floor at the far end of the room. I saw at least three men and two women there. What got me was there were two kids: a boy who looked no older than Ethan, and a slightly older girl. I never found out how or why they were there. From their position, the gunmen could easily cover them without being jumped. Thing was that I didn't see any other gunmen, just the two and the way they stood guard suggested they were not in charge.

Jenny reported everything I saw to Remington and he passed the information on to the infiltration team. I could pick up the chatter from them asking how I got the information, and where I was. I moved around a bit more to check out the next room, but instead of moving a ceiling board, I managed to peek through a slit between the air-conditioning duct and the ceiling board. It wasn't much, but I could pick up three voices in a hushed yet intense discussion. It wasn't difficult for Jenny to listen in as well, and I had to keep her calm when there was mention of a bomb.

We also picked up the motives behind these men's actions, but Remington advised me against writing it out. Given the small group of hostages, you can probably draw your own conclusions. It didn't matter anyway. There was a bomb, yield unknown, and the men were willing to use if they didn't get what they wanted. I couldn't get a sense of where the bomb was, unless I was willing to probe a little deeper and get into one of those men's minds. The most I got was that it was in a box nearby. Either the men were willing to die, or they were planning to be far away when the bomb went off. It meant we had some time. And there were kids among the hostages.

I checked with Remington on what he wanted me to do, and I made it clear I was not going to let the kids be harmed. Of course, the sensible course of action for me was to get out; my task was done and I had provided the information required. He knew I would be reluctant to pick the leader's brains for more information about the bomb, so he asked if I had any plans to ensure the children's safety. I quickly relayed a plan to take out the two gunmen and secure the hostages. Remington was silent for a while, but it felt much longer before he agreed to let me proceed. A little coordination would be needed with the infiltration team and, obviously, no negotiations.

I told Jenny I would be silent for a while, wanting to focus on the task at hand. She would maintain contact as best as she could manage, and she would be silent until I made contact again. I honestly did not know how all this network stuff would work given that my focus was going to be elsewhere, but I trusted Jenny. If she picked up anything, she wasn't going to blab or distract me – at least, I hoped, at that time.

Using my TK, I moved the ceiling board directly above the two guards enough to let the stun pike drop and, still using my TK to control the pike, zap the two at the head, one after the other in rapid succession. It took a lot of concentration to move the pike, and then hold the two guards from dropping too quickly and making noise, which thankfully they didn't when they got zapped. I lowered them to the floor as gently as I could manage before moving the ceiling board the rest of the way, so that I could lower myself into the room. The hostages, who also thankfully kept quiet, looked stunned as I quickly floated down so it didn't look too odd, appearing to fall slower than normal. I held a finger to my lips, hoping they understood to remain quiet... which they did.

I took the rifles off the gunmen and quickly checked for other guns. I found only an additional Glock and took it with me. I left the men lying on the ground and made my way to the hostages. I made sure the kids were okay first and then got Jenny to send the message to the infiltration team informing them what happened. I was then told there was one more hostage with the other gunmen, although I didn't notice one when I looked in the other room. Well, I did have limited visual scope from the ceiling. It might have been someone else who didn't seem like a hostage. I quickly relayed that information as well, minus my opinion even though Remington asked how I missed that. I wasn't scanning minds, so I couldn't really have known.

I got word from Remington that the Infiltration team had made their way to the room, so I ushered the hostages to the door and quickly got them out.

The team was there to meet us. I briefly mentioned the likelihood of one more hostage in the next room and a bomb somewhere. I handed over the weapons, too. I still had my pike with me. The team leader instructed me to get the people out quickly. I led the way to the stairwell and we scrambled down the stairs. I kept my focus on getting the kids out safely.

Five floors down, and the sound of gunfire echoed through the stairwell. They were short bursts, it didn't sound like wild gunfire. I hurried the kids along, getting the grown-ups to move as well. If there was truly a bomb, I hoped it didn't go off while we were making our way down the stairs. The kids did well, and if they were tired, they didn't show it as much as the grown-ups when we finally got out of the building. The police and paramedics took over from there and I quickly made my way back to Remington who was standing next to the van with Sophie and Paul. It was only when I got close enough did I get to hear there actually was a bomb, and it was ticking.

"They're trying to defuse it now," Remington said.

"How much time do they have?" I asked.

"They?" Paul remarked. "Don't we have to evacuate?"

Remington checked with the team leader, then he turned to us. "Five minutes," he said giving me a grim look, enough to get me to make up my mind about my rules. Both Remington and Sophie knew me well enough to note when my mind was made up without me having to say anything.

"I'm going with you," Sophie suddenly spoke up. I gave her a look and she said, "You're going back in to probe the guy's mind, right? I'm going with you."

Remington agreed before I could say anything. He said she could watch out for me, so I wouldn't go too far. Jenny would still be in contact as well. "You don't have time to argue this, Jeannie," he said. "Get going."

I turned, looked up at the building, and took off upward into the darkness. Sophie followed close behind me, keeping up as best as she could. I was flying upwards fast, hoping to not be caught on some camera. Sophie wasn't exactly wearing the same safety gear I was, but the big black jacket might hide her enough, although she was wearing a pair of greenish longs. It took us less than twenty seconds to get to the upper floor, and I had to use my TK to break a window (tough window, by the way) for us to get into the building.

Once inside, we quickly made our way to the infiltration team. The captain was surprised to see me and said I should have left the building already. It was likely if the bomb went off, it was taking the top four floors. The guy who was ragging me earlier was the one working the bomb. The other members of the team were watching over the 'terrorists'. I said Sophie and I were there to help, and then asked which of the bad guys was the one who made the bomb.

I was already scanning by that time so it didn't matter to me which one the captain pointed to. I picked up on the thoughts straightaway and turned my attention to that individual. The captain insisted he was pointing to the leader, but I countered I was paying attention to the one who had assembled the bomb. By then, we had about three minutes.

"I really don't want to do this, but you really need to tell me about the bomb, especially how to defuse it," I said to the individual I focussed on. I kept dropping hints into his mind, pushing his thoughts a little towards the construction of the bomb and how to defuse it. He may have been aware of what I was trying to do like they do in movies and TV shows, get the guy talking about the bomb, maybe he'll let slip on how to defuse; which wire to cut and all that. I could sense Sophie probing as well, and she commented that these 'terrorists' were quite willing to die.

He kept talking about their agenda and all while I kept driving the conversation back to the bomb. I was picking up images and ideas on the construction, and I quietly got Sophie to pick up on what were lies and what were truths within the design. She stood by the bomb, and occasionally looked down at the device to make comparisons between what she was picking up and what she was looking at.

It's a little confusing, I know, but thoughts in these situations are rarely straight-forward and the bomb was intricately designed. Sophie was good. She could understand the electronics and the wiring, and she discreetly started pointing out the way the bomb's system was working to the team member who was working to defuse it. He picked up what she was doing and they worked on cutting off the power supply of the bomb without letting it go off. While I did my part in pushing the guy's mind for information, I couldn't make sense of it all, not the way Sophie did and even though I was reluctant to have her along, I was glad that she came.

We got the bomb deactivated with more than thirty seconds to spare.

The bomb-maker was baffled at how we managed to deactivate his bomb, as were members of the Infiltration team. Sophie simply said we were trained in reading micro expressions; picking up information while talking to the bomb-maker and watching his reactions. To prove it, I spilled all the other information I picked up from his mind to the rest of the team, about his true feelings regarding the 'mission' he and his 'friends' were on, and how things got blown so out of proportion that led to this whole affair. The shocked and shamed expression on the bomb-maker's face was enough to impress the infiltration team.

"Just one thing," the captain said, "how did you get back up so quickly?"

"Oh, we practically flew getting up here," Sophie said in a joking manner, adding a chuckle. The captain gave us this look like he was wondering if he should take us seriously or not. I swear I could sense Jenny letting out a sigh of relief.

Sophie and I made our way to the elevators; I wasn't in the mood to take the stairs. The danger was over, so it was safe enough. I picked up the equipment I left behind earlier. She voiced her opinion then, saying it was a nasty thing I did at the end, revealing all that information.

I agreed and kept quiet after that, feeling a little off about the whole affair. It was a little out of character for me and yet, it felt exactly like something I'd do if the mood struck me. It felt wrong and right at the same time, but I tried not to dwell on it too much. Sophie noticed my mood and I know Jenny, still connected via the network, picked up on it as well. I quietly asked her to leave me to my thoughts, and she complied without saying anything more. I felt the connection between us break-off.

Sophie and I got to the ground floor, made our way out of the building through a side exit and discreetly headed for the van. Remington ushered us in and closed the door after he got in. The van started up and headed back towards The Facility.

While I stayed quiet the whole way back, Remington quietly handed me my glasses. Nakato felt it was good example of using our abilities in the field during such a situation, even though Paul technically didn't do anything. He was pretty jazzed about how Sophie and I flew up the side of the building though.

Anyway, Nakato remarked what we did had a purpose. It was to prove to the Board we could apply our abilities to manage certain situations within a given guideline without violating certain morals to the extreme. It was even stressed that what I did at the end was only mildly invasive, compared to what could have been accomplished if I threw morals out the window and forcibly extracted the required information as certain Board Members would have preferred. I could imagine which Board Member Nakato might have been referring to, although I am sure there were several Board Members who would have preferred us using our abilities as if they were weapons.

I stayed silent. Remington asked if I was okay, and I simply nodded with a weak smile. I felt cold and wrapped my arms around myself. I wasn't looking, but I could sense Remington eyeing me, probably out of concern. I felt an arm go around my back and noticed Sophie sidling up to me on one side. This was soon followed on the other side by Jenny. I looked at Sophie and then at Jenny, and gave them each a smile as best as I could. And that's how the trip back to The Facility was... the three of us together.

It wasn't too late by the time we got back to The Facility and we were pretty hungry. I dropped by the gym first, but Keiko had already finished the kendo class and left. John was still there and asked about the get-up I was wearing. I realised I hadn't changed back to my clothes and may have left them in the van. I told him it was 'a long story' and then excused myself, heading off to the cafeteria. The others were already having their dinner and I noticed Walker was there waiting for me. He took the liberty of ordering a few of my favourite dishes for me once he knew I was back. Sophie filled him in a little about what happened and he ended being my rock for the night. Sophie also had my clothes from the van, which she handed over to me.

It's not I wasn't willing to do what I had to do. It wasn't even I was against doing what I had to do. It's that small part of me enjoying it a little; that bit of the darkness welling up just a little, and I could feel it. It took a bit of effort to stop myself from going too far. It was why I felt cold; nothing to do with the weather. So, spending the night with Walker helped settle my nerves a little.

The next couple of days was settling back into routine, something Sophie had a little problem doing as well. It wasn't her first situation, but it has been the most intense for her, given the situation with the bomb. She pushed herself a little more during our network session, so much so she gave me a headache and I had to calm her down a little. It helped me a little in dealing with my anxiety too.

This is a little difficult to put into words and I'm not quite clear on how to deal with my feelings in this area, especially given the other emotions I have to deal with at the moment. Y'know, with both Walker and Becca leaving soon…

And I'm kinda pooped out right now after all this writing and recalling all that stuff. So, I'm turning in for now.

Dec 7

Kinda got carried away with the last entry, so catching up a little here.

I met with Linda for my monthly review and the main concern was Colleen. I haven't done anything there since I handed my work-room key to her. There's still a part of Colleen in there, the core program, but a lot of the system and memory files making up that core program are now backed up elsewhere. No, I'm not telling where although Remington has guessed. I think Linda knows too, but she didn't push me on it. I compiled most of my notes, at least the ones I made throughout the process of putting Colleen together, and passed them to Linda to have them reviewed. I filled in some blanks as best as I could so it would appear to be complete. She assured me I would get them back and if the desire arose elsewhere to build a similar system, I would be informed and given the opportunity to participate. In fact, she guaranteed it, which I thought seemed odd. I suppose it's fair I get informed if my work is being put into use.

We also covered the few little odds and ends, like how I was doing in classes. I'm all caught up again and managing to keep apace with the others. I haven't slacked off too much on my spaceship design, still constantly making changes or adding stuff to it as I pick up new things in class. It has three main propulsion systems with four back up systems for different situations, such as proximity of a sun, or a planet, or within nebulas, or if there are asteroids or even micro meteorites and other situations. It wasn't just making sure the hull can withstand the rigours of space travel but turning it into a power source as well. Yeah, it's all kinda out there, but I've had Walker double checking my work while he's pushing me to consider all sorts of alternatives; not to mention assistance from Ehrmer, Corogi, a little help from Sophie and others. Apparently, it also pays to work well with others and not go at it whole hog on my own, like I did when I first started out on this. Only thing that fell to the wayside was my piloting lessons on the flight simulator. Haven't been putting in as much time as I should, but it should be like riding a complex and expensive massive bicycle. One session and I could get back into the swing of things. As I was writing that out, I went over the take off and landing procedures, and check-lists, all in my head. Don't think I missed anything, it's practically a habit.

One thing Linda was concerned about was my mentoring, particularly with Kadi and Ethan. Granted my focus hasn't really been on them, and when I do check up with them, they seem to be doing okay. Ethan's taken to hanging with John and his friends, even out of gym. Kadi and Rain are getting along fairly well, with Rain picking up a bit of Kadi's language. I help out there where I can, while translating and helping Kadi with English, although not as much as I really need to. With Becca leaving, it'll be down to me to watch over Kadi as needed. I don't see any problems there. Kadi's gotten used to life – and the food – around here already. It's pretty much what Linda discussed with me where all that was concerned.

And she gave me back my key to my workroom today.

Then on Saturday afternoon, I took a trip into the Dreaming. Ethan said he had started making trips back and was rebuilding his village. According to him, there didn't seem to be borders; no separation between realms or lands like before. If he was right, there was no such thing as my lands or his lands. I got curious enough to take the trip that afternoon.

It was a bit of an effort to get in but not as difficult this time around. The more trips I make to this new version, the easier it'll be to slip in. I was on the bed with my eyes closed, then imagined I slipped through the bed and was falling. This sensation continued and I felt the air rushing around me. When I opened my eyes, it was blue sky above. I turned in mid-air and saw the ground below rushing towards me. It wasn't much of an effort to even slow down as I approached the ground and landed safely in a small open space surrounded by trees. If I didn't know better, it might have been where a tavern once stood. My clothes were pretty much the same as every other trip I made to the Dream-world before, although I did notice some minor changes.

The minor changes didn't stop with my clothes. The Dream-world seemed different from when I was last in it with Sophie. It felt a lot like the original iteration when I first started building my Dream-world. My version had a kind of fantasy feel built more on European fables and legends. It might have been based on my memories of travelling through Western Asia or Eastern Europe before, but not now. The forest didn't seem as dense as before and there appeared to be pathways through them. There was nothing to inform my decision, so I picked the path before me, and started walking.

I took in the sights, as much as a forest path could be considered some sights to see. The hills and mountains in the distance seemed wrong as were some of the trees. I caught sight of a few creatures, but no people. It didn't seem like the Dream-world I was familiar with, and yet not,… but there was something familiar in the air.

It took more than a day of hiking, spending the night under a tree by a stream, before I came across a village. It was an empty village, so I figured it might be the same one Ethan said he was building up. Because some of the buildings or homes looked half built, I wasn't sure if they were just that way or if he was actually building the village himself. Being there invoked a sense of déjà vu. The feeling of unease made me decide I needed a different perspective, so I took off, straight up to get a bird's eye view of the place.

When I reached a comfortable height, I stopped ascending and took a look. The land still looked vast and far reaching. There wasn't a coastline in sight although several rivers cut through the land, starting from snow covered mountains and ending or passing through lakes. Oddly, several mountain lakes were giving off steam. It wasn't something easily noticed, but one of them was begging for attention. The cloudy plume looked like wispy vapours off a mountain side, but not something suggesting volcanic activity. The closer I got, the more it looked like normal steam rising from some little pond – a hot spring. The overflow created a little stream, resulting in a river flowing down a mountain. I landed next to the hot spring, and the heat was enough to fend off the cold of the mountain. The hot spring itself was an oddity, something completely new and unique to this Dream-world, and there were several just on this one mountainside.

My excursion into the Dreaming was to check out what Ethan was up to, out of responsibility and curiosity. Taking a dip in the hot spring was just for the heck of it. In all, it was probably no more than a full day in the Dreaming and about three odd hours in reality.

I slept fairly early on Saturday night – if half past two in the morning can be considered early – and was up by five in the morning. Sunday was spent in review classes and things were pretty mundane today. So, I'm off to the pool for now.

Dec 10

Busy Busy Busy and there's a lot happening, I haven't had time to write it up. Even now, it's not likely I can write everything without going on too long again. So, highlights(!) and keeping it brief would be in order. Let's see if I can manage that.

My sleeping times are now more or less what they were before I came to The Facility; I tend to have quite a bit of time on my hands at nights. When I do get some sleep, it's because I feel like it. Even then, it's no more than a couple of hours each time. I'm not getting any headaches; I'm not having any hallucinations; no emotional problems; nothing that plagued me before, and I don't feel a need to go into the Dreaming for a break. Not quite sure when the change or adjustment happened, but there you go. Colleen doesn't require much attention since she off-loaded her memory and main program – the gateway is still open and I'm sure The Facility is trying to track it – so I've been spending more time at the Flight Simulator and the Spaceship design. For a break, I run through a simulation, be it one of the jets I was training on or a Viper scramble.

A couple of nights back in the simulator, Walker came to me with some data to check. It was unusual because I thought he had turned in for the night after our swim. He plugged a data disk into the flight simulator's system, and showed me a stream of partially familiar looking data over the monitors. I recognised some of it as being the data stream from Tomas' transmission, but more scrambled and denser than before. He asked how I could recognise it so quickly, and I pointed out the various code markers in the data stream. They marked the beginning and end points of certain transmissions.

"Except, there are a lot of markers overlapping each other now," I said, studying the stream. I had spent months identifying the various markers during my time in the Operations Center. It wasn't just one pattern, but several, and I knew the computers could identify those markers. My part was to visually double check and occasionally help to recode the stream into normal data be it text, or more often, visual information. Then the data started overlapping and the computers couldn't find the normal markers. Those IASC fellas thought it was a glitch in the programming and when I voiced my opinion, I got booted from the Operations Center.

So, my conclusion was, "Tommy gave these to you to show me," I said to Walker.

He smiled. "Do you think you can adapt the program to sift through the data and sort things out?"

"Might take a while. These look really dense like there are four or five overlaps now. Maybe more."

"What would be your take for the overlap?" he paused, searching for the right phrasing. "'Go wild', I think is the term."

I thought for a moment, and then said, "If the signal is overlapping with itself, it could be that Tomas' current signal is stronger than before and taking less time to reach us, arriving the same time as the older signals."

"And...?"

I knew he was pushing me. "His transmissions have been gaining strength? Or he's closer to home now than before so the signals don't have to travel that far? Or there's something else boosting the signals?" He grinned at me. "It could be anything," I whined a little. "Anything could cause each progressive transmission to be denser than before, so we are receiving several transmission signals at the same time."

"They do need you back in there," he said. He ejected the data disc and handed it to me. "The original program is in there too, in addition to what you just saw. Let's see what you can do with it."

"Tommy could have figured this out. It just takes someone who's familiar with the data to examine the markers. Surely someone within the IASC would know this," I said.

"If that were the case, they wouldn't have come to me for solutions"

"You know they won't be happy you came to me."

He smiled, then left without saying anything more.

I spent the next day sifting through the program's code, checking the syntax and analysing areas where changes could be made. I needed it to behave a little more intelligently, to adapt as needed if the signal overlapped again. The likelihood of a full rewrite seemed inevitable, and not preferred. I considered running the program through Colleen, and teaching her how to read the data stream, what to look for and how to isolate the markers to match with their corresponding formats. Without an A.I. to adapt accordingly to the shifting nature of the data, a normal computer OS was not going to make heads or tails of the data stream by relying on the markers. Colleen is a consideration I haven't acted on, as I still have classes, mentoring, kendo and other things to get through – yea, that briefly covers it all.

Then earlier today while in class, I get a comms from Remington to meet him and Linda in her office. Mr Hardy wasn't too pleased about it.

Pete was in Linda's office as well. I was told to have a seat, which I did without saying anything, and wondering what kind of trouble I was in this time. I was certain I hadn't done anything lately to warrant this kind of sudden attention, especially with Pete there. He started by assuring I wasn't in any trouble. Walker had put in a recommendation to have me back in the Operations Center, and this meeting was to check if I was interested in taking up the part-time job again. I admitted still being interested in the mission itself, especially Tomas' well-being, but I didn't quite say "Yes" directly. This was noticed by Remington.

"There are times when your confidence comes through and you really can shine in what you do," he said, "especially when you know what you're gunning for. You have all that potential, but, Jeannie, you're holding yourself back a lot."

I clarified that it wasn't so much a confidence thing as it was a genuine fear of losing control, of succumbing to the darkness within myself. Pete felt it was just an excuse, and my confidence in myself wavered from time to time depending on the situation I found myself in. Often enough, I would eventually step up, but after struggling with my doubts and insecurities.

"Yes, most of the Board Members are concerned over your potential for evil given your genetic disposition and your psyche profile, and while you have occasionally gotten me worried I was wrong about you, you've shown great strength of character by choosing to do the right thing. Granted, there were not always easy choices, but you have set quite an example among your peers and friends whether you're aware of it or not," Pete said.

The mention of my psyche profile grabbed my attention. I didn't even know I had taken a psyche evaluation. Pete then said he would recommend getting me back into the Operations Center and promptly left the room before I had a chance to respond.

I wanted to ask about my psyche profile then, but didn't. Remington, however, asked if I was free for a while. I didn't say anything. He gave Linda a slight nod and she smiled, pulling out a folder from her desk drawer and handed it to me. As my G/C, it made sense she would have a copy of my psyche profile. I doubt she could share it with me, whether Pete was in the room or not.

Suffice to say, I'm supposedly quite psychotic bordering on being a sociopath. I noticed a question mark next to a word, 'Oneirophrenia'. I haven't had time to look it up yet. Everything pointed to the fact that I could be a really nasty person if I were so inclined, and notations of my actions, behaviours and even journal entries were listed as examples to point towards the conclusions listed. Remington picked up on what I was thinking, and said, "It doesn't matter what that says, it's just gives us something to watch out for."

"From what I know about you," Linda started, "you have a good heart, but with a mean streak that occasionally rears its head. The way you were with Walter late last year and trying to deal with Ethan, taking him down the way you did…" She trailed off there, like she didn't want to say what was on her mind, or she didn't want to upset me. Remington told her to be open and straight with me. "I think that dark part of you that you're so scared of, is also the best part of you, especially with the control you have over it."

Remington backed her up by saying, "You do have more control over it than you give yourself credit for. I know you pulled back a lot after that last confrontation with Phillip, but that deal with the bomb-maker, it was more so Sophie wasn't the one who did the probing, right?"

I stayed quiet. I didn't have any particular answer. I suppose if I didn't do it, he would have gotten Sophie to do the mind probe anyway, and she would have been more than willing to try. We would never really know.

"It's been a tough year, I think," said Linda. "Just be yourself. Despite this 'darkness' that you worry about, it's counterbalanced by your conscience, your empathy and your friends; your support system."

That was pretty much it, a little more than what Pete told me last year although there was some overlap. I got dismissed from her office, led out by Remington. It made the whole day seem weird. I didn't even go back to class; skipped lunch and sat by myself in the little garden, mulling things over. Walker turned up, didn't say anything and simply sat with me. In the space of a few minutes, everything seemed right again.

I'm really gonna miss him when he leaves.

Dec 12

Trying to create a semi-intelligent algorithm for the data analysis program was a tough nut to crack, even with assistance from Nik. The programming language used allowed for modifications, and it should have provided some inroads through the programme's structure and syntax to allow for some form of intelligent analysis. However, incorporating the modifications proved far more difficult than it needed to be.

Nik suggested starting from scratch; an easier, though a far more time consuming option. Heck, Colleen could solve this problem faster if I was allowed to incorporate the original program into her. As her core program wasn't the same as the one used by The Facility or the IASC, I wasn't really allowed to do that. That whole music recognition program rearing its head.

I got Nik's help because I needed someone else to take up the slack where time was concerned. I had the network sessions to monitor and my other work to give some time to. Reworking the analysis program became too time consuming. I approached him to consult first, and when he offered some ideas, I suggested collaborating. Then I had to find out what that entailed and thankfully, there wasn't any red tape; a quick word or two with our G/C's, and he was officially on board.

Nik went full-on at the program yesterday while I monitored a network session run by Bastian and Kevin, backed up by Ethan monitoring for leaks and 'lag-time'; what we call it when someone's mind wandered or got distracted from his or her assigned work, distracting other participants. It's like when you're in a study session, someone starts humming some familiar tune. It gets into everybody else's head, like ear-worms. When it hits us within the network, everyone gets distracted really fast.

So, Nik did a chunk of programming yesterday, and I did some review with him today. We've been trying to develop an intuitive rudimentary AI system into the analysis program, but it's proving to be too massive an addendum with insufficient variables to work with. The restriction came from those IASC boys when I presented my plan on Thursday night – or Friday morning, take your pick what half past one in the morning would qualify for. They even reminded me of the beat recognition software I used, which they still don't agree was a valid reference program. Pete did really quick work and by dinner on Thursday night, I was asked to prepare a short presentation. It was great to see Tommy again after a long while.

I know, I jumped around a bit on the timeline there. So, to be clear, I was asked to do the presentation around dinner on Thursday, which I did a few hours later. I caught up with Nik on Friday morning in class. Within an hour, he was raring to go and I had cleared it with our G/C's soon after. I had the network session in the afternoon, sparring with Keiko in the evening, dinner with Walker, Sophie and Will, and catching up with Nik again only this morning. He showed me what he had done, we worked out what else needed to be done and what it would take. Starting from scratch really did not seem appealing to either of us. He did make an alternate suggestion, something I had considered... But I'm not writing it down here. Not until after we've done our presentation tonight.

I have to admit, it's kinda cool working with Nik on a project like this and it gave me an opportunity to practise my Malay. Rusty as I was, he was patient and understanding in indulging me, but I think he was glad to have someone to converse with in Malay. It's the same with Kadi when I'm speaking to her in her own language, although she would still comment on my atrocious dialect. I've also been managing the occasional sentences in Walker's language, although he discourages me from using it. It always makes him laugh, but in that embarrassing way.

Working with Nik has also given rise to a few new rumours Carol was more than willing to share over lunch. I've gotten to the point where tuning her out for those portions is an automatic thing now, but it is a little hard to ignore it outright.

Meanwhile, Becca's almost done with her packing with the main basic necessities in use left to be packed. It's still under a couple of weeks before she leaves, and there are four crates of cargo ready to be shipped ahead by Monday. Walker's got two crates. These 'crates' are specialised light-weight containers, about 3x3x3 feet, filled with mostly memento, some equipment, personal project work and other bits either brought over initially or to be taken back and shared with their respective civilisations. Walker's suite is almost empty save for the furniture. He didn't have much since the fire and water damaged most of his stuff. I gave him the little holographic projector I had; the one with a few images of Mikey, a few of which had me in them. The battery should last a year or so, and it is rechargeable. He's got some time to create a recharger or new power source when he gets home.

That's it, this is making me feel really bummed out. I'm gonna stop here and head off to the gym, trash some of this... depression... out of my system.

Dec 15

Something weird just happened. It wasn't weird when it was happening, it just seems weird when I think back on it and how it's lingering in my thoughts. I had a dream, but I can't tell if it was an actual dream, which would have been fleeting and gone in a while, or if it was a sudden unexpected trip into the Dreaming, which would account for its vividness and lingering afterthought.

I was doing some work on Colleen in my workroom and I kinda dozed off. It was just for a little while. Even Colleen's clock showed that I was asleep for barely ten minutes. That is, if I actually did fall asleep. That's something that Colleen can't verify. But it was rather late, about three in the morning, and my eyes were feeling a little strained from the work I was doing. I took my glasses off and rested my eyes a little, and next thing I knew, I was in some tavern that looked like Kinstein's Kitchen, but at the same time it wasn't.

I was seated at a table in this medieval looking tavern, not thinking if anything was out of place. I was aware I felt comfortable and safe despite suddenly being in this odd place. It didn't occur to me I was dreaming, not even when Keitaro sat down at the table placing a hot beverage before me. I thanked him without a second thought, and proceeded to sip at the drink. Oddly, I can't recall what drink it was except that it was hot. Everything else seems clear, as I type this out on Colleen's console.

Keitaro and I caught up with each other. He asked how I was getting along, sorting out the garbled signal I had been focussing on over the last couple of days. I wasn't letting it dominate my time although it did take up a reasonable chunk. I then asked how he was doing with his work, and he said he was reworking an older design in his robotics work to accommodate the equipment he has to work with now. The whole conversation was as casual as could be. I somehow felt compelled to ask how he was doing in general, what with being dispersed to the winds and all by Phillip. He casually replied that it hurt at first, but it wasn't as bad as it seemed. It sounded like a joke and I chuckled a little before asking when he would be coming back.

"I need to check with my sister about that first," was his reply. "Could you help out with that?"

"I don't think she's too keen to talk to me about you," I said. "I think she still holds me responsible for what happened."

You'd think I should have noticed the odd turn our conversation took, but it all still felt normal. I'm still surprised I can recall the conversation in detail because his reply was, "She has to know, whatever happened was all my choice and it's best I explain it to her myself. You just have to get her to me."

"Not if she's unwilling."

"Then force it."

"I can't. It wouldn't be right and it might make things worse between us. Also, I don't like using my abilities to force someone to do things they may not want to do."

He laughed at that and said, "You're actually worried about how I would convince her that you didn't force me to help you when you have to force her to meet with me."

The way he said it did make me laugh along although it really wasn't a joke in hindsight. I then jolted awake. A shiver ran up my spine and I felt really weird. While the conversation was vivid for me to write most of what was said almost verbatim, most of the other details seem fuzzy, like the tavern itself, the drink and other patrons who may or may not have been there around us. I'm sure the table we sat at was wooden, but I can't recall if it was like rough wood like it had been in Kinstein's place or treated wood like it is in some replica tavern. I think we also alternated between stools and chairs, or did we sit on the floor, Japanese style? And if it was simply a dream, should I take Keitaro's request to meet with his sister seriously? If so, where am I supposed to take her to meet him? Just drag her into the Dreaming and hope for the best?

The Dreaming isn't what it used to be, and I don't think I had any actual control before. As much as I could manipulate a few things, I couldn't control everything; not Michelle, not what happened to Keitaro and not what Phillip did. Not at all.

Or am I just over thinking things?

Somehow, I need to convince Keiko about Keitaro and get them to meet up.

Dec 18

You know those shows where some pro goes rogue, and the master is called in to help take the pro down. The master says something like, "I taught him everything he knows, but I didn't teach him everything I know," then someone would say, "Maybe he's picked up some new things you don't know."

When I did come up with an idea how to get Keiko to meet with Keitaro, I needed to get her to agree to the idea first. It was not the best idea, but it was something she could respect if I was successful.

I challenged her to a kendo match.

When we spar in kendo during practice, the hits I make are usually because she lets me get those hits against her. To say she's really good at kendo is a massive understatement. Even during those kendo meets with those masters and *sensei*, they greet her with high regard. So challenging her might be more than foolhardy, but it got her attention enough to agree to the stakes. If I won, she would allow me to link her up with Keitaro. If I lost, the subject was dropped forever and I'll never bug her about it ever again. Those were high stakes, for both of us.

Or perhaps she was curious if I improved enough to face her in kendo; not in practice or as exercise, but a true confrontation. It's the only weapon style in which I can't beat her, out of all the other weapons we've used on each other, including the *bokkun*. We discussed certain issues, such as requiring some assurances and *shinpan*, i.e. referees. Referees weren't too difficult because Nakato was a *YonDan* (4th level Dan) in kendo – I didn't know that – and Kadi has improved well enough that Keiko suggested having her be a second judge. The assurance was to make sure I wouldn't be using my TP abilities to anticipate her moves, and that's despite our experiment earlier this year. That wasn't easy since in her eyes, I've got most of the TPs on my side. So, I recommended Callie and Carl. Carl had no interest in helping me whatsoever, and he was more than willing to participate. Callie was impartial where I was concerned. And to make sure those two would be fair, I wanted Jenny as well. It's not that I didn't want Sophie, but Jenny was a better choice in keeping tabs on Callie. So that was that, and today, Keiko and I faced off in the VR Arena that had been configured to a kendo ring.

The lead up to the fight was eventful in itself. Everyone was aware that it was a case of student (me) against master (Keiko), but no one was sure what the stakes were. I've been in enough fights around The Facility – like the last beat down with John – to attract attention, not to mention the whispers of odds. Of course, the lunch group knew there were stakes and Carol did her best to weasel some info out of me. I only said it was between Keiko and myself. The way she and Helen went on tho, it was obvious the rumour mill was churning overtime, raising my anxiety levels.

That's where Walker came through again, taking me through his form of mind clearing meditation in the pool. He got me floating on my back, keeping my mouth and nose above the water level. He tilted my head back so that my ears and eyes were below the water level, and he helped to keep me in that arched position. Wasn't that easy at first, but once I got my breathing to the rhythm he tapped on my back, I found myself relaxing and the tension ebbing away with the water flowing about me. My thoughts quieted down, and the sensation of drifting came over me. I could still sense his fingers tapping on my back and my breathing followed that slow rhythm. I don't think I'll be able to do this on my own, not without him supporting me and keeping me from sinking.

He slowly brought me out of that state as well. He must have known when I was at the most relaxed, probably by feeling those vibes in the water. He then suggested staying away from Carol until after the match. After we got out of the pool, I ended up working a while on Colleen and then dozing off for an hour or so at her console. I probably should have gotten some proper sleep, but in the end it didn't really have much impact on my performance.

So back to that quote at the beginning, Keiko did teach me most of what I know about kendo, but not everything that she knows, and boy, was that an eye-opener. I think even Nakato was surprised at some of the moves Keiko pulled during the fight. And to that counter-point, I did learn something from those session of facing off against different opponents during my grading, and also from coaching the juniors on my own for a couple of weeks. It's mostly that self-realisation of how certain moves or strikes are supposed to work. I may not know what those moves are called, but there's the sense of when it goes so right; the simple weight shifts on the feet, the movement of the shoulders, the arc of the swing, the feeling you get when you hit the sweet spot on the *men* or the *koté* or the *do...*

Keiko and I were suited up when we entered the arena a little after ten this morning, pausing at the entrance to bow to the hall, paying respect to it. Nakato and Kadi did the same, as did our other trainees. Most of the spectators who followed us in to witness the match followed suit as well. Callie, Carl and Jenny sat at various place around the ring, not together. Sophie was there as well. I had to reason with her why I picked Jenny, and she didn't mind. There were other TPs there as well and it was Sophie's plan to have them monitor the fight too.

After all our rituals were done, Keiko and I took our spots across each other just outside of the ring, and we proceeded to put the rest of the armour on securely. Nakato briefed Kadi on her responsibilities, and they took their positions just outside the ring. When we were ready, Keiko and I bowed to each other. We took three strides into the ring and drew our *shinai*. The fight began.

In my time sparring with Keiko, I noted how she would attack and defend herself – on the rare occasion when she pulled a defensive move. She was deadly with every strike and she had a preference for striking the *koté* more often; not the easiest thing since it's the least stationary target. Going for the *do* was second choice and the *men* strike was a third option. I always figured that since she started really young, the *koté* and *do* strikes were the best choices if a small kid were to face off against an adult. It also didn't mean that her *men* strikes weren't dangerous either. This was also the first time I got the full force of her *kiai*. It was really intimidating, so much so that she easily scored the first strike against me which I barely saw coming. I swear, I felt my head rattle first before I heard anything else when she went for the *men* hit. Even the roar of the audience got drowned out following that strike.

The thing is, our match wasn't a conventional match where you simply score the best of three strikes within five minutes. It was more of a round of five sets, with each set lasting a full five minutes. A time-keeper wasn't needed, only a counter with a buzzer. You could score as many strikes within each set during those five minutes. Person with the most strikes wins the set. And while we agreed to a best-of-five-sets, we were also going for all five sets. If I was going to lose, it was going to be a full loss across the five sets. We weren't stopping even if one of us was already ahead by three sets.

That first round was all hers, her speed and stamina really shining through, and she didn't even ease up on her strikes. She came at me fast and furious, I could barely react at first. Thing is, towards the end of that set, I managed to clock her speed. My focus snapped back into place even as I managed to get my *shinai* to barely counter her strike. She still got the *men* hit, but I got her speed. When we took a couple of minutes rest between the sets, we knelt at opposite ends facing each other. Neither of us removed our armour. I could feel my head pounding a little, and my right wrist was throbbing from the hits it took. I took the time to reflect on her attacks and what I might be able to do in the next set, not that it helped much. But when we got back to the centre of the ring at the start of the second set, I think she knew we had a real showdown going on.

I had my eyes closed when we took the three strides to the centre of the ring, and as I drew my *shinai*, my focussed deepened. I opened my eyes as we stood facing each other and I felt the corners of my mouth forming a slight smile while looking at my opponent. Everything else faded away. We loosed our *kiai* at almost the same time, the tips of our *shinai* tapping against each other. She didn't attack straight away this time, probably realising the circumstances had changed ever so slightly in facing me. She pulled a couple of feints, her forward foot taking a half step forward and opening her guard to draw me in. On her third feint, I took the opportunity to strike, but she leaned back and I missed the *men* hit, overextending myself. She stepped in with a solid *do* hit. With that, the second set started going the way of the first set. At least, I wasn't holding back anymore, taking more attempts at making a strike even if she was blocking every attempt I made. Even as I was ramping up to her speed, I couldn't read her moves enough to block in time. She was even making strikes without much of a follow through, unlike how she kept drilling me as well as the juniors.

By the third set, my head was aching quite a bit and my wrist hurt enough to make a proper grip with the *koté* on, problematic. In the few minutes I had before starting the third set, I struggled to refocus my mind, ignoring the several aches and pain as best as I could. With my eyes closed, I got to my feet and took the three strides to the centre, only opening my eyes as I drew my *shinai* once more. Again, everything around me faded away. Instead of waiting, I started attacking first, as fast as I could. I think it surprised her because I made a hit. It wasn't a solid hit so it wasn't a scoring strike, but still, I got to her. It was enough to have her step back for the first time in the match. I quickly pressed on and she started attacking as well, suddenly pulling moves I had never seen before. Like when I went for the *men* again but, in amazing speed, she brushed my *shinai* aside as she raised her *shinai* while moving just a little to my left and scored a *men* strike single-handedly. Even Nakato was so impressed that it took him a moment to flag the point. Kadi wasn't even sure if it was a legit strike.

I was momentarily stunned by the impressive move, but I didn't let it faze me for too long as we immediately continued. I took most of what she had been doing throughout the match by then and started attempting them; the shorter swings, the reflex strikes; less follow-through so I didn't have to waste time running past her and having to turn around like I was taught to do; striking with a wrist movement instead of the full arm swings; and especially the blocking, reflecting her strikes, and those small quick shifts that would keep her from striking the *men* or *koté*. Just enough so even if she did make a hit, it wasn't a proper solid strike. It was stuff she didn't teach, but I was learning really fast. Fast enough that she didn't score as many points in the third set as she did in the first two. Fast enough that I started scoring a few points of my own before the five minutes were up. By the end, she got the three sets out of five, but we weren't done.

I felt winded and was panting a bit, but I could also notice her breathing a little harder from across the ring as we knelt, waiting for the next set. It was the first time I was seeing her stamina weakening during kendo. Even in our sparring, she barely breaks a sweat, but now...

This was different. She might be seriously intense during our practice, but not up to this level. With me fighting back for real, it was pushing her a little more than usual. Still, I could sense the calmness about her, that serenity she always has when it comes to kendo; that respectability. That composure. I could feel her gaze reaching across the ring and I straightened myself, calmed my mind and, again, got everything else to fade away. I think as far as we were concerned, there was no ring; no arena anymore. Just the two of us, on the field of battle.

That suited me just fine.

The call back to the centre sounded more like a whisper in the wind. I didn't close my eyes this time, I didn't need to. I was already focussed on her. Sophie later said it was akin to watching a nature documentary with two alpha beasts approaching each other in a battle for dominance, cooler than any other sword fight in any movie she had seen. If that was what she said she saw, then that's what she saw, but it wasn't anything like that to me. Right from the start, and quite often through the fourth set, Keiko started favouring a high-guard, holding her *shinai* up in the striking position instead of the usual defensive (*kamae,* or *en garde*) position. Her high-guard opened up only two striking points, which were the *do* and *tsuki* – a thrust for the throat – the latter being a tougher and dangerous move. It also meant if I rushed in, she was already half a step ahead for a *men* strike. In keeping up my attack, I moved in anyway.

Anticipating a *men* strike, I went for a block and she went for my *do* instead, taking the point. I pressed another attack but pulled a feint instead, stepping back and acknowledging the hit she had made. Thing is, she didn't even flinch or try to block. It was like she knew I would realise what I was doing and would stop myself from actually hitting her. We quickly got back to our centre positions and started again. She took the high-guard again, but instead of being wary, I moved in and attacked anyway going straight for the *men* strike. The moment she managed the block, I closed the gap between us quickly, denying her the proper striking distance for a scoring hit. We ended up pushing against each other, *koté* to *koté*. She gave a hard push and we parted as she brought the *shinai* down for a *men* strike while I made for a *do* strike. I tilted my head slightly to the left and I felt her *shinai* make a glancing blow off the right side of my *men*, right as I got the *do* hit and the point. It impressed her enough to give me something that looked like a salute with her *shinai*.

I continued pressing my attack throughout the set as she alternated between the high-guard and the normal stance. I realised she never tilted her head to avoid a hit the way I did. She would subtly shift her position with quick small steps. In a way, her form never wavered. From the top of her head down the torso to the legs, her body was always in a straight line, centrally balanced.

Never swayed or swerved the way I did. Aside from the *kiai*, which may have sounded like random screeching to the audience, she kept her composure well. In the end, she took the fourth set, but by only three strikes ahead. I wasn't winning, but at least I was losing with a little dignity now, compared to that first set.

Utilising what I was picking up and adapting as best as I could, the final set was more of a proper kendo battle between us. I was moving faster, barely standing still in one place for too long, compared to that first set, and making more attacks, even managing a few scoring hits while effectively blocking against her strikes. Not all though, as she still landed quite a few hits. I treated the first round as if I was in a grading match against someone who might be my equal, or maybe just a little bit better. I got bashed good and proper for my mistake. Going up against Keiko proper was so different from our usual sparring in the gym during practice. She still took the fifth set, but only by one strike more than me. After we finished paying our respects and started removing the *men* and *koté* did I notice her composure sag a little, taking a long cleansing breath. She appeared tired, but not as tired as I was. Five sets of five minutes each was really intense, especially with the *men* remaining on throughout it all.

People were filing out of the arena when we started taking off our *men*. There were a few left when Carl came by. He muttered under his breath, "Guess you can fight fair," and walked on by, over to Keiko. He leaned over as if to say something. She gave a short, curt nod in response, and he left. I noticed Sophie and Jenny sitting with Walker, who gave a wave. I waved back. I got to my feet, feeling a little wobbly, as Nakato came over. He was impressed with the speed I was picking up things. He commented on several aspects of the match, pointing out a few things needing a little more work, and what impressed him. I thanked him, and he then went over to Keiko. She was still in the kneeling position, so Nakato knelt before her and they bowed to each other. They appeared to be chatting, so I walked over to Sophie, Jenny and Walker. I passed Kadi along the way and thanked her for being a referee. She felt she actually learnt a lot more than from a normal class.

Sophie and Jenny confirmed what Carl had inferred, that I never used my TP abilities to anticipate Keiko's moves. Walker notice the various bruises on my forearm and asked if I was okay. I only said that my head was still aching from the hits I took, distracting my attention from my arm or wrist. On his way out of the arena, Nakato told Keiko and me to make sure we had a check up with Ms. Phillips. He would follow up with her by the end of the day to make sure we complied. By this point, Keiko came over to our small group.

I told her I would honour our agreement since she had won, keeping it short, simple and without mentioning Keitaro. To my surprise, she agreed to meet up with her brother in the Dreaming since I had put up a valiant effort, especially in the final set. "At least, it is my decision now," she said. "And I have nothing more to teach you, but I still expect you to help train our juniors."

I smiled at that and gave her an affirmative response. She then picked up her equipment and left the arena. The rest of us followed suit. I collected my equipment and made sure to reset the Arena's programming. After cleaning up, I did as Nakato requested and checked in with Ms. Phillips, although I was pretty hungry by then. She did a cursory check-up, checking the bruised areas. I wasn't the most cooperating patient, so she dismissed me and had me check in after I had my lunch. As I was leaving, Keiko came in for her check-up after having had her lunch first.

Lunch was with the usual gang filled with the usual questions regarding the fight. The true purpose for the duel still eluded Carol, likely until she reads this or the previous entry. After lunch, it was back to the Infirmary, and Ms. Phillips' thorough examination took the rest of the afternoon. By the time she was done, I had time to check in with Keiko at the gym to deal with our juniors who had tons of questions about our duel.

I've been typing this up since dinner and now, I'm heading to the pool.

Dec 20

The trip with Keiko took a little more time than expected. It was odd, given we didn't seem to have spent much time on the other side of reality. She didn't delay, and suggested making the attempt at contacting Keitaro on Saturday night as she needn't skip her afternoon classes and kendo.

I spent my day in classes and then checking in with Nik on our little project. That's going smoothly although I suspect those IASC folks aren't going to be ecstatic with our solution. I have been keeping Walker and Tommy in the loop, so at least they know where we're heading with decrypting the signal, to which I'll mention here as a two point approach and leave it at that. At best, we should have some preliminary results in a few days. Nik is really showing off his programming skills with the project.

I had dinner with Keiko, explained how we were going to make contact with Keitaro and what to expect if all went well in our attempt. She was a little apprehensive and it was more to do with the whole telepathy thing. It wasn't an assurance, but I told her I wasn't going to be poking about in her head, and it wasn't likely I was gong to glean anything from her mind. It was going to be, "a consciousness sharing experience of sorts, nothing more than lucid dreaming at best." I supposed I could have gotten Helen to talk to her about it first, since she was one of the few non-telepaths who I took into the Dreaming; Keitaro and Walker being the others. Still, she was a little nervous.

Keitaro had been moved into a separate room, the one which had been used to house the critters before. Ms. Phillips turned it into an extra ward for any of her patients that needed extra attention and isolation away from the usual Infirmary area. Will said it was set up so Ethan had someplace quiet to do his trips to the Dreaming.

Will had set up a couple of chairs next to Keitaro's bed for Keiko and myself. We sat across each other with Keitaro between us. Following the plan I laid out earlier, we held each other's hand as well as Keitaro's hands. It was a little for show, but it also showed a willingness and openness on Keiko's part to the whole thing. It made linking up with her a little easier, even though I still felt a little resistance. There have been incidences where physical contact with someone in the Dreaming resulted in immediate connection. Granted, those cases usually involved me pulling someone else in, which was why Ms. Phillips preferred having either Will or, as a last resort, Sophie use their TK ability in handling me if I fell asleep in the occasional odd place. In any case, I did hope that physical contact with Keitaro would have allowed us to make contact easily.

No such luck.

I made a few attempts to make contact, before trying to get into the Dreaming instead. That required me to slip in by changing our perception of the Infirmary. Keiko reacted immediately when the plants started sprouting around us. In reality, it looked like we fell asleep next to Keitaro. To her, the world started changing around us, overwhelming the Infirmary and practically tearing down the walls around us. The bed Keitaro was on changed around him. Honestly, I expected him to disappear with reality, but he remained with us. It might have been because Keiko and I remained in physical contact with him, holding his hands, but it might not have been likely. Once everything had settled and the forest was around us, he sat up and greeted us. Even I was completely taken aback by that.

Keiko was skeptical if the person with us was even her brother, and I didn't blame her. It felt too easy; the way we simply slipped into the Dreaming with his comatose body and he wakes up, like its no big deal.

If took a few rounds of questions and answers for us to be sure we were meeting the real Keitaro. Even I couldn't guarantee the Keitaro we met wasn't a complete construct from Keiko's and my imaginations simply because he could answer all our questions; because in our minds, we knew the answers anyway. We had to go on faith. He didn't have any memories from the last few months, from since he was dissipated by Phillip until the end of the previous Dream-world in any case. He was somewhat aware of this particular Dream-world taking shape and said he could influence a few things, before asking how much I enjoyed the hot springs.

I didn't answer but Keiko noticed me blushing and said so. It was weird for me because I'm usually not too concerned with being caught with my pants down, so to speak. Maybe it was simply the idea that Keitaro was the one watching me?

Anyway...
I took the opportunity to take a walk and leave the siblings to their personal matter. I do not know what they talked about, I didn't ask Keiko and she didn't offer to share. Whatever it was, they appeared to be more than done when I got back to them about an hour later. I didn't wander far, but enough to do some exploring and be out of earshot. She looked happy and calm when I got back, so I guess we did find Keitaro after all.

I asked the same question as before, if he was coming back. He wanted to, but said there was something he needed to do in this new Dream-world. I looked at Keiko and she had this sly smile indicating some kind of understanding. Neither of them told me anymore and after eyeing them suspiciously, I shrugged and dropped the matter. Keiko was offered a look around the place, maybe check out a hot-spring, but she declined. So, Keiko and I said good-bye to Keitaro and we left, waking up approximately five hours after we went in.

On the outside, Keiko had a private word with Ms. Phillips, who was already on duty so early in the morning. I guess it had to do with Keitaro's status. I learnt he would be remaining within the Infirmary for now. Apparently, she had planned to have her brother sent home. She then thanked me for forcing the issue of meeting with her brother. With that, we parted for the day. I found out she made a call home, probably to update her parents.

She seemed more like herself after all these months of sullenness. I didn't see her for the rest of today either and she didn't turn up for kendo. I carried on with our juniors anyway. Will informed me she dropped by the Infirmary to check on Keitaro sometime in the evening, probably during the kendo training.

Anyway, I guess that's about it. I'm heading off to the pool for now and catch up with Walker.

Dec 23

Several things have come together over the last few days. The last network test was carried out yesterday and we've had some resounding success. This current team of participants want to utilise the Learning Network for study groups. Remington's given the go ahead, provided we have TPs who are willing to run with it. It's extremely beneficial to those who are participating in the Network itself, but the downside is we TPs running the network don't have as high a retention rate as the participants. If a Teep wants to fully be part of the learning network, they can't be the one running the network. Callie and Toni made it possible for us Teeps to have retention within the network, maybe they can improve it further.

Otherwise, Bastian, Kevin and Ethan are doing well enough as a team with their participants pulling a solid average of 95% retention from their varied materials, even with the F.E.P.'s among them. They're more often the wild cards, but not lately.

On the project front, Nik finished a preliminary working model to sift through the convoluted data from Tomas' transmission in a serviceable way. Even then, the process will still take weeks, maybe months to sort the data into the proper packets, given the unrefined nature of the program as it is. We presented this to Tommy and the IASC folks and still stressed the need for a proper A.I. to handle the variable and evolving nature of the data stream. When we were asked about the timeline needed to come up with such a system, that's when we played our ace.

Nik took the lead saying we had already fed the data stream into an A.I. system, and in the time it had taken to create the preliminary program, Colleen had already sorted two data packets from the messed up data I received from Walker. Tommy backed us up by verifying the validity of the data. All felt it was best I didn't say anything at first, especially since the IASC folks had no idea who Colleen was. Of course, they had to question the system, and that was when I provided a basic and simple explanation about the nature of Colleen and her origins. None of them believed I had assembled Colleen from discarded spare parts, much less programmed a viable Artificial Intelligent machine using said parts, and then taught it how to recognised the markers with the data stream in order to extract the data packets with precision (whew). It also brought up the whole beat recognition program debacle again.

"Whatever arguments you guys want to bring up, the point is we have a program that works in sorting the data stream," Tommy told them. "It may be working independently as a stand-alone system, but it works. We should focus on this instead of wasting more time while the data continues to stream in."

That got their attention, enough to grudgingly agree we had a point in our favour. It also made us at the Operations Center far more valuable to the whole program than we had been. Before, we only had to validate the data as it streamed in. With Colleen's help, assisted by Nik and me, we were now at the forefront of untangling the mass of backed up data while the folks at the IASC would have to assist with the data validation. It was a nice reversal; an opinion I didn't voice out there and then. I really wanted to rub it in, but didn't. Gotta show some respect, right?

So, I'm back in the Operations Center three nights a week. Nik will have the weekends at his convenience and will also get work credit. He's excited about getting to work in the Operations Center. Colleen will still do the heavy lifting while Nik and I will share the workload of verifying the cleared data before sending it off to the IASC folks for them to double-check (which was my job before) and compile the information. They do seem satisfied with the two data packets we decoded.

Walker and Becca have shipped their packing and they'll be leaving in a couple of days, heading off to the site of the next launch for the ISS. I don't know where or when that'll happen, but it's within the week. I've been sorting things with Becca on how to handle Kadi on certain cultural aspects, just in case. This has been going on over dinners until I have to catch up with Walker later in the night. He's been pushing me a little more on the aqua-acrobatic routines, emphasising his half of the routine, so I can take Sunee and Corogi to the end of their current routine. Since I have to take over teaching them, I've got to know his half of the routine. In addition to taking me through the routine, we have visual footage for my reference as well.

With Walker's knowledge and approval, Sophie's been helping to record the routine. I've also gotten permission to access the security footage from the security camera watching the pool area; only for the routine and nothing else. With the various angles and the footage, I used Colleen to extrapolate a three dimensional holographic video of the routine, in addition to dealing with the transmission data. It might be a weird thing to hear from her, but she's happy to be of some proper use instead of sitting idly in the room, doing nothing much for days and weeks at a stretch.

We've been doing all that over these past few days, starting since Saturday night. It didn't occur to him earlier that Sunee and Corogi would need someone to help them with their routine. It seemed odd to me the whole thing slipped his mind until lately, but it also gave me a nice excuse to be with him a little more before he leaves.

Speaking of which, I should be getting to the pool now.

Dec 25

If this were some movie, there would have been some kind of bittersweet moment where Walker and I would have embraced as he left. Then in those final moments, something would have clicked. Either he would decide to stay or I would decide to go with him, and we would be together. Or he would still have left and I would discover that I'm carrying his child, something to remind me of him always. Some kind of Christmas miracle maybe.

But, no.

My life isn't like the movies and shows I've seen, or the stories I've read. Both Walker and Becca have left The Facility, and I'm on my own, more or less. Sure I spent the night with Walker in his suite. It was empty of his possessions, and we discussed what few responsibilities I had to carry on. It was mostly to help Sunee and Corogi with their aqua-acrobatics, and not screw up being back in the Operations Center. He had prepared a few notes for me on what else he thought I could follow through at the Center as well. Then he gave me a little box wrapped with Christmas wrapping paper, saying I wasn't allowed to open it until tonight. I gushed a little because I didn't even think about getting him a Christmas present. He said the holographic unit I gave him earlier was already his Christmas present.

We didn't sleep last night, and I'm leaving it at that. We also didn't go to the pool either, but I did make it back to my suite to catch Becca. We caught up a little and she was leaving a few things for me, particularly a few dresses she felt would look good on me. We had breakfast together and Walker joined us too, as did Jenny, Sophie and Hank. After that, Jenny, Sophie and I had to report to the VR Arena for the field trip, so I said my final goodbyes to both Walker and Becca there and then.

And that was it.

They left sometime during the field trip.

I got to meet with our guest tutors from the various agencies who were leading the various groups on the field trip. They were different from last year, but the new guy from the IASC said he had heard about me from his predecessor. Apparently, so did the lady from JAXA. I smiled and thanked them in return, not really sure for what. They asked which team I was accompanying, but I wasn't on the field trip this time. My part was to observe the network from the control booth, as I had some responsibilities to cover where the network and the trip were concerned.

When it was time for the field trip back to Serenity Compound to start, I made my way to the Arena's control room. The supervision of the field trip was usually done by Remington. As he was accompanying Becca and Walker, he asked me to take his place, providing me a list to duties to carry out. On the bright side, I could still overhear the various lectures going on during the trip even if I wasn't part of the network. Any questions I had would have to wait until after the field trip was done.

Still, I was learning in my own way, working in the control room. The tech assisting me, Roy, was incredibly helpful because I ran into quite a few blind alleys and didn't know what to do. I didn't realise maintaining a consistently shifting simulation to accommodate the four groups was such a task. Being in the simulation itself, meant you weren't always aware of what another group was up to. Within the network, you got a sense of what they were being taught, but you would still be with your own group in your particular location. The full size of the Compound wouldn't have fit within the Arena, so there were short-cuts to accommodate the various sizes of the locations. The Compound itself looked so different from last year with most of the buildings completed and a few smaller ones still being constructed. We could see the implemented wiring and plumbing systems. I jotted questions on a little notepad whenever they popped into my head and quickly got back to helping with the VR integrity, while occasionally checking in on the network.

Kevin and Bastian did a good job with keeping things going leaving Ethan nothing much to do as a back-up. Sophie did her part in monitoring and got Ethan to pitch in when a few of the participants started having their thoughts drift from their lessons. I could sense Jenny was pleased with how things were working out. While she wasn't officially part of the field trip, she got a pass as being the main supervisor for the network TPs. She even took a moment to check with me, asking if I was okay with my own tasks, then chided me for checking on the network like a mother hen. That was her job for today.

I stopped interfering on the network after that.

Both Kevin and Bastian showed no signs of fatigue as the field trip pressed on to its third hour. They've come a long way, as have Sophie and Ethan. Jenny too, the way she could supervise them all. And I wondered if I had improved in any way...

Maybe it was Becca and Walker leaving, or my working in the Arena's control room instead of being on the network and part of the field trip. In that moment, it suddenly felt like I needed to do some stock-taking of my own life. I was closing three years of this life at The Facility and probably with lots more to come. Most of the lessons have been a struggle and life in particular hasn't been easy. Not that it was any easier before, but it sure wasn't this eventful and pretty much locked to one place. I've been told my presence hasn't been a cakewalk for The Facility either, but I'm still here. And then my thoughts drifted to Mikey and what I was going to do about him. This year in particular wasn't the best we've had and our relationship was a little damaged, unlikely to be fixed in the near future.

So, had I changed?

I couldn't really tell or say on my own account.

I got pulled out of my thoughts by Roy, and he got me to focus on my 'job' at hand. I apologised for being distracted and the rest of the field trip had my full attention. In all, the field trip lasted three hours and forty minutes with a twenty minute Q&A session within the Arena, continuing into the Luncheon as well. I took the opportunity there to put forth my own questions, and our guest tutors were more than happy to accommodate. Serenity Compound was still a year or so from being populated. There were still a few tests to be carried out, like having a building inspector make sure that the Compound is habitable. One little mistake and lives would be lost, never mind the pristine conditions of the plumbing and electrical systems I asked about.

Linda was at the Luncheon to check on me. She also informed me then that Becca and Walker were gone from The Facility, and I could take the afternoon off if I wanted. I didn't, opting to attend the physics class in the afternoon. Keiko called off our training session today due to the dinner in a while. I took the extra time to write this up instead, here, alone in my room and suite. It never felt this quiet.

Anyway, Hank is supposed to make sure I attend the Christmas dinner although I do have another plan for later tonight. I suppose it's like a date thing, planned for after the dinner. I've got about another twenty minutes before Hank comes by. Guess I should take a shower and change.

Dec 27

According to Linda, acts of bravery and stupidity are indistinguishable until the results of said acts are determined. If the initial voyages of discoveries failed, then those pioneers might have been considered idiotic for trying in the first place. You've got to be either really brave or utterly idiotic to strap yourself to a machine loaded with tons of explosive materials just to go into space. Then again, considering the results and consequences of those early pioneers, we look at them as brave people. Heroes, even.

According to her, you could apply it to almost any act of bravery or stupidity. You just had to look and analyse the end result and what benefits there were. Of course, she shared that little bit of unconventional wisdom with me when she found what I had done. It was either a very brave or a very stupid thing that I did, but that had yet to be determined once we would know what the actual repercussions are, and right now, it was leaning way into the stupid zone.

I had released Phillip.

Brave?
Or stupid?

After the Christmas gathering, I spent a few hours in Keitaro's company. I had loaded a digital copy of "Tokyo Godfathers" onto my console and then set it up for us to watch it. Well, I watched it in his company since he was still in a coma, but I felt it was something I should do with him since I knew it was an annual tradition for him. In watching the show and seeing all the coincidental miracles happen to the main characters in their attempts to do the right thing, no matter the obstacles in their way, I was kinda hoping for a small little miracle myself, and Keitaro would wake up.

Again, no such luck. I had to resign to the realisation that miracles happen in stories, and it wasn't likely to happen here. But I had to hope things would somehow work out.

And sometimes, you had to contribute a little effort in making some miracles happen.. Maybe I was reading too much into the movie, but that's how I felt about it this year. It seemed strange I had a different view of the movie, this being the third time I was watching it. I know some books have different... feel(?)... when I read them again at different times. I guess some movies would do too; give you different insights each time you view it.

When I decided to do what I did, it wasn't on a whim and it wasn't because of Keitaro. I also didn't have any really good reason for my actions. It seemed the right thing to do. Not at the time, but...

Okay, I'm beginning to feel like a proper git of an idiot about it now.

It's just, there was a debate in Sociology class, and it kinda made sense while it was going on. We were discussing criminal and justice systems, and how civilised societies should handle their undesirables; to what extent should a death penalty be acceptable and would we recognise if individuals are inherently evil with no chance of redemption. Would two wrongs make a right? Could we justify the death of one individual who had committed the act of killing someone else? The discussion was animated and difficult, and we even touched on the actions of soldiers during war and peacetime; the fallout of killing during battle on the psyche of a soldier when the war is over.

If it came down to someone like Phillip, would killing him be justifiable? I was convinced I had done that already, only for him to return... The guilt haunted me the last few years prior to his return; not so much the guilt of killing him, but that I did it so easily without much of a second thought at the time. And I came so damn close to doing it again, because of what he tried to do to Walker, and what he did to Keitaro.

For the few who argued for a death penalty, I kept raising the question of doing the actual killing itself. A small handful didn't mind the idea of taking the life of a guilty individual, but I remarked they had never been put into the position of killing for real. I was questioned as to how I would know what the real situation was like; to be responsible for extinguishing a life you held in your hands.

For the last few years, I had lived with the knowledge I had taken a life. While leaving out a lot of details, I reluctantly talked about the circumstances in which I dispersed Phillip's consciousness within the Dream-world, and effectively killing him in reality. He was pronounced brain-dead even though his body was kept on life-support. Granted, he came back recently to cause more havoc in my life, and I consequently imprisoned him, after a fashion.

An argument was raised pointing to his body being still alive meant I never killed him at all. Surprisingly, I was backed up by Jenny first, and then Jo. Once Jo spoke up, things took a more serious turn as if any doubters in the class suddenly realised what I was saying was true. Maybe the incident a couple of years back involving her, Callie, Jenny and Toni was more common knowledge than I would've guessed, or Jo had some reputation for being taken seriously.

One guy then pointed out that since I mentioned Phillip coming back, it negated the fact I killed him in the first place. John argued a mistake being erased, didn't mean the mistake didn't happen.

"Killing him wasn't '*a mistake*' in the first place," I grumbled.

Corogi then said, "If what you've been telling us is accepted as true, that this Phillip is truly evil, and you are now holding his consciousness captive, what are you going to do with him? It would be highly unlikely you would contain him for long."

"I honestly don't know what to do with him," I said.

The tutor pointed out that long term incarceration had two possible outcomes; it would either lead to repentance, or retribution. If repentance wasn't at all likely, then a more permanent solution needed to be considered. It really got me thinking. Perhaps it was the season, coupled with a few other things making me feel I needed to work things out with Phillip to see where we stood; if I needed to consider the permanent solution.

So, after lunch, I made a phone call from Linda's office. She was curious as to what I was up to because, against policy, I requested she didn't leave her office during the call. It would have been recorded anyway, but I asked her to stay. I called M (Phillip's brother) and asked him what he would do if he were to face Phillip again. He was unsure of what I was asking, and I then informed him what had happened where Phillip was concerned. I asked him to check on his brother and keep an eye on him for a while. It was a precaution, because I was going to attempt making contact with Phillip. He agreed, we said our good-byes and I hung up. Linda questioned if it was a wise move, and I said I needed to work some things out.

I then went to the Infirmary, informing the attending nurse I was going for a Dream-walk (but not really), and then went deep into the darkness of my soul to seek out my demonic prisoner. The fact it didn't faze me the slightest to be in that darkness occurred to me. I didn't feel cold or afraid, and I didn't even hesitate in the slightest. It was almost as if I was comfortable with the darkness.

I threw Phillip deep into it, if it even had a depth. I wasn't sure if I could find him, but it turned out to be fairly easy; I can't explain how. He looked emaciated; like something had drained out of him. He probably felt that way, or simply imagined it. On this psychic plane, he wouldn't be wasting away in any physical way, no matter how he appeared. His personality didn't change much, proclaiming I was there to gloat over him when I turned up. Even with darkness around us, we could see each other clearly. He appeared curled up in a foetal position, and I may have seemed to be standing over him, but there wasn't any floor.

"Just quit it," I said. "You know as well as I do our physical appearances have no relevance here."

He let out a slight chuckle and appeared to stand, his form filling out to look like his normal self. "As far as prisons go, this is pretty effective," he said. "You're really all around me, watching and judging. I can feel it. And there's no where to go as far as I can see or sense." I didn't say anything. "So, what do you want?"

"I don't really know," I said. "I took part in a discussion today about how society should deal with evil."

"That's simple. You eradicate it." He looked at me as I remained quiet. "Ah, but how would you determine what exactly is evil? You're thinking if eradicating me would make you an evil person. That conscience of yours still bothering you? What's the point of having the ability to do something with your power if you're not going to use it?"

His language was a little more colourful; it did get to me. And he wasn't the first person I've met who thought that way. He's the first person I've met who went all the way in using his abilities the way he did. In the time I've known him, he had mentally enslaved others, manipulated the thoughts of his own parents, and there's what he did to Keitaro. Let's not forget what he did to me. If there was ever a perfect example of power corrupting absolutely, he'd be the encyclopaedic reference.

"You know, where the rest of the world is concerned, you're already dead. Officially. Your body is practically a vegetable. And you're right. It is entirely within my power to kill you here and now; no one would know. You already don't exist." It may have seemed like bravado, and in reality, I probably would have been shaking, saying such things, but I found myself chillingly calm and serious.

"Ah, but you'd know," he teased.

"True. I've already lived with it for the last few years. Doing it again, to you, isn't really going to bother me in the least." I did think if I was lying or not, there and then. The look on his face suggested he took it seriously. "It is, as you said, within my power to do it."

"Yes, it is. And given the chance, I would do the same to you."

I felt myself smile. "You did have your chance and you missed." Something else crossed my mind there and then, and my smile felt a little crooked.

"Then, do it already. Just kill me."

"You know what else is within my power to do?"

"What?"

I gave him a hug and said, "I forgive you." With that, I could feel something radiating from inside me.

At first, he said, "Bullshit!" Well, in a more colourful way.

I didn't let go and held tighter, my head resting on his shoulder, eyes closed. I felt that crooked smile balancing out. Then he said, "You're glowing."

That's when I loosened a little and leaned back a bit, still holding on to him. I just said, "I'm not asking for any forgiveness from you, but for everything that you have done, I forgive you." I hugged him again and then stepped back, widening the distance between us.

Why I said and did what I said and did, I'm not really sure. It felt like the right thing to do, and before you jump to *that* conclusion, it wasn't likely he got into my head and dropped the idea there. I'm certain he didn't get into my head. His reaction was genuine, and I would have sensed if he was lying or faking it. He cursed vehemently and said, "I don't want your forgiveness. I don't need it. You're the one who should apologise."

I laughed at his reaction. "Well, that's not going to happen because it serves no purpose. Want it or not, need it or not, I forgive you." I gave him another sly smile and then said, "And I'm sending you home. Consider it a Christmas gift." And I gave him a wink. His silent, bewildered reaction said a lot, like he didn't believe me. I had an idea of what to do, but I wasn't sure it was going to work.

It was a tricky problem. Phillip's consciousness had been separated from his physical form for a really long time now. Think of it as an abnormal out of body experience, his consciousness drifting around, unattached to his physical body, probably existing sparsely within the subconscious realms of other people's dreams. I figured it was how he managed to take control of Keitaro's body, but only after he got rid of Keitaro's consciousness. I think for most of us psychics, going into another persons mind is often a sharing thing. We're often in our heads, picking up thoughts, voices or noises from another person.

These Dream-walks I take are different from the usual TP experience. Still, I never thought I was actually separated from my body in reality despite the experiences I've had in the Dream-world. This thing with Phillip, as far as I could tell, was something entirely different. Whether I was dealing with him, his mind, his spirit or his soul, I didn't know for sure.

But I knew where his body was, and I knew who was with him at the moment. So, from where I was within the dark recesses of my being, I reached out to M. I felt his surprise when I made contact. We had linked up before so it wasn't too troubling for him. I quickly explained what I was going to do, needing him to focus on his brother. That gave me line of sight to make a bridge between the Phillip in my head and his body.

Link established, I grabbed hold of Phillip, who protested, and literally flung him, like I was tossing a sack of *dren*. I sent him through the link, closed it, left M's mind and woke up in the Infirmary sometime past midnight on Sunday. I tidied up the bed and left for a snack at the café after checking with the nurse on duty. And that was it.

While I was having a late supper, I was joined by Tommy. We caught up on a few things, he told me how Nik was doing with his work at the Operations Center, and a little after one in the morning, my comms went off with a message from Linda informing me to report to her office. Tommy and I parted ways; he returned to Operations Center while I headed to Linda's office.

I always figured the G/Cs stayed within the building with us trainees, and Linda being in her office at one in the morning, not exactly dressed as professionally as she normally does, kinda confirmed it. A phone call from M was routed to her office, and it was unusual he managed to call back. Again, Linda remained in the office while I took the call. M said Phillip's EEG monitor started giving a weak reading suggesting brain activity, not long after I broke psychic contact with him. If what I tried worked, Phillip's mind was back in his own body, but I couldn't say to what extent the state of his mind was. When he asked me to explain, I could only speculate that given the amount of time Phillip had his mind and body apart, there might be some imbalance between mind and body, as well as some cognitive issues. M was studying to be a doctor, although I'm not sure in what field; it wouldn't tax him to understand what I was talking about.

This was when Linda found out what I had done about Phillip.

M asked if I would be willing to go over and verify it was indeed Phillip's consciousness in his own body. I was willing, but I needed to get clearance. Even as I said it, I looked over to Linda who didn't seem too pleased. I did want to meet with him in person to discuss Mikey as well. He said he would wait for my call to confirm, and then we ended the call.

I explained to Linda in detail what happened – pretty much everything I've written here – and that's when she gave me that whole bit about acts of bravery and stupidity. "The judgment's out on letting him go like that, it might be a really foolish thing to do, but forgiving him? Considering what I know about you and him? I'd say that was brave of you," she said. "You're not worried he'll do something to get back at you?"

"He might try," I said. "But I'm not going to worry about it for now. I think I've got that part of my life under control. If I need to deal with him again, I'll do what's necessary to deal with him. And I think he knows it too; that I'm not afraid of him anymore."

Linda watched me silently. I didn't read her mind, but I guess she was deciding what to make of my statements. She moved towards me and guided me towards her office's door. "Well, it sounds like you had a long day. Get some rest and send me a report before the end of the day. I'll get you some time off for this little errand of yours," she said as we left her office.

After that, I managed to get some sleep; an hour or so. It still feels weird having the whole suite to myself and I miss Becca's company. I've been typing this out on my console while sitting on the couch in the living room area; the TV on, the volume low just to provide some white noise. It's almost six now.

I was looking out the window and thinking about it all again. The cold darkness outside seemed like the darkness within me, but there was something different now. I know Phillip did say I was glowing at one point. Maybe it's not just darkness within me, but there is some light as well now.

If it's a small miracle of some kind, I'll take it.

Dec 29

As I am leaving for a spell in a few days, there's a lot to get done to make sure all my responsibilities will be covered. I'm doing okay with classes, but there are the projects that need updating, work with Nik and Colleen has to be on track, not to mention coaching time in kendo and aqua-acrobatics, as well as meeting with Ethan and Kadi on separate basis. I never realised how much of my time was taken up in the evening, especially since Walker left. I always had time with him, but now, I don't see how I managed to squeeze him in. My schedule hasn't changed much, just my activities and responsibilities shifted in those areas.

Like with kendo, I'm now working in tandem with Keiko in training our juniors. Two newbies joined since our duel and it was left to me to help them with the basics, while Keiko carried on with the others. After an hour or so, we move on to common practice involving all, encouraging our juniors to spar with each other while Keiko and I keep watch. Keiko and I would then spar, sometimes in kendo, sometimes in other forms of martial arts, be it bare-handed or with the wooden weapons. Kadi has voiced some interests in other fighting styles as well and showed us a self-defence style unique to her race. Becca mentioned something about it long ago, but she never learnt it, so she couldn't demonstrate anything for us. Kadi was training in it since she was a child. I couldn't even write the name of the fighting style, much less pronounce it.

And then with Sunee and Corogi, I would need to review the footage on Walker's part as a refresher before I can carry on with those two. I know my half down pat and most of Walker's half of the routine, but I don't perform his part, so teaching it isn't easy without some reference. Otherwise, I think I've got everything covered.

Then, there was this meeting I had today, and I learnt a new word: 'noosphere'. Apparently, that word describes what some people believe to be the next level, or stage, of existence. The stage we're in, where all the physical living beings, including all life on our planet at the moment, exists in the biosphere. The noosphere is presumed to be the realm of consciousness; of the mind. A space where minds and consciousness come together, and there is no real, physical embodiment... Sounds a lot like cyberspace to me.

Anyway, in some weird roundabout way, I ended up in a meeting with a couple of people who somehow assumed I was an expert on the noosphere. The meeting was supervised by Remington and Linda. Seriously, when I got the page on my comms unit from Remington and he told me what the meeting was about, I had to ask how I got regarded as an expert on something I wasn't entirely aware of. It turned out, I do know something about it.

We've been using the 'network' on our last few field trips. I even talked about it to some of our guest tutors, explaining what we were doing and how it worked. Apparently, some of them shared it with some colleagues who discussed it with fellow researchers and so on. A question was raised about it, and back it went up the chain, coming back to The Facility. The initial inquiries were directed to those running the network at first, and then to Callie, since she developed the current system we use for the network. Then they heard about the Dream-world and 'Eureka!', the network wasn't what they were looking for in the first place. This led them to Ethan, who was with Jenny, who then pointed them in my direction along with the suggestion of talking to Remington first. See? Roundabout.

During the meeting, these two – Mr. Reiger and Ms. Irons, who are part of the ESA – kept asking about the noosphere and it took me a while to realise they were referring to the Dream-world. They asked how it was created, where it existed, in what form it existed; if one had to be a telepath or psychic to have to go there; if there was any independent intelligent life there.

Before that, they started by getting a feel for me. They asked about my background. Linda said I wasn't required to share anything I wasn't comfortable sharing. Their probing questions led me to sharing some thoughts on what I believed in. It gave them a slight idea about me. I blithely admitted that despite studying and learning new stuff at The Facility for the last three years, I really knew nothing much. At all.

For all the craziness around the various sciences thrown at me in classes, it was a lot of dry information in my perception. There were a lot of theories being shared; some could be proven by experiments but most could not, and I compared them to religious beliefs. When it came down to it, in my view, science and religion have their belief systems, and each of their followers resorted to faith in the end. How did we, as humans, come to be on this world? Did God create us? Or did we evolve? Or are we truly some lost colony of other distant worlds? There is no actual evidence that I've seen or been shown to me, personally, to convince me anybody has the right story. So, that's all they are to me in the end – stories. Theories. To lean in any particular direction requires faith, and I've never felt the need to lean in any particular direction.

Heck, there are times when I'm not even sure if what I perceive as reality is really real, given how real my "other worlds" have appeared to me. For all I know, I'm already in some noosphere and everything I perceive is simply illusion – and yeah, the idea of '*The Matrix*' did pop into my mind.

And I've digressed.

But not by much as it's the gist of what I rambled on nervously to the two guests. Ms. Irons found me fascinating and wanted to discuss my take on theology, but her colleague reminded her why they were there. In the end, Remington suggested I take them on a trip into the Dreaming. I reminded him of trouble getting in there these days, and the Dreaming is currently a different place than before. I wasn't sure what we would find there as I haven't had time to explore. He suggested taking Ethan along since we both knew he was still making regular trips into the Dreaming. I reluctantly agreed.

Remington then got Linda to take the guests to have a check up with Ms. Phillips, and to have them sign some forms and waivers. After they left the room, Remington eyed me curiously and then asked if I felt I was making progress here at The Facility.

"Isn't that for you and Linda to decide?" I asked.

"Just getting a feel after everything you just said."

"Every time I learn something, it makes me realise I know nothing at all."

"And yet, you still manage to put what you learn to decent practical use," he said. "And more importantly, you get to pass it on."

He then suggested I get ready for tonight. When I agreed to take Mr. Reiger and Ms. Irons into the Dreaming, it was going to be tonight. I still had my session with Keiko, followed by dinner. After this, I'm off to the pool to meet with Sunee and Corogi and then, it's off to the Dream-world.

We'll see what's what when, and if, I get those two in there...

Dec 31

Getting Mr. Reiger and Ms. Irons into the Dreaming turned out to be an easier task than expected. To make things simple, Ethan 'carried' Mr. Reiger in while I had Ms. Irons. I briefed Ethan on how to link his passenger, as he's never pulled anyone into the Dream-world on his own before; none I know of. He managed it easily. Surprisingly, it wasn't too difficult for me to get there either, given the problems I had before. I guess the trip was a success where Mr. Reiger and Ms. Irons are concerned.

Ms. Irons was the one who was a little more open with me about the nature of their investigation. Apparently, she had time to check up on me too, as I found out during the trip. It was something I was unprepared for. I mean, Linda said I didn't have to share any personal information, but she didn't mention they, or at least, Ms. Irons, would have access to to my journal from within The Facility. Or that Ms. Phillips could share limited data associated with my journeys into the Dreaming, such as my brain scan readings. It somehow wasn't in violation of any personal information. The information on my journal was meant to be public anyway, and the EEG readings, which had nothing to do with any actual medical records, were for their research.

Ms. Irons said she only wanted to get to know me better, and we had a lengthy discussion during our time in the Dream-world. In some weird way, it felt therapeutic to talk with this stranger, not that writing out my thoughts here was any different.

It took a while for Ms. Phillips to hook everyone to EEG machines; everyone except me as they already had my readings on file. It had been decided that those readings were sufficient, and could be treated as a baseline for comparison to the readings being recorded this trip. Besides, I used my usual bed.

Mr. Reiger was a bit skeptical if it was actually possible for the four of us to share the same dream-space. It struck me as odd considering his purpose coming to The Facility in the first place. Ms. Phillips assured him that I had done this with several others before, without mentioning other specific incidents.

In any case, you can imagine Mr. Reiger's surprise when we did meet up in the Dream-world. I can't say what Ethan did, but he got Mr. Reiger in. I took Ms. Irons by the hand, I got her to close her eyes and started describing the environment of the Dream-world to her, imagining the world popping up around me within the Infirmary. It worked well enough last time. This time, it was easier to make the world appear and we slipped in like that. Ms. Irons was impressed at the ease of getting to the Dreaming. The slight snag was since I didn't follow Ethan in, Ms. Irons and I didn't turn up at the same place where Ethan and Mr. Reiger were. It took a while to make the trek to Ethan's new village; the one I saw half-built before.

Not long after we started hiking, Ms. Irons asked how I knew where I was going. I said, "We'll get where we're going simply because it's where we want to go and where we're meant to be. It's always worked that way."

"Sounds like dream-logic," she said. Then she asked about the world itself. How big it was? Did it have any basis in reality? Why was it a forest and not something else, like some urban setting? It was a while before she noticed our clothes had changed and then asked how that happened. She queried her more contemporary set of clothes opposed to my more old-fashioned fantasy realm style attire.

In relation to my clothes, I explained about the previous version of the Dream-world, and the tasks I had to do. I mentioned having met other people from around the world who found their way into the Dreaming. I couldn't prove anything there, save for actually meeting one person in reality, after meeting said person in the Dream-world. And it wasn't Phillip.

She had read about Phillip, my experiences with him, as well as what I had done a few days back. She seemed sympathetic about it, remarking that I had done a courageous thing; to forgive him and set him free, given everything he had done. While I was taken by surprise by how much she knew, I admitted feeling unsure about it. I was going to check on him in a couple of days, to confirm if he was truly back in his own body.

As we continued our trek through the forest, she poked and she probed, and I opened up about almost everything from Phillip to Michelle, from Keitaro being hurt to Walker leaving, and how I felt about it all. She simply… listened. No advice; no comfort; no judgment. Before we knew it, Ethan's village was in view and the 'therapy session' was over. Before we headed into the village, she said, "We are all formed by our past, the good and the bad parts. And we have to accept it all because all that makes us who we are. We are informed by it, we learn from it and we even use it in order to live here in the present and plan for the future, whatever that future may be."

"I really have no clear idea what my future is going to be right now," I said. "I thought I did when I started studying and living here, but now, I really don't know anymore. Feels like I'm treading water."

She then said the weirdest thing. "Then stop treading and like Dory says, 'just keep swimming'."

I know I gave her a suspicious look. "You're quoting a fish."

"Yes, I am," she said proudly. "My little girl loves that movie."

I laughed, hard and full, and she laughed with me. It felt really good.

We headed into the village and I have to say, Ethan has been busy there. It was populated, and there was farming going on, as well as a bustling market place. I noticed Mr. Reiger looking around excitedly, touching things and talking to people. He didn't notice us approaching until Ms. Irons reached out and grabbed his arm. The village was not unlike the previous version. I was curious where the people came from. They definitely suited the locale and the world. Mr. Reiger himself seemed dressed to blend in.

It took a while, but I found Ethan helping out at a river bank, working with some of the villagers on an irrigation issue. For all the technological stuff we cover at The Facility, it was strange that Ethan, the youngster he is, would be so low-tech in this place. But, he seemed happy and at ease with it, perhaps it's a good thing. In a way, I guess he found a balance in his life. Despite the bustle around here, it was generally peaceful and quiet, contrary to what was going on in his head when he first came to The Facility last year.

We spent a few hours in the village and around dusk, I took Ms. Irons for a flight for her get a look at the lay of the land. I encouraged her to fly by herself. She managed to float for a brief moment before I had to catch her. You can do anything you want in a dream, and it's the same for the Dream-world. The problem is you're conscious about it all, and it's hard to break the rules of reality in your mind.

By the time we got back to the Infirmary, it had been over fifteen hours since we started. Mr. Reiger claimed he felt it had not been more than five, maybe six hours he spent in there. Ethan felt it was more like three. Ms. Irons felt it was more than twelve hours or so, since we were trekking for a while before spending time in the village, and it was nightfall when we left. All I could say was, based on experience, time passed differently in there than out here, although I never checked if different people had a different sense of time passing. This was the first time we verified the difference.

Ethan was thanked for his help. He then left, while I hung back a little longer. Mr. Reiger and Ms. Irons looked over the readings from the EEGs and made comparisons. Ms. Phillips had marked a few points with notes indicating what was going on with our bodies during the session. Mr. Reiger was particularly interested in the readings between the delta and theta wave activity in various parts of the brain that would not usually register such readings. Ms. Irons pointed out the unusually high activity on the gamma and beta waves at several points, which wouldn't be there in normal dream sleep. Still, with up to fifteen hours of data from various parts of the brain being monitored, it was a lot of data to sift through. Mr. Reiger said despite me calling it a Dream-world or a Dreaming session, it was more likely we weren't dreaming at all. Ultimately, none of it mattered much to me. I took my leave then, and Ms. Irons said she would like to keep in touch with me. I was agreeable, and I thanked her before leaving the Infirmary.

I spent the rest of the day catching up on some stuff and going around doing what I had been doing the last few days prior to the Dream-trip. I touched bases with all my tutors today. I still have dinner with Sophie tomorrow and then I'm heading home on Saturday. For whatever else it's worth, I'll settle what needs to be settled and 'just keep swimming'.

heh...

Jan 1

Hey mom,

It's probably easier and faster if I made a call, but it just seemed right this should be written down instead. After all, this whole journal did start as reports home, sort of a semi-daily letter, albeit one scrutinised and probably edited before being posted somewhere on the Internet. That was the arrangement after all. It took a life of its own and eventually became a journal of sorts for me to write into.

And after some thought and consideration, this will be the final entry. I mean, I am heading home to settle a few things and then, I will be coming back to The Facility. After three years and the occasional meeting or phone call, I think we're on an even keel where these matters are concerned now. Of course, we'll discuss it when I get home.

You pretty much know what I'm up to and I'm sure Remington is keeping you well informed. I don't think it's going to vary much except that my focus will be streamlined a little more to where my skill-set lies. You've met my friends and some of the staff, so you are aware of the company I'm keeping. While he may not be my counsellor anymore, Remington still keeps an eye on me and occasionally gets me involved in some situations where he believes my abilities or talents will be of use. He's not pushing me into doing things I'm not uncomfortable with. It's more about me discovering what I'm capable of in a given situation. I know I had reservations over what I did with that bomb-maker, but I do understand it's something I need to deal with. If I didn't do what I did, more people would have most likely died.

It's not justification, it was a choice.

My choice at that. My decision, for good or ill. And I'm at peace with that now, just as I'm at peace with my actions involving Phillip. I'll leave it at that.

Speaking of which, I intend to let Mikey stay with his dad. Given the situation between Mikey and I, it seems it is time for Mikey to spend some time with his dad. If he decides he wants to stay with Karen instead, and if Karen and Rick are willing, I'll work things out. I'll find something that's fair to Mikey, but I feel he should get to know his father.

They can be hard decisions, right? How many of these decisions did you have with Rick and me? How do we know when these decisions are really the right ones? Maybe, coming to The Facility three years ago wasn't really the right decision after all and maybe it was the right decision from the beginning. Would I have confronted and dealt with all these issues I've faced over the last three years in the same way? Would I have even confronted them at all?

One thing I can be sure of is, I am comfortable with who I am now. The realisation didn't suddenly come to me, I think it's always been there. I just needed a little perspective; who I was, who I am... Who I can be. It wasn't just talking things out with Ms. Irons, or even discussing that conversation with Sophie, Helen and Carol over dinner last night. Or maybe it was all of it, and everything else.

In any case, it's not really an ending or a beginning, this being a new year already. Life goes on and I'll have to do as best as I can manage, and get on with it. Sure, it would have been nice and neat if I had some closure over some issues. In retrospect, if my journal was a collection of vignettes encompassing my life, a sense of closure would be great, but I've accepted such closure may never come, even when my life ends. Like all else, we hope for the best and make do, and we press on.

I might get to fly a jet plane from take-off to landing someday. I might even get my spaceship built too; or set foot on either the Serenity Compound or Olympus Base. Maybe I'll get to physically meet Peter there, or Tomas, if he gets home, or get back with Walker, or visit Becca. Or I might meet someone and settle into a more quiet life, working here at The Facility or the IASC or any of those agencies.

Whatever my future may be, I honestly don't know.
It'll be interesting to find out though.

I'll see you soon, mom.
With love,
- Syndicessca Jeannie
- Jan 1, ----

Printed in the United States
By Bookmasters